P9-DCJ-341

NEW KID

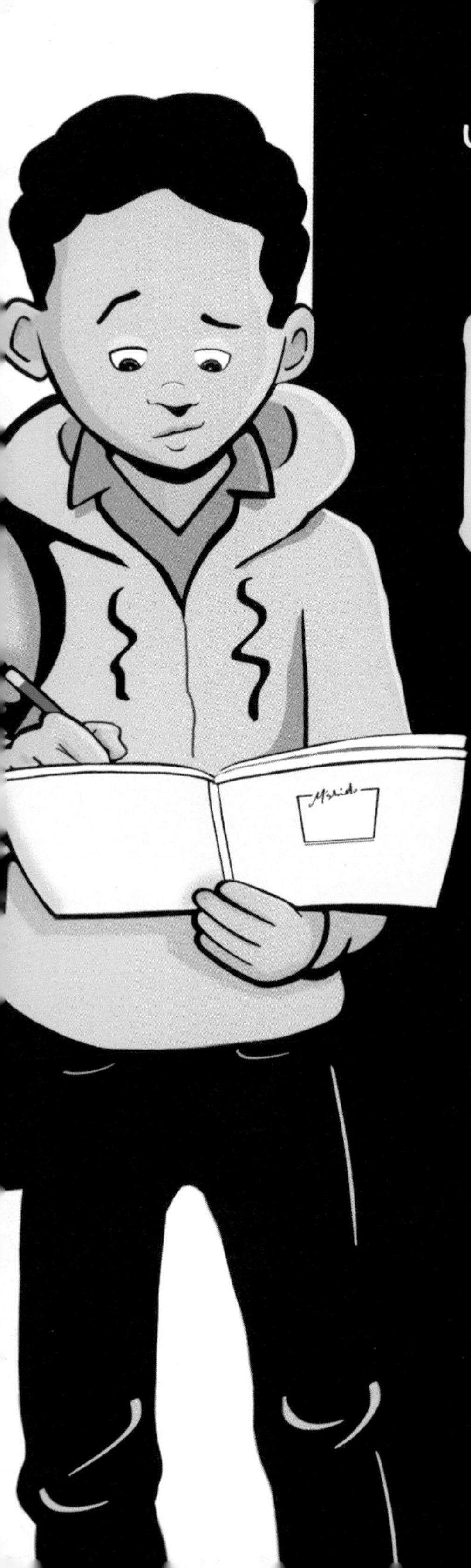

JERRY CRAFT

NEW KID

WITH COLOR BY
JIM CALLAHAN

HARPER
An Imprint of HarperCollinsPublishers

New Kid
Copyright © 2019 by Jerry Craft
All rights reserved. Manufactured in the U.S.A.
No part of this book may be used or reproduced in any manner
whatsoever without written permission except in the case of
brief quotations embodied in critical articles and reviews.
For information address HarperCollins Children's Books,
a division of HarperCollins Publishers,
195 Broadway, New York, NY 10007.
www.harpercollinschildrens.com

Library of Congress Control Number: 2018938256
ISBN 978-0-06-269119-4 (paperback) - ISBN 978-0-06-269120-0
(hardcover)

20 21 22   PC/LSCC   10 9 8 7 6 5
❖
First Edition

To the Jordan Banks in all of us

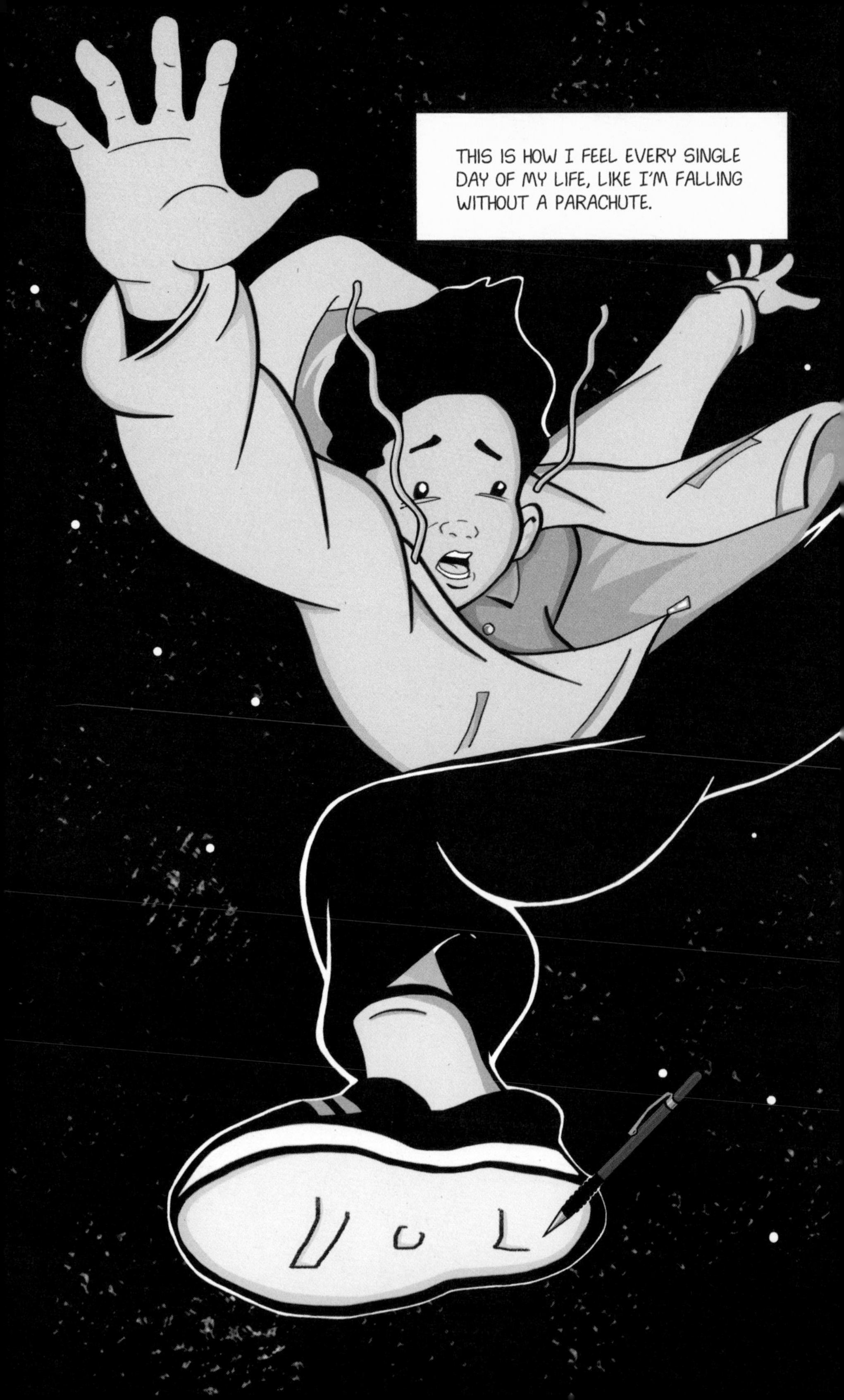
THIS IS HOW I FEEL EVERY SINGLE DAY OF MY LIFE, LIKE I'M FALLING WITHOUT A PARACHUTE.

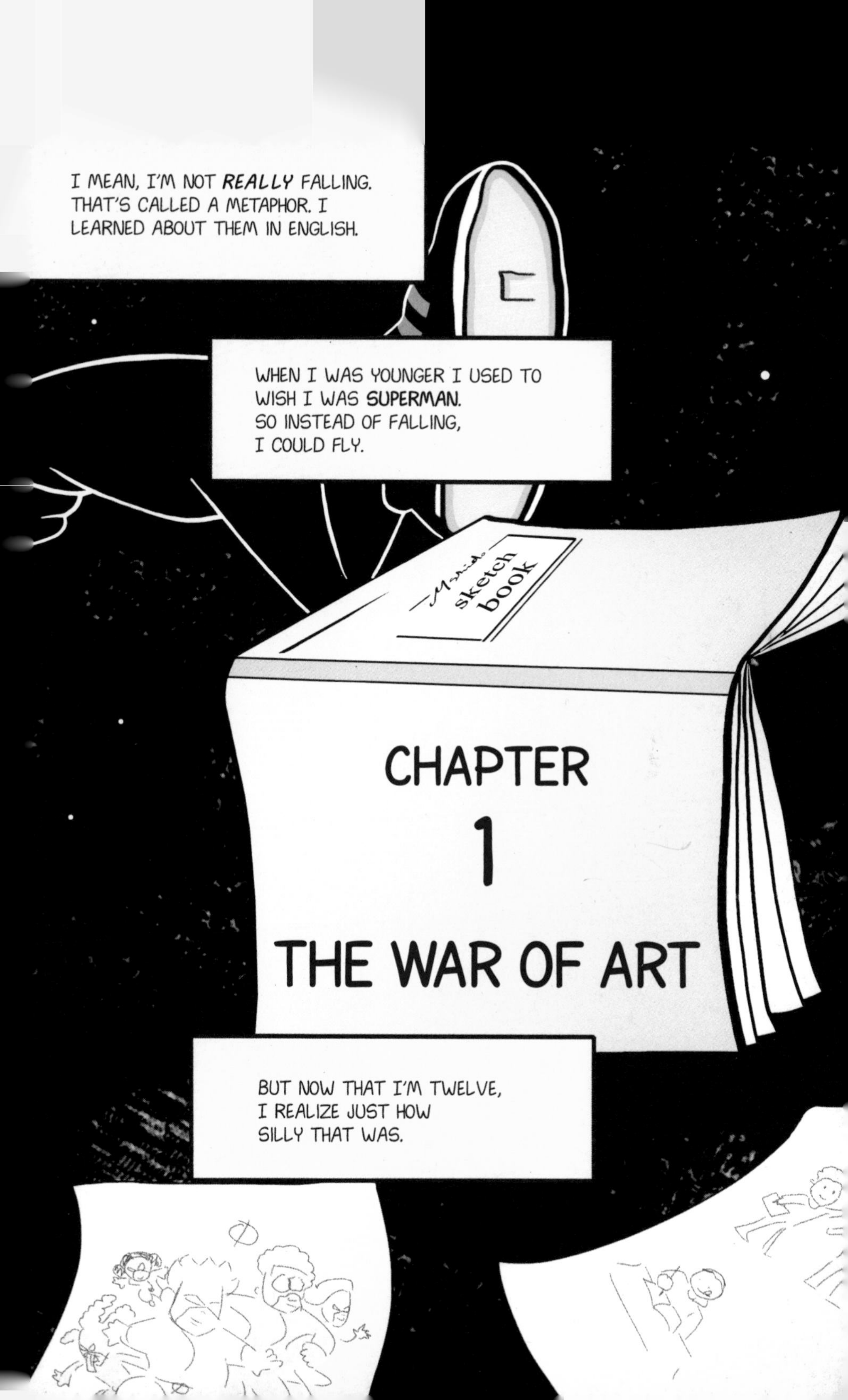
I MEAN, I'M NOT REALLY FALLING. THAT'S CALLED A METAPHOR. I LEARNED ABOUT THEM IN ENGLISH.
WHEN I WAS YOUNGER I USED TO WISH I WAS SUPERMAN. SO INSTEAD OF FALLING, I COULD FLY.
sketch book
CHAPTER 1 THE WAR OF ART
BUT NOW THAT I'M TWELVE, I REALIZE JUST HOW SILLY THAT WAS.

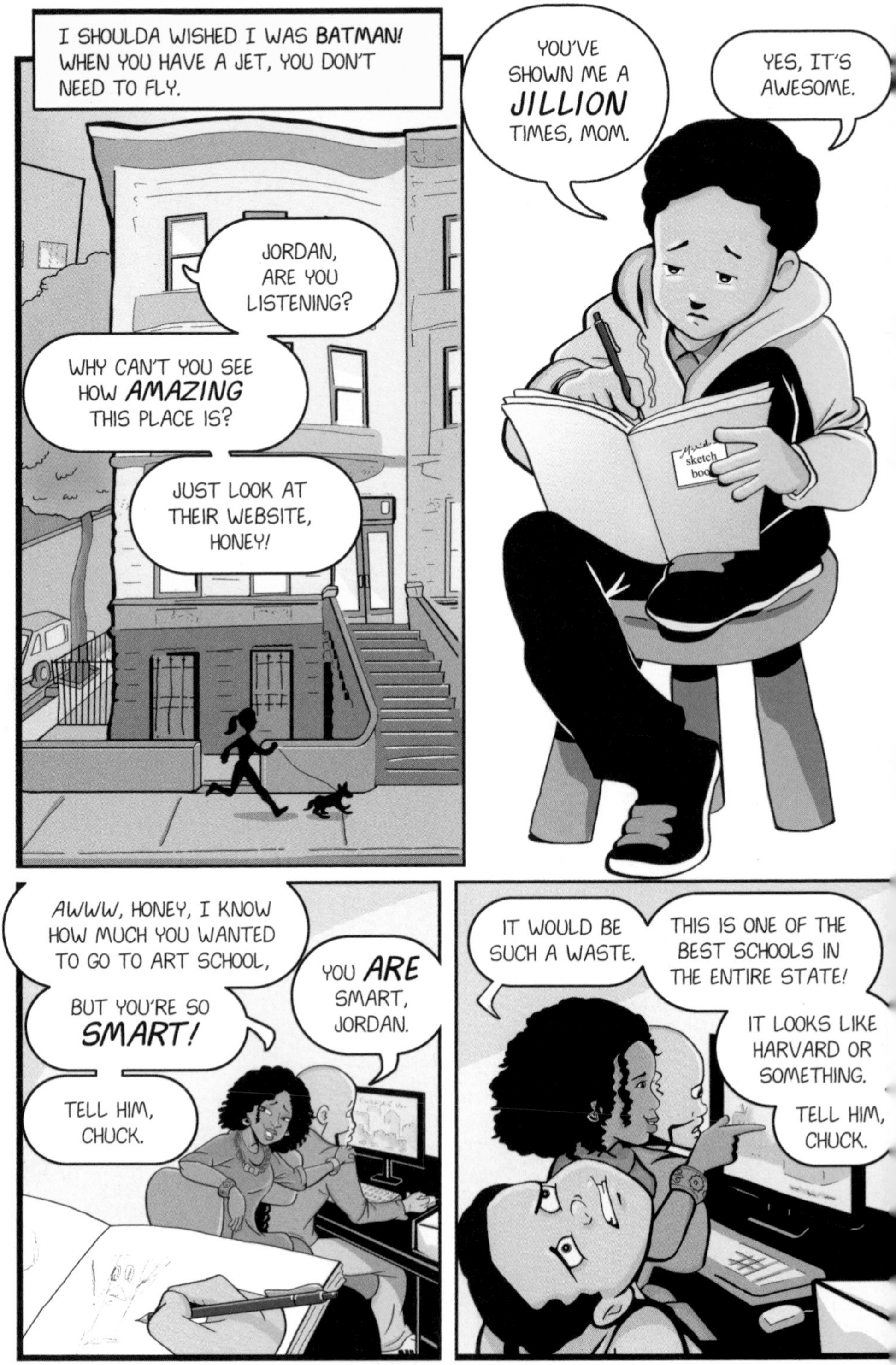
I SHOULDA WISHED I WAS **BATMAN!** WHEN YOU HAVE A JET, YOU DON'T NEED TO FLY.
JORDAN, ARE YOU LISTENING?
WHY CAN'T YOU SEE HOW *AMAZING* THIS PLACE IS?
JUST LOOK AT THEIR WEBSITE, HONEY!
YOU'VE SHOWN ME A *JILLION* TIMES, MOM.
YES, IT'S AWESOME.
sketch
AWWW, HONEY, I KNOW HOW MUCH YOU WANTED TO GO TO ART SCHOOL,
BUT YOU'RE SO *SMART!*
TELL HIM, CHUCK.
YOU *ARE* SMART, JORDAN.
IT WOULD BE SUCH A WASTE.
THIS IS ONE OF THE BEST SCHOOLS IN THE ENTIRE STATE!
IT LOOKS LIKE HARVARD OR SOMETHING.
TELL HIM, CHUCK.

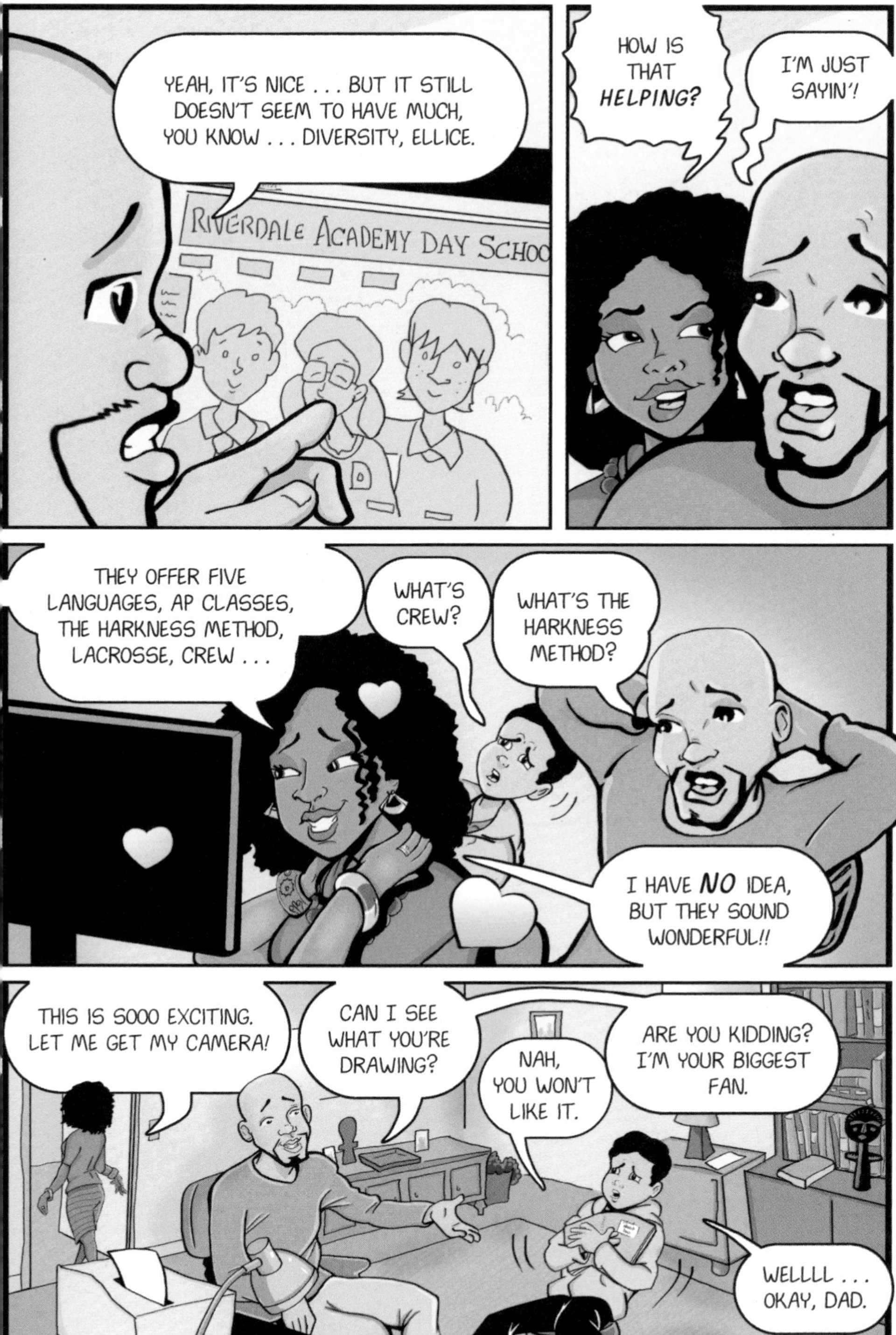
YEAH, IT'S NICE . . . BUT IT STILL DOESN'T SEEM TO HAVE MUCH, YOU KNOW . . . DIVERSITY, ELLICE.
RIVERDALE ACADEMY DAY SCHOO
HOW IS THAT *HELPING?*
I'M JUST SAYIN'!
THEY OFFER FIVE LANGUAGES, AP CLASSES, THE HARKNESS METHOD, LACROSSE, CREW . . .
WHAT'S CREW?
WHAT'S THE HARKNESS METHOD?
I HAVE **NO** IDEA, BUT THEY SOUND WONDERFUL!!
THIS IS SOOO EXCITING. LET ME GET MY CAMERA!
CAN I SEE WHAT YOU'RE DRAWING?
NAH, YOU WON'T LIKE IT.
ARE YOU KIDDING? I'M YOUR BIGGEST FAN.
WELLLL . . . OKAY, DAD.

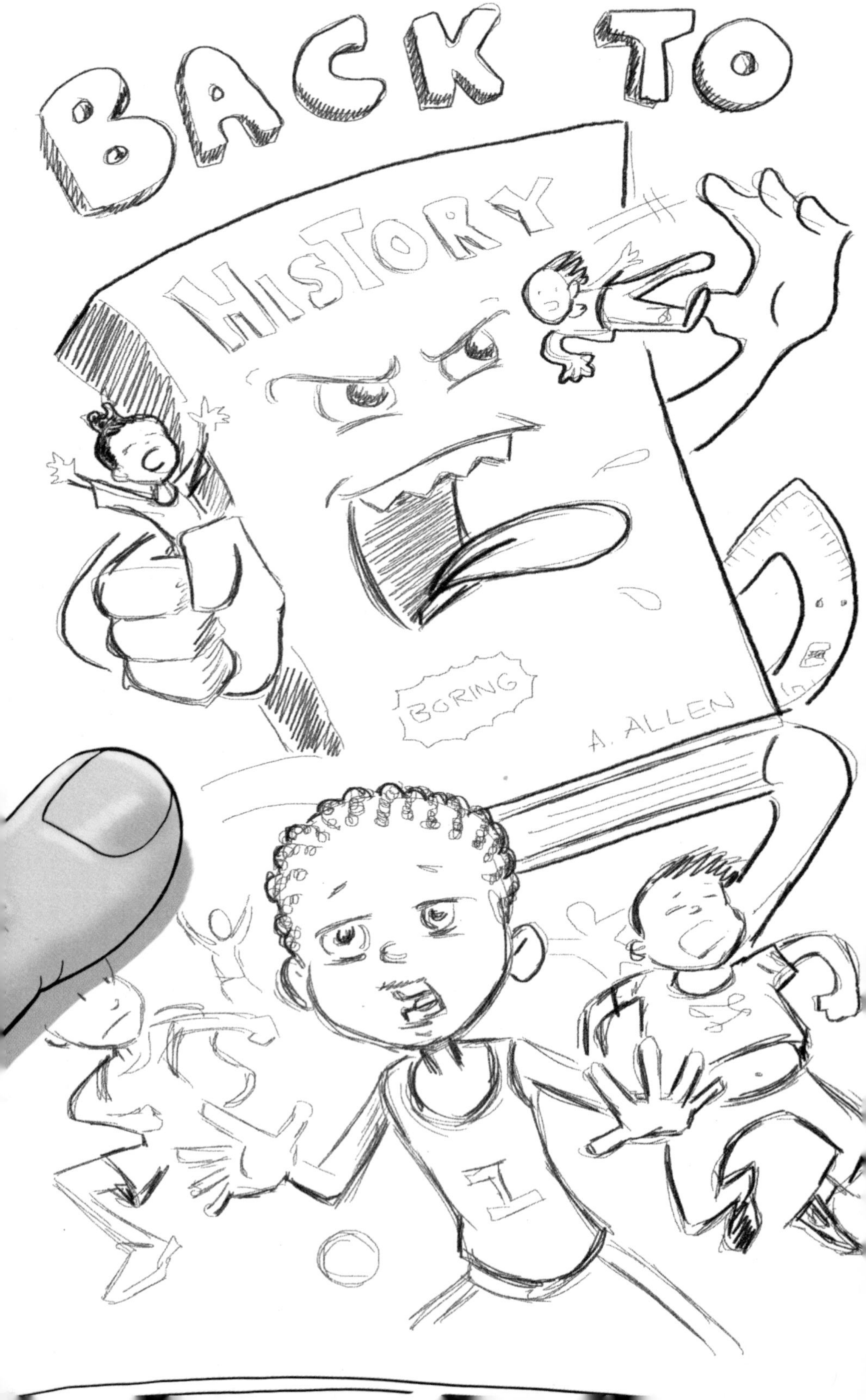
BACK TO
HISTORY
BORING
A. ALLEN

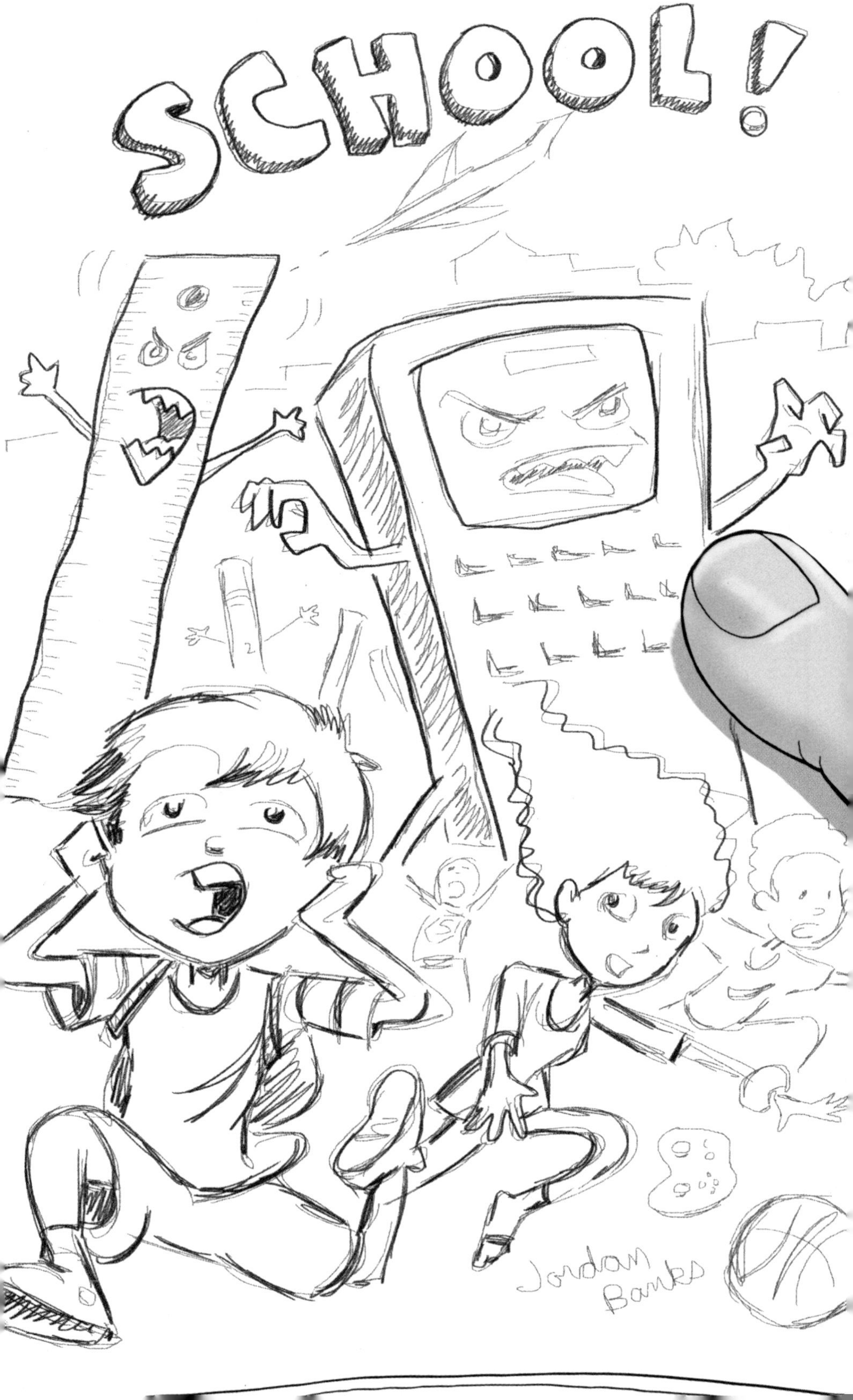
SCHOOL!
Jordan Banks

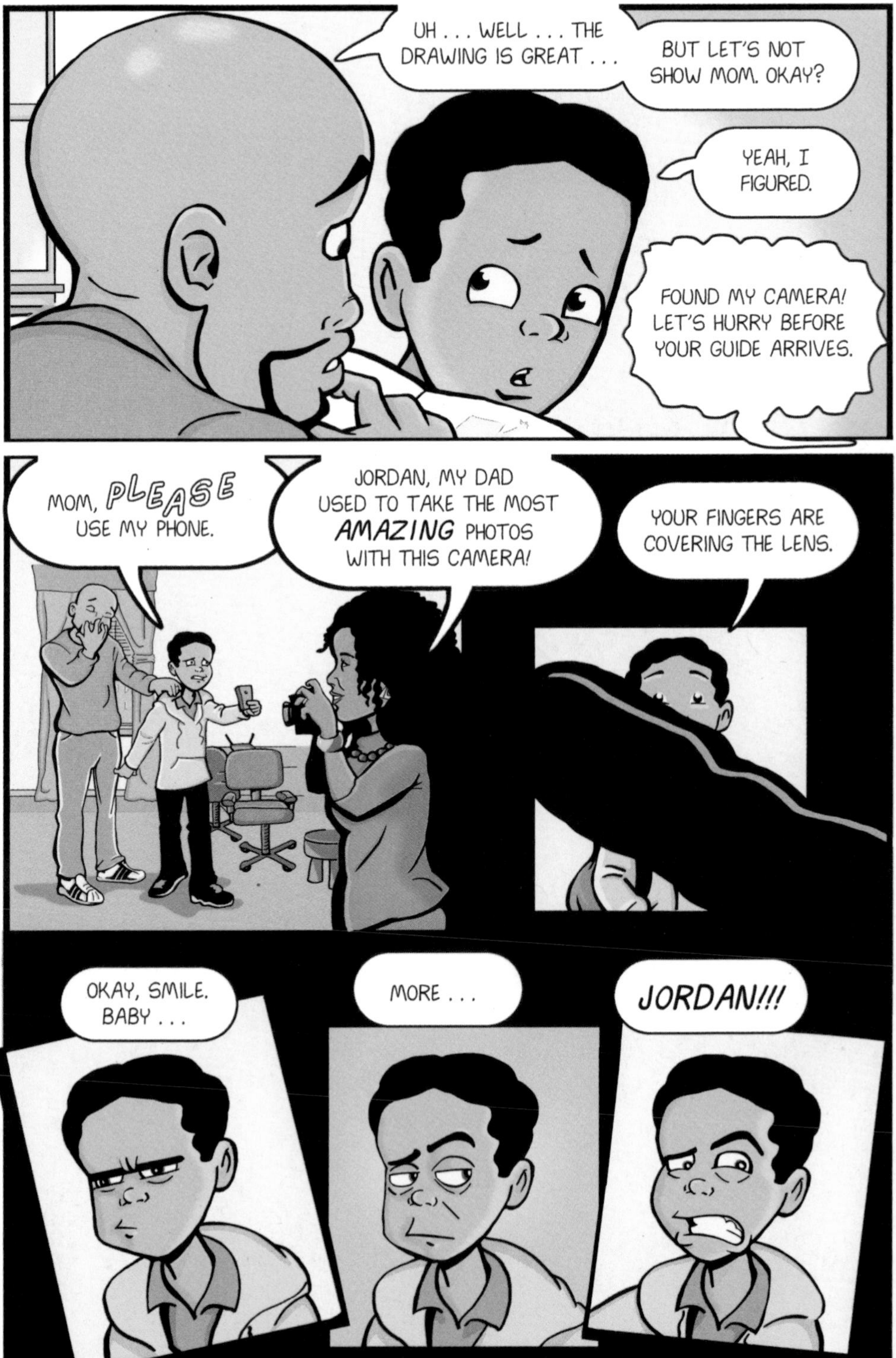
UH . . . WELL . . . THE DRAWING IS GREAT . . .
BUT LET'S NOT SHOW MOM. OKAY?
YEAH, I FIGURED.
FOUND MY CAMERA! LET'S HURRY BEFORE YOUR GUIDE ARRIVES.
MOM, PLEASE USE MY PHONE.
JORDAN, MY DAD USED TO TAKE THE MOST AMAZING PHOTOS WITH THIS CAMERA!
YOUR FINGERS ARE COVERING THE LENS.
OKAY, SMILE. BABY . . .
MORE . . .
JORDAN!!!

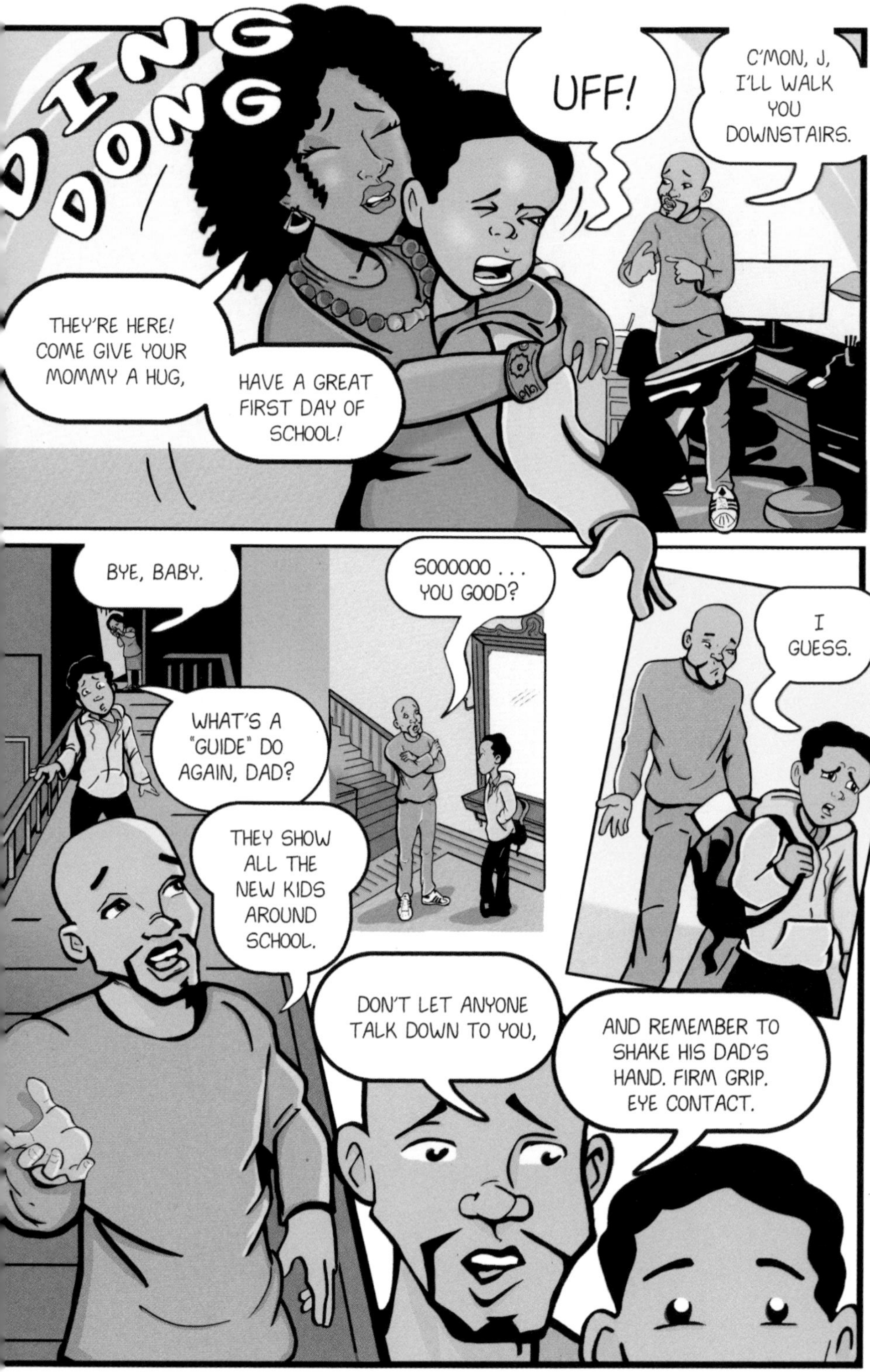
DING DONG
UFF!
C'MON, J, I'LL WALK YOU DOWNSTAIRS.
THEY'RE HERE! COME GIVE YOUR MOMMY A HUG,
HAVE A GREAT FIRST DAY OF SCHOOL!
BYE, BABY.
WHAT'S A "GUIDE" DO AGAIN, DAD?
THEY SHOW ALL THE NEW KIDS AROUND SCHOOL.
SOOOOOO . . . YOU GOOD?
I GUESS.
DON'T LET ANYONE TALK DOWN TO YOU,
AND REMEMBER TO SHAKE HIS DAD'S HAND. FIRM GRIP. EYE CONTACT.

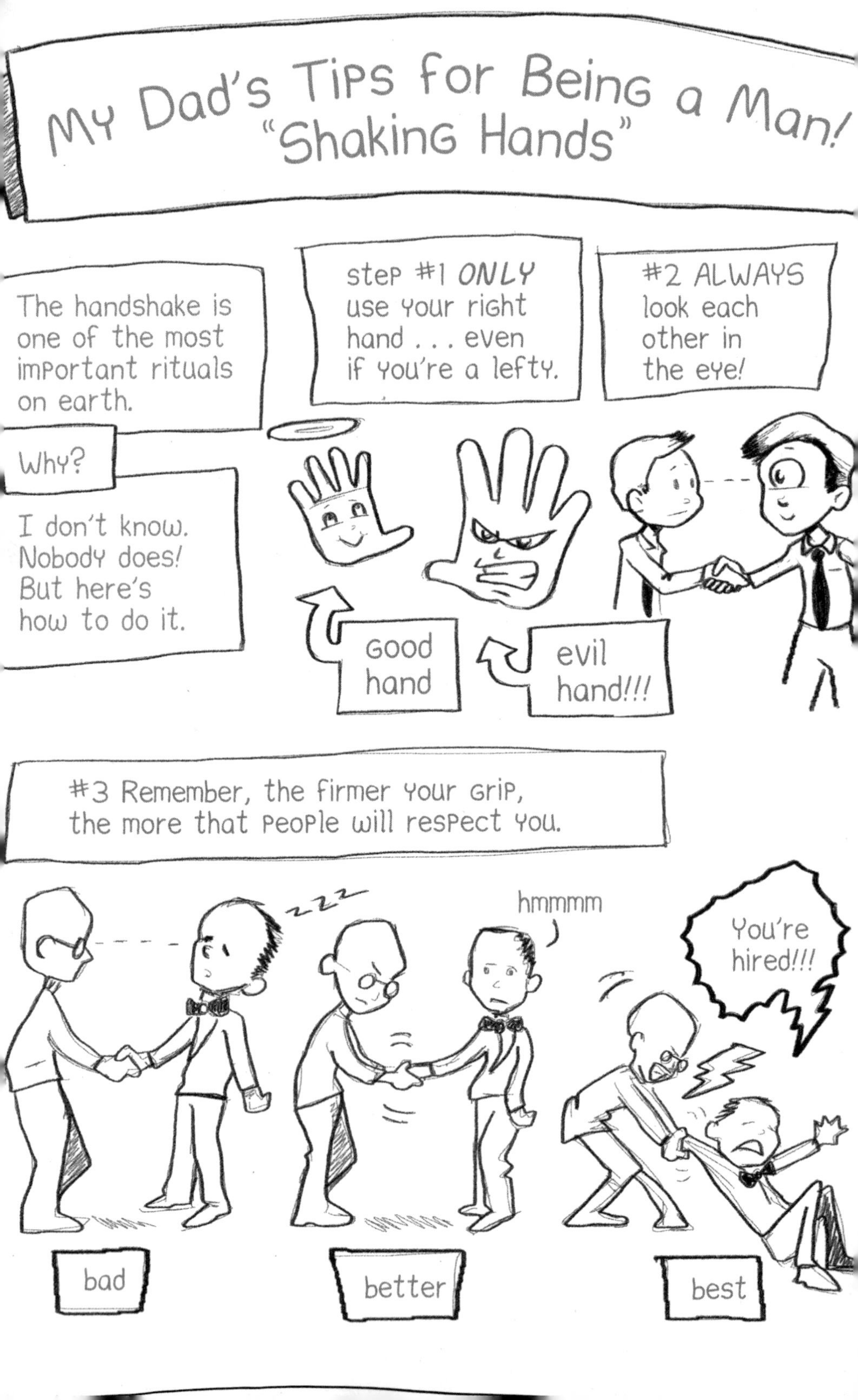

My Dad's Tips for Being a Man!
"Shaking Hands"
The handshake is one of the most important rituals on earth.
Why?
I don't know. Nobody does! But here's how to do it.
step #1 ONLY use your right hand . . . even if you're a lefty.
good hand
evil hand!!!
#2 ALWAYS look each other in the eye!
#3 Remember, the firmer your grip, the more that people will respect you.
z z z
hmmmm
You're hired!!!
bad
better
best

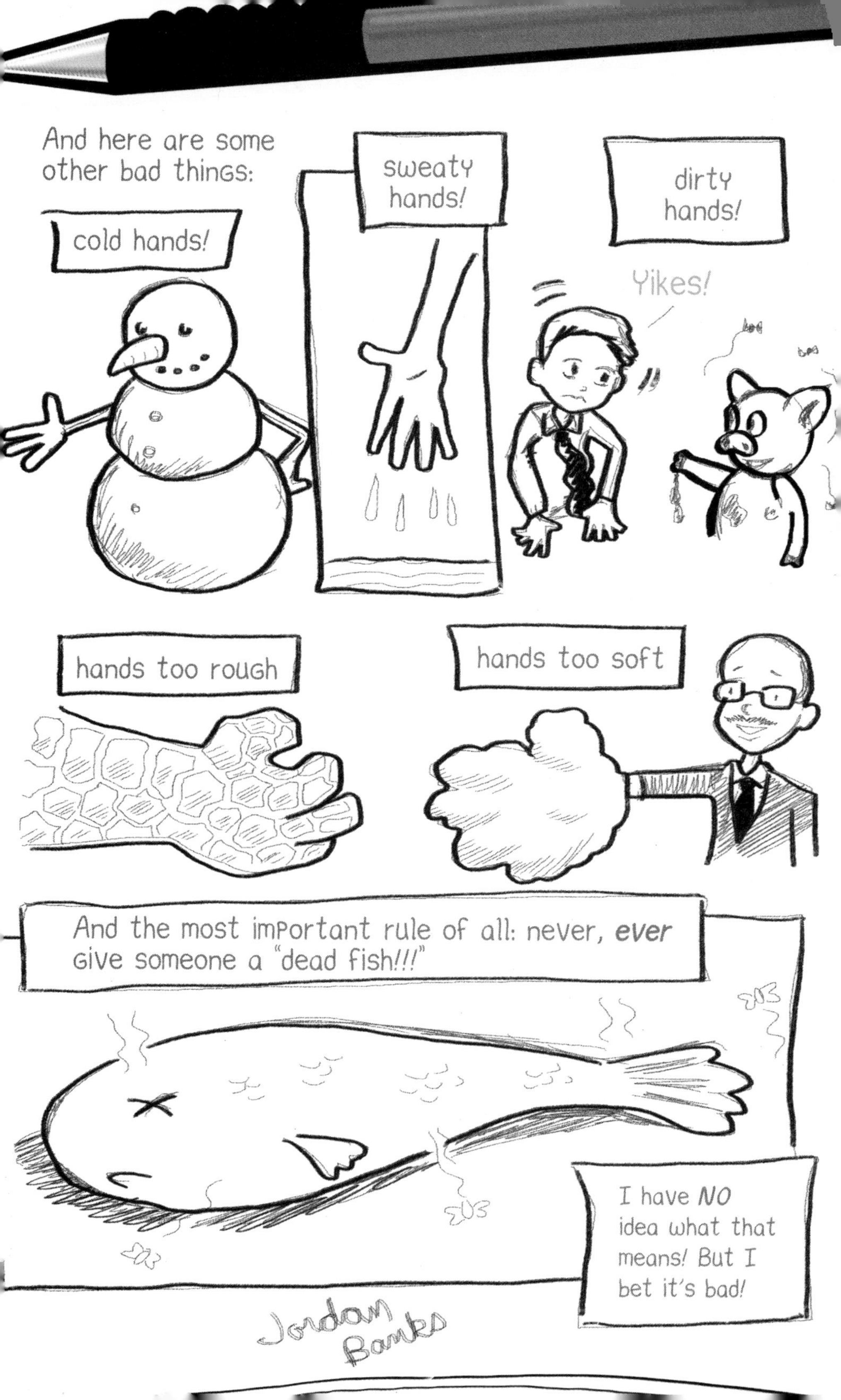

And here are some other bad things:
cold hands!
sweaty hands!
dirty hands!
Yikes!
hands too rough
hands too soft
And the most important rule of all: never, *ever* give someone a "dead fish!!!"
I have *NO* idea what that means! But I bet it's bad!
Jordan Banks

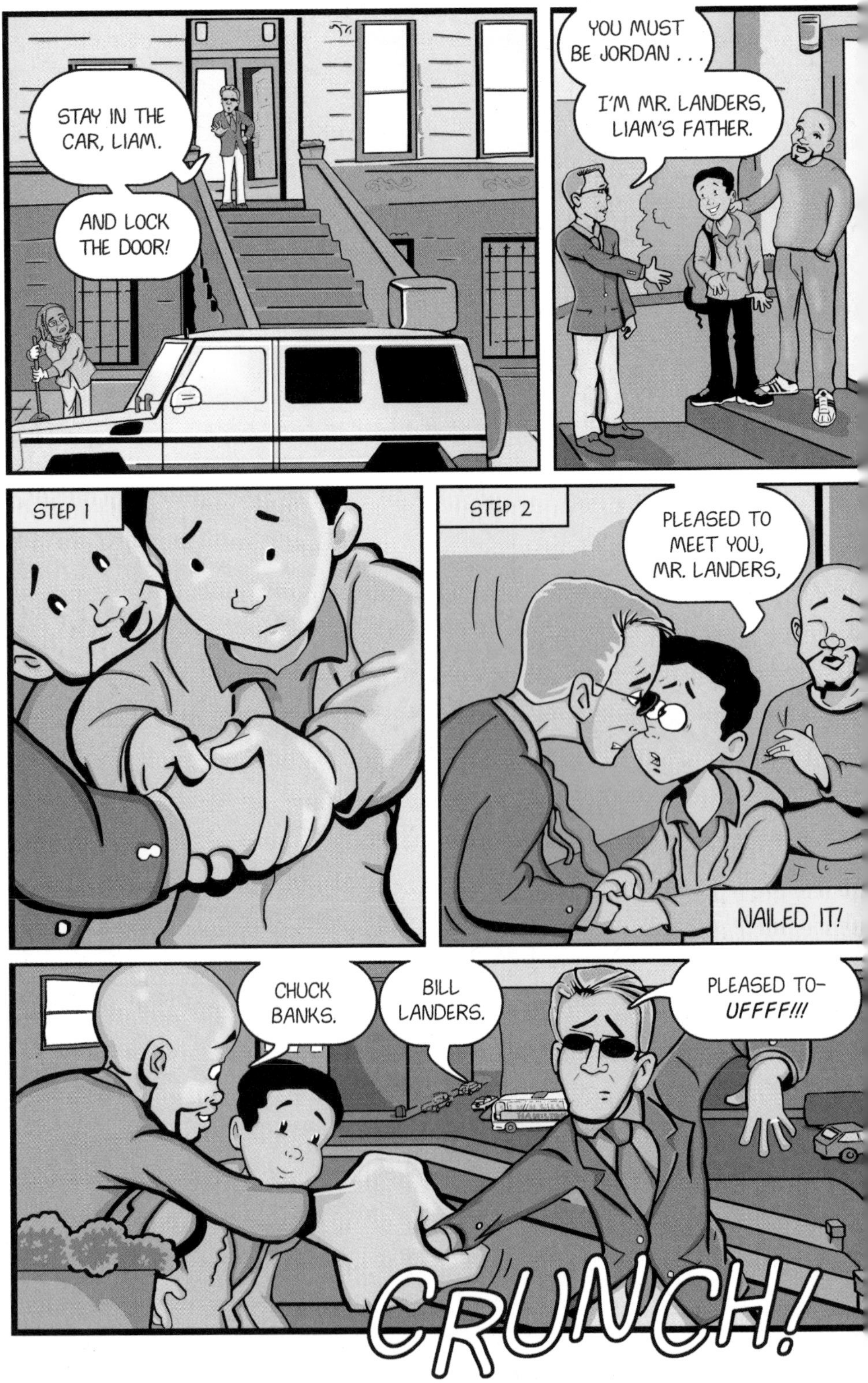
STAY IN THE CAR, LIAM.
AND LOCK THE DOOR!
YOU MUST BE JORDAN . . .
I'M MR. LANDERS, LIAM'S FATHER.
STEP 1
STEP 2
PLEASED TO MEET YOU, MR. LANDERS,
NAILED IT!
CHUCK BANKS.
BILL LANDERS.
PLEASED TO– UFFFF!!!
CRUNCH!

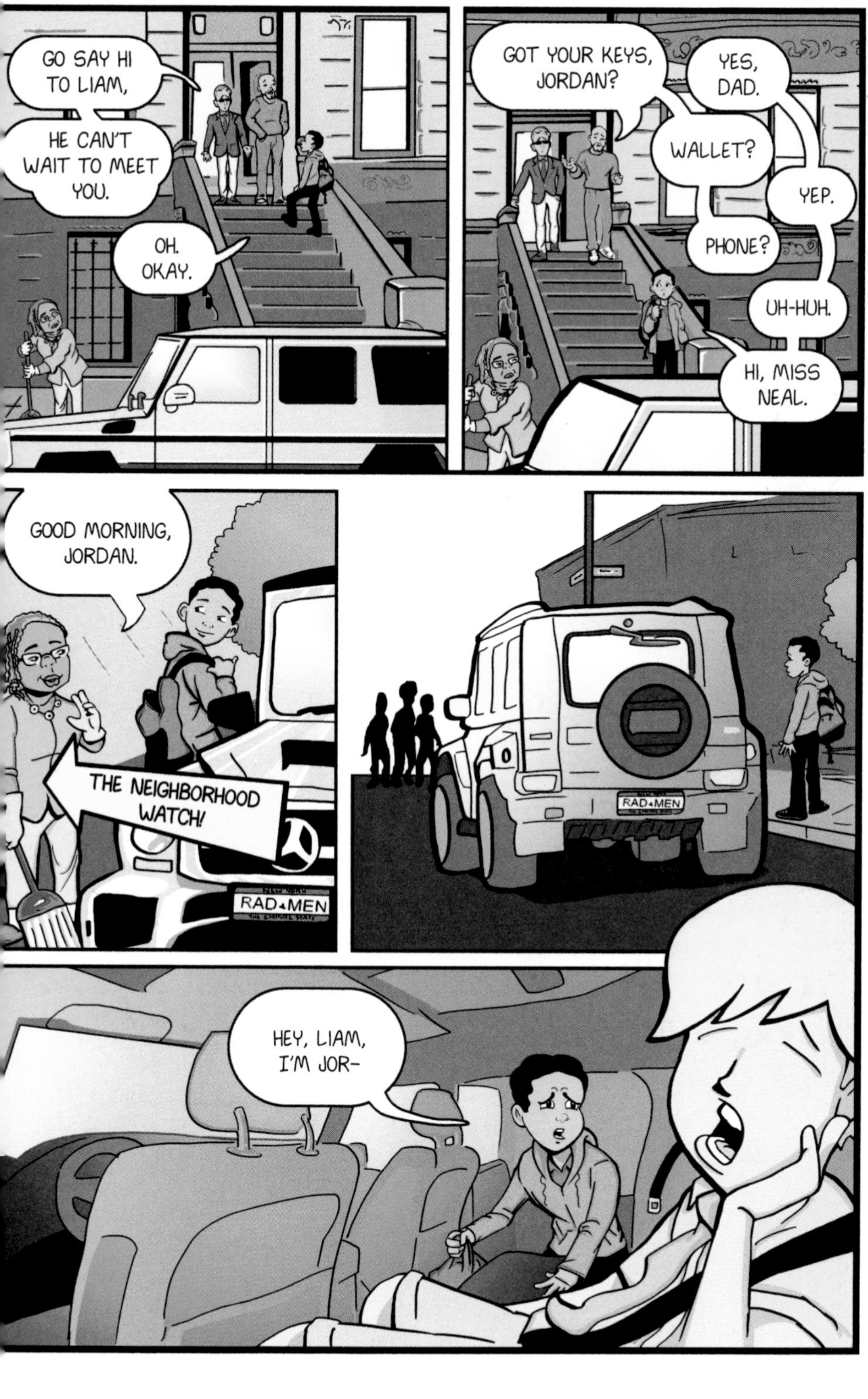
GO SAY HI TO LIAM,
HE CAN'T WAIT TO MEET YOU.
OH. OKAY.
GOT YOUR KEYS, JORDAN?
YES, DAD.
WALLET?
YEP.
PHONE?
UH-HUH.
HI, MISS NEAL.
GOOD MORNING, JORDAN.
THE NEIGHBORHOOD WATCH!
RAD▲MEN
RAD▲MEN
HEY, LIAM, I'M JOR-

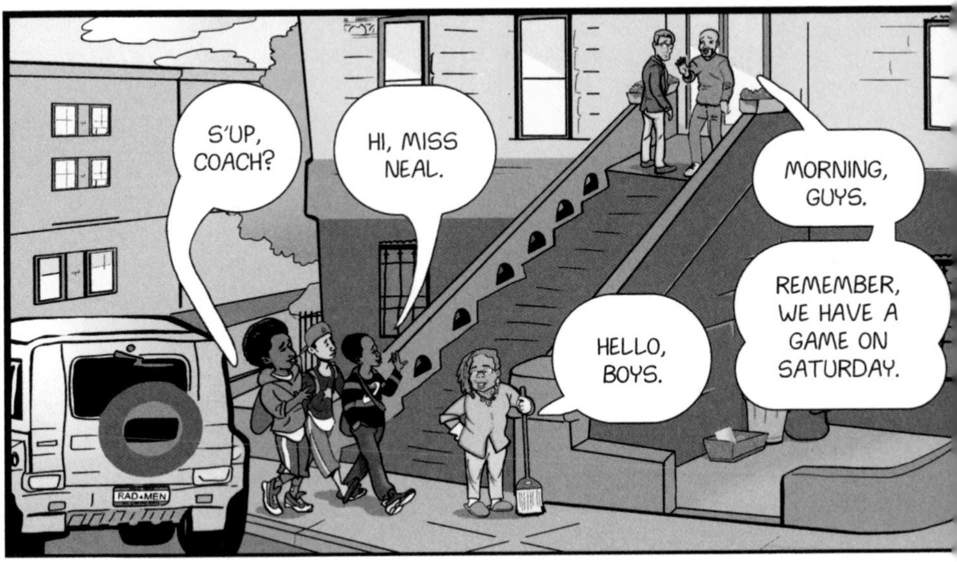
S'UP, COACH?
HI, MISS NEAL.
MORNING, GUYS.
REMEMBER, WE HAVE A GAME ON SATURDAY.
HELLO, BOYS.
RAD-MEN

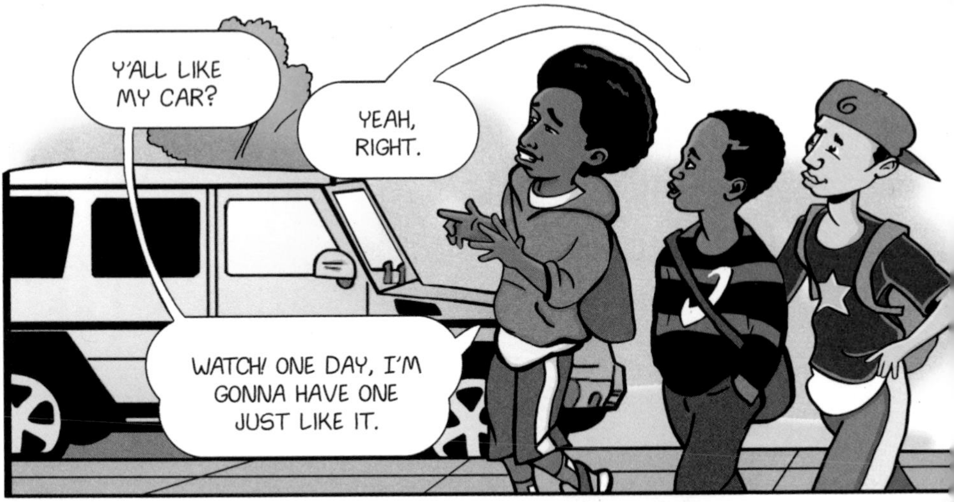
Y'ALL LIKE MY CAR?
YEAH, RIGHT.
WATCH! ONE DAY, I'M GONNA HAVE ONE JUST LIKE IT.

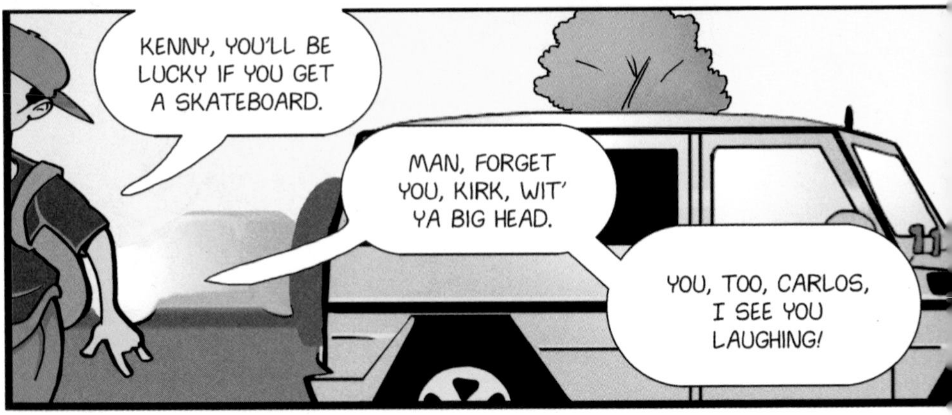
KENNY, YOU'LL BE LUCKY IF YOU GET A SKATEBOARD.
MAN, FORGET YOU, KIRK, WIT' YA BIG HEAD.
YOU, TOO, CARLOS, I SEE YOU LAUGHING!

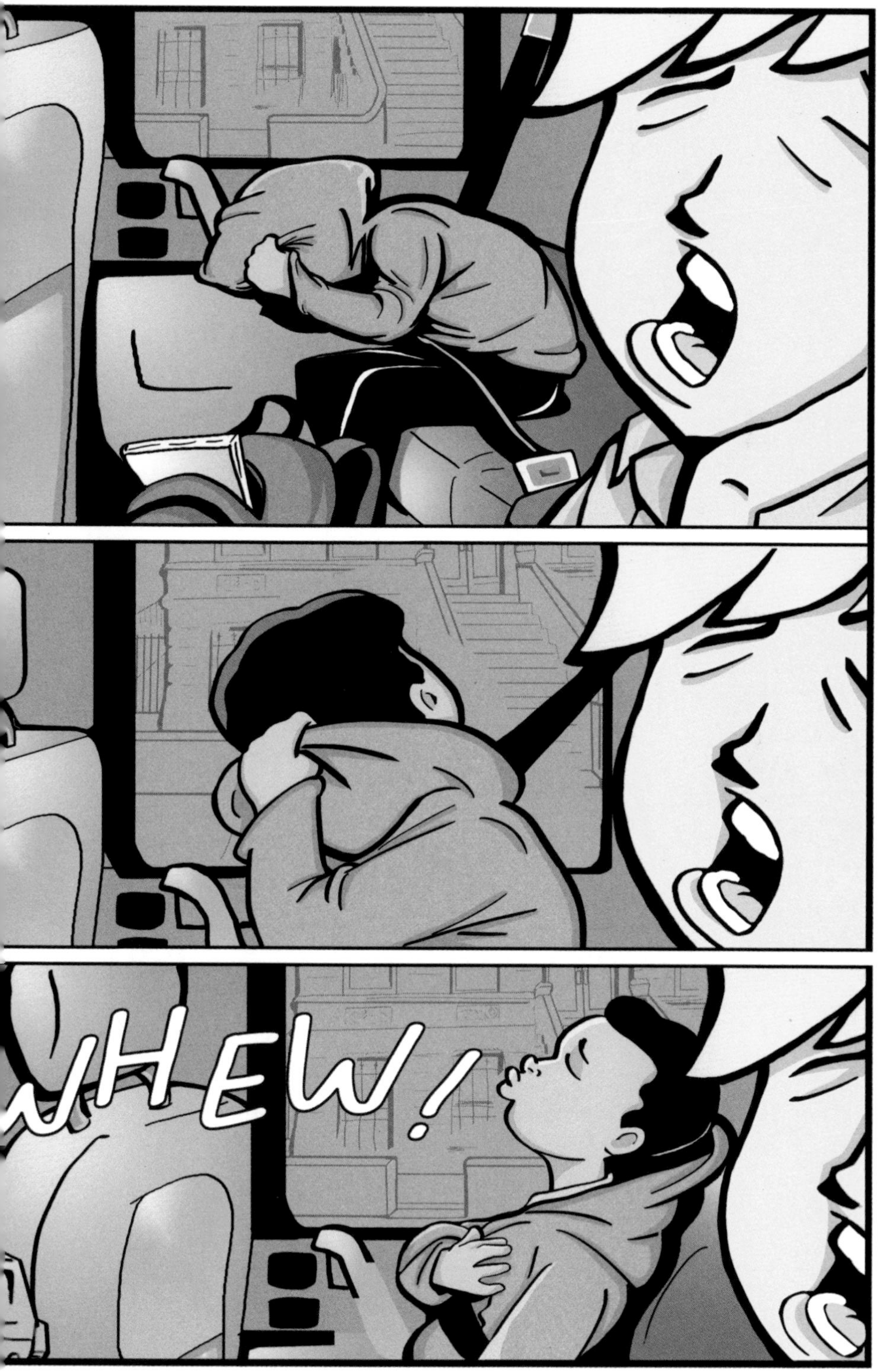
WHEW!

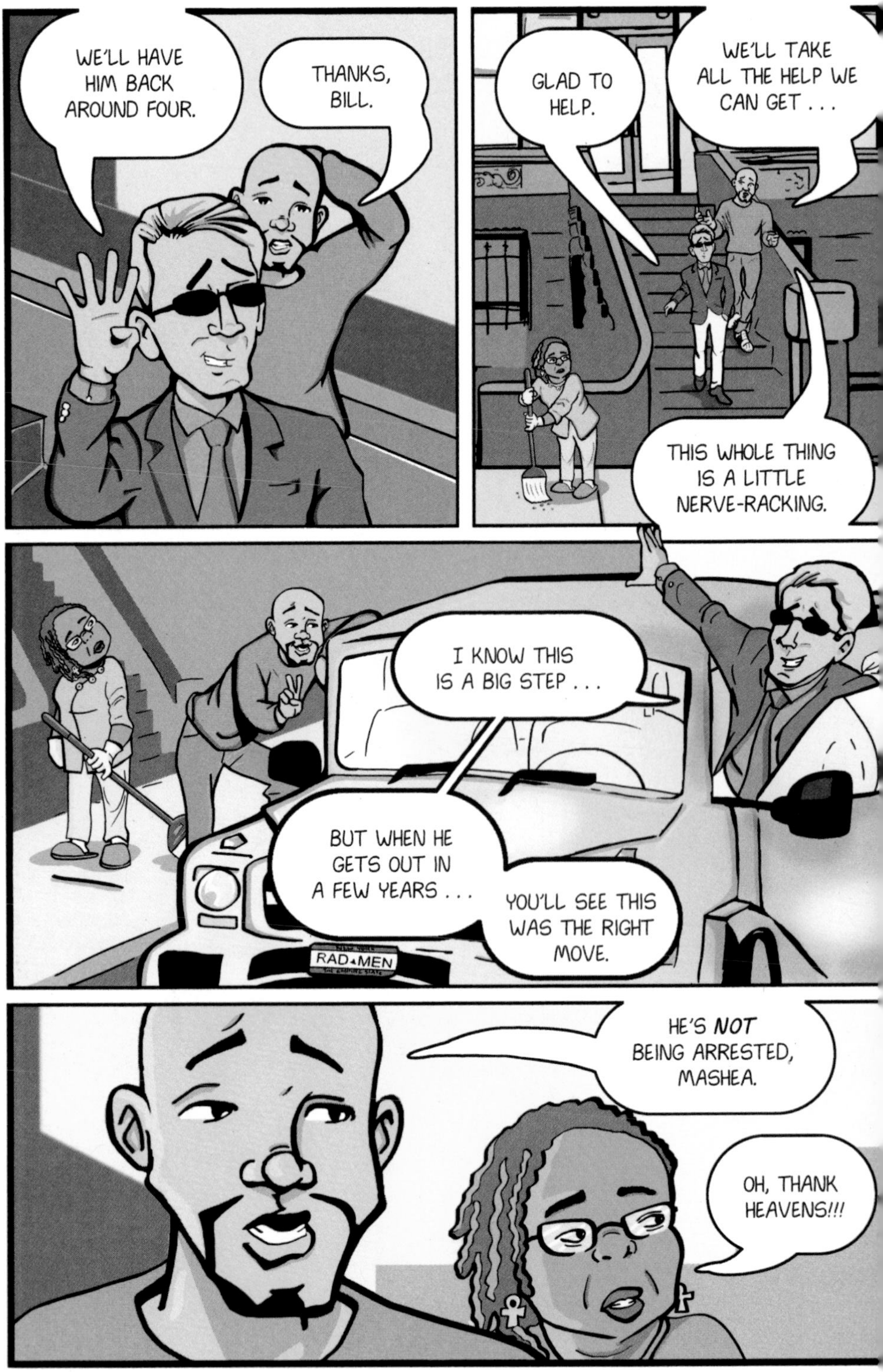
WE'LL HAVE HIM BACK AROUND FOUR.
THANKS, BILL.
GLAD TO HELP.
WE'LL TAKE ALL THE HELP WE CAN GET . . .
THIS WHOLE THING IS A LITTLE NERVE-RACKING.
I KNOW THIS IS A BIG STEP . . .
BUT WHEN HE GETS OUT IN A FEW YEARS . . .
YOU'LL SEE THIS WAS THE RIGHT MOVE.
RAD MEN
HE'S **NOT** BEING ARRESTED, MASHEA.
OH, THANK HEAVENS!!!

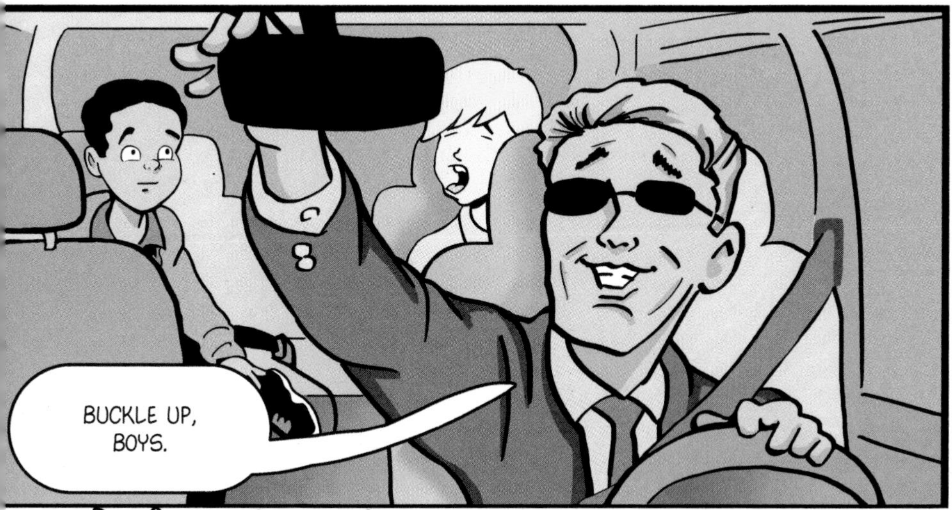
BUCKLE UP, BOYS.

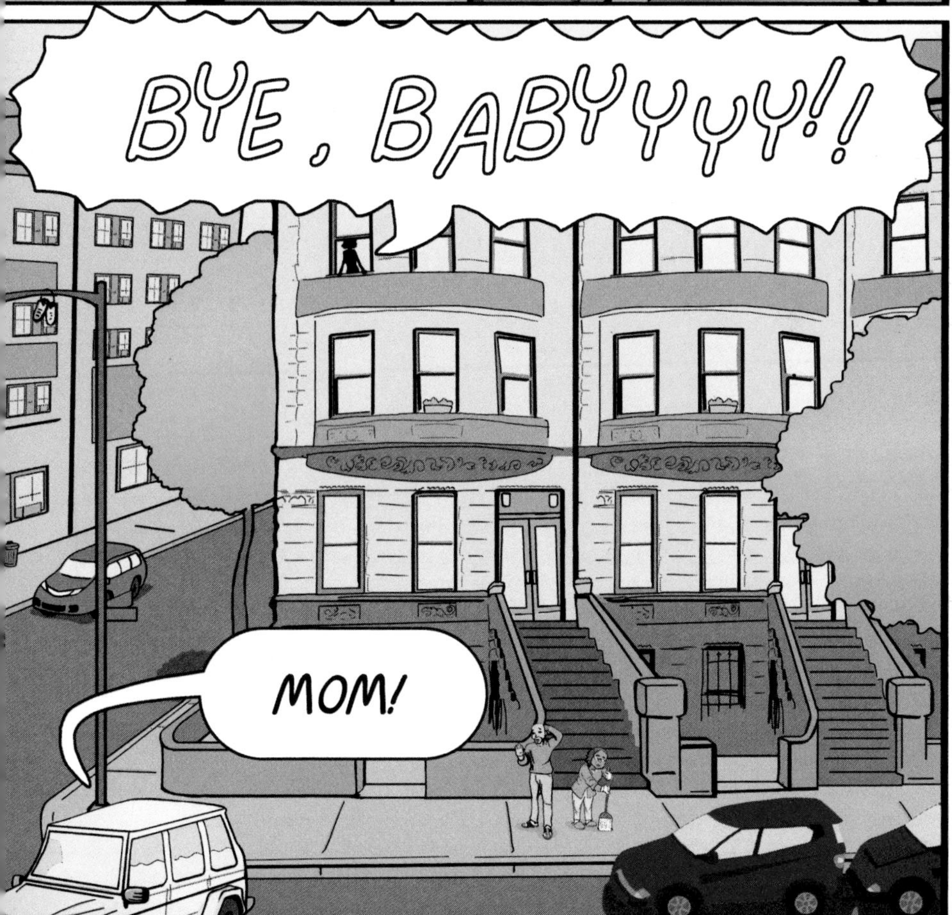
BYE, BABYYYY!!
MOM!

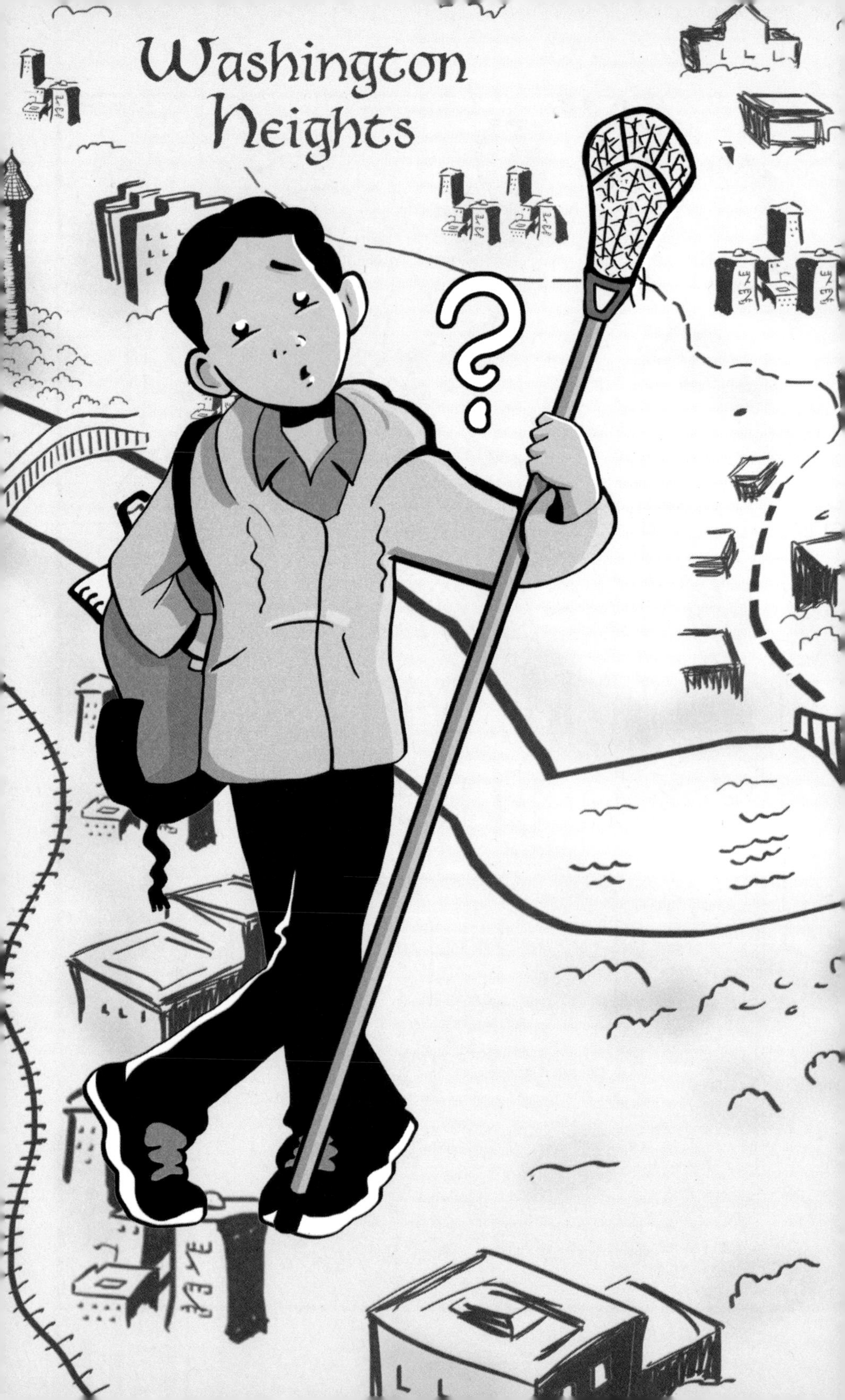
Washington
Heights

Chapter 2

The Road to Riverdale — There and Back Again

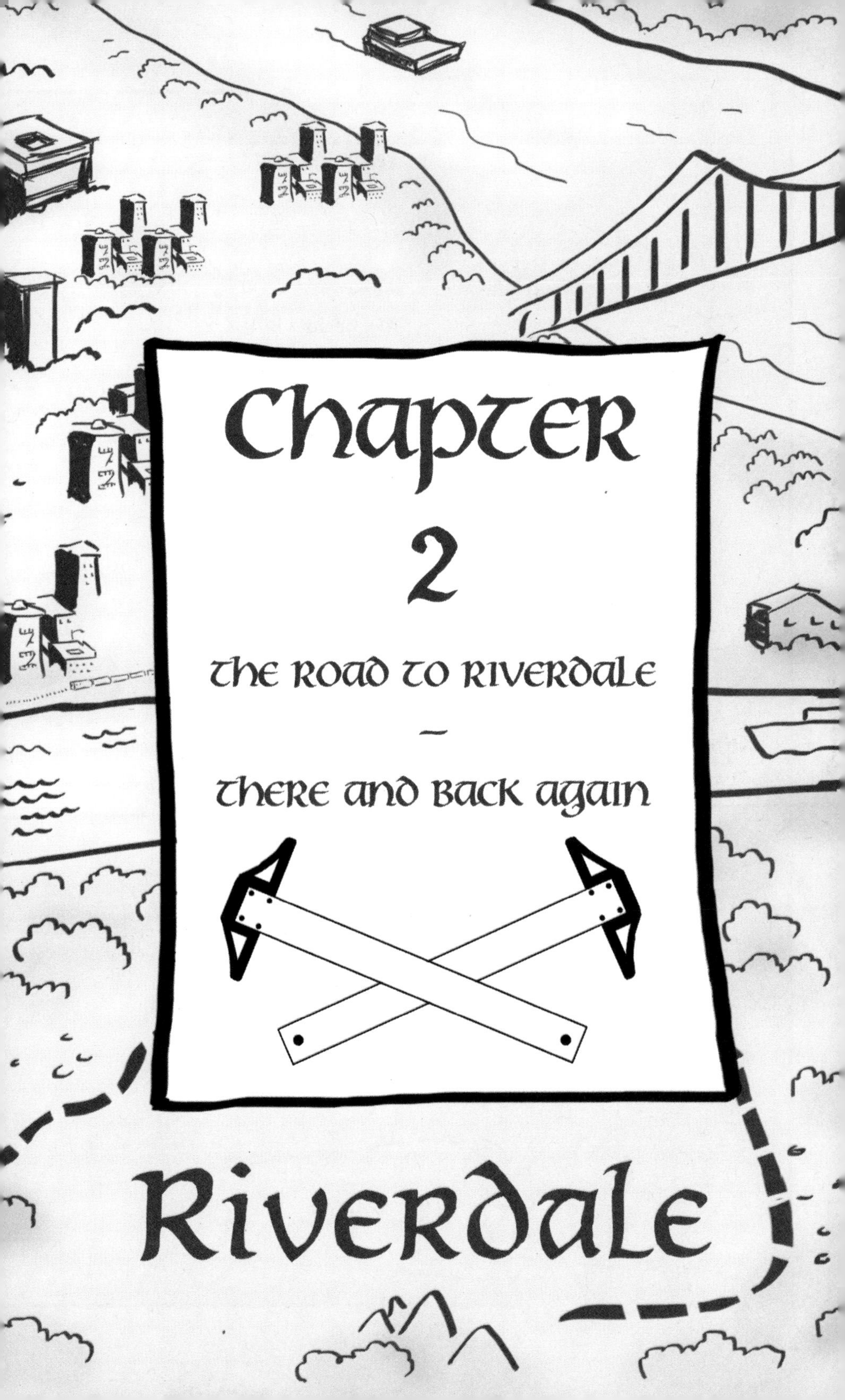
Riverdale

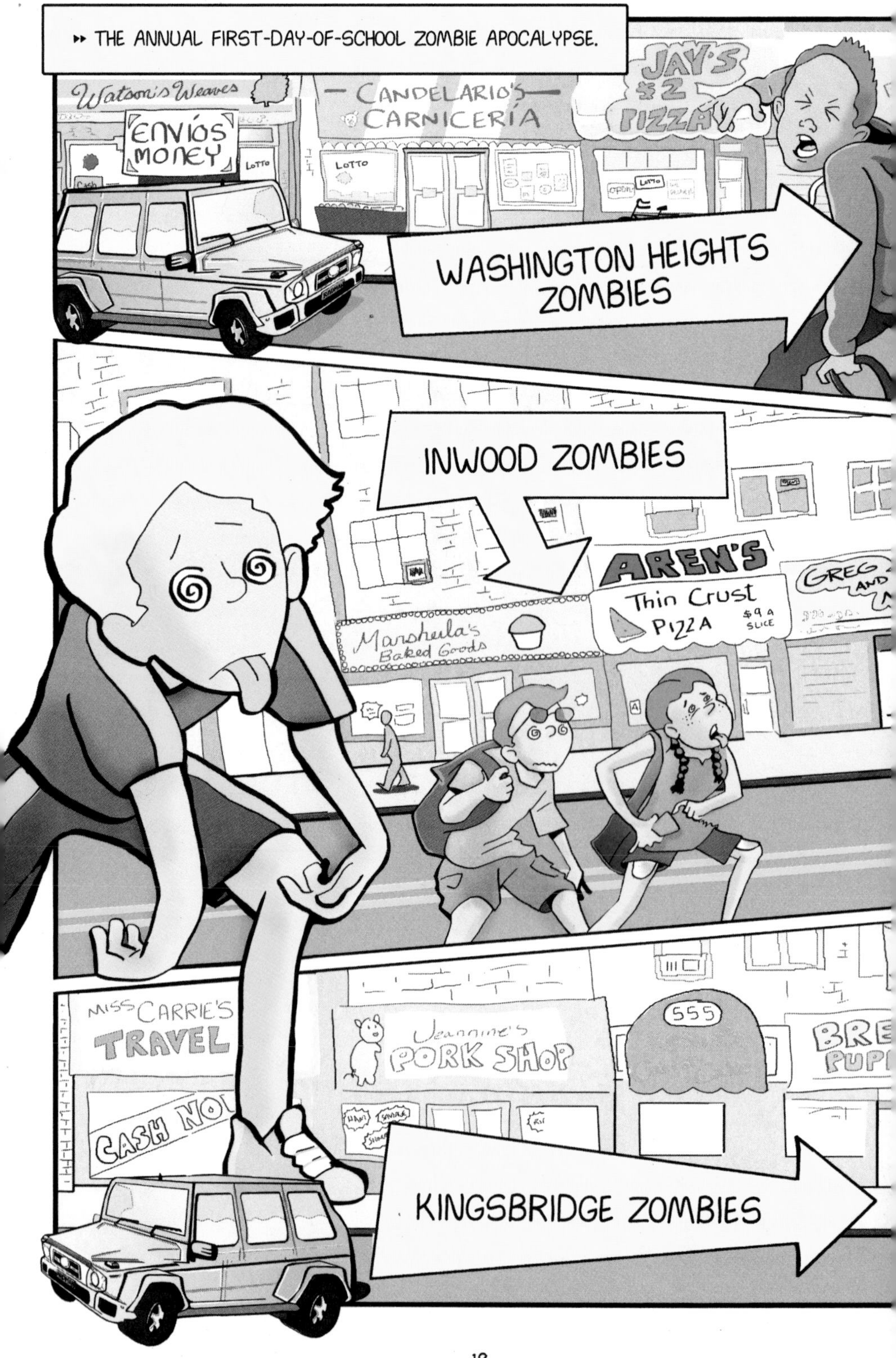
▸▸ THE ANNUAL FIRST-DAY-OF-SCHOOL ZOMBIE APOCALYPSE.
Watson's Weaves
CANDELARIO'S CARNICERÍA
JAY'S $2 PIZZA
ENVÍOS MONEY
LOTTO
LOTTO
WASHINGTON HEIGHTS ZOMBIES
INWOOD ZOMBIES
AREN'S
Thin Crust PIZZA
$9 A SLICE
Marsheila's Baked Goods
MISS CARRIE'S TRAVEL
CASH NOW
Jeannine's PORK SHOP
555
KINGSBRIDGE ZOMBIES

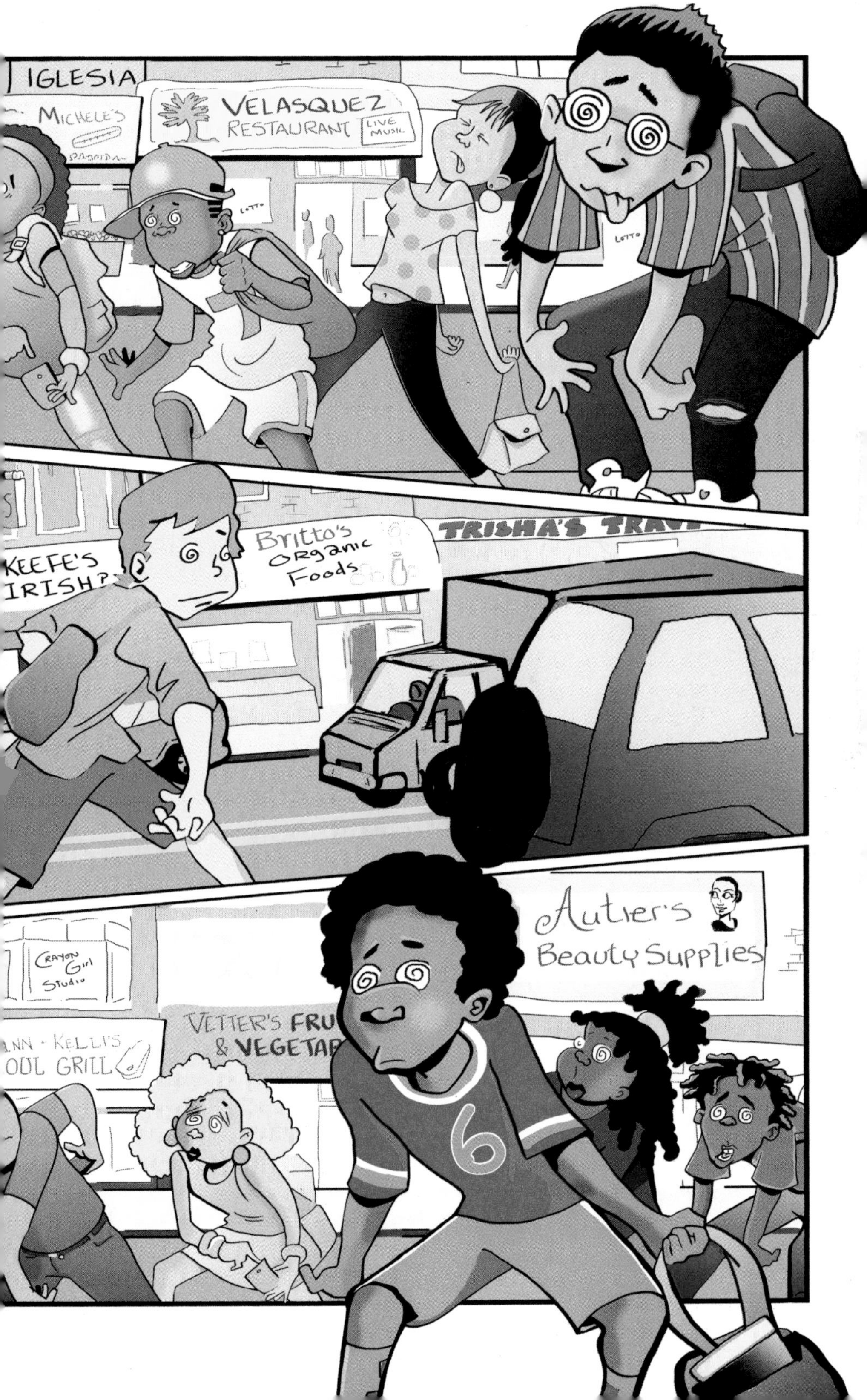
IGLESIA
MICHELE'S
VELASQUEZ RESTAURANT
LIVE MUSIC
LOTTO
LOTTO
KEEFE'S
Britto's Organic Foods
TRISHA'S
Crayon Girl Studio
Autier's Beauty Supplies
VETTER'S
KELLI'S

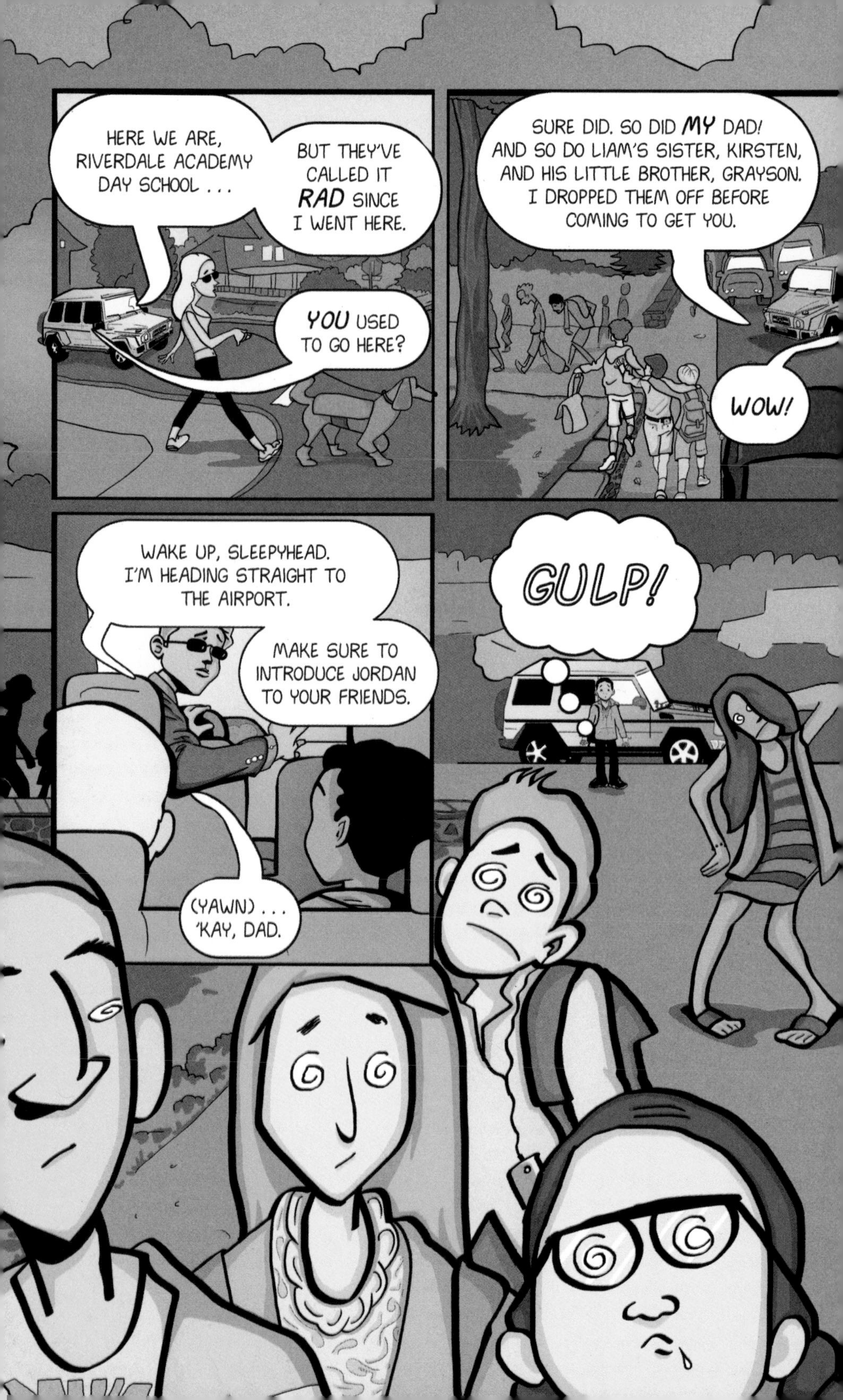
HERE WE ARE, RIVERDALE ACADEMY DAY SCHOOL . . .
BUT THEY'VE CALLED IT **RAD** SINCE I WENT HERE.
YOU USED TO GO HERE?
SURE DID. SO DID ***MY*** DAD! AND SO DO LIAM'S SISTER, KIRSTEN, AND HIS LITTLE BROTHER, GRAYSON. I DROPPED THEM OFF BEFORE COMING TO GET YOU.
WOW!
WAKE UP, SLEEPYHEAD. I'M HEADING STRAIGHT TO THE AIRPORT.
MAKE SURE TO INTRODUCE JORDAN TO YOUR FRIENDS.
(YAWN) . . . 'KAY, DAD.
GULP!

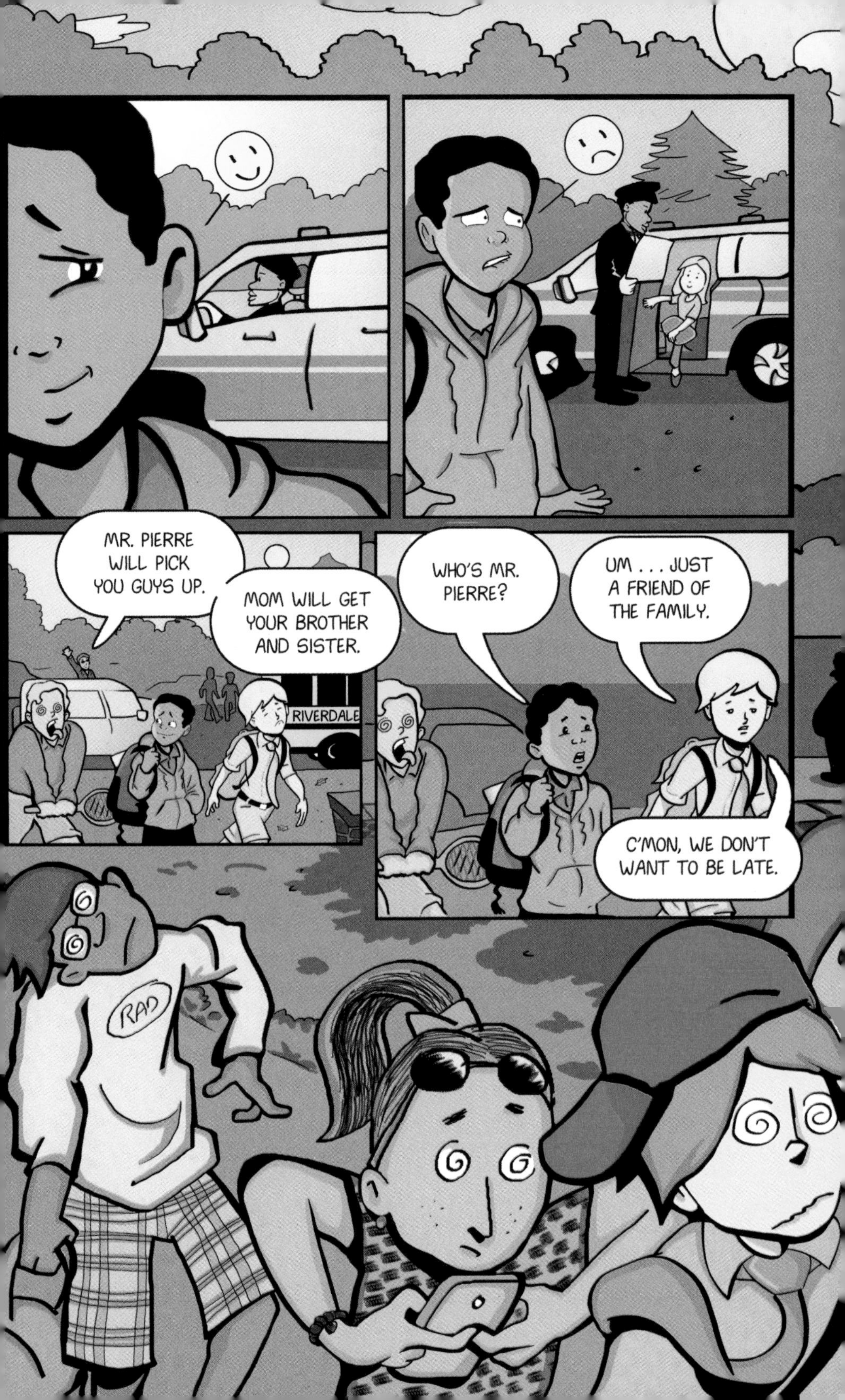
MR. PIERRE WILL PICK YOU GUYS UP.
MOM WILL GET YOUR BROTHER AND SISTER.
RIVERDALE
WHO'S MR. PIERRE?
UM . . . JUST A FRIEND OF THE FAMILY.
C'MON, WE DON'T WANT TO BE LATE.
RAD

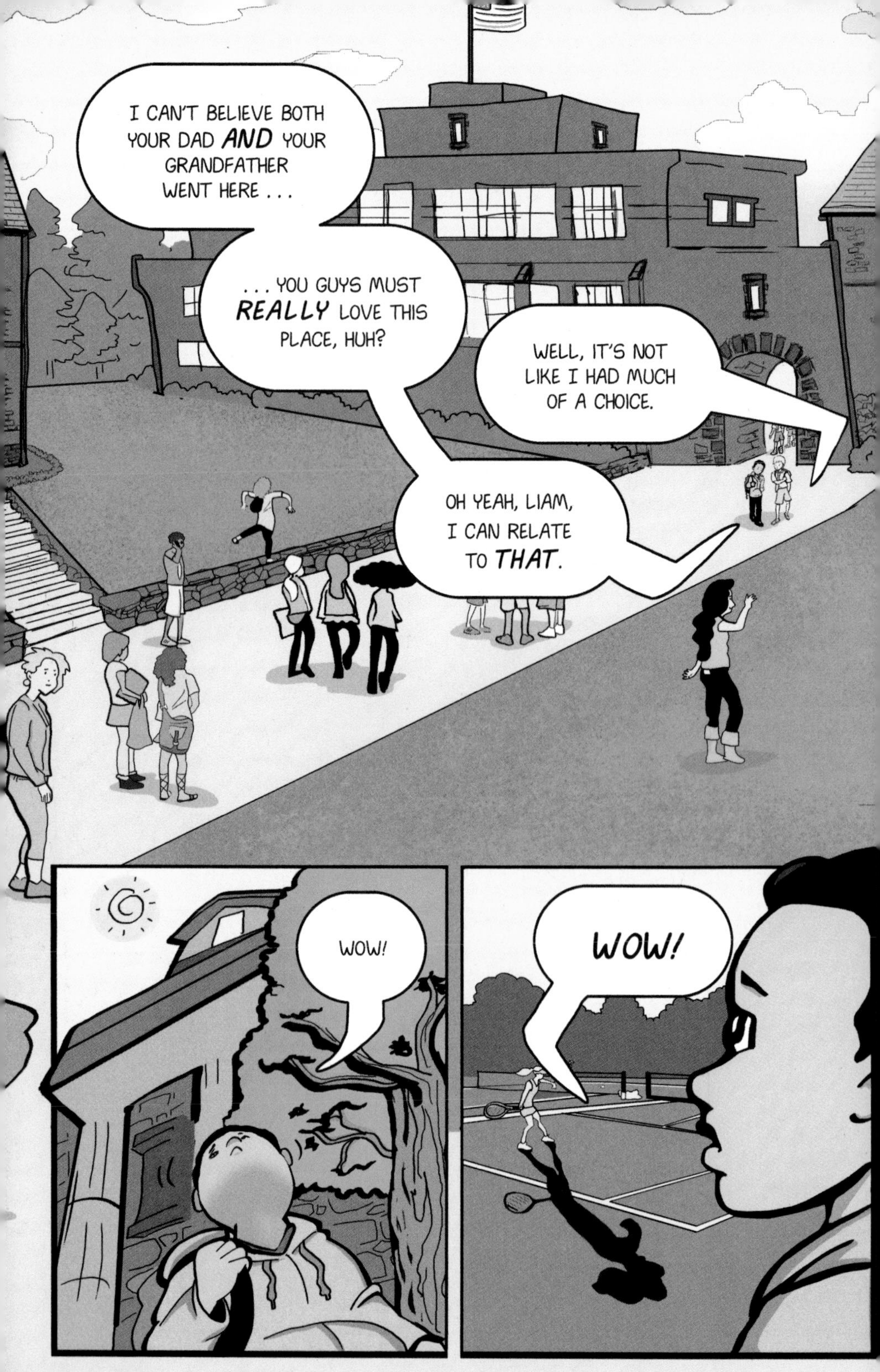
I CAN'T BELIEVE BOTH YOUR DAD AND YOUR GRANDFATHER WENT HERE . . .
. . . YOU GUYS MUST REALLY LOVE THIS PLACE, HUH?
WELL, IT'S NOT LIKE I HAD MUCH OF A CHOICE.
OH YEAH, LIAM, I CAN RELATE TO THAT.
WOW!
WOW!

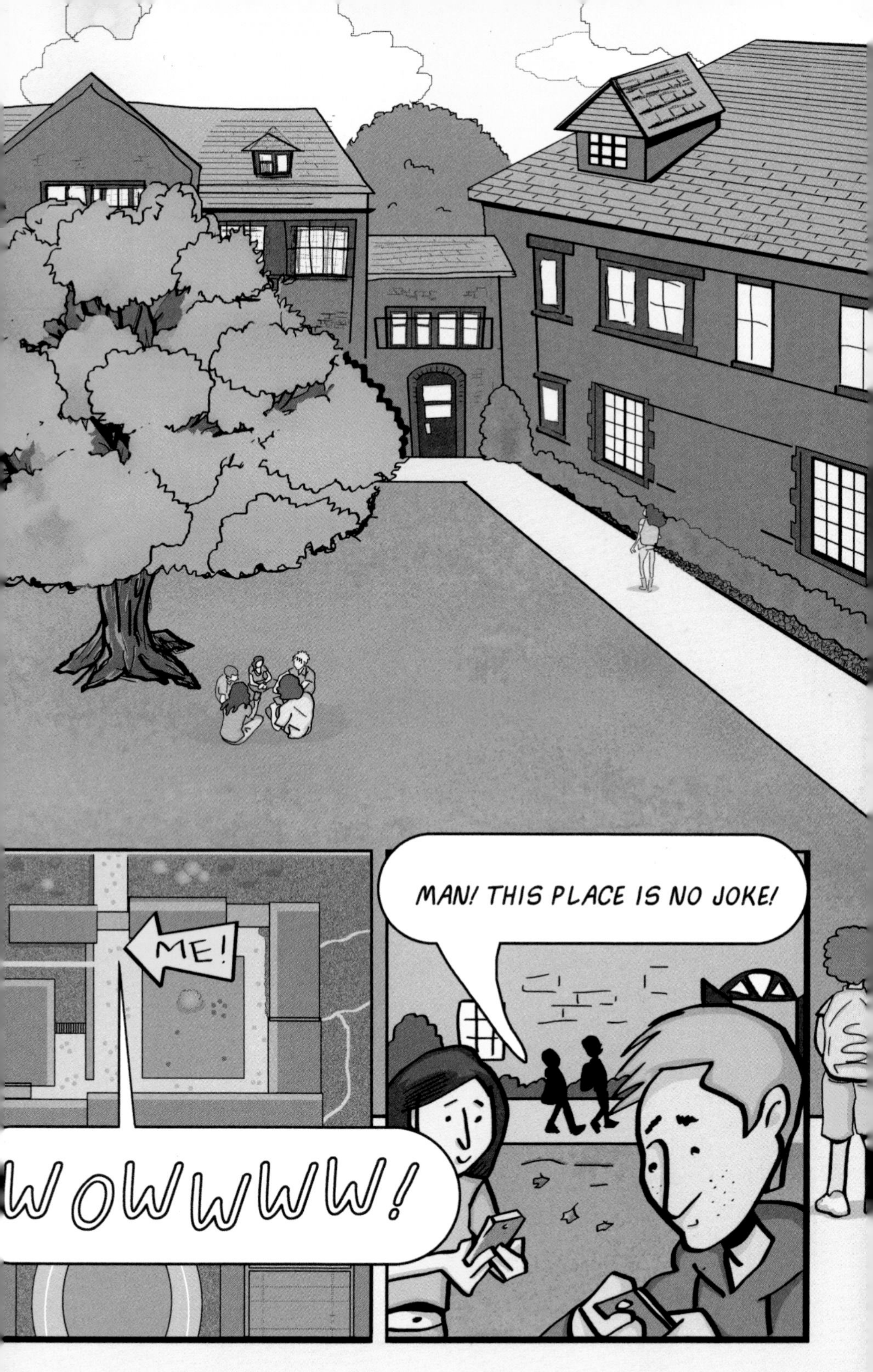
ME!
WOWWWW!
MAN! THIS PLACE IS NO JOKE!

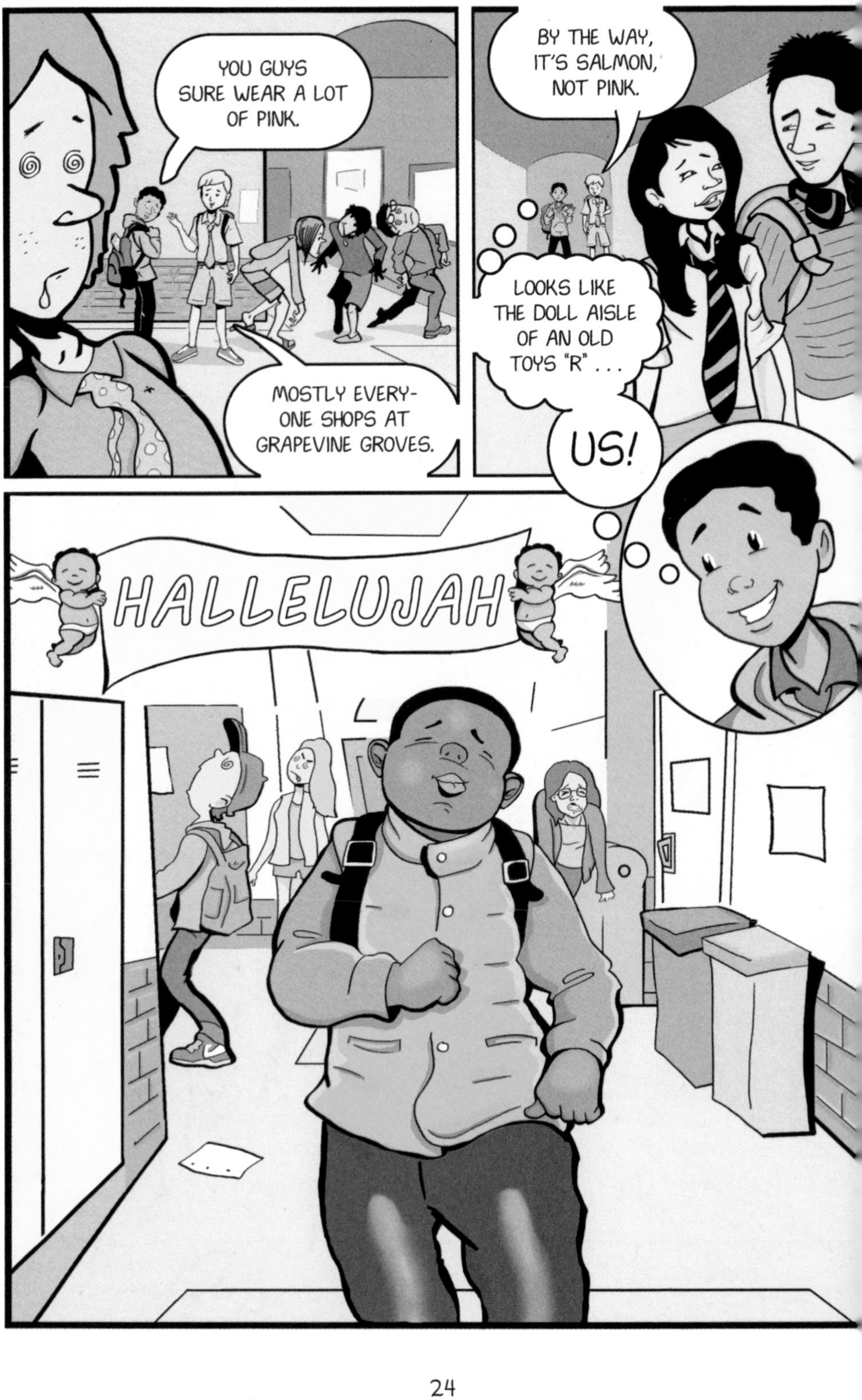
YOU GUYS SURE WEAR A LOT OF PINK.
MOSTLY EVERY-ONE SHOPS AT GRAPEVINE GROVES.
BY THE WAY, IT'S SALMON, NOT PINK.
LOOKS LIKE THE DOLL AISLE OF AN OLD TOYS "R" . . .
US!
HALLELUJAH

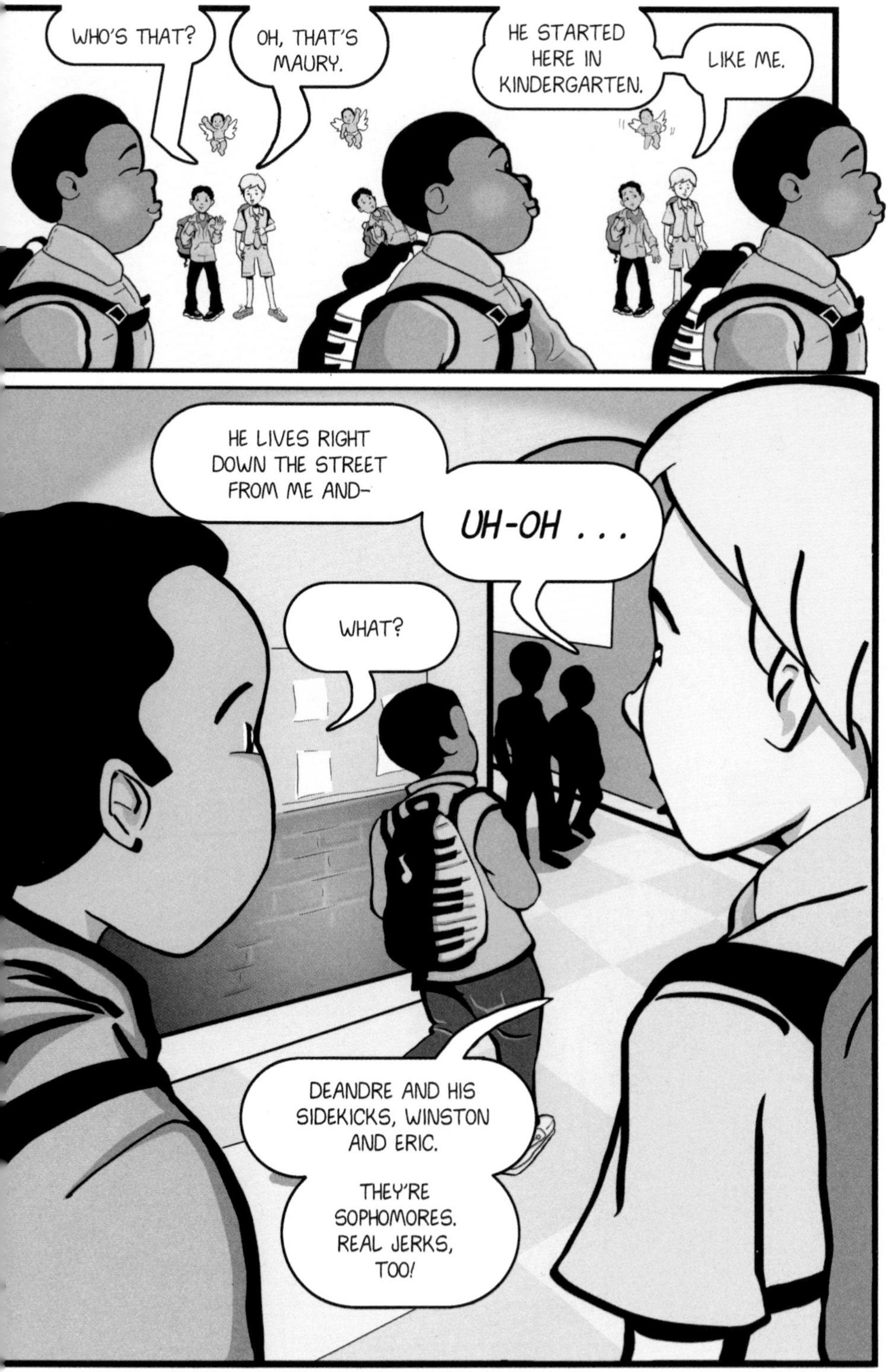
WHO'S THAT?
OH, THAT'S MAURY.
HE STARTED HERE IN KINDERGARTEN.
LIKE ME.
HE LIVES RIGHT DOWN THE STREET FROM ME AND-
UH-OH . . .
WHAT?
DEANDRE AND HIS SIDEKICKS, WINSTON AND ERIC.
THEY'RE SOPHOMORES. REAL JERKS, TOO!

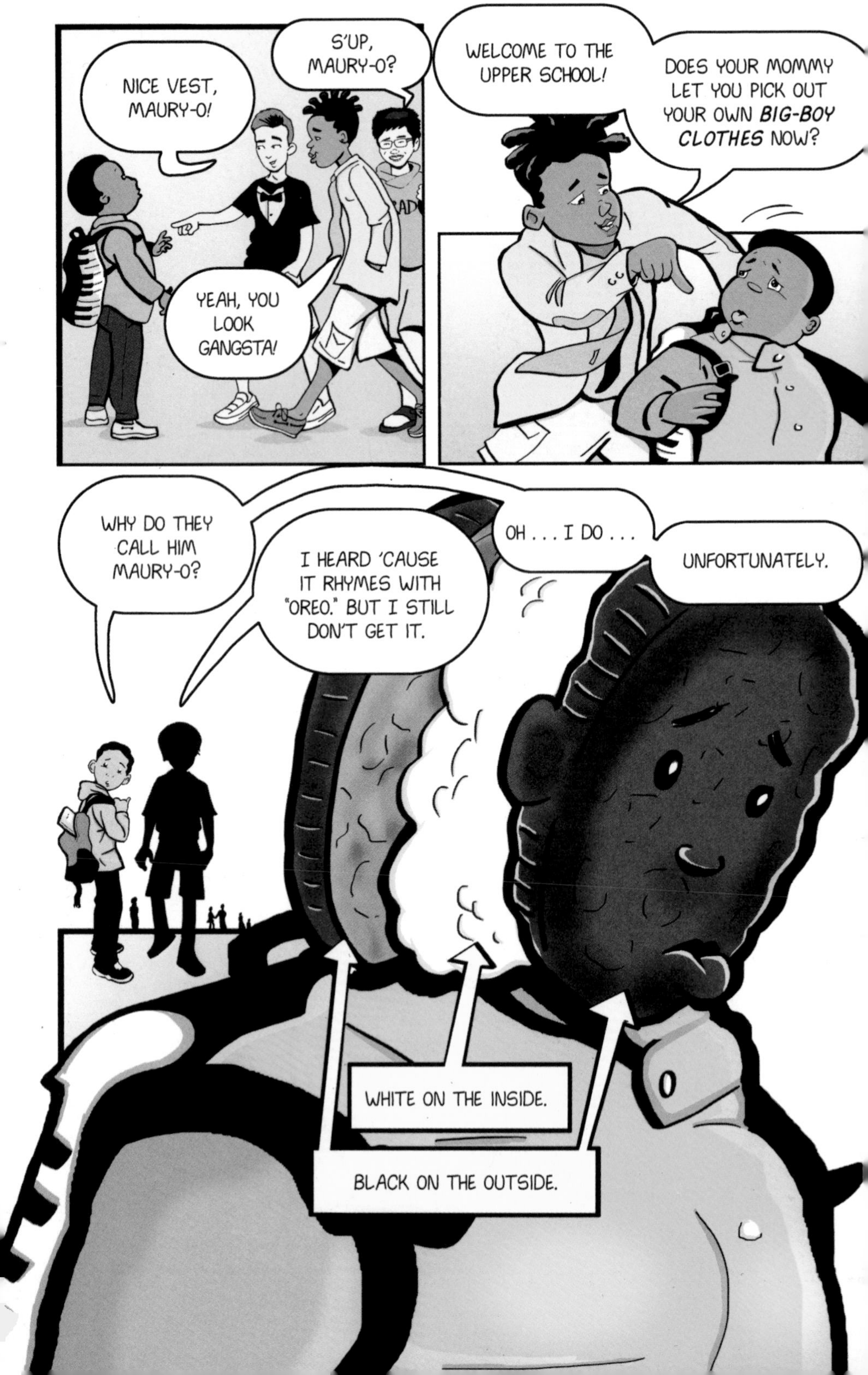
NICE VEST, MAURY-O!
S'UP, MAURY-O?
YEAH, YOU LOOK GANGSTA!
WELCOME TO THE UPPER SCHOOL!
DOES YOUR MOMMY LET YOU PICK OUT YOUR OWN BIG-BOY CLOTHES NOW?
WHY DO THEY CALL HIM MAURY-O?
I HEARD 'CAUSE IT RHYMES WITH "OREO." BUT I STILL DON'T GET IT.
OH . . . I DO . . .
UNFORTUNATELY.
WHITE ON THE INSIDE.
BLACK ON THE OUTSIDE.

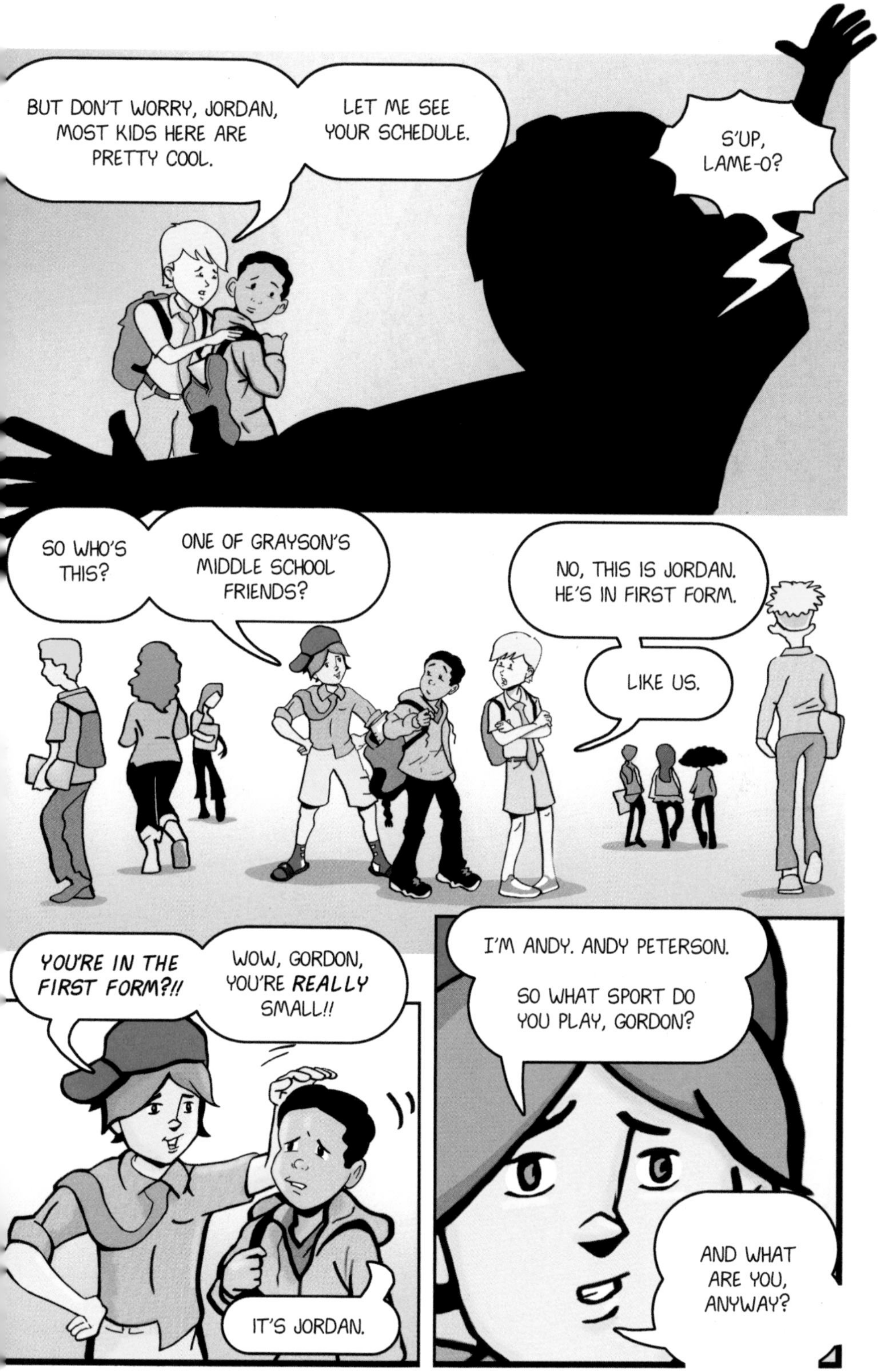
BUT DON'T WORRY, JORDAN, MOST KIDS HERE ARE PRETTY COOL.
LET ME SEE YOUR SCHEDULE.
S'UP, LAME-O?
SO WHO'S THIS?
ONE OF GRAYSON'S MIDDLE SCHOOL FRIENDS?
NO, THIS IS JORDAN. HE'S IN FIRST FORM.
LIKE US.
YOU'RE IN THE FIRST FORM?!!
WOW, GORDON, YOU'RE ***REALLY*** SMALL!!
IT'S JORDAN.
I'M ANDY. ANDY PETERSON.
SO WHAT SPORT DO YOU PLAY, GORDON?
AND WHAT ARE YOU, ANYWAY?

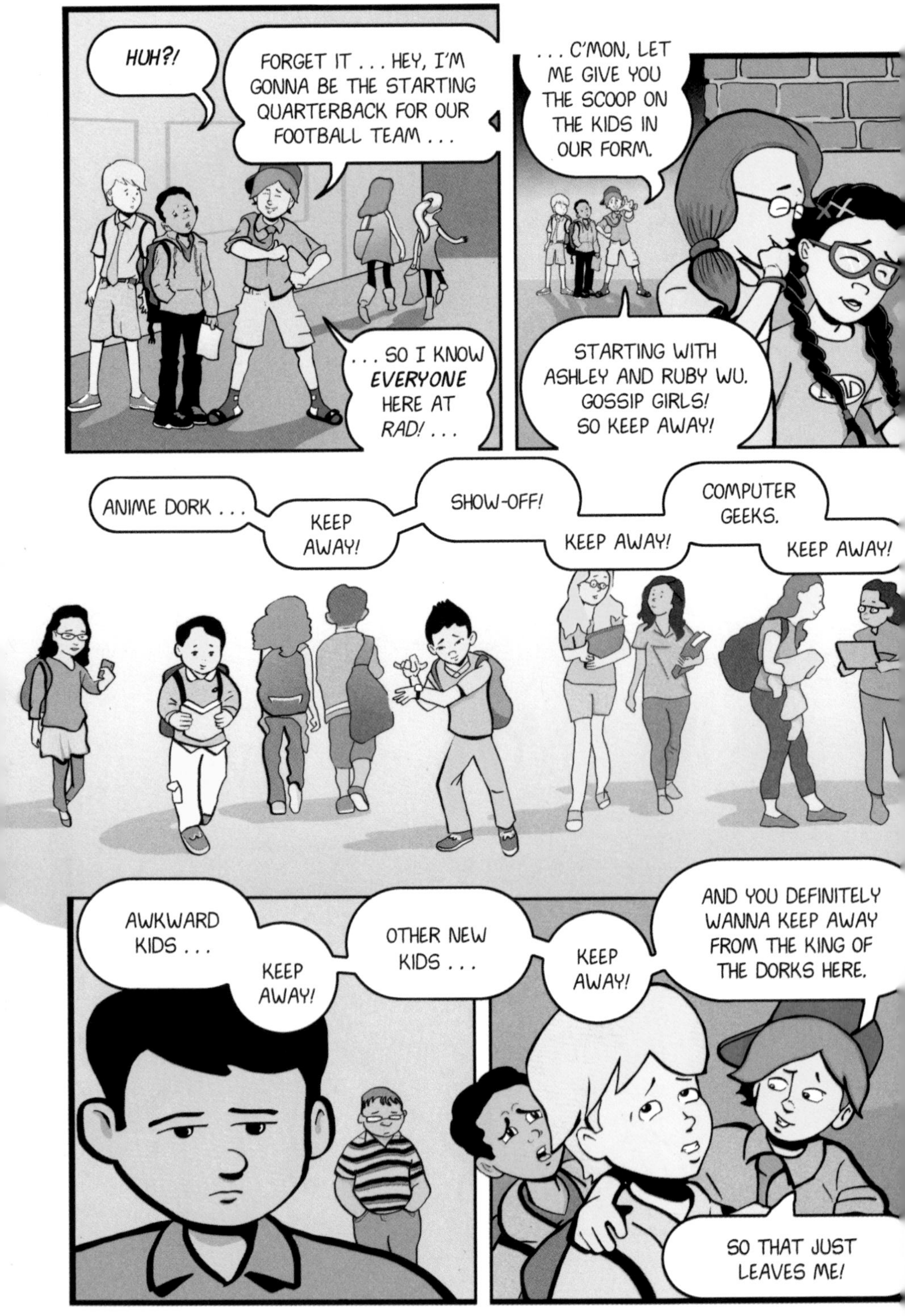
HUH?!
FORGET IT . . . HEY, I'M GONNA BE THE STARTING QUARTERBACK FOR OUR FOOTBALL TEAM . . .
. . . SO I KNOW EVERYONE HERE AT RAD! . . .
. . . C'MON, LET ME GIVE YOU THE SCOOP ON THE KIDS IN OUR FORM.
STARTING WITH ASHLEY AND RUBY WU. GOSSIP GIRLS! SO KEEP AWAY!
ANIME DORK . . .
KEEP AWAY!
SHOW-OFF!
KEEP AWAY!
COMPUTER GEEKS.
KEEP AWAY!
AWKWARD KIDS . . .
KEEP AWAY!
OTHER NEW KIDS . . .
KEEP AWAY!
AND YOU DEFINITELY WANNA KEEP AWAY FROM THE KING OF THE DORKS HERE.
SO THAT JUST LEAVES ME!

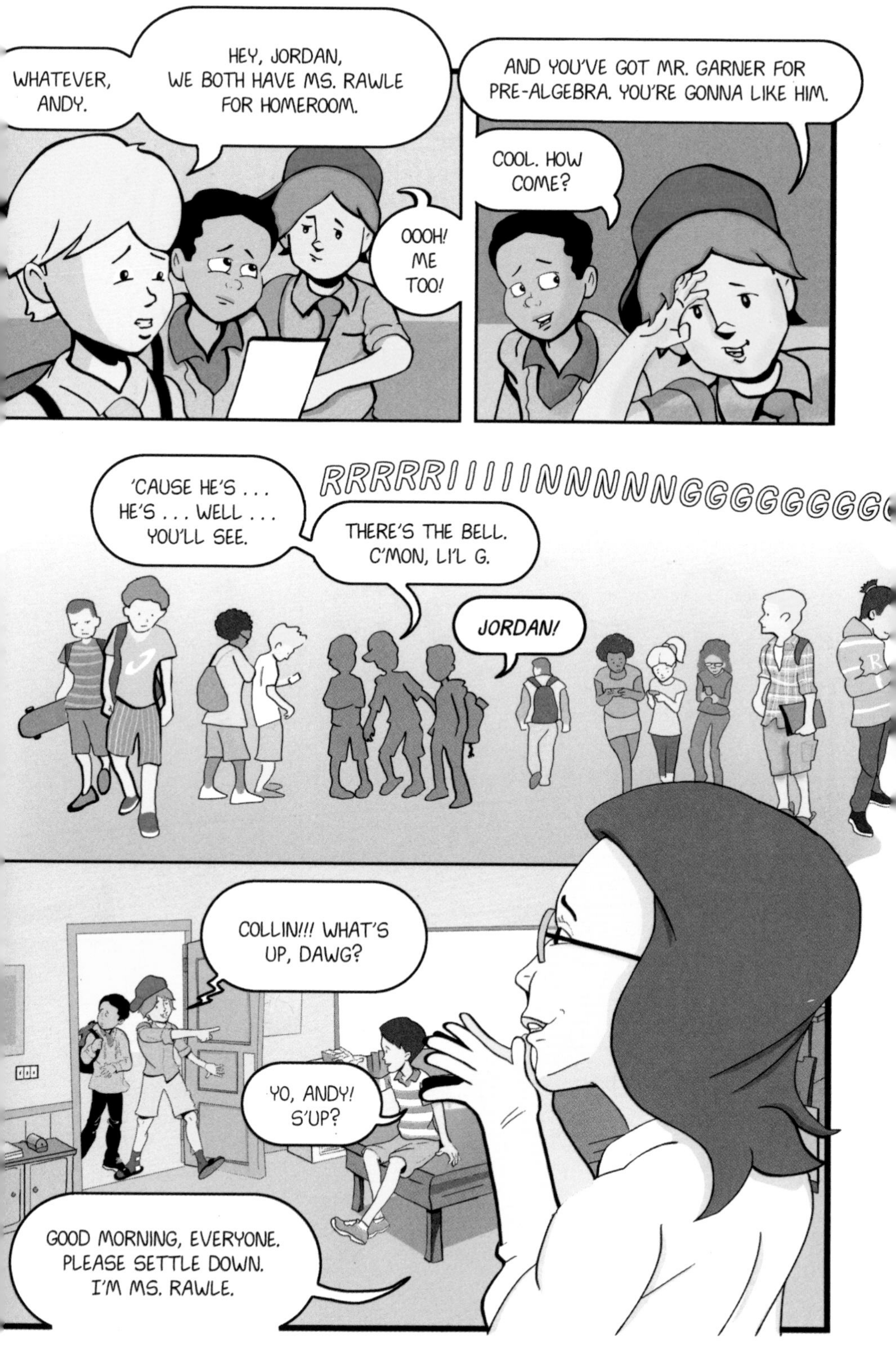
WHATEVER, ANDY.
HEY, JORDAN, WE BOTH HAVE MS. RAWLE FOR HOMEROOM.
OOOH! ME TOO!
AND YOU'VE GOT MR. GARNER FOR PRE-ALGEBRA. YOU'RE GONNA LIKE HIM.
COOL. HOW COME?
'CAUSE HE'S . . . HE'S . . . WELL . . . YOU'LL SEE.
RRRRRIIIIINNNNNGGGGGGGG
THERE'S THE BELL. C'MON, LI'L G.
JORDAN!
COLLIN!!! WHAT'S UP, DAWG?
YO, ANDY! S'UP?
GOOD MORNING, EVERYONE. PLEASE SETTLE DOWN. I'M MS. RAWLE.

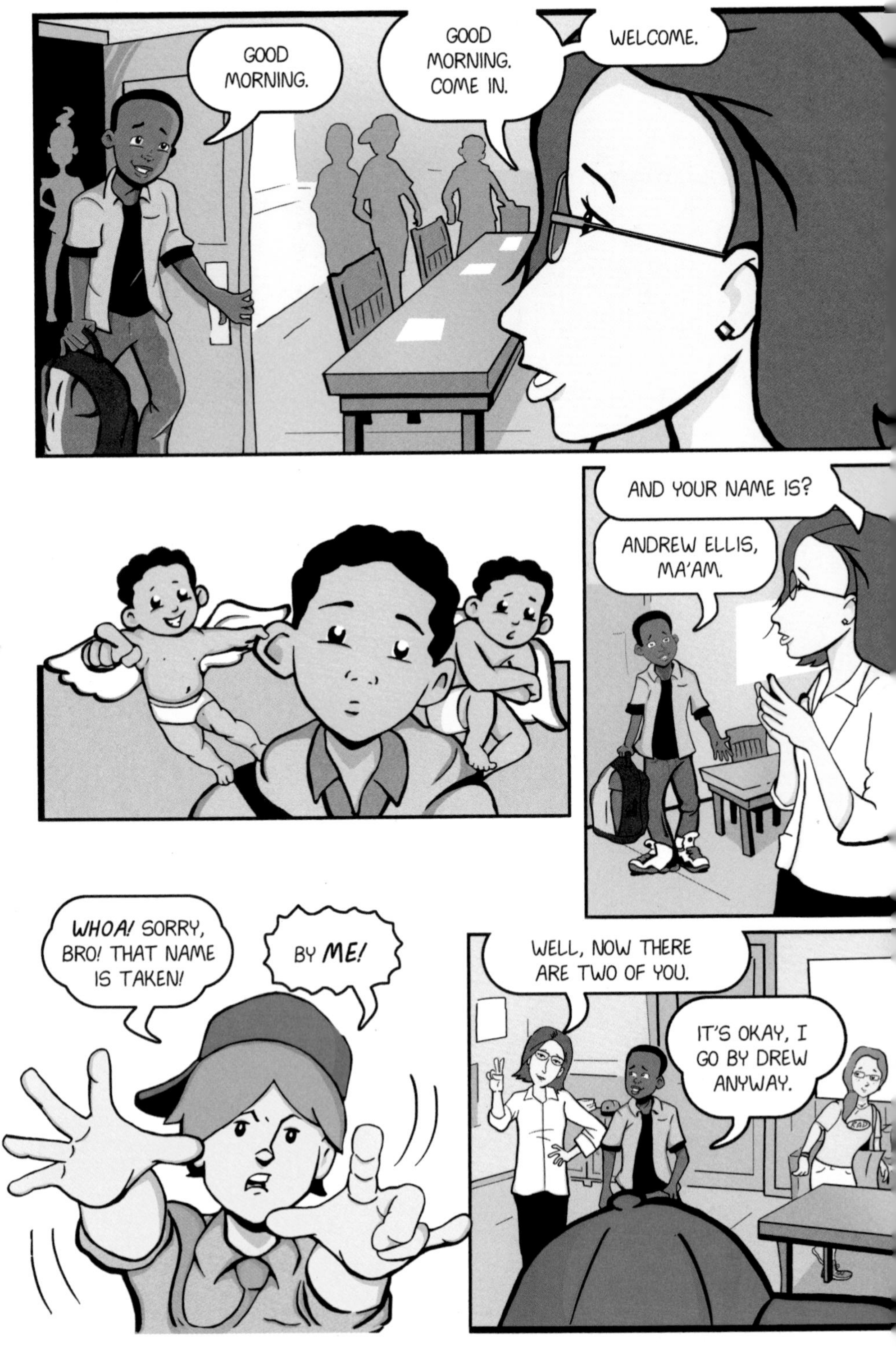
GOOD MORNING.
GOOD MORNING. COME IN.
WELCOME.
AND YOUR NAME IS?
ANDREW ELLIS, MA'AM.
WHOA! SORRY, BRO! THAT NAME IS TAKEN!
BY ME!
WELL, NOW THERE ARE TWO OF YOU.
IT'S OKAY, I GO BY DREW ANYWAY.

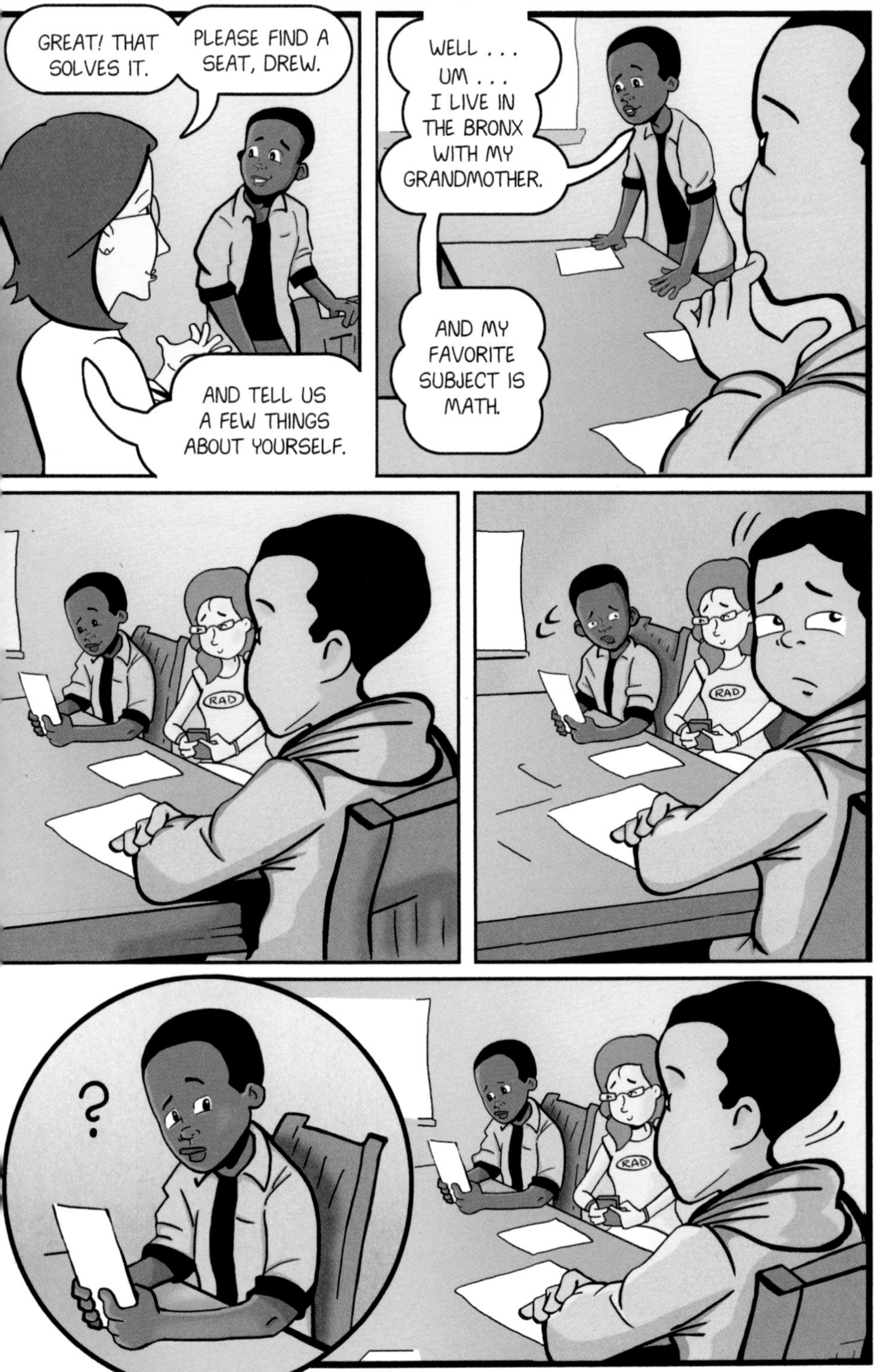
GREAT! THAT SOLVES IT.
PLEASE FIND A SEAT, DREW.
AND TELL US A FEW THINGS ABOUT YOURSELF.
WELL . . . UM . . . I LIVE IN THE BRONX WITH MY GRANDMOTHER.
AND MY FAVORITE SUBJECT IS MATH.
RAD
RAD
RAD
?

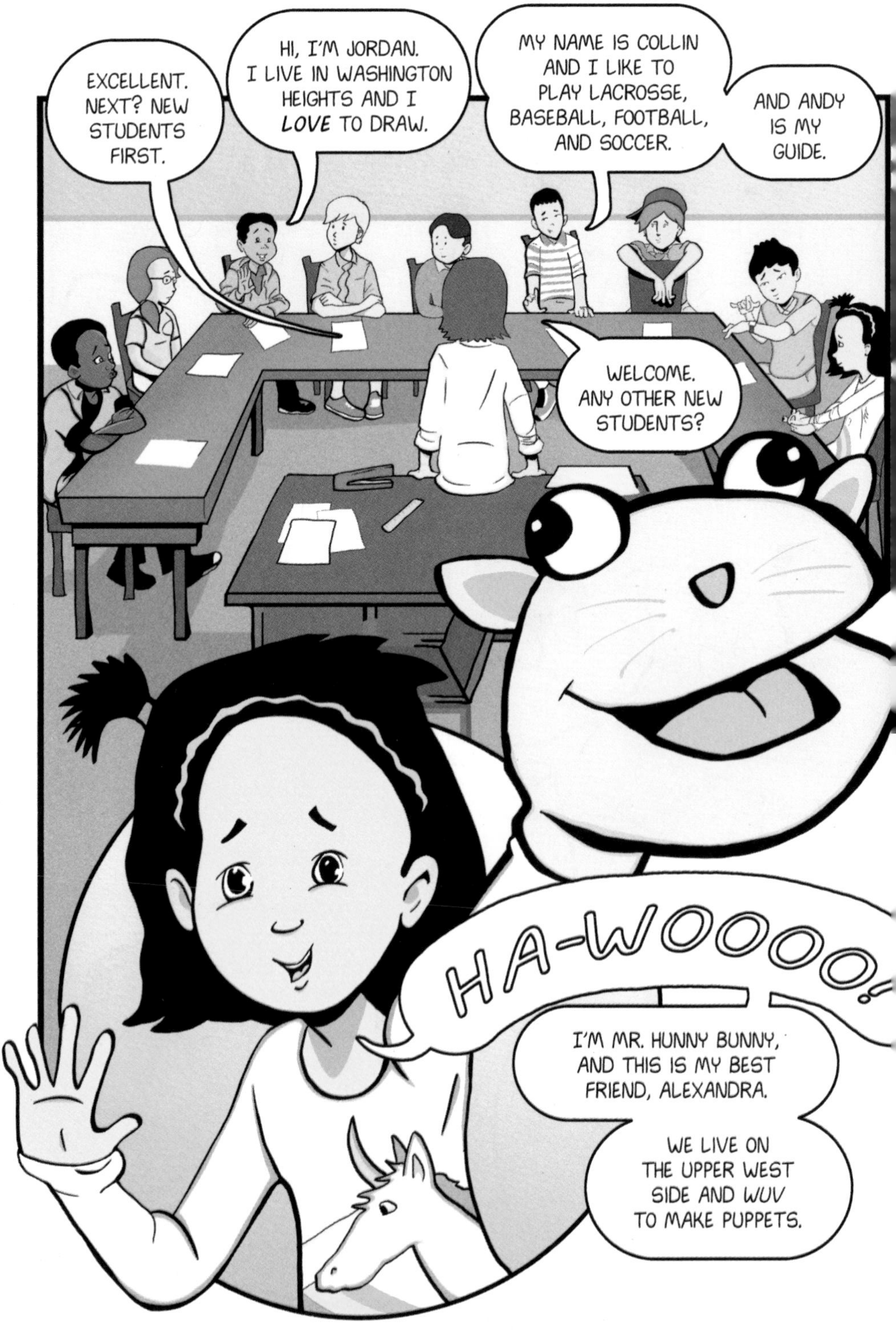
EXCELLENT. NEXT? NEW STUDENTS FIRST.
HI, I'M JORDAN. I LIVE IN WASHINGTON HEIGHTS AND I LOVE TO DRAW.
MY NAME IS COLLIN AND I LIKE TO PLAY LACROSSE, BASEBALL, FOOTBALL, AND SOCCER.
AND ANDY IS MY GUIDE.
WELCOME. ANY OTHER NEW STUDENTS?
HA-WOOOO!
I'M MR. HUNNY BUNNY, AND THIS IS MY BEST FRIEND, ALEXANDRA.
WE LIVE ON THE UPPER WEST SIDE AND WUV TO MAKE PUPPETS.

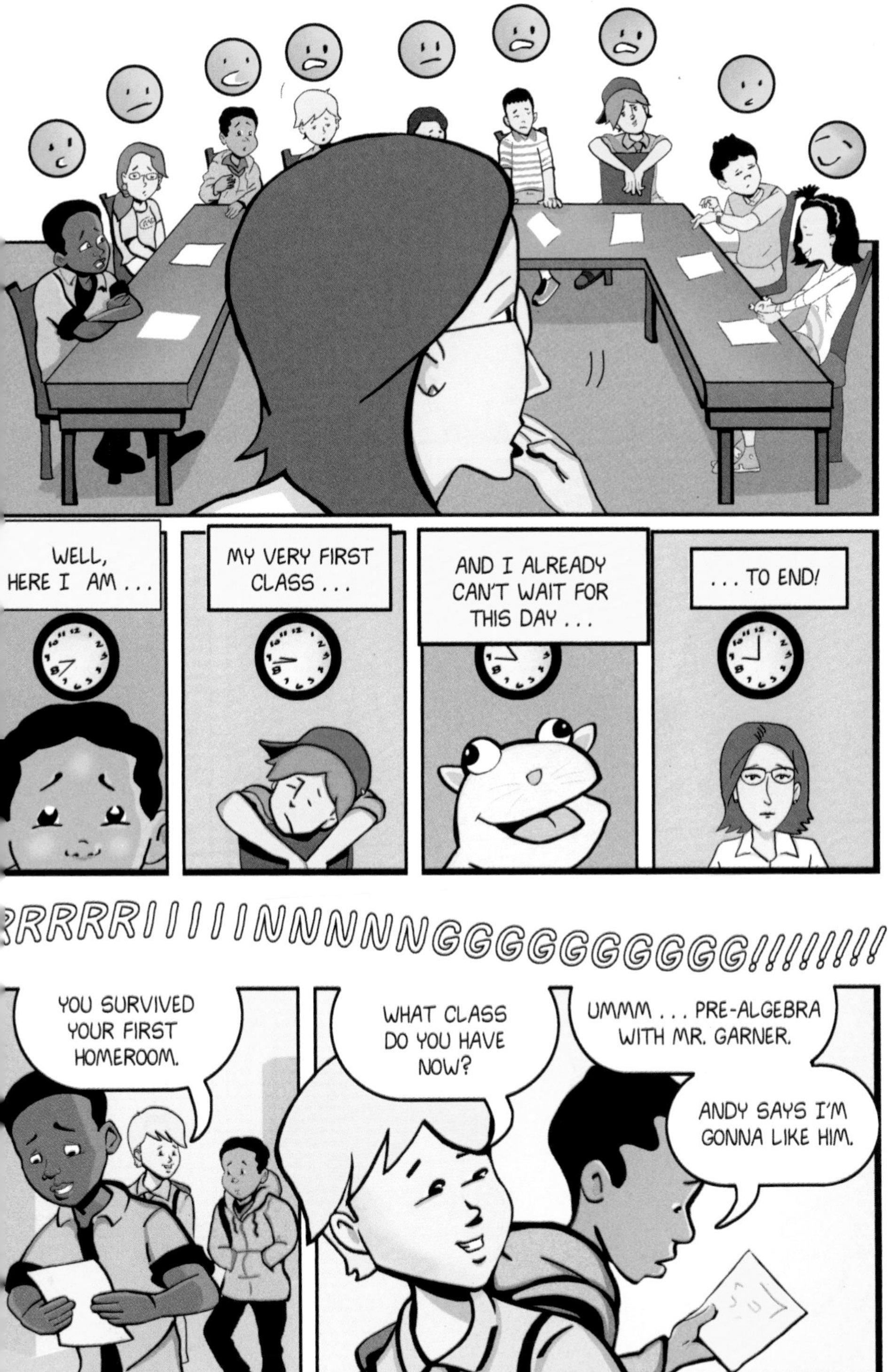

WELL, HERE I AM . . .
MY VERY FIRST CLASS . . .
AND I ALREADY CAN'T WAIT FOR THIS DAY . . .
. . . TO END!
RRRRRIIIIINNNNNNGGGGGGGGGG!!!!!!!!
YOU SURVIVED YOUR FIRST HOMEROOM.
WHAT CLASS DO YOU HAVE NOW?
UMMM . . . PRE-ALGEBRA WITH MR. GARNER.
ANDY SAYS I'M GONNA LIKE HIM.

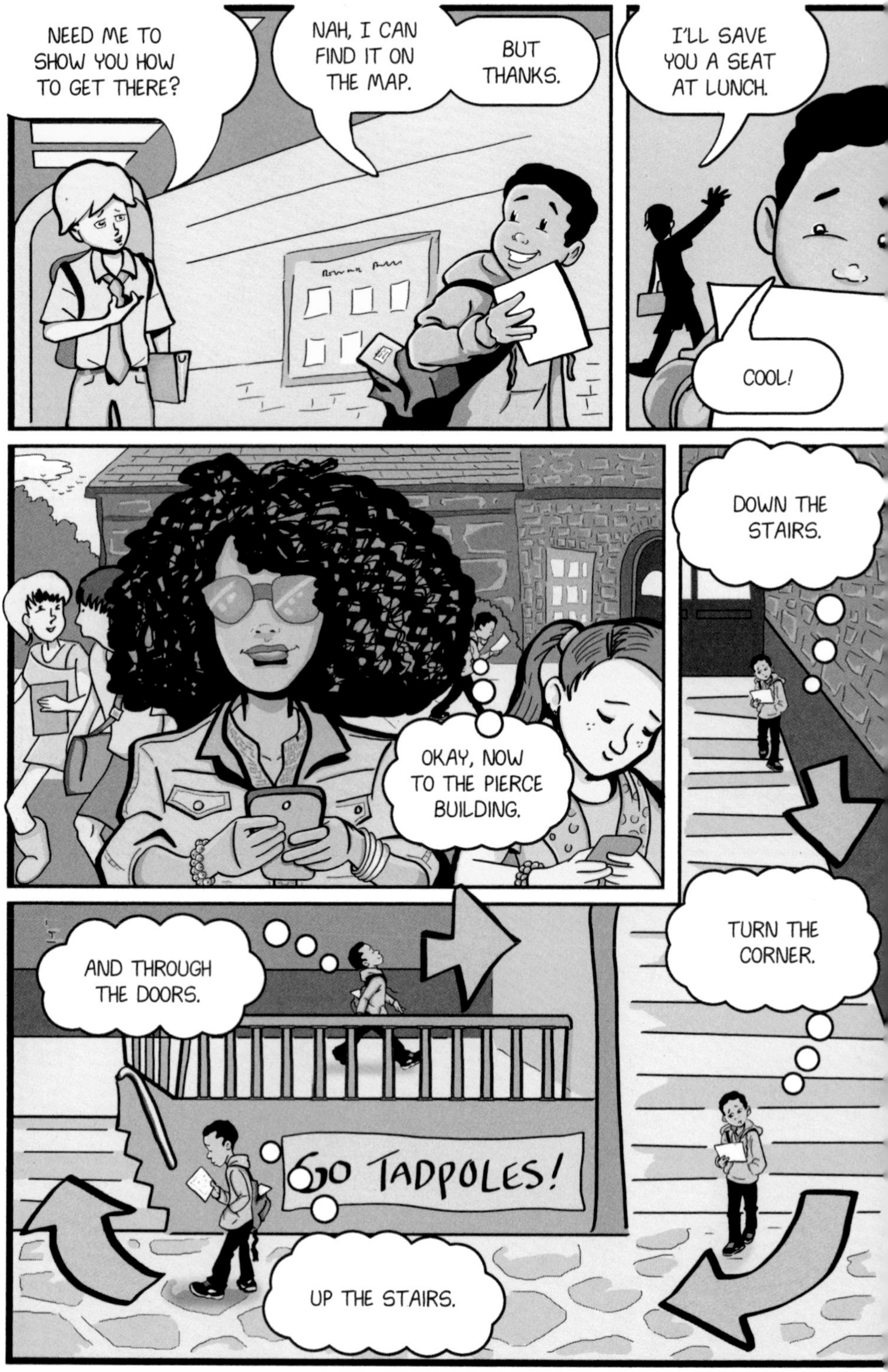
NEED ME TO SHOW YOU HOW TO GET THERE?
NAH, I CAN FIND IT ON THE MAP.
BUT THANKS.
I'LL SAVE YOU A SEAT AT LUNCH.
COOL!
OKAY, NOW TO THE PIERCE BUILDING.
DOWN THE STAIRS.
TURN THE CORNER.
AND THROUGH THE DOORS.
GO TADPOLES!
UP THE STAIRS.

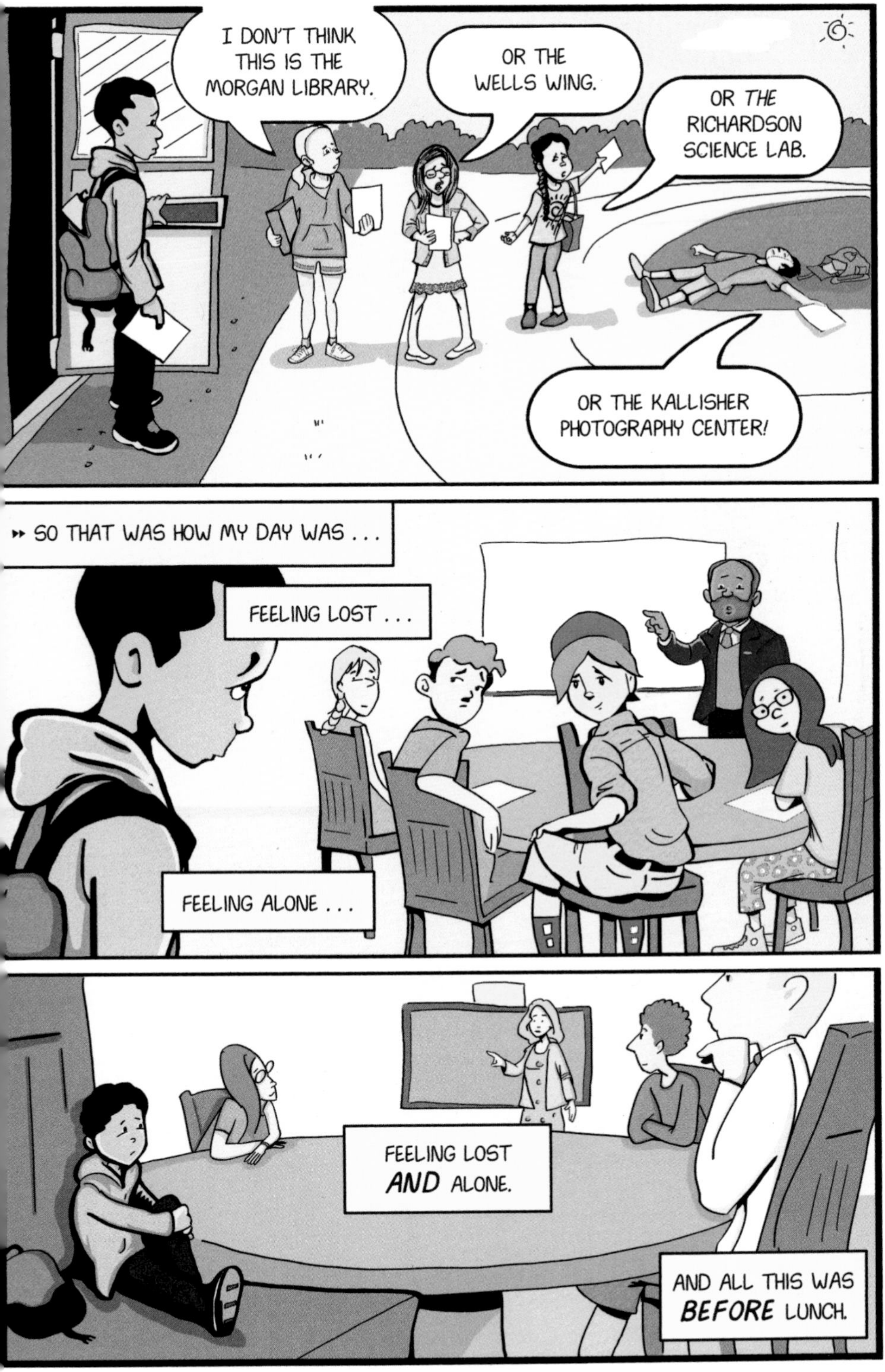
I DON'T THINK THIS IS THE MORGAN LIBRARY.
OR THE WELLS WING.
OR THE RICHARDSON SCIENCE LAB.
OR THE KALLISHER PHOTOGRAPHY CENTER!
SO THAT WAS HOW MY DAY WAS . . .
FEELING LOST . . .
FEELING ALONE . . .
FEELING LOST AND ALONE.
AND ALL THIS WAS BEFORE LUNCH.

CHAPTER 3

THE HUNGRY GAMES: STOP MOCKING J

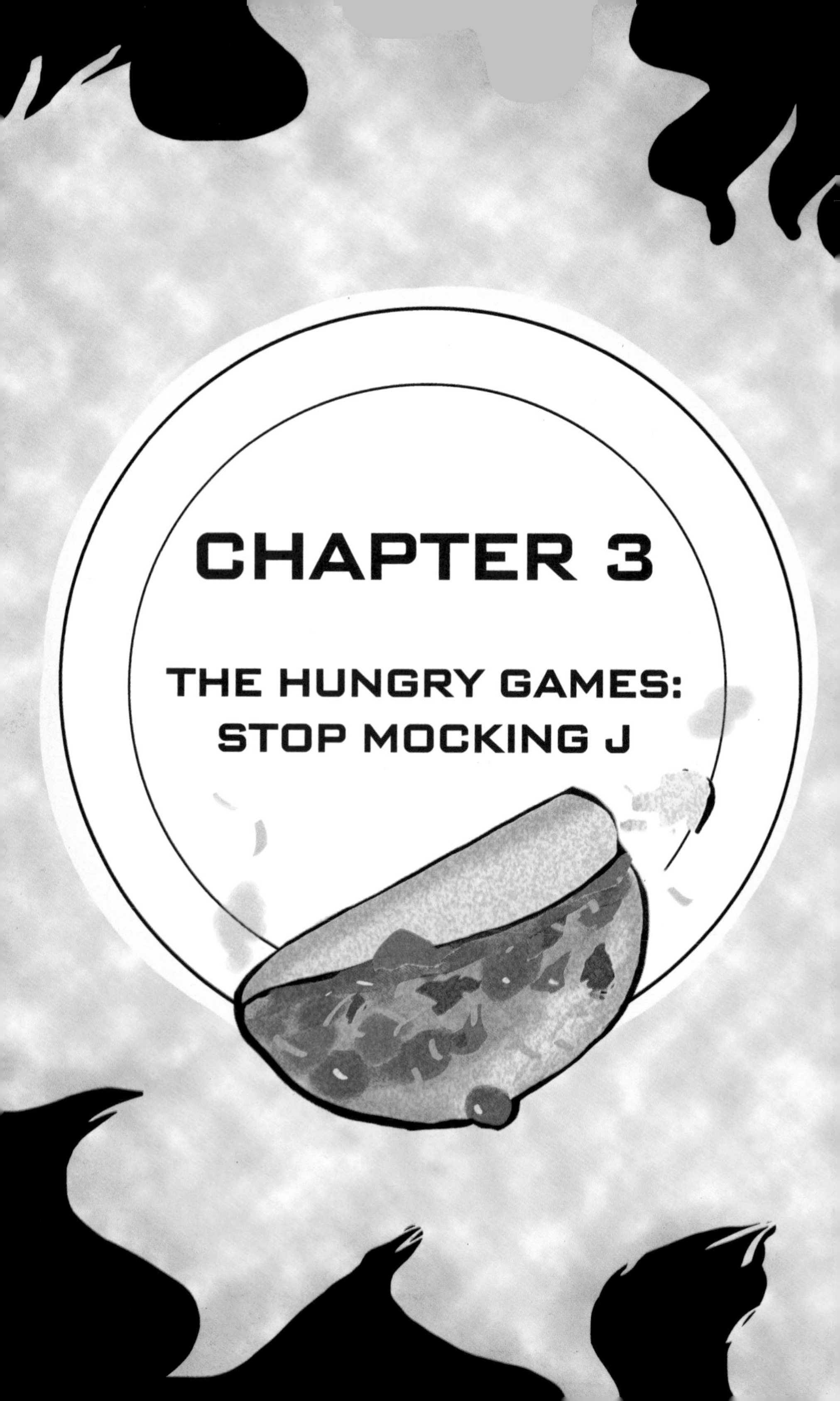

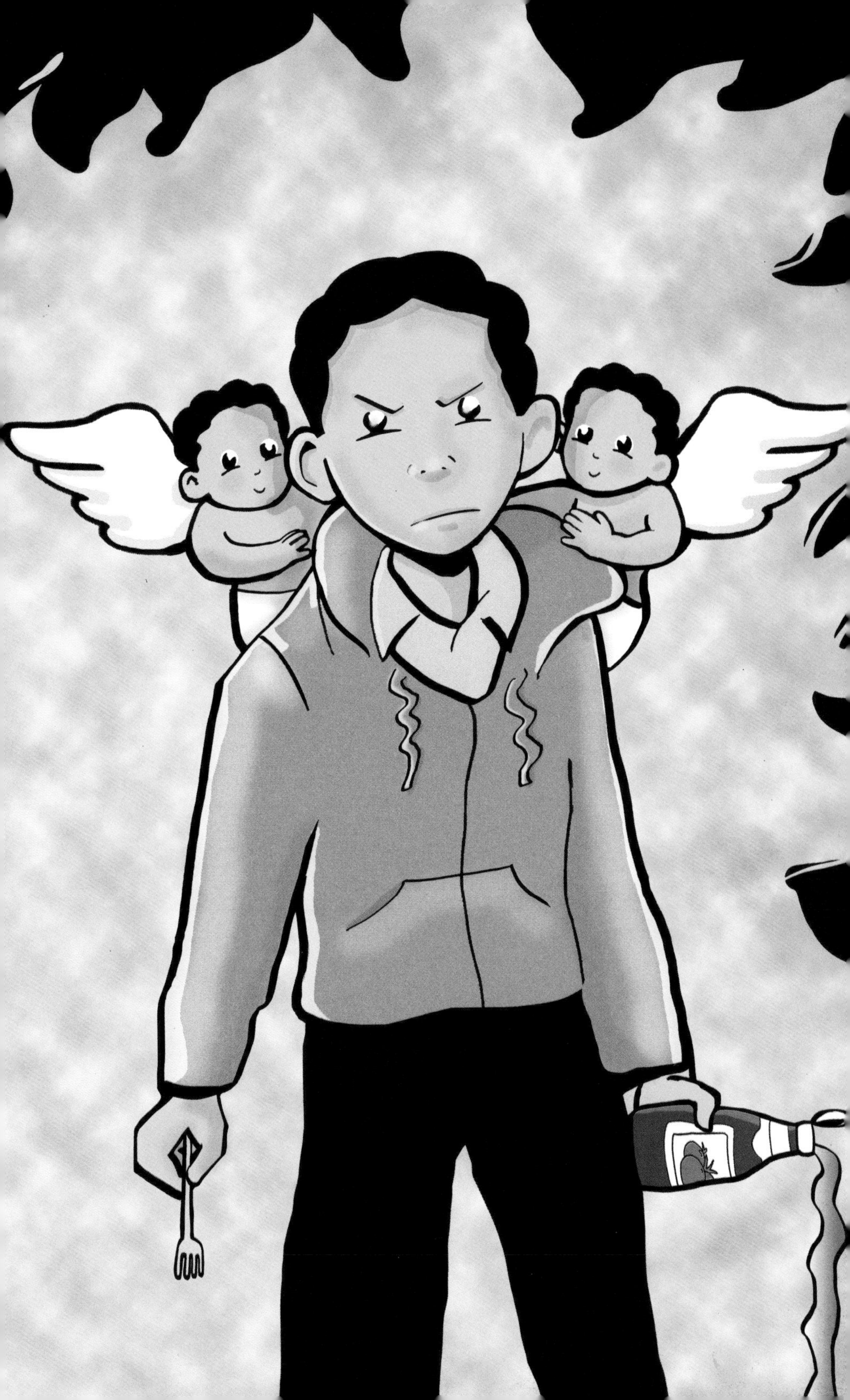

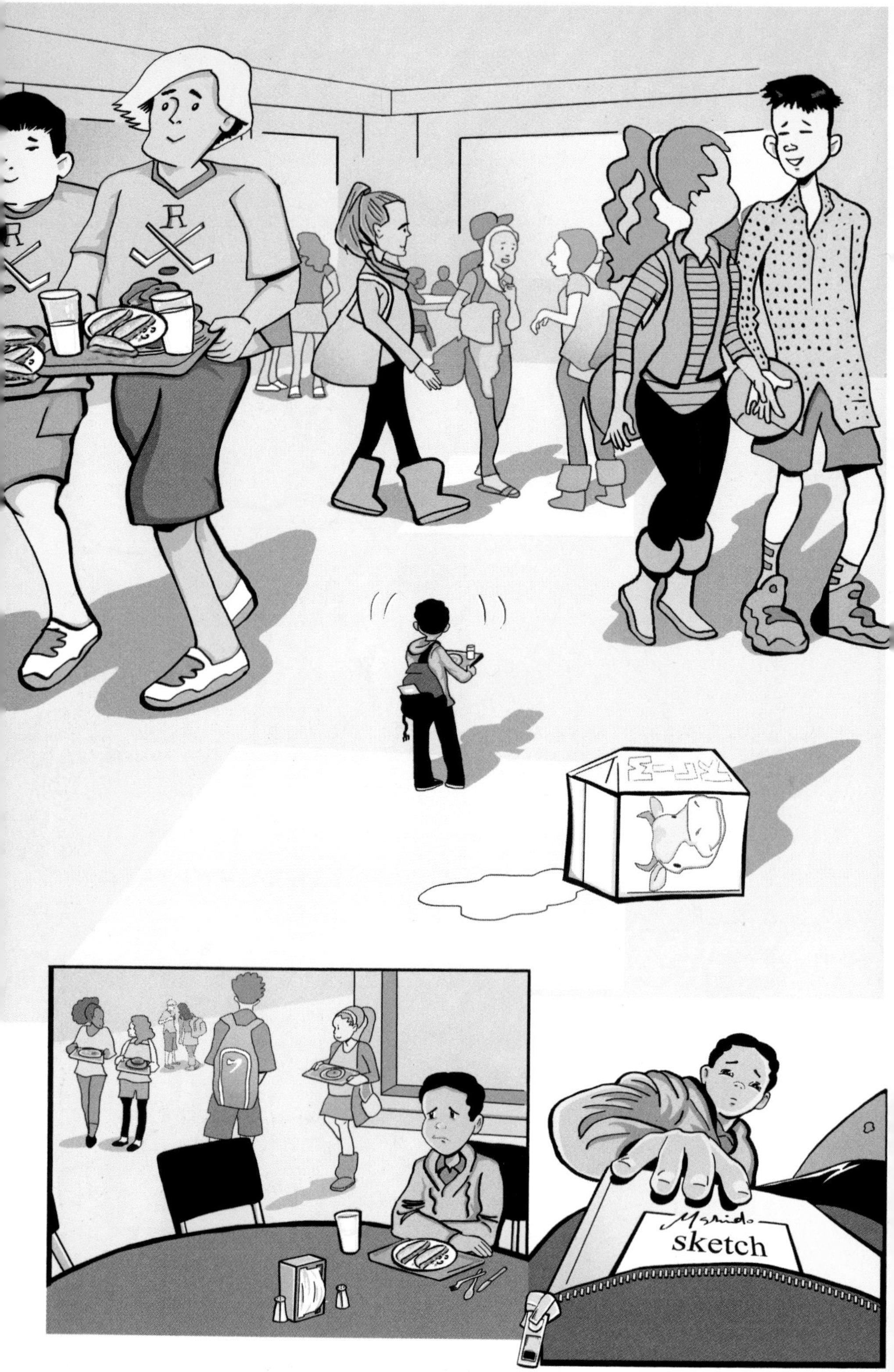
sketch

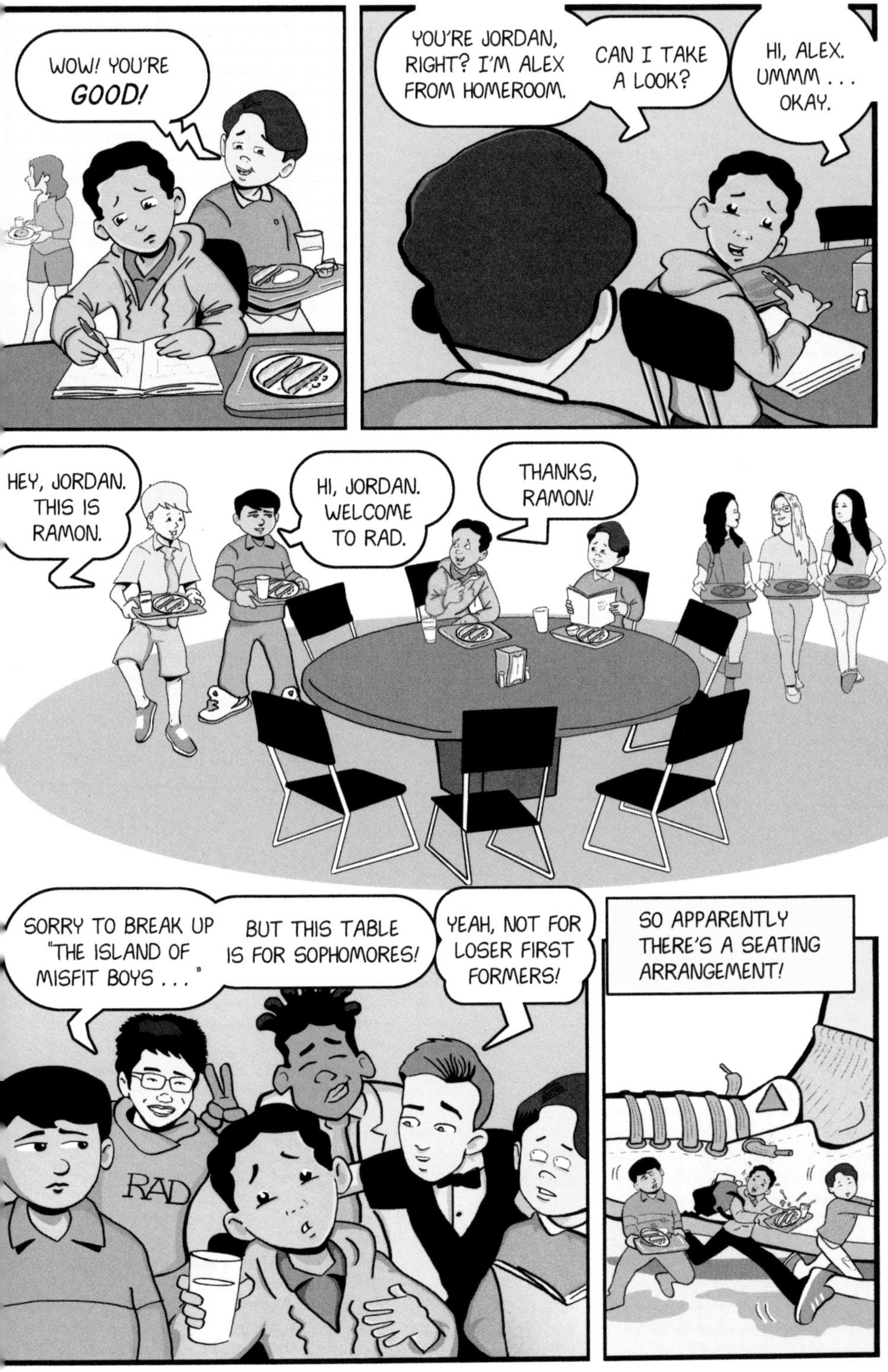
WOW! YOU'RE *GOOD!*
YOU'RE JORDAN, RIGHT? I'M ALEX FROM HOMEROOM.
CAN I TAKE A LOOK?
HI, ALEX. UMMM . . . OKAY.
HEY, JORDAN. THIS IS RAMON.
HI, JORDAN. WELCOME TO RAD.
THANKS, RAMON!
SORRY TO BREAK UP "THE ISLAND OF MISFIT BOYS . . ."
BUT THIS TABLE IS FOR SOPHOMORES!
YEAH, NOT FOR LOSER FIRST FORMERS!
RAD
SO APPARENTLY THERE'S A SEATING ARRANGEMENT!

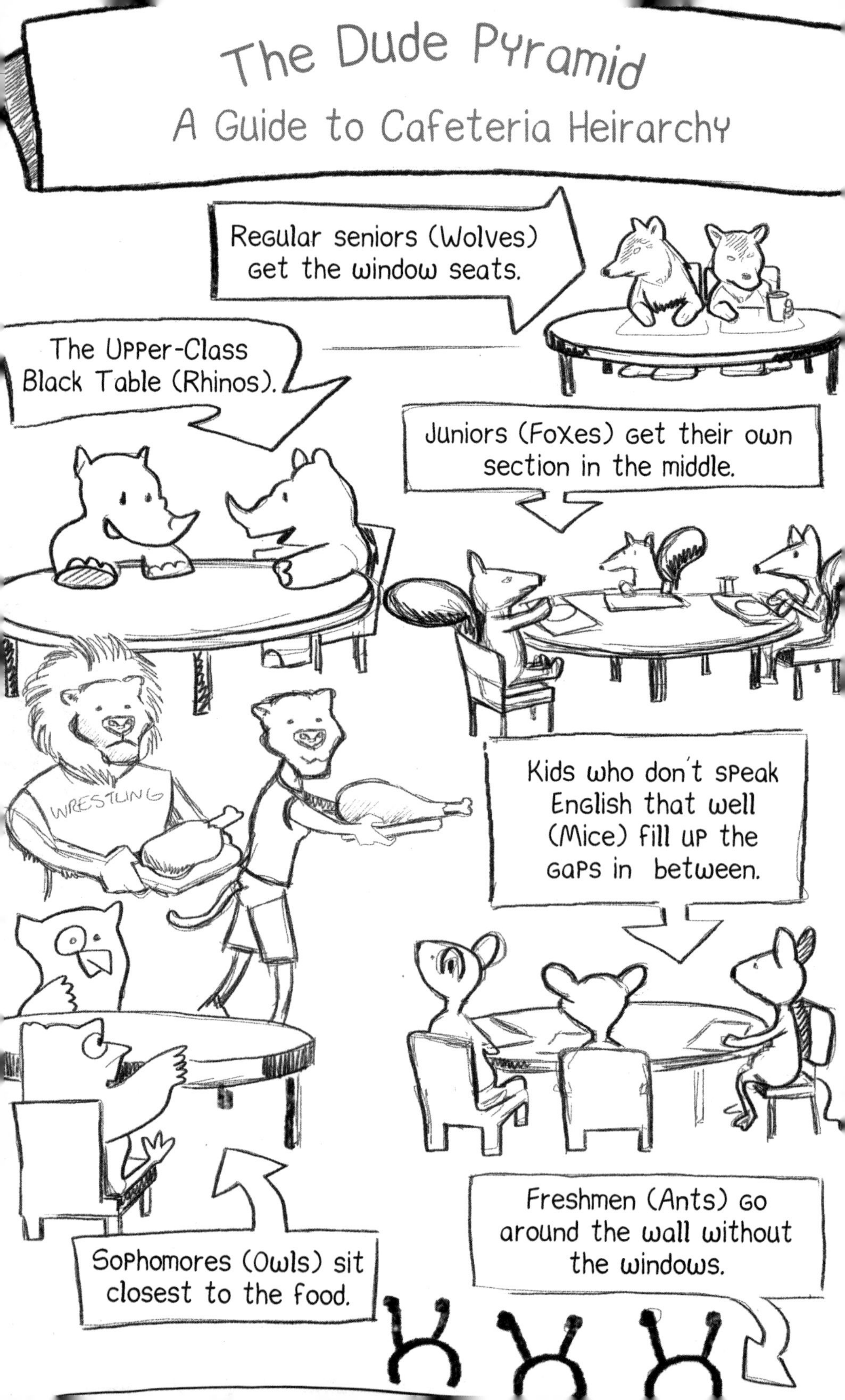
The Dude Pyramid
A Guide to Cafeteria Heirarchy
Regular seniors (Wolves) get the window seats.
The Upper-Class Black Table (Rhinos).
Juniors (Foxes) get their own section in the middle.
WRESTLING
Kids who don't speak English that well (Mice) fill up the gaps in between.
Freshmen (Ants) go around the wall without the windows.
Sophomores (Owls) sit closest to the food.

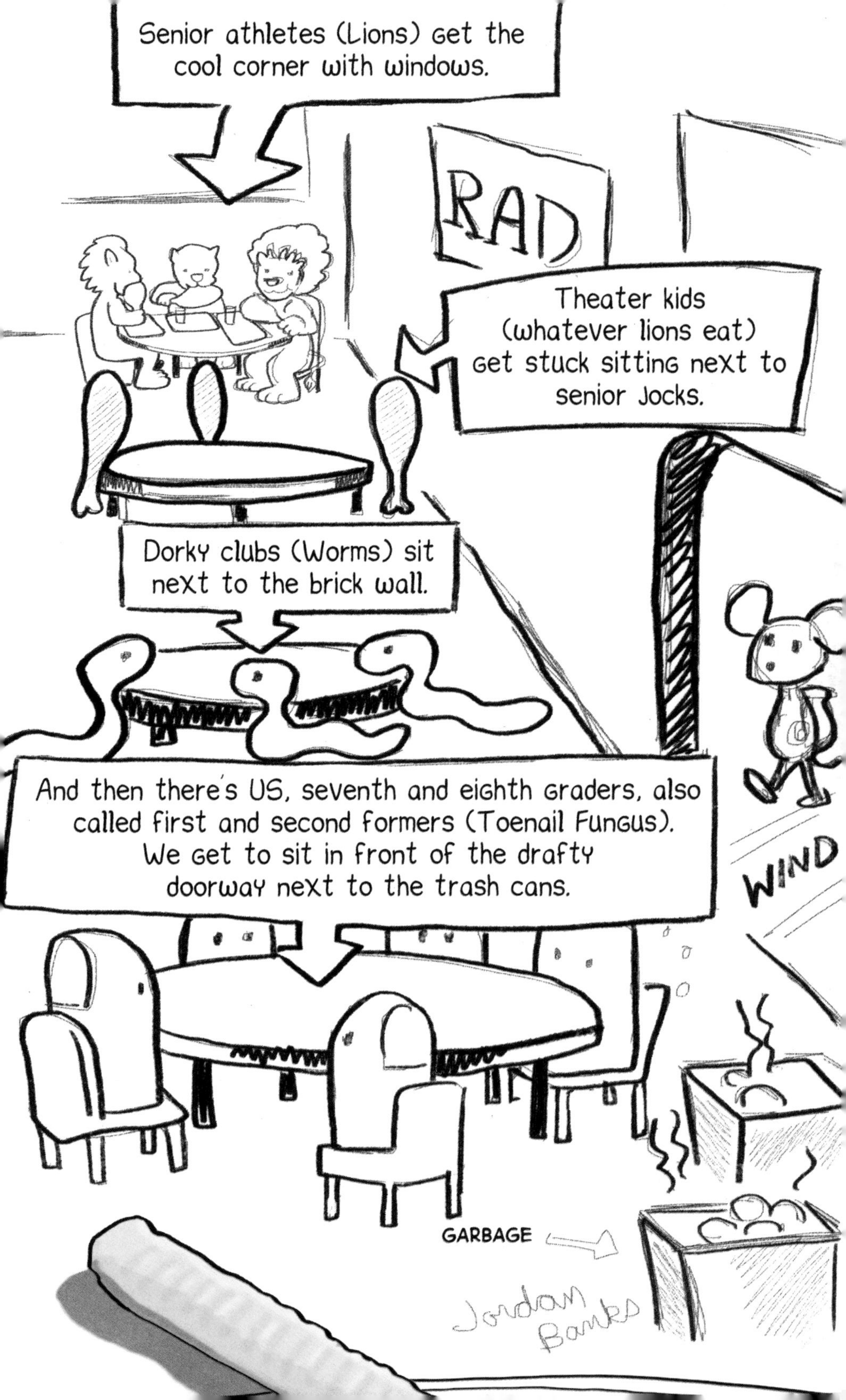
Senior athletes (Lions) get the cool corner with windows.
RAD
Theater kids (whatever lions eat) get stuck sitting next to senior jocks.
Dorky clubs (Worms) sit next to the brick wall.
And then there's US, seventh and eighth graders, also called first and second formers (Toenail Fungus). We get to sit in front of the drafty doorway next to the trash cans.
WIND
GARBAGE
Jordan Banks

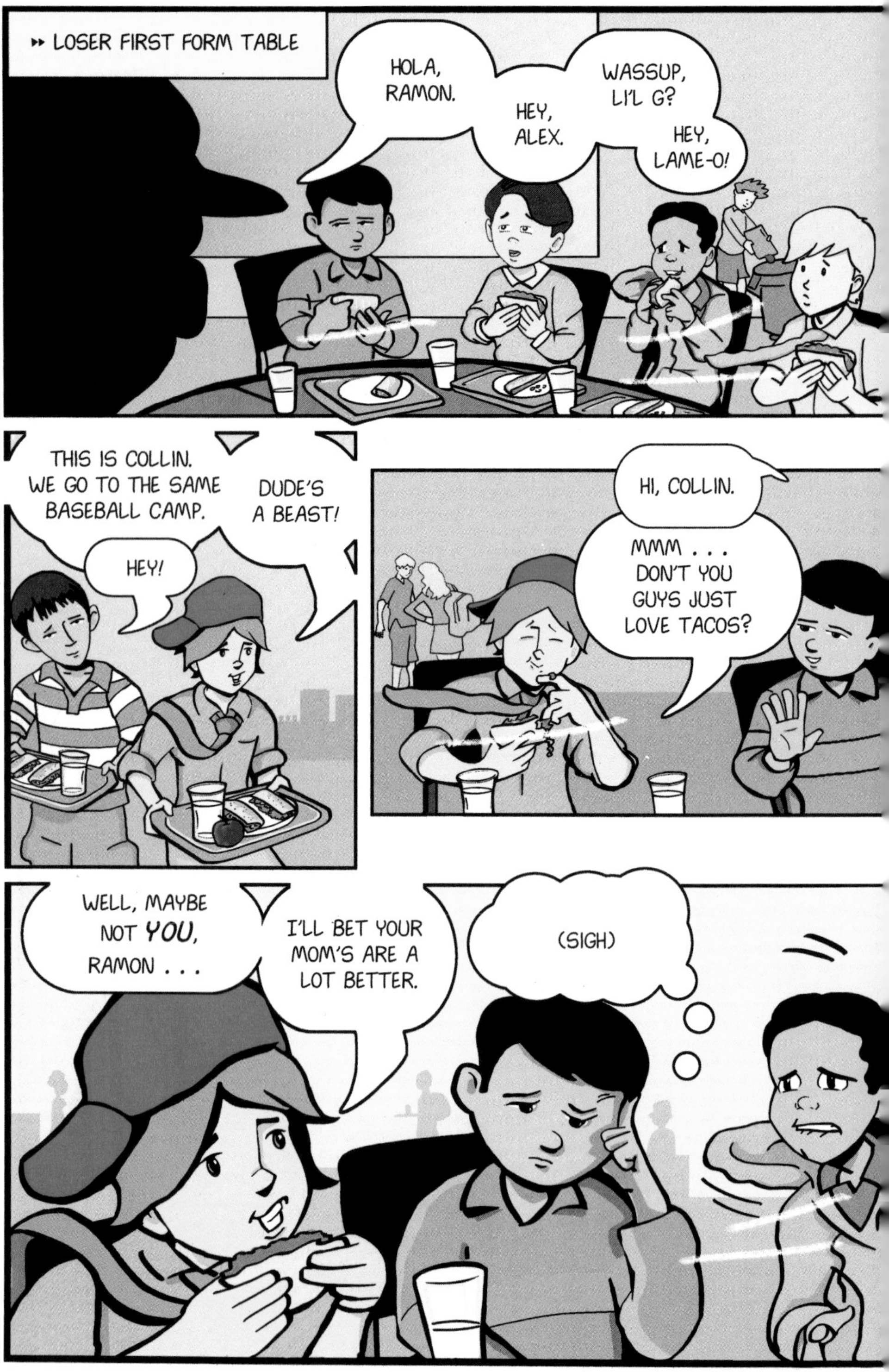
▸▸ LOSER FIRST FORM TABLE
HOLA, RAMON.
HEY, ALEX.
WASSUP, LI'L G?
HEY, LAME-O!
THIS IS COLLIN. WE GO TO THE SAME BASEBALL CAMP.
DUDE'S A BEAST!
HEY!
HI, COLLIN.
MMM . . . DON'T YOU GUYS JUST LOVE TACOS?
WELL, MAYBE NOT *YOU*, RAMON . . .
I'LL BET YOUR MOM'S ARE A LOT BETTER.
(SIGH)

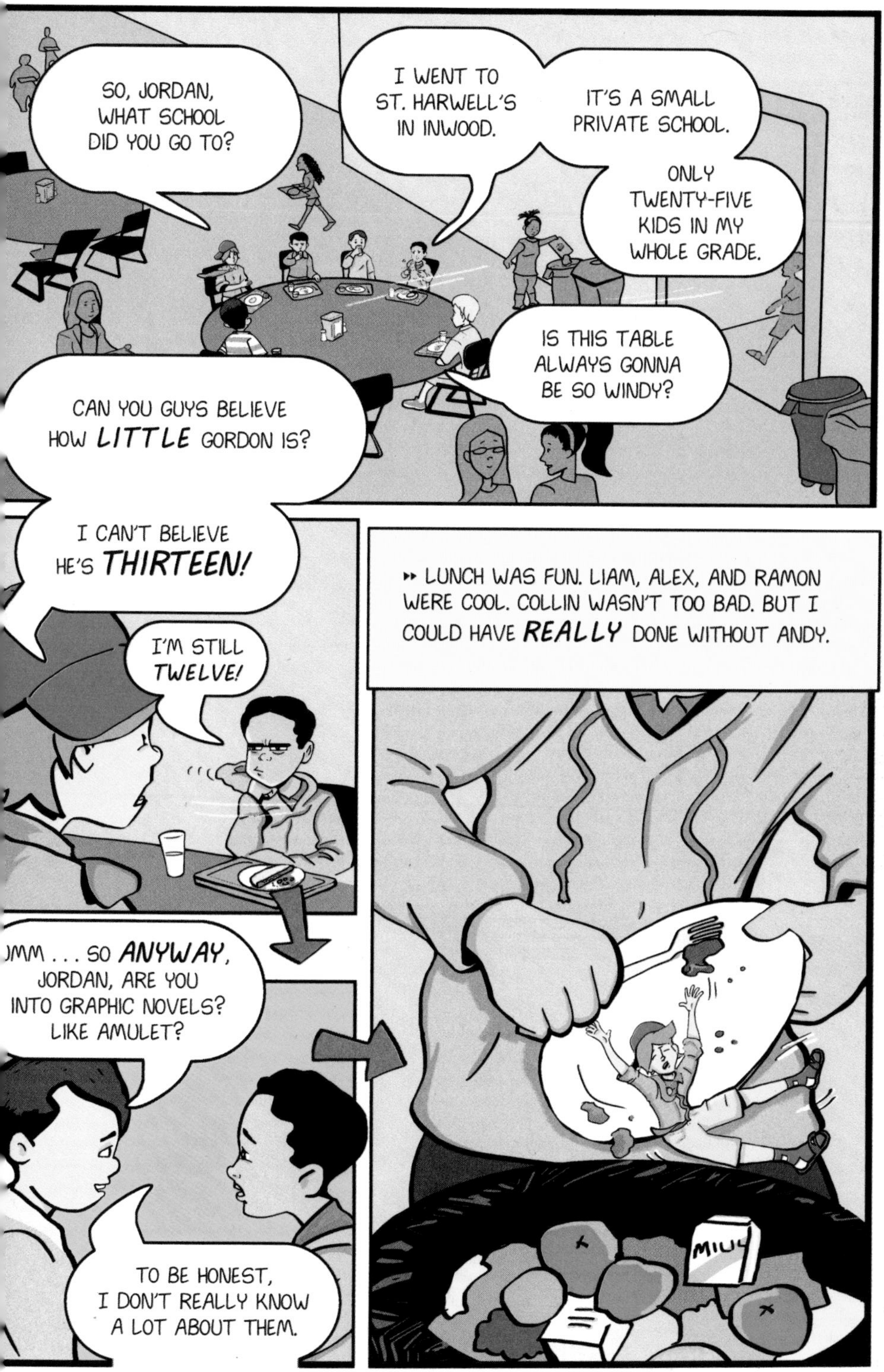
SO, JORDAN, WHAT SCHOOL DID YOU GO TO?
I WENT TO ST. HARWELL'S IN INWOOD.
IT'S A SMALL PRIVATE SCHOOL.
ONLY TWENTY-FIVE KIDS IN MY WHOLE GRADE.
IS THIS TABLE ALWAYS GONNA BE SO WINDY?
CAN YOU GUYS BELIEVE HOW LITTLE GORDON IS?
I CAN'T BELIEVE HE'S THIRTEEN!
I'M STILL TWELVE!
LUNCH WAS FUN. LIAM, ALEX, AND RAMON WERE COOL. COLLIN WASN'T TOO BAD. BUT I COULD HAVE REALLY DONE WITHOUT ANDY.
UMM . . . SO ANYWAY, JORDAN, ARE YOU INTO GRAPHIC NOVELS? LIKE AMULET?
TO BE HONEST, I DON'T REALLY KNOW A LOT ABOUT THEM.
MILK

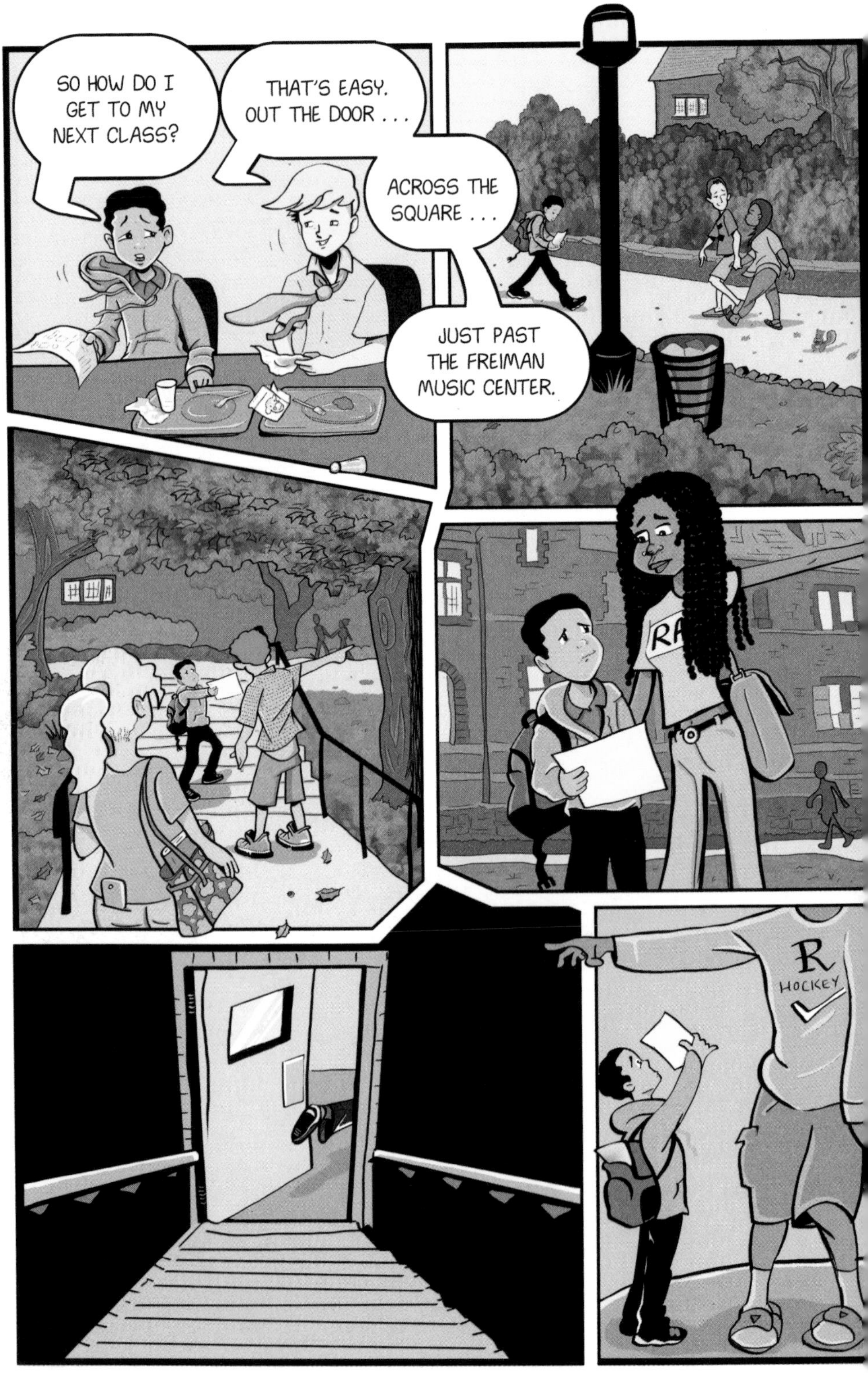
SO HOW DO I GET TO MY NEXT CLASS?
THAT'S EASY. OUT THE DOOR . . .
ACROSS THE SQUARE . . .
JUST PAST THE FREIMAN MUSIC CENTER.
RA
R
HOCKEY

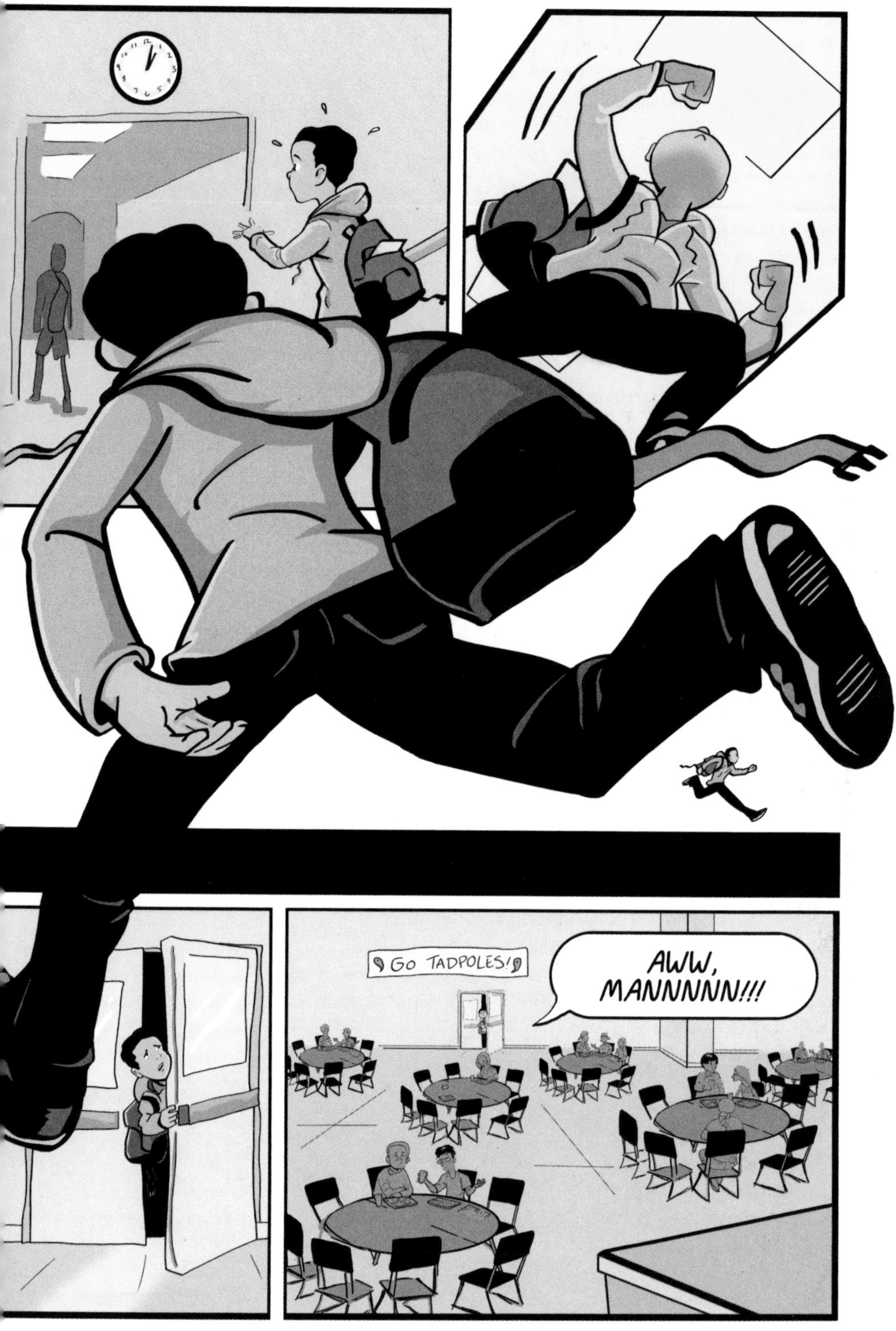
GO TADPOLES!
AWW, MANNNNN!!!

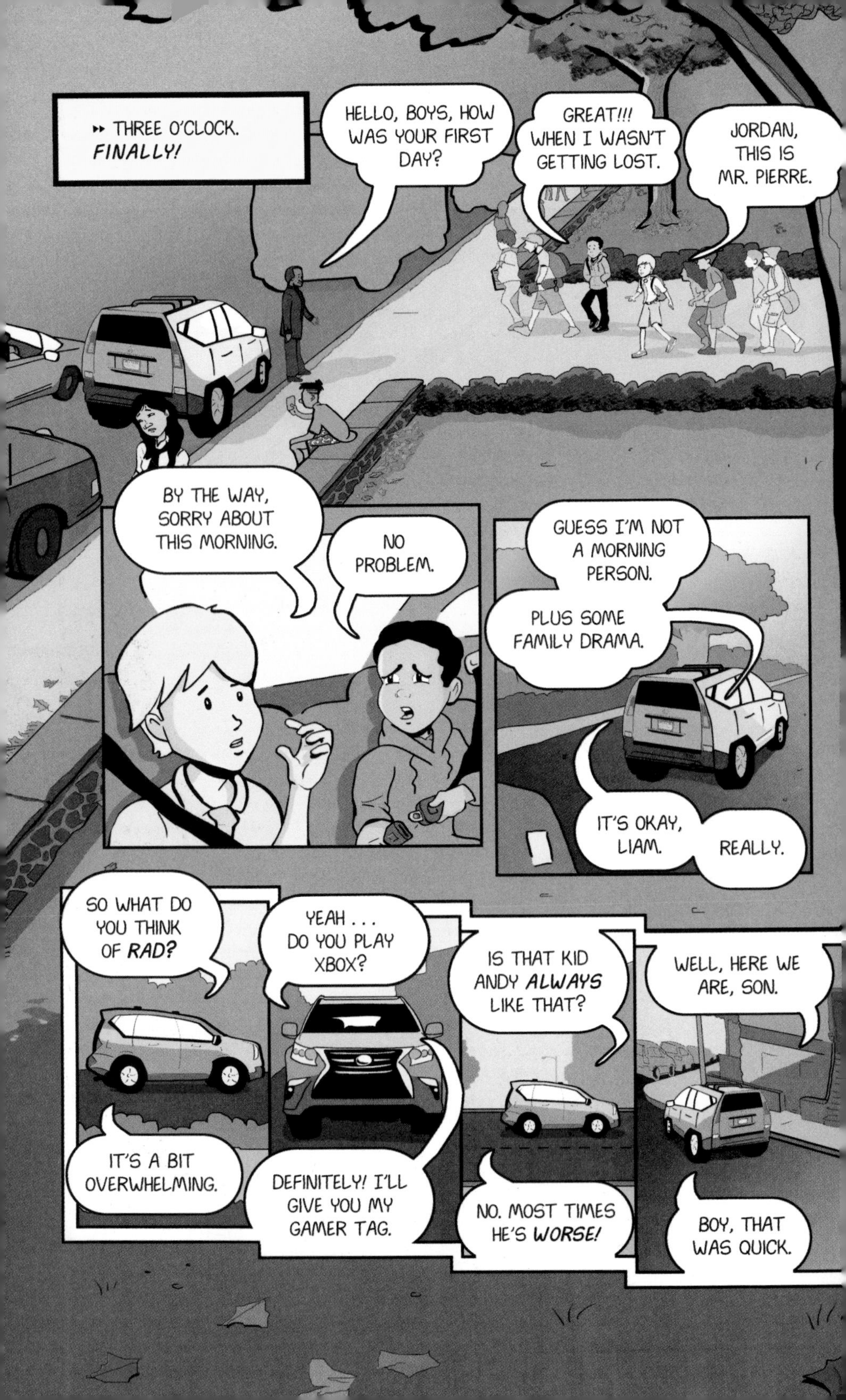
THREE O'CLOCK. *FINALLY!*
HELLO, BOYS, HOW WAS YOUR FIRST DAY?
GREAT!!! WHEN I WASN'T GETTING LOST.
JORDAN, THIS IS MR. PIERRE.
BY THE WAY, SORRY ABOUT THIS MORNING.
NO PROBLEM.
GUESS I'M NOT A MORNING PERSON.
PLUS SOME FAMILY DRAMA.
IT'S OKAY, LIAM.
REALLY.
SO WHAT DO YOU THINK OF *RAD?*
IT'S A BIT OVERWHELMING.
YEAH . . . DO YOU PLAY XBOX?
DEFINITELY! I'LL GIVE YOU MY GAMER TAG.
IS THAT KID ANDY *ALWAYS* LIKE THAT?
NO. MOST TIMES HE'S *WORSE!*
WELL, HERE WE ARE, SON.
BOY, THAT WAS QUICK.

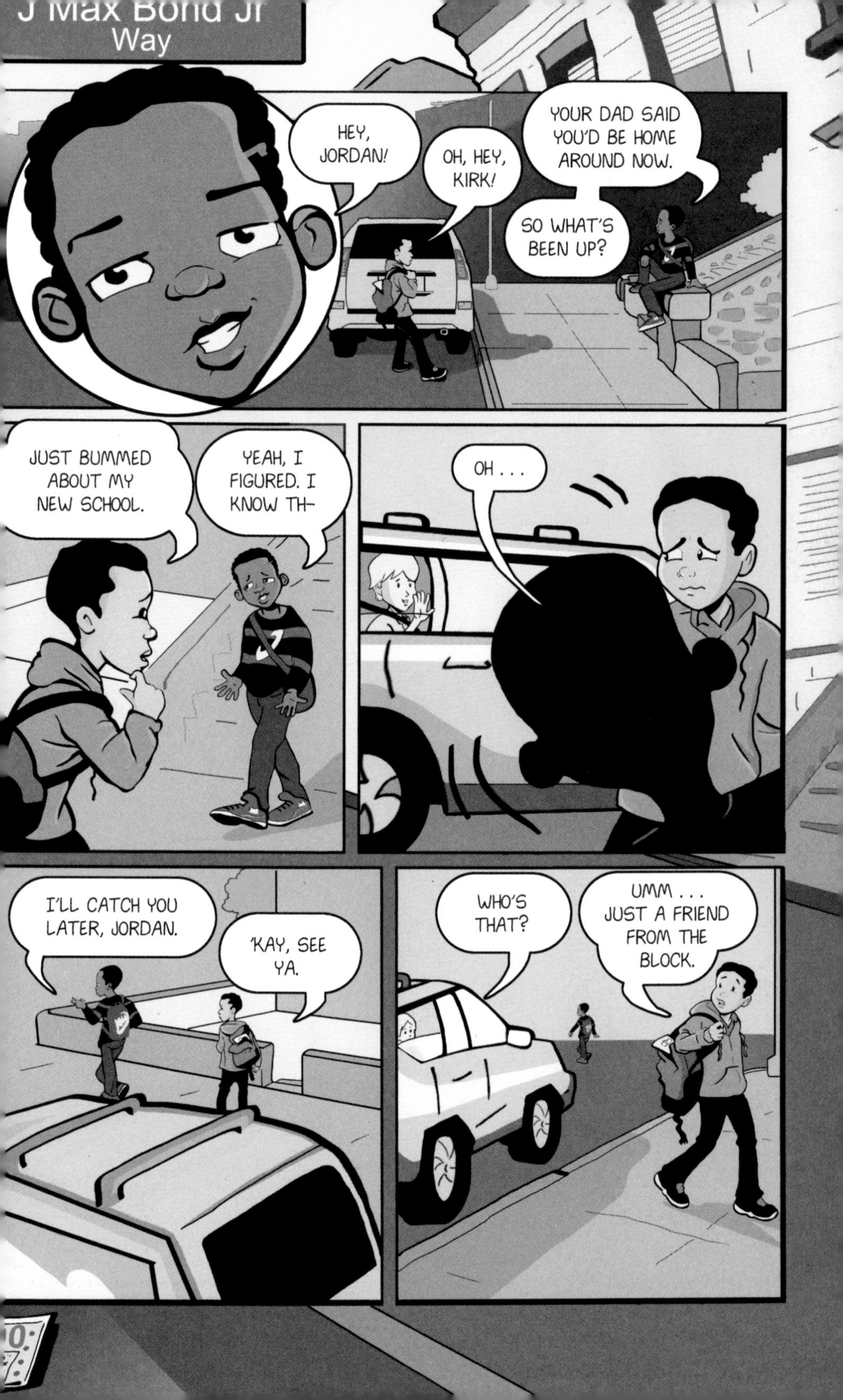
J Max Bond Jr Way
HEY, JORDAN!
OH, HEY, KIRK!
YOUR DAD SAID YOU'D BE HOME AROUND NOW.
SO WHAT'S BEEN UP?
JUST BUMMED ABOUT MY NEW SCHOOL.
YEAH, I FIGURED. I KNOW TH-
OH . . .
I'LL CATCH YOU LATER, JORDAN.
'KAY, SEE YA.
WHO'S THAT?
UMM . . . JUST A FRIEND FROM THE BLOCK.

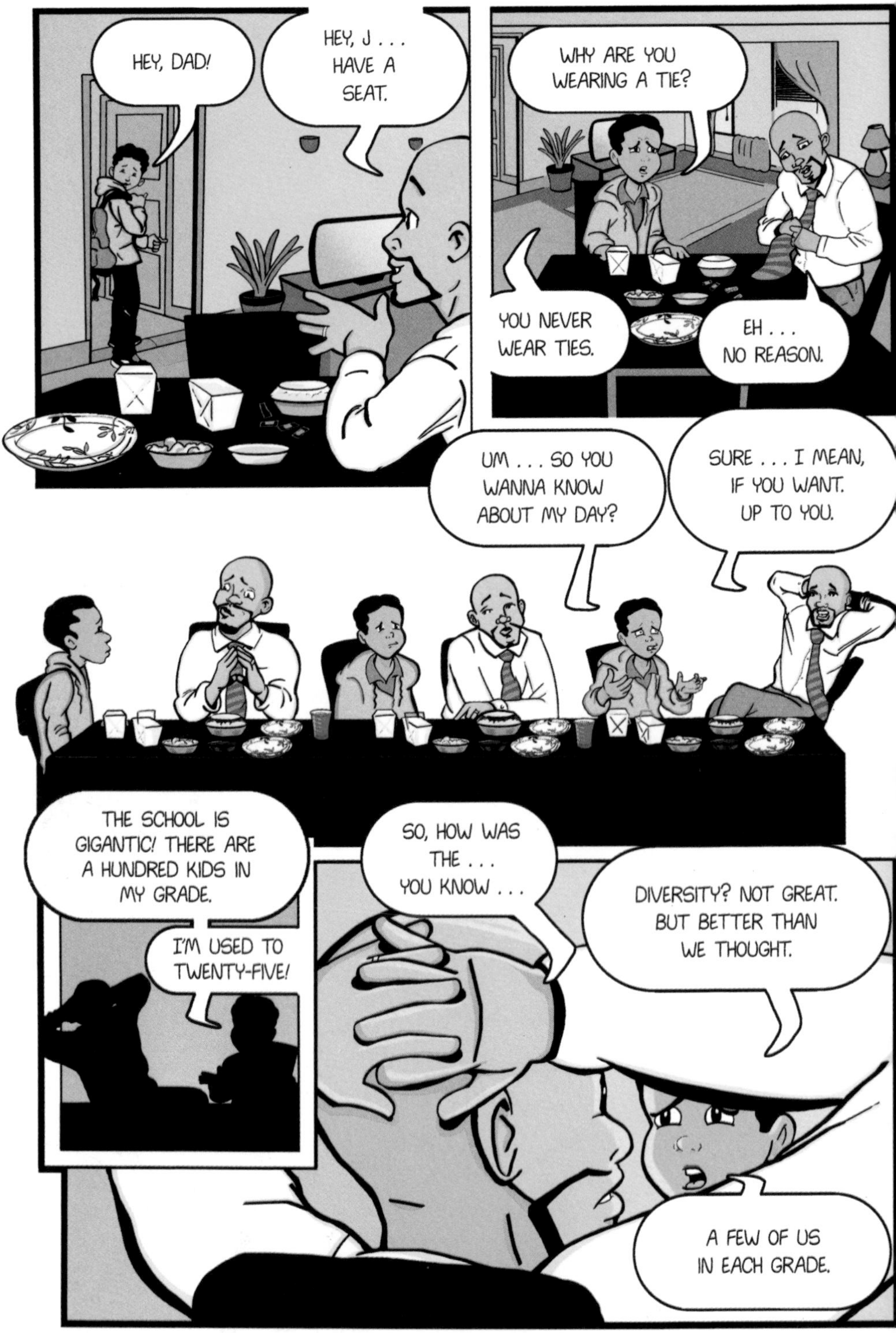
HEY, DAD!
HEY, J . . . HAVE A SEAT.
WHY ARE YOU WEARING A TIE?
YOU NEVER WEAR TIES.
EH . . . NO REASON.
UM . . . SO YOU WANNA KNOW ABOUT MY DAY?
SURE . . . I MEAN, IF YOU WANT. UP TO YOU.
THE SCHOOL IS GIGANTIC! THERE ARE A HUNDRED KIDS IN MY GRADE.
I'M USED TO TWENTY-FIVE!
SO, HOW WAS THE . . . YOU KNOW . . .
DIVERSITY? NOT GREAT. BUT BETTER THAN WE THOUGHT.
A FEW OF US IN EACH GRADE.

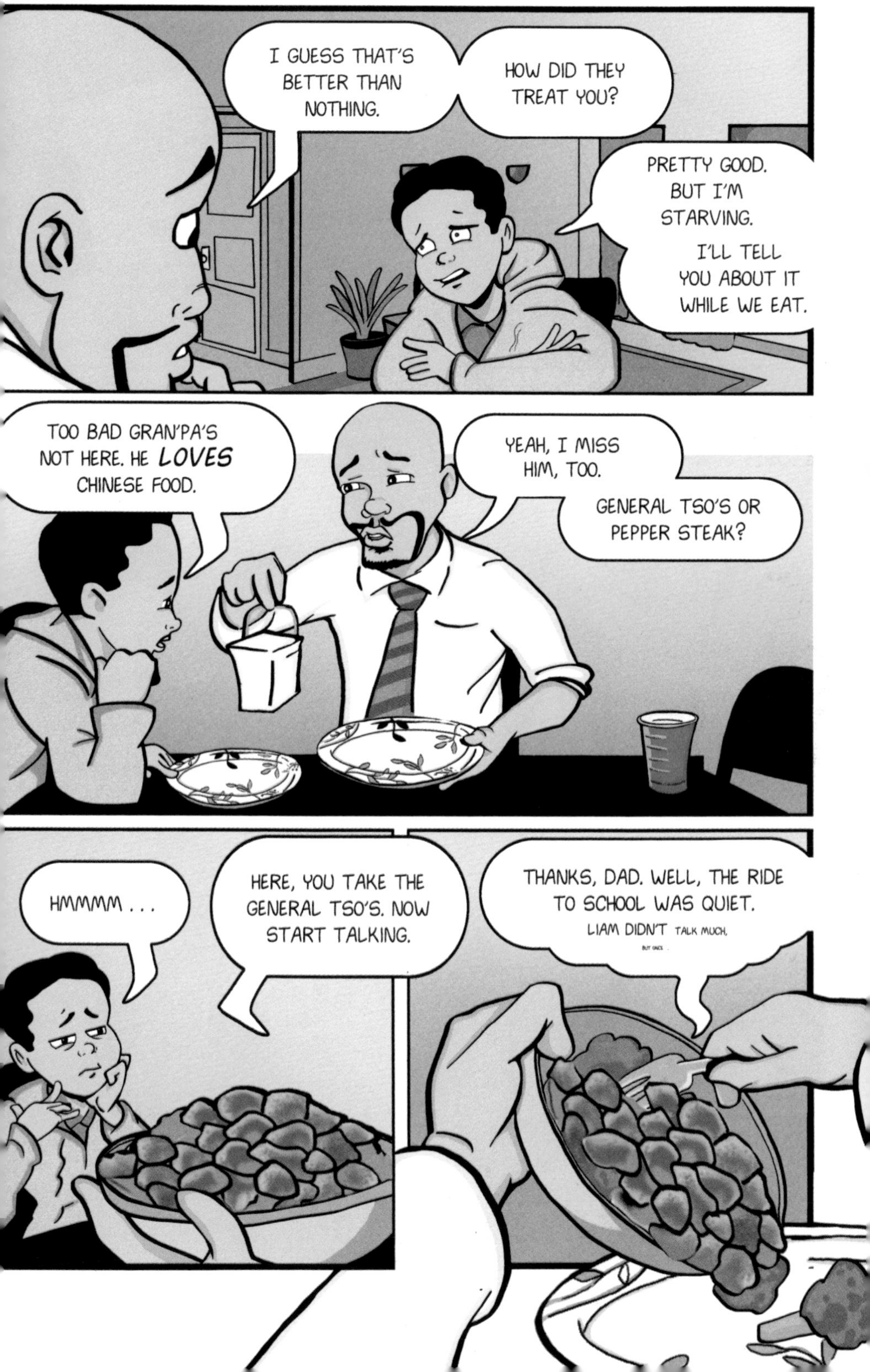

I GUESS THAT'S BETTER THAN NOTHING.
HOW DID THEY TREAT YOU?
PRETTY GOOD. BUT I'M STARVING.
I'LL TELL YOU ABOUT IT WHILE WE EAT.
TOO BAD GRAN'PA'S NOT HERE. HE LOVES CHINESE FOOD.
YEAH, I MISS HIM, TOO.
GENERAL TSO'S OR PEPPER STEAK?
HMMMM . . .
HERE, YOU TAKE THE GENERAL TSO'S. NOW START TALKING.
THANKS, DAD. WELL, THE RIDE TO SCHOOL WAS QUIET.
LIAM DIDN'T TALK MUCH,
BUT ONCE .

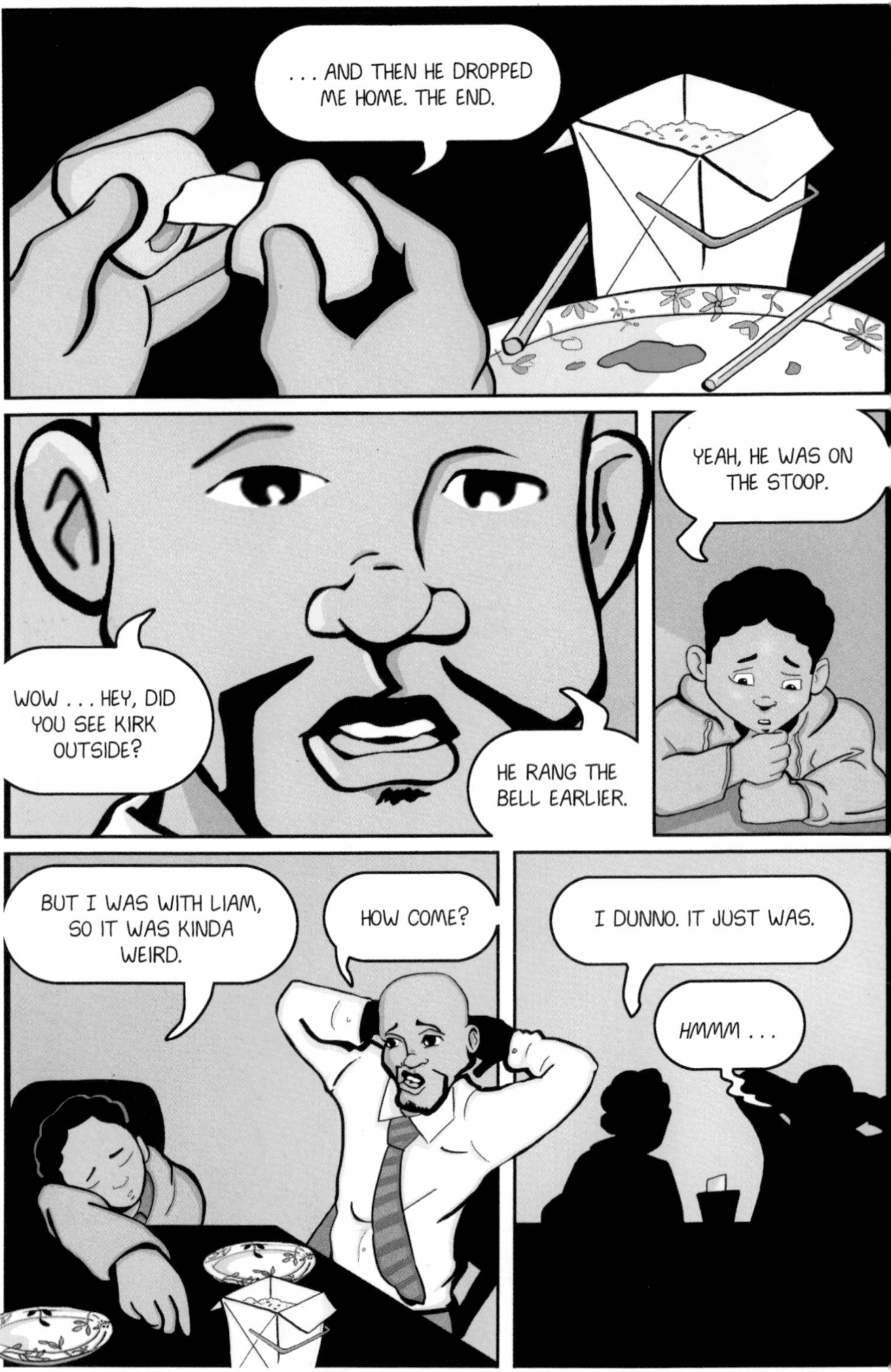
. . . AND THEN HE DROPPED ME HOME. THE END.
WOW . . . HEY, DID YOU SEE KIRK OUTSIDE?
HE RANG THE BELL EARLIER.
YEAH, HE WAS ON THE STOOP.
BUT I WAS WITH LIAM, SO IT WAS KINDA WEIRD.
HOW COME?
I DUNNO. IT JUST WAS.
HMMM . . .

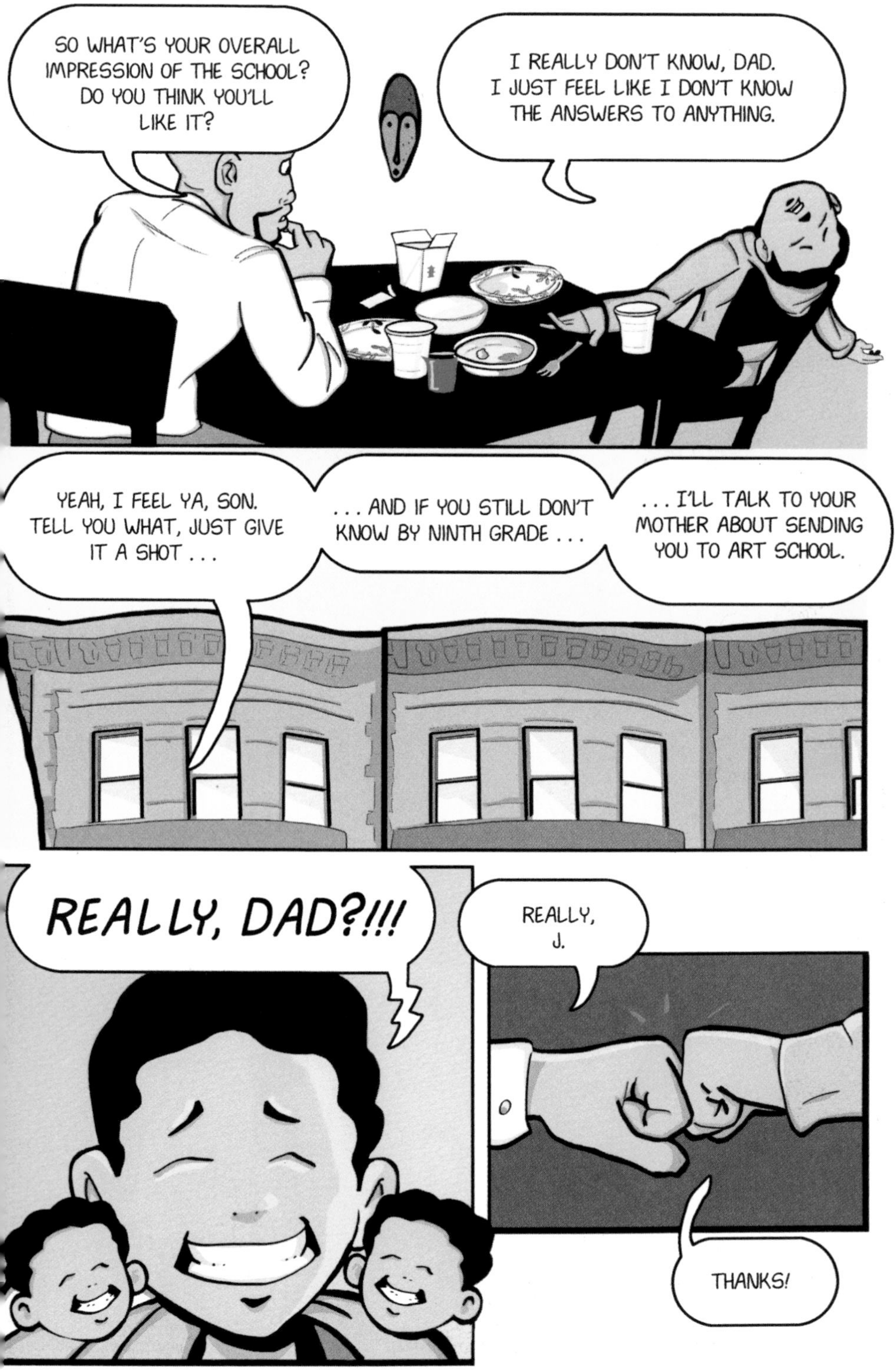
SO WHAT'S YOUR OVERALL IMPRESSION OF THE SCHOOL? DO YOU THINK YOU'LL LIKE IT?
I REALLY DON'T KNOW, DAD. I JUST FEEL LIKE I DON'T KNOW THE ANSWERS TO ANYTHING.
YEAH, I FEEL YA, SON. TELL YOU WHAT, JUST GIVE IT A SHOT . . .
. . . AND IF YOU STILL DON'T KNOW BY NINTH GRADE . . .
. . . I'LL TALK TO YOUR MOTHER ABOUT SENDING YOU TO ART SCHOOL.
REALLY, DAD?!!!
REALLY, J.
THANKS!

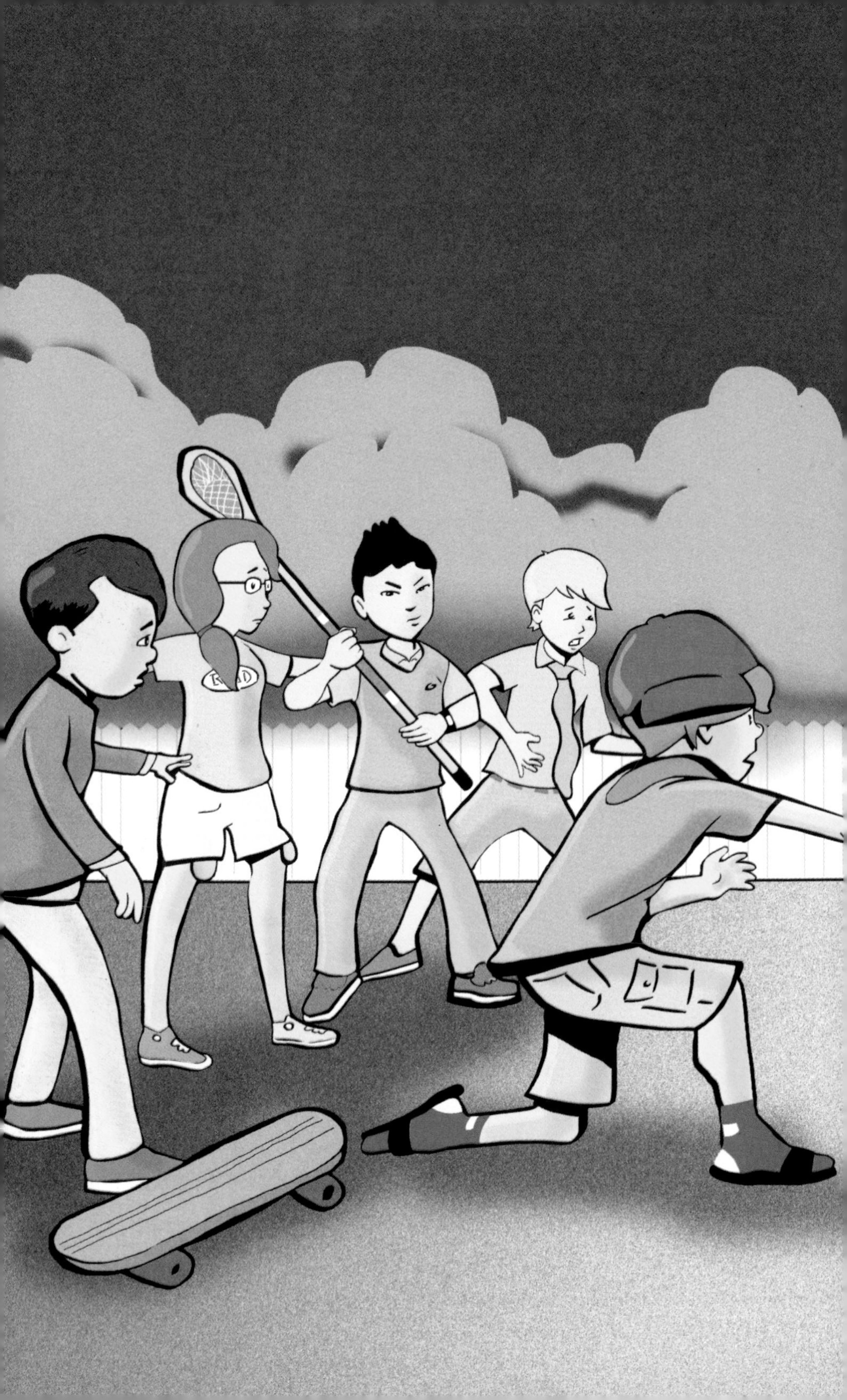

CHAPTER 4

UPPER, UPPER WEST SIDE STORY

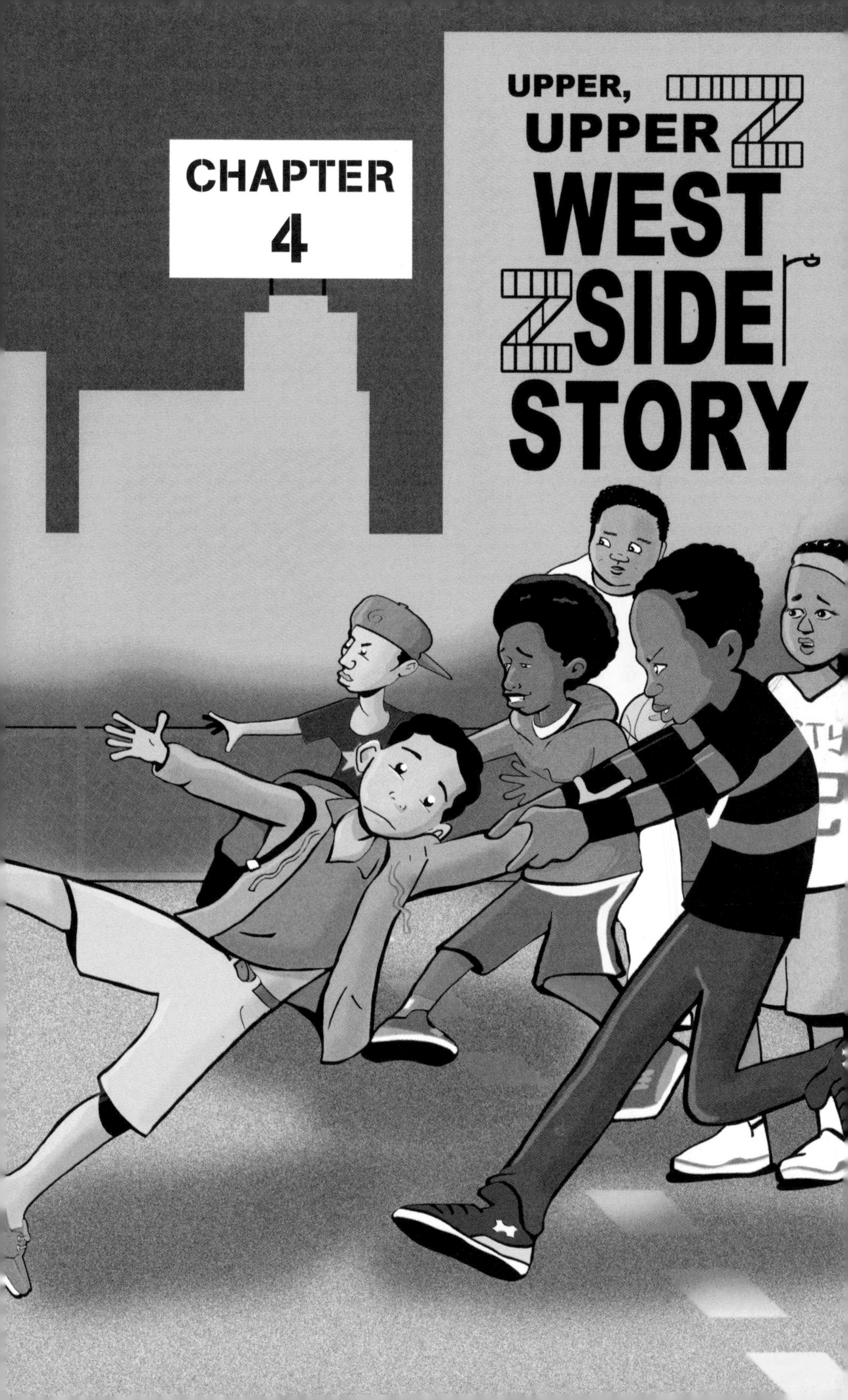

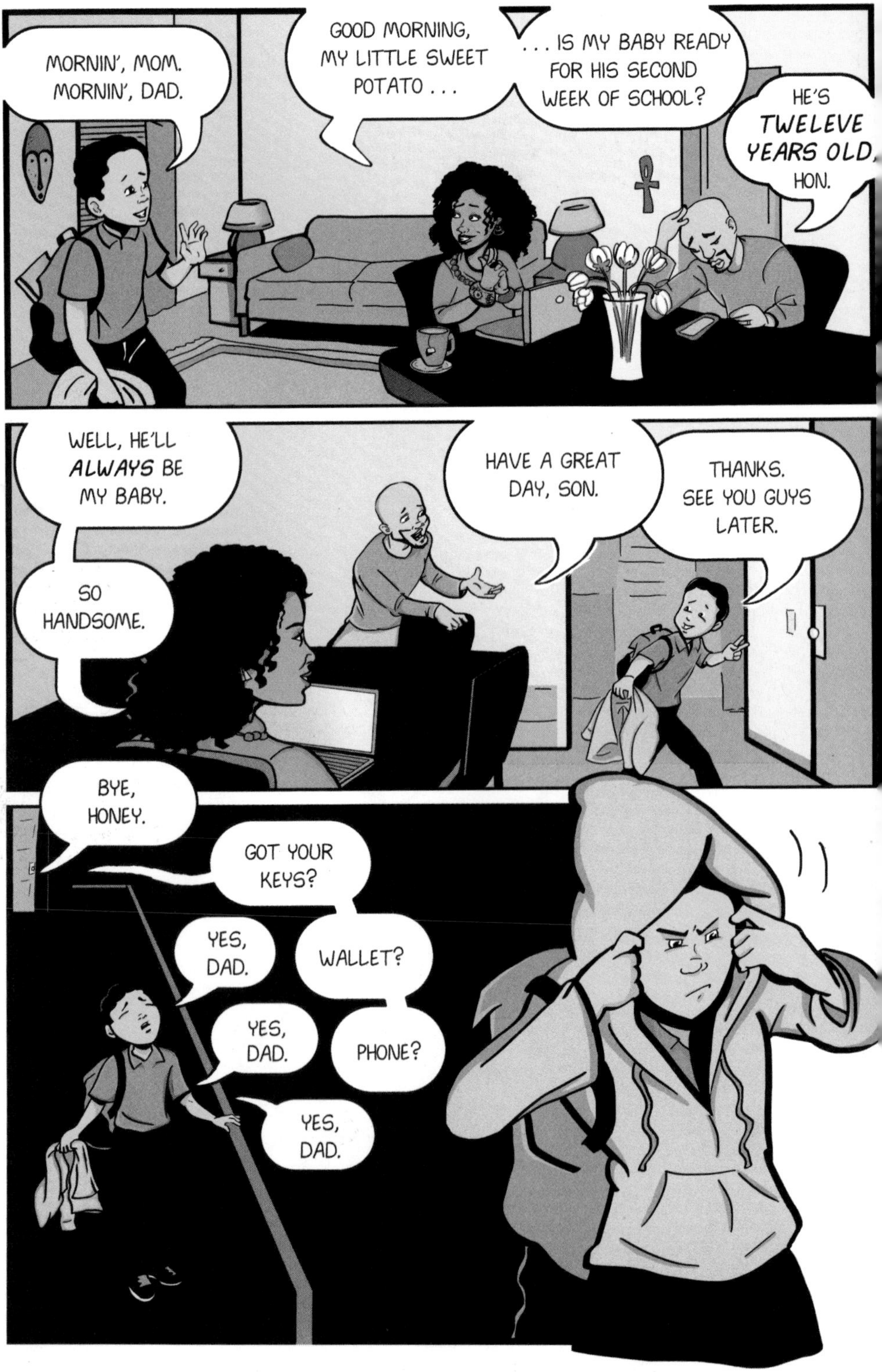
MORNIN', MOM. MORNIN', DAD.
GOOD MORNING, MY LITTLE SWEET POTATO . . .
. . . IS MY BABY READY FOR HIS SECOND WEEK OF SCHOOL?
HE'S ***TWELEVE YEARS OLD***, HON.
WELL, HE'LL ***ALWAYS*** BE MY BABY.
SO HANDSOME.
HAVE A GREAT DAY, SON.
THANKS. SEE YOU GUYS LATER.
BYE, HONEY.
GOT YOUR KEYS?
YES, DAD.
WALLET?
YES, DAD.
PHONE?
YES, DAD.

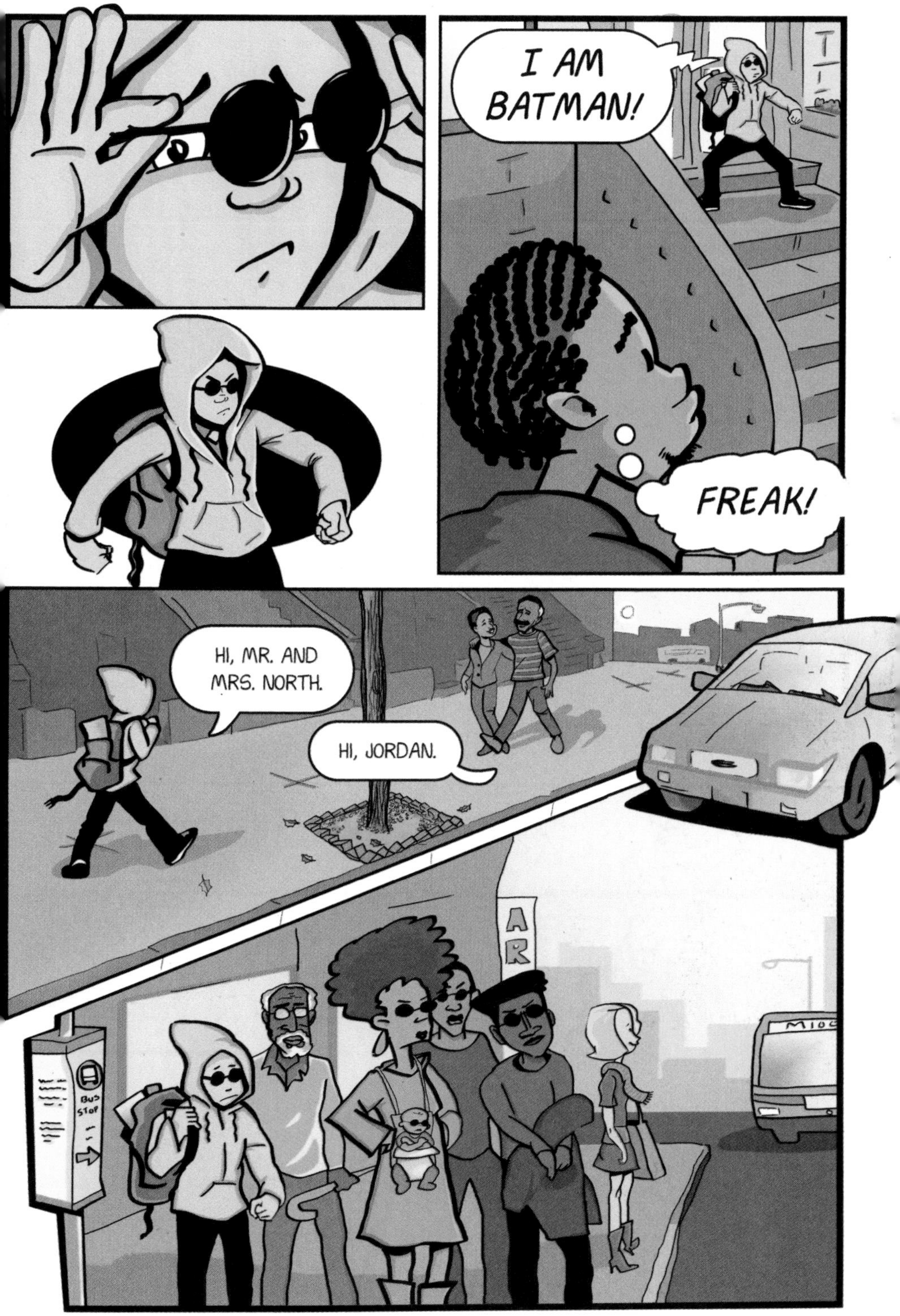
I AM BATMAN!
FREAK!
HI, MR. AND MRS. NORTH.
HI, JORDAN.
BUS STOP
M10

Jordan's Tips for Taking the Bus

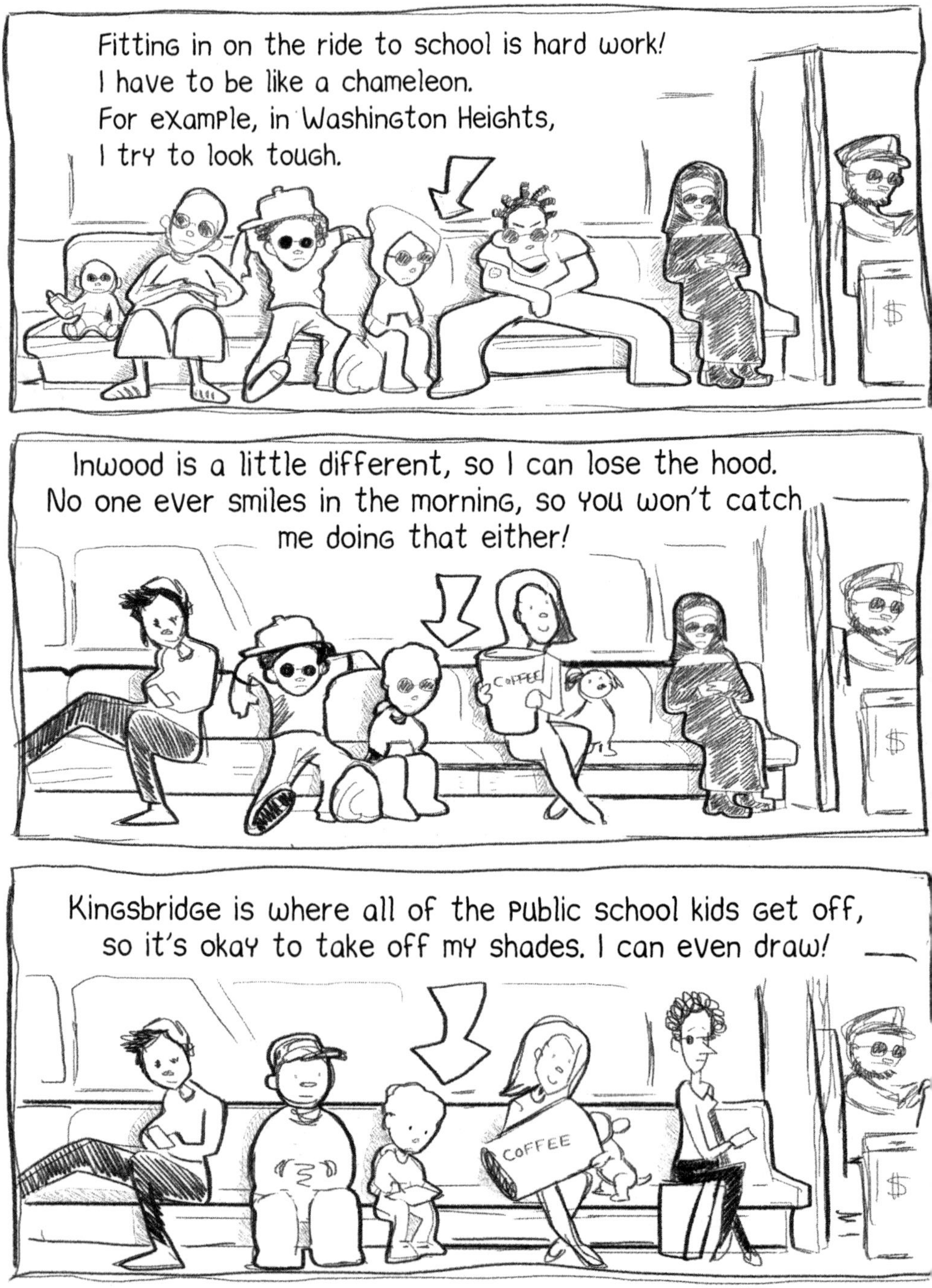
Fitting in on the ride to school is hard work! I have to be like a chameleon. For example, in Washington Heights, I try to look tough.
Inwood is a little different, so I can lose the hood. No one ever smiles in the morning, so you won't catch me doing that either!
COFFEE
Kingsbridge is where all of the public school kids get off, so it's okay to take off my shades. I can even draw!
COFFEE

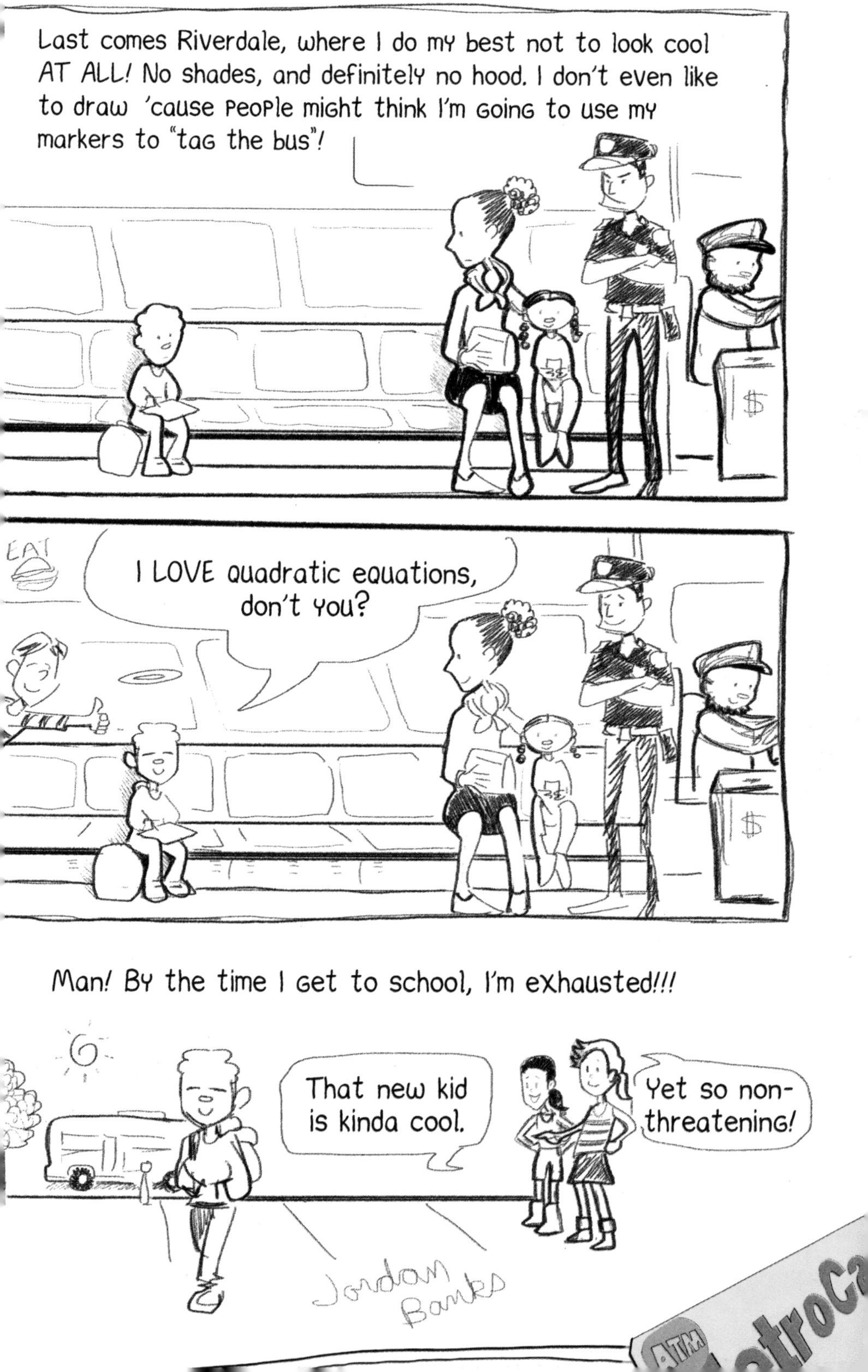
Last comes Riverdale, where I do my best not to look cool AT ALL! No shades, and definitely no hood. I don't even like to draw 'cause people might think I'm going to use my markers to "tag the bus"!
$
EAT
I LOVE quadratic equations, don't you?
$
Man! By the time I get to school, I'm exhausted!!!
That new kid is kinda cool.
Yet so non-threatening!
Jordan Banks
ATM

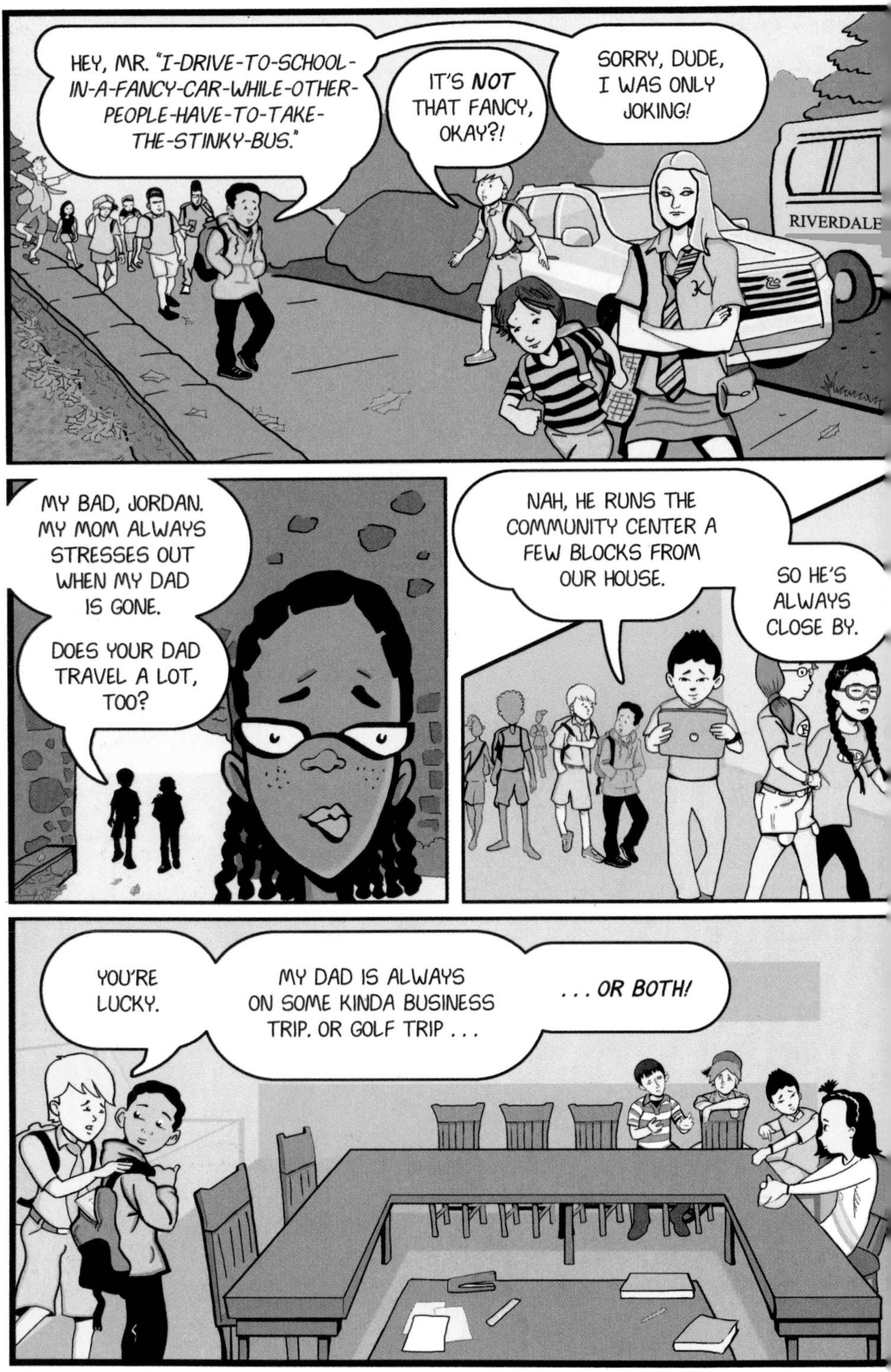
HEY, MR. "I-DRIVE-TO-SCHOOL-IN-A-FANCY-CAR-WHILE-OTHER-PEOPLE-HAVE-TO-TAKE-THE-STINKY-BUS."
IT'S **NOT** THAT FANCY, OKAY?!
SORRY, DUDE, I WAS ONLY JOKING!
RIVERDALE
MY BAD, JORDAN. MY MOM ALWAYS STRESSES OUT WHEN MY DAD IS GONE.
DOES YOUR DAD TRAVEL A LOT, TOO?
NAH, HE RUNS THE COMMUNITY CENTER A FEW BLOCKS FROM OUR HOUSE.
SO HE'S ALWAYS CLOSE BY.
YOU'RE LUCKY.
MY DAD IS ALWAYS ON SOME KINDA BUSINESS TRIP. OR GOLF TRIP . . .
. . . **OR BOTH!**

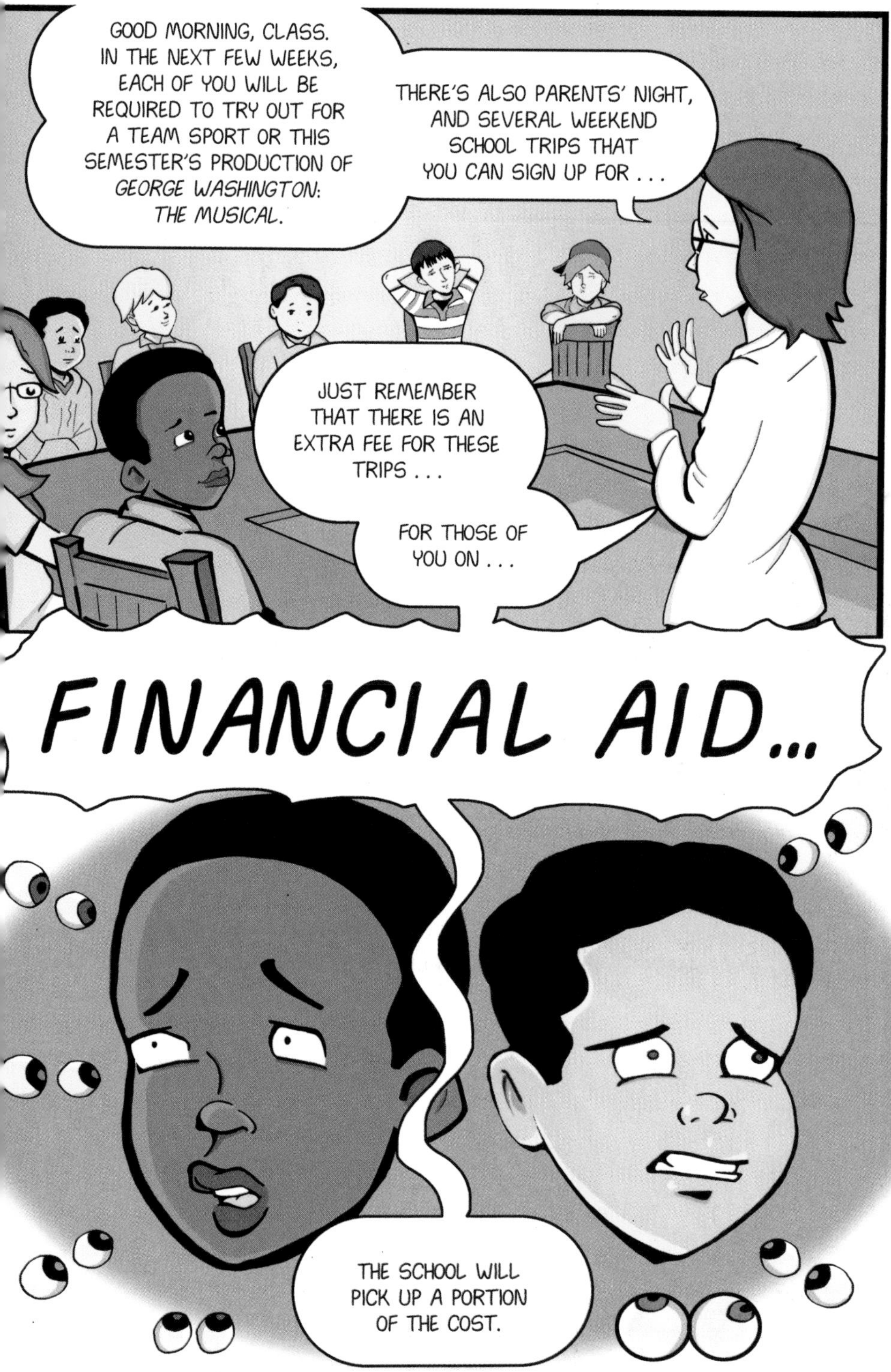
GOOD MORNING, CLASS. IN THE NEXT FEW WEEKS, EACH OF YOU WILL BE REQUIRED TO TRY OUT FOR A TEAM SPORT OR THIS SEMESTER'S PRODUCTION OF *GEORGE WASHINGTON: THE MUSICAL*.
THERE'S ALSO PARENTS' NIGHT, AND SEVERAL WEEKEND SCHOOL TRIPS THAT YOU CAN SIGN UP FOR . . .
JUST REMEMBER THAT THERE IS AN EXTRA FEE FOR THESE TRIPS . . .
FOR THOSE OF YOU ON . . .
FINANCIAL AID...
THE SCHOOL WILL PICK UP A PORTION OF THE COST.

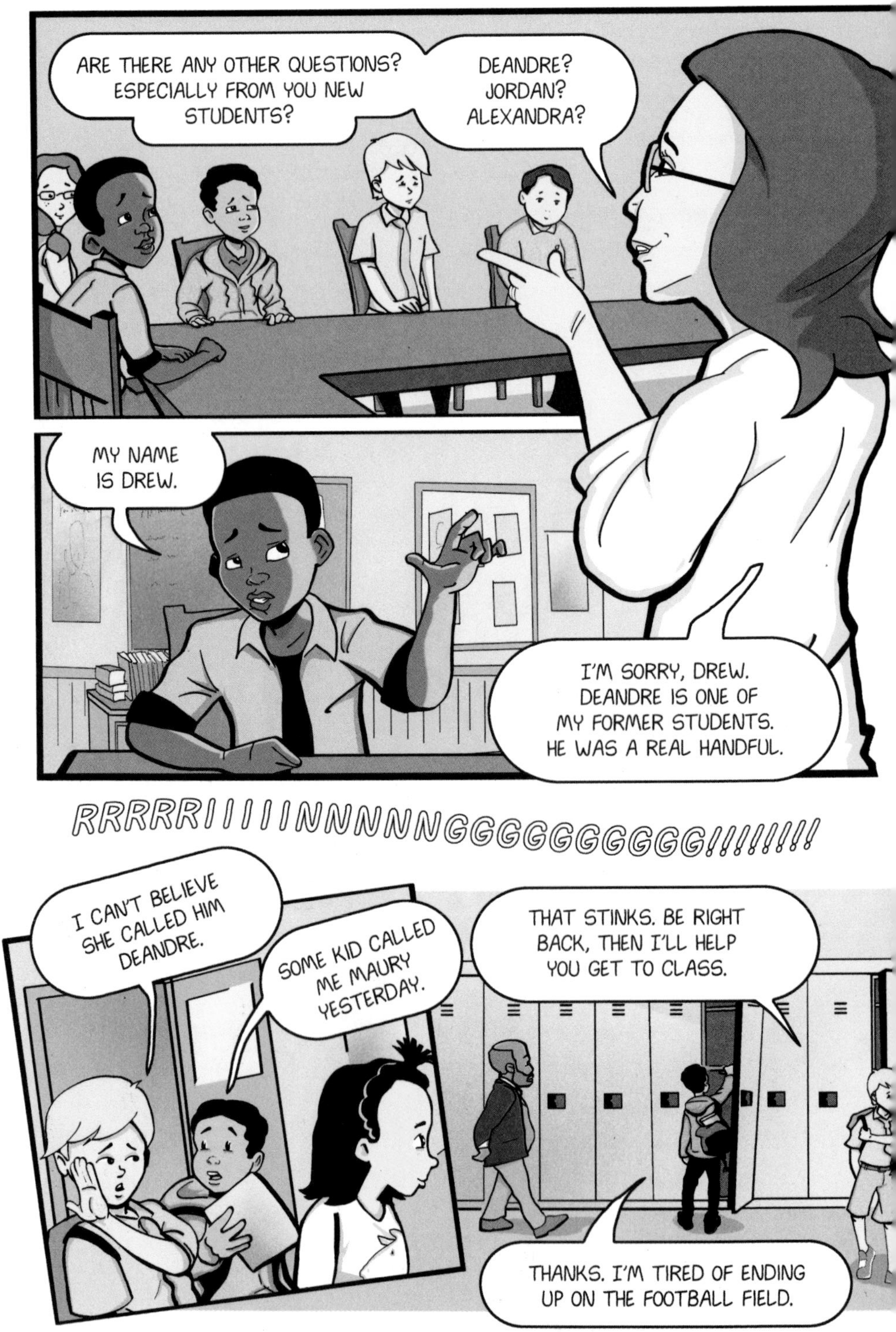
ARE THERE ANY OTHER QUESTIONS? ESPECIALLY FROM YOU NEW STUDENTS?
DEANDRE? JORDAN? ALEXANDRA?
MY NAME IS DREW.
I'M SORRY, DREW. DEANDRE IS ONE OF MY FORMER STUDENTS. HE WAS A REAL HANDFUL.
RRRRRIIIIINNNNNGGGGGGGGG!!!!!!!!
I CAN'T BELIEVE SHE CALLED HIM DEANDRE.
SOME KID CALLED ME MAURY YESTERDAY.
THAT STINKS. BE RIGHT BACK, THEN I'LL HELP YOU GET TO CLASS.
THANKS. I'M TIRED OF ENDING UP ON THE FOOTBALL FIELD.

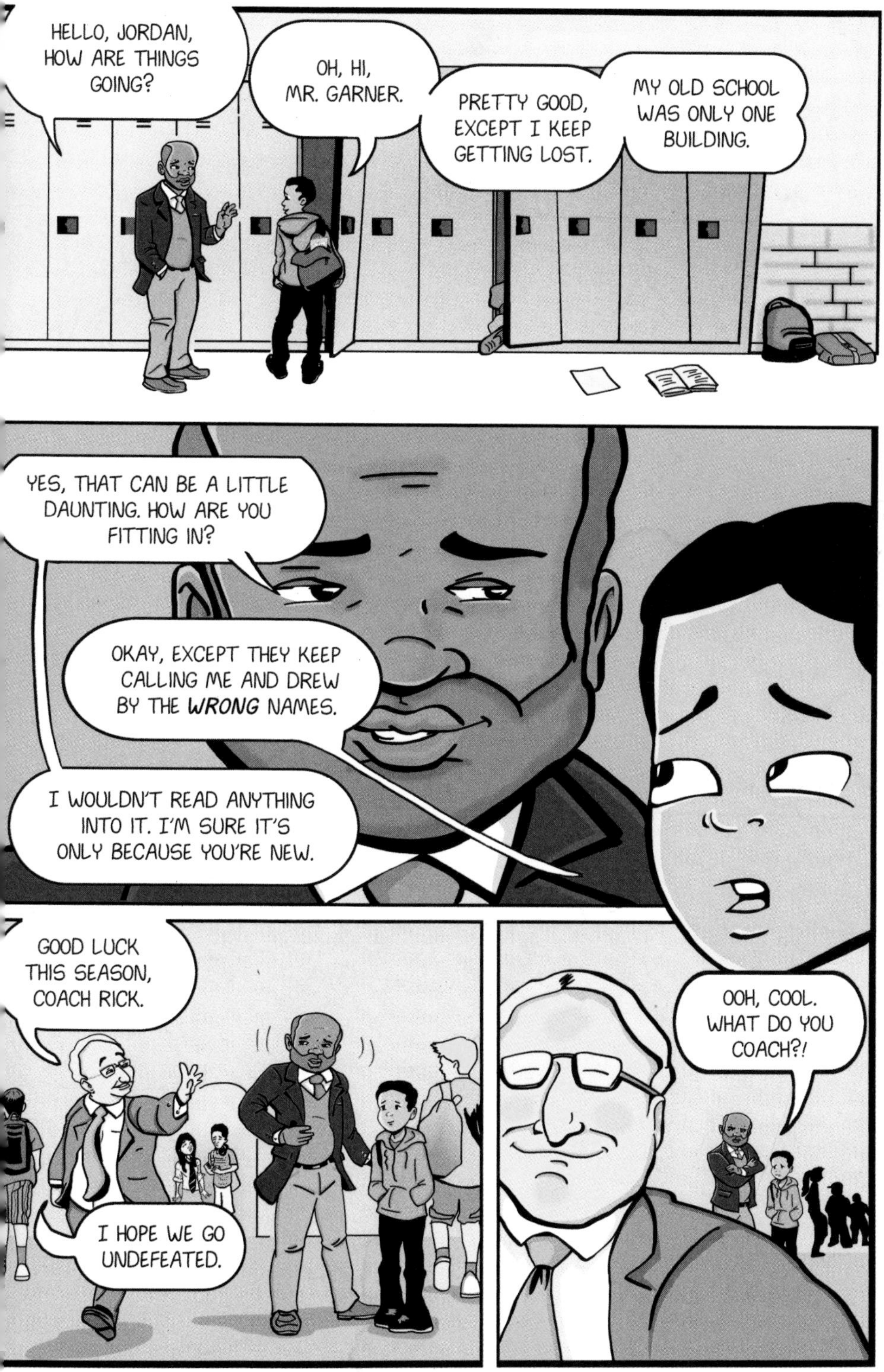
HELLO, JORDAN, HOW ARE THINGS GOING?
OH, HI, MR. GARNER.
PRETTY GOOD, EXCEPT I KEEP GETTING LOST.
MY OLD SCHOOL WAS ONLY ONE BUILDING.
YES, THAT CAN BE A LITTLE DAUNTING. HOW ARE YOU FITTING IN?
OKAY, EXCEPT THEY KEEP CALLING ME AND DREW BY THE *WRONG* NAMES.
I WOULDN'T READ ANYTHING INTO IT. I'M SURE IT'S ONLY BECAUSE YOU'RE NEW.
GOOD LUCK THIS SEASON, COACH RICK.
I HOPE WE GO UNDEFEATED.
OOH, COOL. WHAT DO YOU COACH?!

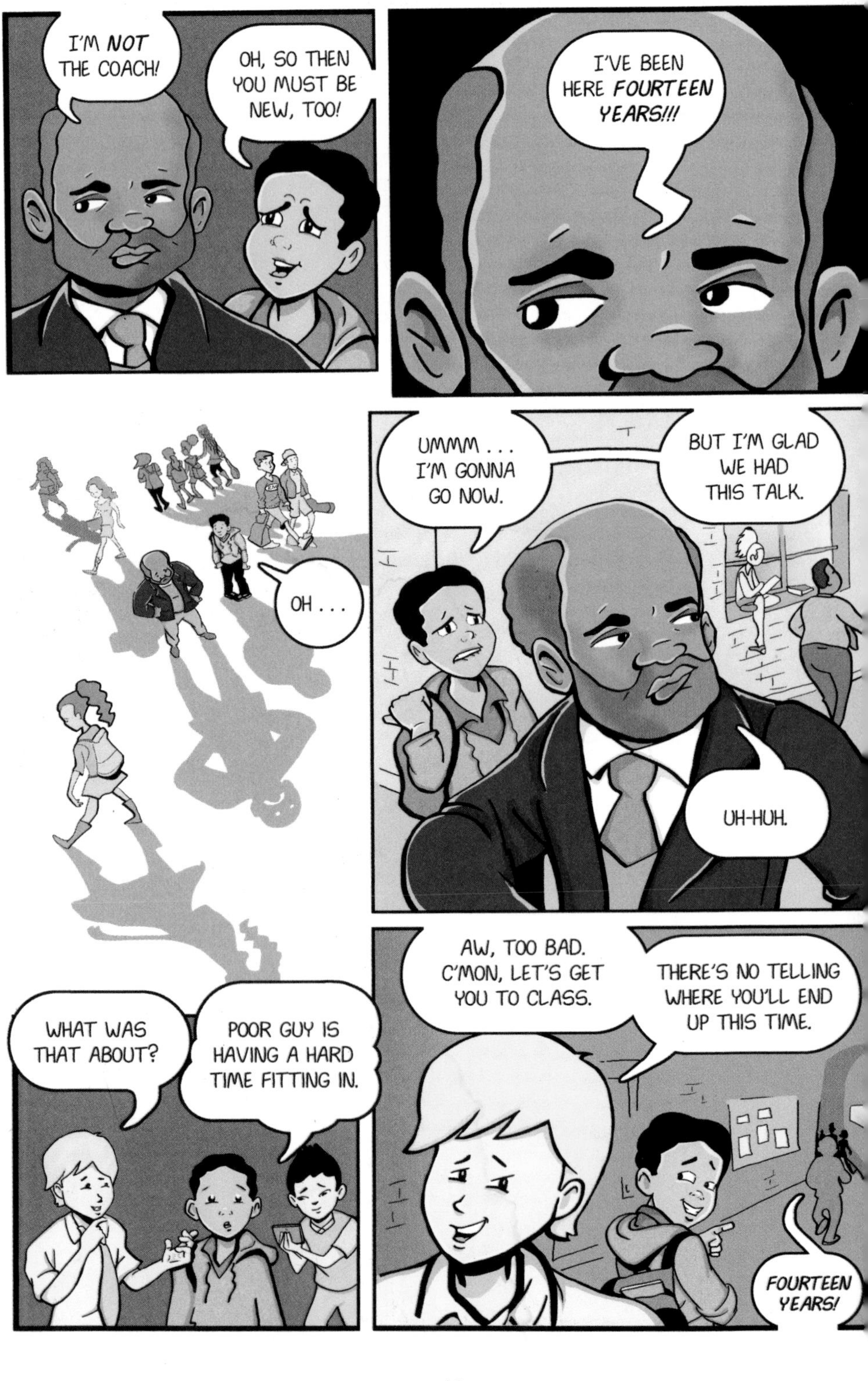
I'M NOT THE COACH!
OH, SO THEN YOU MUST BE NEW, TOO!
I'VE BEEN HERE FOURTEEN YEARS!!!
OH . . .
UMMM . . . I'M GONNA GO NOW.
BUT I'M GLAD WE HAD THIS TALK.
UH-HUH.
WHAT WAS THAT ABOUT?
POOR GUY IS HAVING A HARD TIME FITTING IN.
AW, TOO BAD. C'MON, LET'S GET YOU TO CLASS.
THERE'S NO TELLING WHERE YOU'LL END UP THIS TIME.
FOURTEEN YEARS!

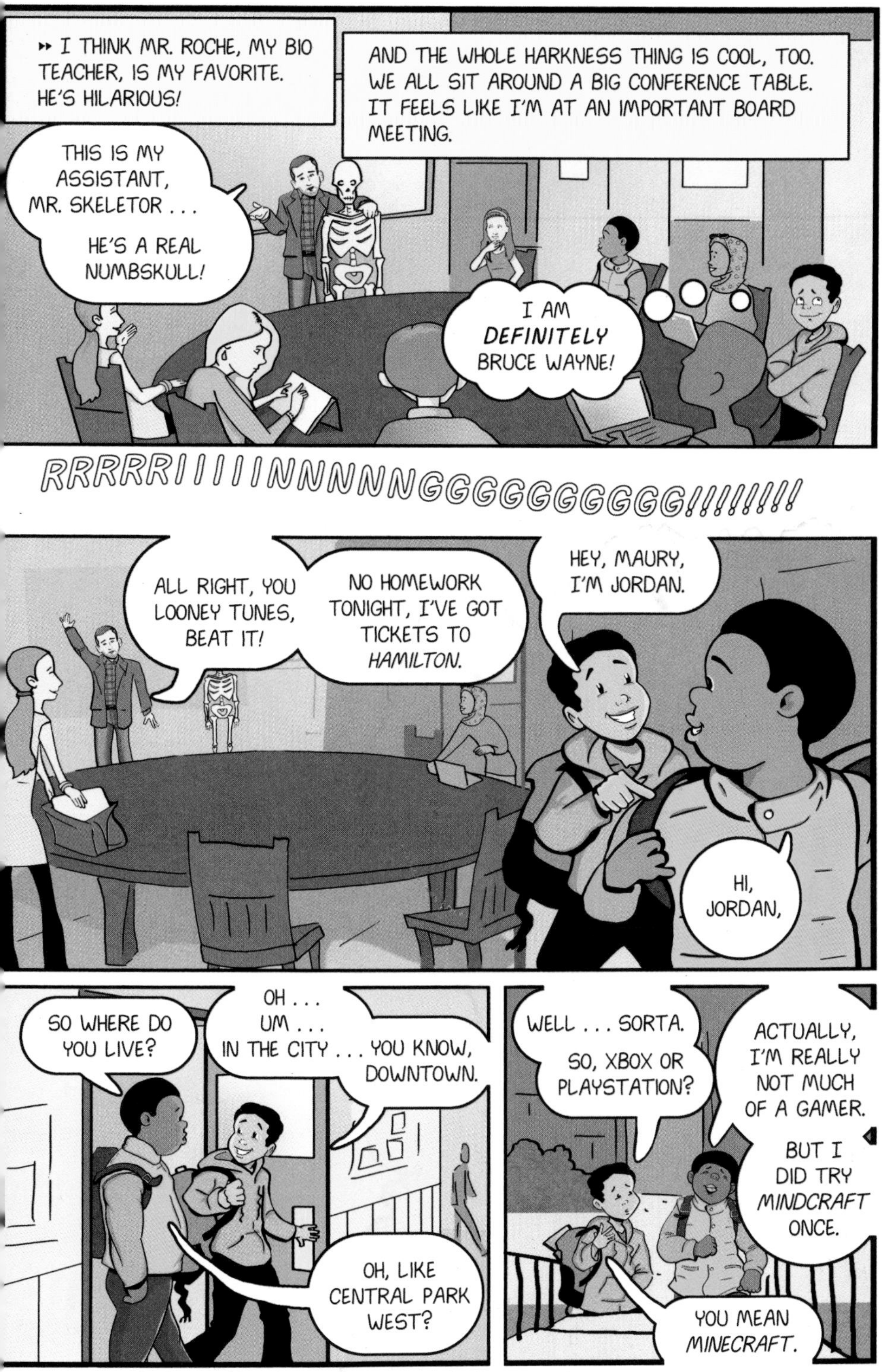
▸▸ I THINK MR. ROCHE, MY BIO TEACHER, IS MY FAVORITE. HE'S HILARIOUS!
AND THE WHOLE HARKNESS THING IS COOL, TOO. WE ALL SIT AROUND A BIG CONFERENCE TABLE. IT FEELS LIKE I'M AT AN IMPORTANT BOARD MEETING.
THIS IS MY ASSISTANT, MR. SKELETOR . . .
HE'S A REAL NUMBSKULL!
I AM **DEFINITELY** BRUCE WAYNE!
RRRRRIIIIINNNNNGGGGGGGGGG!!!!!!!
ALL RIGHT, YOU LOONEY TUNES, BEAT IT!
NO HOMEWORK TONIGHT, I'VE GOT TICKETS TO *HAMILTON.*
HEY, MAURY, I'M JORDAN.
HI, JORDAN.
SO WHERE DO YOU LIVE?
OH . . . UM . . . IN THE CITY . . . YOU KNOW, DOWNTOWN.
OH, LIKE CENTRAL PARK WEST?
WELL . . . SORTA.
SO, XBOX OR PLAYSTATION?
ACTUALLY, I'M REALLY NOT MUCH OF A GAMER.
BUT I DID TRY *MINDCRAFT* ONCE.
YOU MEAN *MINECRAFT.*

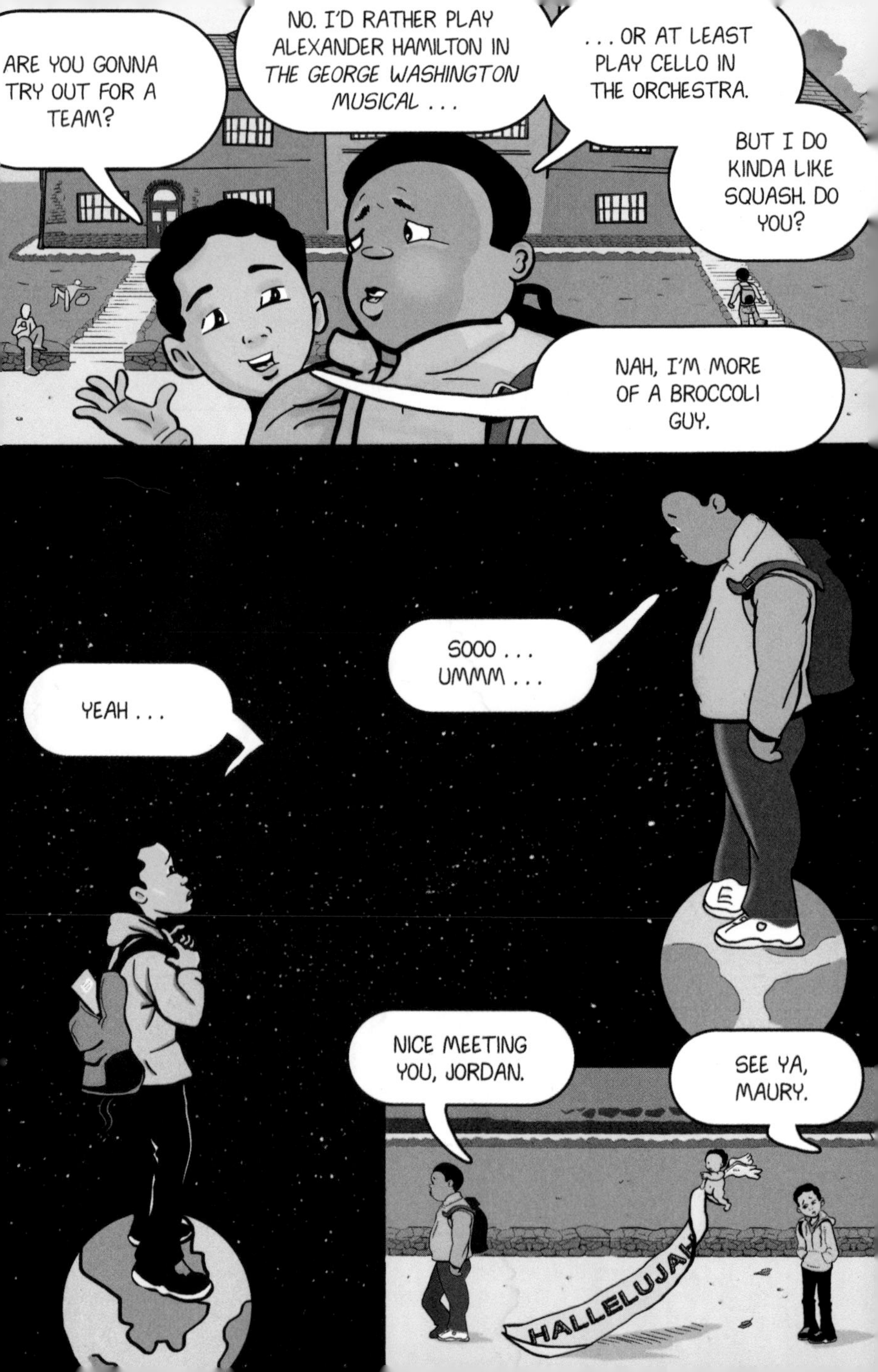
ARE YOU GONNA TRY OUT FOR A TEAM?
NO. I'D RATHER PLAY ALEXANDER HAMILTON IN *THE GEORGE WASHINGTON MUSICAL* . . .
. . . OR AT LEAST PLAY CELLO IN THE ORCHESTRA.
BUT I DO KINDA LIKE SQUASH. DO YOU?
NAH, I'M MORE OF A BROCCOLI GUY.
SOOO . . . UMMM . . .
YEAH . . .
NICE MEETING YOU, JORDAN.
SEE YA, MAURY.
HALLELUJAH

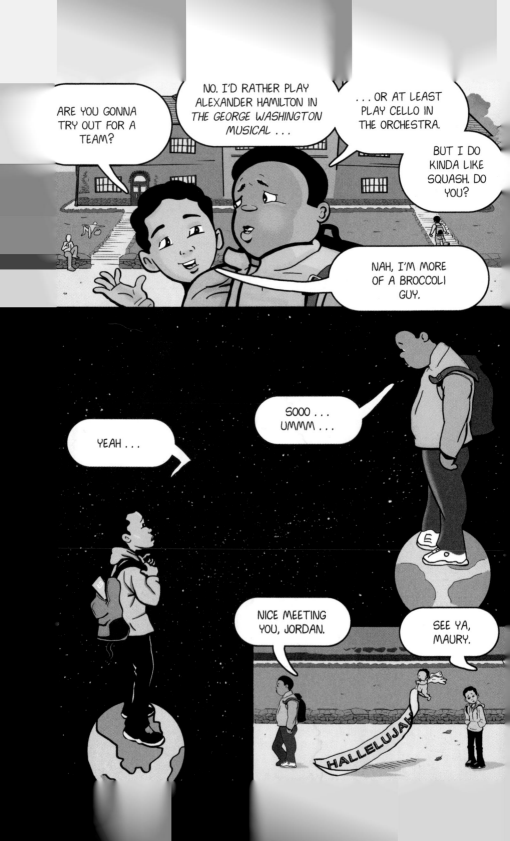

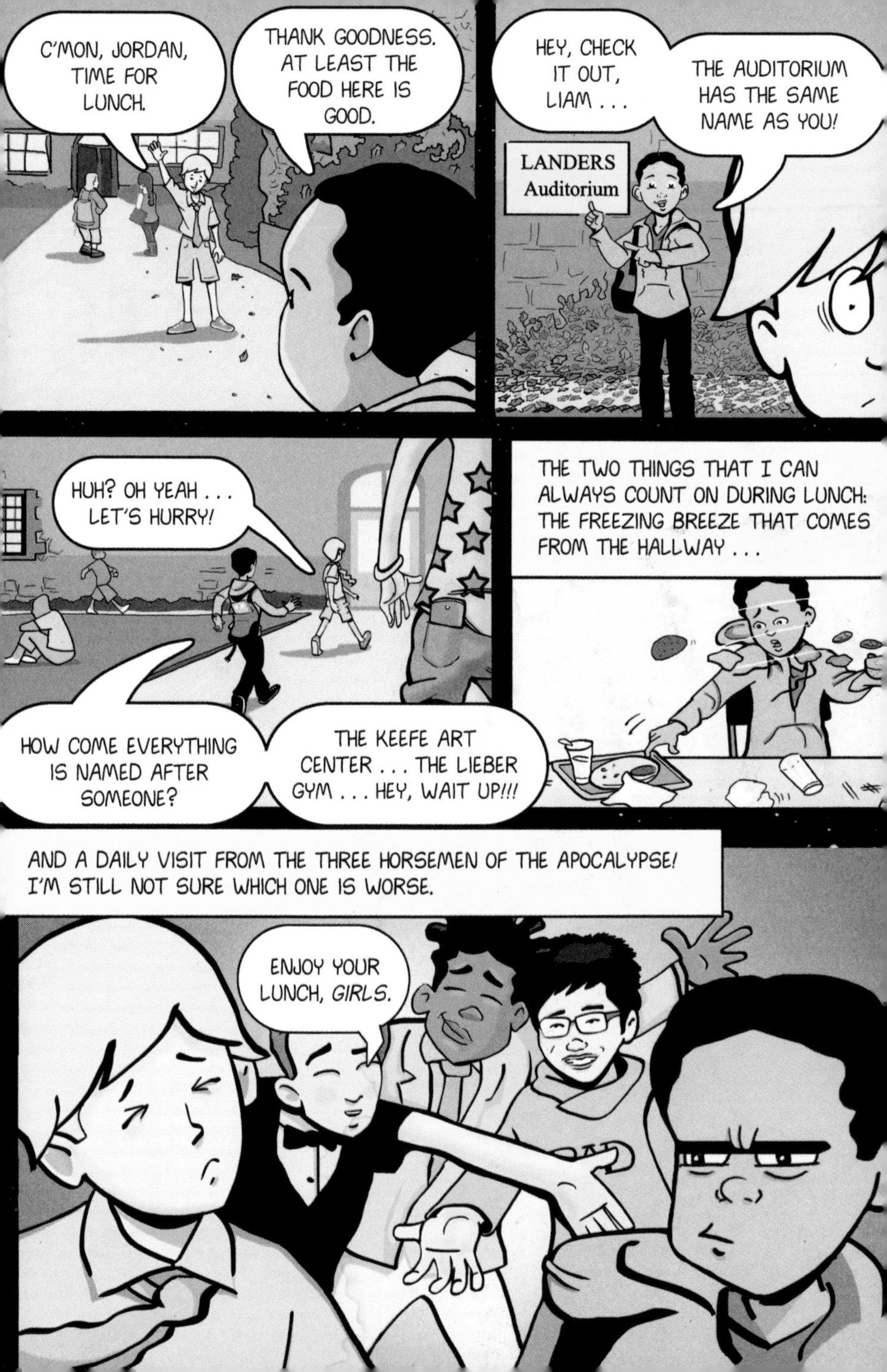
C'MON, JORDAN, TIME FOR LUNCH.
THANK GOODNESS. AT LEAST THE FOOD HERE IS GOOD.
HEY, CHECK IT OUT, LIAM . . .
THE AUDITORIUM HAS THE SAME NAME AS YOU!
LANDERS Auditorium
HUH? OH YEAH . . . LET'S HURRY!
HOW COME EVERYTHING IS NAMED AFTER SOMEONE?
THE KEEFE ART CENTER . . . THE LIEBER GYM . . . HEY, WAIT UP!!!
THE TWO THINGS THAT I CAN ALWAYS COUNT ON DURING LUNCH: THE FREEZING BREEZE THAT COMES FROM THE HALLWAY . . .
AND A DAILY VISIT FROM THE THREE HORSEMEN OF THE APOCALYPSE! I'M STILL NOT SURE WHICH ONE IS WORSE.
ENJOY YOUR LUNCH, *GIRLS*.

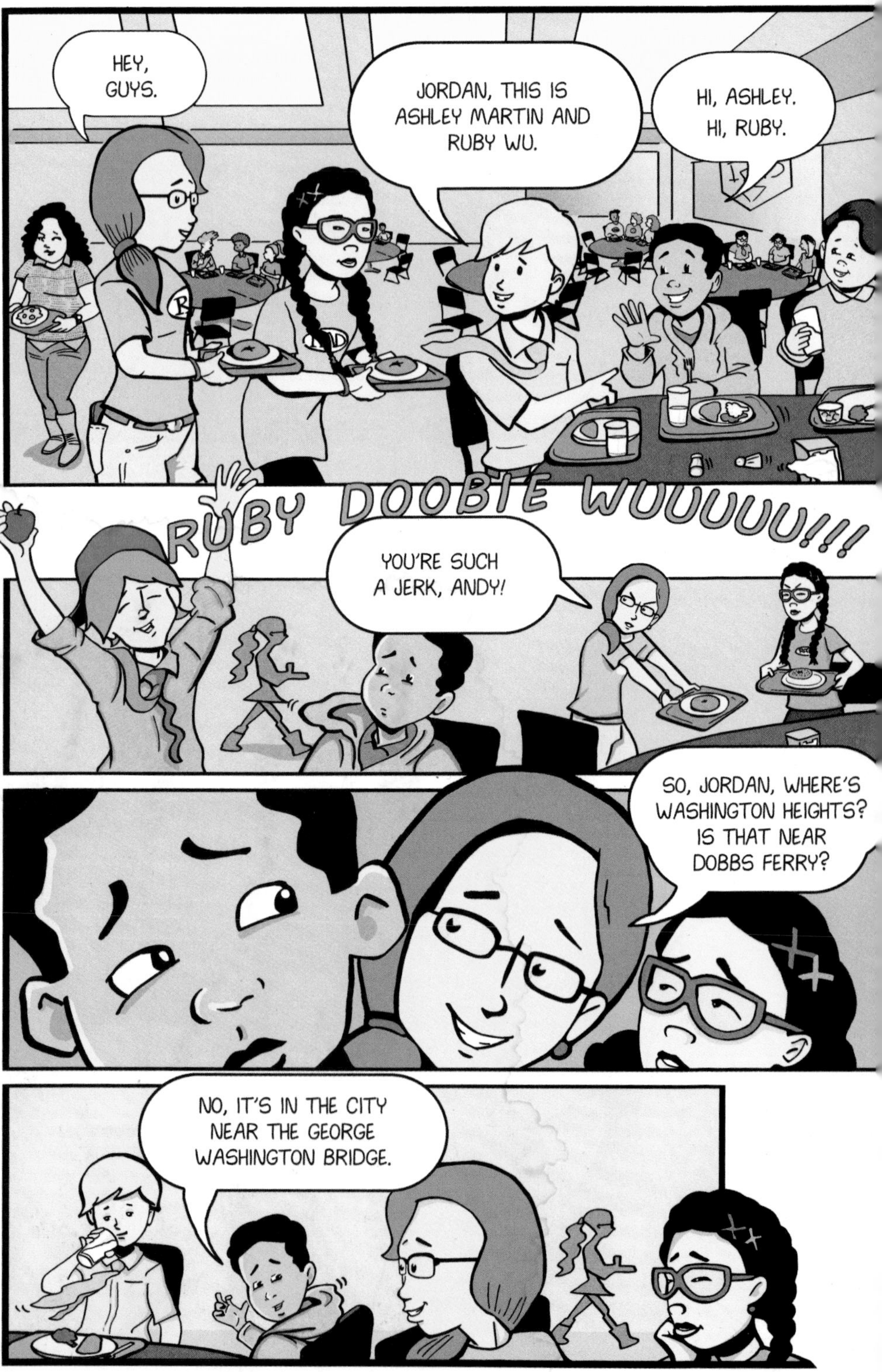
HEY, GUYS.
JORDAN, THIS IS ASHLEY MARTIN AND RUBY WU.
HI, ASHLEY. HI, RUBY.
RUBY DOOBIE WUUUUUU!!!
YOU'RE SUCH A JERK, ANDY!
SO, JORDAN, WHERE'S WASHINGTON HEIGHTS? IS THAT NEAR DOBBS FERRY?
NO, IT'S IN THE CITY NEAR THE GEORGE WASHINGTON BRIDGE.

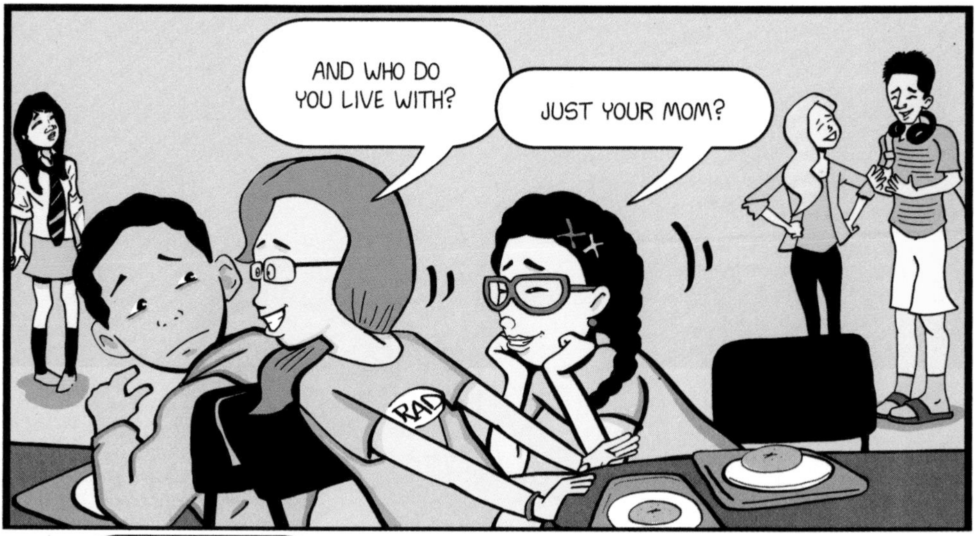
AND WHO DO YOU LIVE WITH?
JUST YOUR MOM?

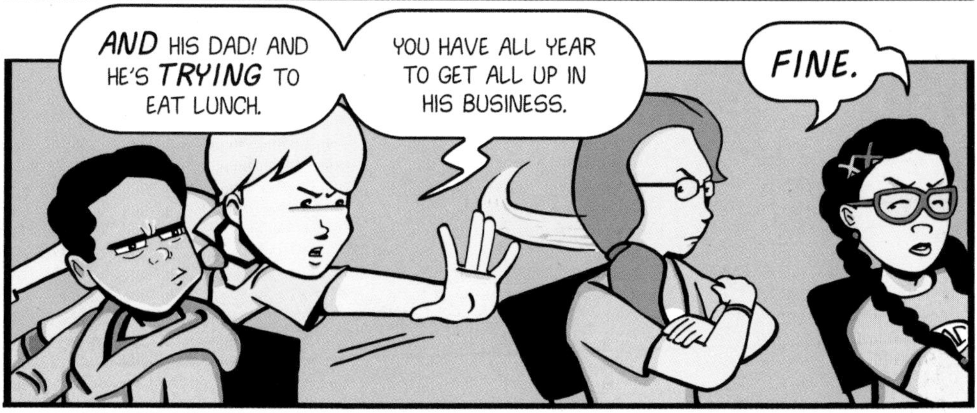
AND HIS DAD! AND HE'S TRYING TO EAT LUNCH.
YOU HAVE ALL YEAR TO GET ALL UP IN HIS BUSINESS.
FINE.

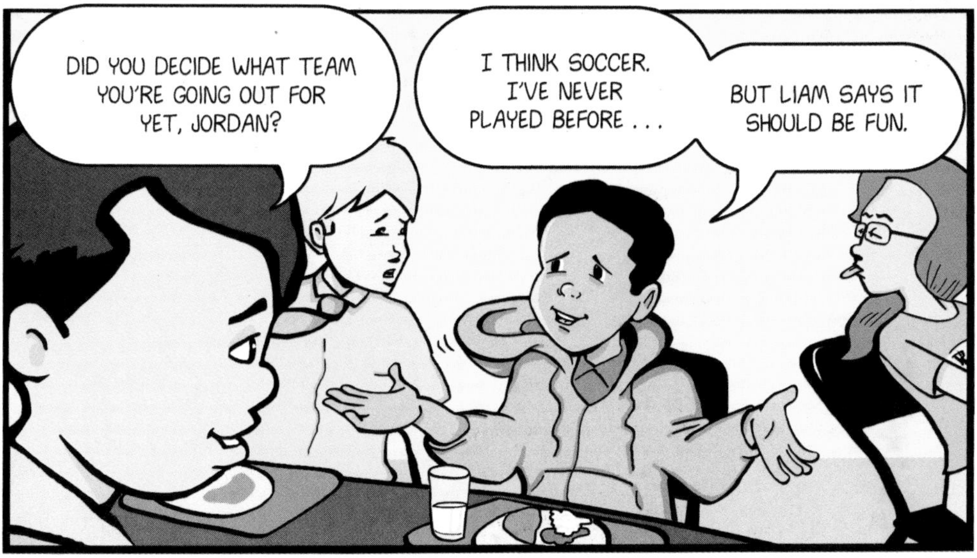
DID YOU DECIDE WHAT TEAM YOU'RE GOING OUT FOR YET, JORDAN?
I THINK SOCCER. I'VE NEVER PLAYED BEFORE . . .
BUT LIAM SAYS IT SHOULD BE FUN.

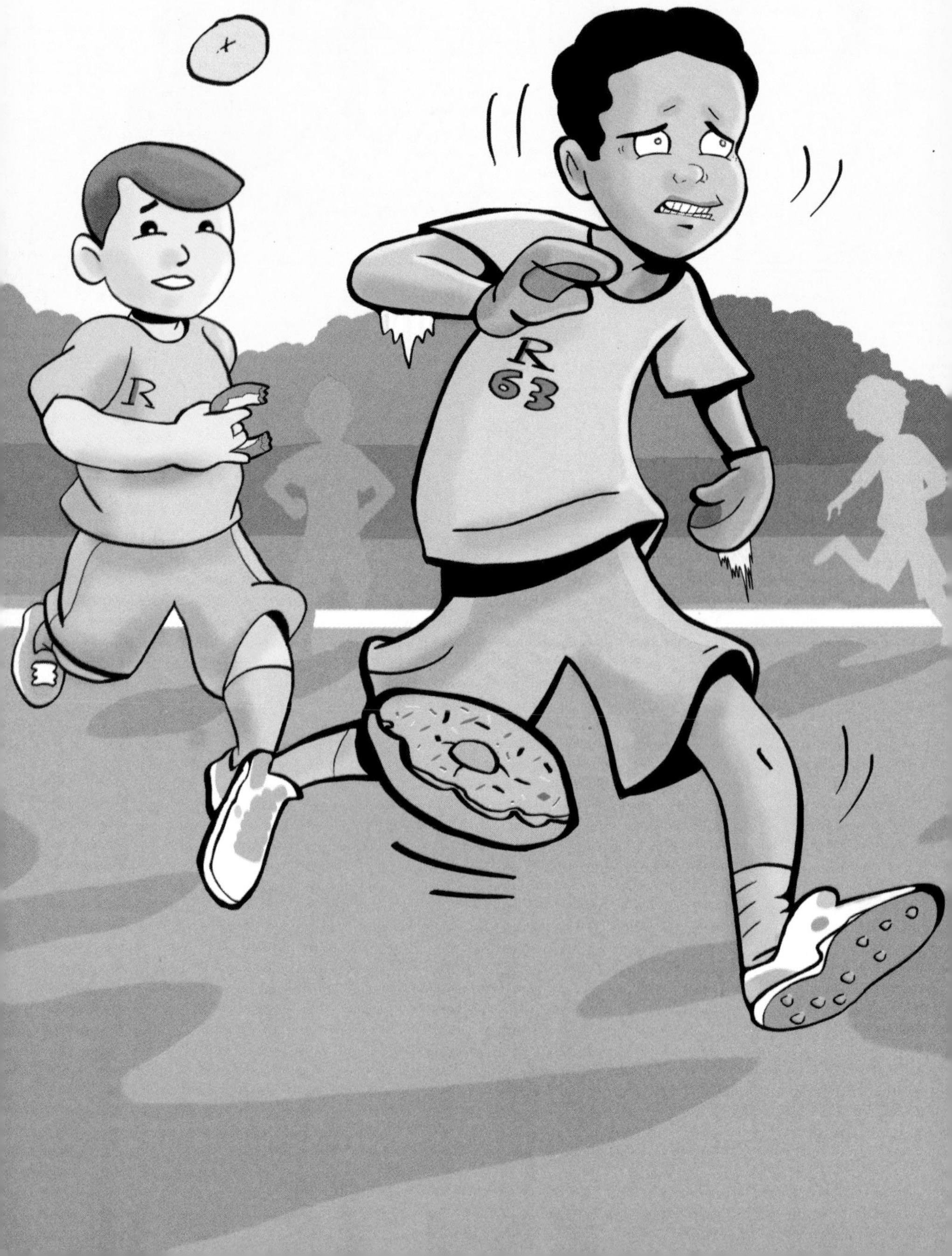
R
R
63

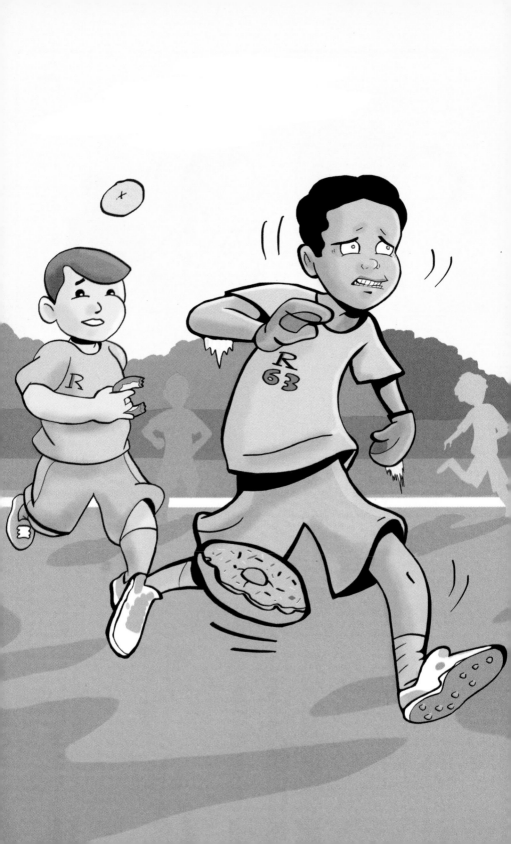

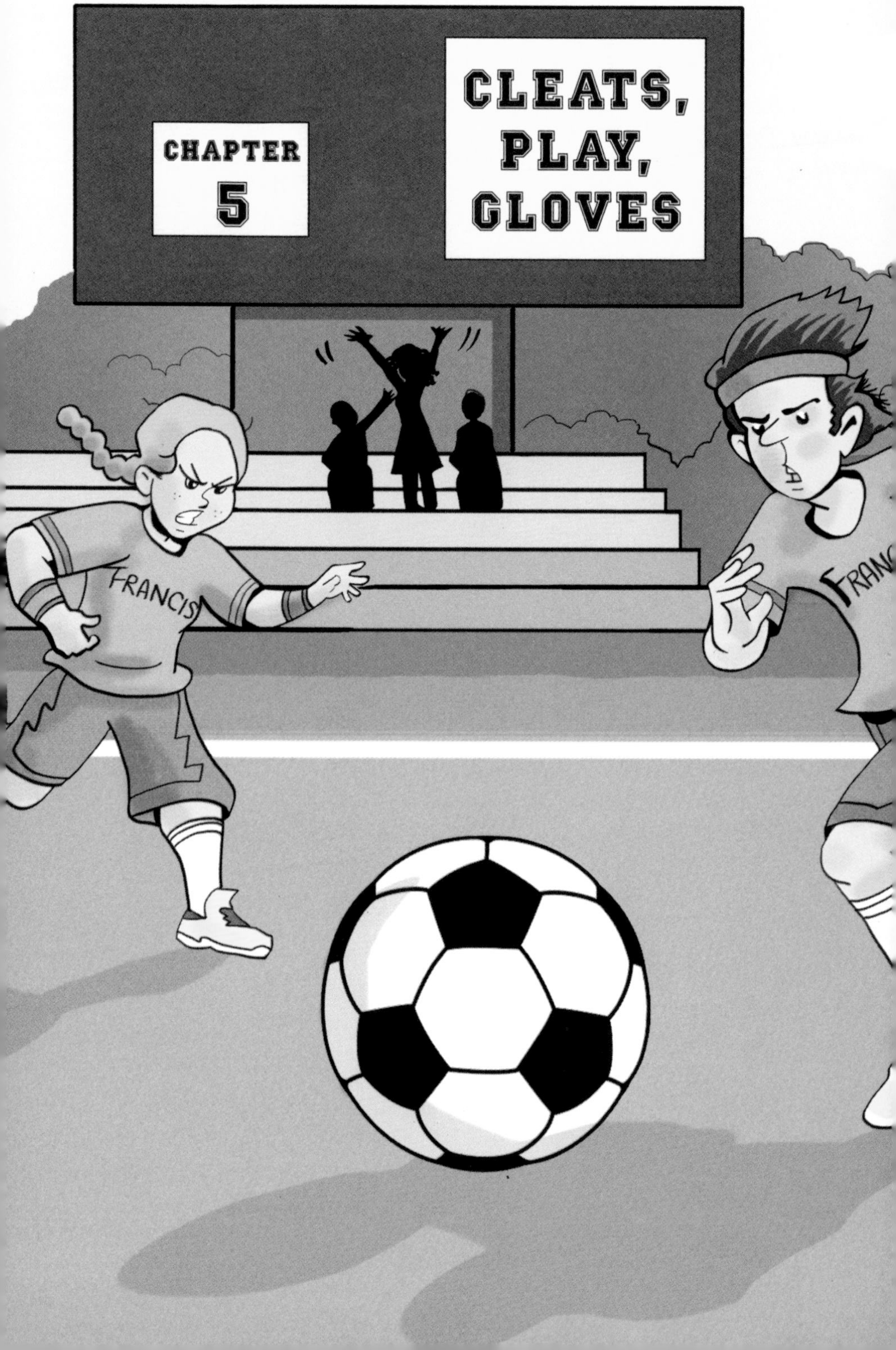
CHAPTER
5
CLEATS, PLAY, GLOVES
FRANCIS

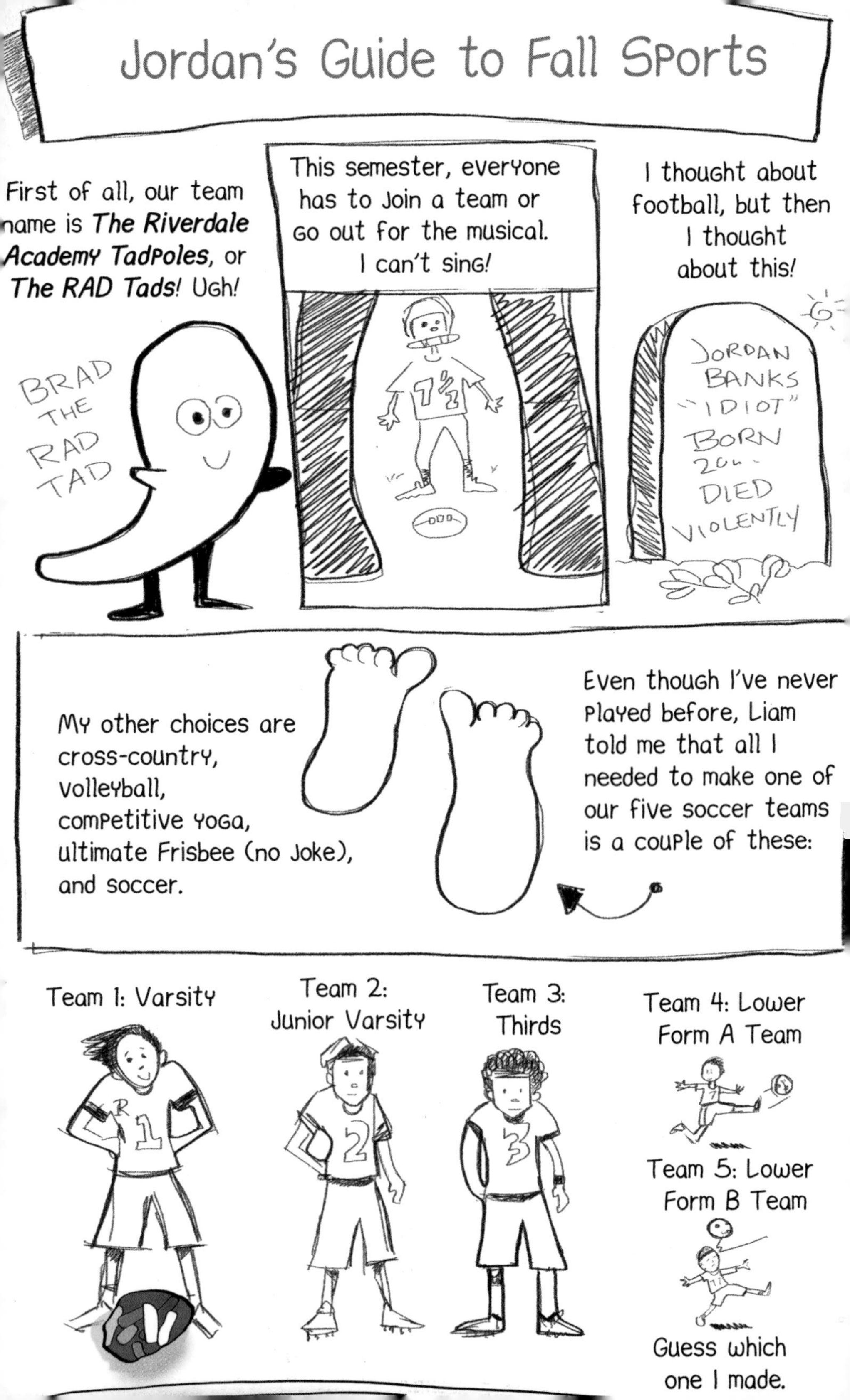
Jordan's Guide to Fall Sports
First of all, our team name is *The Riverdale Academy Tadpoles*, or *The RAD Tads*! Ugh!
BRAD THE RAD TAD
This semester, everyone has to join a team or go out for the musical. I can't sing!
I thought about football, but then I thought about this!
JORDAN BANKS
"IDIOT"
BORN
DIED VIOLENTLY
My other choices are cross-country, volleyball, competitive yoga, ultimate Frisbee (no joke), and soccer.
Even though I've never played before, Liam told me that all I needed to make one of our five soccer teams is a couple of these:
Team 1: Varsity
Team 2: Junior Varsity
Team 3: Thirds
Team 4: Lower Form A Team
Team 5: Lower Form B Team
Guess which one I made.

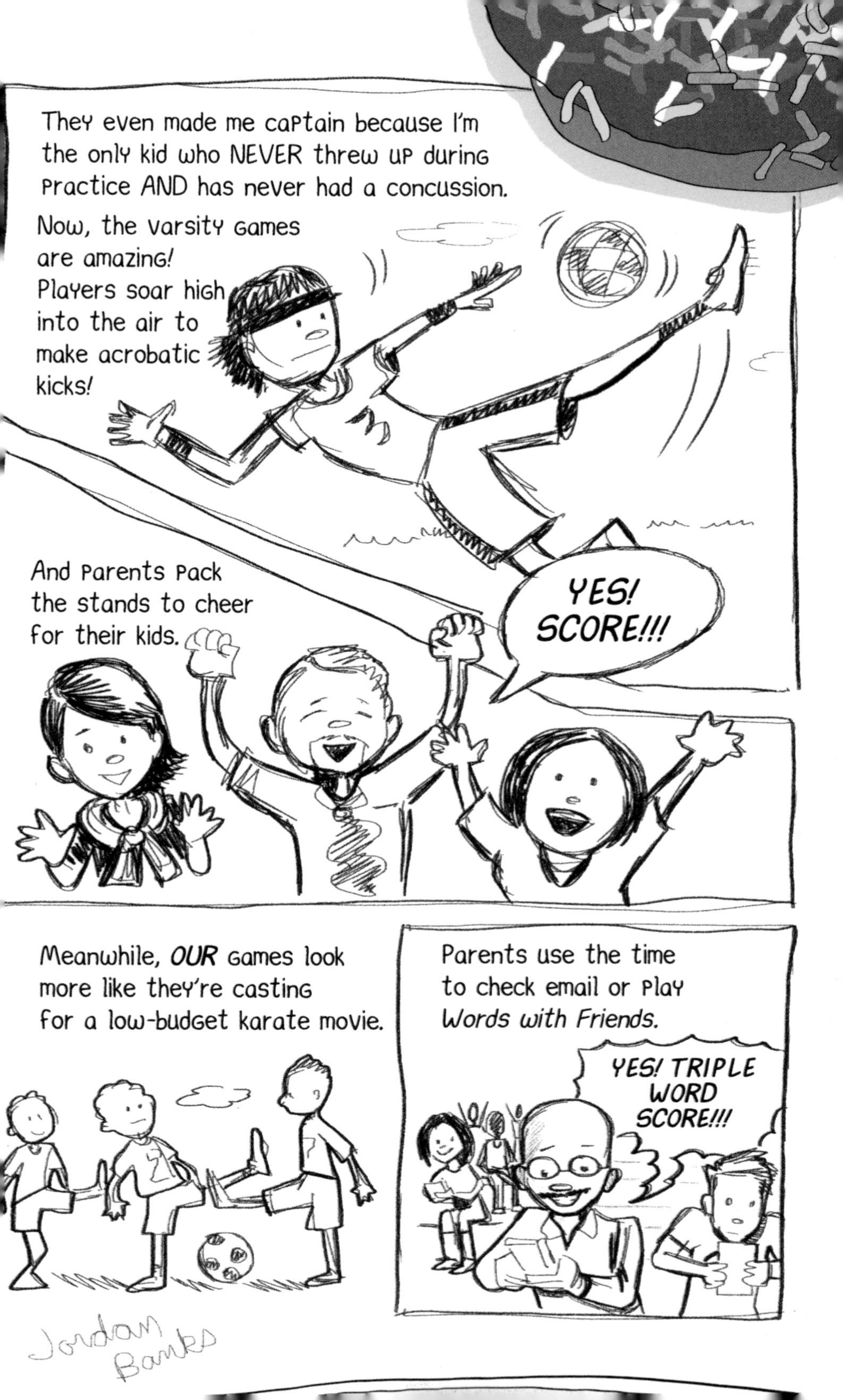

They even made me captain because I'm the only kid who NEVER threw up during practice AND has never had a concussion.
Now, the varsity games are amazing! Players soar high into the air to make acrobatic kicks!
And parents pack the stands to cheer for their kids.
YES! SCORE!!!
Meanwhile, OUR games look more like they're casting for a low-budget karate movie.
Parents use the time to check email or play Words with Friends.
YES! TRIPLE WORD SCORE!!!
Jordan Banks

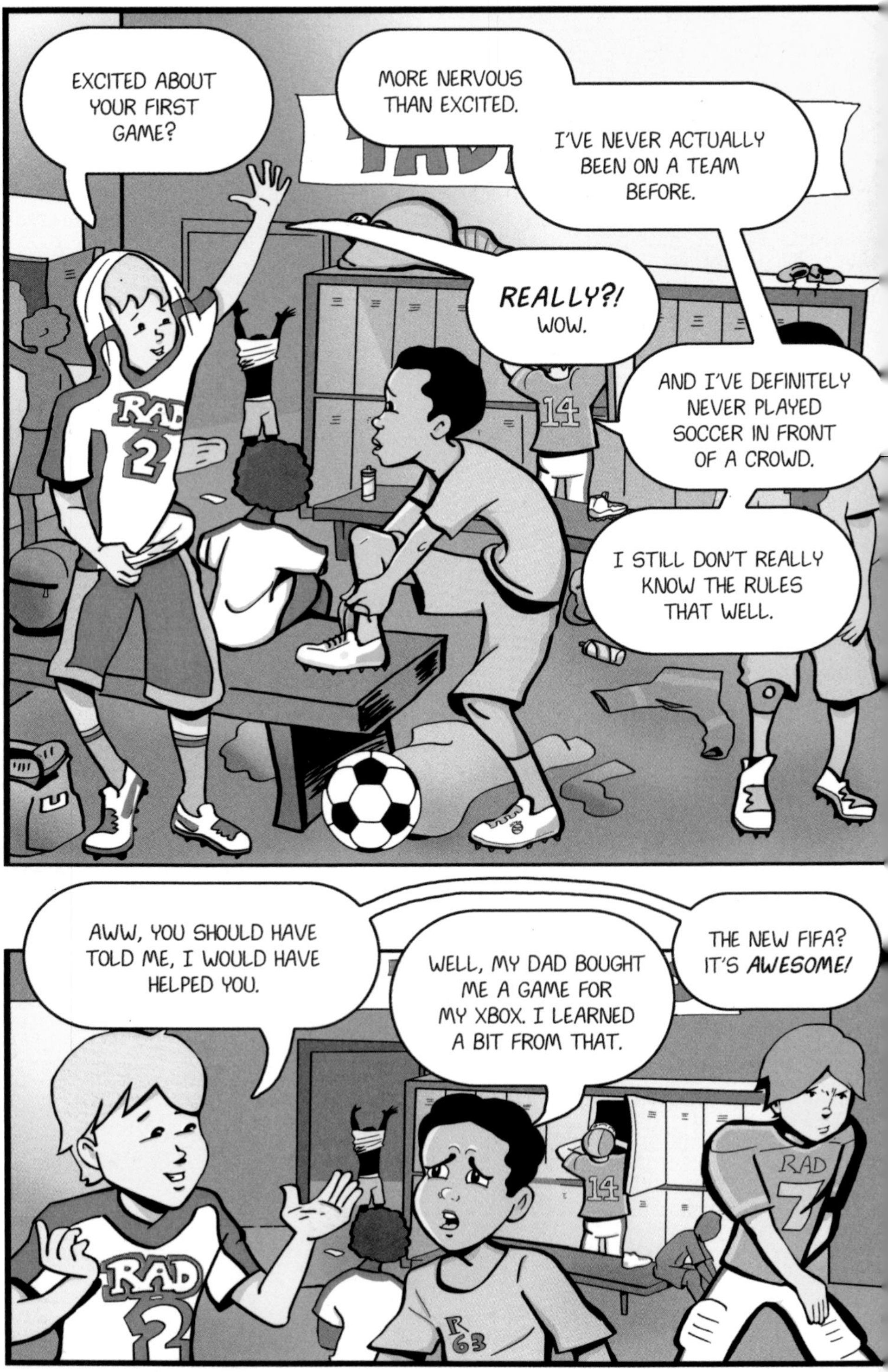
EXCITED ABOUT YOUR FIRST GAME?
MORE NERVOUS THAN EXCITED.
I'VE NEVER ACTUALLY BEEN ON A TEAM BEFORE.
REALLY?! WOW.
AND I'VE DEFINITELY NEVER PLAYED SOCCER IN FRONT OF A CROWD.
I STILL DON'T REALLY KNOW THE RULES THAT WELL.
AWW, YOU SHOULD HAVE TOLD ME, I WOULD HAVE HELPED YOU.
WELL, MY DAD BOUGHT ME A GAME FOR MY XBOX. I LEARNED A BIT FROM THAT.
THE NEW FIFA? IT'S ***AWESOME!***

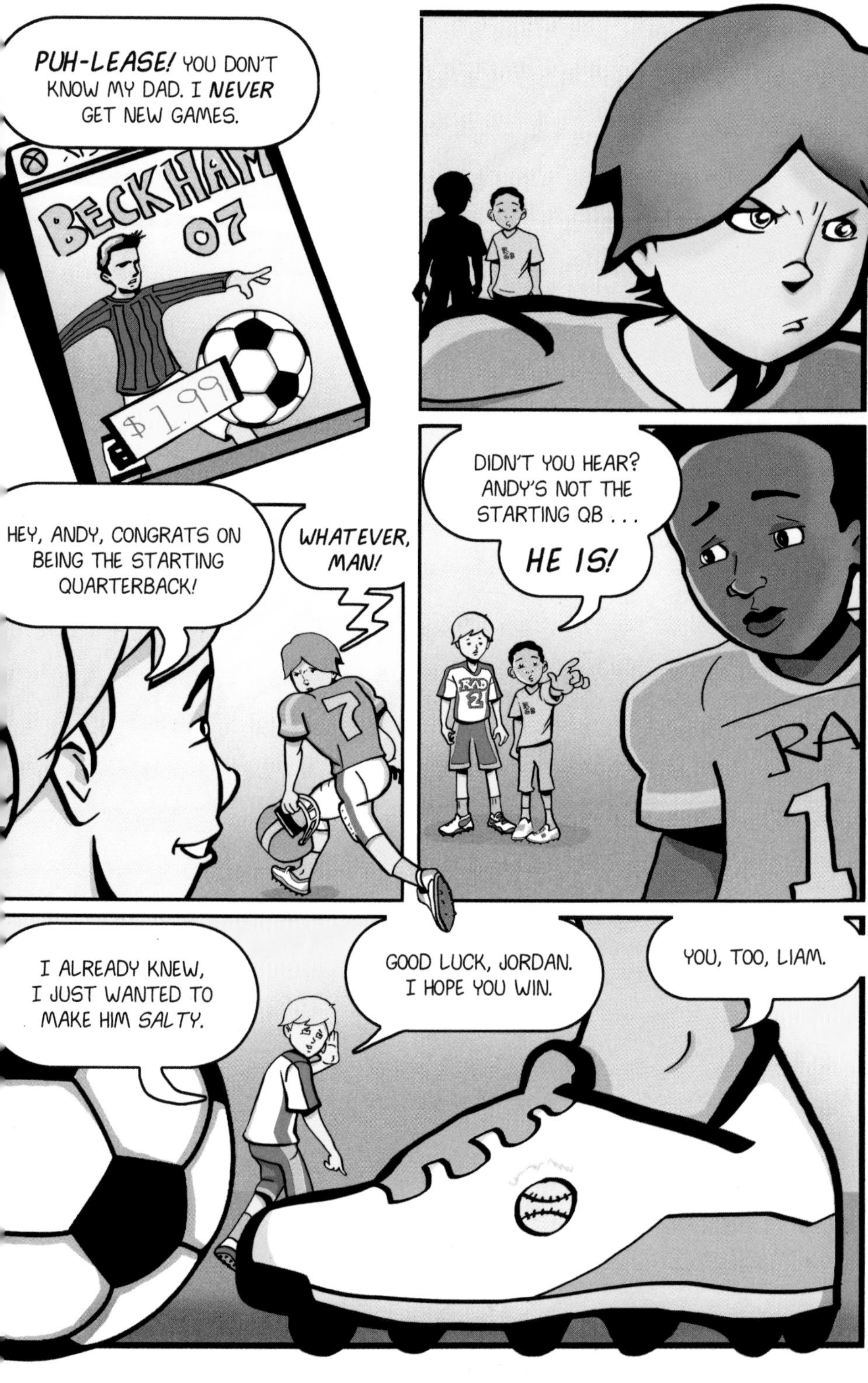
PUH-LEASE! YOU DON'T KNOW MY DAD. I NEVER GET NEW GAMES.
BECKHAM 07
$1.99
HEY, ANDY, CONGRATS ON BEING THE STARTING QUARTERBACK!
WHATEVER, MAN!
DIDN'T YOU HEAR? ANDY'S NOT THE STARTING QB . . .
HE IS!
I ALREADY KNEW, I JUST WANTED TO MAKE HIM SALTY.
GOOD LUCK, JORDAN. I HOPE YOU WIN.
YOU, TOO, LIAM.

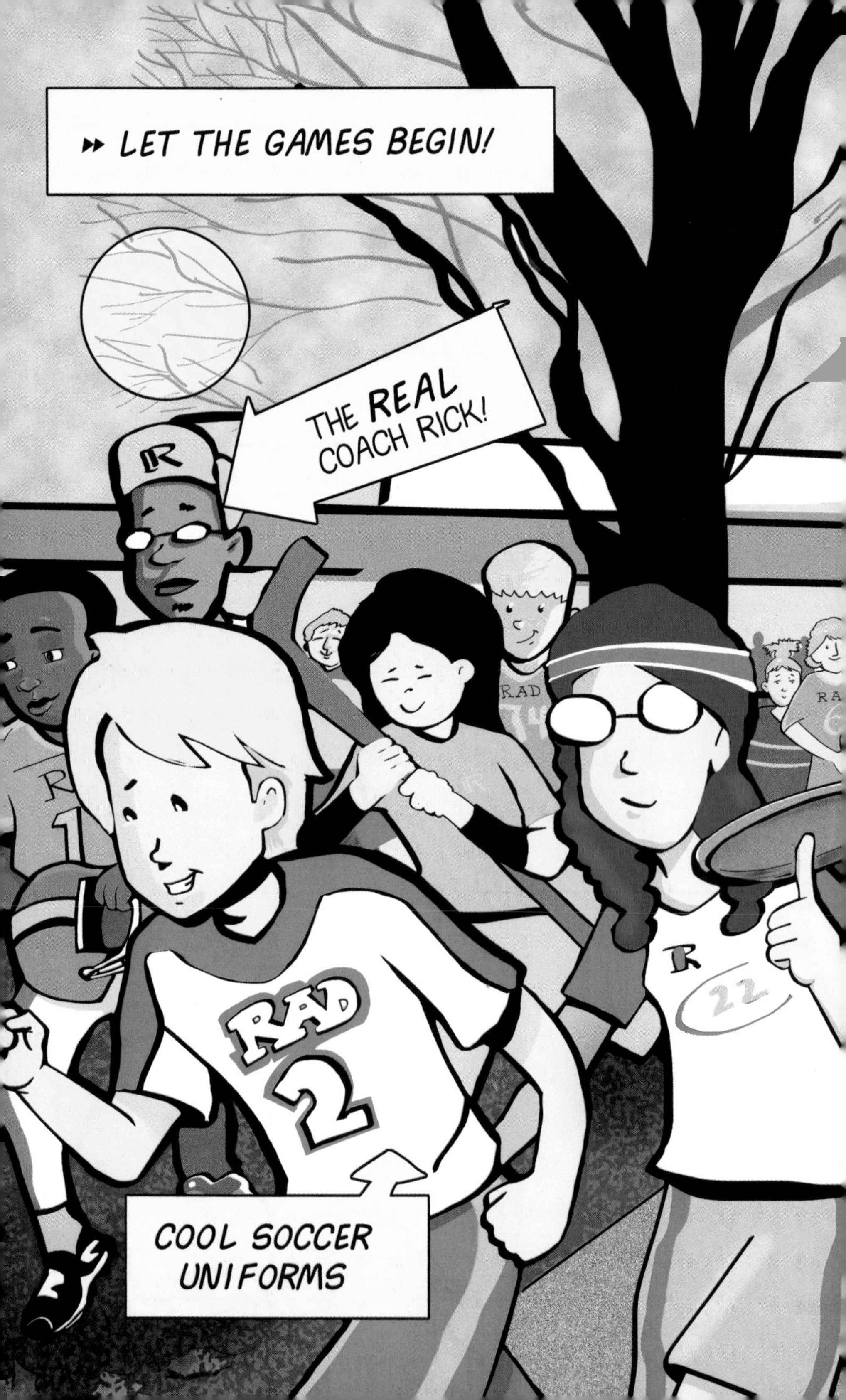

▸▸ LET THE GAMES BEGIN!
THE REAL COACH RICK!
COOL SOCCER UNIFORMS

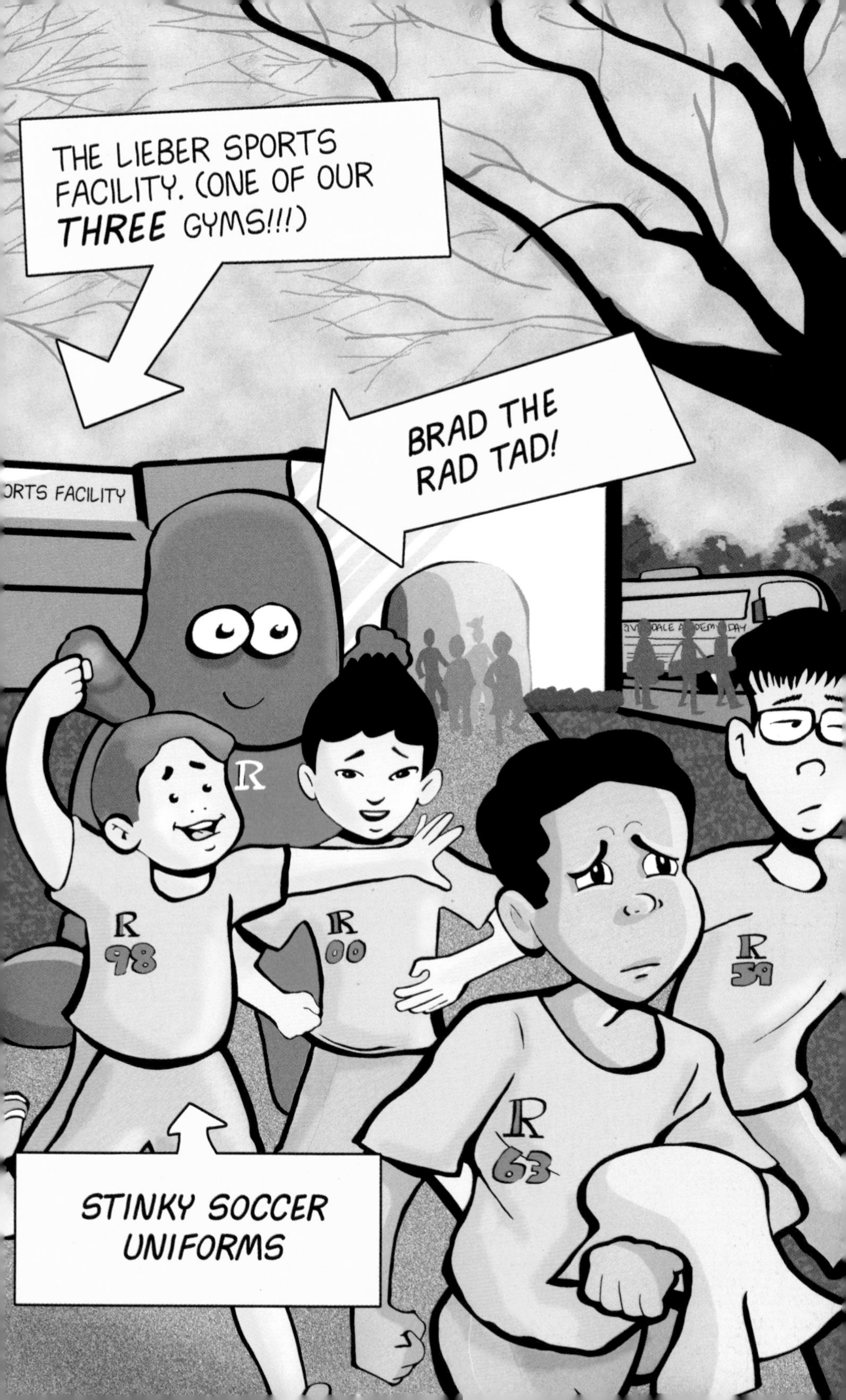
THE LIEBER SPORTS FACILITY. (ONE OF OUR **THREE** GYMS!!!)
BRAD THE RAD TAD!
ORTS FACILITY
STINKY SOCCER UNIFORMS

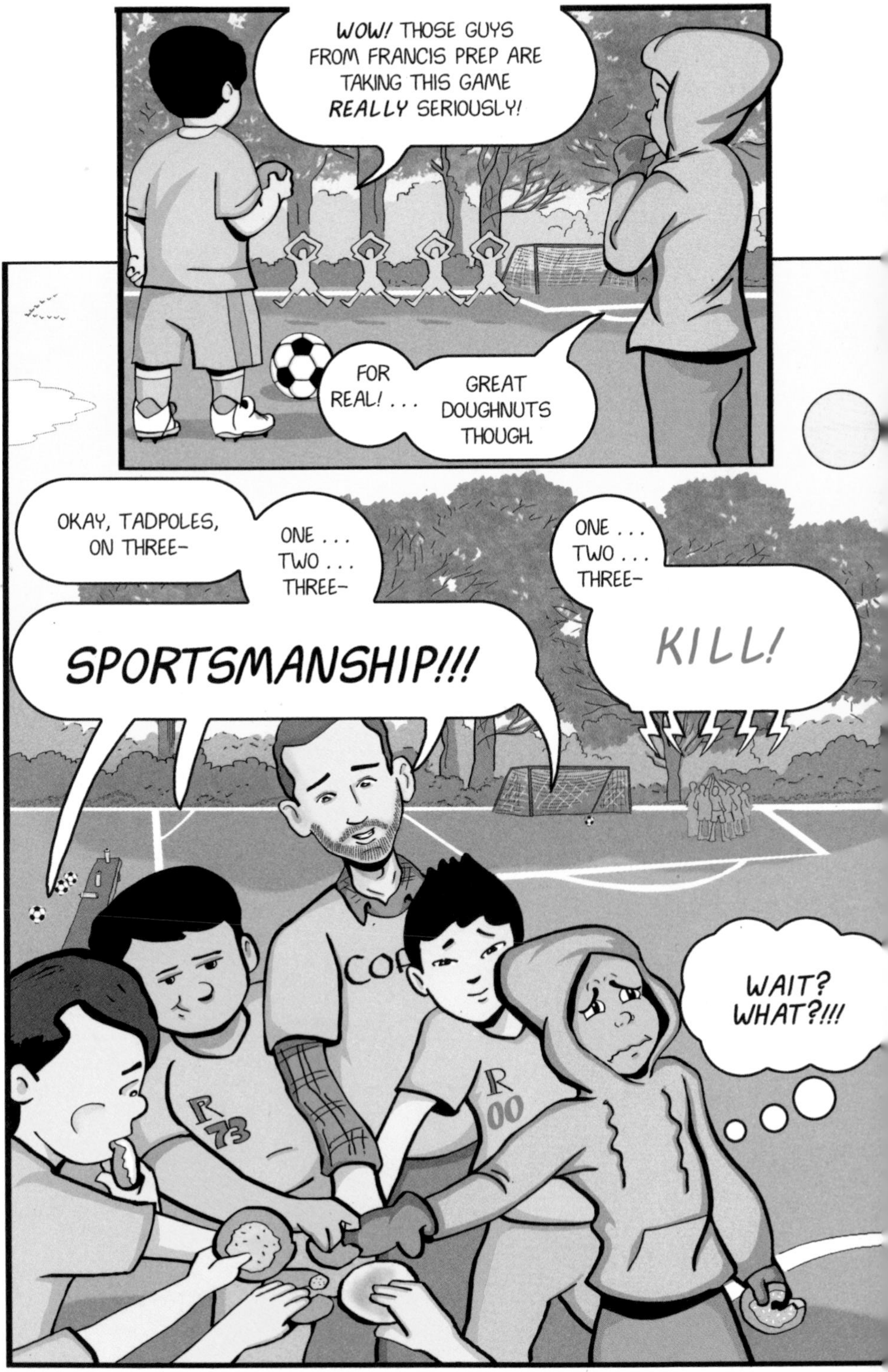
WOW! THOSE GUYS FROM FRANCIS PREP ARE TAKING THIS GAME REALLY SERIOUSLY!
FOR REAL! . . .
GREAT DOUGHNUTS THOUGH.
OKAY, TADPOLES, ON THREE-
ONE . . . TWO . . . THREE-
ONE . . . TWO . . . THREE-
SPORTSMANSHIP!!!
KILL!
WAIT? WHAT?!!!

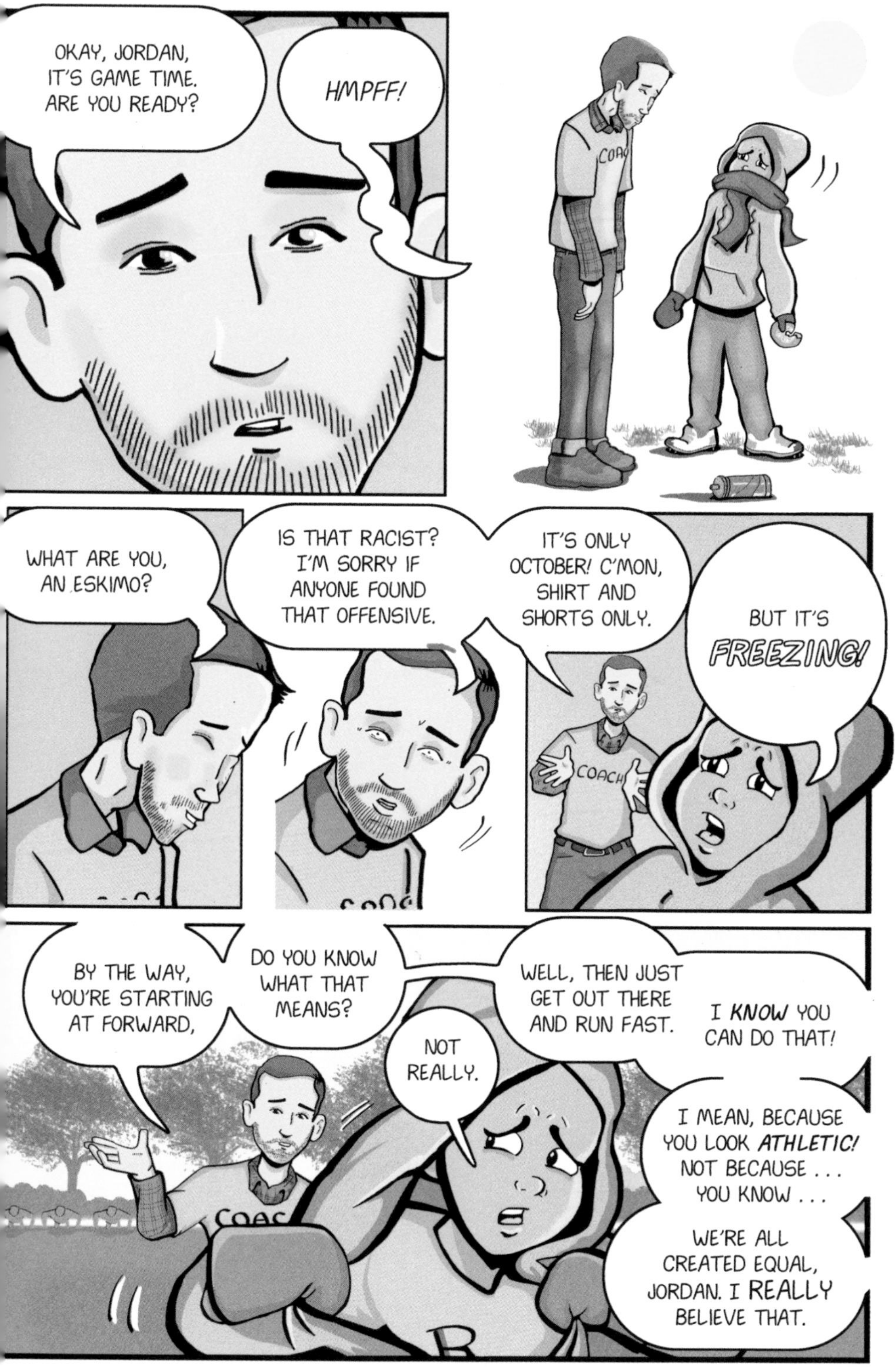
OKAY, JORDAN, IT'S GAME TIME. ARE YOU READY?
HMPFF!
COACH
WHAT ARE YOU, AN ESKIMO?
IS THAT RACIST? I'M SORRY IF ANYONE FOUND THAT OFFENSIVE.
IT'S ONLY OCTOBER! C'MON, SHIRT AND SHORTS ONLY.
BUT IT'S FREEZING!
COACH
BY THE WAY, YOU'RE STARTING AT FORWARD,
DO YOU KNOW WHAT THAT MEANS?
NOT REALLY.
WELL, THEN JUST GET OUT THERE AND RUN FAST.
I KNOW YOU CAN DO THAT!
I MEAN, BECAUSE YOU LOOK ATHLETIC! NOT BECAUSE . . . YOU KNOW . . .
WE'RE ALL CREATED EQUAL, JORDAN. I REALLY BELIEVE THAT.

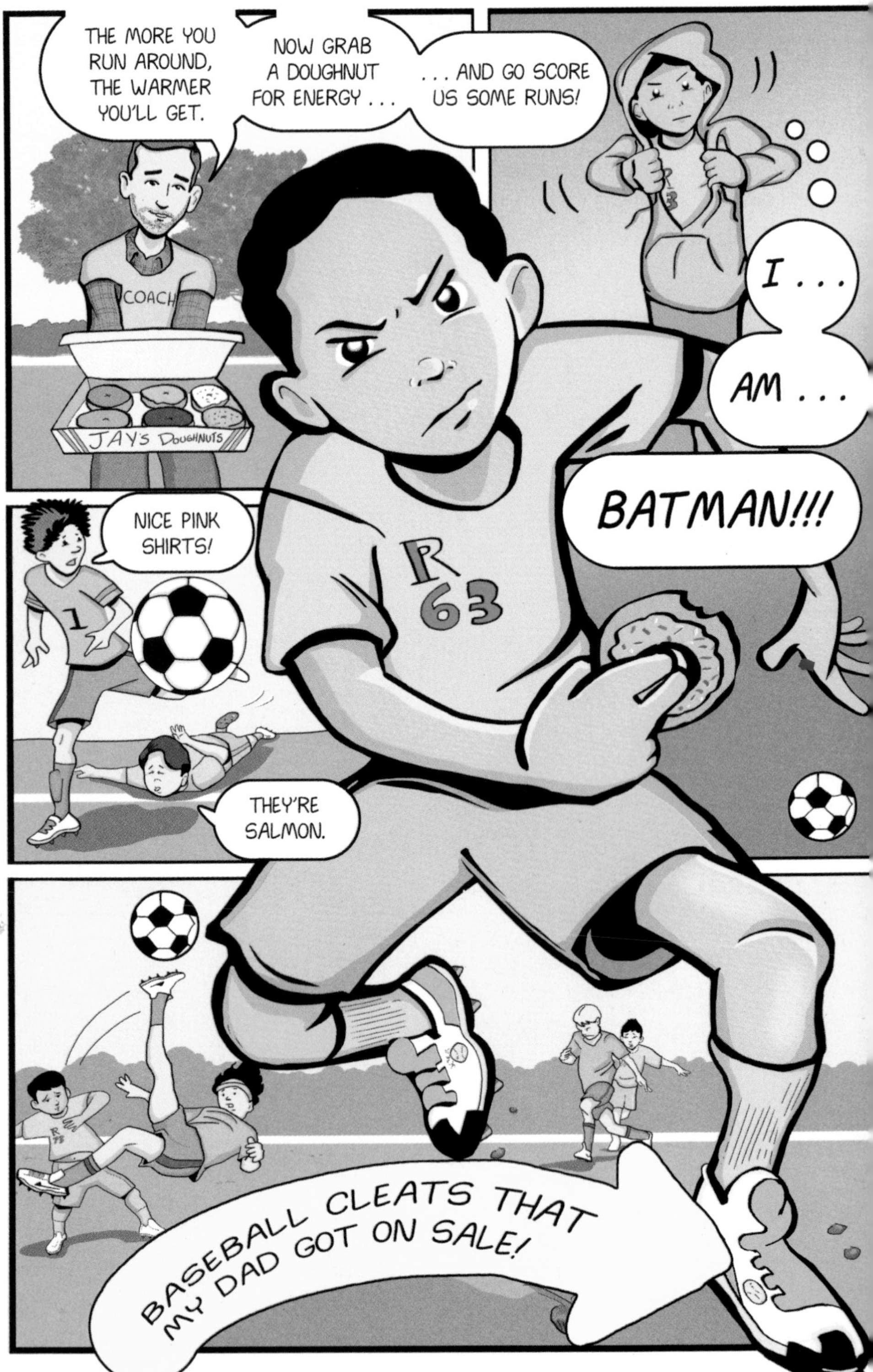
THE MORE YOU RUN AROUND, THE WARMER YOU'LL GET.
NOW GRAB A DOUGHNUT FOR ENERGY . . .
. . . AND GO SCORE US SOME RUNS!
COACH
JAY'S DOUGHNUTS
I . . .
AM . . .
BATMAN!!!
NICE PINK SHIRTS!
THEY'RE SALMON.
BASEBALL CLEATS THAT MY DAD GOT ON SALE!

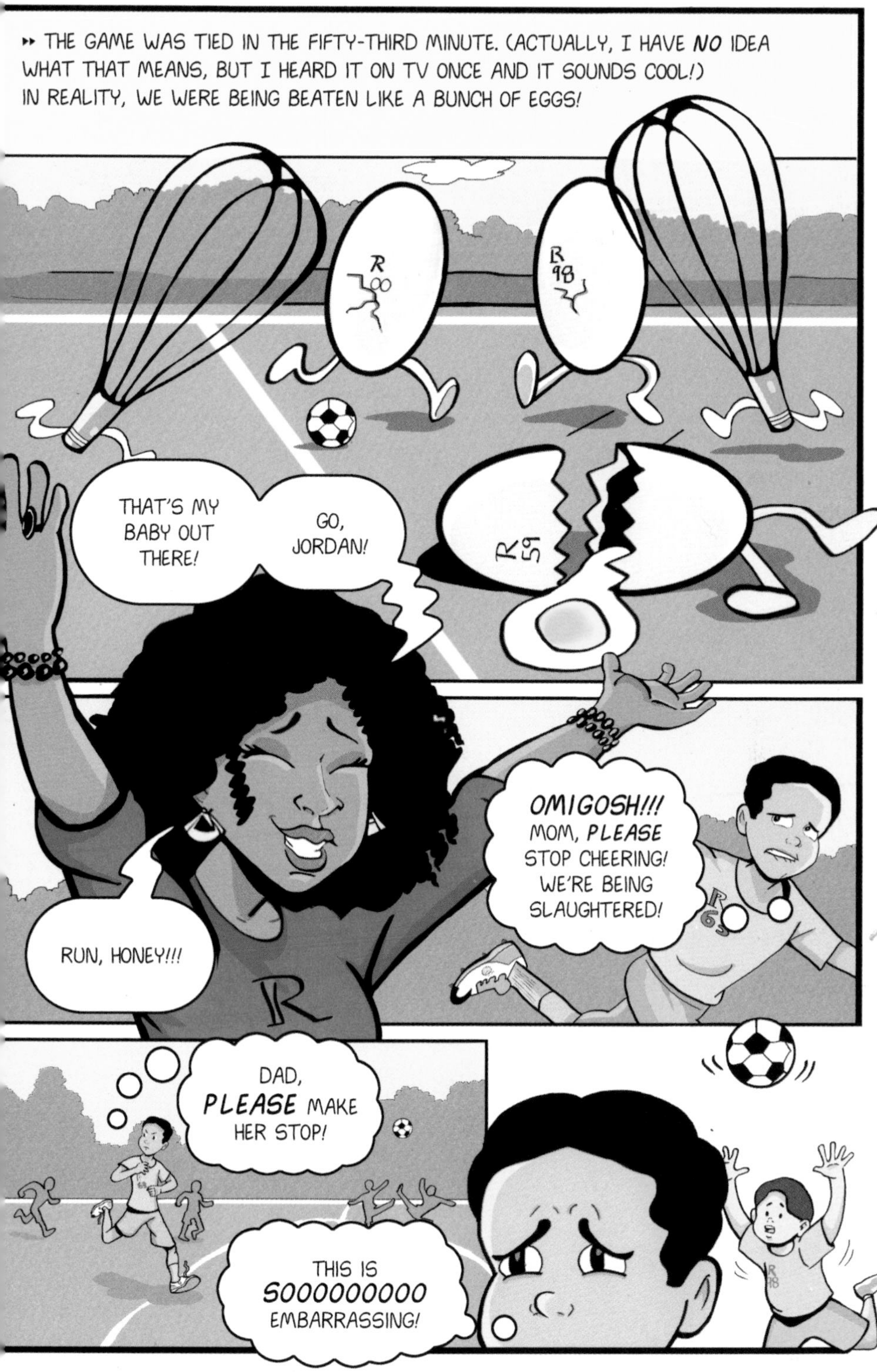
▸▸ THE GAME WAS TIED IN THE FIFTY-THIRD MINUTE. (ACTUALLY, I HAVE *NO* IDEA WHAT THAT MEANS, BUT I HEARD IT ON TV ONCE AND IT SOUNDS COOL!) IN REALITY, WE WERE BEING BEATEN LIKE A BUNCH OF EGGS!
THAT'S MY BABY OUT THERE!
GO, JORDAN!
OMIGOSH!!! MOM, *PLEASE* STOP CHEERING! WE'RE BEING SLAUGHTERED!
RUN, HONEY!!!
DAD, *PLEASE* MAKE HER STOP!
THIS IS *SOOOOOOOOO* EMBARRASSING!

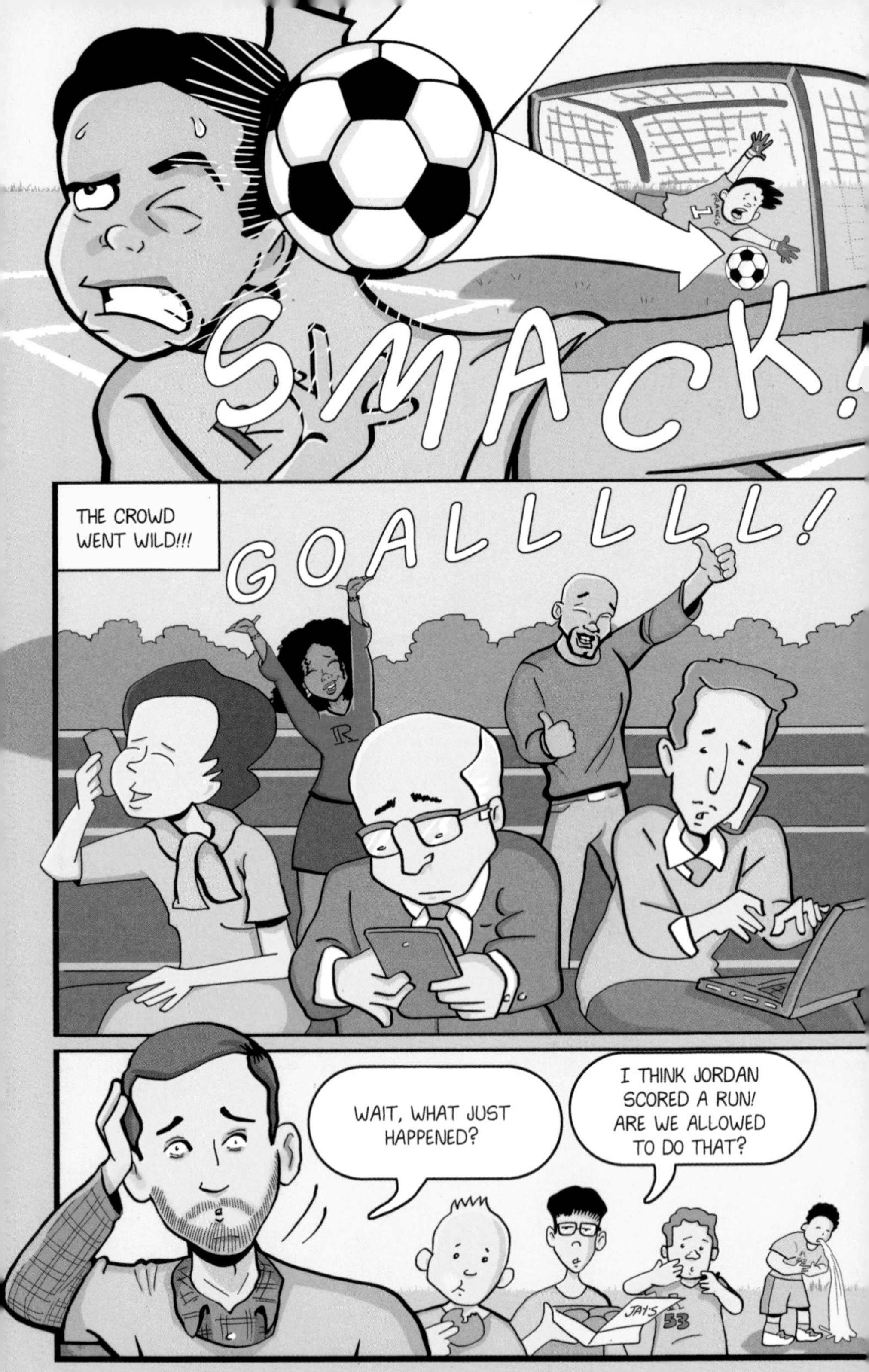
SMACK!
THE CROWD WENT WILD!!!
GOALLLLL!
WAIT, WHAT JUST HAPPENED?
I THINK JORDAN SCORED A RUN! ARE WE ALLOWED TO DO THAT?
JAY'S
53

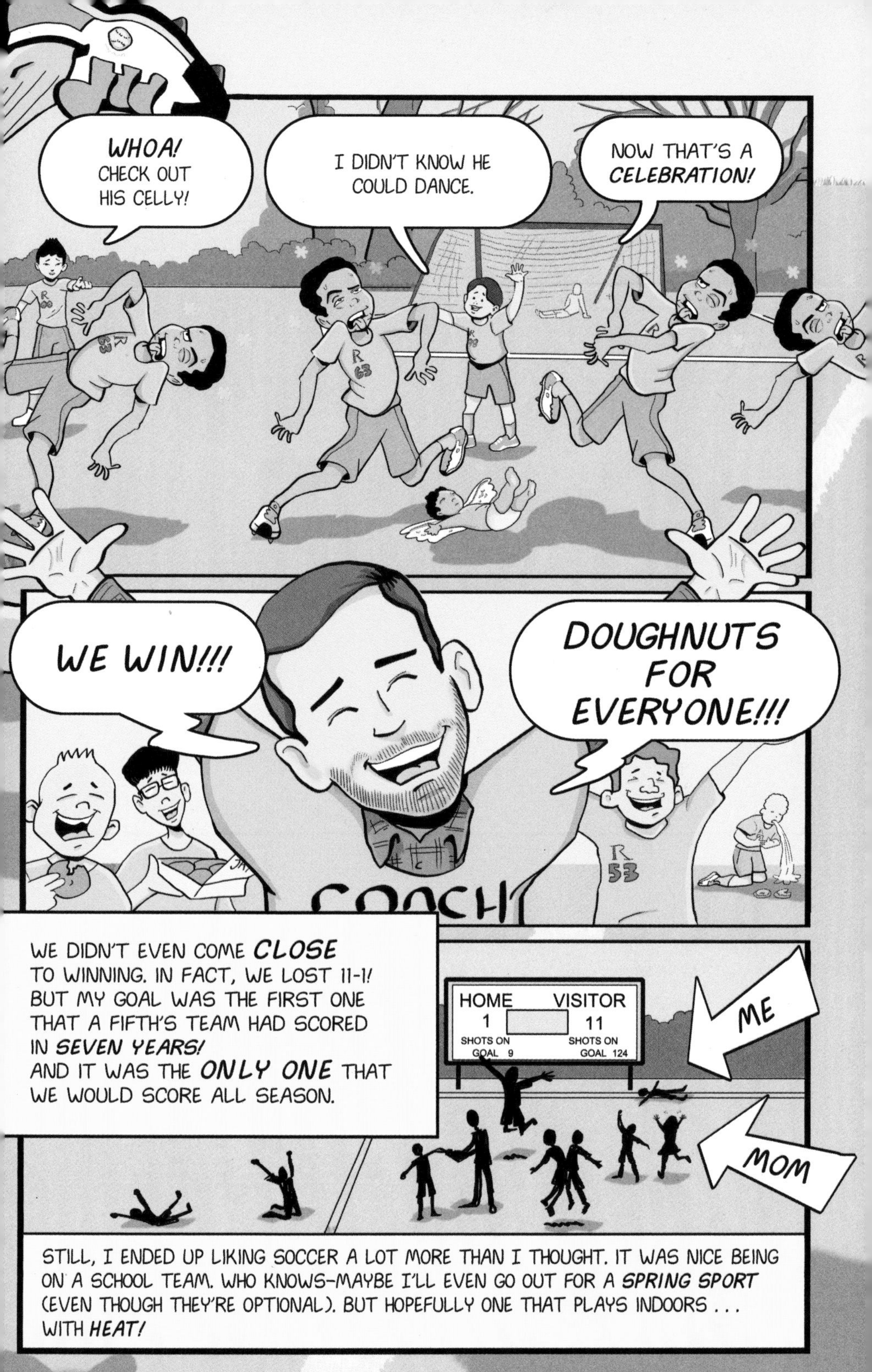
WHOA! CHECK OUT HIS CELLY!
I DIDN'T KNOW HE COULD DANCE.
NOW THAT'S A CELEBRATION!
WE WIN!!!
DOUGHNUTS FOR EVERYONE!!!
COACH
WE DIDN'T EVEN COME CLOSE TO WINNING. IN FACT, WE LOST 11-1! BUT MY GOAL WAS THE FIRST ONE THAT A FIFTH'S TEAM HAD SCORED IN SEVEN YEARS! AND IT WAS THE ONLY ONE THAT WE WOULD SCORE ALL SEASON.
HOME
1
SHOTS ON GOAL 9
VISITOR
11
SHOTS ON GOAL 124
ME
MOM
STILL, I ENDED UP LIKING SOCCER A LOT MORE THAN I THOUGHT. IT WAS NICE BEING ON A SCHOOL TEAM. WHO KNOWS—MAYBE I'LL EVEN GO OUT FOR A SPRING SPORT (EVEN THOUGH THEY'RE OPTIONAL). BUT HOPEFULLY ONE THAT PLAYS INDOORS . . . WITH HEAT!

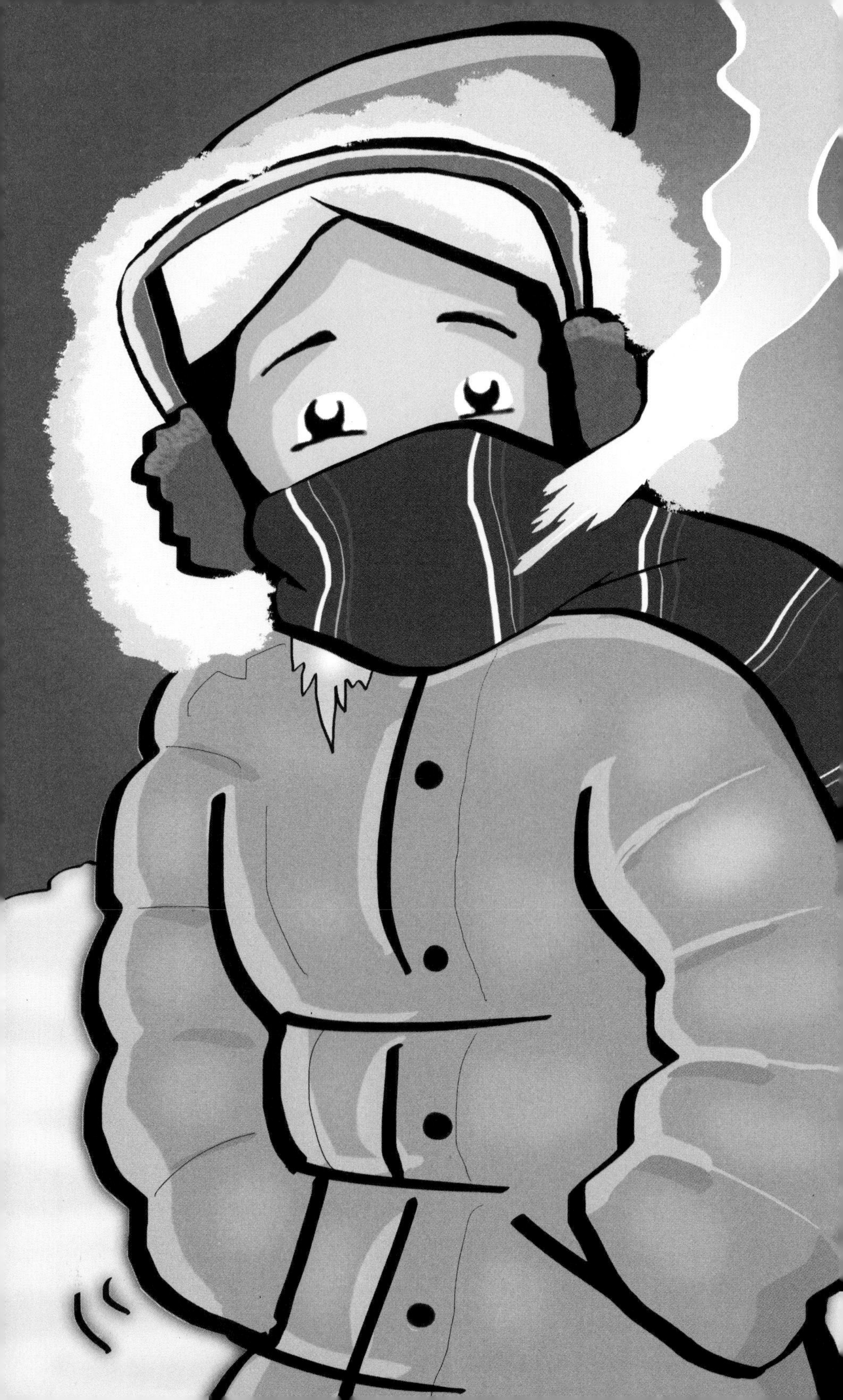

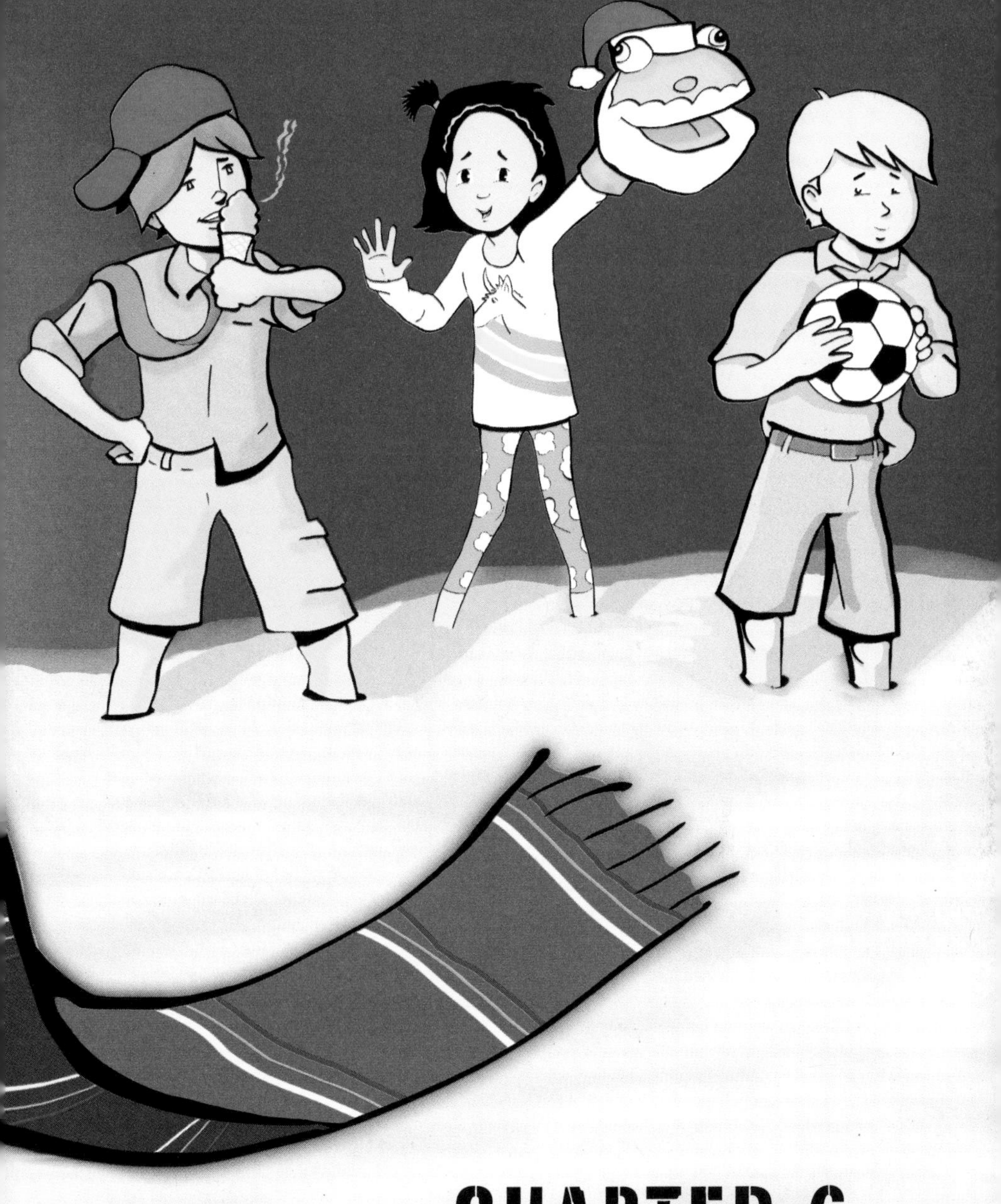

CHAPTER 6

JORDAN BANKS: THE NON-WINTER SOLDIER

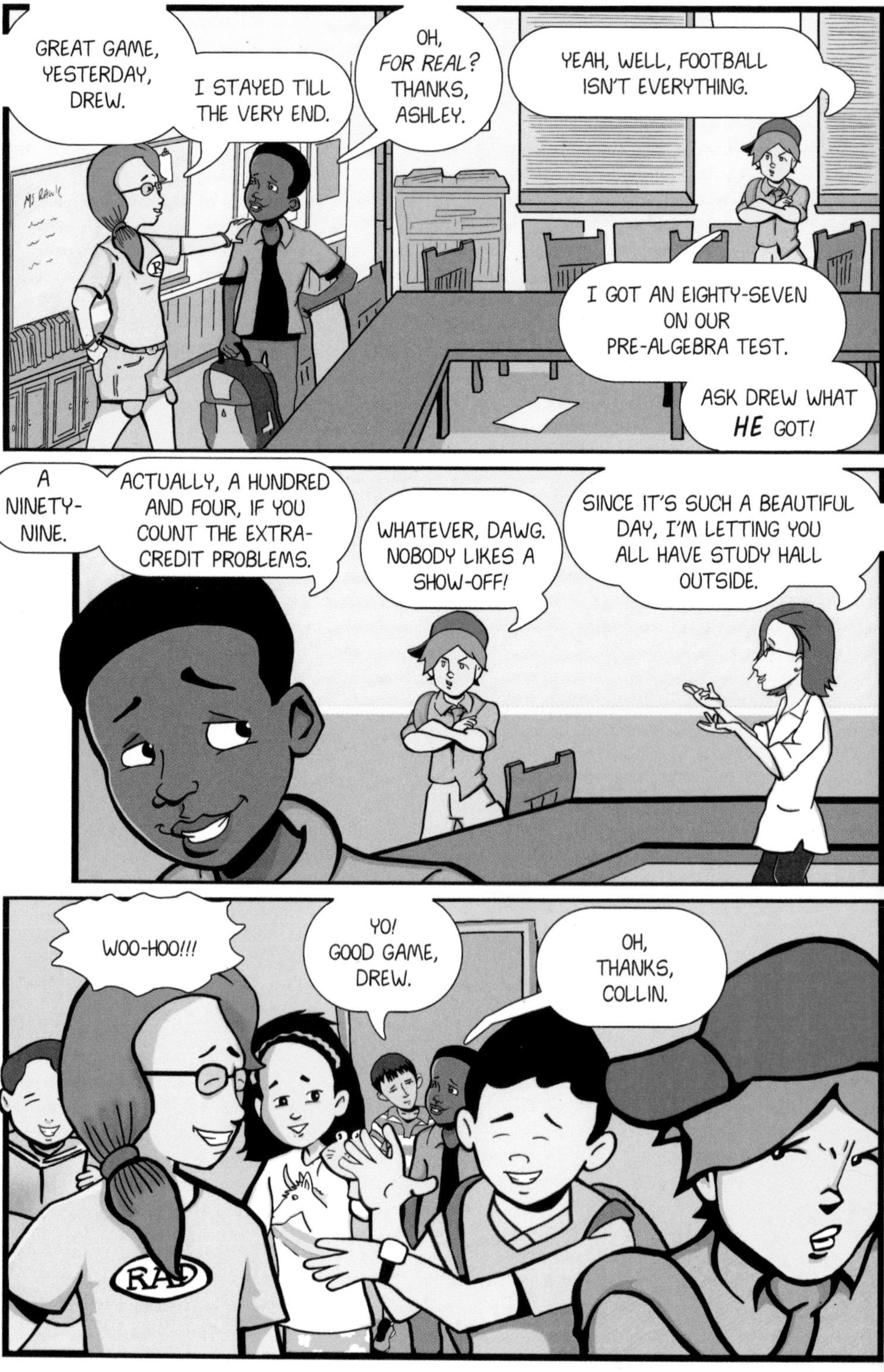
GREAT GAME, YESTERDAY, DREW.
I STAYED TILL THE VERY END.
OH, FOR REAL? THANKS, ASHLEY.
YEAH, WELL, FOOTBALL ISN'T EVERYTHING.
I GOT AN EIGHTY-SEVEN ON OUR PRE-ALGEBRA TEST.
ASK DREW WHAT HE GOT!
A NINETY-NINE.
ACTUALLY, A HUNDRED AND FOUR, IF YOU COUNT THE EXTRA-CREDIT PROBLEMS.
WHATEVER, DAWG. NOBODY LIKES A SHOW-OFF!
SINCE IT'S SUCH A BEAUTIFUL DAY, I'M LETTING YOU ALL HAVE STUDY HALL OUTSIDE.
WOO-HOO!!!
YO! GOOD GAME, DREW.
OH, THANKS, COLLIN.

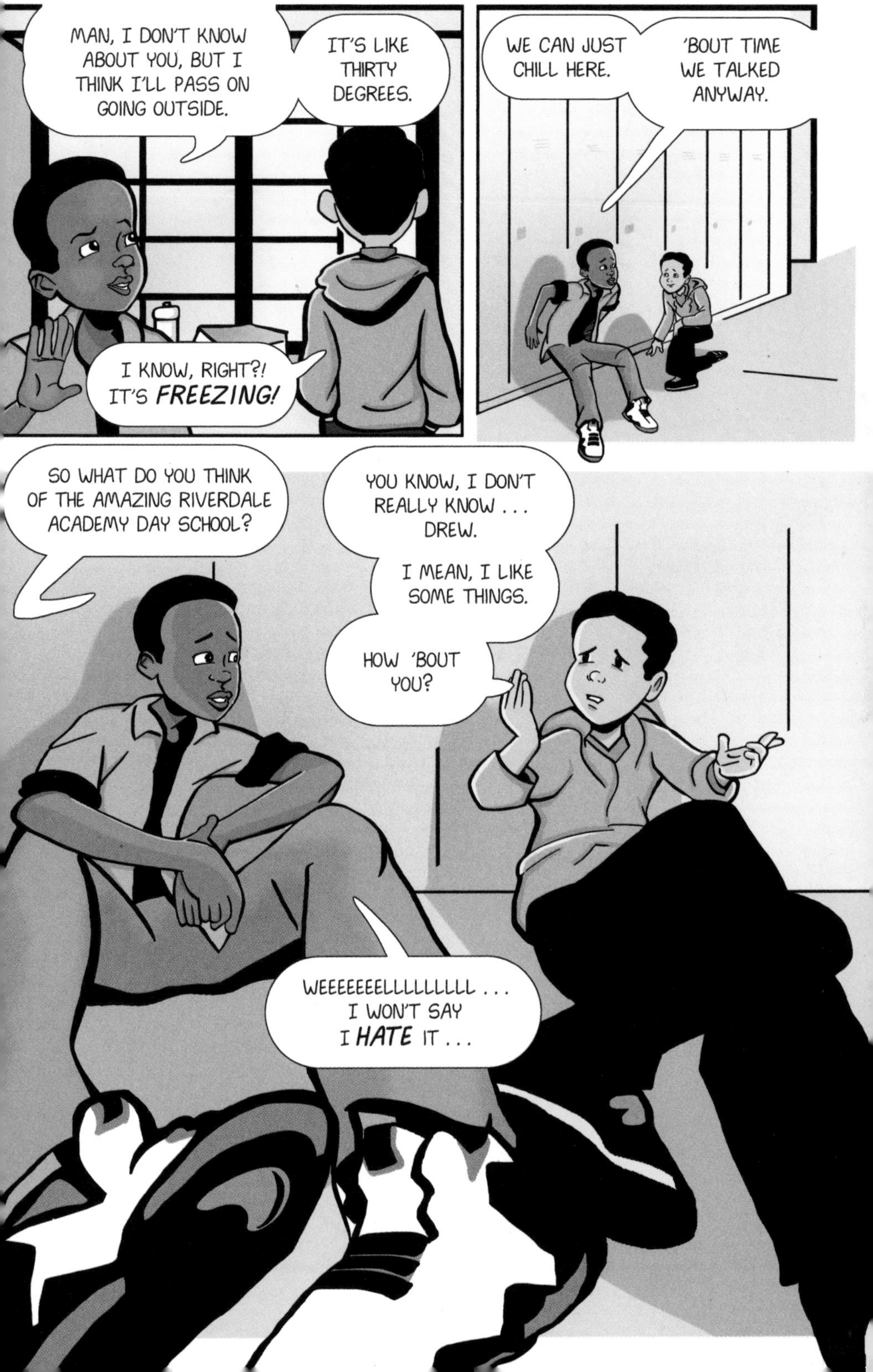
MAN, I DON'T KNOW ABOUT YOU, BUT I THINK I'LL PASS ON GOING OUTSIDE.
IT'S LIKE THIRTY DEGREES.
I KNOW, RIGHT?! IT'S **FREEZING!**
WE CAN JUST CHILL HERE.
'BOUT TIME WE TALKED ANYWAY.
SO WHAT DO YOU THINK OF THE AMAZING RIVERDALE ACADEMY DAY SCHOOL?
YOU KNOW, I DON'T REALLY KNOW . . . DREW.
I MEAN, I LIKE SOME THINGS.
HOW 'BOUT YOU?
WEEEEEEELLLLLLLLL . . . I WON'T SAY I **HATE** IT . . .

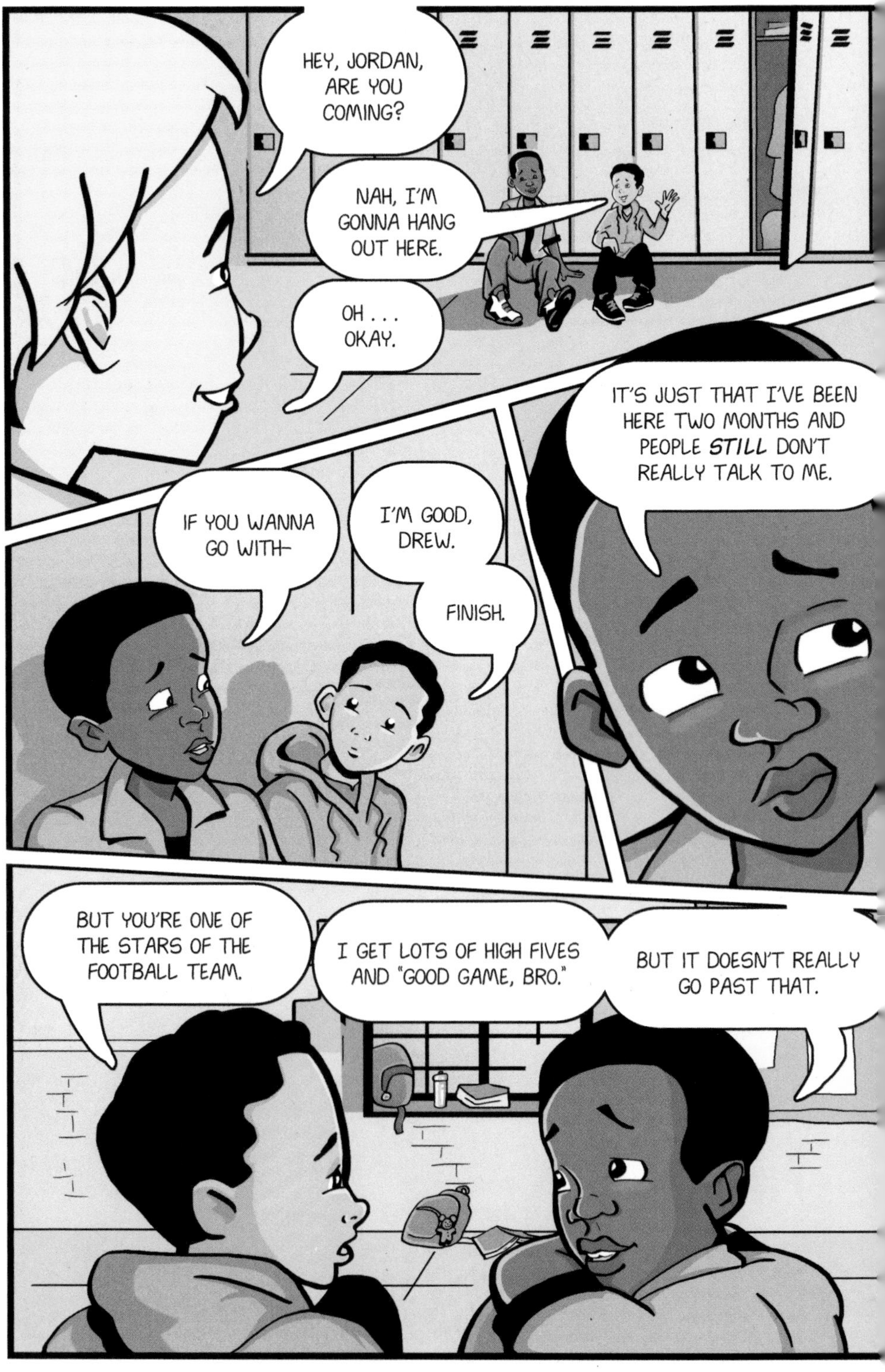
HEY, JORDAN, ARE YOU COMING?
NAH, I'M GONNA HANG OUT HERE.
OH . . . OKAY.
IF YOU WANNA GO WITH—
I'M GOOD, DREW.
FINISH.
IT'S JUST THAT I'VE BEEN HERE TWO MONTHS AND PEOPLE STILL DON'T REALLY TALK TO ME.
BUT YOU'RE ONE OF THE STARS OF THE FOOTBALL TEAM.
I GET LOTS OF HIGH FIVES AND "GOOD GAME, BRO."
BUT IT DOESN'T REALLY GO PAST THAT.

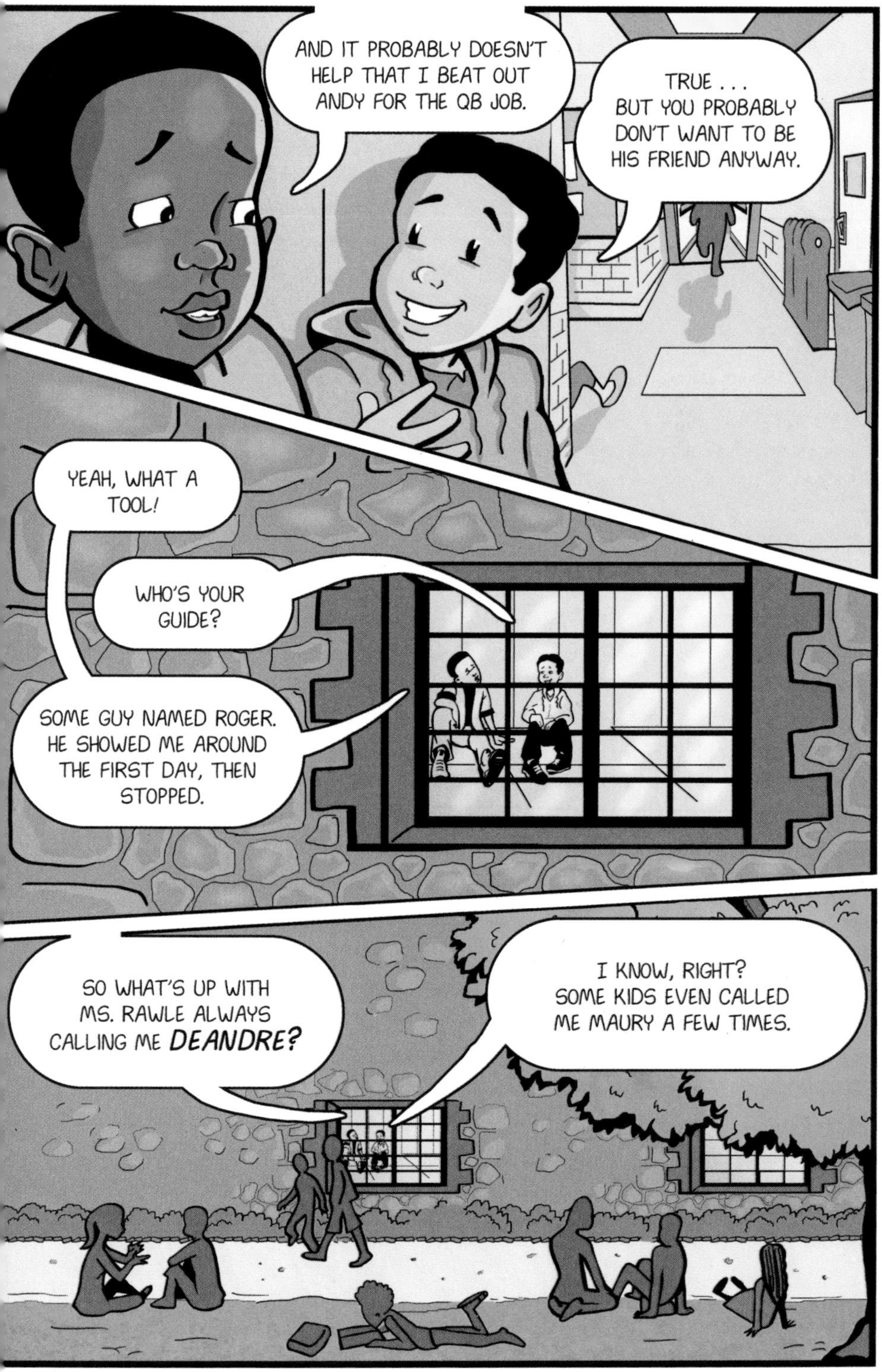
AND IT PROBABLY DOESN'T HELP THAT I BEAT OUT ANDY FOR THE QB JOB.
TRUE . . . BUT YOU PROBABLY DON'T WANT TO BE HIS FRIEND ANYWAY.
YEAH, WHAT A TOOL!
WHO'S YOUR GUIDE?
SOME GUY NAMED ROGER. HE SHOWED ME AROUND THE FIRST DAY, THEN STOPPED.
SO WHAT'S UP WITH MS. RAWLE ALWAYS CALLING ME DEANDRE?
I KNOW, RIGHT? SOME KIDS EVEN CALLED ME MAURY A FEW TIMES.

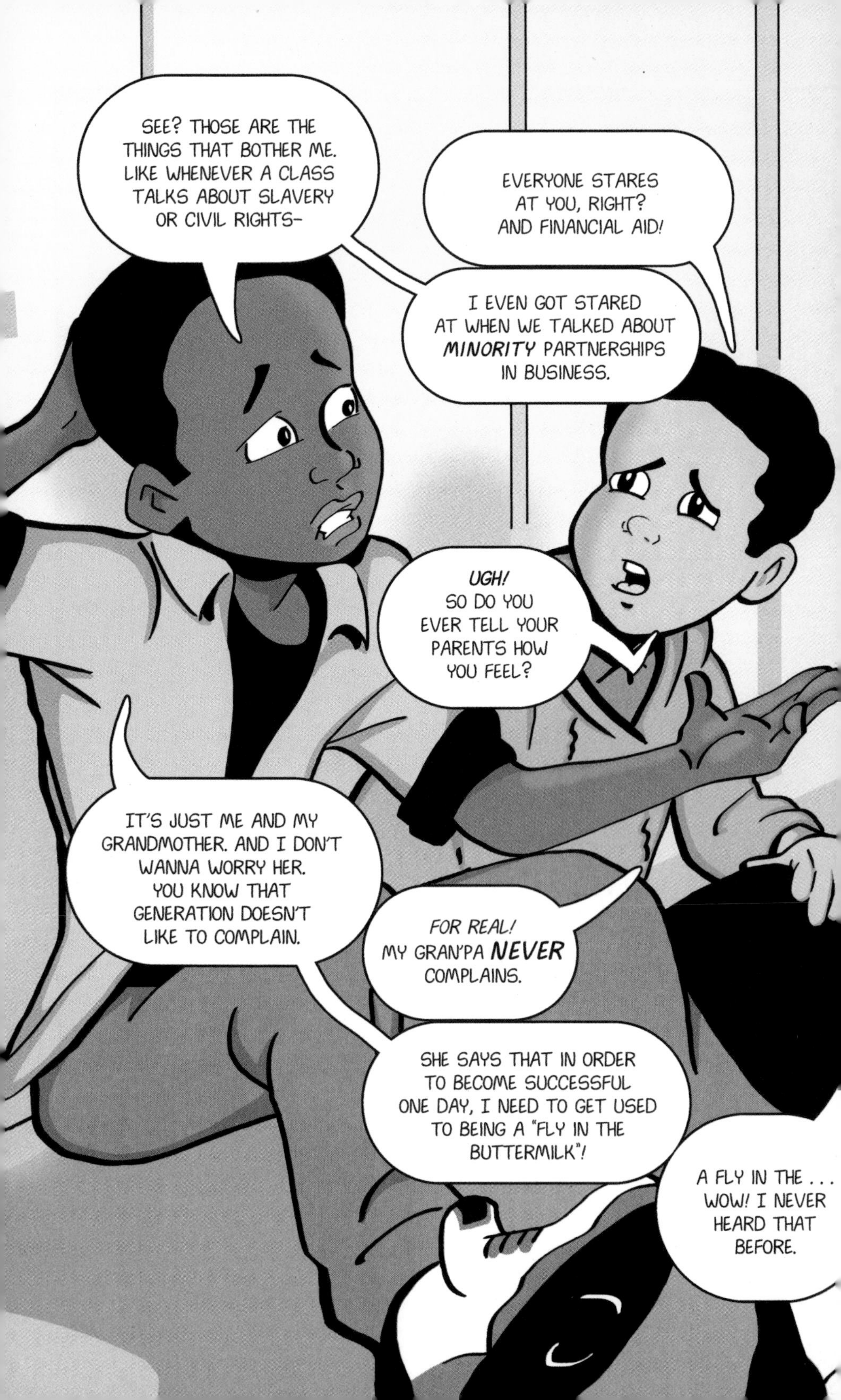
SEE? THOSE ARE THE THINGS THAT BOTHER ME. LIKE WHENEVER A CLASS TALKS ABOUT SLAVERY OR CIVIL RIGHTS–
EVERYONE STARES AT YOU, RIGHT? AND FINANCIAL AID!
I EVEN GOT STARED AT WHEN WE TALKED ABOUT *MINORITY* PARTNERSHIPS IN BUSINESS.
UGH! SO DO YOU EVER TELL YOUR PARENTS HOW YOU FEEL?
IT'S JUST ME AND MY GRANDMOTHER. AND I DON'T WANNA WORRY HER. YOU KNOW THAT GENERATION DOESN'T LIKE TO COMPLAIN.
FOR REAL! MY GRAN'PA ***NEVER*** COMPLAINS.
SHE SAYS THAT IN ORDER TO BECOME SUCCESSFUL ONE DAY, I NEED TO GET USED TO BEING A "FLY IN THE BUTTERMILK"!
A FLY IN THE . . . WOW! I NEVER HEARD THAT BEFORE.

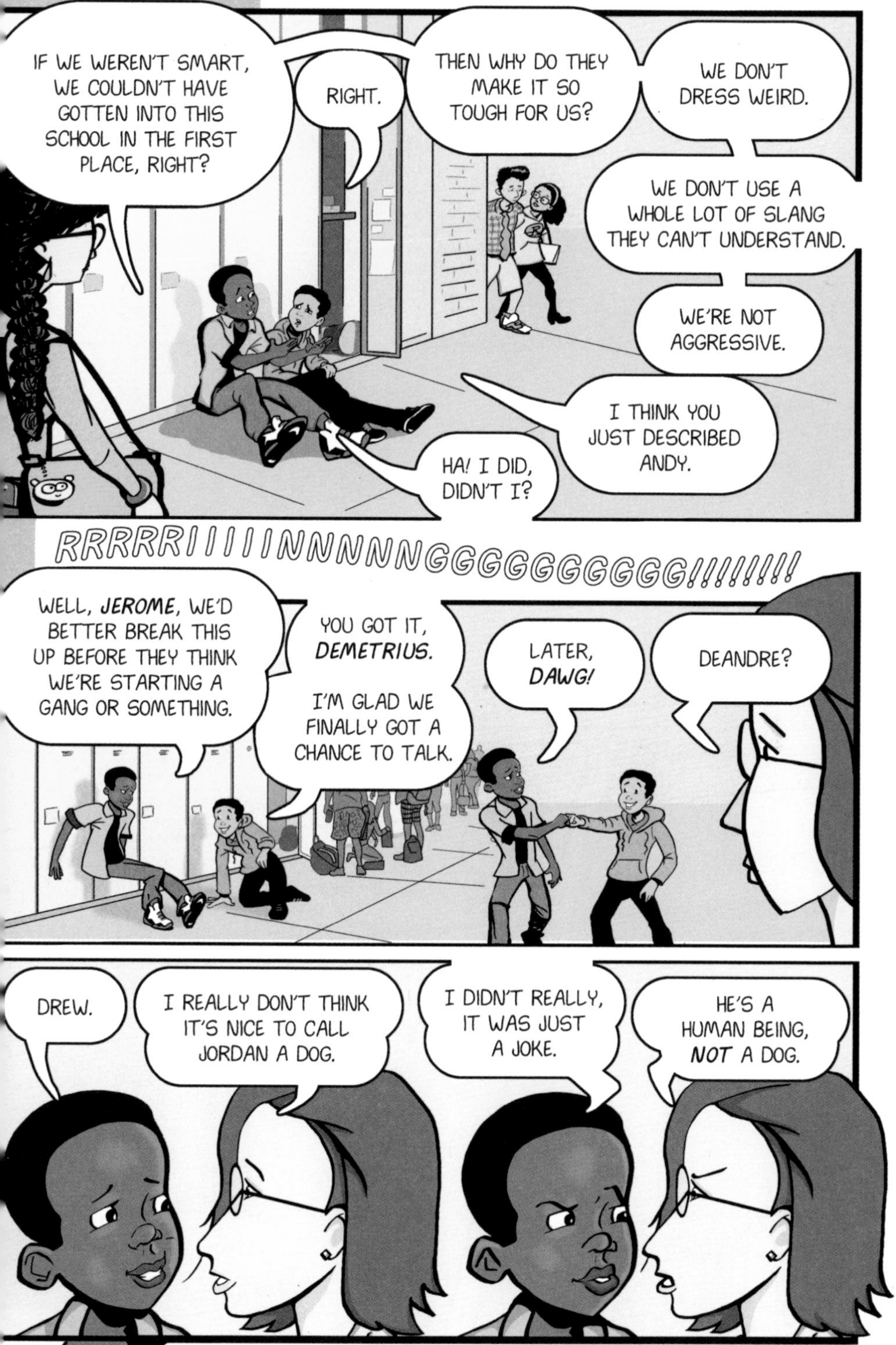
IF WE WEREN'T SMART, WE COULDN'T HAVE GOTTEN INTO THIS SCHOOL IN THE FIRST PLACE, RIGHT?
RIGHT.
THEN WHY DO THEY MAKE IT SO TOUGH FOR US?
WE DON'T DRESS WEIRD.
WE DON'T USE A WHOLE LOT OF SLANG THEY CAN'T UNDERSTAND.
WE'RE NOT AGGRESSIVE.
I THINK YOU JUST DESCRIBED ANDY.
HA! I DID, DIDN'T I?
RRRRRIIIIINNNNNGGGGGGGGGG!!!!!!!!
WELL, **JEROME**, WE'D BETTER BREAK THIS UP BEFORE THEY THINK WE'RE STARTING A GANG OR SOMETHING.
YOU GOT IT, **DEMETRIUS.**
I'M GLAD WE FINALLY GOT A CHANCE TO TALK.
LATER, **DAWG!**
DEANDRE?
DREW.
I REALLY DON'T THINK IT'S NICE TO CALL JORDAN A DOG.
I DIDN'T REALLY, IT WAS JUST A JOKE.
HE'S A HUMAN BEING, **NOT** A DOG.

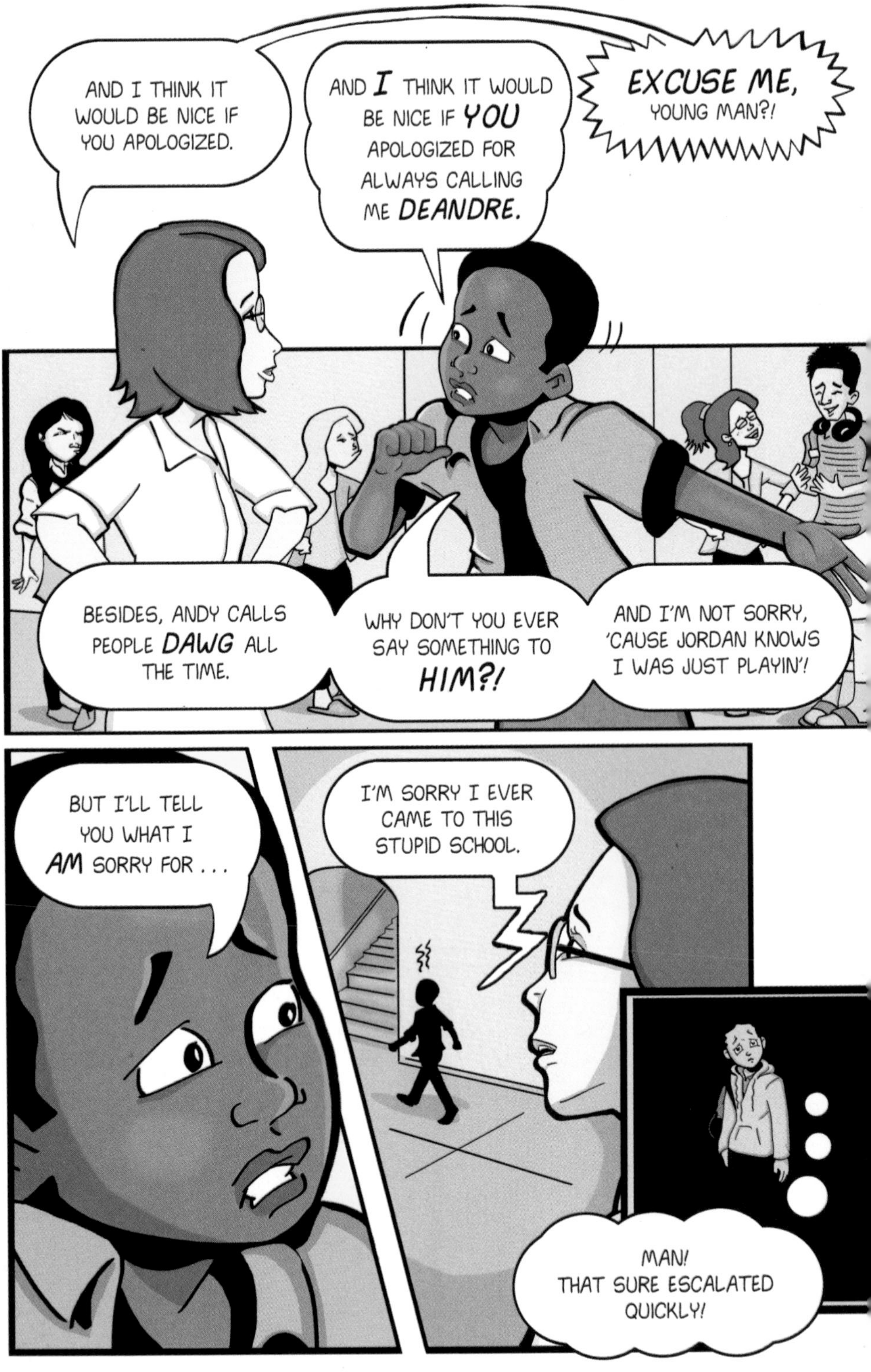
AND I THINK IT WOULD BE NICE IF YOU APOLOGIZED.
AND I THINK IT WOULD BE NICE IF YOU APOLOGIZED FOR ALWAYS CALLING ME DEANDRE.
EXCUSE ME, YOUNG MAN?!
BESIDES, ANDY CALLS PEOPLE DAWG ALL THE TIME.
WHY DON'T YOU EVER SAY SOMETHING TO HIM?!
AND I'M NOT SORRY, 'CAUSE JORDAN KNOWS I WAS JUST PLAYIN'!
BUT I'LL TELL YOU WHAT I AM SORRY FOR . . .
I'M SORRY I EVER CAME TO THIS STUPID SCHOOL.
MAN! THAT SURE ESCALATED QUICKLY!

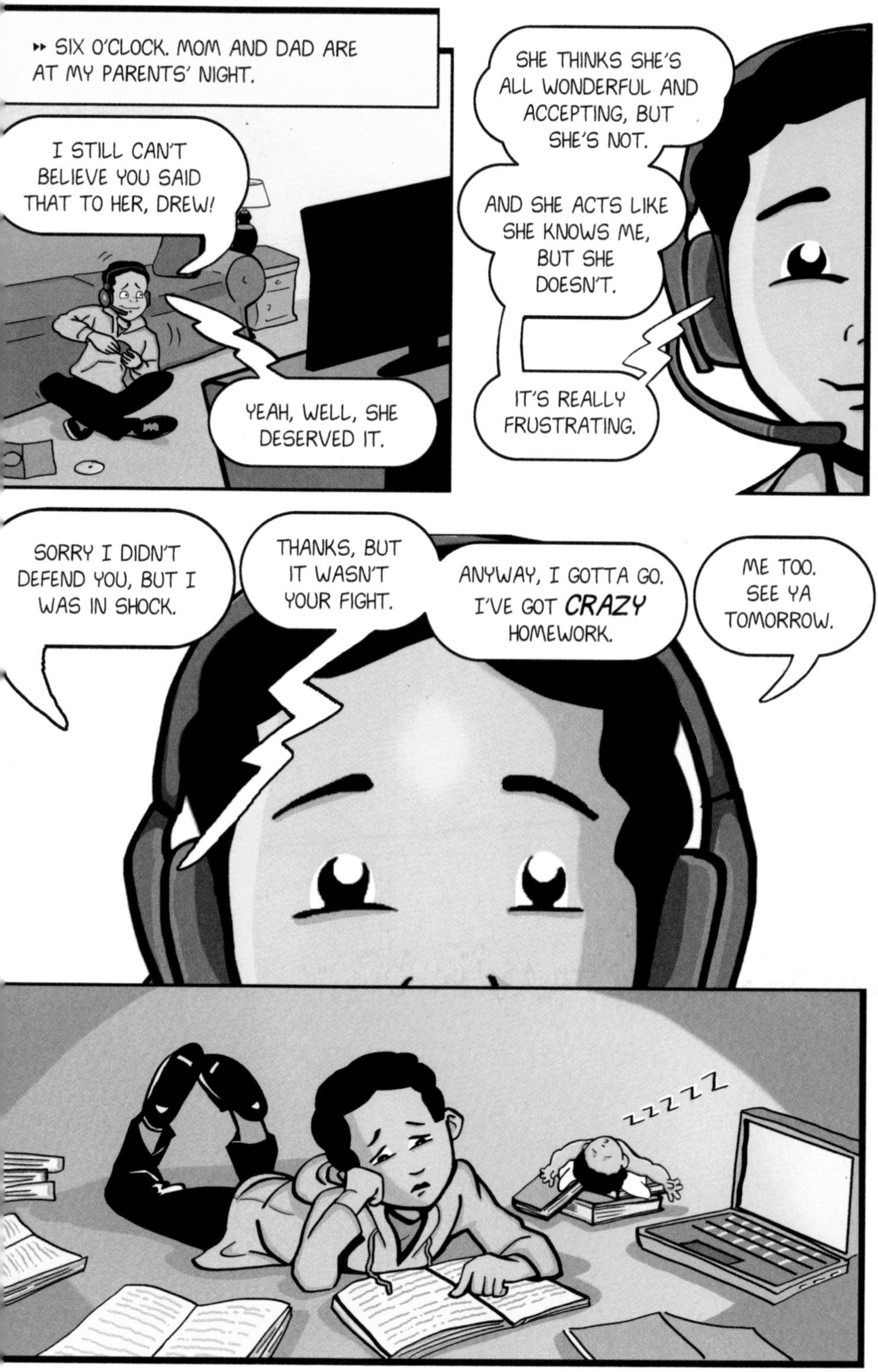
▸▸ SIX O'CLOCK. MOM AND DAD ARE AT MY PARENTS' NIGHT.
I STILL CAN'T BELIEVE YOU SAID THAT TO HER, DREW!
YEAH, WELL, SHE DESERVED IT.
SHE THINKS SHE'S ALL WONDERFUL AND ACCEPTING, BUT SHE'S NOT.
AND SHE ACTS LIKE SHE KNOWS ME, BUT SHE DOESN'T.
IT'S REALLY FRUSTRATING.
SORRY I DIDN'T DEFEND YOU, BUT I WAS IN SHOCK.
THANKS, BUT IT WASN'T YOUR FIGHT.
ANYWAY, I GOTTA GO. I'VE GOT CRAZY HOMEWORK.
ME TOO. SEE YA TOMORROW.
ZZZZZ

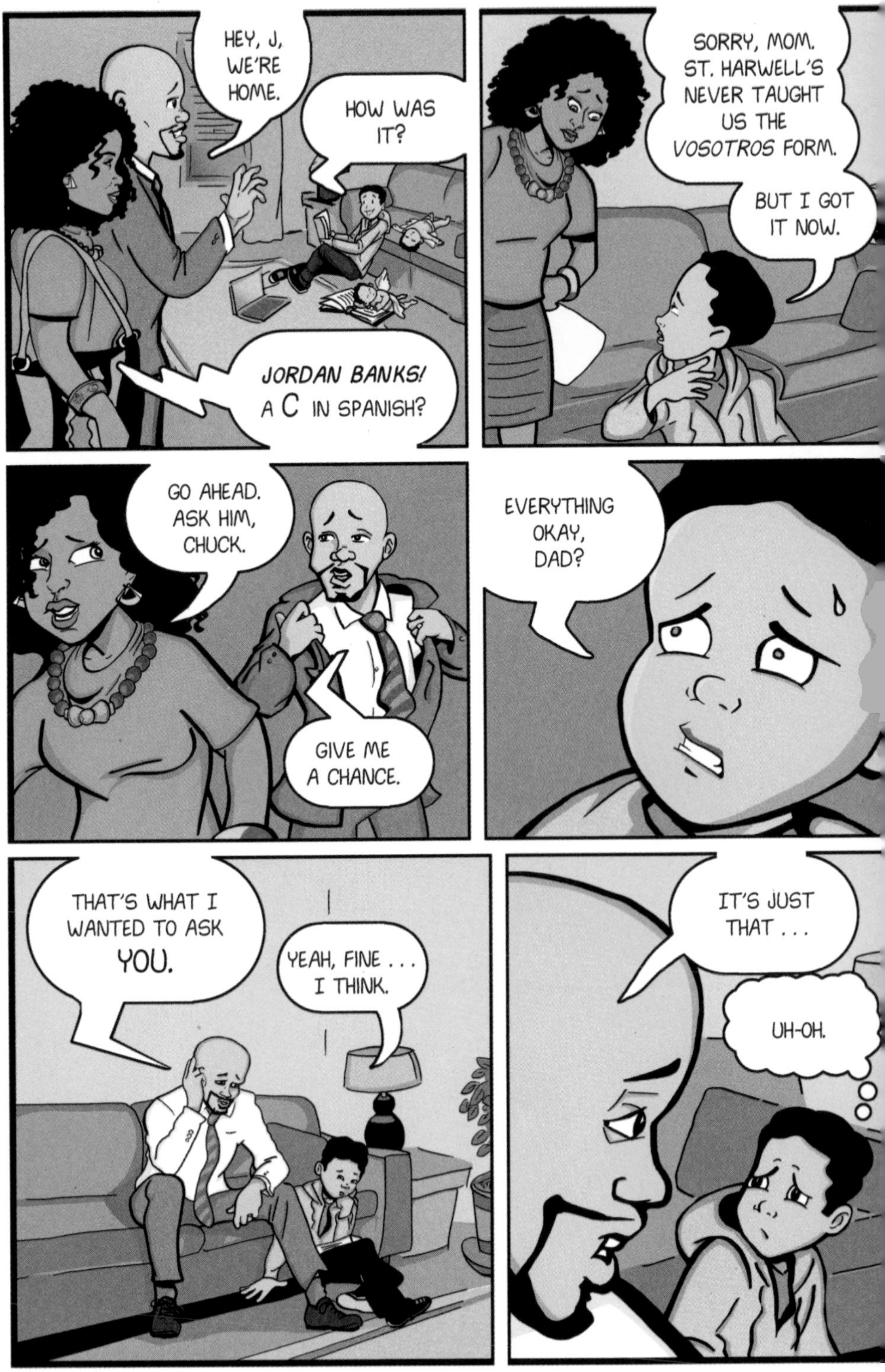
HEY, J, WE'RE HOME.
HOW WAS IT?
JORDAN BANKS! A C IN SPANISH?
SORRY, MOM. ST. HARWELL'S NEVER TAUGHT US THE VOSOTROS FORM.
BUT I GOT IT NOW.
GO AHEAD. ASK HIM, CHUCK.
GIVE ME A CHANCE.
EVERYTHING OKAY, DAD?
THAT'S WHAT I WANTED TO ASK YOU.
YEAH, FINE . . . I THINK.
IT'S JUST THAT . . .
UH-OH.

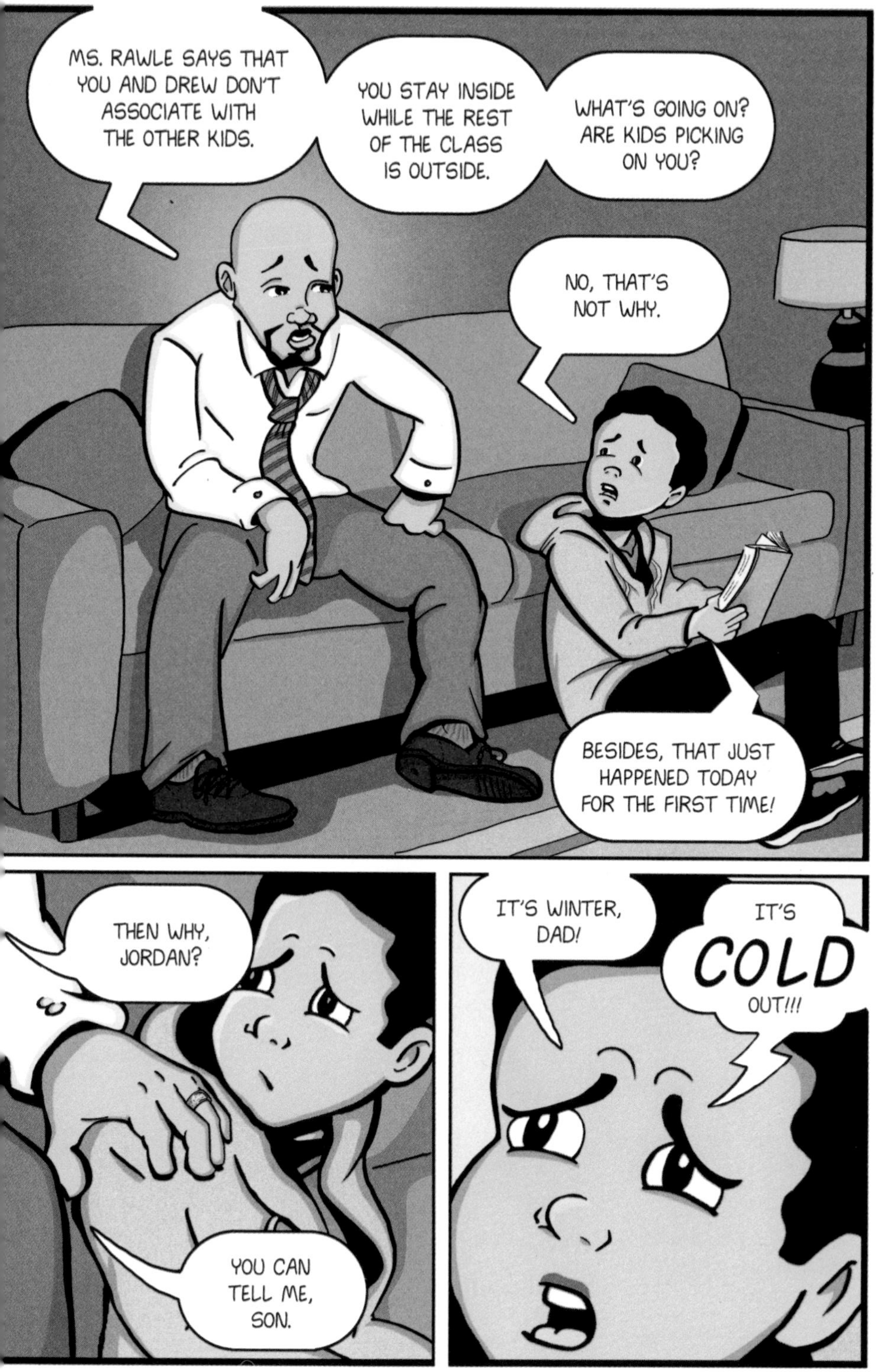
MS. RAWLE SAYS THAT YOU AND DREW DON'T ASSOCIATE WITH THE OTHER KIDS.
YOU STAY INSIDE WHILE THE REST OF THE CLASS IS OUTSIDE.
WHAT'S GOING ON? ARE KIDS PICKING ON YOU?
NO, THAT'S NOT WHY.
BESIDES, THAT JUST HAPPENED TODAY FOR THE FIRST TIME!
THEN WHY, JORDAN?
YOU CAN TELL ME, SON.
IT'S WINTER, DAD!
IT'S COLD OUT!!!

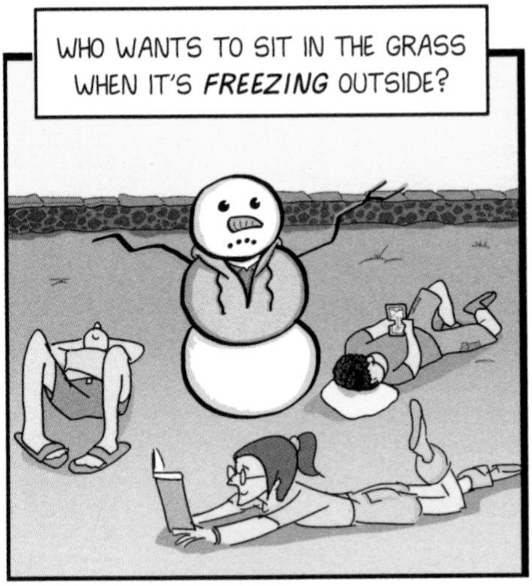
WHO WANTS TO SIT IN THE GRASS WHEN IT'S *FREEZING* OUTSIDE?

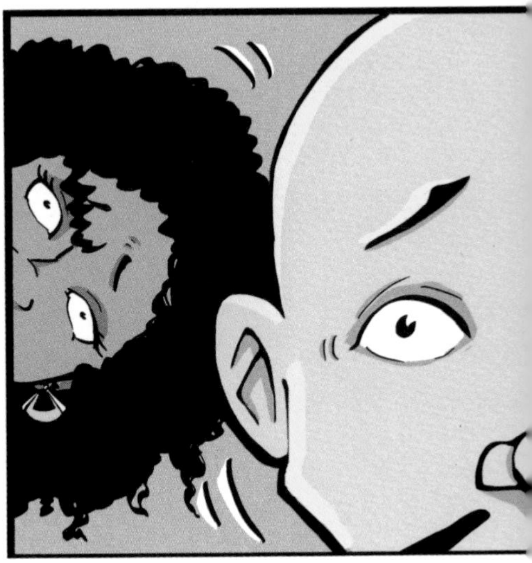

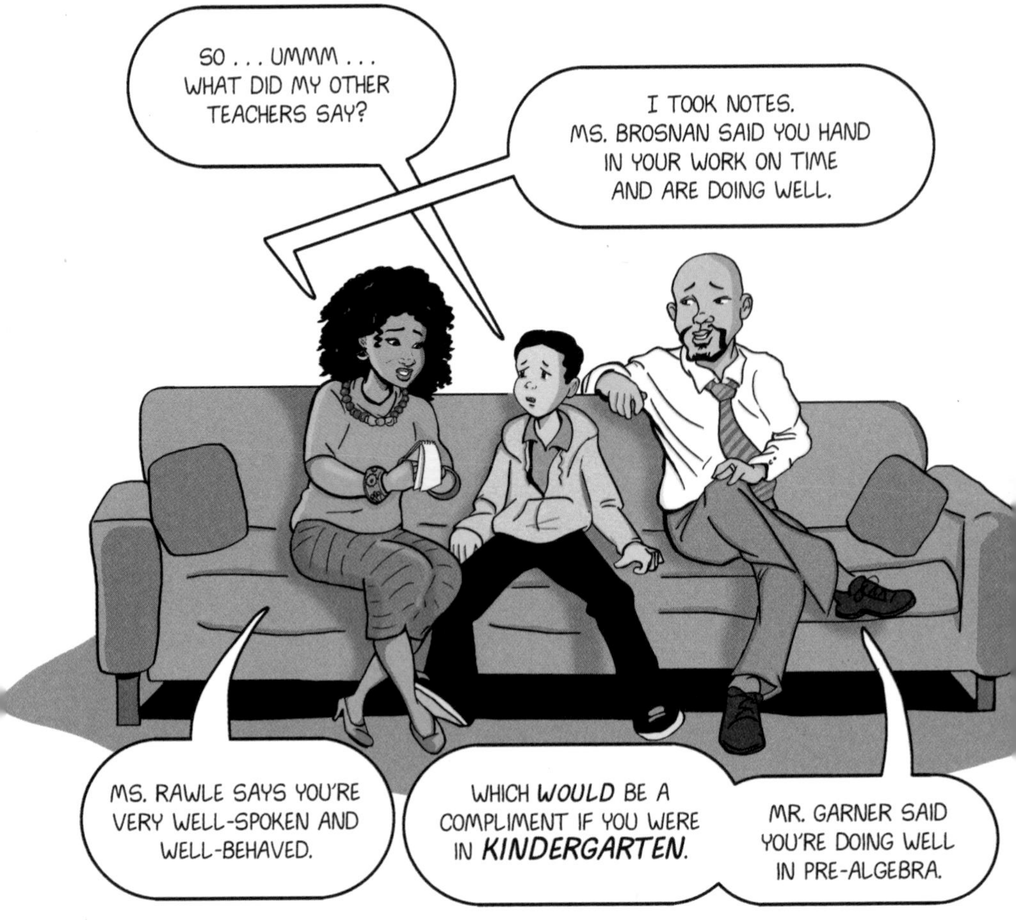
SO . . . UMMM . . . WHAT DID MY OTHER TEACHERS SAY?
I TOOK NOTES. MS. BROSNAN SAID YOU HAND IN YOUR WORK ON TIME AND ARE DOING WELL.
MS. RAWLE SAYS YOU'RE VERY WELL-SPOKEN AND WELL-BEHAVED.
WHICH *WOULD* BE A COMPLIMENT IF YOU WERE IN *KINDERGARTEN*.
MR. GARNER SAID YOU'RE DOING WELL IN PRE-ALGEBRA.

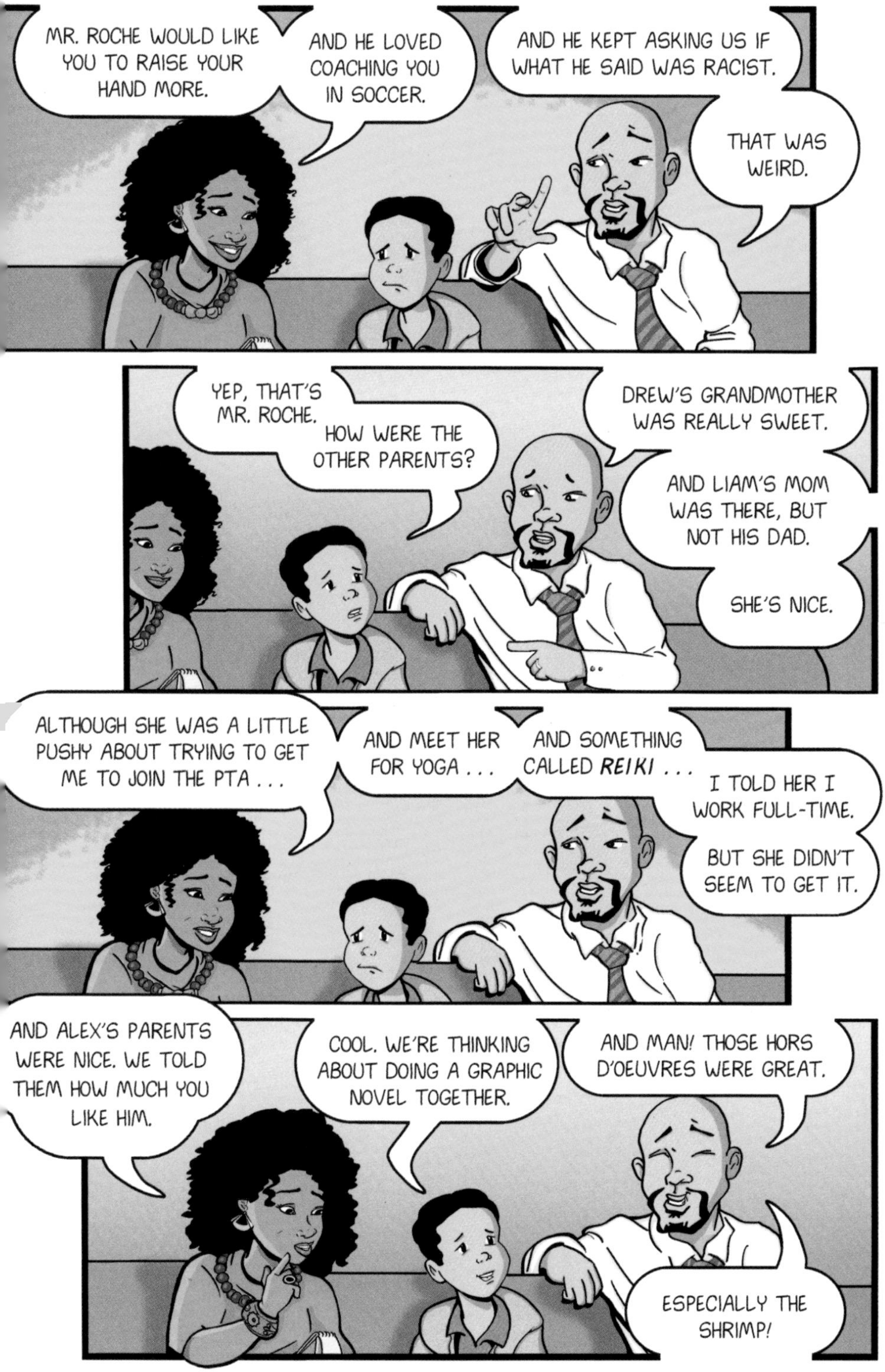
MR. ROCHE WOULD LIKE YOU TO RAISE YOUR HAND MORE.
AND HE LOVED COACHING YOU IN SOCCER.
AND HE KEPT ASKING US IF WHAT HE SAID WAS RACIST.
THAT WAS WEIRD.
YEP, THAT'S MR. ROCHE.
HOW WERE THE OTHER PARENTS?
DREW'S GRANDMOTHER WAS REALLY SWEET.
AND LIAM'S MOM WAS THERE, BUT NOT HIS DAD.
SHE'S NICE.
ALTHOUGH SHE WAS A LITTLE PUSHY ABOUT TRYING TO GET ME TO JOIN THE PTA . . .
AND MEET HER FOR YOGA . . .
AND SOMETHING CALLED *REIKI* . . .
I TOLD HER I WORK FULL-TIME.
BUT SHE DIDN'T SEEM TO GET IT.
AND ALEX'S PARENTS WERE NICE. WE TOLD THEM HOW MUCH YOU LIKE HIM.
COOL. WE'RE THINKING ABOUT DOING A GRAPHIC NOVEL TOGETHER.
AND MAN! THOSE HORS D'OEUVRES WERE GREAT.
ESPECIALLY THE SHRIMP!

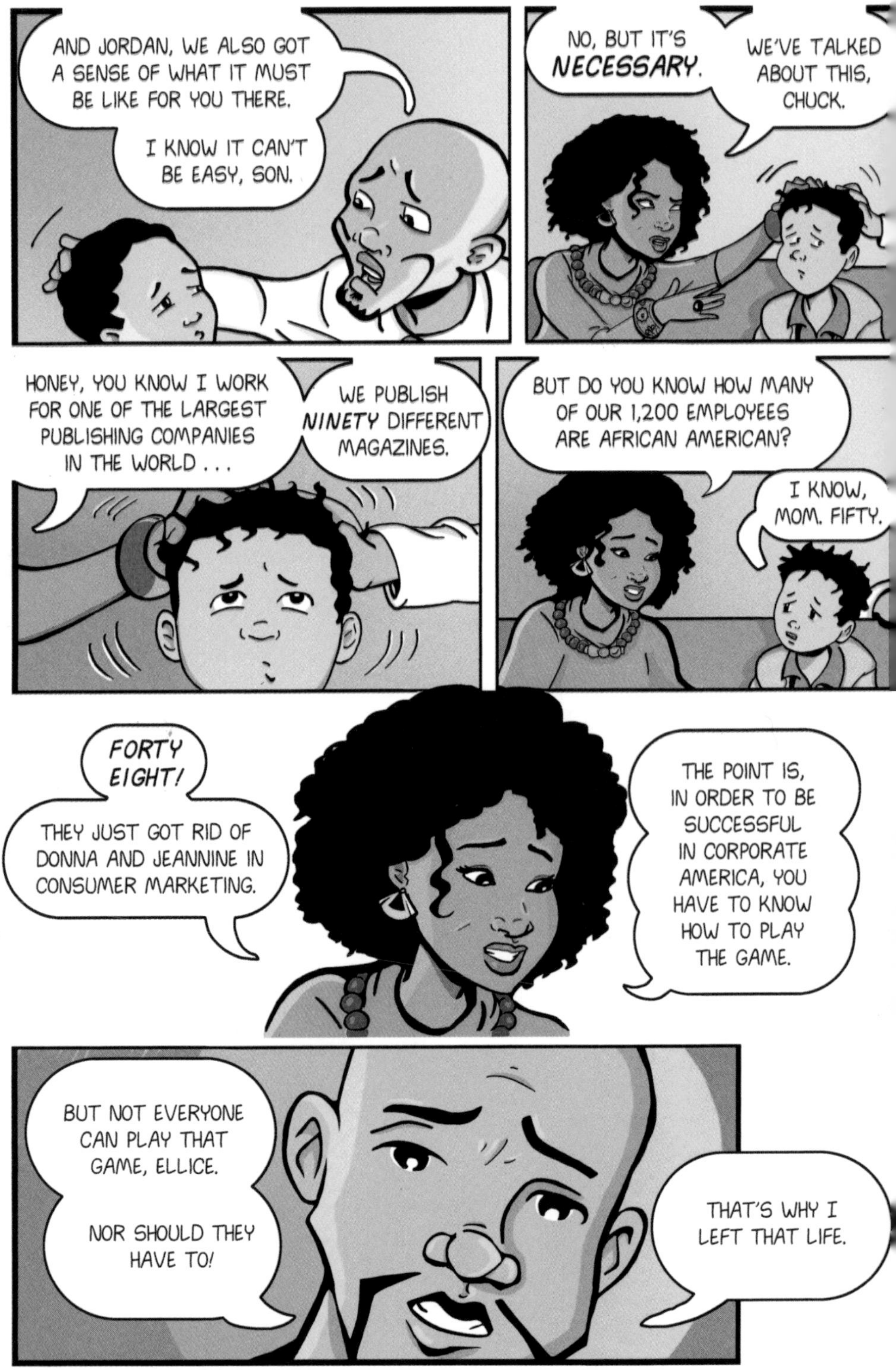
AND JORDAN, WE ALSO GOT A SENSE OF WHAT IT MUST BE LIKE FOR YOU THERE.
I KNOW IT CAN'T BE EASY, SON.
NO, BUT IT'S NECESSARY.
WE'VE TALKED ABOUT THIS, CHUCK.
HONEY, YOU KNOW I WORK FOR ONE OF THE LARGEST PUBLISHING COMPANIES IN THE WORLD . . .
WE PUBLISH NINETY DIFFERENT MAGAZINES.
BUT DO YOU KNOW HOW MANY OF OUR 1,200 EMPLOYEES ARE AFRICAN AMERICAN?
I KNOW, MOM. FIFTY.
FORTY EIGHT!
THEY JUST GOT RID OF DONNA AND JEANNINE IN CONSUMER MARKETING.
THE POINT IS, IN ORDER TO BE SUCCESSFUL IN CORPORATE AMERICA, YOU HAVE TO KNOW HOW TO PLAY THE GAME.
BUT NOT EVERYONE CAN PLAY THAT GAME, ELLICE.
NOR SHOULD THEY HAVE TO!
THAT'S WHY I LEFT THAT LIFE.

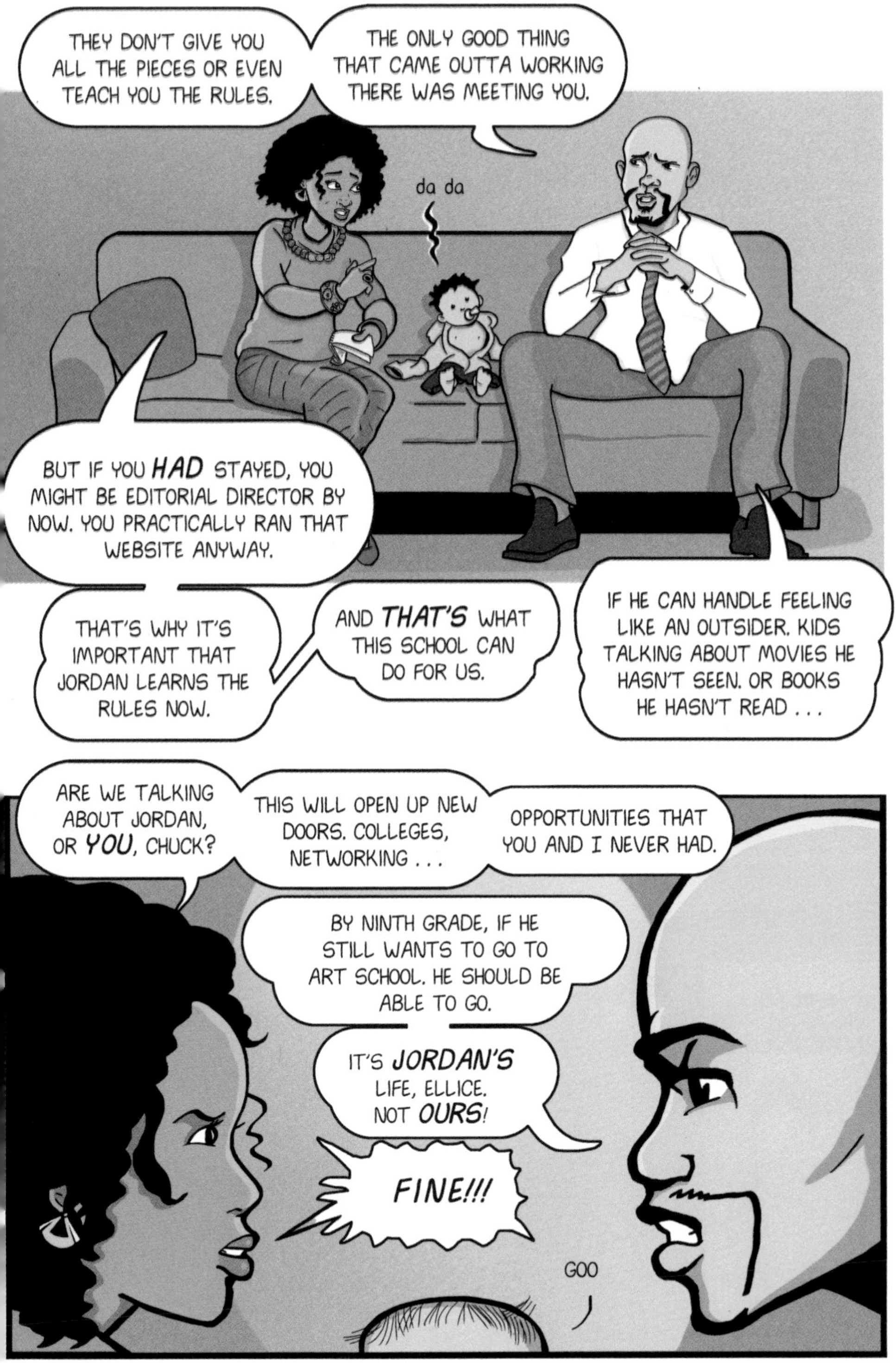
THEY DON'T GIVE YOU ALL THE PIECES OR EVEN TEACH YOU THE RULES.
THE ONLY GOOD THING THAT CAME OUTTA WORKING THERE WAS MEETING YOU.
da da
BUT IF YOU **HAD** STAYED, YOU MIGHT BE EDITORIAL DIRECTOR BY NOW. YOU PRACTICALLY RAN THAT WEBSITE ANYWAY.
THAT'S WHY IT'S IMPORTANT THAT JORDAN LEARNS THE RULES NOW.
AND **THAT'S** WHAT THIS SCHOOL CAN DO FOR US.
IF HE CAN HANDLE FEELING LIKE AN OUTSIDER. KIDS TALKING ABOUT MOVIES HE HASN'T SEEN. OR BOOKS HE HASN'T READ . . .
ARE WE TALKING ABOUT JORDAN, OR **YOU**, CHUCK?
THIS WILL OPEN UP NEW DOORS. COLLEGES, NETWORKING . . .
OPPORTUNITIES THAT YOU AND I NEVER HAD.
BY NINTH GRADE, IF HE STILL WANTS TO GO TO ART SCHOOL. HE SHOULD BE ABLE TO GO.
IT'S **JORDAN'S** LIFE, ELLICE. NOT **OURS**!
FINE!!!
GOO

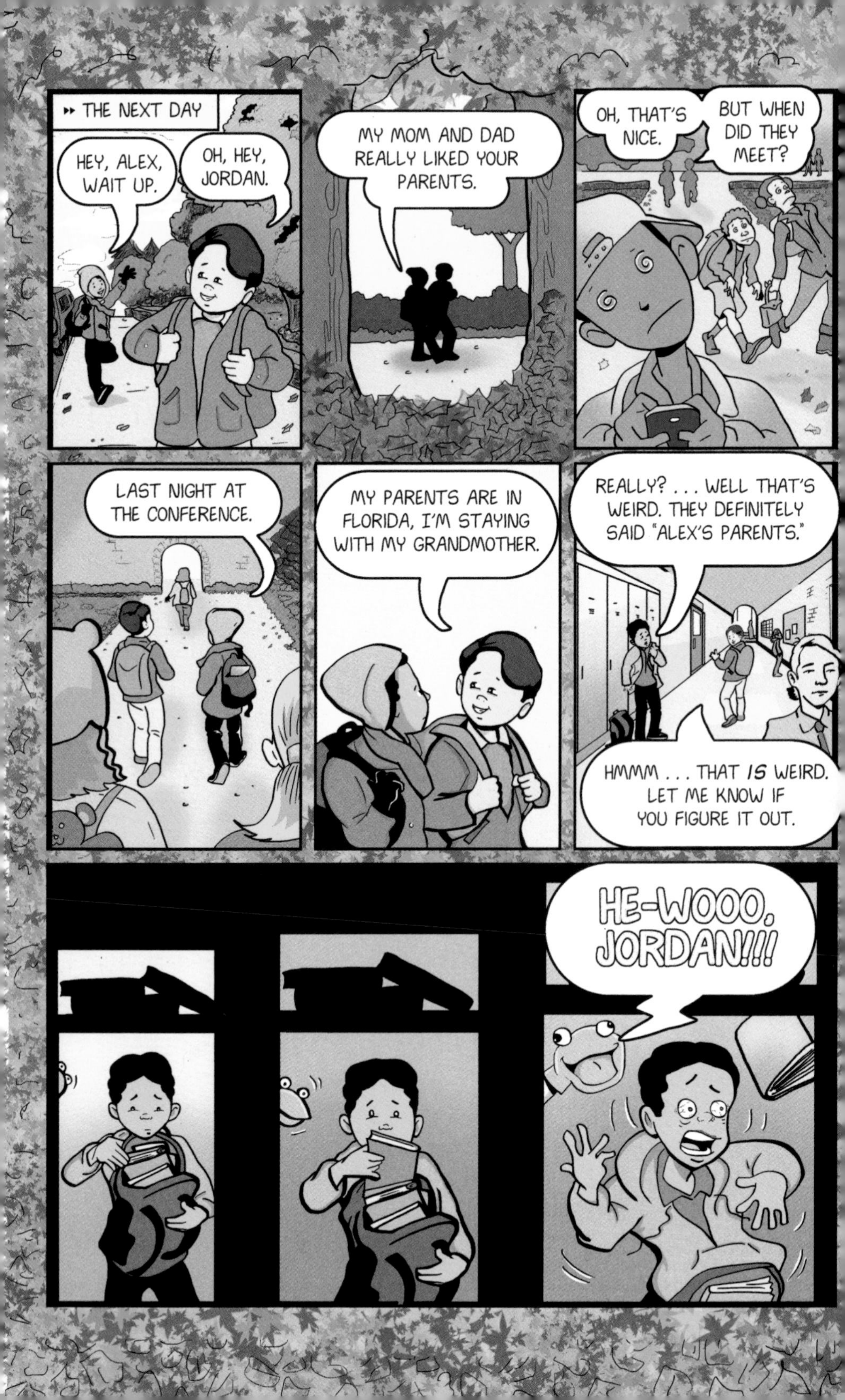
THE NEXT DAY
HEY, ALEX, WAIT UP.
OH, HEY, JORDAN.
MY MOM AND DAD REALLY LIKED YOUR PARENTS.
OH, THAT'S NICE.
BUT WHEN DID THEY MEET?
LAST NIGHT AT THE CONFERENCE.
MY PARENTS ARE IN FLORIDA, I'M STAYING WITH MY GRANDMOTHER.
REALLY? . . . WELL THAT'S WEIRD. THEY DEFINITELY SAID "ALEX'S PARENTS."
HMMM . . . THAT *IS* WEIRD. LET ME KNOW IF YOU FIGURE IT OUT.
HE-WOOO, JORDAN!!!

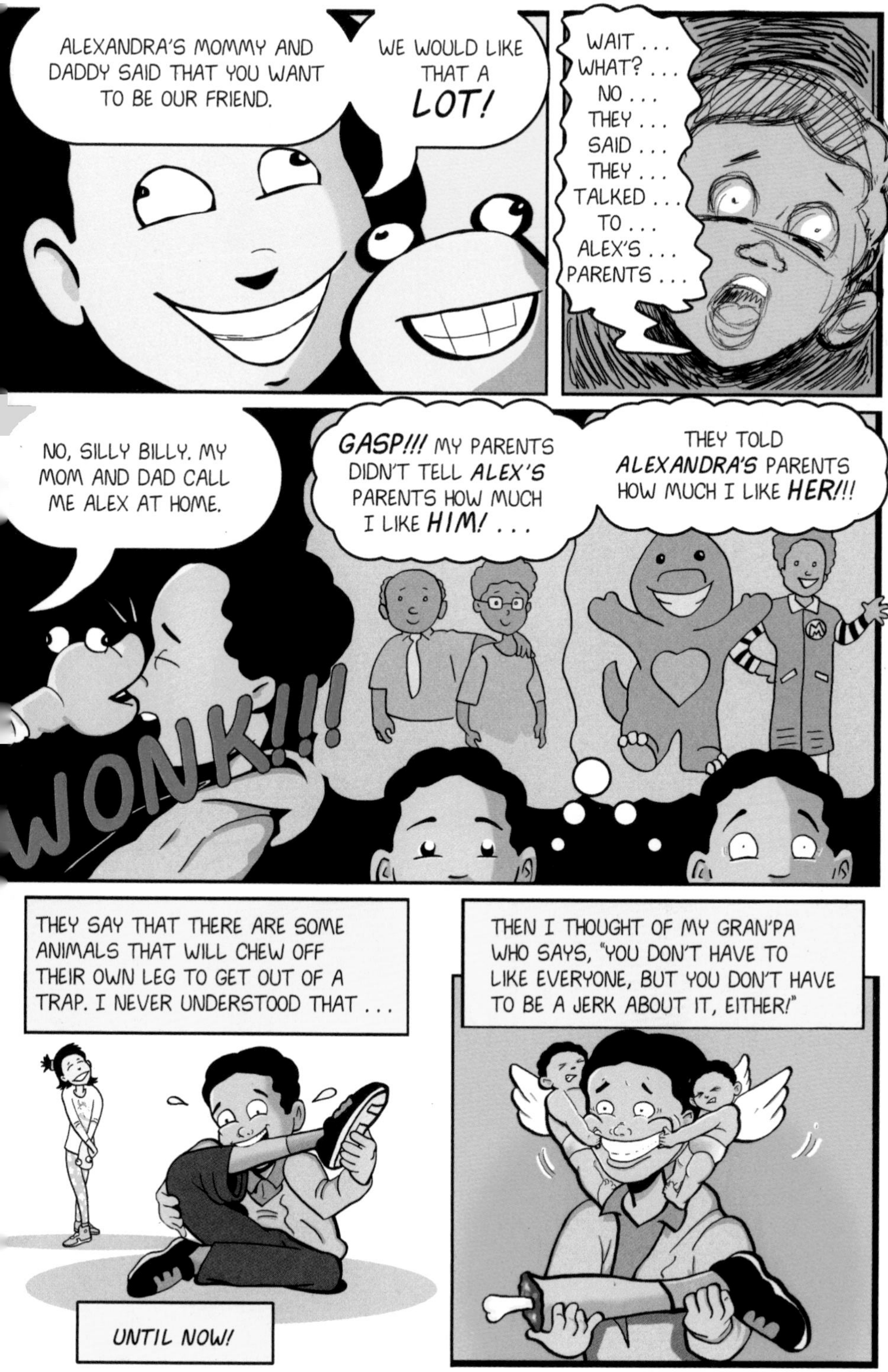
ALEXANDRA'S MOMMY AND DADDY SAID THAT YOU WANT TO BE OUR FRIEND.
WE WOULD LIKE THAT A LOT!
WAIT . . . WHAT? . . . NO . . . THEY . . . SAID . . . THEY . . . TALKED . . . TO . . . ALEX'S . . . PARENTS . . .
NO, SILLY BILLY. MY MOM AND DAD CALL ME ALEX AT HOME.
WONK!!!
GASP!!! MY PARENTS DIDN'T TELL ALEX'S PARENTS HOW MUCH I LIKE HIM! . . .
THEY TOLD ALEXANDRA'S PARENTS HOW MUCH I LIKE HER!!!
THEY SAY THAT THERE ARE SOME ANIMALS THAT WILL CHEW OFF THEIR OWN LEG TO GET OUT OF A TRAP. I NEVER UNDERSTOOD THAT . . .
UNTIL NOW!
THEN I THOUGHT OF MY GRAN'PA WHO SAYS, "YOU DON'T HAVE TO LIKE EVERYONE, BUT YOU DON'T HAVE TO BE A JERK ABOUT IT, EITHER!"

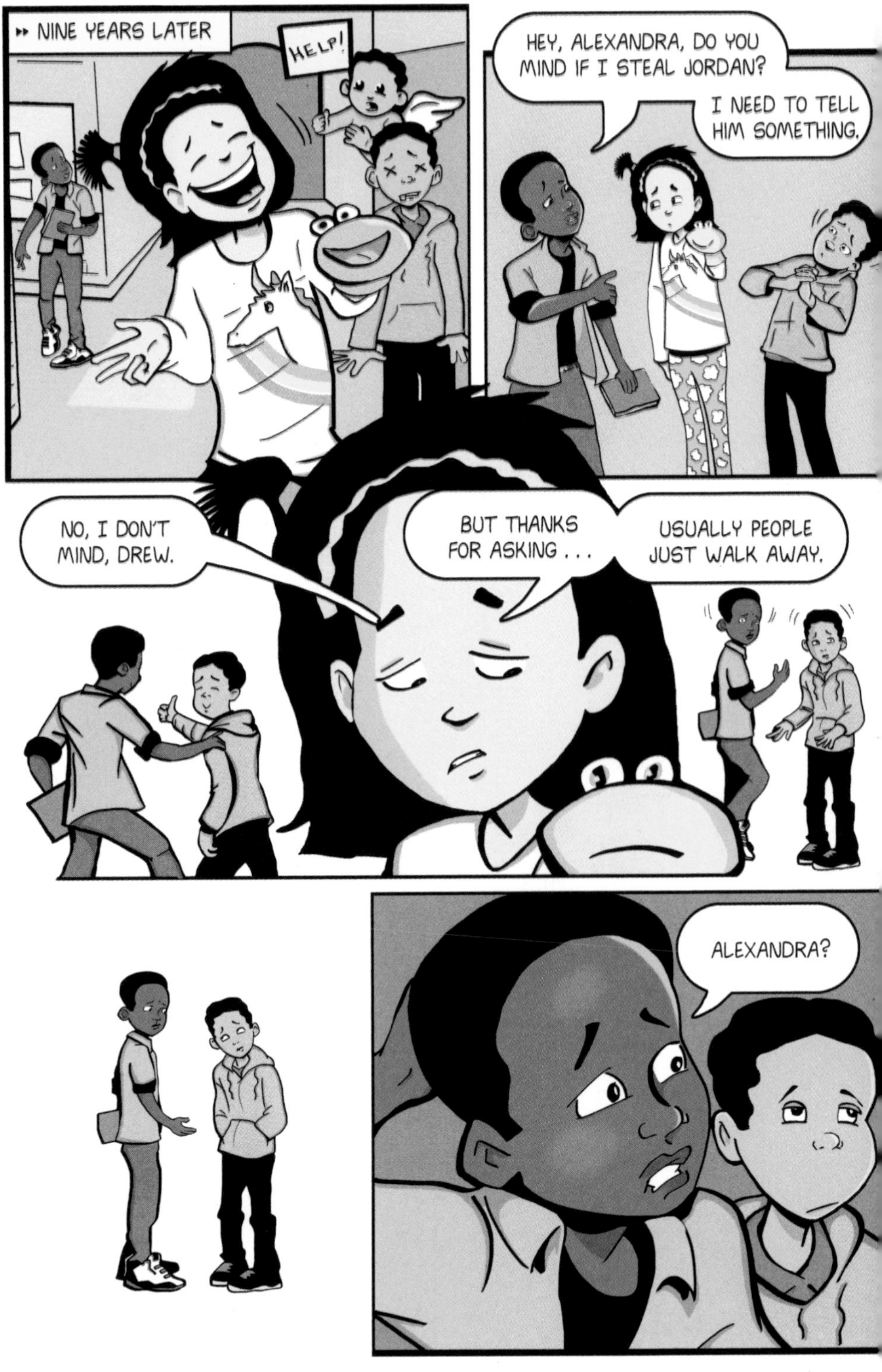

NINE YEARS LATER
HELP!
HEY, ALEXANDRA, DO YOU MIND IF I STEAL JORDAN?
I NEED TO TELL HIM SOMETHING.
NO, I DON'T MIND, DREW.
BUT THANKS FOR ASKING . . .
USUALLY PEOPLE JUST WALK AWAY.
ALEXANDRA?

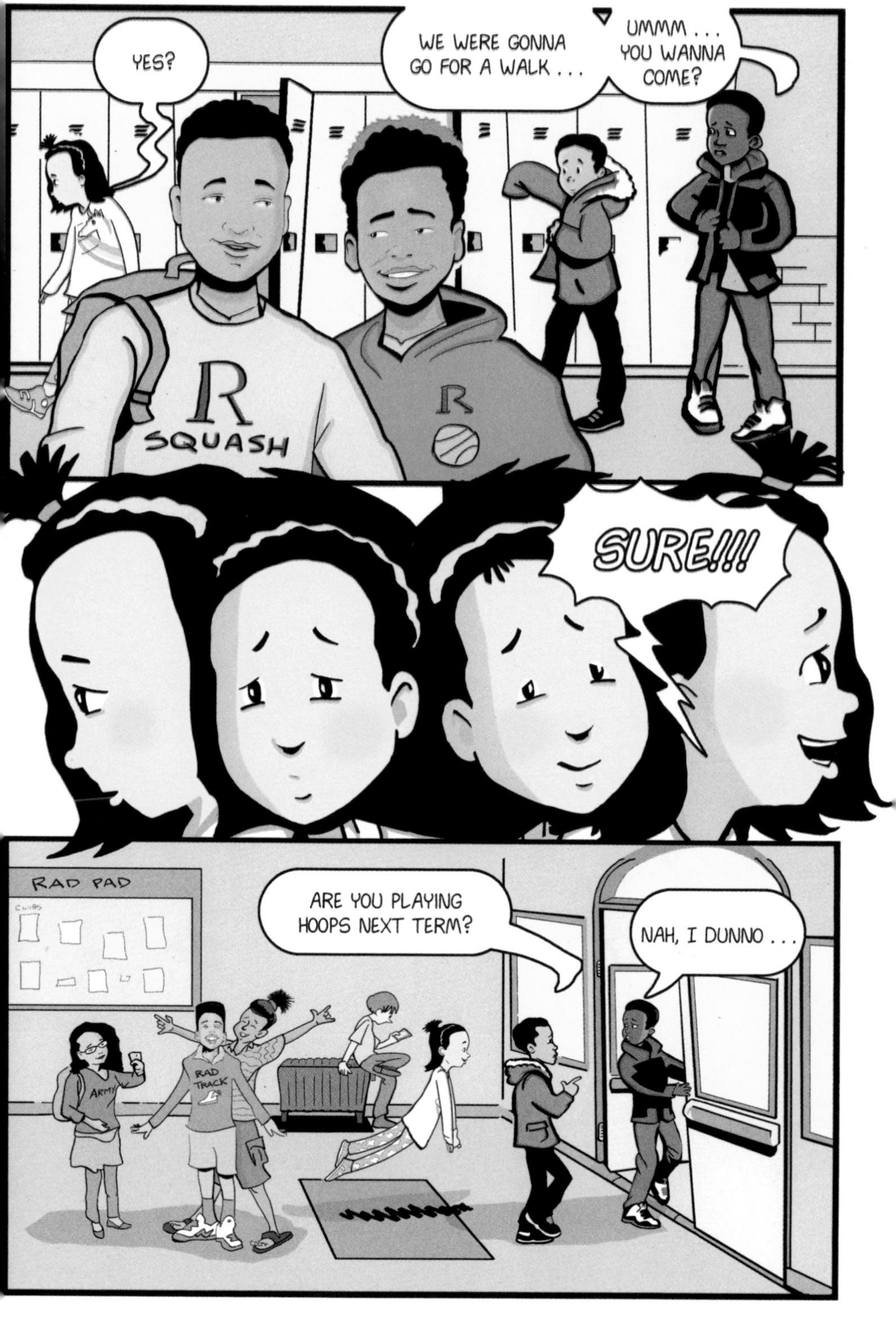
YES?
WE WERE GONNA GO FOR A WALK . . .
UMMM . . . YOU WANNA COME?
R SQUASH
R
SURE!!!
RAD PAD
ARE YOU PLAYING HOOPS NEXT TERM?
NAH, I DUNNO . . .
ARMY
RAD TRACK

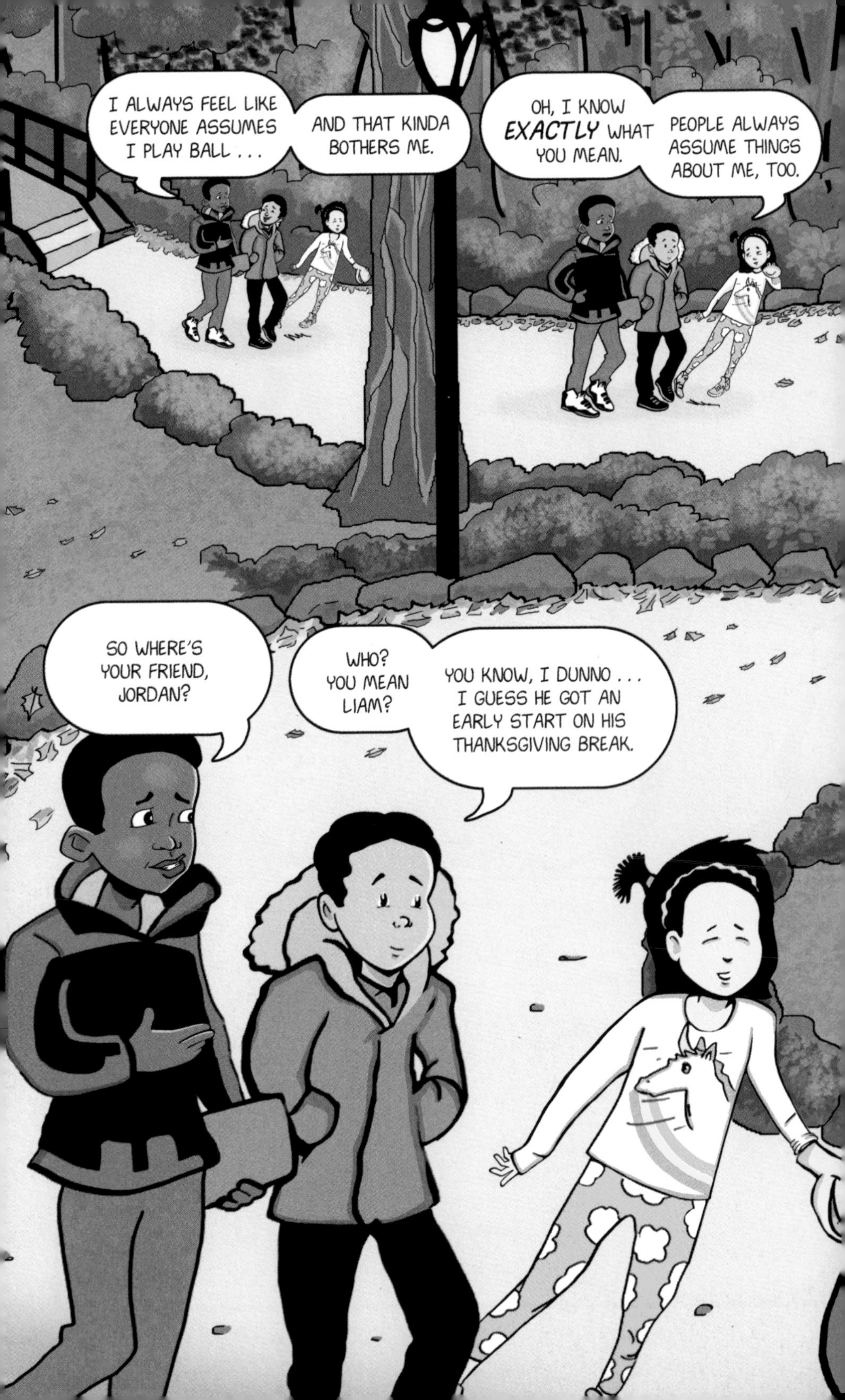
I ALWAYS FEEL LIKE EVERYONE ASSUMES I PLAY BALL . . .
AND THAT KINDA BOTHERS ME.
OH, I KNOW *EXACTLY* WHAT YOU MEAN.
PEOPLE ALWAYS ASSUME THINGS ABOUT ME, TOO.
SO WHERE'S YOUR FRIEND, JORDAN?
WHO? YOU MEAN LIAM?
YOU KNOW, I DUNNO . . . I GUESS HE GOT AN EARLY START ON HIS THANKSGIVING BREAK.

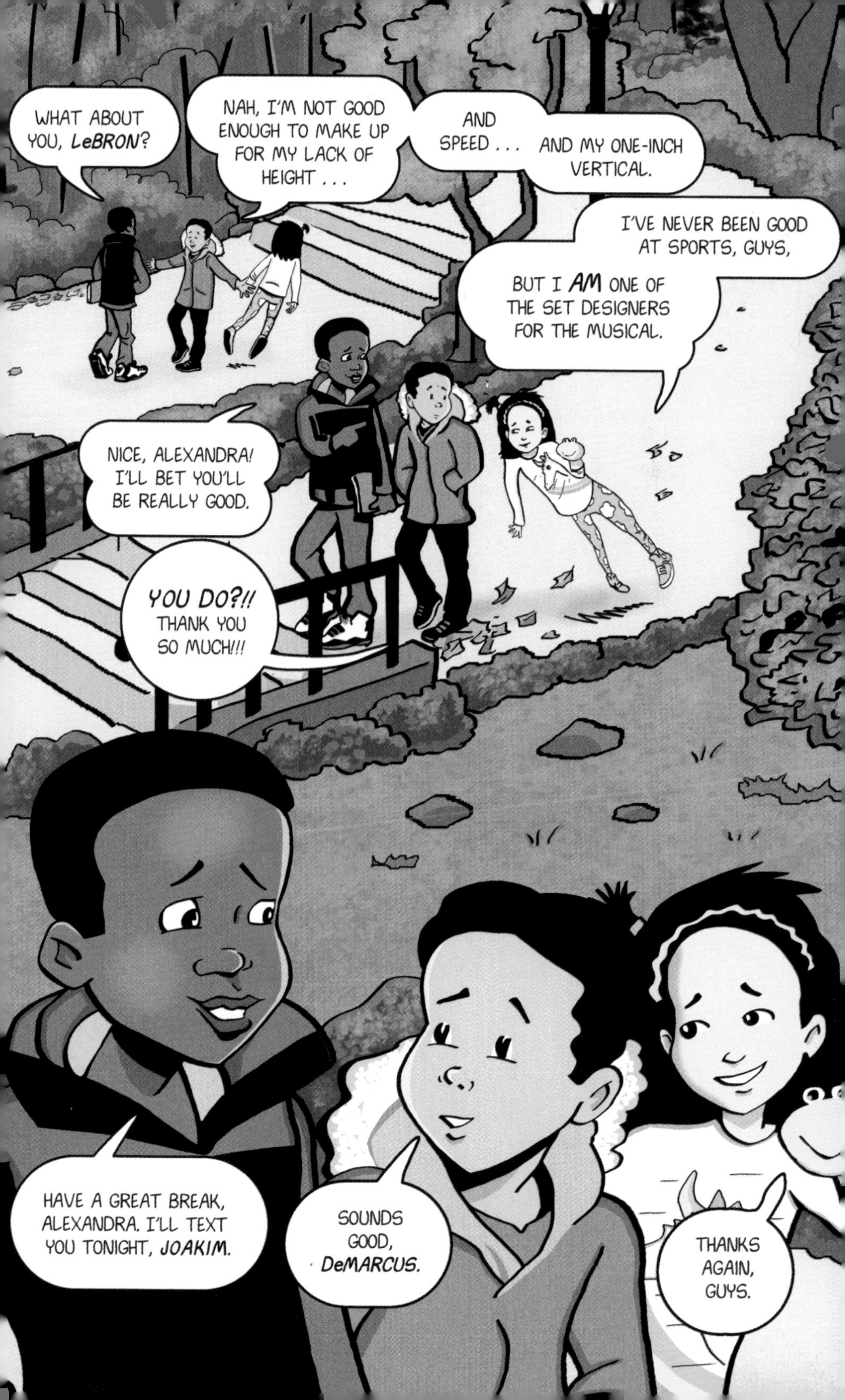
WHAT ABOUT YOU, LeBRON?
NAH, I'M NOT GOOD ENOUGH TO MAKE UP FOR MY LACK OF HEIGHT . . .
AND SPEED . . .
AND MY ONE-INCH VERTICAL.
I'VE NEVER BEEN GOOD AT SPORTS, GUYS,
BUT I AM ONE OF THE SET DESIGNERS FOR THE MUSICAL.
NICE, ALEXANDRA! I'LL BET YOU'LL BE REALLY GOOD.
YOU DO?!! THANK YOU SO MUCH!!!
HAVE A GREAT BREAK, ALEXANDRA. I'LL TEXT YOU TONIGHT, JOAKIM.
SOUNDS GOOD, DeMARCUS.
THANKS AGAIN, GUYS.

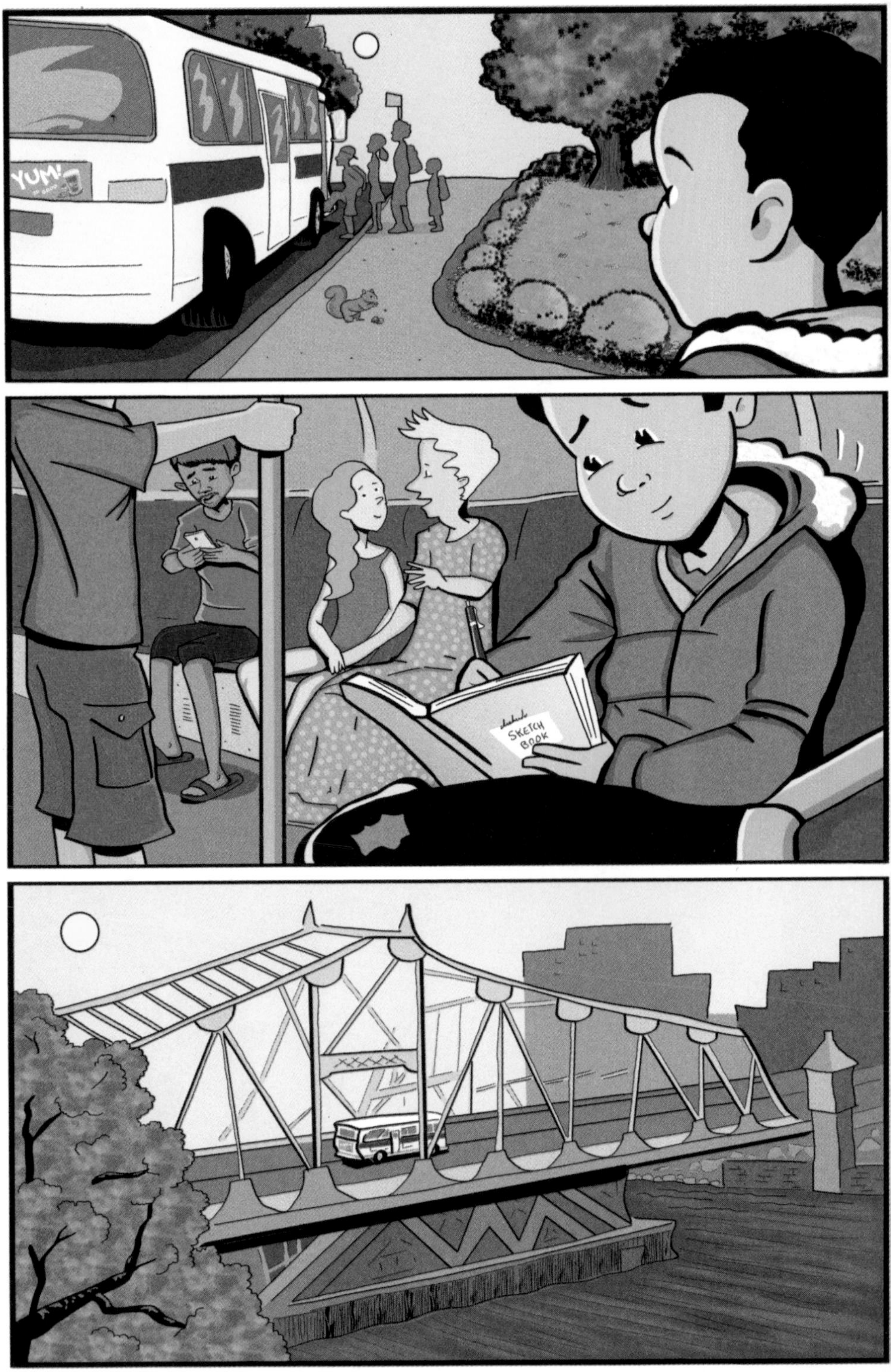
YUM!
SKETCH BOOK

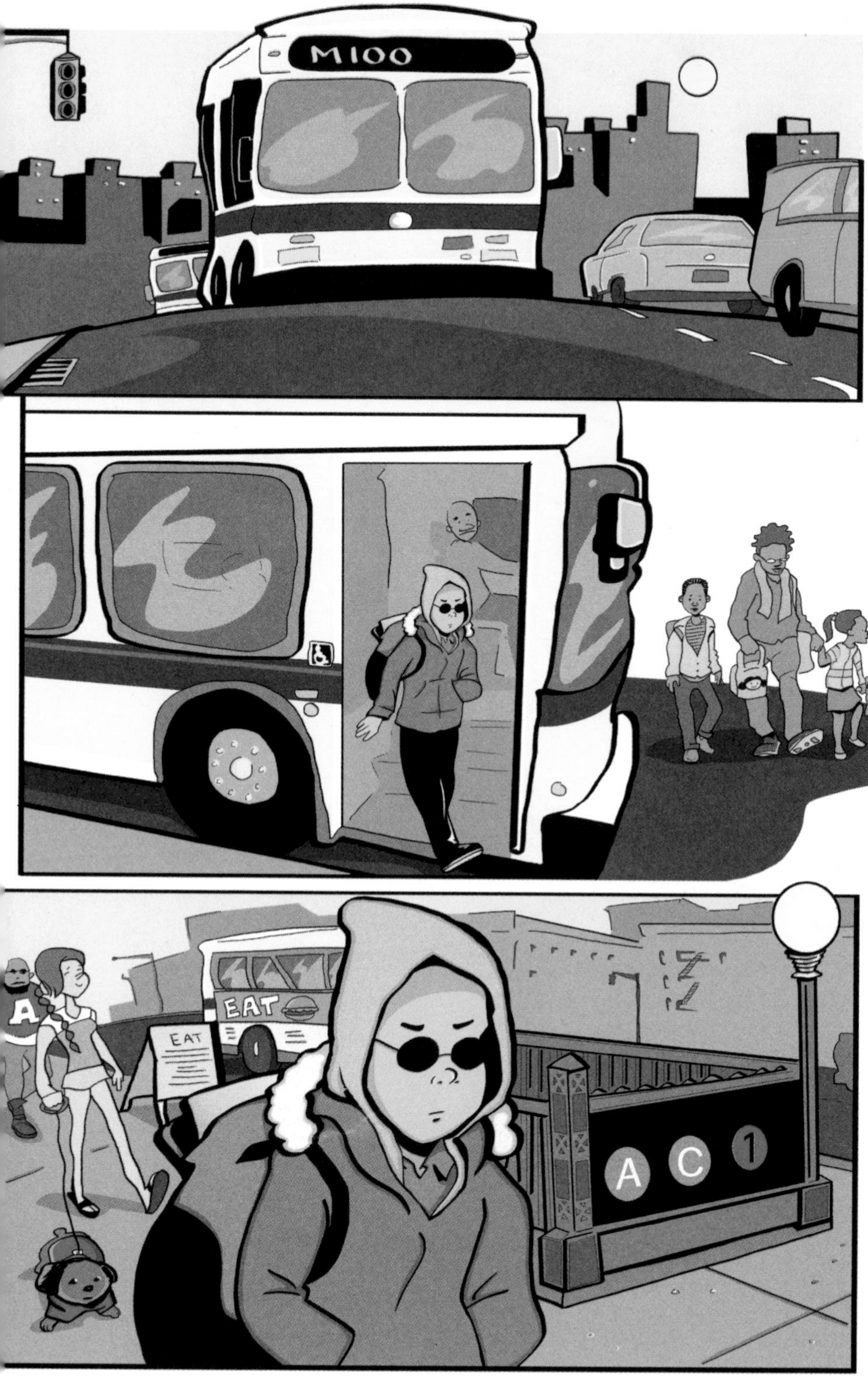
M100
EAT
EAT
A
A C 1

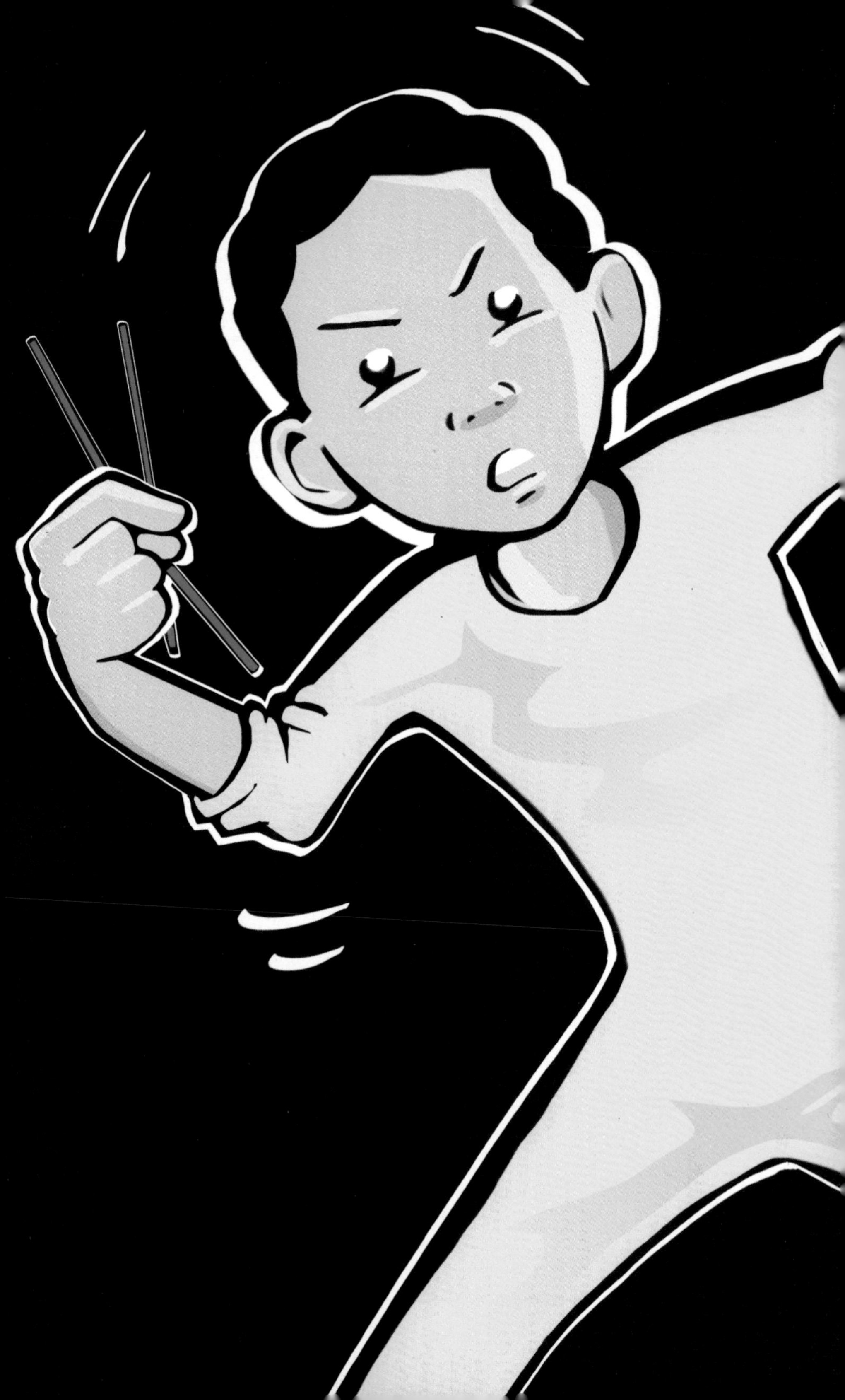

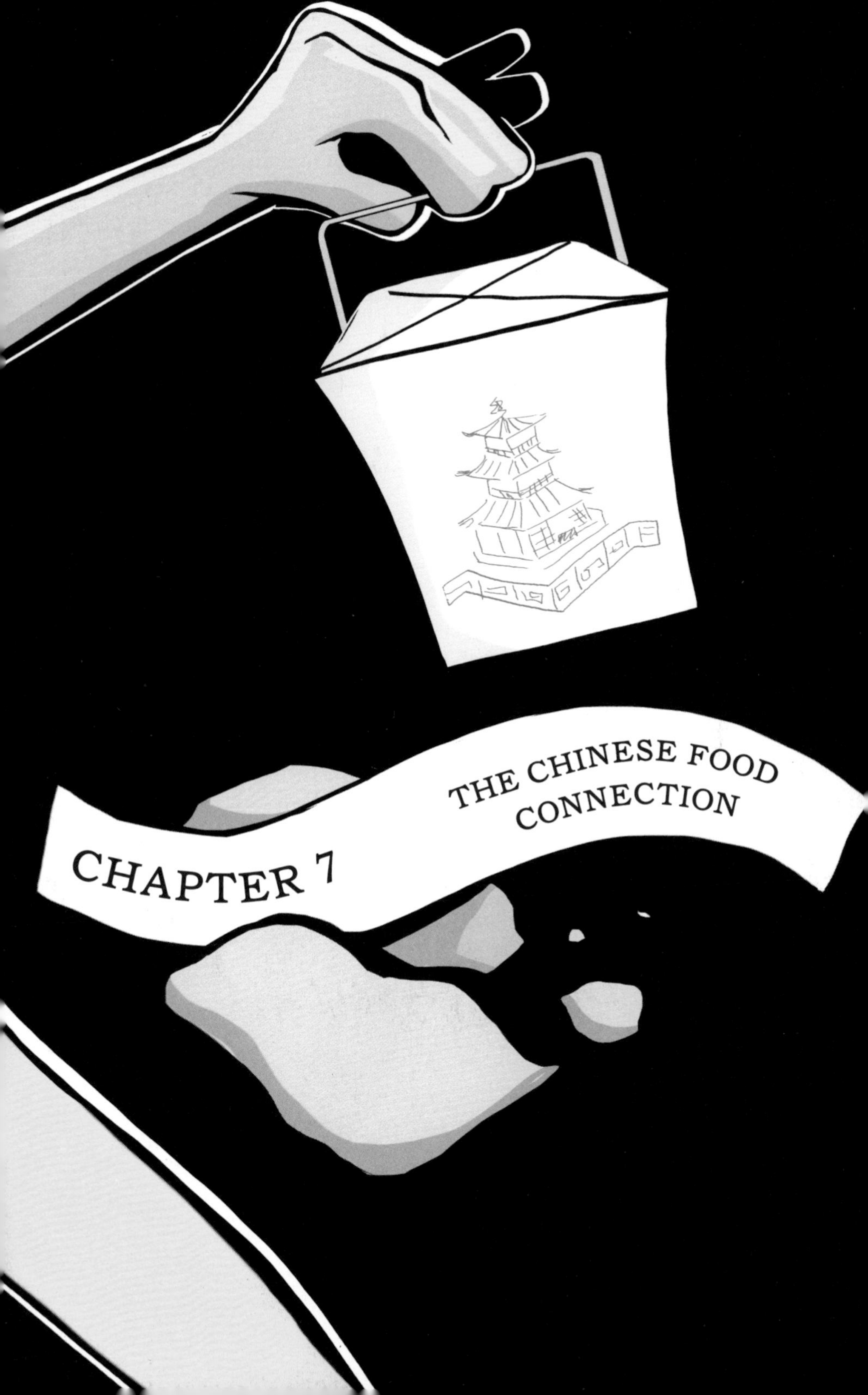
THE CHINESE FOOD
CONNECTION
CHAPTER 7

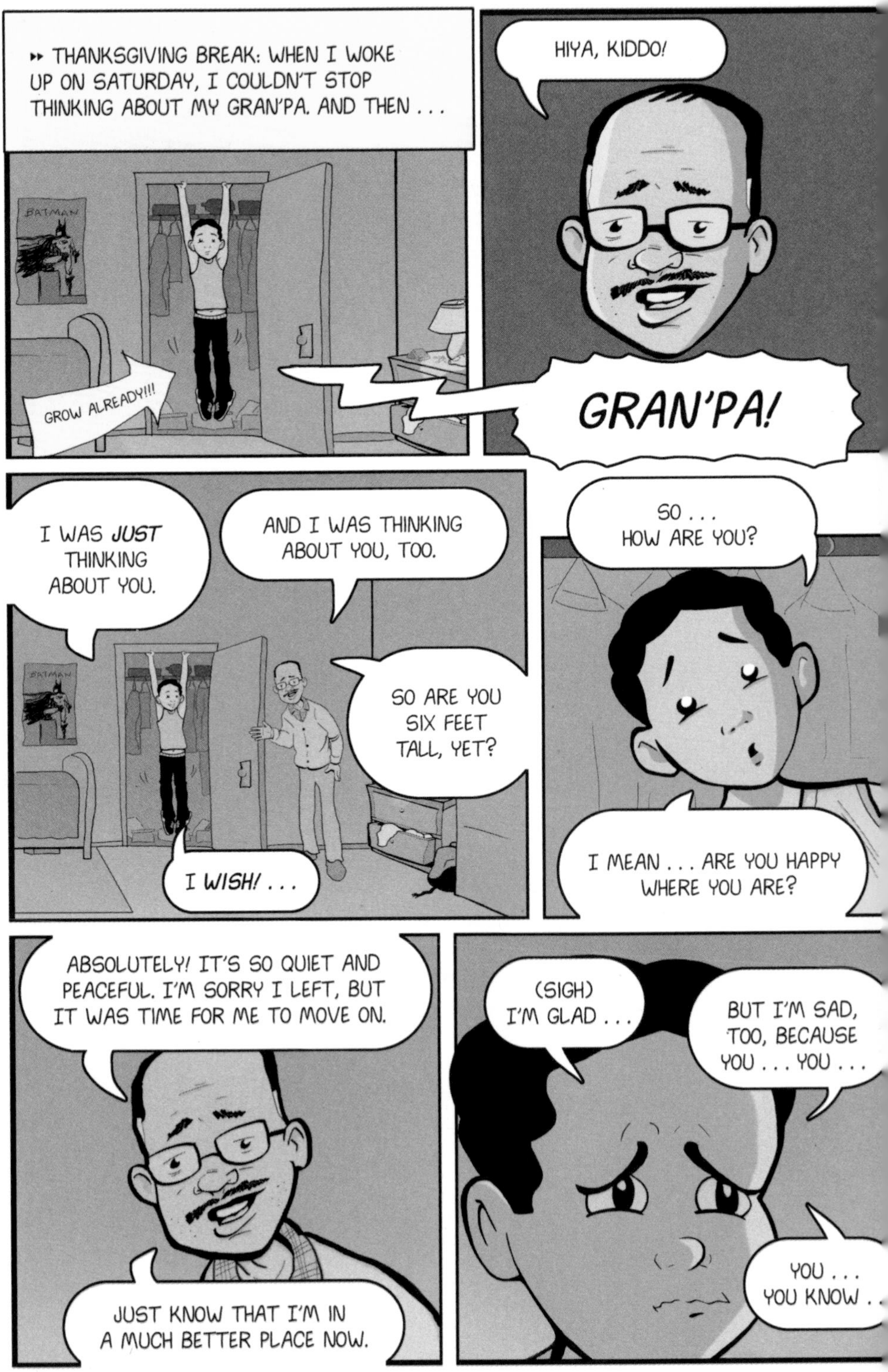
▸▸ THANKSGIVING BREAK: WHEN I WOKE UP ON SATURDAY, I COULDN'T STOP THINKING ABOUT MY GRAN'PA. AND THEN . . .
BATMAN
GROW ALREADY!!!
HIYA, KIDDO!
GRAN'PA!
I WAS *JUST* THINKING ABOUT YOU.
AND I WAS THINKING ABOUT YOU, TOO.
BATMAN
SO ARE YOU SIX FEET TALL, YET?
I *WISH!* . . .
SO . . . HOW ARE YOU?
I MEAN . . . ARE YOU HAPPY WHERE YOU ARE?
ABSOLUTELY! IT'S SO QUIET AND PEACEFUL. I'M SORRY I LEFT, BUT IT WAS TIME FOR ME TO MOVE ON.
JUST KNOW THAT I'M IN A MUCH BETTER PLACE NOW.
(SIGH) I'M GLAD . . .
BUT I'M SAD, TOO, BECAUSE YOU . . . YOU . . .
YOU . . . YOU KNOW . .

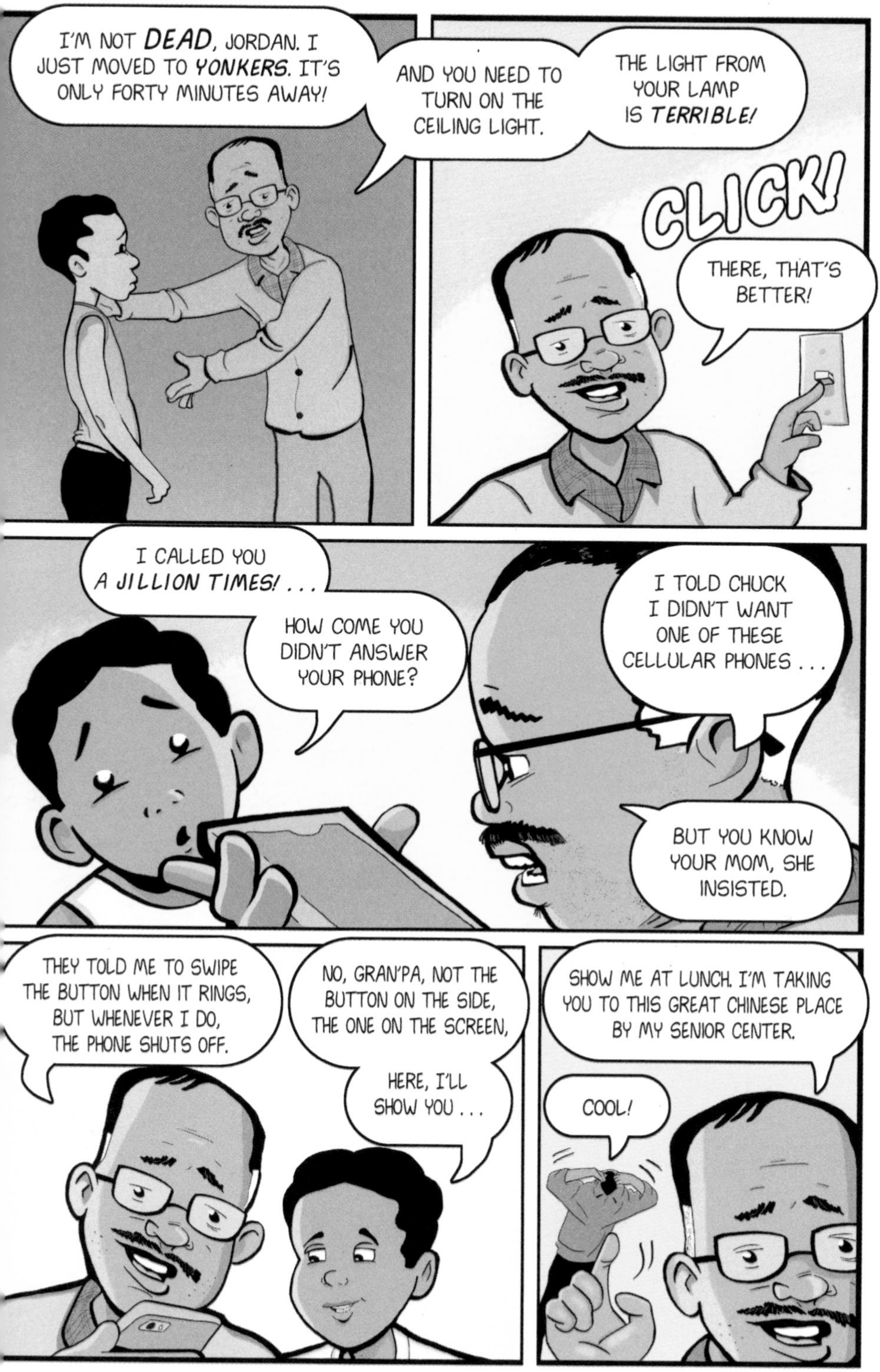

I'M NOT DEAD, JORDAN. I JUST MOVED TO YONKERS. IT'S ONLY FORTY MINUTES AWAY!
AND YOU NEED TO TURN ON THE CEILING LIGHT.
THE LIGHT FROM YOUR LAMP IS TERRIBLE!
CLICK!
THERE, THAT'S BETTER!
I CALLED YOU A JILLION TIMES! . . .
HOW COME YOU DIDN'T ANSWER YOUR PHONE?
I TOLD CHUCK I DIDN'T WANT ONE OF THESE CELLULAR PHONES . . .
BUT YOU KNOW YOUR MOM, SHE INSISTED.
THEY TOLD ME TO SWIPE THE BUTTON WHEN IT RINGS, BUT WHENEVER I DO, THE PHONE SHUTS OFF.
NO, GRAN'PA, NOT THE BUTTON ON THE SIDE, THE ONE ON THE SCREEN,
HERE, I'LL SHOW YOU . . .
SHOW ME AT LUNCH. I'M TAKING YOU TO THIS GREAT CHINESE PLACE BY MY SENIOR CENTER.
COOL!

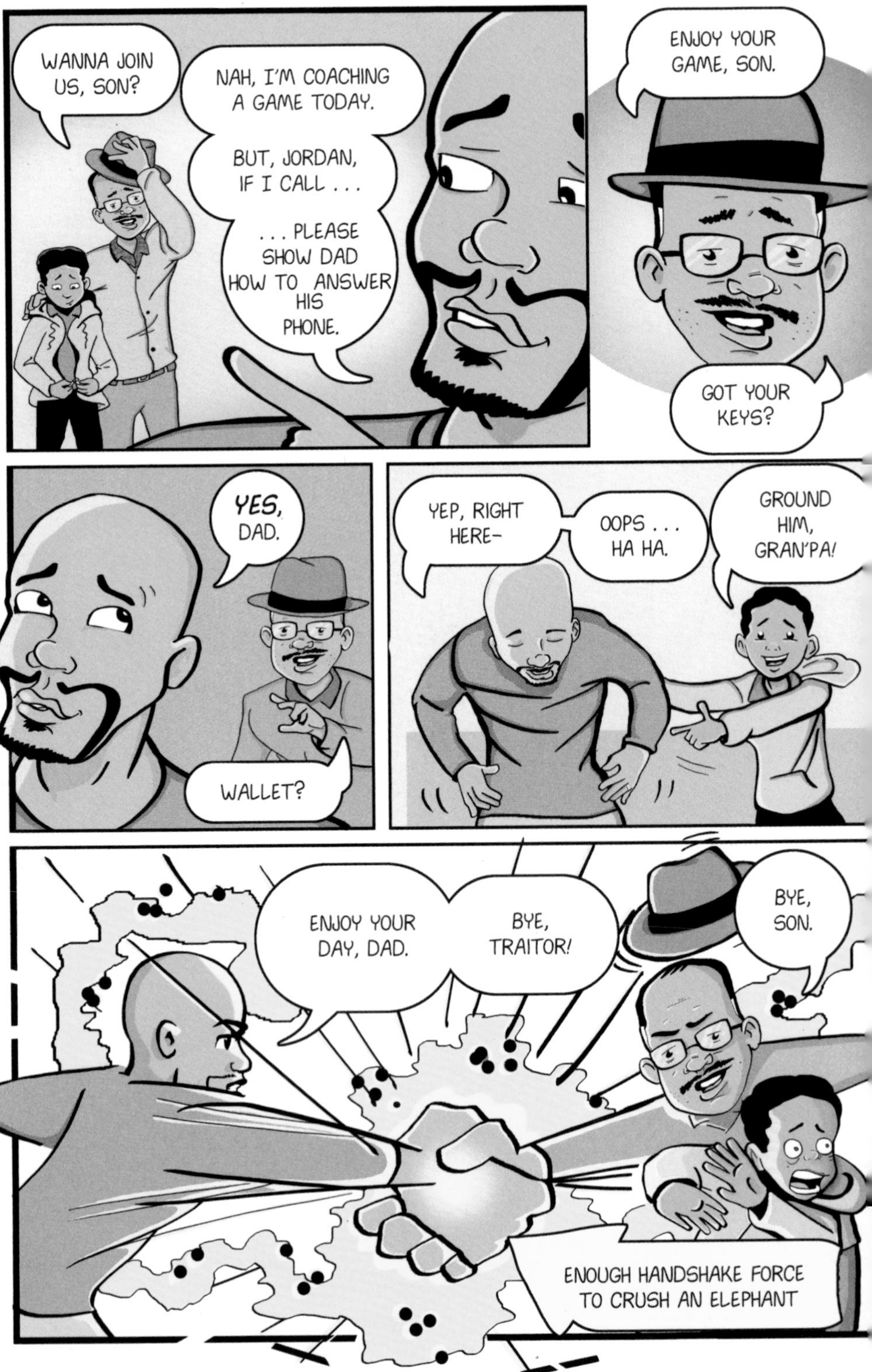
WANNA JOIN US, SON?
NAH, I'M COACHING A GAME TODAY.
BUT, JORDAN, IF I CALL . . .
. . . PLEASE SHOW DAD HOW TO ANSWER HIS PHONE.
ENJOY YOUR GAME, SON.
GOT YOUR KEYS?
YES, DAD.
WALLET?
YEP, RIGHT HERE–
OOPS . . . HA HA.
GROUND HIM, GRAN'PA!
ENJOY YOUR DAY, DAD.
BYE, TRAITOR!
BYE, SON.
ENOUGH HANDSHAKE FORCE TO CRUSH AN ELEPHANT

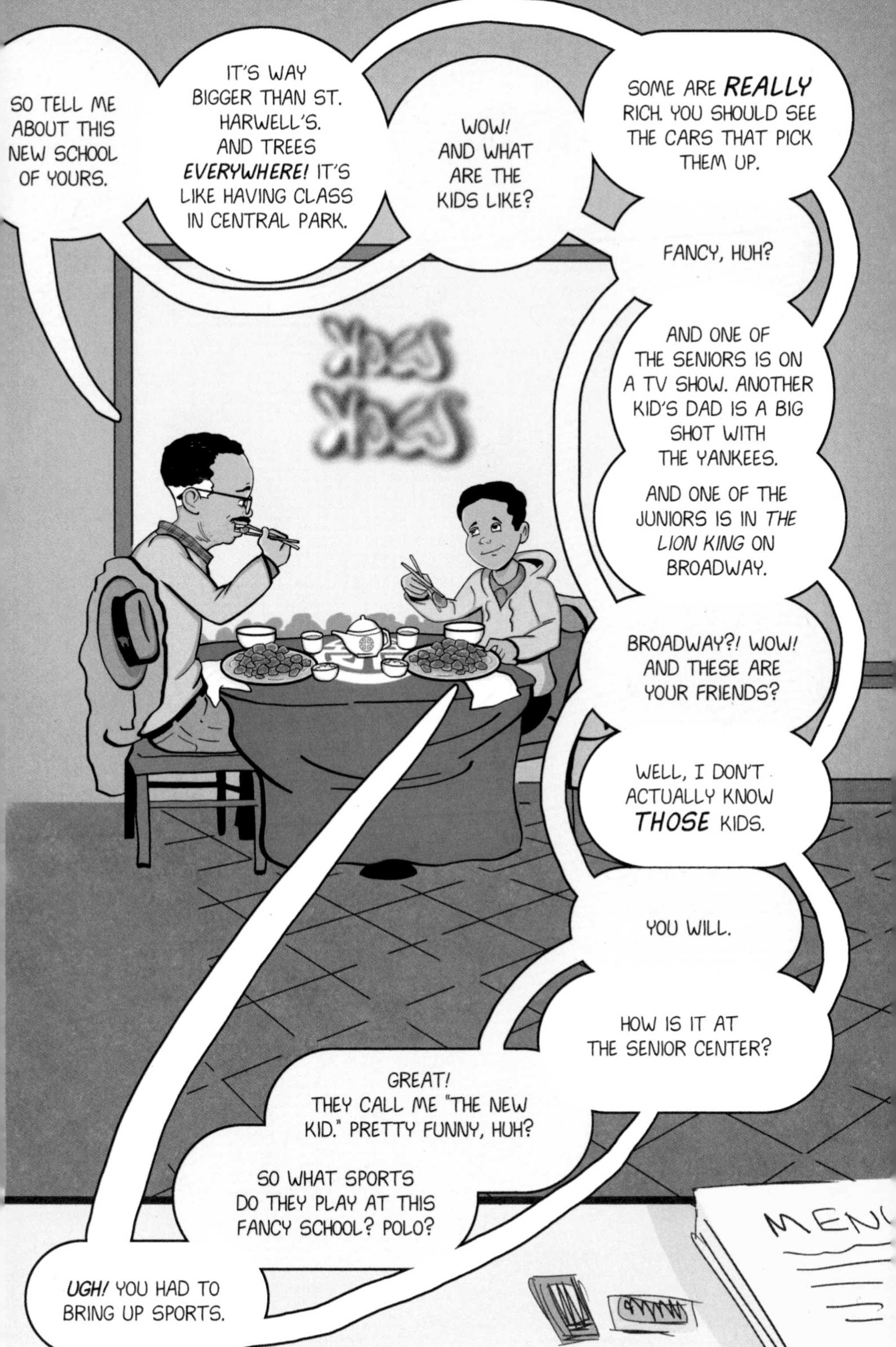
SO TELL ME ABOUT THIS NEW SCHOOL OF YOURS.
IT'S WAY BIGGER THAN ST. HARWELL'S. AND TREES *EVERYWHERE!* IT'S LIKE HAVING CLASS IN CENTRAL PARK.
WOW! AND WHAT ARE THE KIDS LIKE?
SOME ARE **REALLY** RICH. YOU SHOULD SEE THE CARS THAT PICK THEM UP.
FANCY, HUH?
AND ONE OF THE SENIORS IS ON A TV SHOW. ANOTHER KID'S DAD IS A BIG SHOT WITH THE YANKEES.
AND ONE OF THE JUNIORS IS IN *THE LION KING* ON BROADWAY.
BROADWAY?! WOW! AND THESE ARE YOUR FRIENDS?
WELL, I DON'T ACTUALLY KNOW **THOSE** KIDS.
YOU WILL.
HOW IS IT AT THE SENIOR CENTER?
GREAT! THEY CALL ME "THE NEW KID." PRETTY FUNNY, HUH?
SO WHAT SPORTS DO THEY PLAY AT THIS FANCY SCHOOL? POLO?
UGH! YOU HAD TO BRING UP SPORTS.
MEN

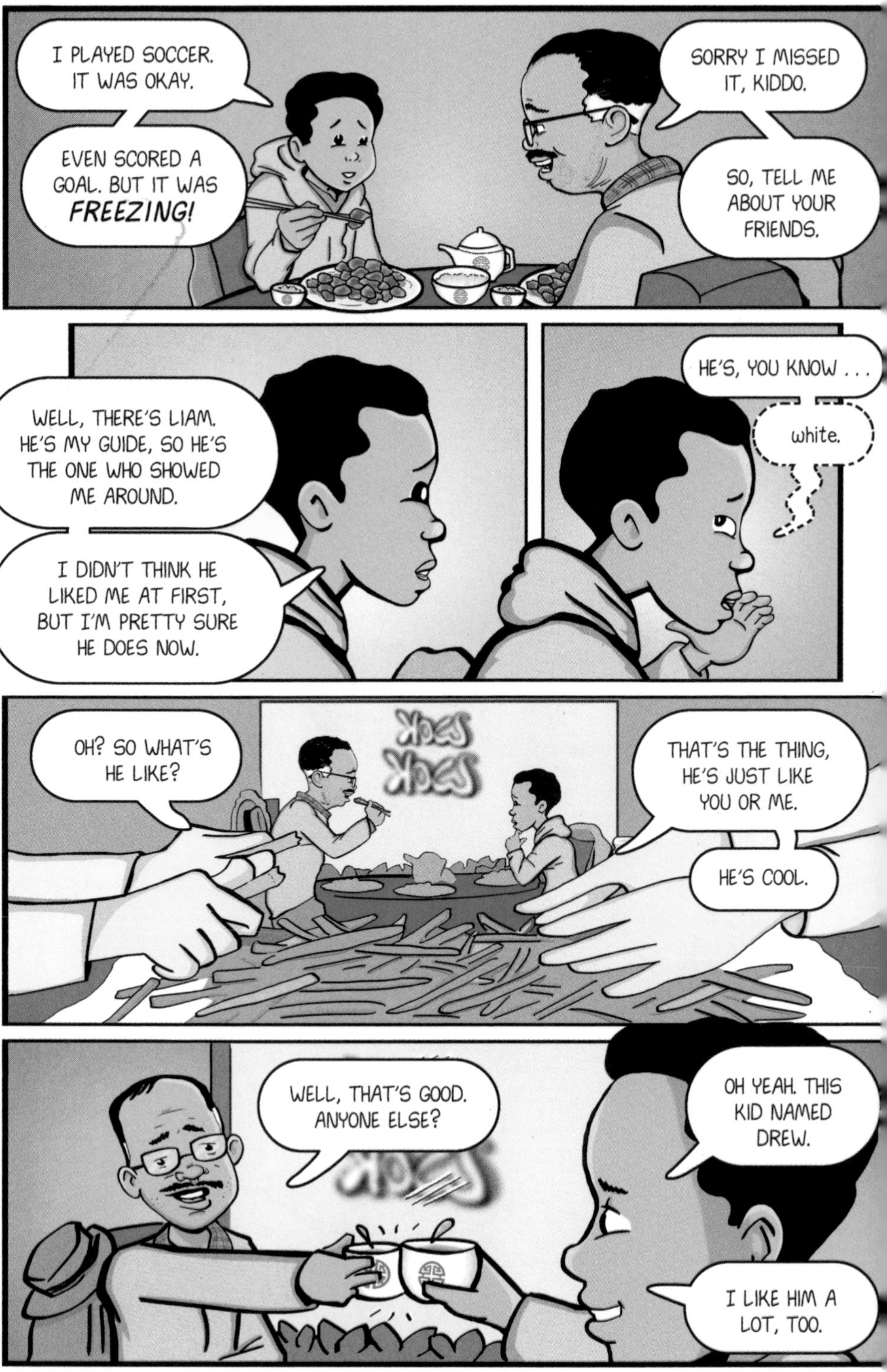
I PLAYED SOCCER. IT WAS OKAY.
EVEN SCORED A GOAL. BUT IT WAS *FREEZING!*
SORRY I MISSED IT, KIDDO.
SO, TELL ME ABOUT YOUR FRIENDS.
WELL, THERE'S LIAM. HE'S MY GUIDE, SO HE'S THE ONE WHO SHOWED ME AROUND.
I DIDN'T THINK HE LIKED ME AT FIRST, BUT I'M PRETTY SURE HE DOES NOW.
HE'S, YOU KNOW . . .
white.
OH? SO WHAT'S HE LIKE?
THAT'S THE THING, HE'S JUST LIKE YOU OR ME.
HE'S COOL.
WELL, THAT'S GOOD. ANYONE ELSE?
OH YEAH. THIS KID NAMED DREW.
I LIKE HIM A LOT, TOO.

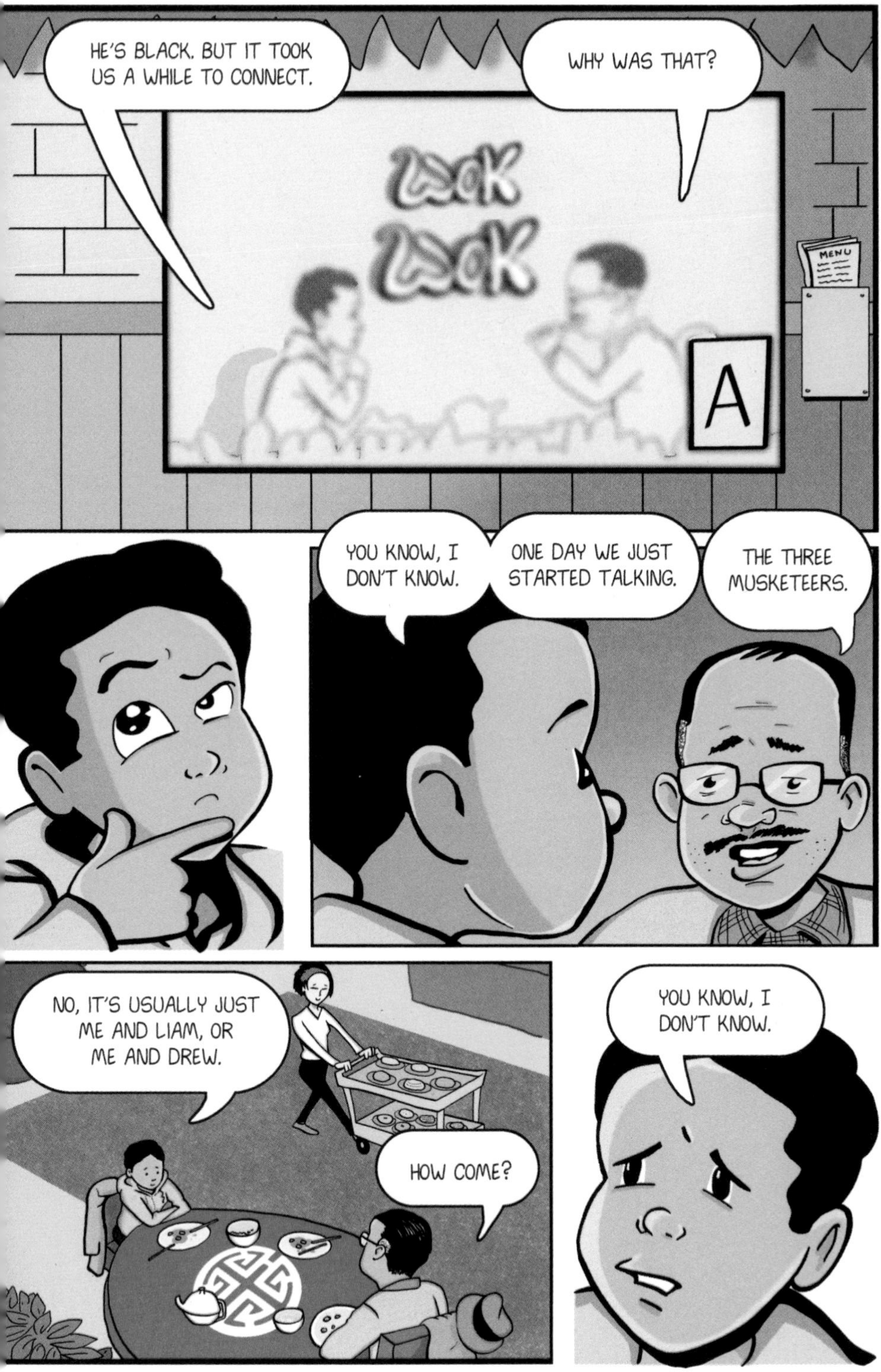
HE'S BLACK. BUT IT TOOK US A WHILE TO CONNECT.
WHY WAS THAT?
YOU KNOW, I DON'T KNOW.
ONE DAY WE JUST STARTED TALKING.
THE THREE MUSKETEERS.
NO, IT'S USUALLY JUST ME AND LIAM, OR ME AND DREW.
HOW COME?
YOU KNOW, I DON'T KNOW.

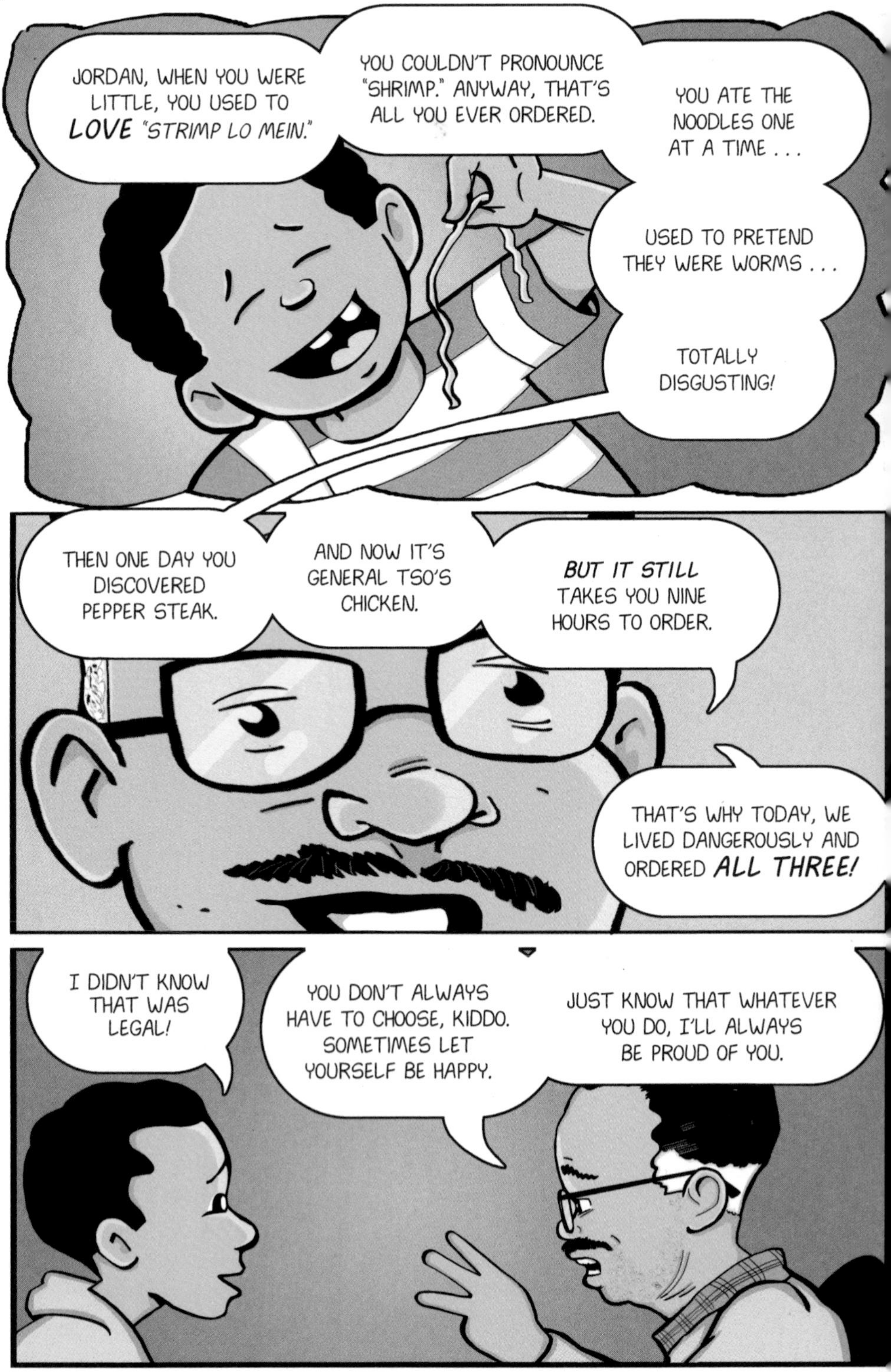
JORDAN, WHEN YOU WERE LITTLE, YOU USED TO **LOVE** "STRIMP LO MEIN."
YOU COULDN'T PRONOUNCE "SHRIMP." ANYWAY, THAT'S ALL YOU EVER ORDERED.
YOU ATE THE NOODLES ONE AT A TIME . . .
USED TO PRETEND THEY WERE WORMS . . .
TOTALLY DISGUSTING!
THEN ONE DAY YOU DISCOVERED PEPPER STEAK.
AND NOW IT'S GENERAL TSO'S CHICKEN.
BUT IT STILL TAKES YOU NINE HOURS TO ORDER.
THAT'S WHY TODAY, WE LIVED DANGEROUSLY AND ORDERED **ALL THREE!**
I DIDN'T KNOW THAT WAS LEGAL!
YOU DON'T ALWAYS HAVE TO CHOOSE, KIDDO. SOMETIMES LET YOURSELF BE HAPPY.
JUST KNOW THAT WHATEVER YOU DO, I'LL ALWAYS BE PROUD OF YOU.

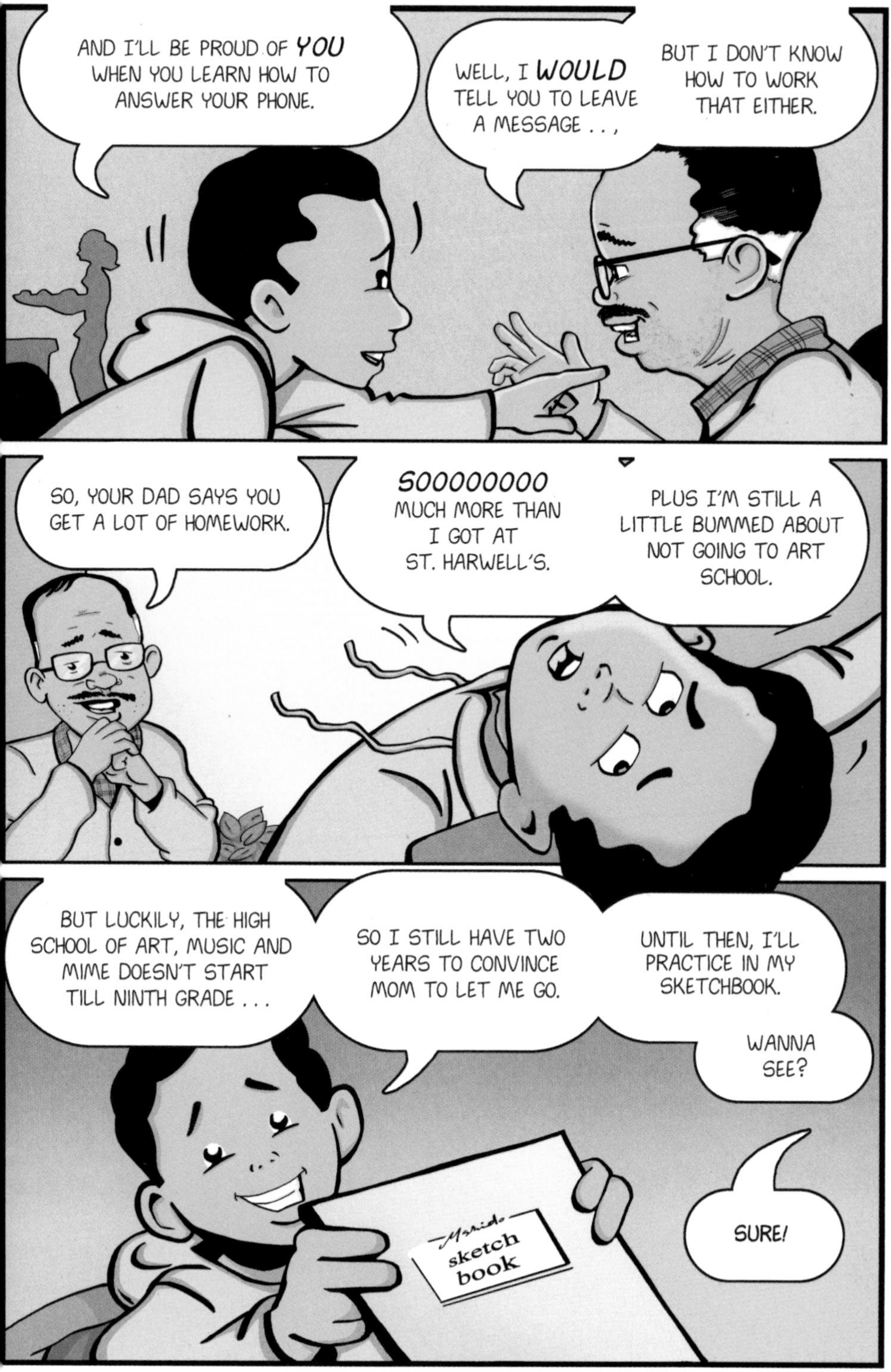
AND I'LL BE PROUD OF *YOU* WHEN YOU LEARN HOW TO ANSWER YOUR PHONE.
WELL, I **WOULD** TELL YOU TO LEAVE A MESSAGE . . . ,
BUT I DON'T KNOW HOW TO WORK THAT EITHER.
SO, YOUR DAD SAYS YOU GET A LOT OF HOMEWORK.
SOOOOOOOO MUCH MORE THAN I GOT AT ST. HARWELL'S.
PLUS I'M STILL A LITTLE BUMMED ABOUT NOT GOING TO ART SCHOOL.
BUT LUCKILY, THE HIGH SCHOOL OF ART, MUSIC AND MIME DOESN'T START TILL NINTH GRADE . . .
SO I STILL HAVE TWO YEARS TO CONVINCE MOM TO LET ME GO.
UNTIL THEN, I'LL PRACTICE IN MY SKETCHBOOK.
WANNA SEE?
SURE!
sketch book

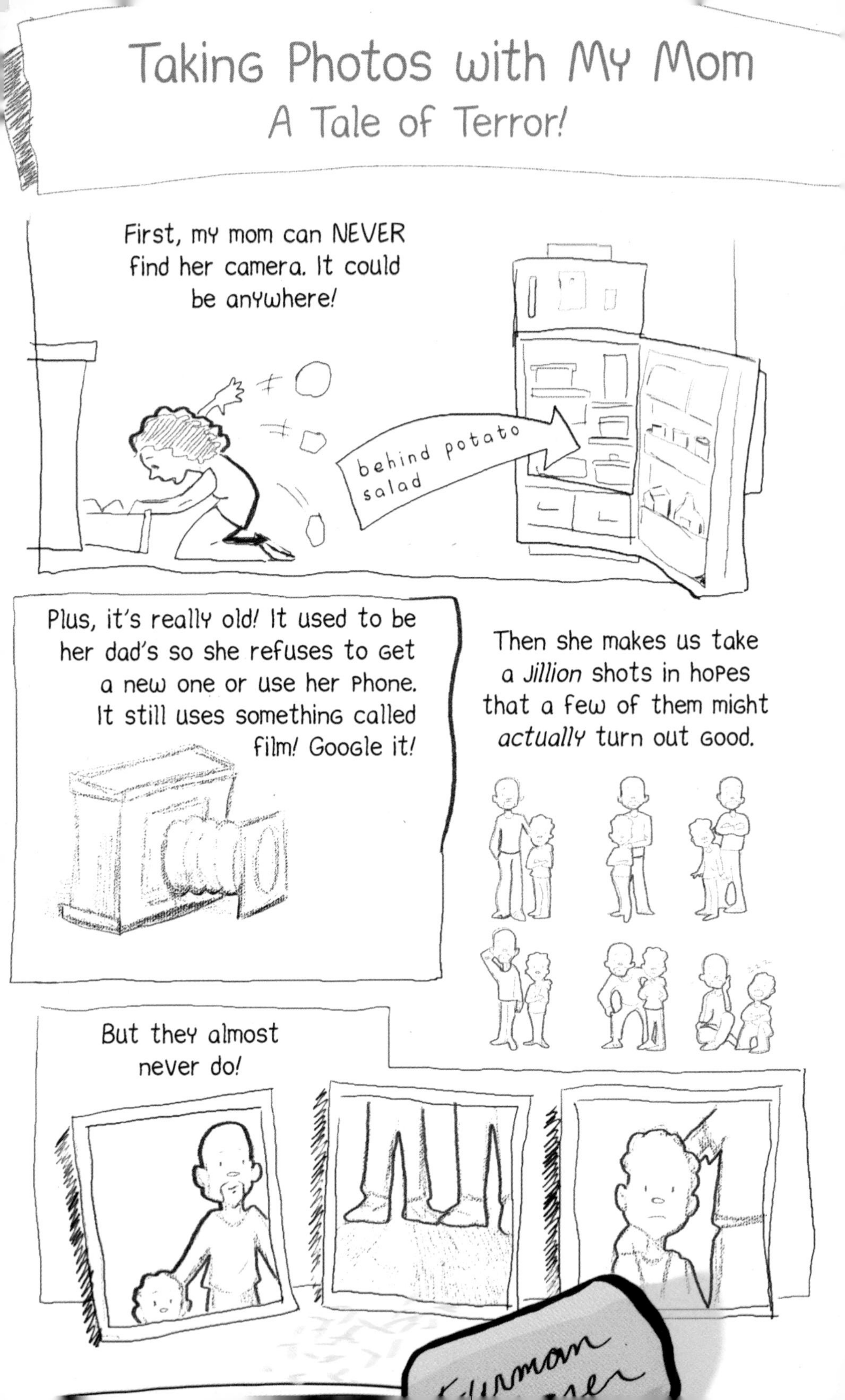
Taking Photos with My Mom
A Tale of Terror!
First, my mom can NEVER find her camera. It could be anywhere!
behind potato salad
Plus, it's really old! It used to be her dad's so she refuses to get a new one or use her phone. It still uses something called film! Google it!
Then she makes us take a *jillion* shots in hopes that a few of them might *actually* turn out good.
But they almost never do!

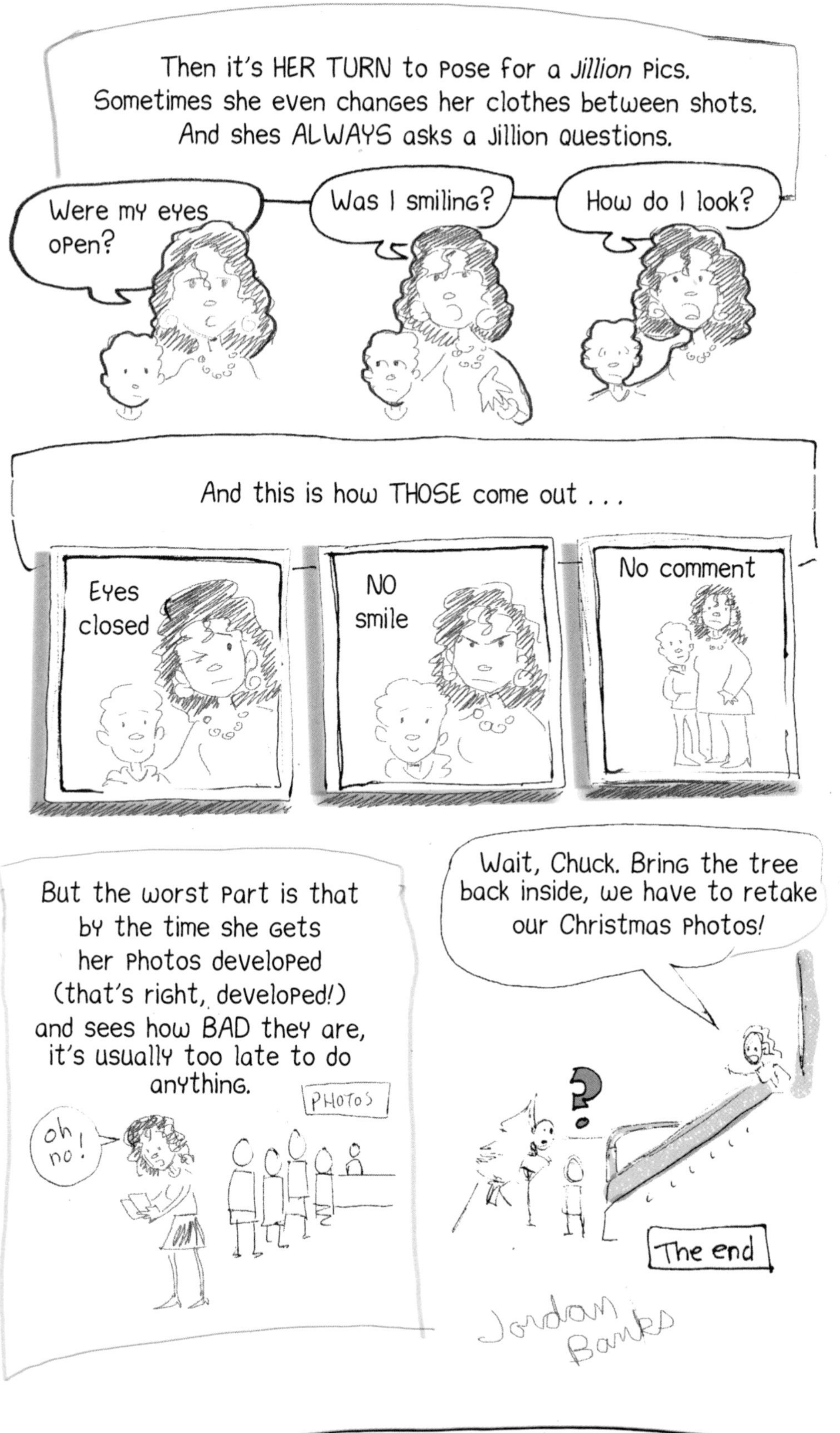

Then it's HER TURN to pose for a *Jillion* pics. Sometimes she even changes her clothes between shots. And shes ALWAYS asks a Jillion questions.
Were my eyes open?
Was I smiling?
How do I look?
And this is how THOSE come out . . .
Eyes closed
NO smile
No comment
But the worst part is that by the time she gets her photos developed (that's right, developed!) and sees how BAD they are, it's usually too late to do anything.
PHOTOS
oh no!
Wait, Chuck. Bring the tree back inside, we have to retake our Christmas photos!
The end
Jordan Banks

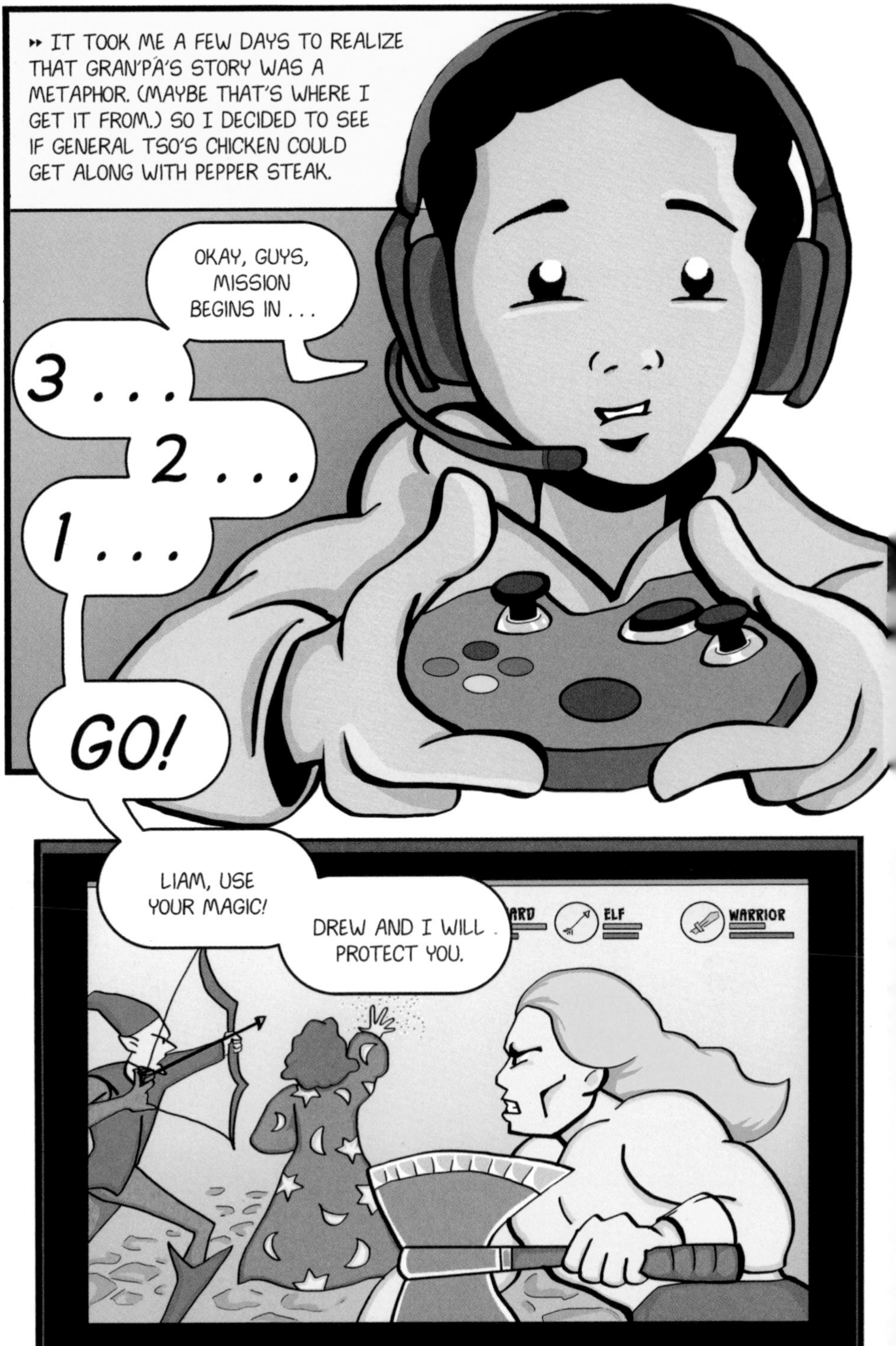
IT TOOK ME A FEW DAYS TO REALIZE THAT GRAN'PA'S STORY WAS A METAPHOR. (MAYBE THAT'S WHERE I GET IT FROM.) SO I DECIDED TO SEE IF GENERAL TSO'S CHICKEN COULD GET ALONG WITH PEPPER STEAK.
OKAY, GUYS, MISSION BEGINS IN . . .
3 . . .
2 . . .
1 . . .
GO!
LIAM, USE YOUR MAGIC!
DREW AND I WILL PROTECT YOU.
ELF
WARRIOR

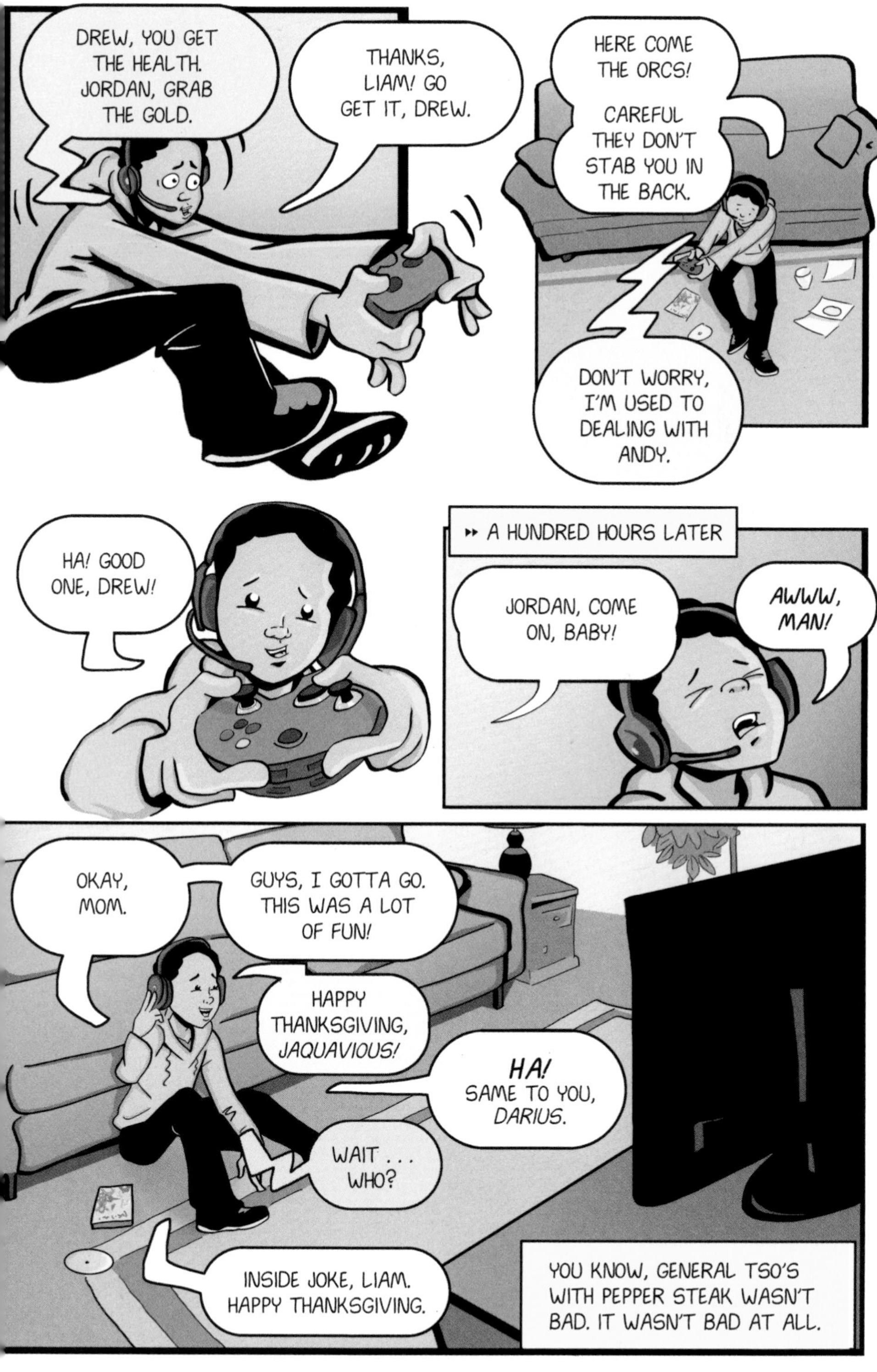
DREW, YOU GET THE HEALTH. JORDAN, GRAB THE GOLD.
THANKS, LIAM! GO GET IT, DREW.
HERE COME THE ORCS!
CAREFUL THEY DON'T STAB YOU IN THE BACK.
DON'T WORRY, I'M USED TO DEALING WITH ANDY.
HA! GOOD ONE, DREW!
A HUNDRED HOURS LATER
JORDAN, COME ON, BABY!
AWWW, MAN!
OKAY, MOM.
GUYS, I GOTTA GO. THIS WAS A LOT OF FUN!
HAPPY THANKSGIVING, JAQUAVIOUS!
HA! SAME TO YOU, DARIUS.
WAIT . . . WHO?
INSIDE JOKE, LIAM. HAPPY THANKSGIVING.
YOU KNOW, GENERAL TSO'S WITH PEPPER STEAK WASN'T BAD. IT WASN'T BAD AT ALL.

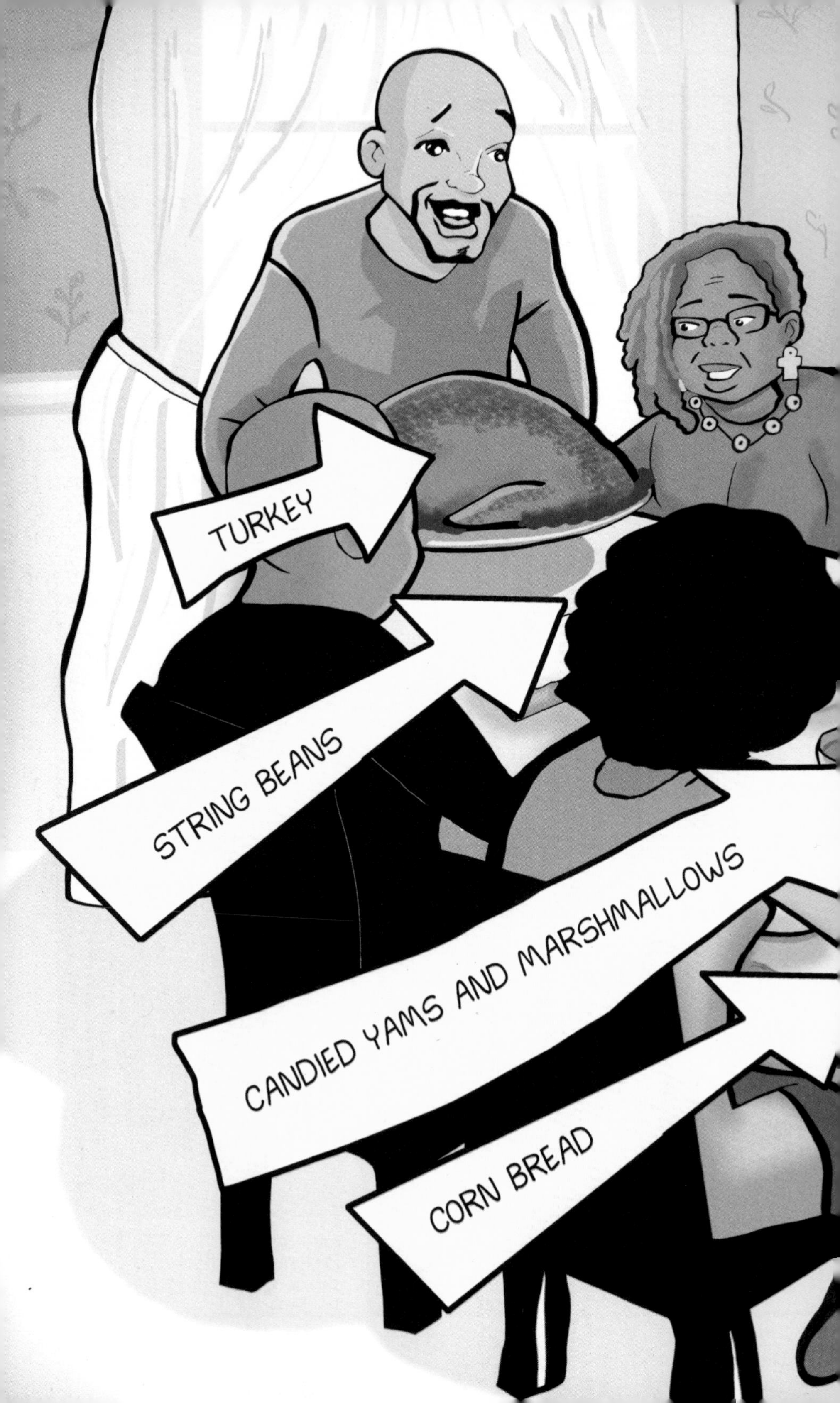
TURKEY
STRING BEANS
CANDIED YAMS AND MARSHMALLOWS
CORN BREAD

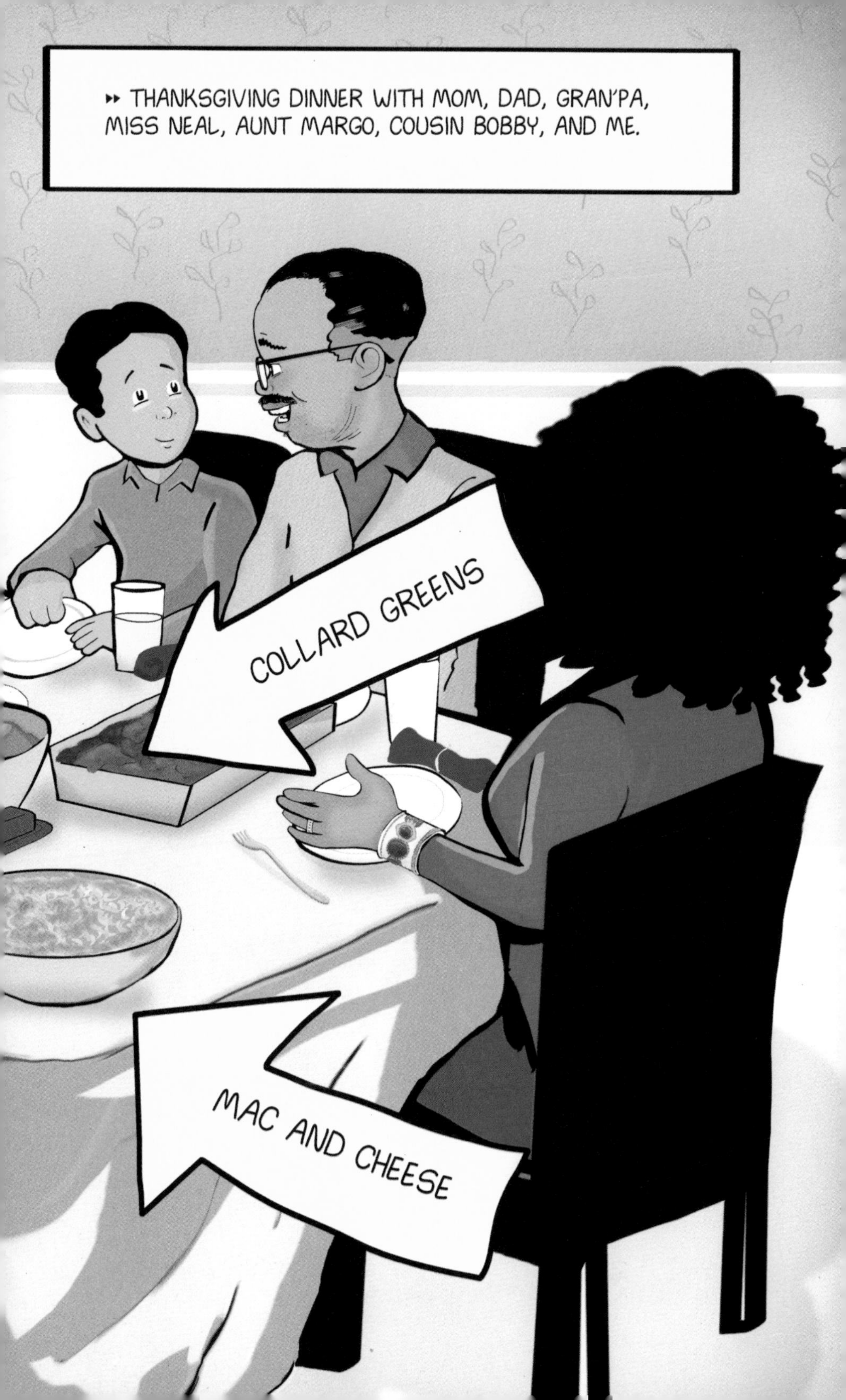
▸▸ THANKSGIVING DINNER WITH MOM, DAD, GRAN'PA, MISS NEAL, AUNT MARGO, COUSIN BOBBY, AND ME.
COLLARD GREENS
MAC AND CHEESE

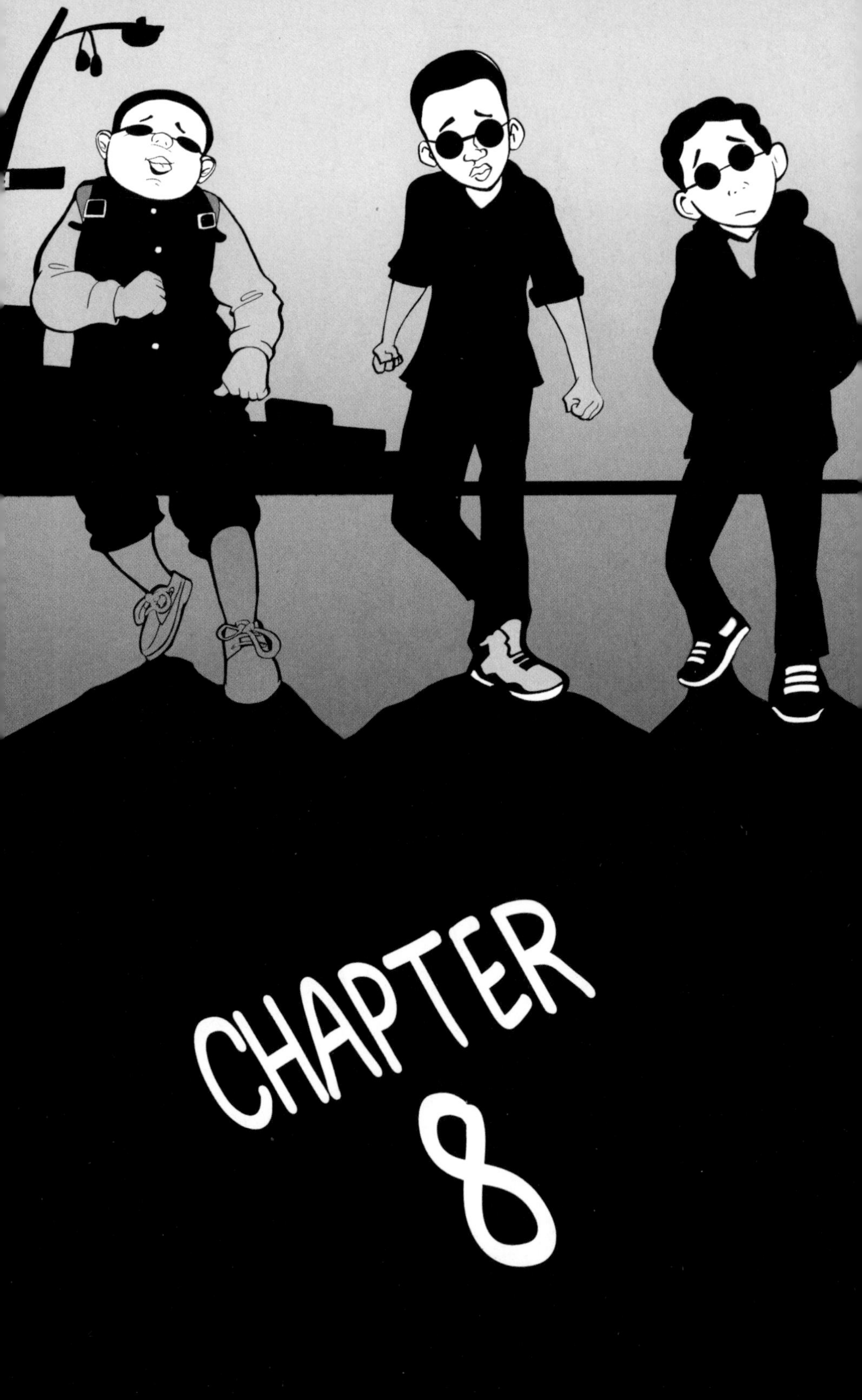

CHAPTER 8

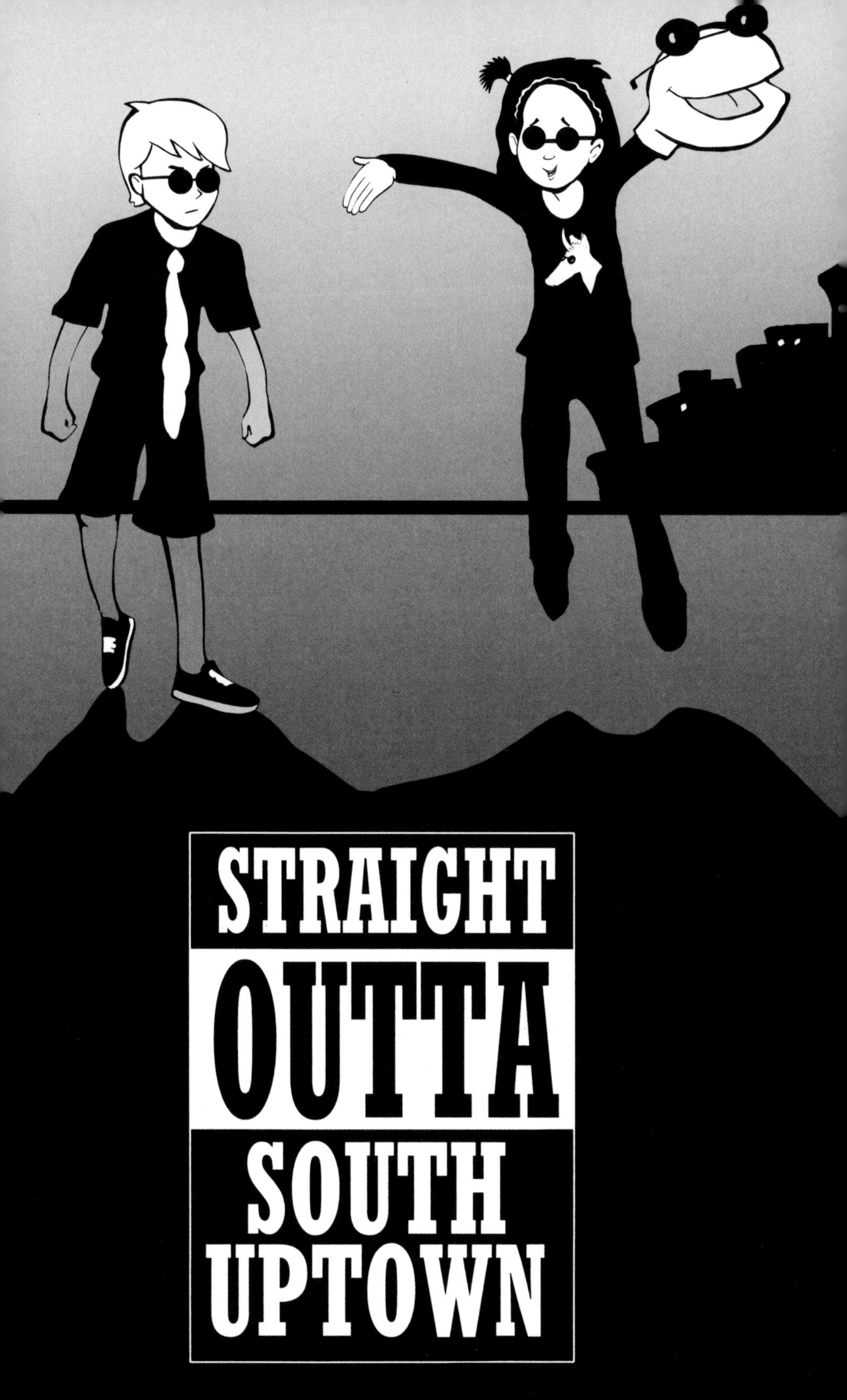
STRAIGHT
OUTTA
SOUTH
UPTOWN

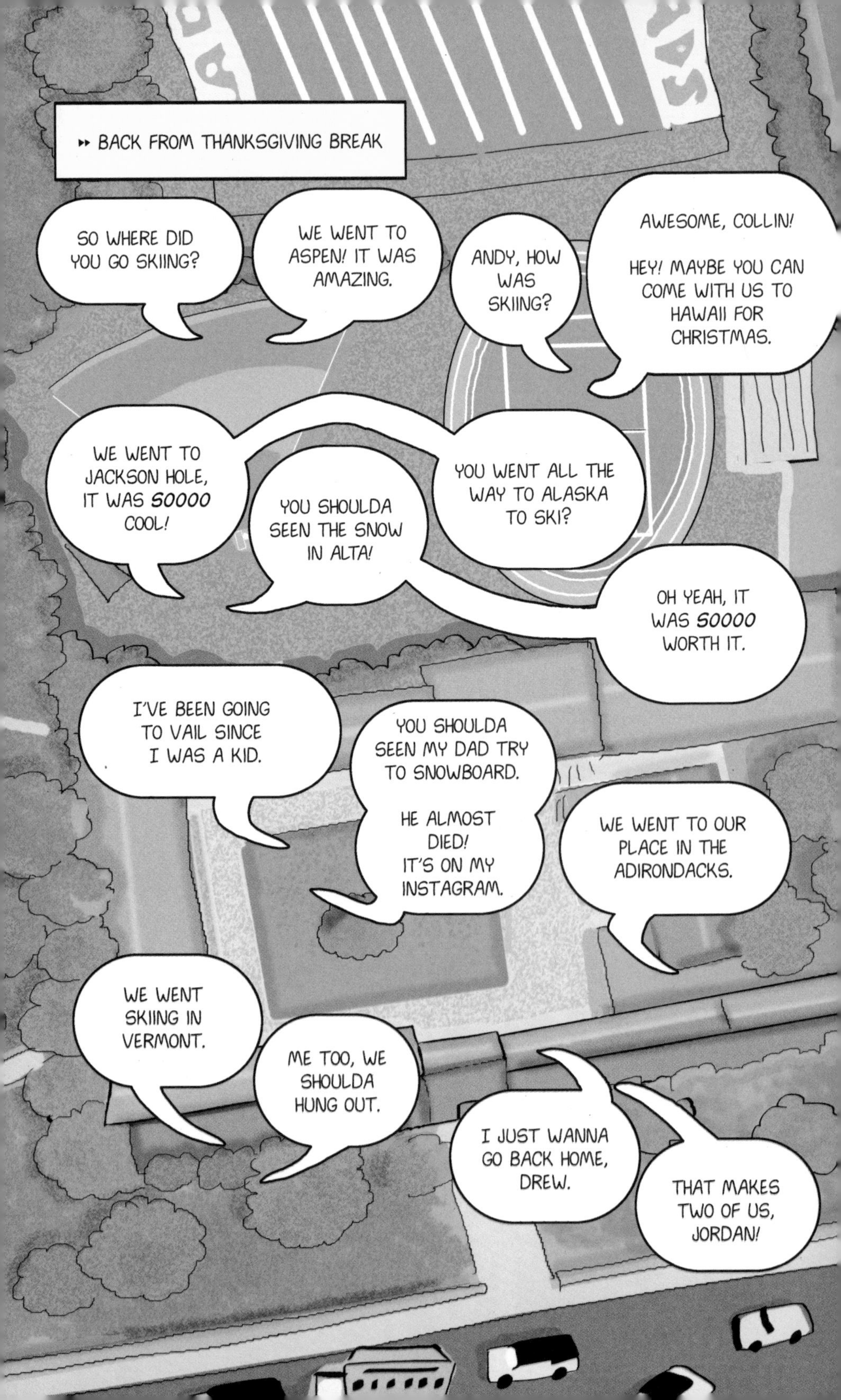
▸▸ BACK FROM THANKSGIVING BREAK
SO WHERE DID YOU GO SKIING?
WE WENT TO ASPEN! IT WAS AMAZING.
ANDY, HOW WAS SKIING?
AWESOME, COLLIN!
HEY! MAYBE YOU CAN COME WITH US TO HAWAII FOR CHRISTMAS.
WE WENT TO JACKSON HOLE, IT WAS *SOOOO* COOL!
YOU SHOULDA SEEN THE SNOW IN ALTA!
YOU WENT ALL THE WAY TO ALASKA TO SKI?
OH YEAH, IT WAS *SOOOO* WORTH IT.
I'VE BEEN GOING TO VAIL SINCE I WAS A KID.
YOU SHOULDA SEEN MY DAD TRY TO SNOWBOARD.
HE ALMOST DIED! IT'S ON MY INSTAGRAM.
WE WENT TO OUR PLACE IN THE ADIRONDACKS.
WE WENT SKIING IN VERMONT.
ME TOO, WE SHOULDA HUNG OUT.
I JUST WANNA GO BACK HOME, DREW.
THAT MAKES TWO OF US, JORDAN!

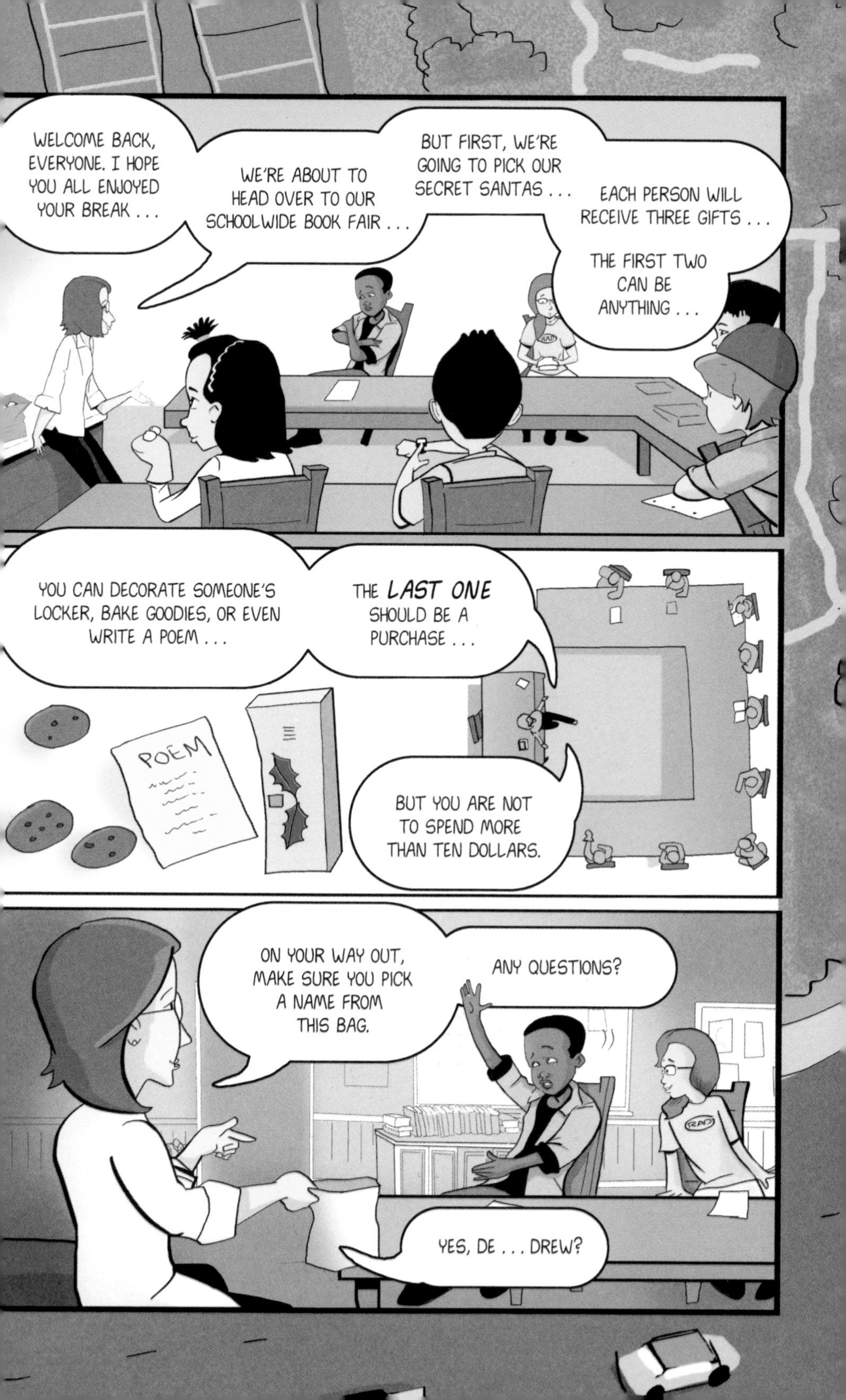
WELCOME BACK, EVERYONE. I HOPE YOU ALL ENJOYED YOUR BREAK . . .
WE'RE ABOUT TO HEAD OVER TO OUR SCHOOLWIDE BOOK FAIR . . .
BUT FIRST, WE'RE GOING TO PICK OUR SECRET SANTAS . . .
EACH PERSON WILL RECEIVE THREE GIFTS . . .
THE FIRST TWO CAN BE ANYTHING . . .
YOU CAN DECORATE SOMEONE'S LOCKER, BAKE GOODIES, OR EVEN WRITE A POEM . . .
THE *LAST ONE* SHOULD BE A PURCHASE . . .
POEM
BUT YOU ARE NOT TO SPEND MORE THAN TEN DOLLARS.
ON YOUR WAY OUT, MAKE SURE YOU PICK A NAME FROM THIS BAG.
ANY QUESTIONS?
YES, DE . . . DREW?

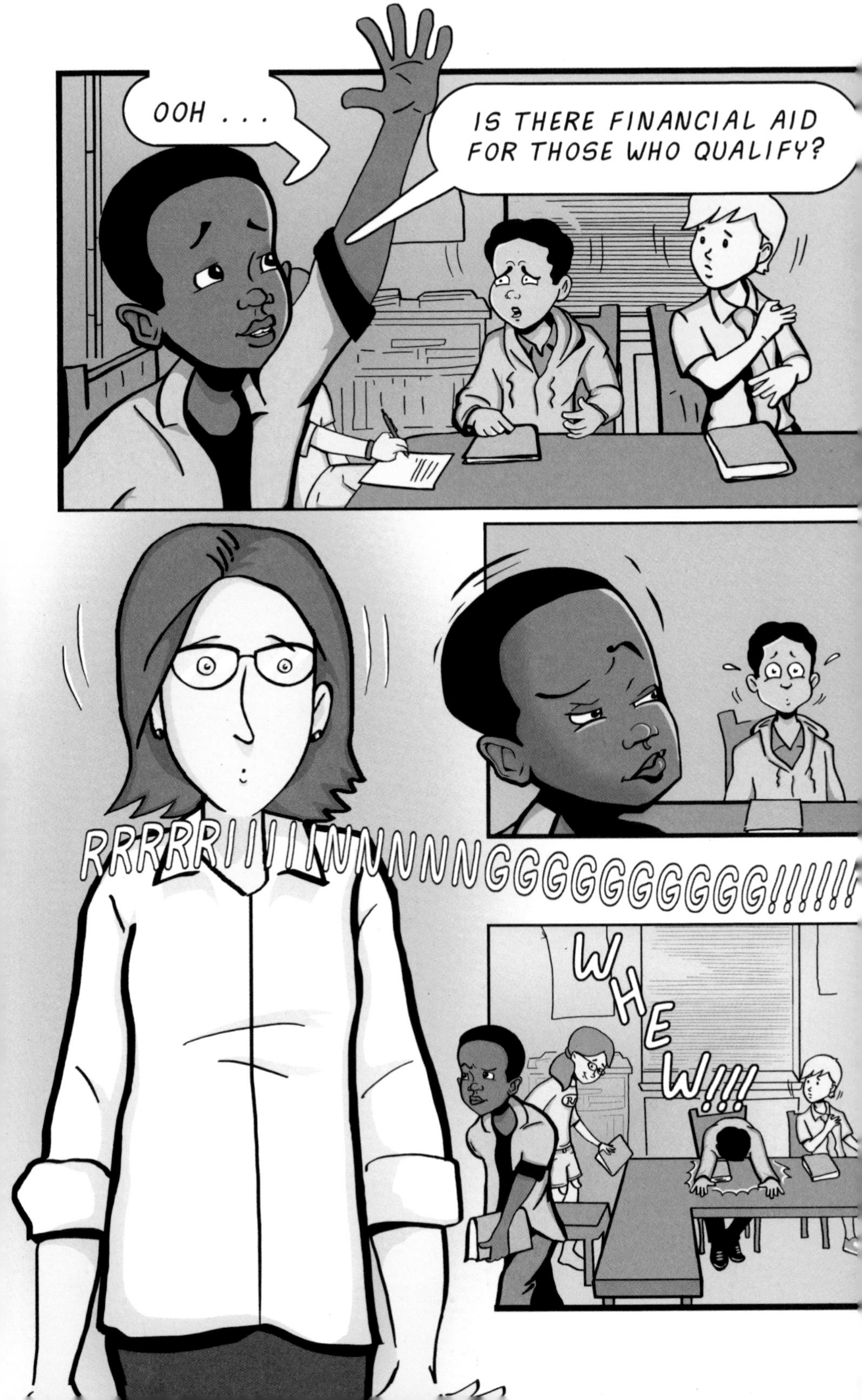
OOH . . .
IS THERE FINANCIAL AID FOR THOSE WHO QUALIFY?
RRRRRIIIIINNNNNNGGGGGGGGGG!!!!!!
WHEW!!!

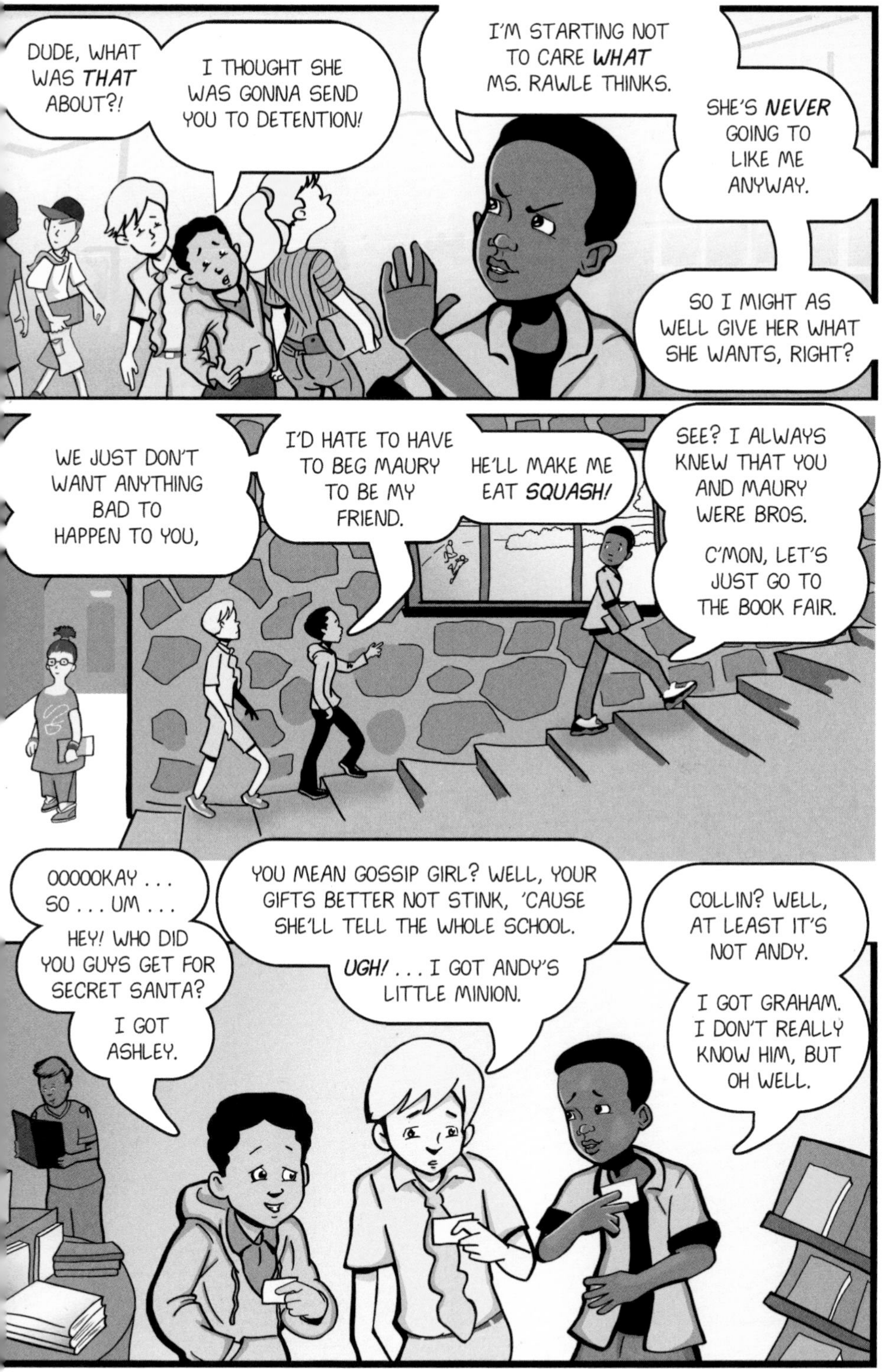

DUDE, WHAT WAS *THAT* ABOUT?!
I THOUGHT SHE WAS GONNA SEND YOU TO DETENTION!
I'M STARTING NOT TO CARE *WHAT* MS. RAWLE THINKS.
SHE'S *NEVER* GOING TO LIKE ME ANYWAY.
SO I MIGHT AS WELL GIVE HER WHAT SHE WANTS, RIGHT?
WE JUST DON'T WANT ANYTHING BAD TO HAPPEN TO YOU,
I'D HATE TO HAVE TO BEG MAURY TO BE MY FRIEND.
HE'LL MAKE ME EAT *SQUASH!*
SEE? I ALWAYS KNEW THAT YOU AND MAURY WERE BROS.
C'MON, LET'S JUST GO TO THE BOOK FAIR.
OOOOOKAY . . . SO . . . UM . . .
HEY! WHO DID YOU GUYS GET FOR SECRET SANTA?
I GOT ASHLEY.
YOU MEAN GOSSIP GIRL? WELL, YOUR GIFTS BETTER NOT STINK, 'CAUSE SHE'LL TELL THE WHOLE SCHOOL.
UGH! . . . I GOT ANDY'S LITTLE MINION.
COLLIN? WELL, AT LEAST IT'S NOT ANDY.
I GOT GRAHAM. I DON'T REALLY KNOW HIM, BUT OH WELL.

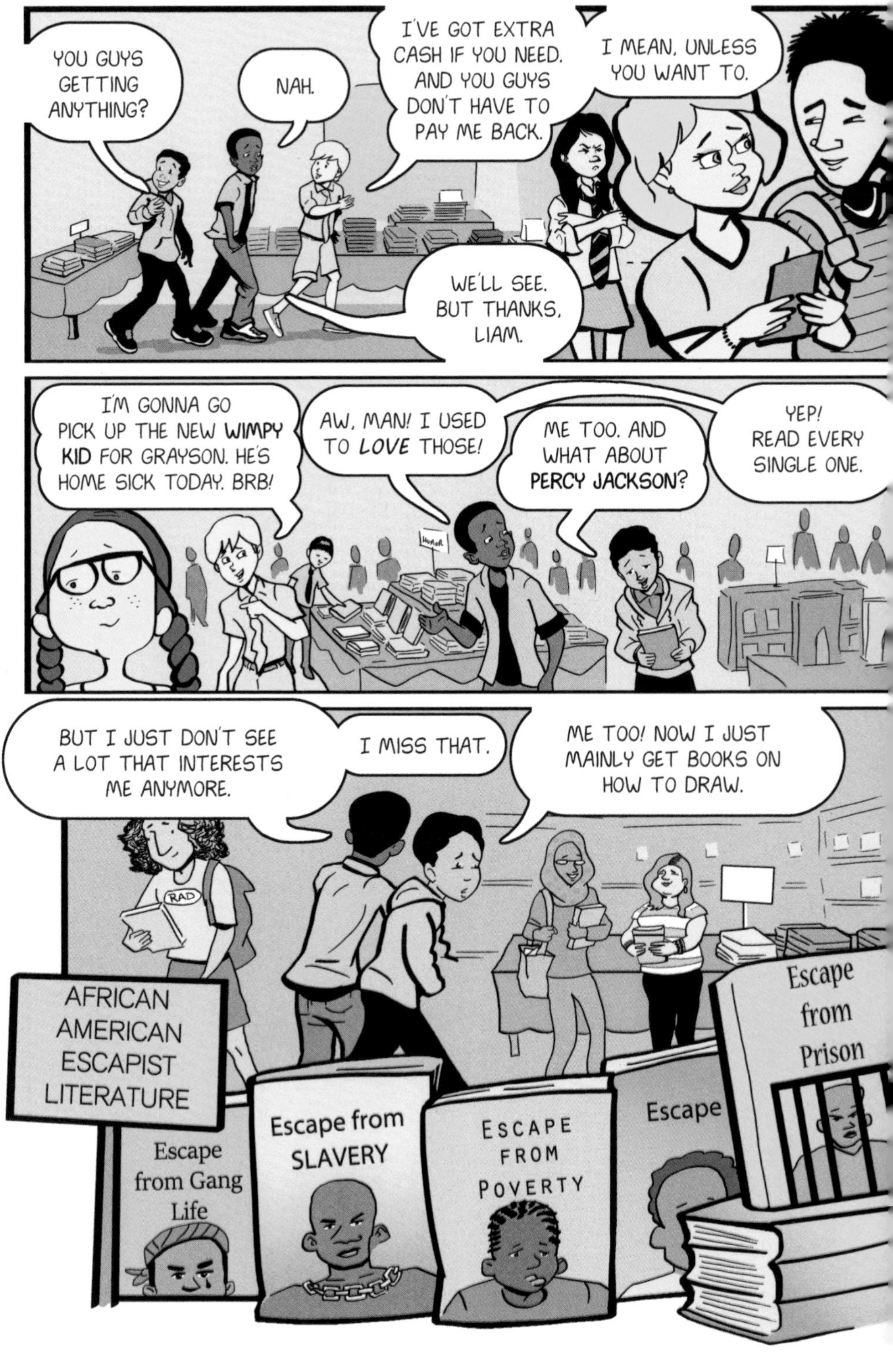

YOU GUYS GETTING ANYTHING?
NAH.
I'VE GOT EXTRA CASH IF YOU NEED. AND YOU GUYS DON'T HAVE TO PAY ME BACK.
I MEAN, UNLESS YOU WANT TO.
WE'LL SEE. BUT THANKS, LIAM.
I'M GONNA GO PICK UP THE NEW **WIMPY KID** FOR GRAYSON. HE'S HOME SICK TODAY. BRB!
AW, MAN! I USED TO ***LOVE*** THOSE!
ME TOO. AND WHAT ABOUT **PERCY JACKSON**?
YEP! READ EVERY SINGLE ONE.
BUT I JUST DON'T SEE A LOT THAT INTERESTS ME ANYMORE.
I MISS THAT.
ME TOO! NOW I JUST MAINLY GET BOOKS ON HOW TO DRAW.
RAD
AFRICAN AMERICAN ESCAPIST LITERATURE
Escape from Gang Life
Escape from SLAVERY
ESCAPE FROM POVERTY
Escape
Escape from Prison

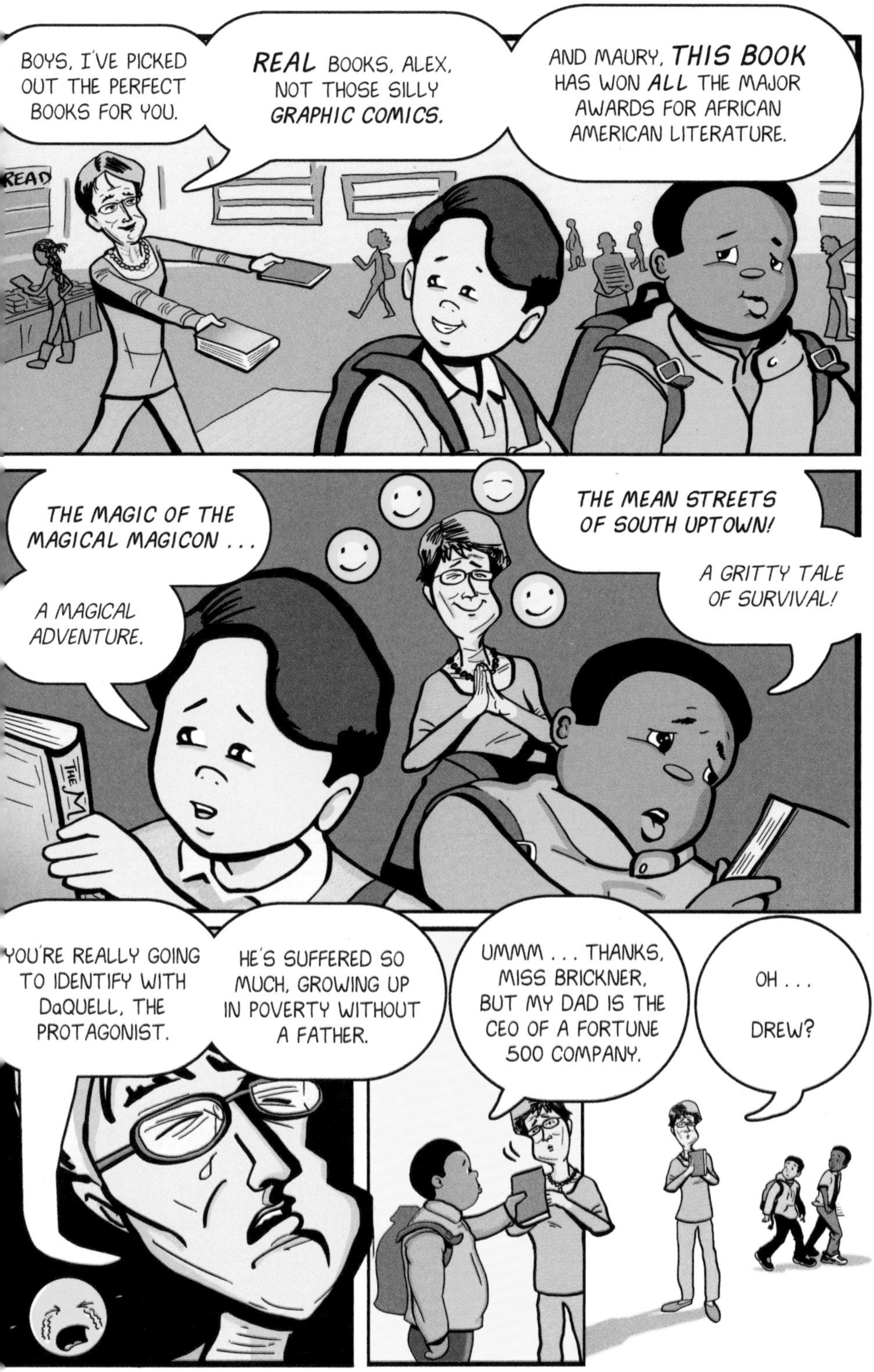
BOYS, I'VE PICKED OUT THE PERFECT BOOKS FOR YOU.
REAL BOOKS, ALEX, NOT THOSE SILLY GRAPHIC COMICS.
AND MAURY, THIS BOOK HAS WON ALL THE MAJOR AWARDS FOR AFRICAN AMERICAN LITERATURE.
READ
THE MAGIC OF THE MAGICAL MAGICON . . .
A MAGICAL ADVENTURE.
THE MEAN STREETS OF SOUTH UPTOWN!
A GRITTY TALE OF SURVIVAL!
THE M
YOU'RE REALLY GOING TO IDENTIFY WITH DaQUELL, THE PROTAGONIST.
HE'S SUFFERED SO MUCH, GROWING UP IN POVERTY WITHOUT A FATHER.
UMMM . . . THANKS, MISS BRICKNER, BUT MY DAD IS THE CEO OF A FORTUNE 500 COMPANY.
OH . . .
DREW?

Judging Kids by the Covers of Their Books!

MAINSTREAM BOOKS

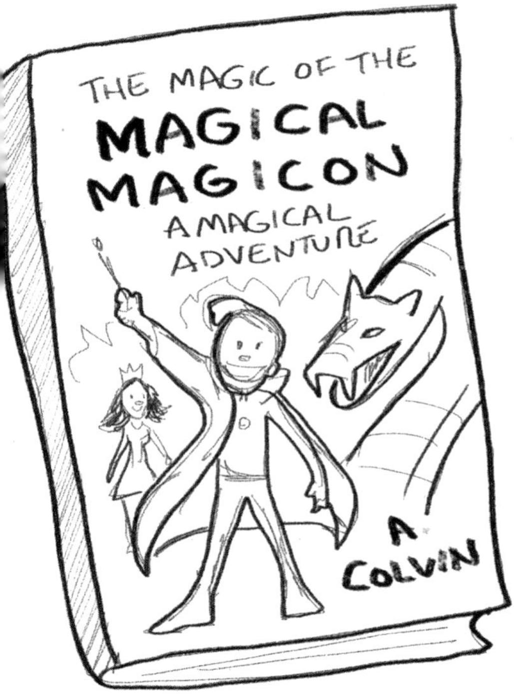
THE MAGIC OF THE
MAGICAL MAGICON
A MAGICAL ADVENTURE
A. COLVIN

AFRICAN AMERICAN BOOKS

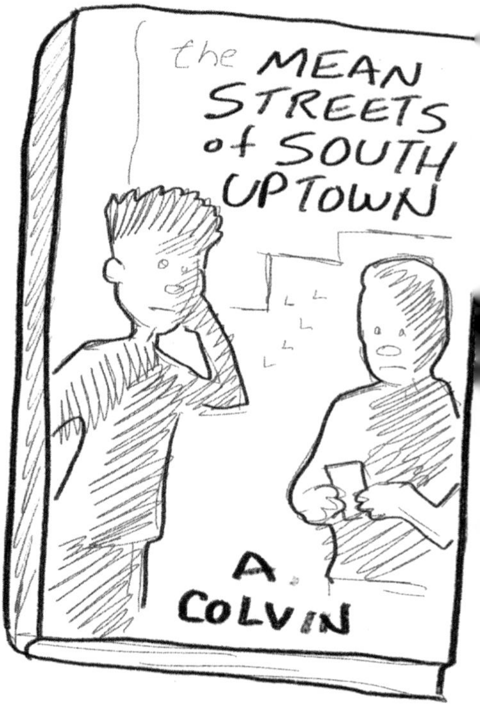
the MEAN STREETS of SOUTH UPTOWN
A. COLVIN

MAINSTREAM BOOK COVERS:

Cool, colorful illustrations full of magic and hope!

MAINSTREAM BOOK PLOTS:

Prince Aimii leaves his dull life to slay a dragon, rescue Princess Brea, and prove to his father that one day he'll make a worthy king.

AFRICAN AMERICAN BOOK COVERS:

A depressing photograph full of realism and hopelessness.

AFRICAN AMERICAN BOOK PLOTS:

After moving to his third city in three years, DaQuell "Scooter" Jackson must decide if he will pursue his dream of being in the NBA or join a notorious gang.

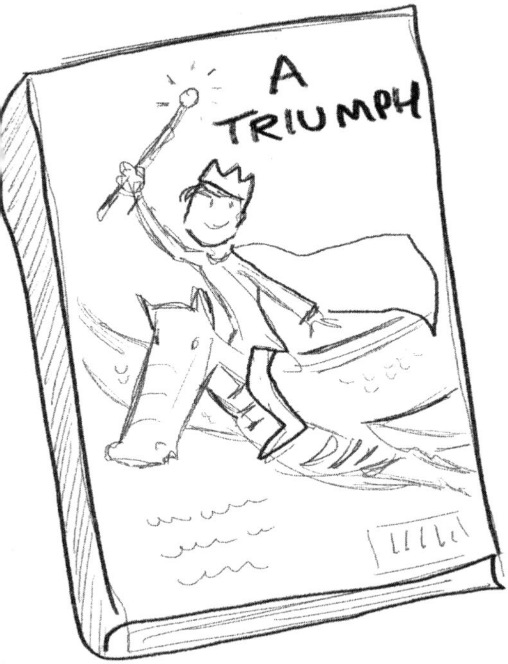
A TRIUMPH

MAINSTREAM BOOK HEROES:

* Lives in a magical kingdom!
* Lives in a stable home!
* Wants to live better!
* His father is king!

REVIEWS:

A thrilling magical tale that is sure to inspire readers of all ages to never give up until they have found the treasure they seek.

–*School Library Journal*

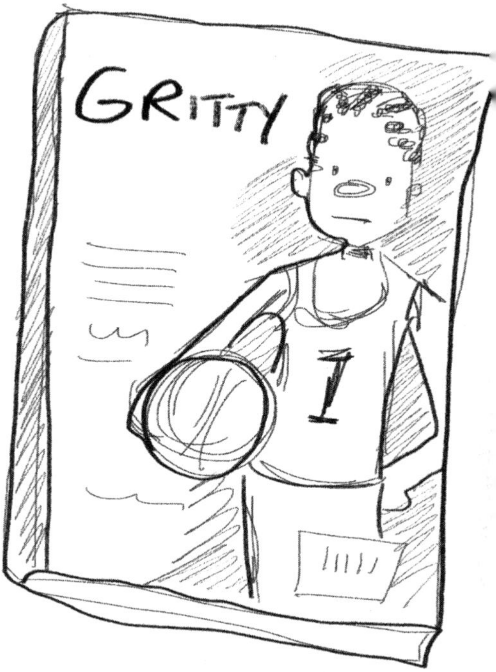
GRITTY
I

AFRICAN AMERICAN BOOK HEROES:

* Lives in the hood!
* Lives in a broken home!
* Just wants to live!
* His father is gone!

REVIEWS:

A gritty, urban reminder of the grit of today's urban grittiness.

–*Jet* magazine

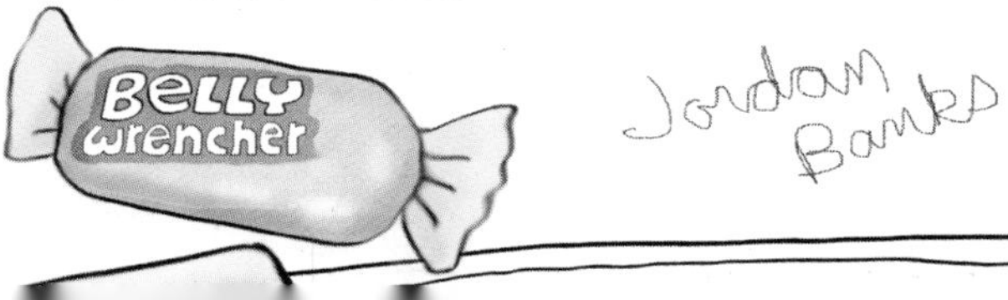
Belly Wrencher
Jordan Banks

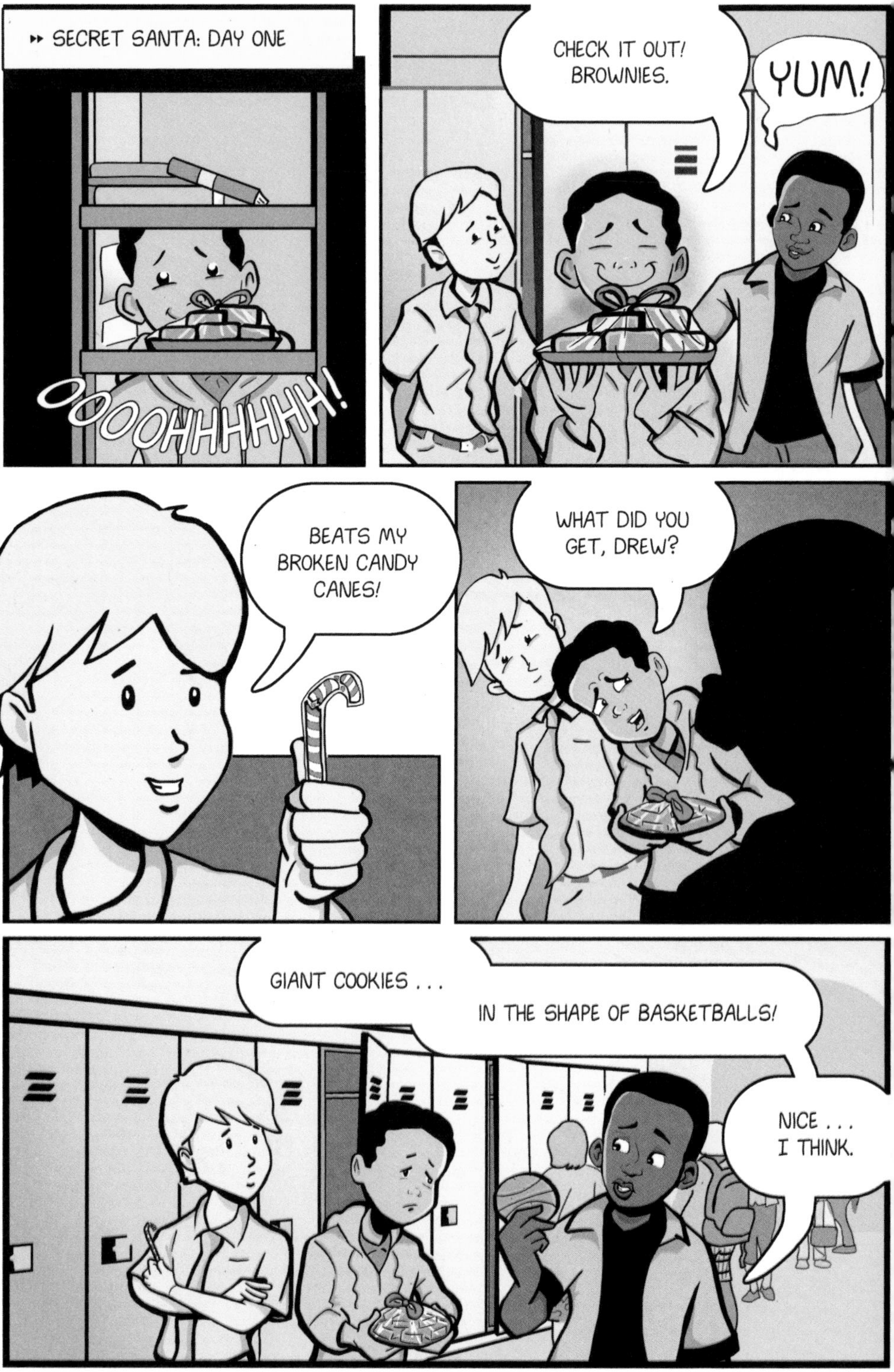

SECRET SANTA: DAY ONE
OOOOHHHHHH!
CHECK IT OUT! BROWNIES.
YUM!
BEATS MY BROKEN CANDY CANES!
WHAT DID YOU GET, DREW?
GIANT COOKIES . . .
IN THE SHAPE OF BASKETBALLS!
NICE . . . I THINK.

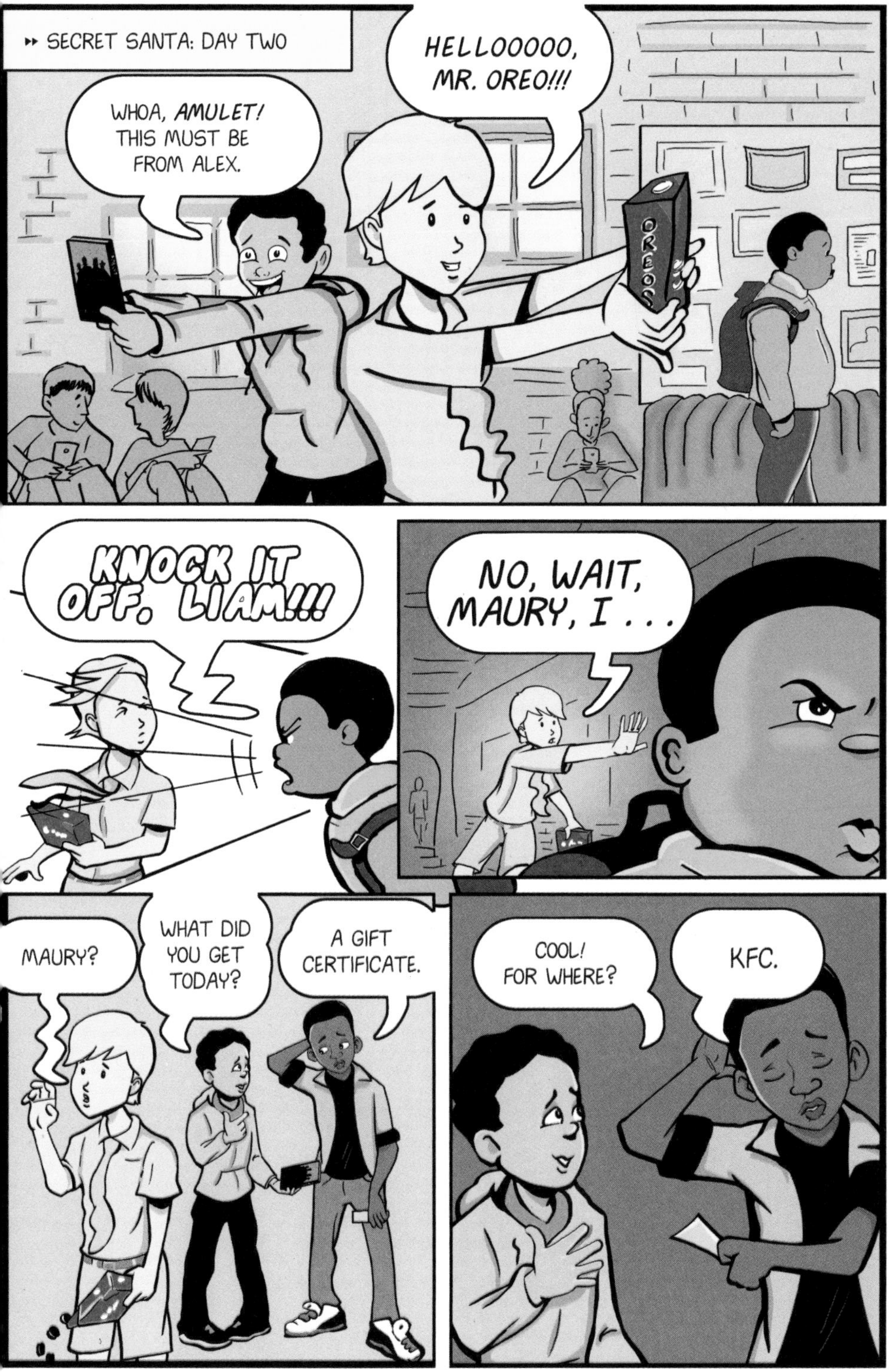

SECRET SANTA: DAY TWO
WHOA, AMULET! THIS MUST BE FROM ALEX.
HELLOOOOO, MR. OREO!!!
OREOS
KNOCK IT OFF, LIAM!!!
NO, WAIT, MAURY, I . . .
MAURY?
WHAT DID YOU GET TODAY?
A GIFT CERTIFICATE.
COOL! FOR WHERE?
KFC.

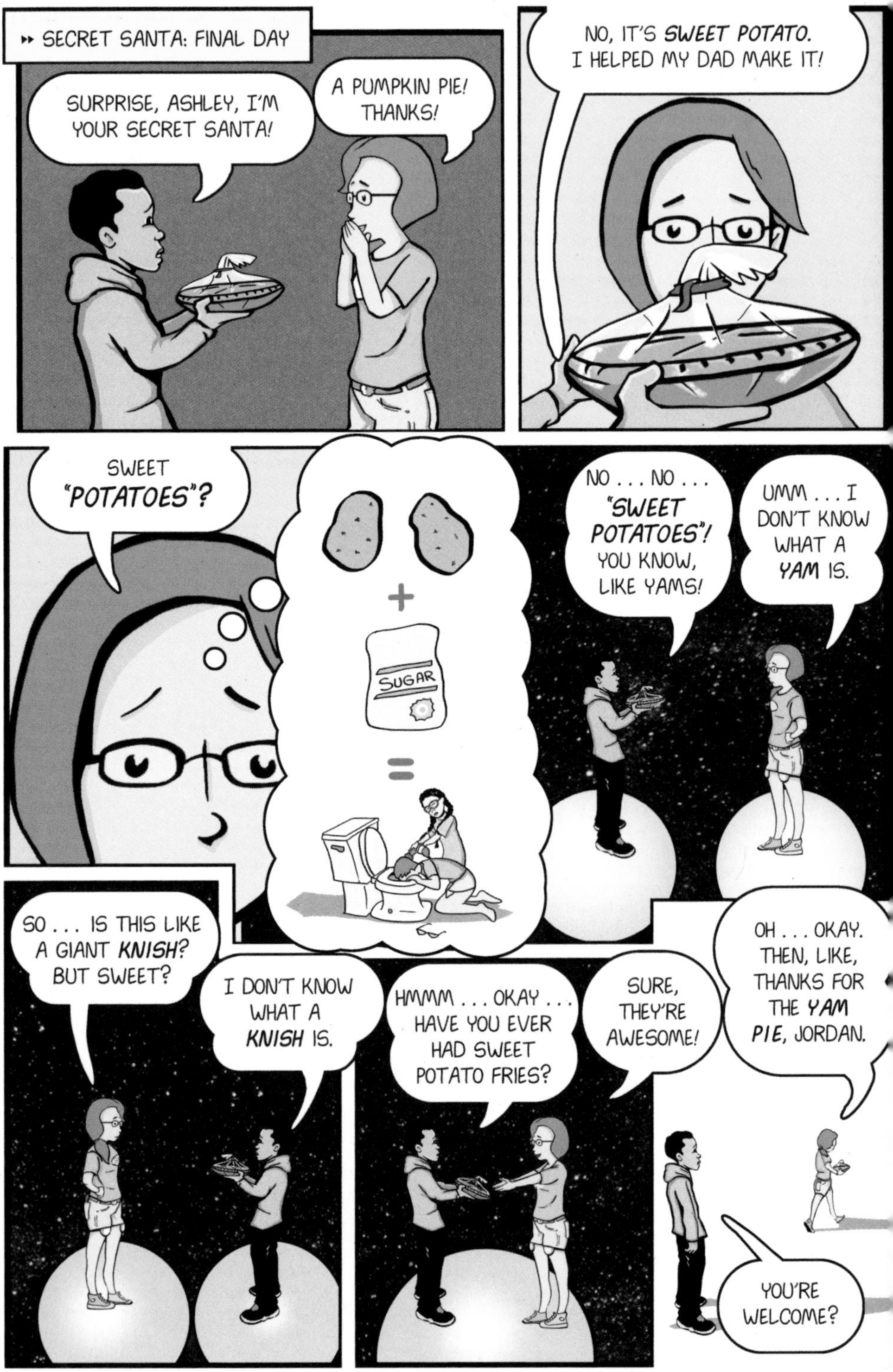
SECRET SANTA: FINAL DAY
SURPRISE, ASHLEY, I'M YOUR SECRET SANTA!
A PUMPKIN PIE! THANKS!
NO, IT'S SWEET POTATO. I HELPED MY DAD MAKE IT!
SWEET "POTATOES"?
SUGAR
NO . . . NO . . . "SWEET POTATOES"! YOU KNOW, LIKE YAMS!
UMM . . . I DON'T KNOW WHAT A YAM IS.
SO . . . IS THIS LIKE A GIANT KNISH? BUT SWEET?
I DON'T KNOW WHAT A KNISH IS.
HMMM . . . OKAY . . . HAVE YOU EVER HAD SWEET POTATO FRIES?
SURE, THEY'RE AWESOME!
OH . . . OKAY. THEN, LIKE, THANKS FOR THE YAM PIE, JORDAN.
YOU'RE WELCOME?

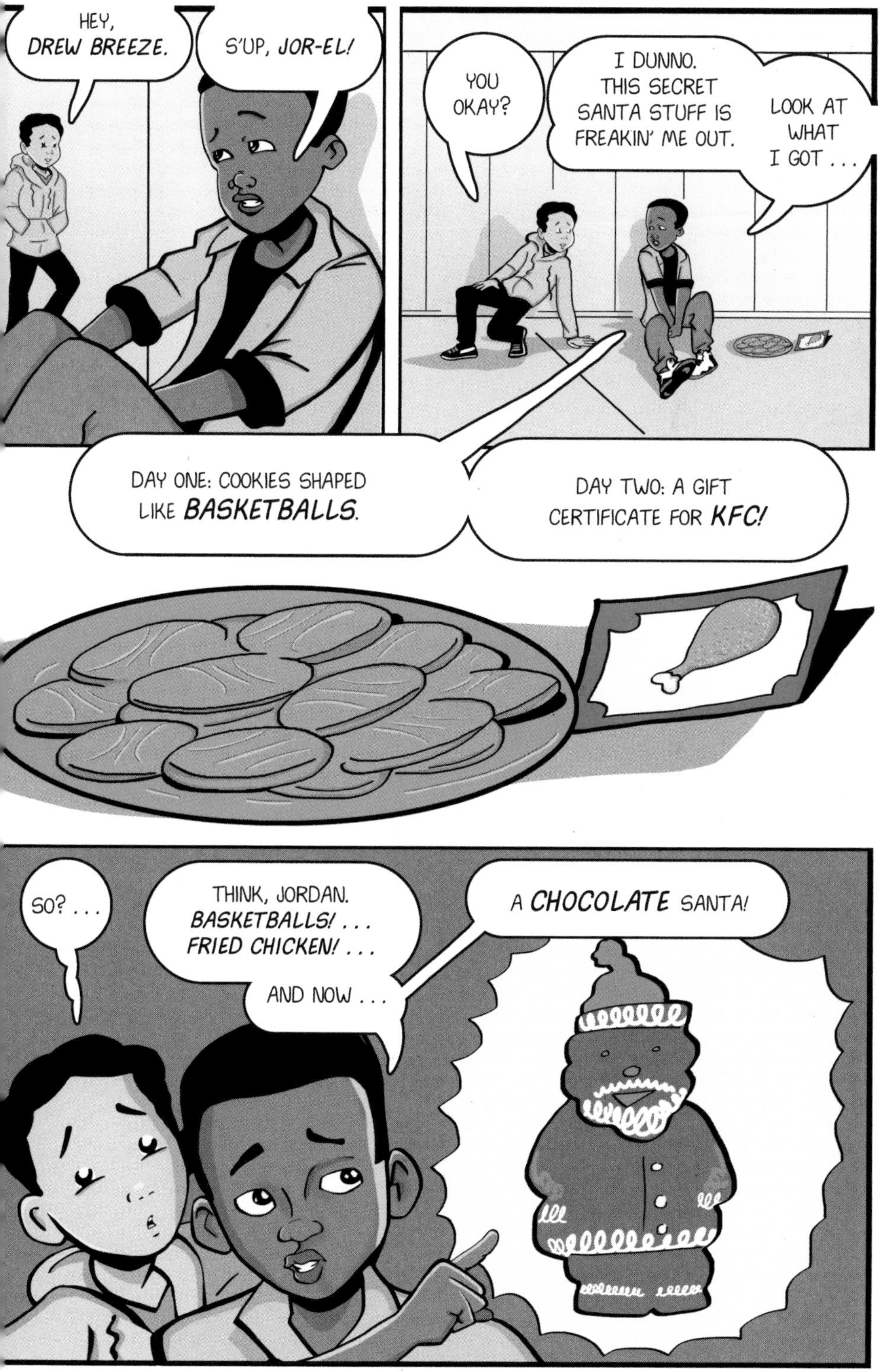
HEY, DREW BREEZE.
S'UP, JOR-EL!
YOU OKAY?
I DUNNO. THIS SECRET SANTA STUFF IS FREAKIN' ME OUT.
LOOK AT WHAT I GOT . . .
DAY ONE: COOKIES SHAPED LIKE BASKETBALLS.
DAY TWO: A GIFT CERTIFICATE FOR KFC!
SO? . . .
THINK, JORDAN. BASKETBALLS! . . . FRIED CHICKEN! . . .
AND NOW . . .
A CHOCOLATE SANTA!

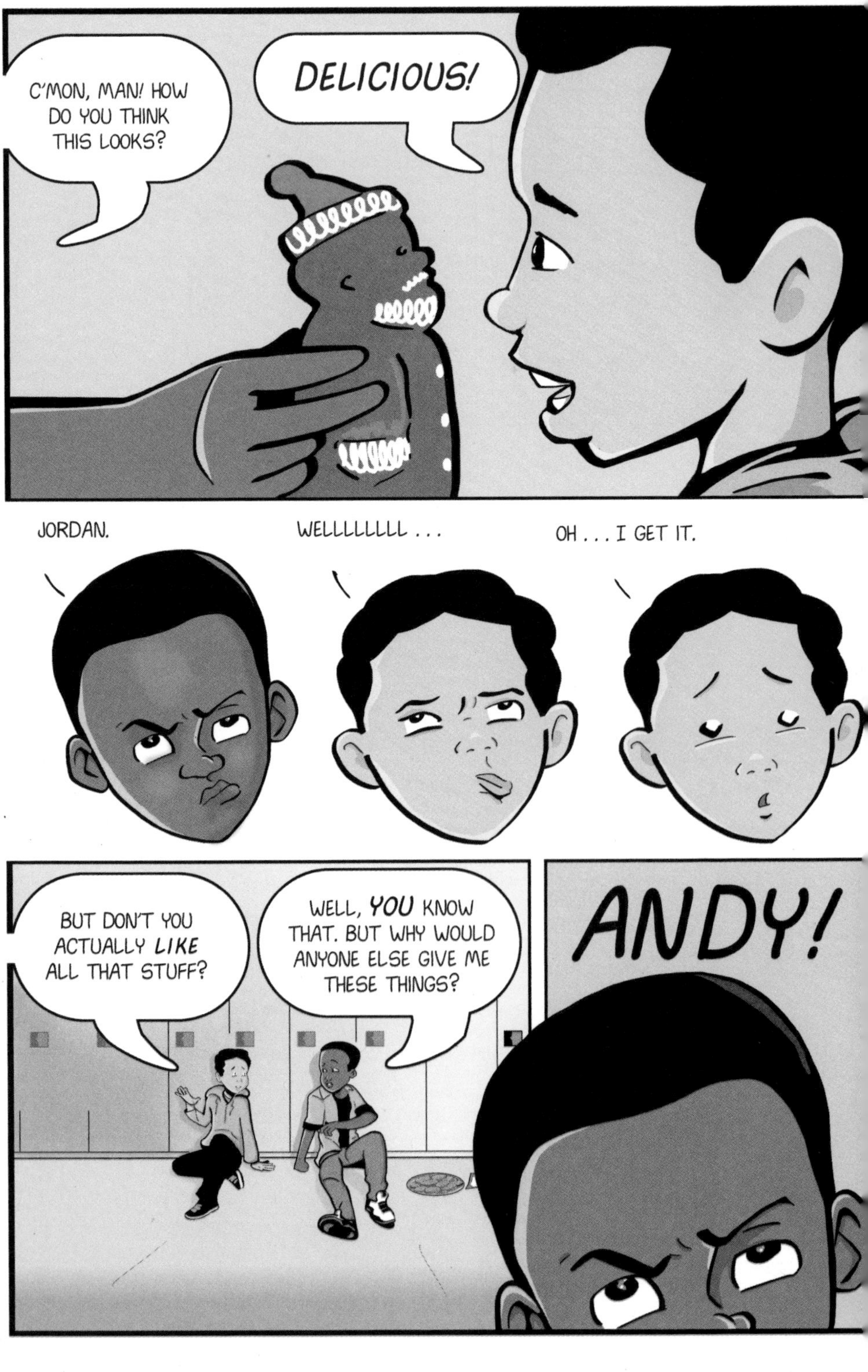
C'MON, MAN! HOW DO YOU THINK THIS LOOKS?
DELICIOUS!
JORDAN.
WELLLLLLLLL . . .
OH . . . I GET IT.
BUT DON'T YOU ACTUALLY LIKE ALL THAT STUFF?
WELL, YOU KNOW THAT. BUT WHY WOULD ANYONE ELSE GIVE ME THESE THINGS?
ANDY!

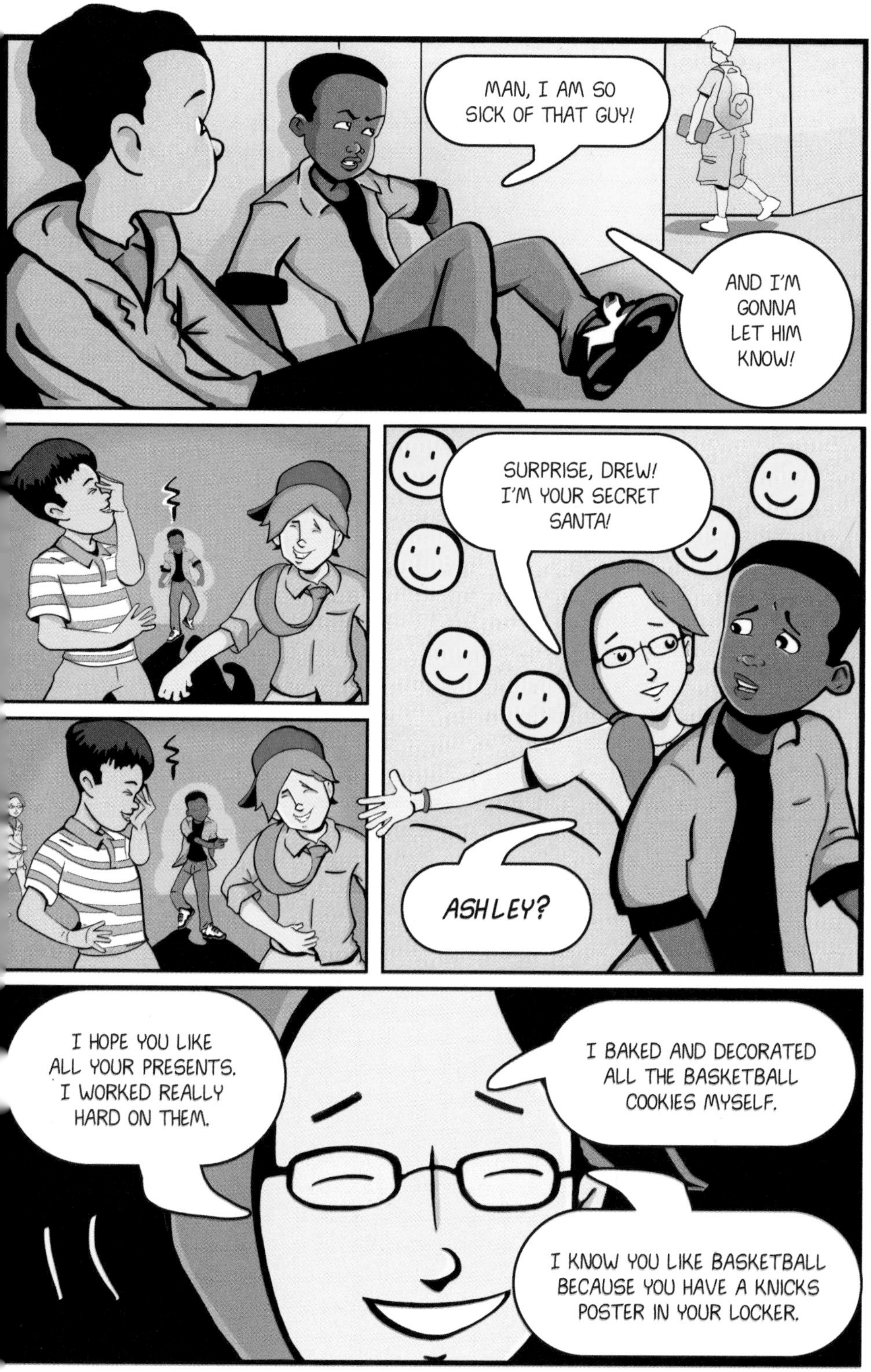
MAN, I AM SO SICK OF THAT GUY!
AND I'M GONNA LET HIM KNOW!
SURPRISE, DREW! I'M YOUR SECRET SANTA!
ASHLEY?
I HOPE YOU LIKE ALL YOUR PRESENTS. I WORKED REALLY HARD ON THEM.
I BAKED AND DECORATED ALL THE BASKETBALL COOKIES MYSELF.
I KNOW YOU LIKE BASKETBALL BECAUSE YOU HAVE A KNICKS POSTER IN YOUR LOCKER.

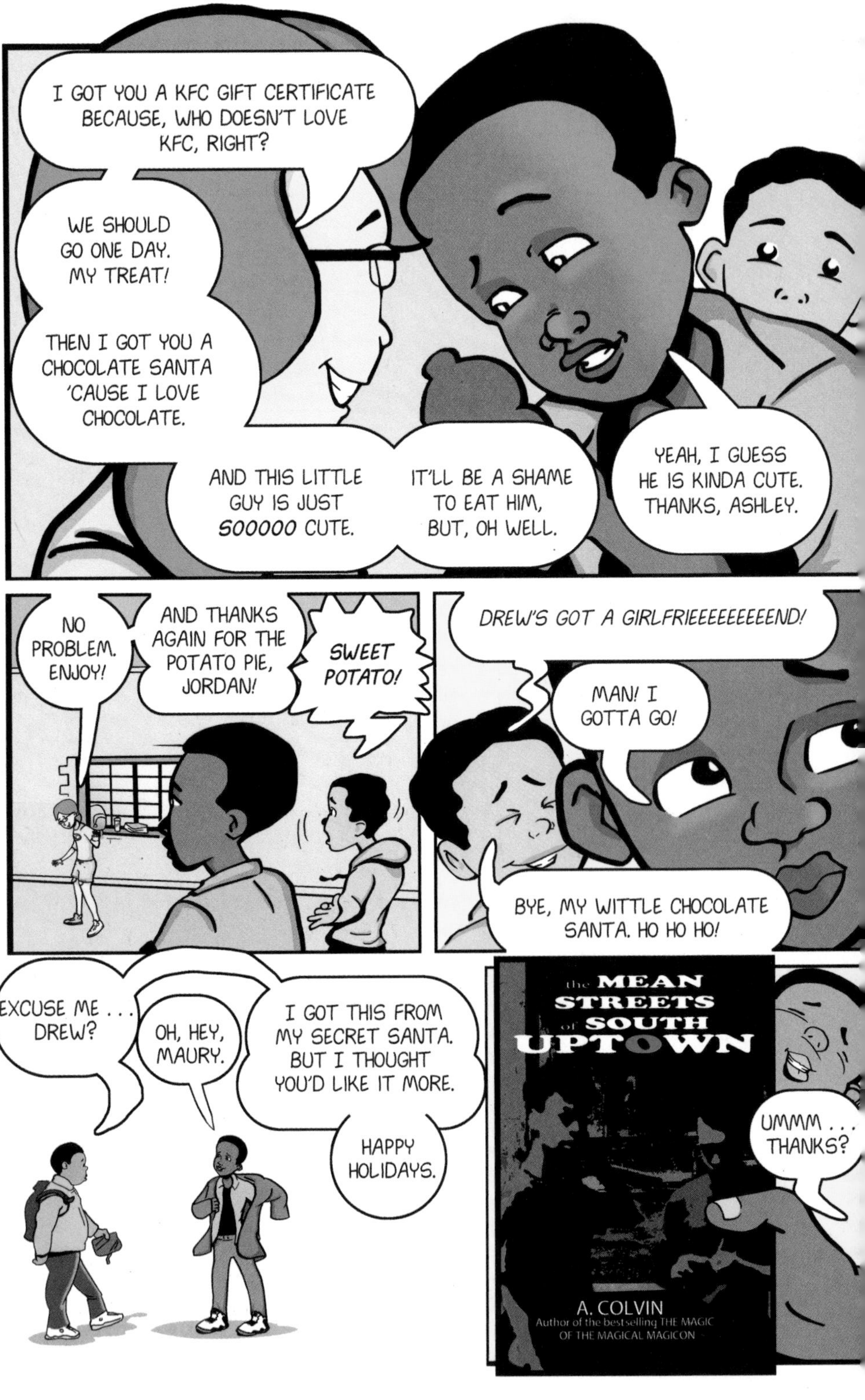
I GOT YOU A KFC GIFT CERTIFICATE BECAUSE, WHO DOESN'T LOVE KFC, RIGHT?
WE SHOULD GO ONE DAY. MY TREAT!
THEN I GOT YOU A CHOCOLATE SANTA 'CAUSE I LOVE CHOCOLATE.
AND THIS LITTLE GUY IS JUST *SOOOOO* CUTE.
IT'LL BE A SHAME TO EAT HIM, BUT, OH WELL.
YEAH, I GUESS HE IS KINDA CUTE. THANKS, ASHLEY.
NO PROBLEM. ENJOY!
AND THANKS AGAIN FOR THE POTATO PIE, JORDAN!
SWEET POTATO!
DREW'S GOT A GIRLFRIEEEEEEEEEEND!
MAN! I GOTTA GO!
BYE, MY WITTLE CHOCOLATE SANTA. HO HO HO!
EXCUSE ME . . . DREW?
OH, HEY, MAURY.
I GOT THIS FROM MY SECRET SANTA. BUT I THOUGHT YOU'D LIKE IT MORE.
HAPPY HOLIDAYS.
the MEAN STREETS of SOUTH UPTOWN
A. COLVIN
Author of the bestselling THE MAGIC OF THE MAGICAL MAGICON
UMMM . . . THANKS?

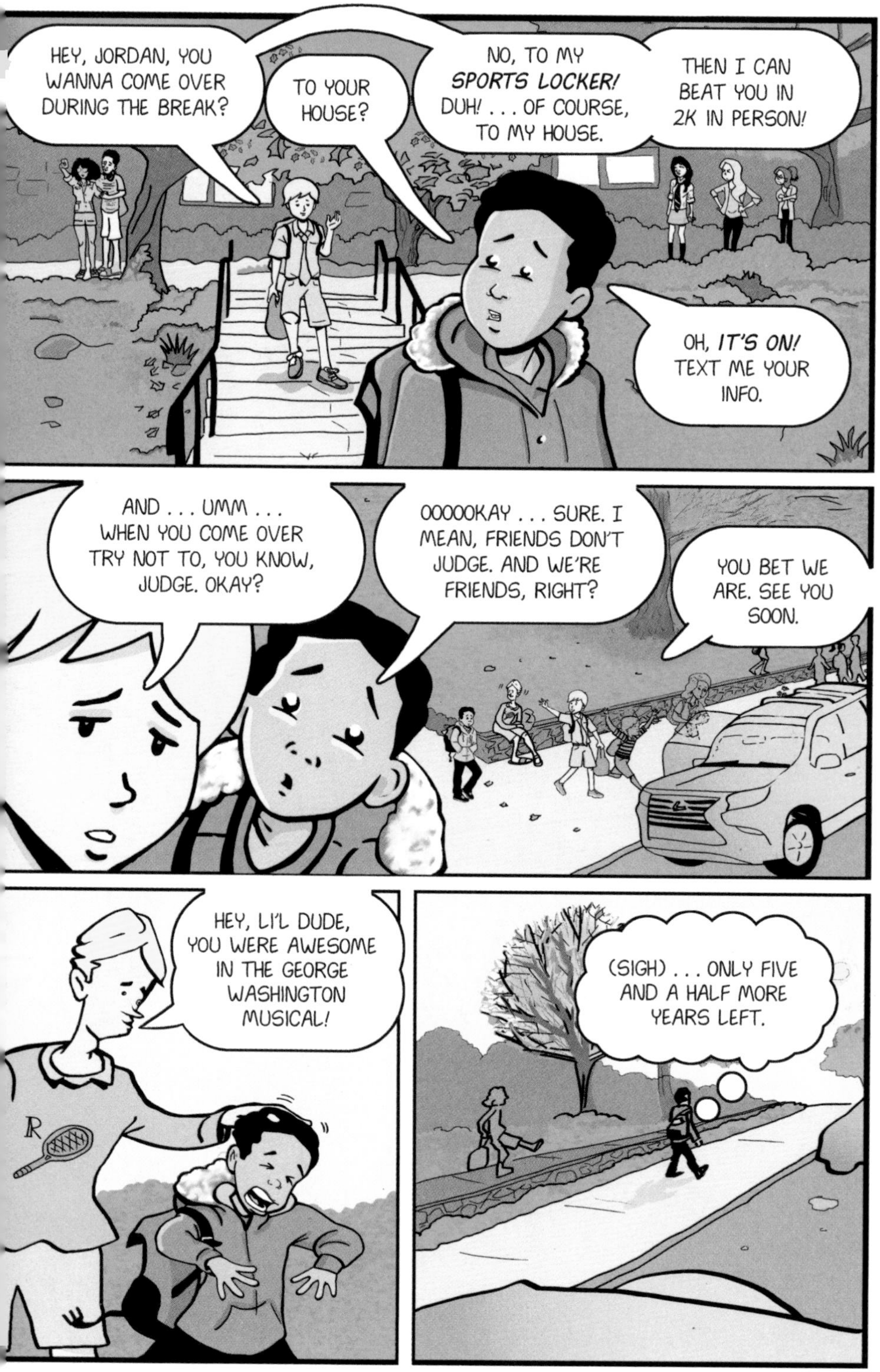
HEY, JORDAN, YOU WANNA COME OVER DURING THE BREAK?
TO YOUR HOUSE?
NO, TO MY **SPORTS LOCKER!** DUH! . . . OF COURSE, TO MY HOUSE.
THEN I CAN BEAT YOU IN 2K IN PERSON!
OH, ***IT'S ON!*** TEXT ME YOUR INFO.
AND . . . UMM . . . WHEN YOU COME OVER TRY NOT TO, YOU KNOW, JUDGE. OKAY?
OOOOOKAY . . . SURE. I MEAN, FRIENDS DON'T JUDGE. AND WE'RE FRIENDS, RIGHT?
YOU BET WE ARE. SEE YOU SOON.
HEY, LI'L DUDE, YOU WERE AWESOME IN THE GEORGE WASHINGTON MUSICAL!
(SIGH) . . . ONLY FIVE AND A HALF MORE YEARS LEFT.

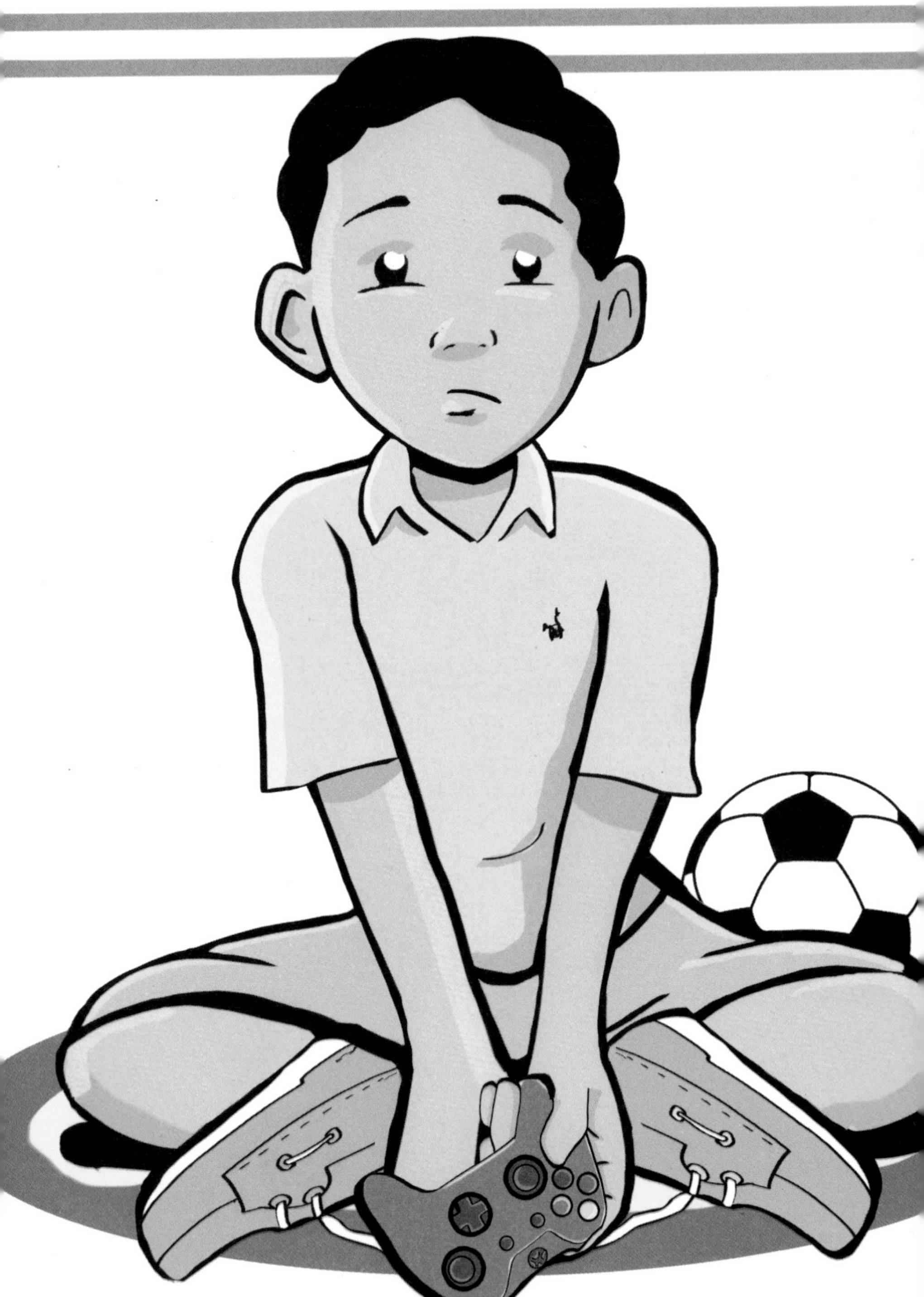

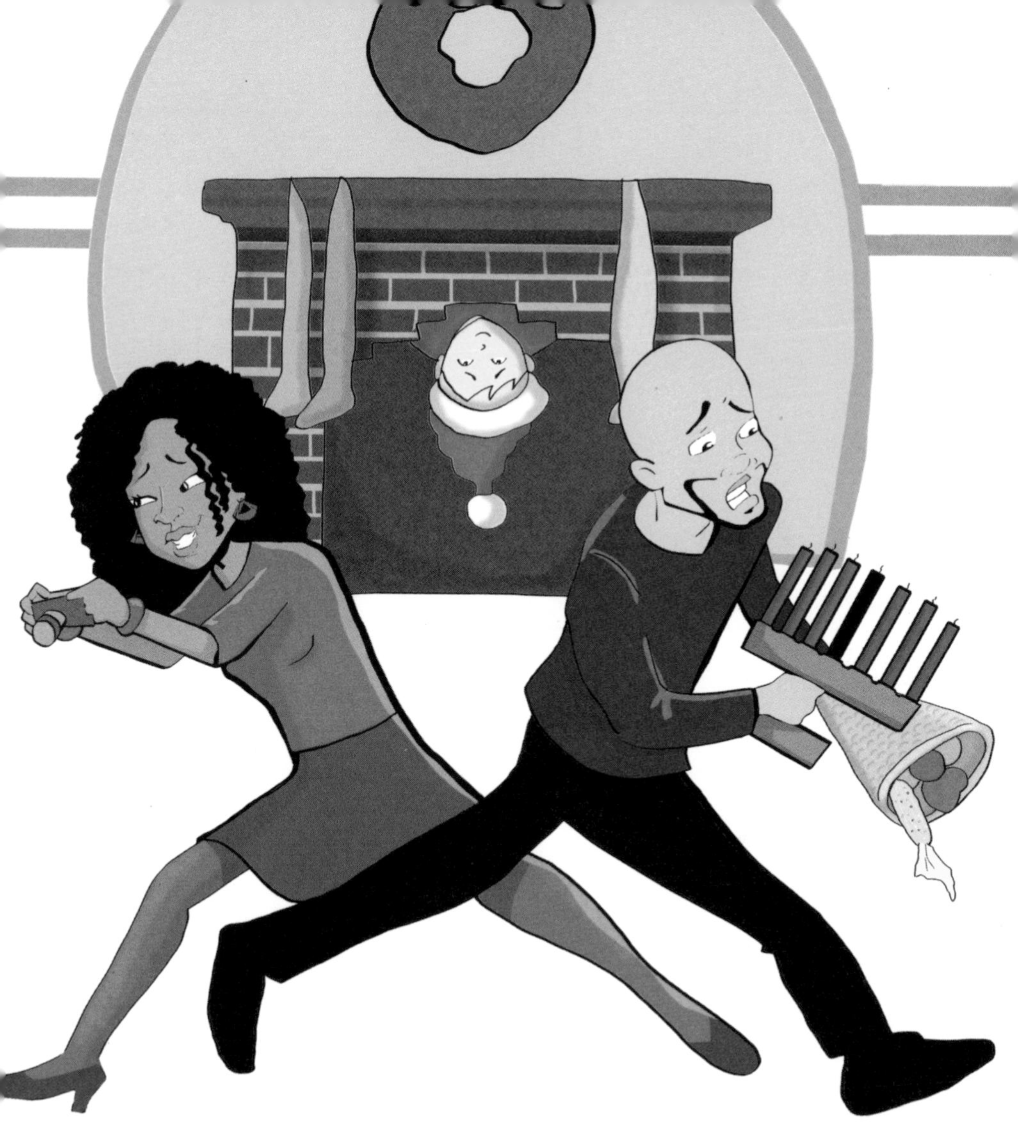

CHAPTER 9

A KWANZAA STORY

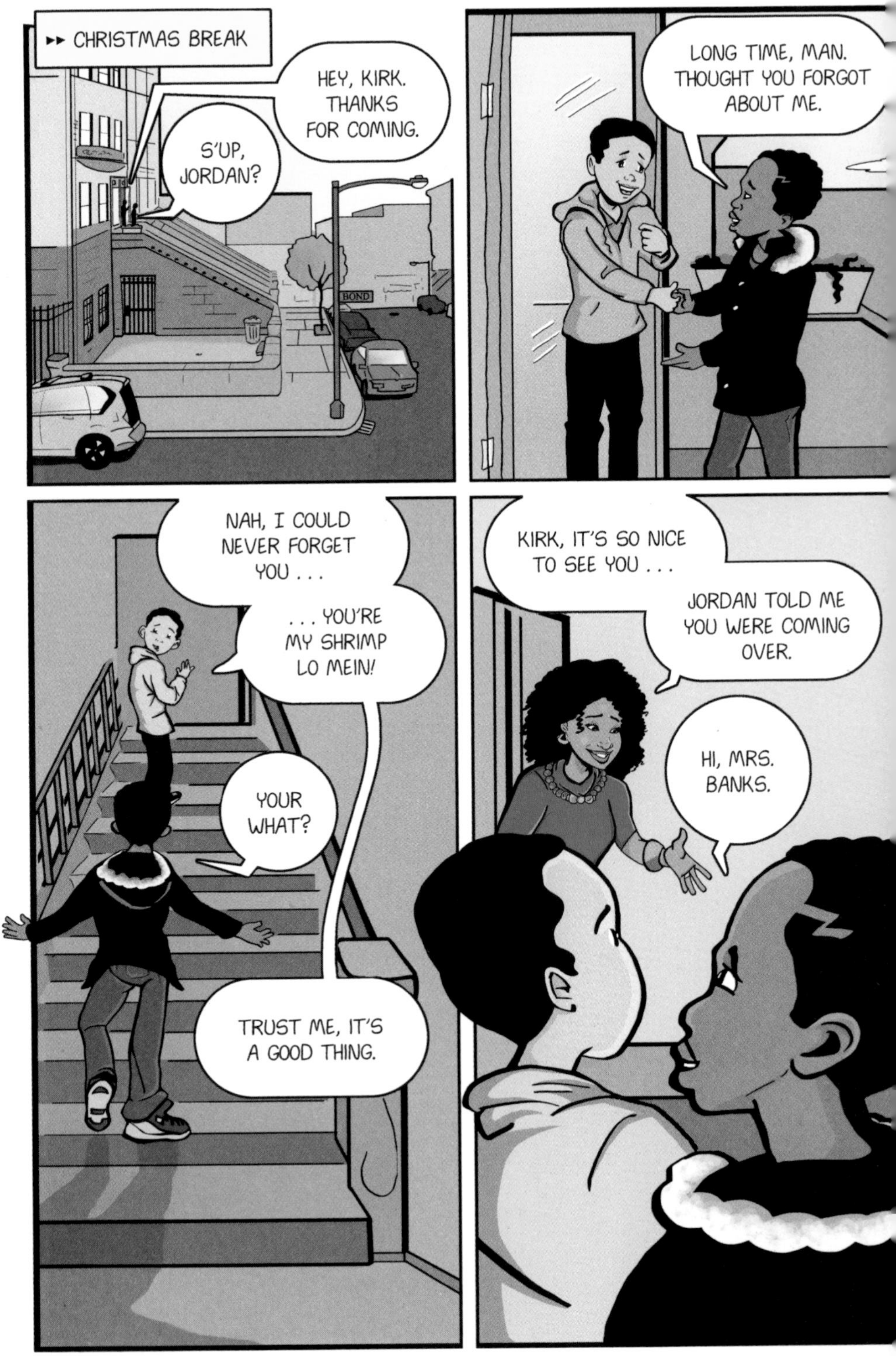
CHRISTMAS BREAK
HEY, KIRK. THANKS FOR COMING.
S'UP, JORDAN?
LONG TIME, MAN. THOUGHT YOU FORGOT ABOUT ME.
NAH, I COULD NEVER FORGET YOU . . .
. . . YOU'RE MY SHRIMP LO MEIN!
YOUR WHAT?
TRUST ME, IT'S A GOOD THING.
KIRK, IT'S SO NICE TO SEE YOU . . .
JORDAN TOLD ME YOU WERE COMING OVER.
HI, MRS. BANKS.

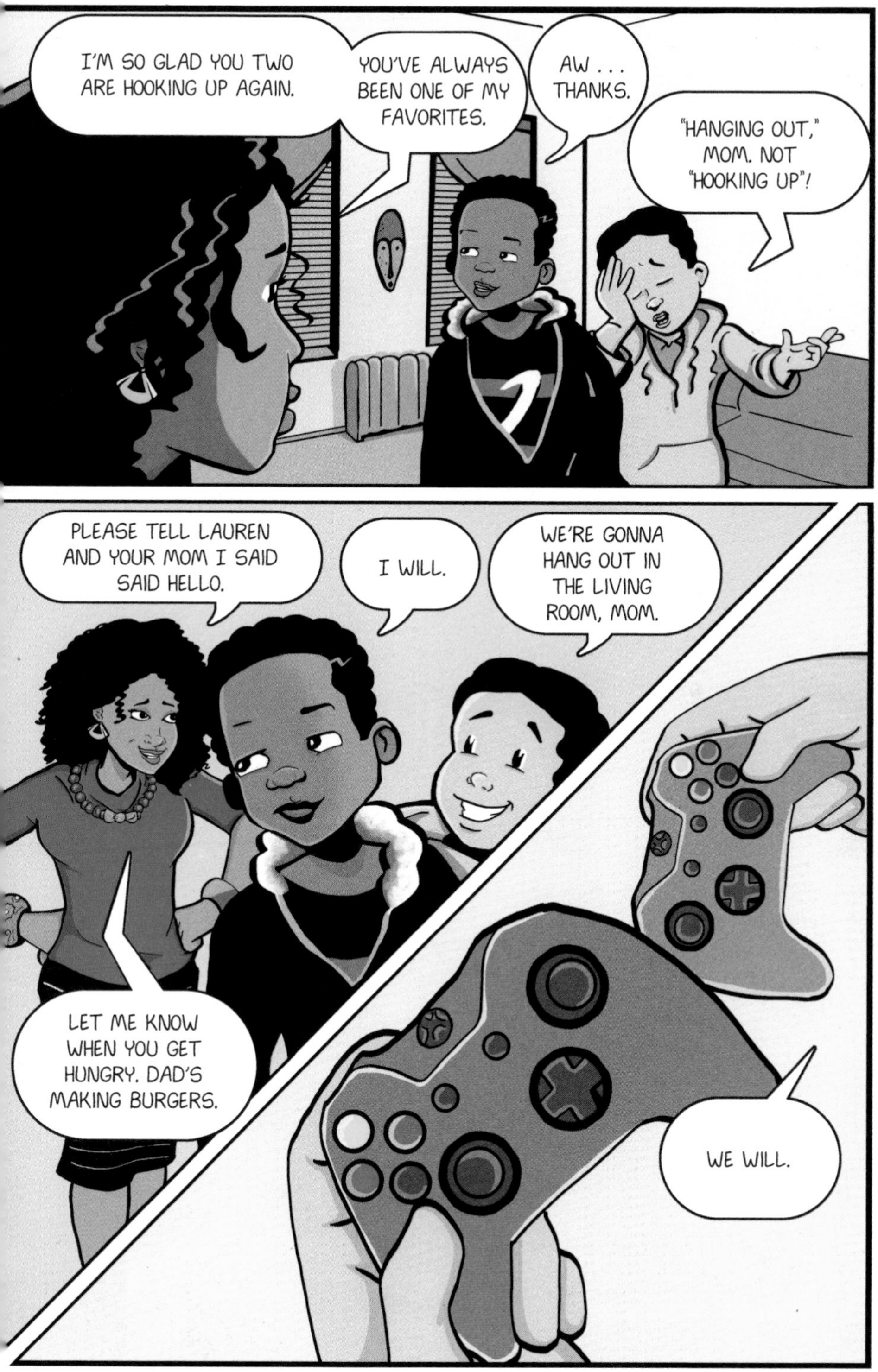
I'M SO GLAD YOU TWO ARE HOOKING UP AGAIN.
YOU'VE ALWAYS BEEN ONE OF MY FAVORITES.
AW . . . THANKS.
"HANGING OUT," MOM. NOT "HOOKING UP"!
PLEASE TELL LAUREN AND YOUR MOM I SAID SAID HELLO.
I WILL.
WE'RE GONNA HANG OUT IN THE LIVING ROOM, MOM.
LET ME KNOW WHEN YOU GET HUNGRY. DAD'S MAKING BURGERS.
WE WILL.

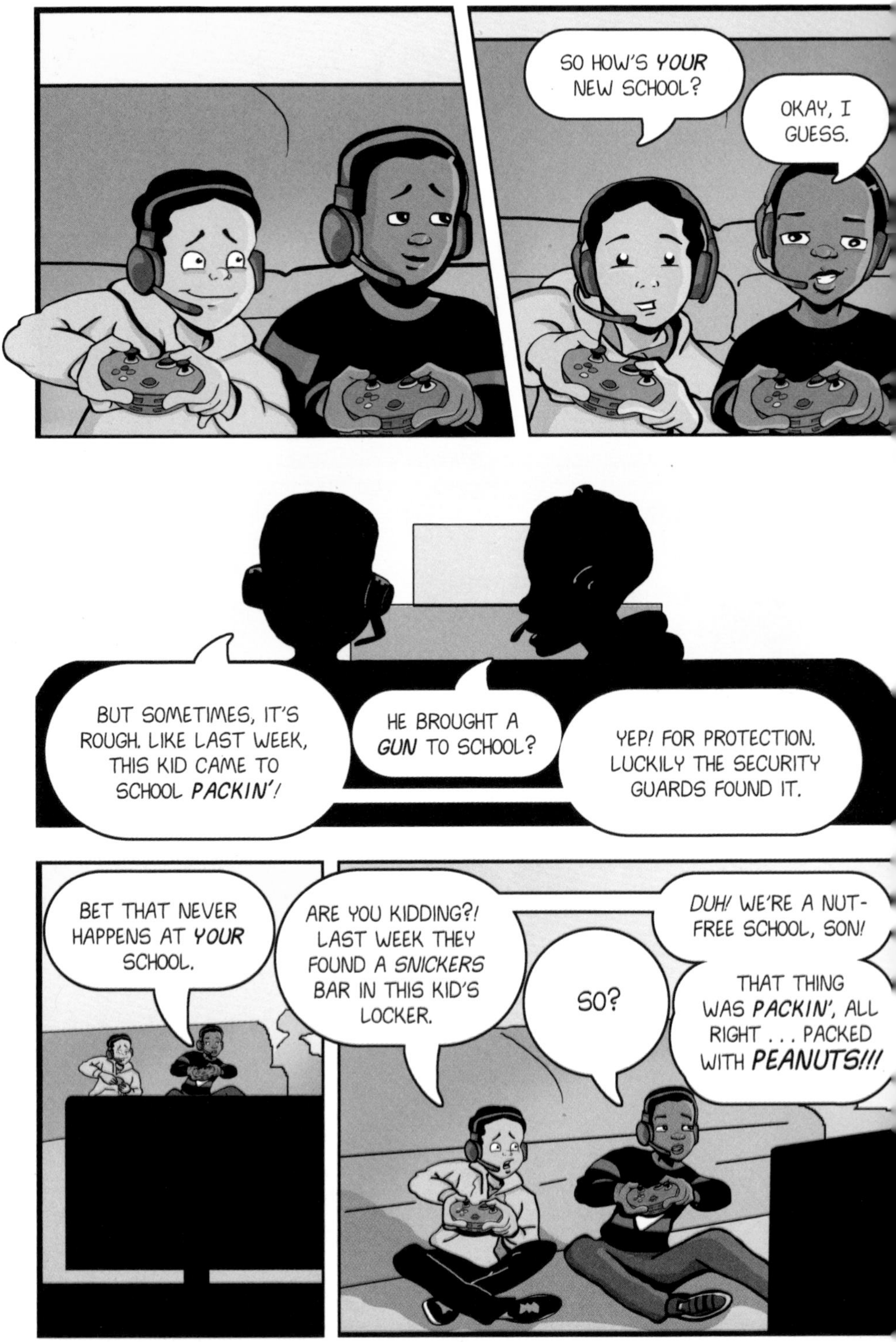
SO HOW'S *YOUR* NEW SCHOOL?
OKAY, I GUESS.
BUT SOMETIMES, IT'S ROUGH. LIKE LAST WEEK, THIS KID CAME TO SCHOOL *PACKIN'*!
HE BROUGHT A *GUN* TO SCHOOL?
YEP! FOR PROTECTION. LUCKILY THE SECURITY GUARDS FOUND IT.
BET THAT NEVER HAPPENS AT *YOUR* SCHOOL.
ARE YOU KIDDING?! LAST WEEK THEY FOUND A *SNICKERS* BAR IN THIS KID'S LOCKER.
SO?
DUH! WE'RE A NUT-FREE SCHOOL, SON!
THAT THING WAS *PACKIN'*, ALL RIGHT . . . PACKED WITH ***PEANUTS!!!***

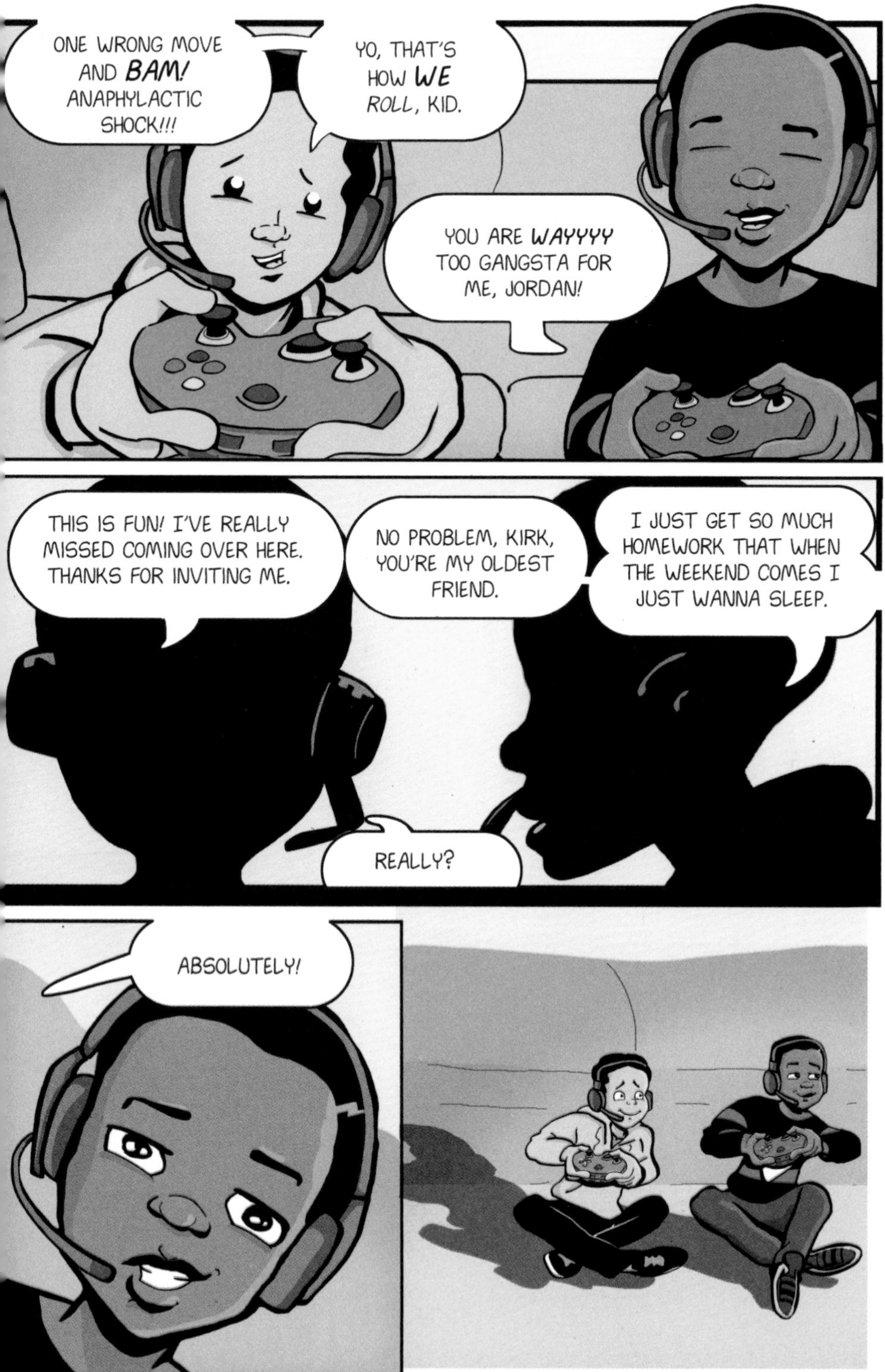
ONE WRONG MOVE AND **BAM!** ANAPHYLACTIC SHOCK!!!
YO, THAT'S HOW **WE** *ROLL*, KID.
YOU ARE **WAYYYY** TOO GANGSTA FOR ME, JORDAN!
THIS IS FUN! I'VE REALLY MISSED COMING OVER HERE. THANKS FOR INVITING ME.
NO PROBLEM, KIRK, YOU'RE MY OLDEST FRIEND.
I JUST GET SO MUCH HOMEWORK THAT WHEN THE WEEKEND COMES I JUST WANNA SLEEP.
REALLY?
ABSOLUTELY!

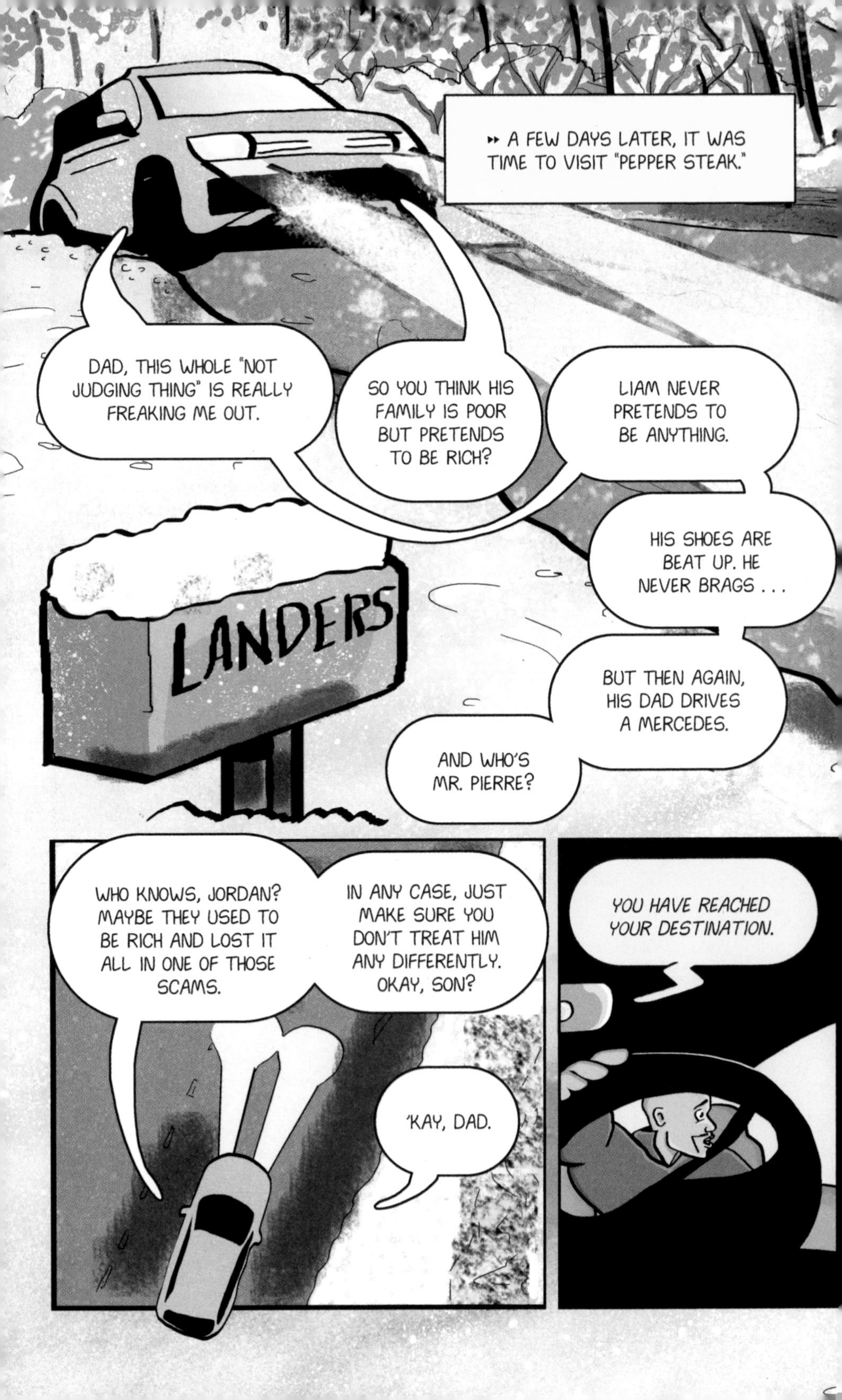
▸▸ A FEW DAYS LATER, IT WAS TIME TO VISIT "PEPPER STEAK."
DAD, THIS WHOLE "NOT JUDGING THING" IS REALLY FREAKING ME OUT.
SO YOU THINK HIS FAMILY IS POOR BUT PRETENDS TO BE RICH?
LIAM NEVER PRETENDS TO BE ANYTHING.
HIS SHOES ARE BEAT UP. HE NEVER BRAGS . . .
BUT THEN AGAIN, HIS DAD DRIVES A MERCEDES.
AND WHO'S MR. PIERRE?
LANDERS
WHO KNOWS, JORDAN? MAYBE THEY USED TO BE RICH AND LOST IT ALL IN ONE OF THOSE SCAMS.
IN ANY CASE, JUST MAKE SURE YOU DON'T TREAT HIM ANY DIFFERENTLY. OKAY, SON?
'KAY, DAD.
YOU HAVE REACHED YOUR DESTINATION.

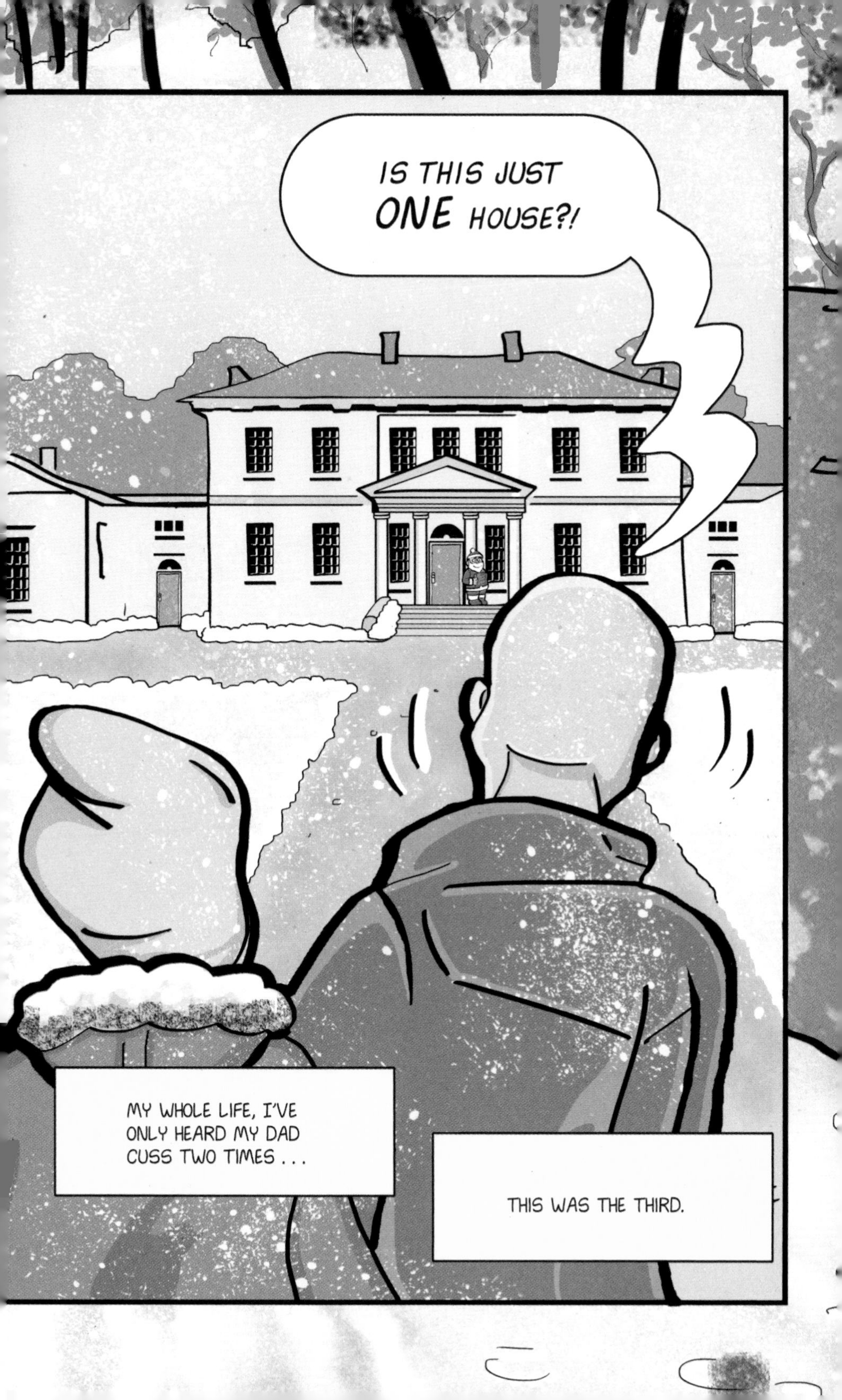
IS THIS JUST ONE HOUSE?!
MY WHOLE LIFE, I'VE ONLY HEARD MY DAD CUSS TWO TIMES . . .
THIS WAS THE THIRD.

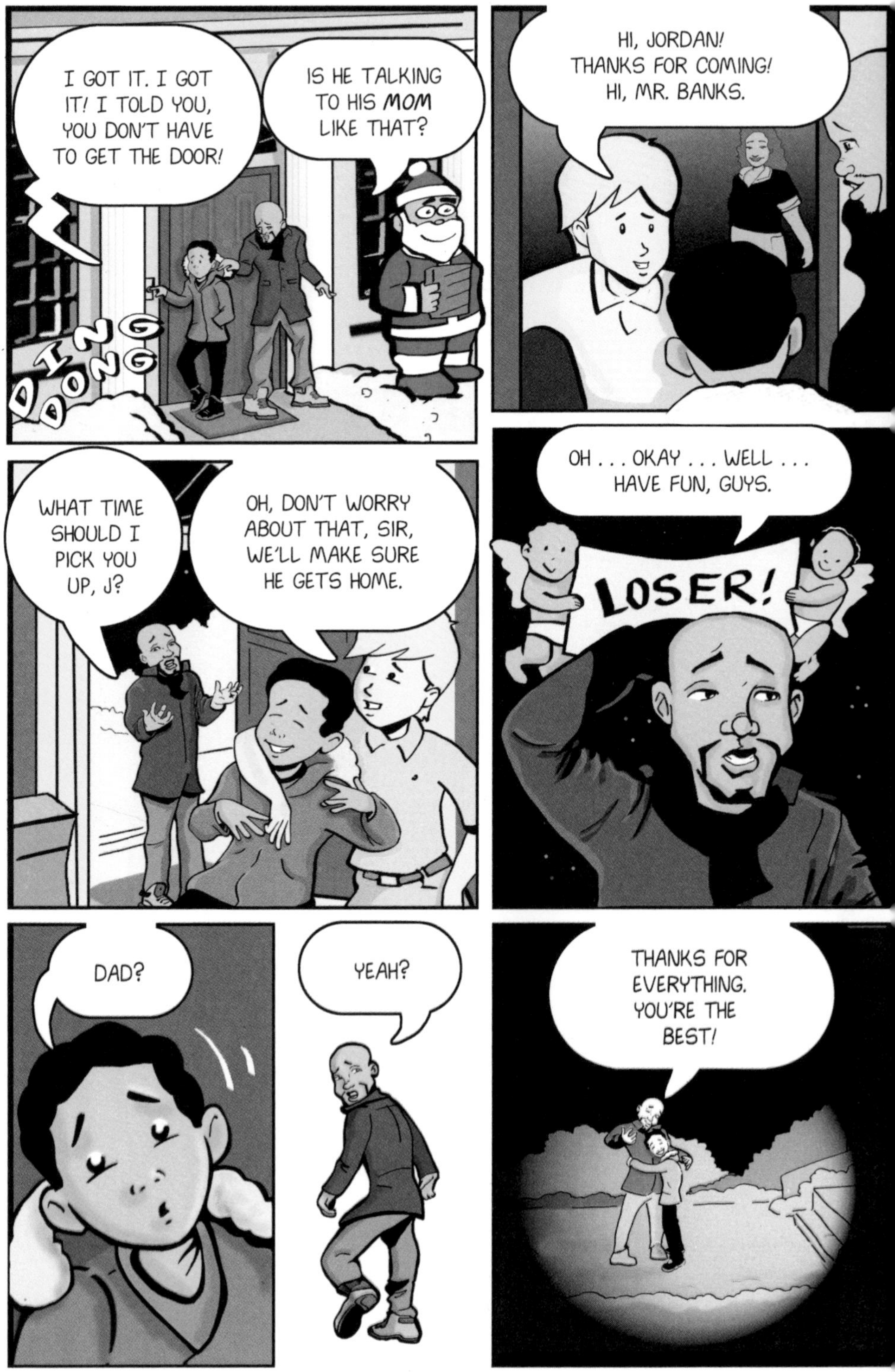
I GOT IT. I GOT IT! I TOLD YOU, YOU DON'T HAVE TO GET THE DOOR!
IS HE TALKING TO HIS MOM LIKE THAT?
DING DONG
HI, JORDAN! THANKS FOR COMING! HI, MR. BANKS.
WHAT TIME SHOULD I PICK YOU UP, J?
OH, DON'T WORRY ABOUT THAT, SIR, WE'LL MAKE SURE HE GETS HOME.
OH . . . OKAY . . . WELL . . . HAVE FUN, GUYS.
LOSER!
DAD?
YEAH?
THANKS FOR EVERYTHING. YOU'RE THE BEST!

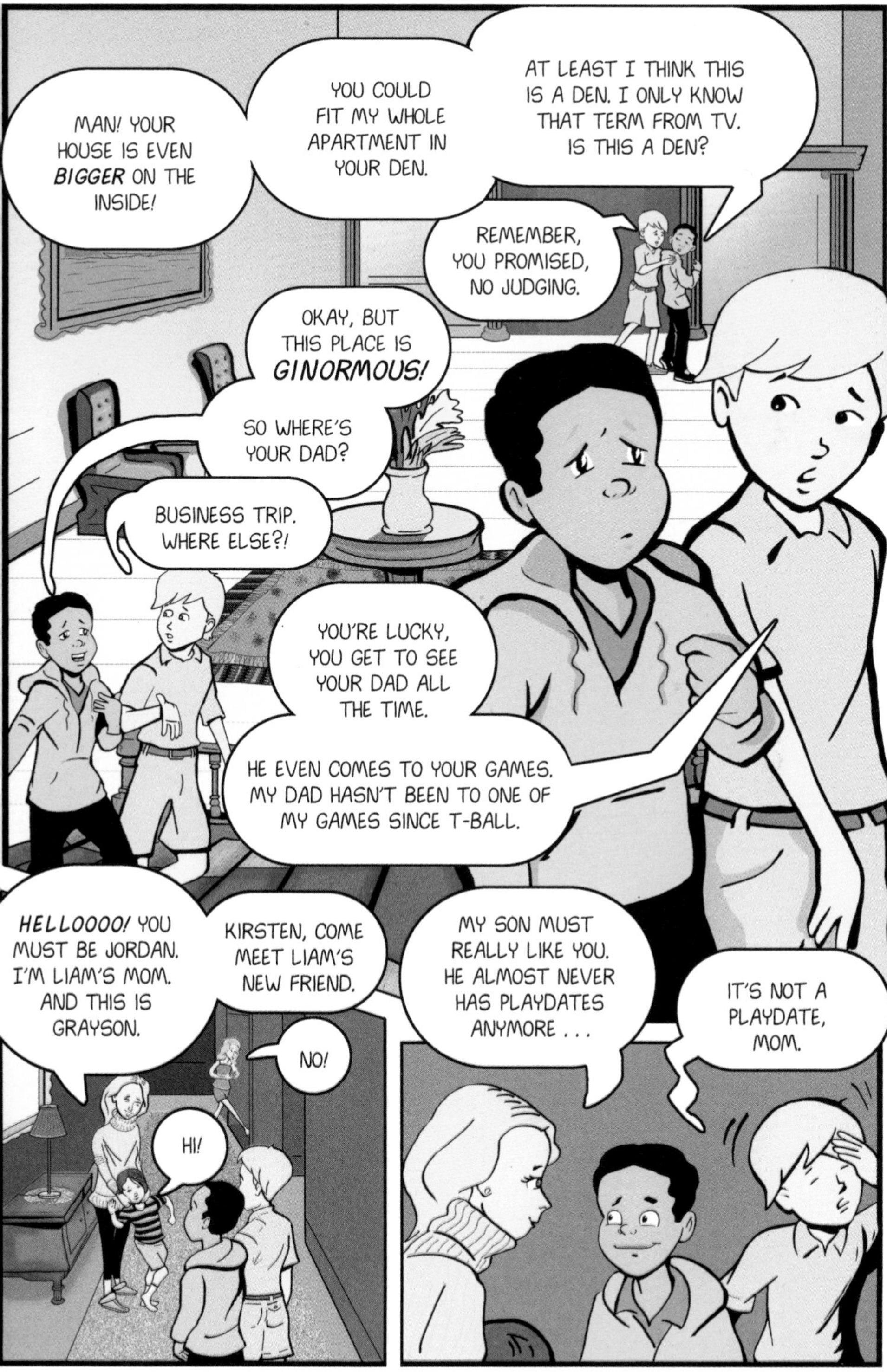
MAN! YOUR HOUSE IS EVEN *BIGGER* ON THE INSIDE!
YOU COULD FIT MY WHOLE APARTMENT IN YOUR DEN.
AT LEAST I THINK THIS IS A DEN. I ONLY KNOW THAT TERM FROM TV. IS THIS A DEN?
REMEMBER, YOU PROMISED, NO JUDGING.
OKAY, BUT THIS PLACE IS *GINORMOUS!*
SO WHERE'S YOUR DAD?
BUSINESS TRIP. WHERE ELSE?!
YOU'RE LUCKY, YOU GET TO SEE YOUR DAD ALL THE TIME.
HE EVEN COMES TO YOUR GAMES. MY DAD HASN'T BEEN TO ONE OF MY GAMES SINCE T-BALL.
HELLOOOO! YOU MUST BE JORDAN. I'M LIAM'S MOM. AND THIS IS GRAYSON.
KIRSTEN, COME MEET LIAM'S NEW FRIEND.
NO!
HI!
MY SON MUST REALLY LIKE YOU. HE ALMOST NEVER HAS PLAYDATES ANYMORE . . .
IT'S NOT A PLAYDATE, MOM.

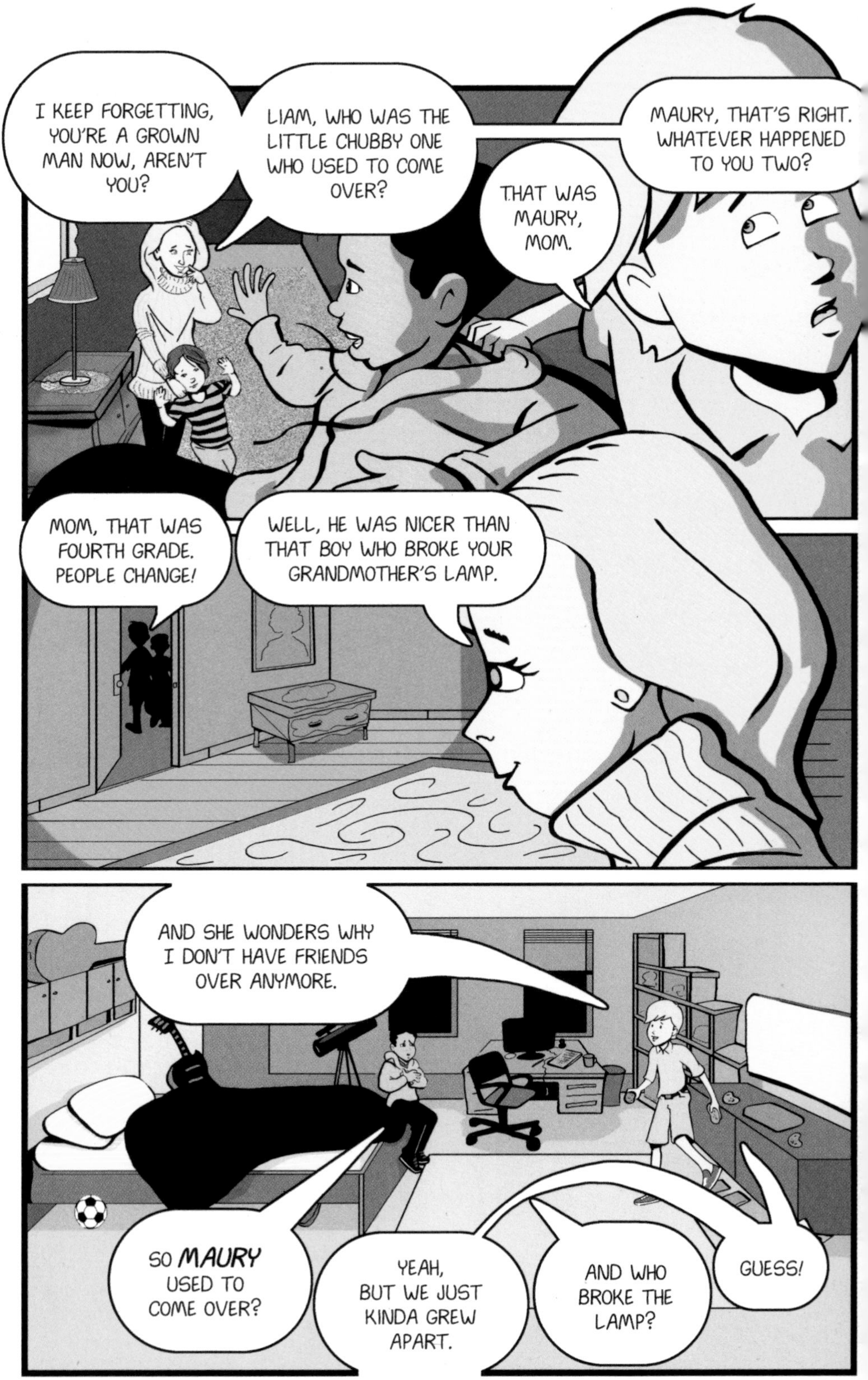
I KEEP FORGETTING, YOU'RE A GROWN MAN NOW, AREN'T YOU?
LIAM, WHO WAS THE LITTLE CHUBBY ONE WHO USED TO COME OVER?
THAT WAS MAURY, MOM.
MAURY, THAT'S RIGHT. WHATEVER HAPPENED TO YOU TWO?
MOM, THAT WAS FOURTH GRADE. PEOPLE CHANGE!
WELL, HE WAS NICER THAN THAT BOY WHO BROKE YOUR GRANDMOTHER'S LAMP.
AND SHE WONDERS WHY I DON'T HAVE FRIENDS OVER ANYMORE.
SO *MAURY* USED TO COME OVER?
YEAH, BUT WE JUST KINDA GREW APART.
AND WHO BROKE THE LAMP?
GUESS!

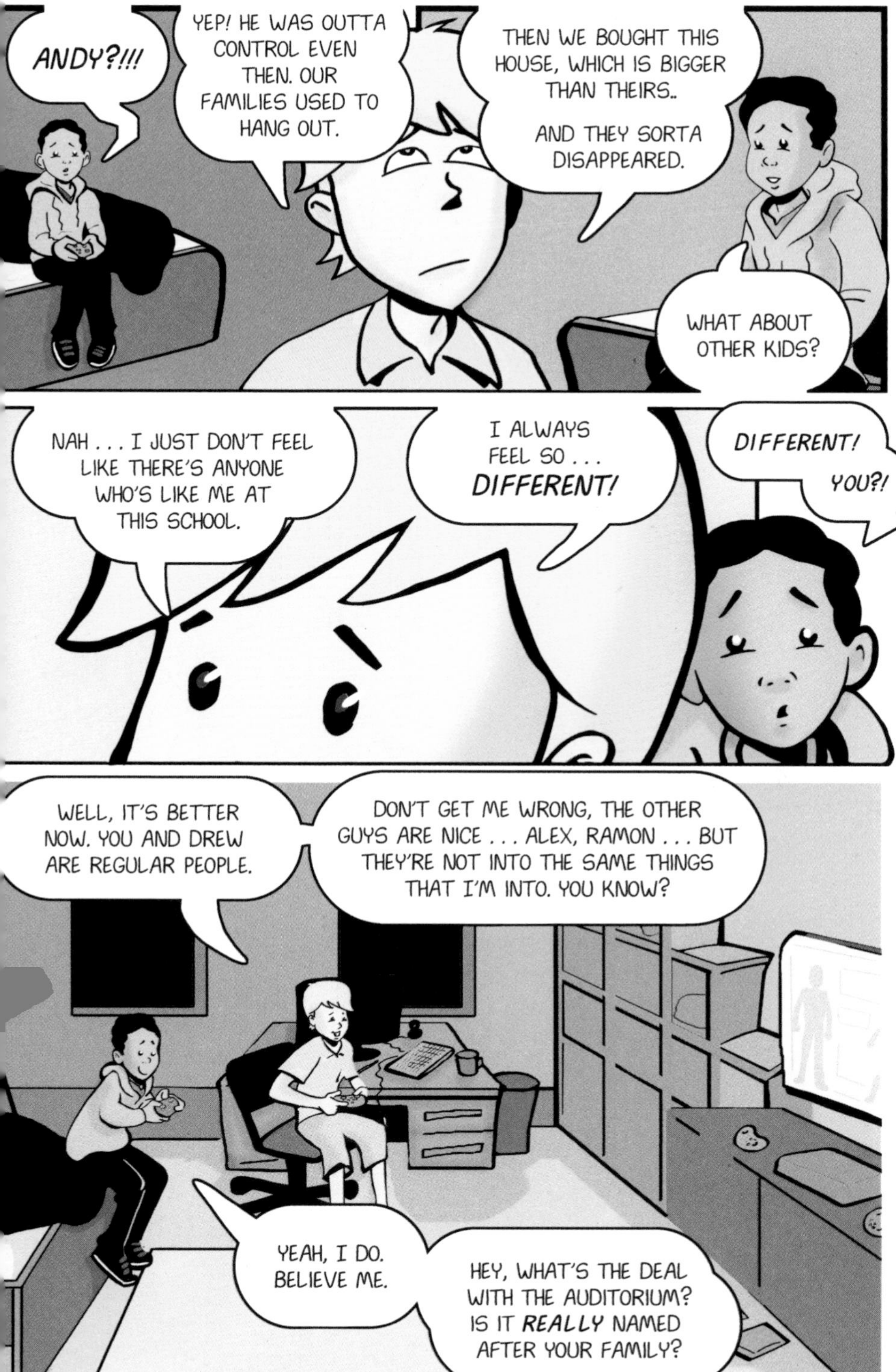
ANDY?!!!
YEP! HE WAS OUTTA CONTROL EVEN THEN. OUR FAMILIES USED TO HANG OUT.
THEN WE BOUGHT THIS HOUSE, WHICH IS BIGGER THAN THEIRS..
AND THEY SORTA DISAPPEARED.
WHAT ABOUT OTHER KIDS?
NAH . . . I JUST DON'T FEEL LIKE THERE'S ANYONE WHO'S LIKE ME AT THIS SCHOOL.
I ALWAYS FEEL SO . . . DIFFERENT!
DIFFERENT!
YOU?!
WELL, IT'S BETTER NOW. YOU AND DREW ARE REGULAR PEOPLE.
DON'T GET ME WRONG, THE OTHER GUYS ARE NICE . . . ALEX, RAMON . . . BUT THEY'RE NOT INTO THE SAME THINGS THAT I'M INTO. YOU KNOW?
YEAH, I DO. BELIEVE ME.
HEY, WHAT'S THE DEAL WITH THE AUDITORIUM? IS IT REALLY NAMED AFTER YOUR FAMILY?

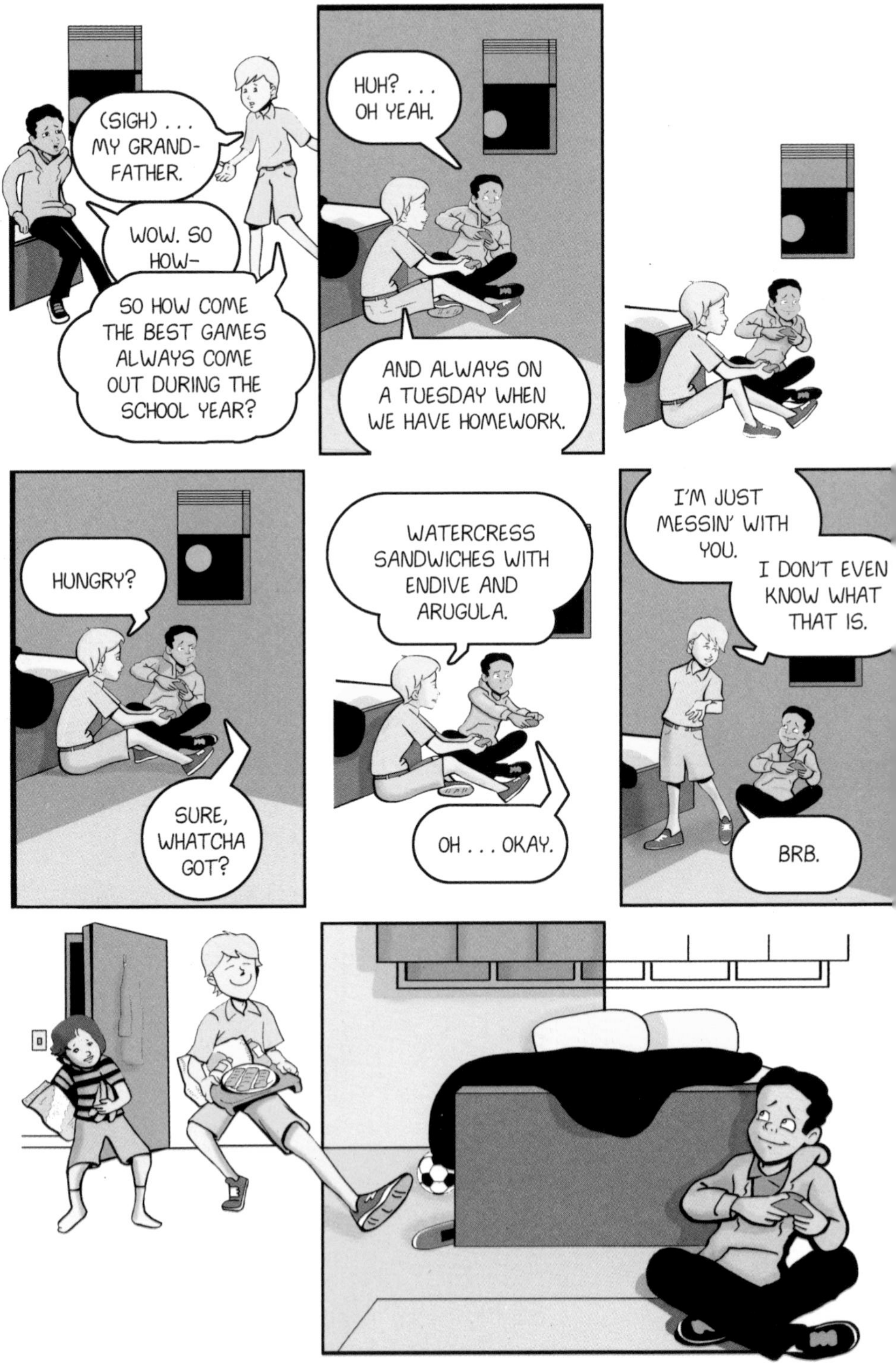
(SIGH) . . . MY GRAND-FATHER.
WOW. SO HOW–
SO HOW COME THE BEST GAMES ALWAYS COME OUT DURING THE SCHOOL YEAR?
HUH? . . . OH YEAH.
AND ALWAYS ON A TUESDAY WHEN WE HAVE HOMEWORK.
HUNGRY?
SURE, WHATCHA GOT?
WATERCRESS SANDWICHES WITH ENDIVE AND ARUGULA.
OH . . . OKAY.
I'M JUST MESSIN' WITH YOU.
I DON'T EVEN KNOW WHAT THAT IS.
BRB.

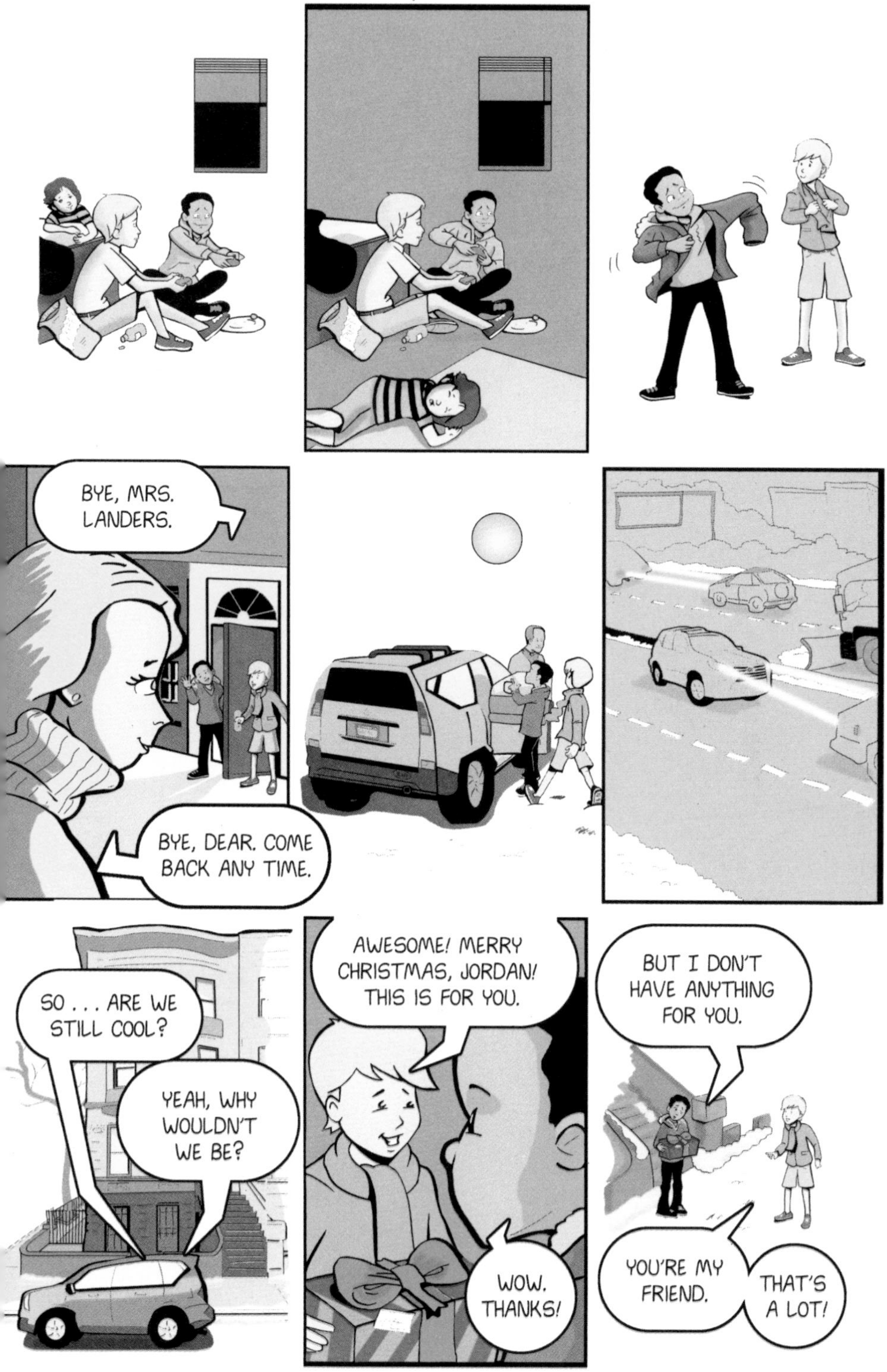
BYE, MRS. LANDERS.
BYE, DEAR. COME BACK ANY TIME.
SO . . . ARE WE STILL COOL?
YEAH, WHY WOULDN'T WE BE?
AWESOME! MERRY CHRISTMAS, JORDAN! THIS IS FOR YOU.
WOW. THANKS!
BUT I DON'T HAVE ANYTHING FOR YOU.
YOU'RE MY FRIEND.
THAT'S A LOT!

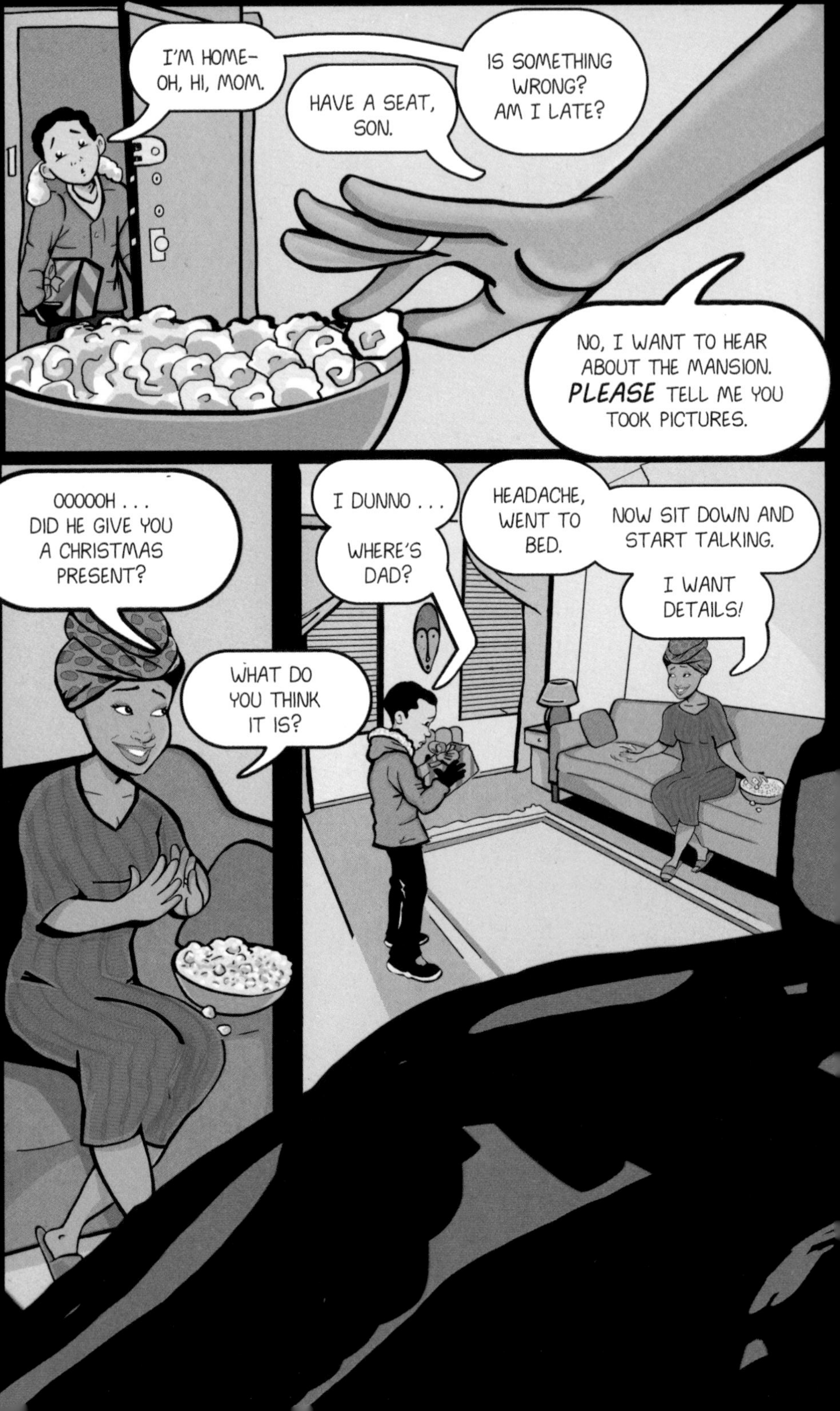
I'M HOME— OH, HI, MOM.
HAVE A SEAT, SON.
IS SOMETHING WRONG? AM I LATE?
NO, I WANT TO HEAR ABOUT THE MANSION. PLEASE TELL ME YOU TOOK PICTURES.
I DUNNO . . .
WHERE'S DAD?
HEADACHE, WENT TO BED.
NOW SIT DOWN AND START TALKING.
I WANT DETAILS!
OOOOOH . . . DID HE GIVE YOU A CHRISTMAS PRESENT?
WHAT DO YOU THINK IT IS?

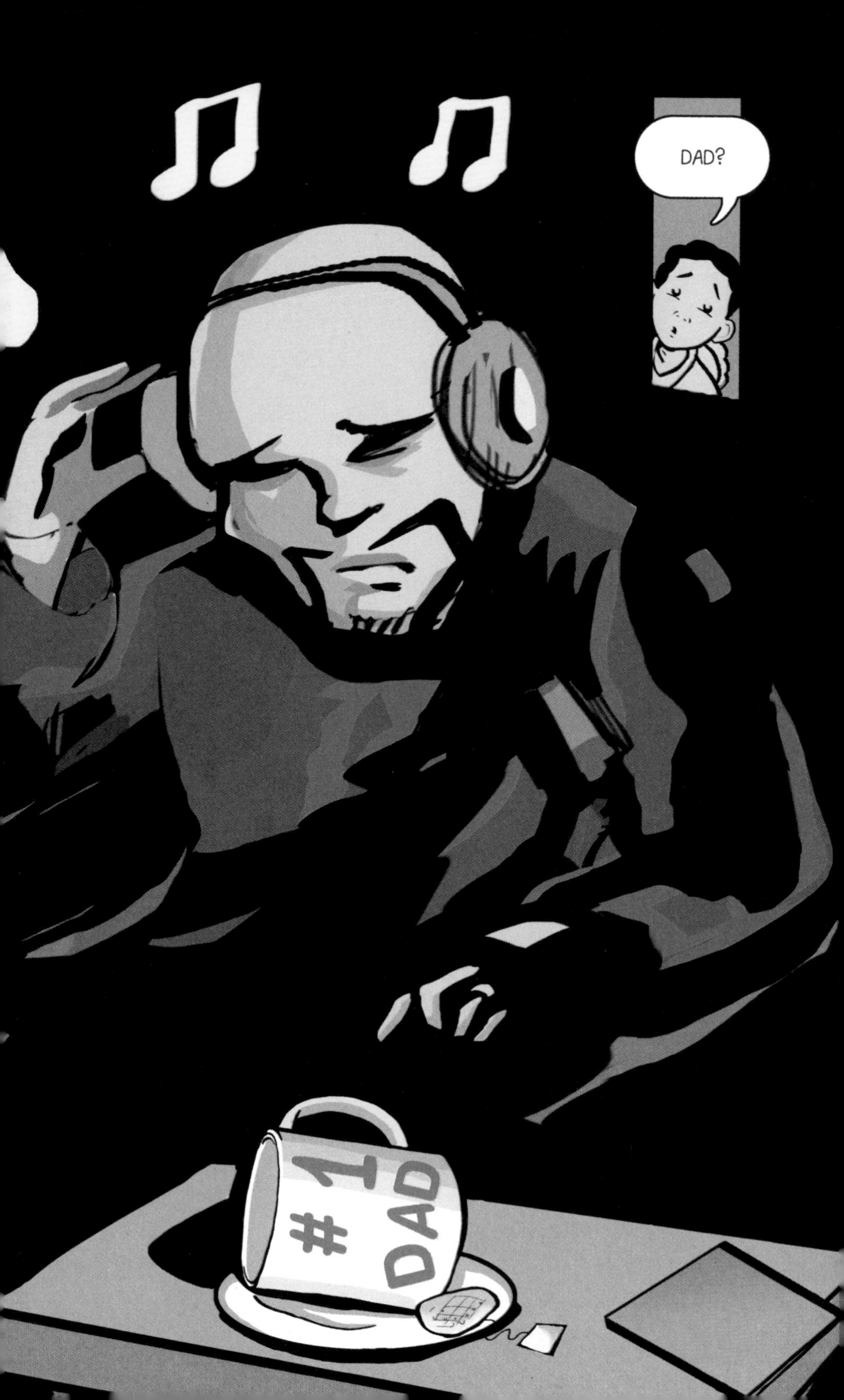
DAD?
#1 DAD

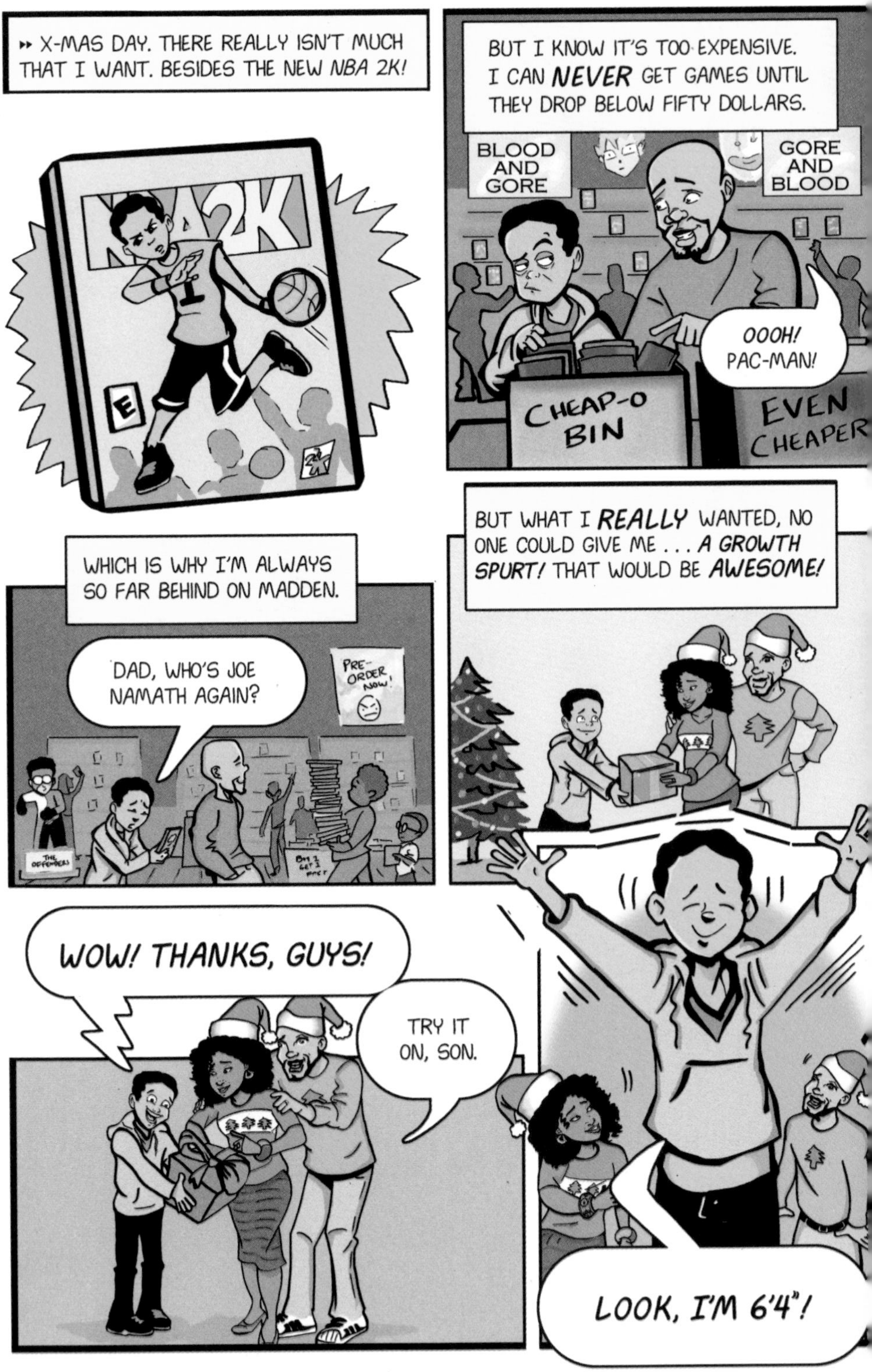
X-MAS DAY. THERE REALLY ISN'T MUCH THAT I WANT. BESIDES THE NEW *NBA 2K*!
2K
BUT I KNOW IT'S TOO EXPENSIVE. I CAN **NEVER** GET GAMES UNTIL THEY DROP BELOW FIFTY DOLLARS.
BLOOD AND GORE
GORE AND BLOOD
OOOH! PAC-MAN!
CHEAP-O BIN
EVEN CHEAPER
WHICH IS WHY I'M ALWAYS SO FAR BEHIND ON MADDEN.
DAD, WHO'S JOE NAMATH AGAIN?
PRE-ORDER NOW!
BUT WHAT I **REALLY** WANTED, NO ONE COULD GIVE ME . . . ***A GROWTH SPURT!*** THAT WOULD BE ***AWESOME!***
WOW! THANKS, GUYS!
TRY IT ON, SON.
LOOK, I'M 6'4"!

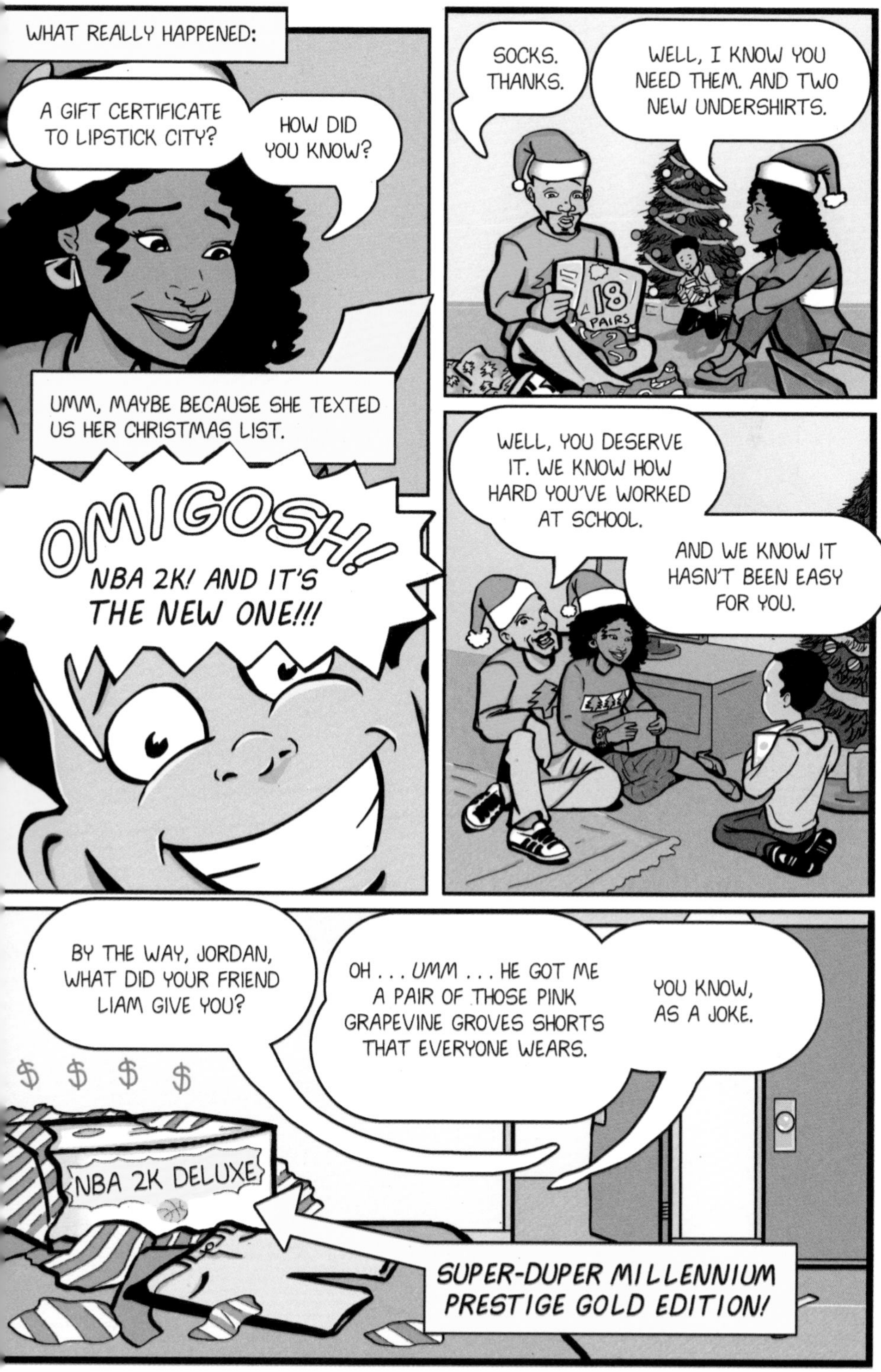
WHAT REALLY HAPPENED:
A GIFT CERTIFICATE TO LIPSTICK CITY?
HOW DID YOU KNOW?
UMM, MAYBE BECAUSE SHE TEXTED US HER CHRISTMAS LIST.
SOCKS. THANKS.
WELL, I KNOW YOU NEED THEM. AND TWO NEW UNDERSHIRTS.
18 PAIRS
OMIGOSH!
NBA 2K! AND IT'S THE NEW ONE!!!
WELL, YOU DESERVE IT. WE KNOW HOW HARD YOU'VE WORKED AT SCHOOL.
AND WE KNOW IT HASN'T BEEN EASY FOR YOU.
BY THE WAY, JORDAN, WHAT DID YOUR FRIEND LIAM GIVE YOU?
OH . . . *UMM* . . . HE GOT ME A PAIR OF THOSE PINK GRAPEVINE GROVES SHORTS THAT EVERYONE WEARS.
YOU KNOW, AS A JOKE.
$ $ $ $
NBA 2K DELUXE
SUPER-DUPER MILLENNIUM PRESTIGE GOLD EDITION!

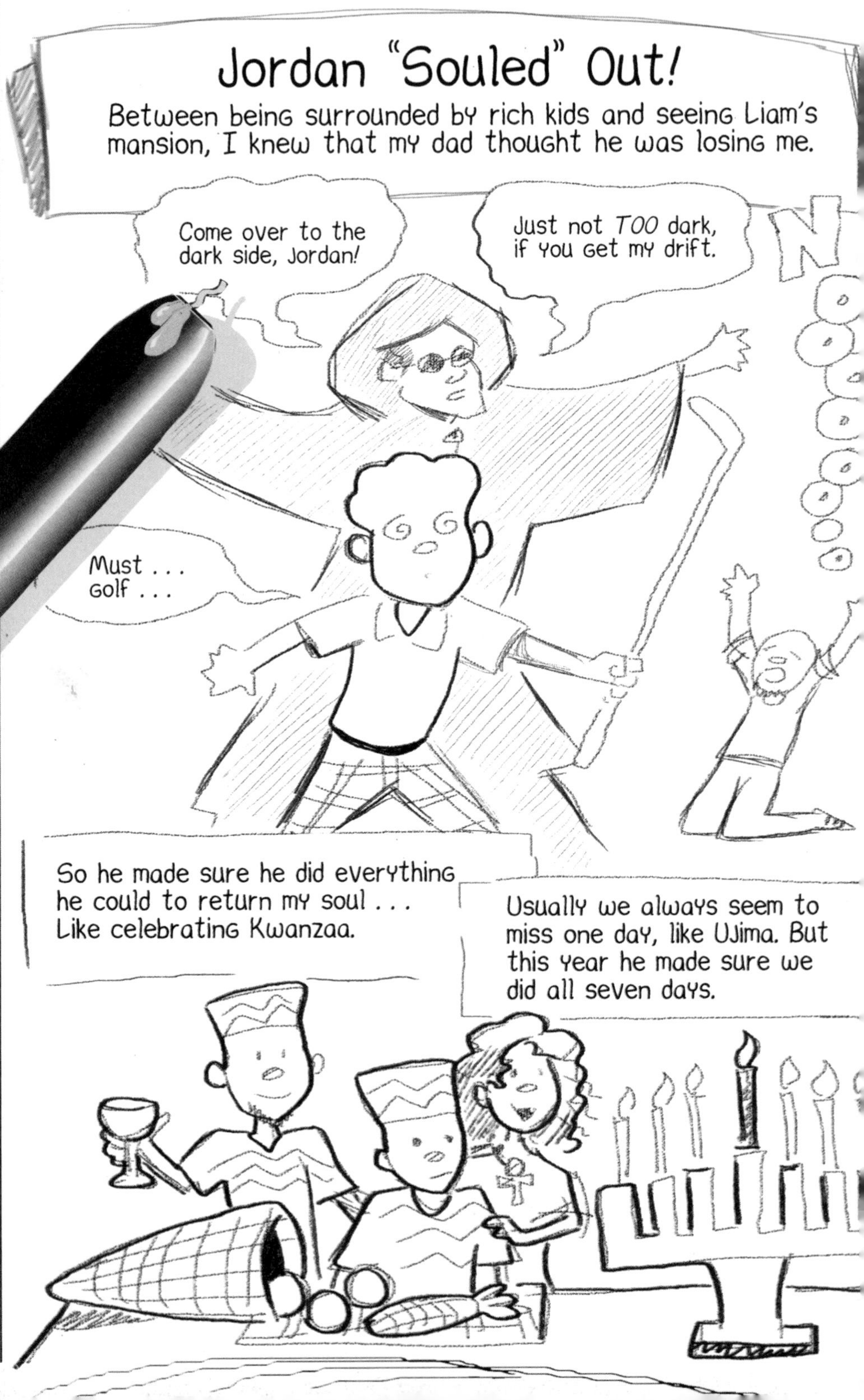
Jordan "Souled" Out!
Between being surrounded by rich kids and seeing Liam's mansion, I knew that my dad thought he was losing me.
Come over to the dark side, Jordan!
Just not *TOO* dark, if you get my drift.
NOOOOOOOOOO
Must . . . golf . . .
So he made sure he did everything he could to return my soul . . . Like celebrating Kwanzaa.
Usually we always seem to miss one day, like Ujima. But this year he made sure we did all seven days.

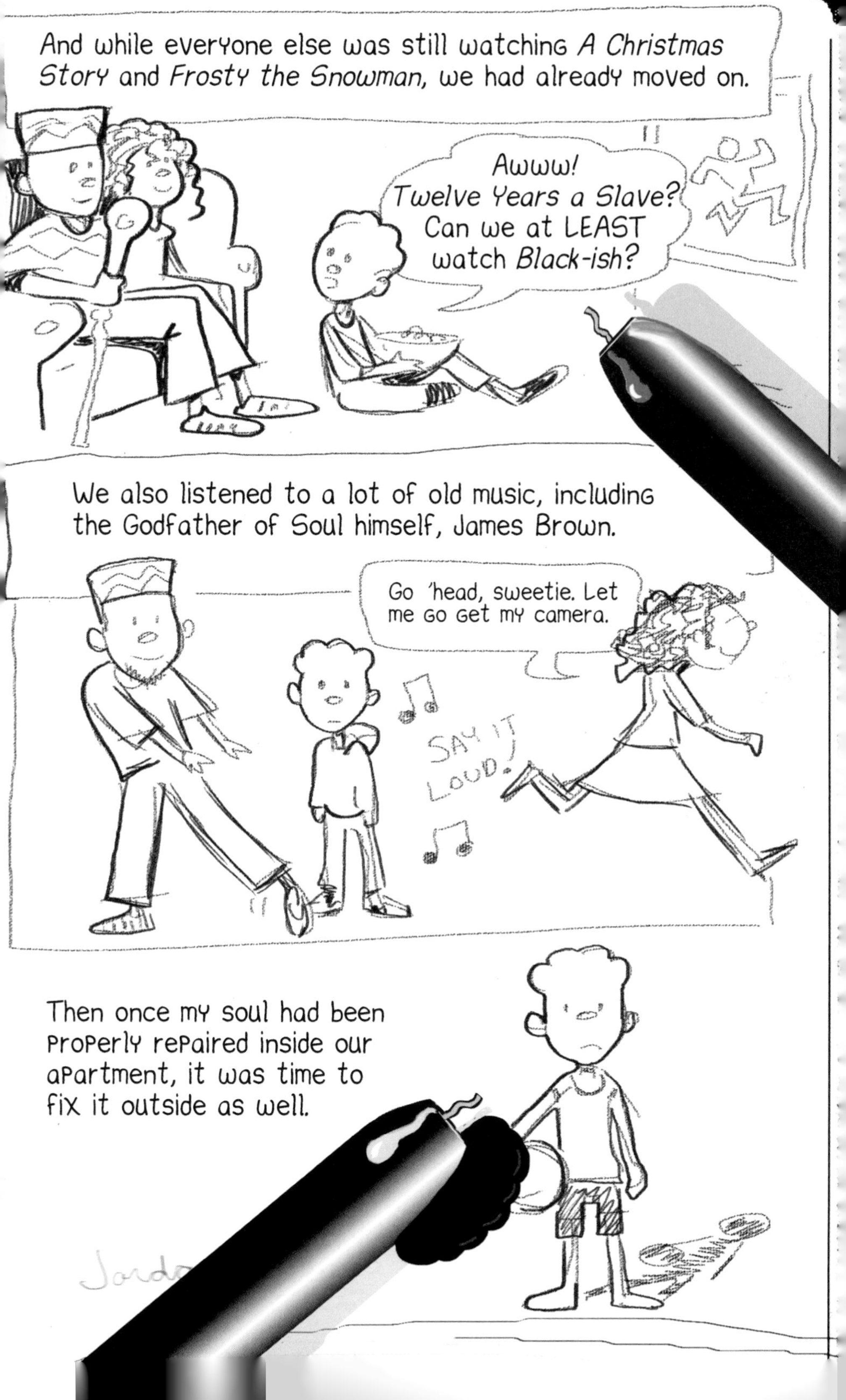
And while everyone else was still watching *A Christmas Story* and *Frosty the Snowman,* we had already moved on.
Awww! *Twelve Years a Slave?* Can we at LEAST watch *Black-ish?*
We also listened to a lot of old music, including the Godfather of Soul himself, James Brown.
Go 'head, sweetie. Let me go get my camera.
SAY IT LOUD!
Then once my soul had been properly repaired inside our apartment, it was time to fix it outside as well.

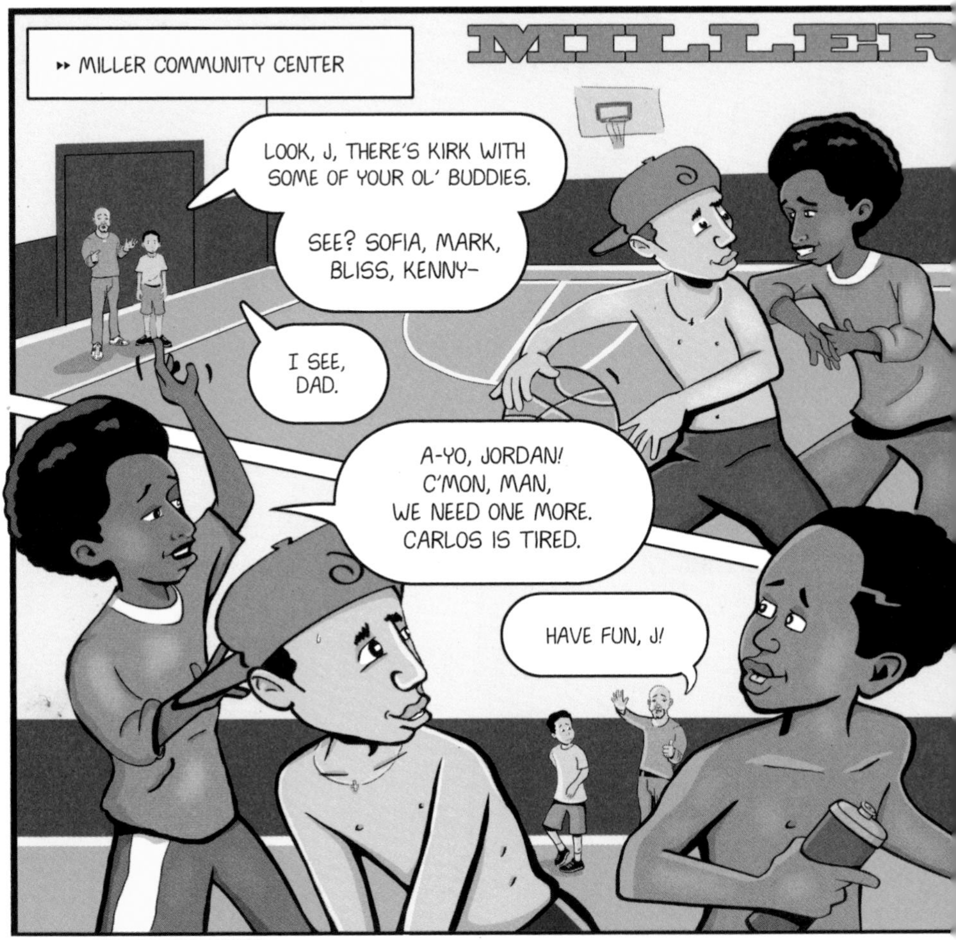
MILLER COMMUNITY CENTER
MILLER
LOOK, J, THERE'S KIRK WITH SOME OF YOUR OL' BUDDIES.
SEE? SOFIA, MARK, BLISS, KENNY–
I SEE, DAD.
A-YO, JORDAN! C'MON, MAN, WE NEED ONE MORE. CARLOS IS TIRED.
HAVE FUN, J!

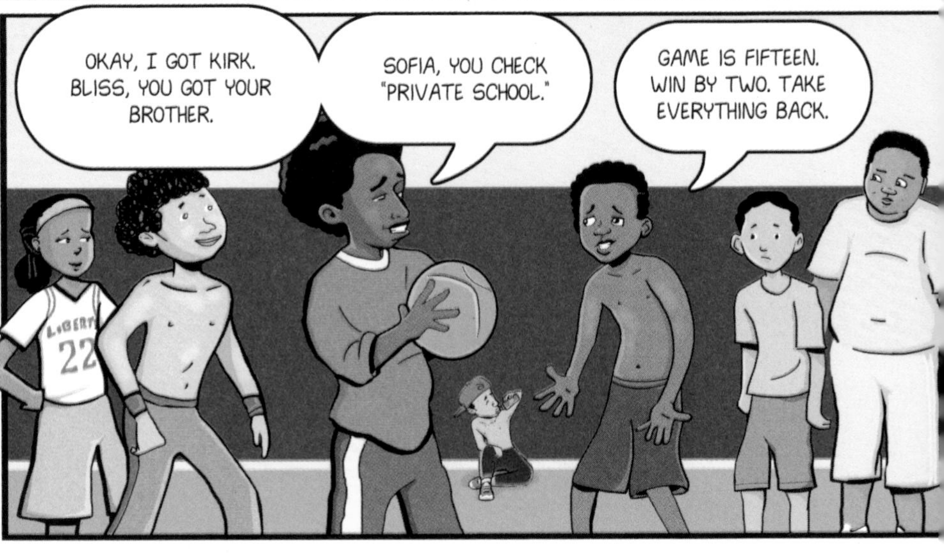
OKAY, I GOT KIRK. BLISS, YOU GOT YOUR BROTHER.
SOFIA, YOU CHECK "PRIVATE SCHOOL."
GAME IS FIFTEEN. WIN BY TWO. TAKE EVERYTHING BACK.
LIBERTY
22

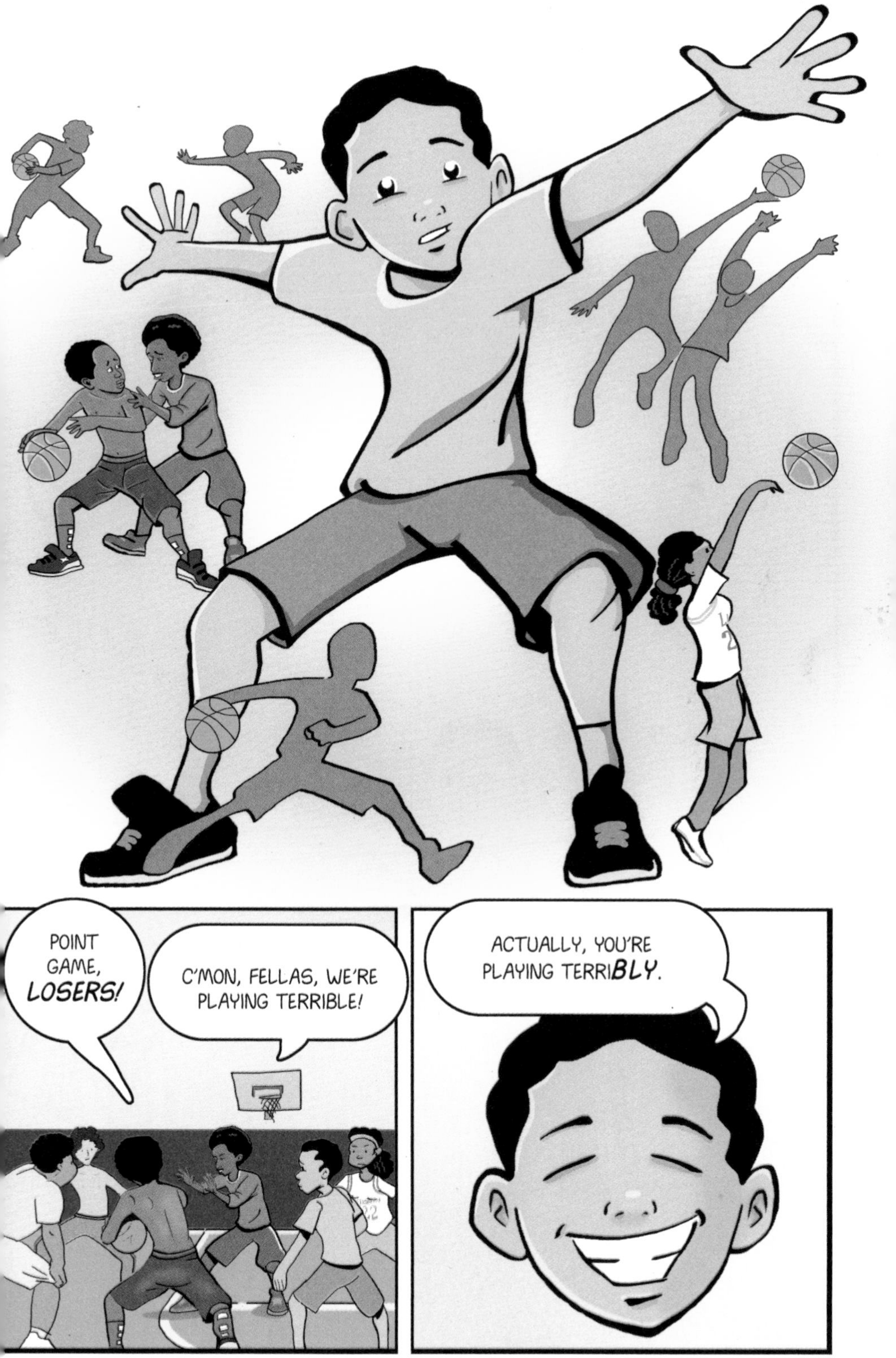
POINT GAME, LOSERS!
C'MON, FELLAS, WE'RE PLAYING TERRIBLE!
ACTUALLY, YOU'RE PLAYING TERRIBLY.

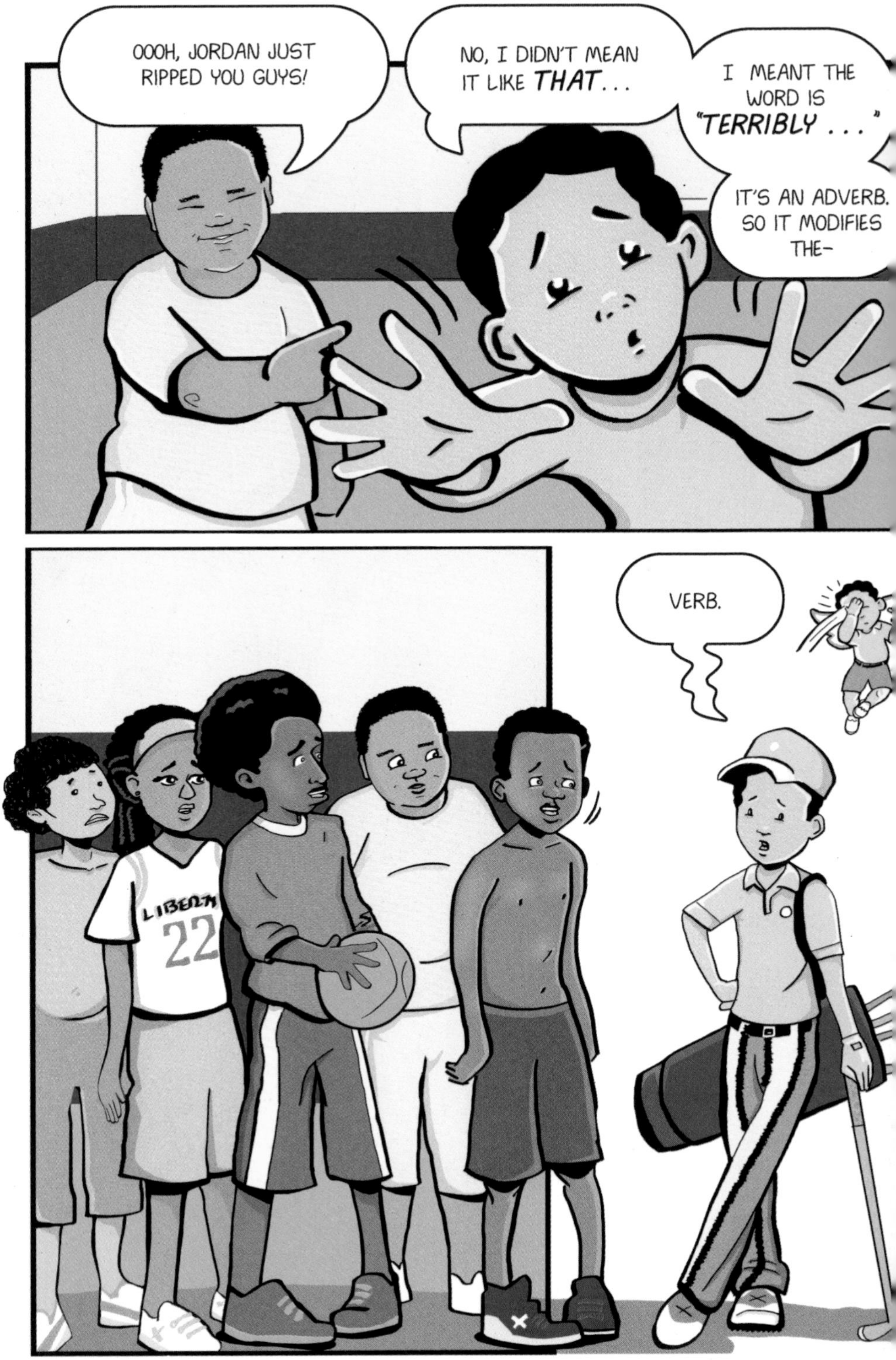
OOOH, JORDAN JUST RIPPED YOU GUYS!
NO, I DIDN'T MEAN IT LIKE THAT...
I MEANT THE WORD IS "TERRIBLY ..."
IT'S AN ADVERB. SO IT MODIFIES THE–
VERB.
LIBERTY
22

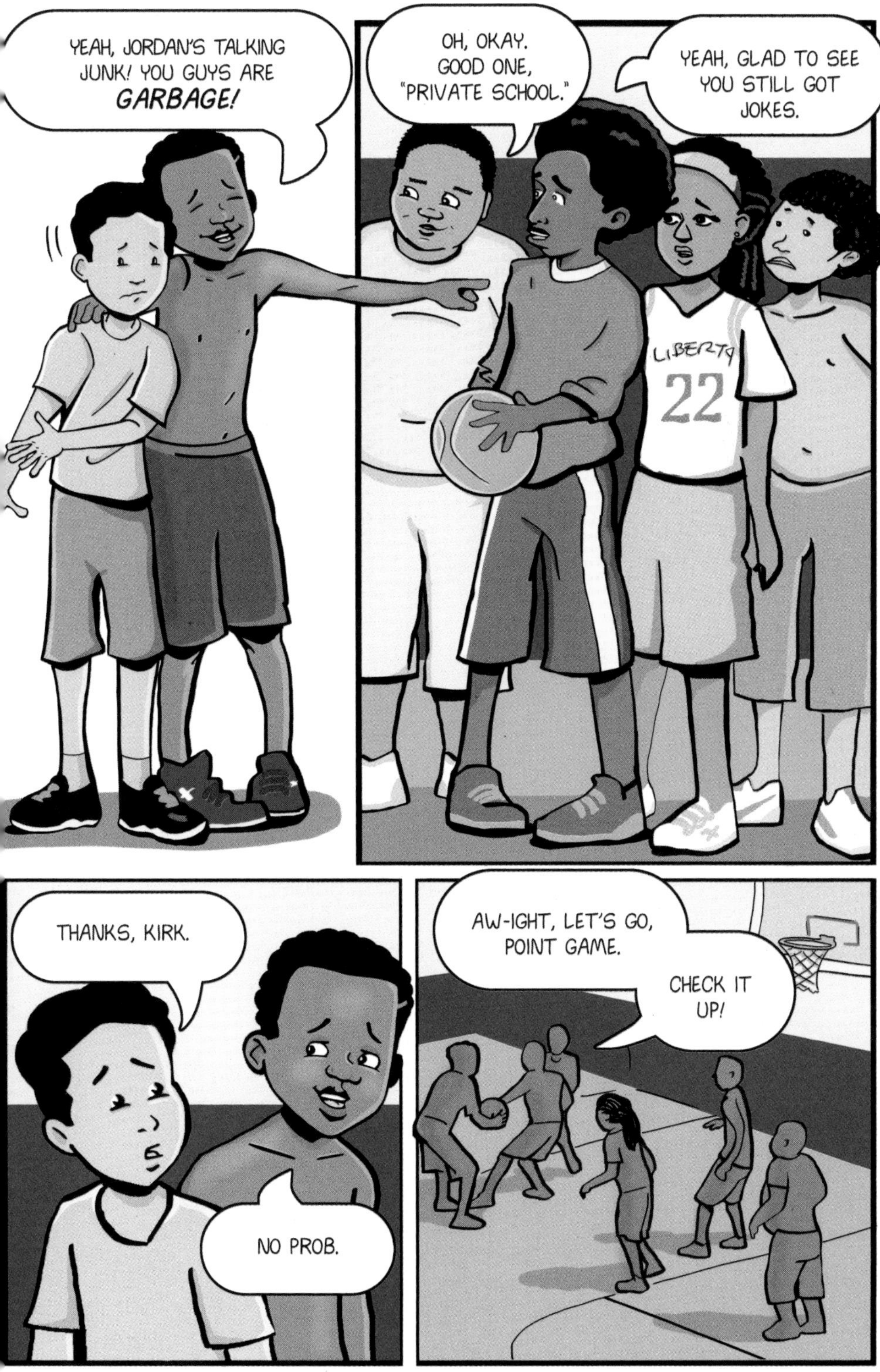
YEAH, JORDAN'S TALKING JUNK! YOU GUYS ARE *GARBAGE!*
OH, OKAY. GOOD ONE, "PRIVATE SCHOOL."
YEAH, GLAD TO SEE YOU STILL GOT JOKES.
LIBERTY
22
THANKS, KIRK.
NO PROB.
AW-IGHT, LET'S GO, POINT GAME.
CHECK IT UP!

THE SOCKY HORROR PICTURE SHOW

CHAPTER 10

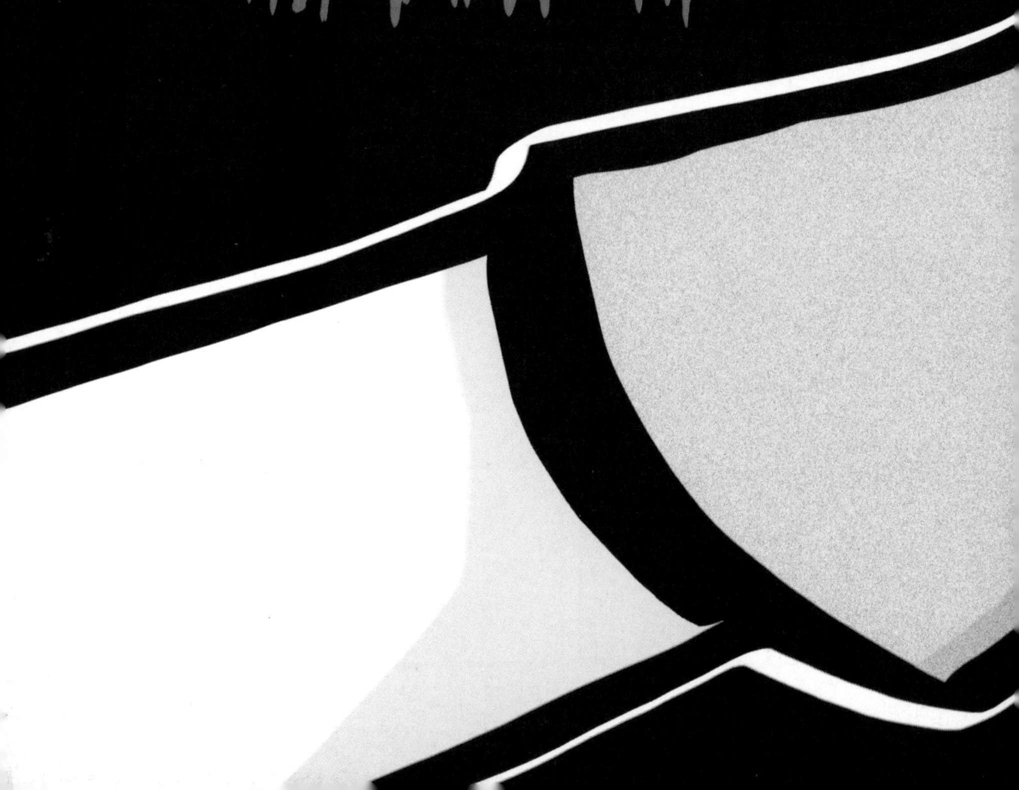

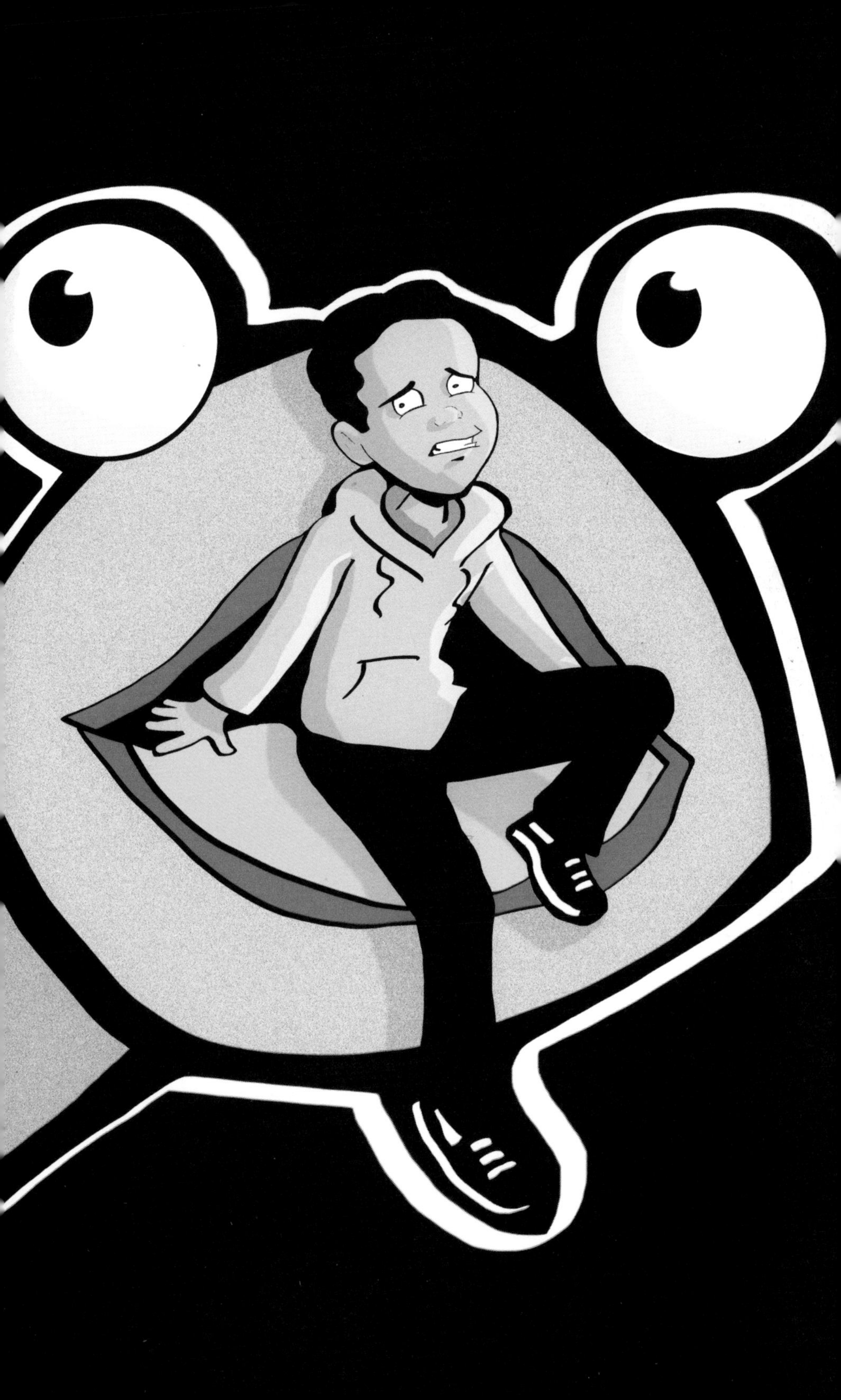

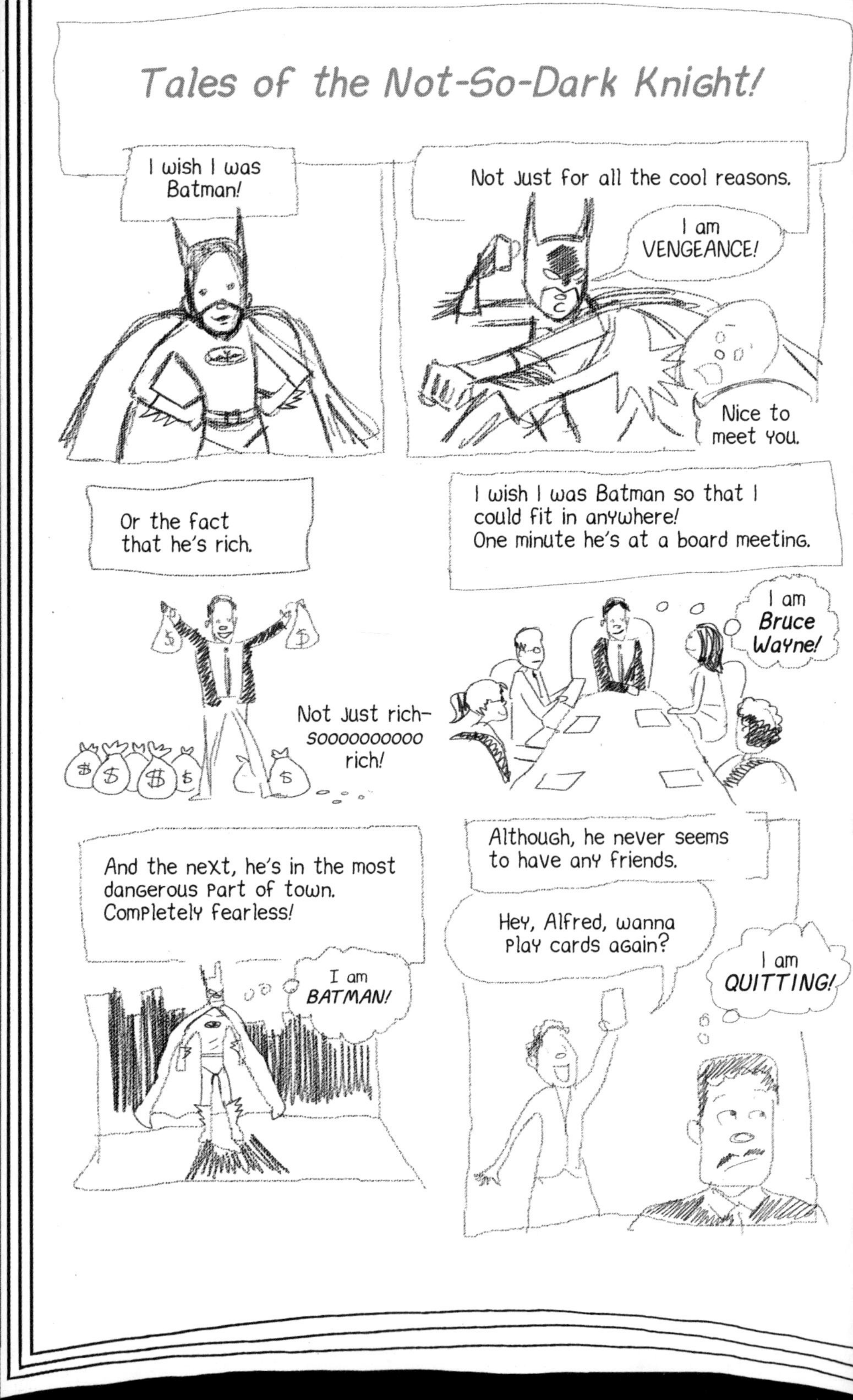
Tales of the Not-So-Dark Knight!
I wish I was Batman!
Not just for all the cool reasons.
I am VENGEANCE!
Nice to meet you.
Or the fact that he's rich.
Not just rich- soooooooooo rich!
I wish I was Batman so that I could fit in anywhere! One minute he's at a board meeting.
I am Bruce Wayne!
And the next, he's in the most dangerous part of town. Completely fearless!
I am BATMAN!
Although, he never seems to have any friends.
Hey, Alfred, wanna play cards again?
I am QUITTING!

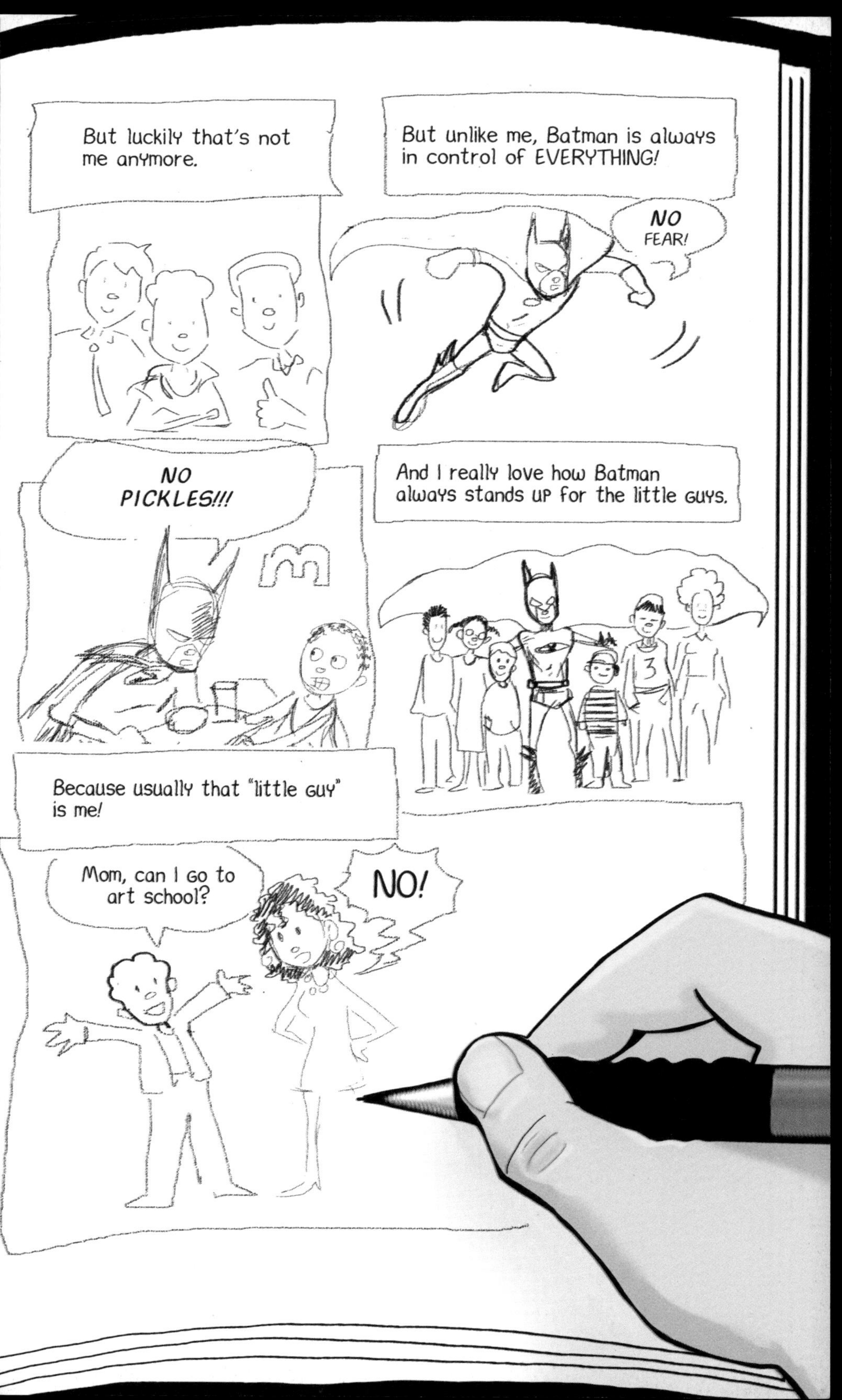

But luckily that's not me anymore.
But unlike me, Batman is always in control of EVERYTHING!
NO FEAR!
NO PICKLES!!!
And I really love how Batman always stands up for the little guys.
Because usually that "little guy" is me!
Mom, can I go to art school?
NO!

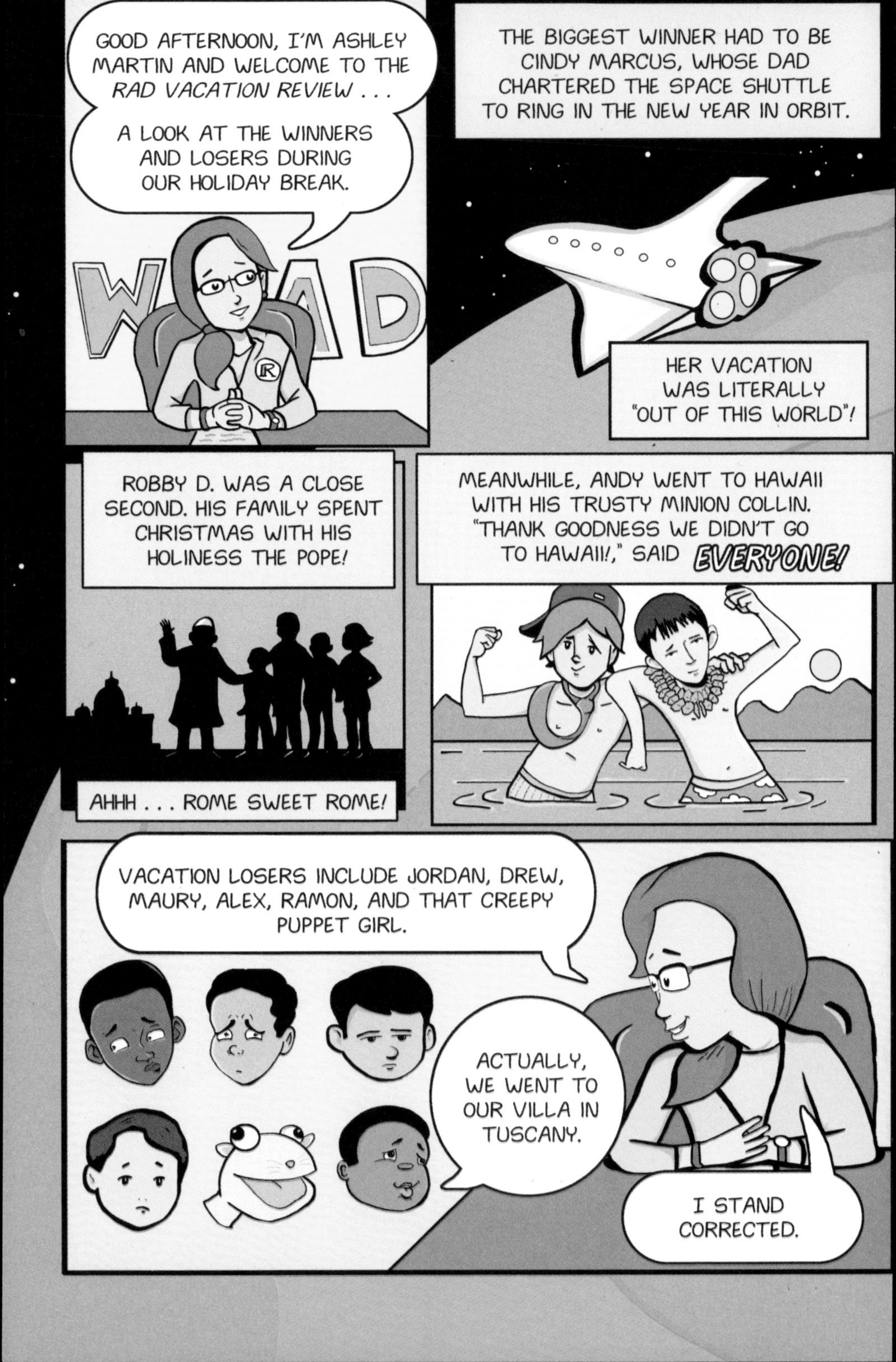
GOOD AFTERNOON, I'M ASHLEY MARTIN AND WELCOME TO THE *RAD VACATION REVIEW* . . .
A LOOK AT THE WINNERS AND LOSERS DURING OUR HOLIDAY BREAK.
THE BIGGEST WINNER HAD TO BE CINDY MARCUS, WHOSE DAD CHARTERED THE SPACE SHUTTLE TO RING IN THE NEW YEAR IN ORBIT.
HER VACATION WAS LITERALLY "OUT OF THIS WORLD"!
ROBBY D. WAS A CLOSE SECOND. HIS FAMILY SPENT CHRISTMAS WITH HIS HOLINESS THE POPE!
AHHH . . . ROME SWEET ROME!
MEANWHILE, ANDY WENT TO HAWAII WITH HIS TRUSTY MINION COLLIN. "THANK GOODNESS WE DIDN'T GO TO HAWAII!," SAID EVERYONE!
VACATION LOSERS INCLUDE JORDAN, DREW, MAURY, ALEX, RAMON, AND THAT CREEPY PUPPET GIRL.
ACTUALLY, WE WENT TO OUR VILLA IN TUSCANY.
I STAND CORRECTED.

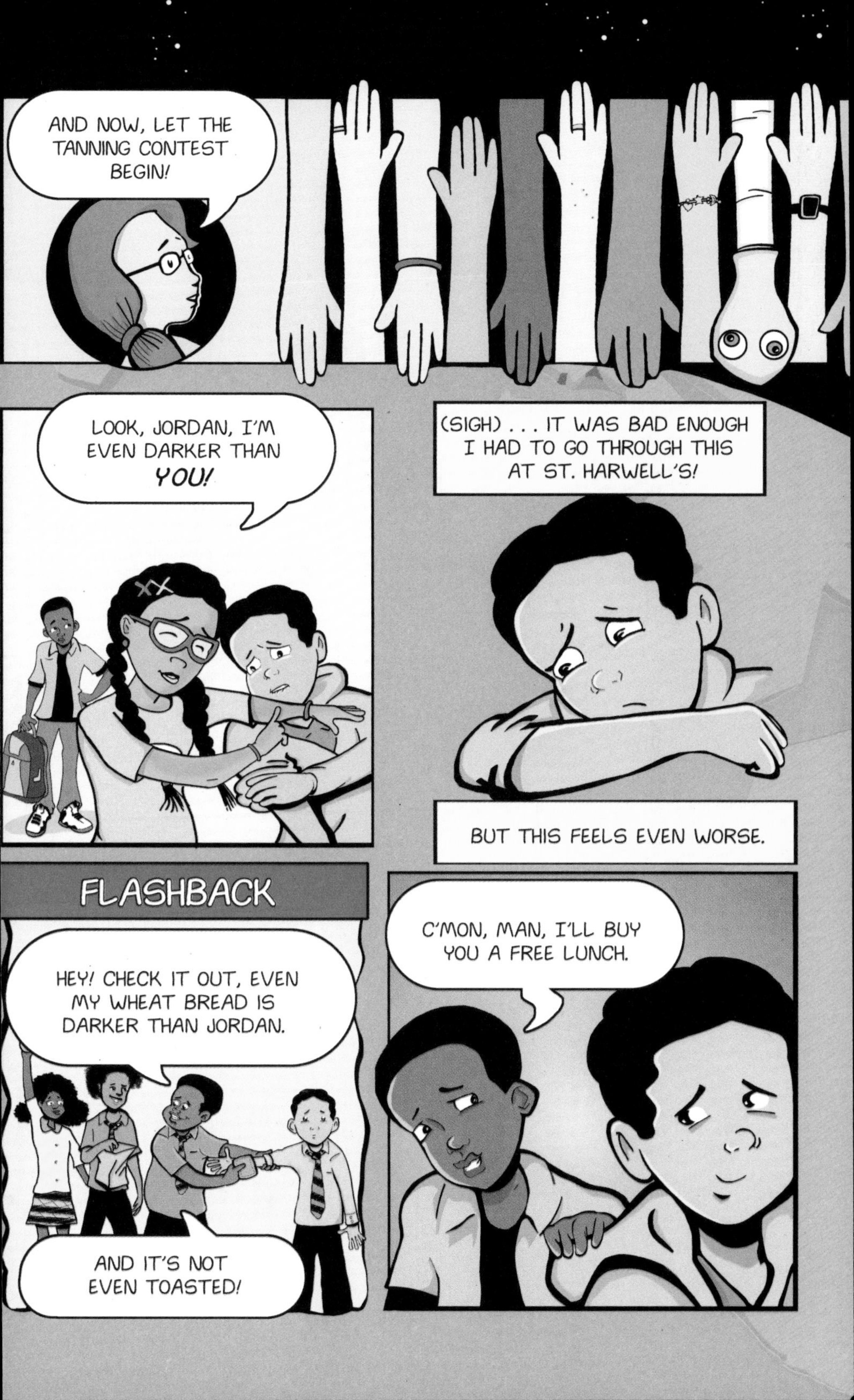
AND NOW, LET THE TANNING CONTEST BEGIN!
LOOK, JORDAN, I'M EVEN DARKER THAN YOU!
(SIGH) . . . IT WAS BAD ENOUGH I HAD TO GO THROUGH THIS AT ST. HARWELL'S!
BUT THIS FEELS EVEN WORSE.
FLASHBACK
HEY! CHECK IT OUT, EVEN MY WHEAT BREAD IS DARKER THAN JORDAN.
AND IT'S NOT EVEN TOASTED!
C'MON, MAN, I'LL BUY YOU A FREE LUNCH.

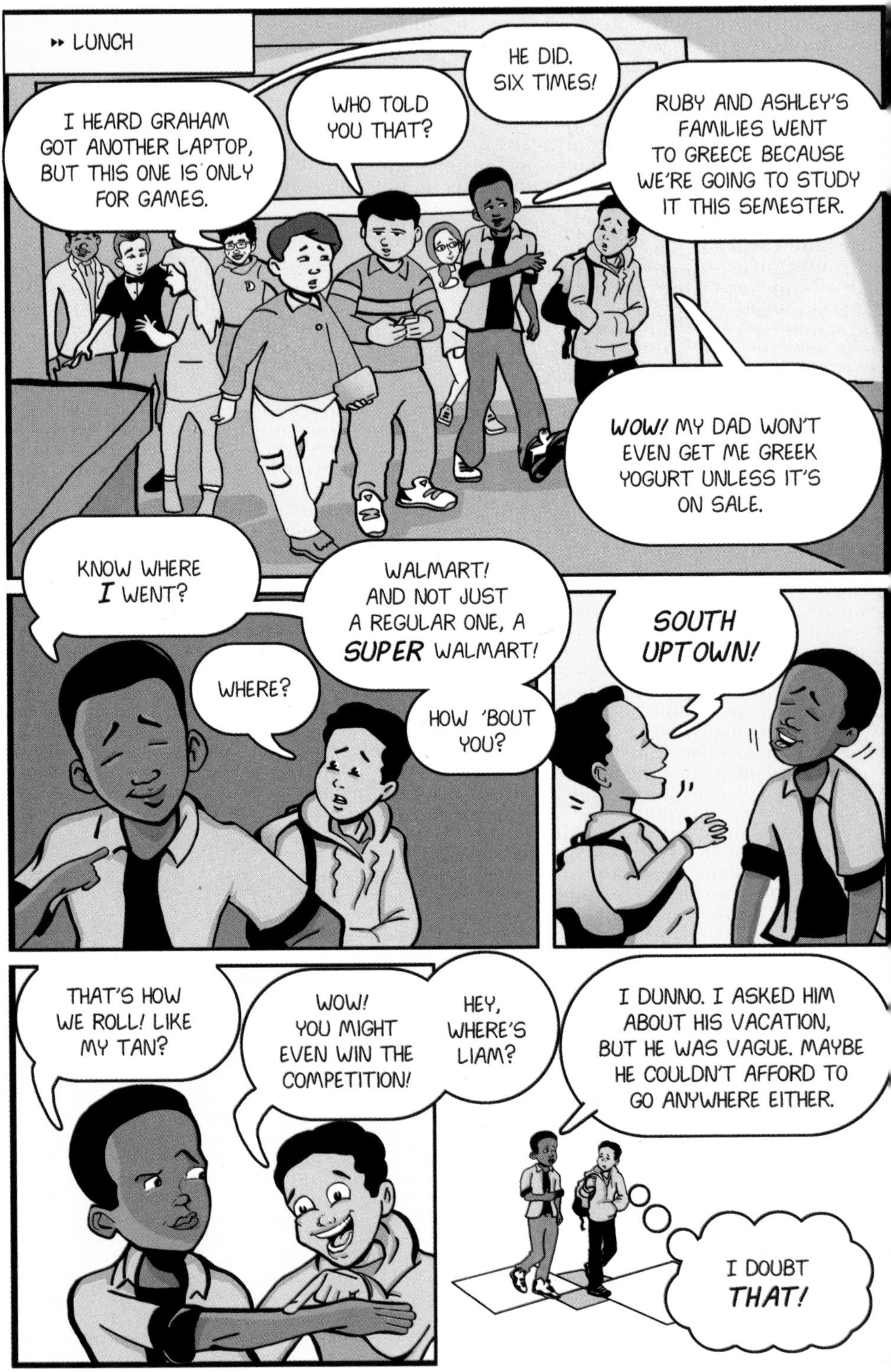
LUNCH
I HEARD GRAHAM GOT ANOTHER LAPTOP, BUT THIS ONE IS ONLY FOR GAMES.
WHO TOLD YOU THAT?
HE DID. SIX TIMES!
RUBY AND ASHLEY'S FAMILIES WENT TO GREECE BECAUSE WE'RE GOING TO STUDY IT THIS SEMESTER.
WOW! MY DAD WON'T EVEN GET ME GREEK YOGURT UNLESS IT'S ON SALE.
KNOW WHERE I WENT?
WHERE?
WALMART! AND NOT JUST A REGULAR ONE, A SUPER WALMART!
HOW 'BOUT YOU?
SOUTH UPTOWN!
THAT'S HOW WE ROLL! LIKE MY TAN?
WOW! YOU MIGHT EVEN WIN THE COMPETITION!
HEY, WHERE'S LIAM?
I DUNNO. I ASKED HIM ABOUT HIS VACATION, BUT HE WAS VAGUE. MAYBE HE COULDN'T AFFORD TO GO ANYWHERE EITHER.
I DOUBT THAT!

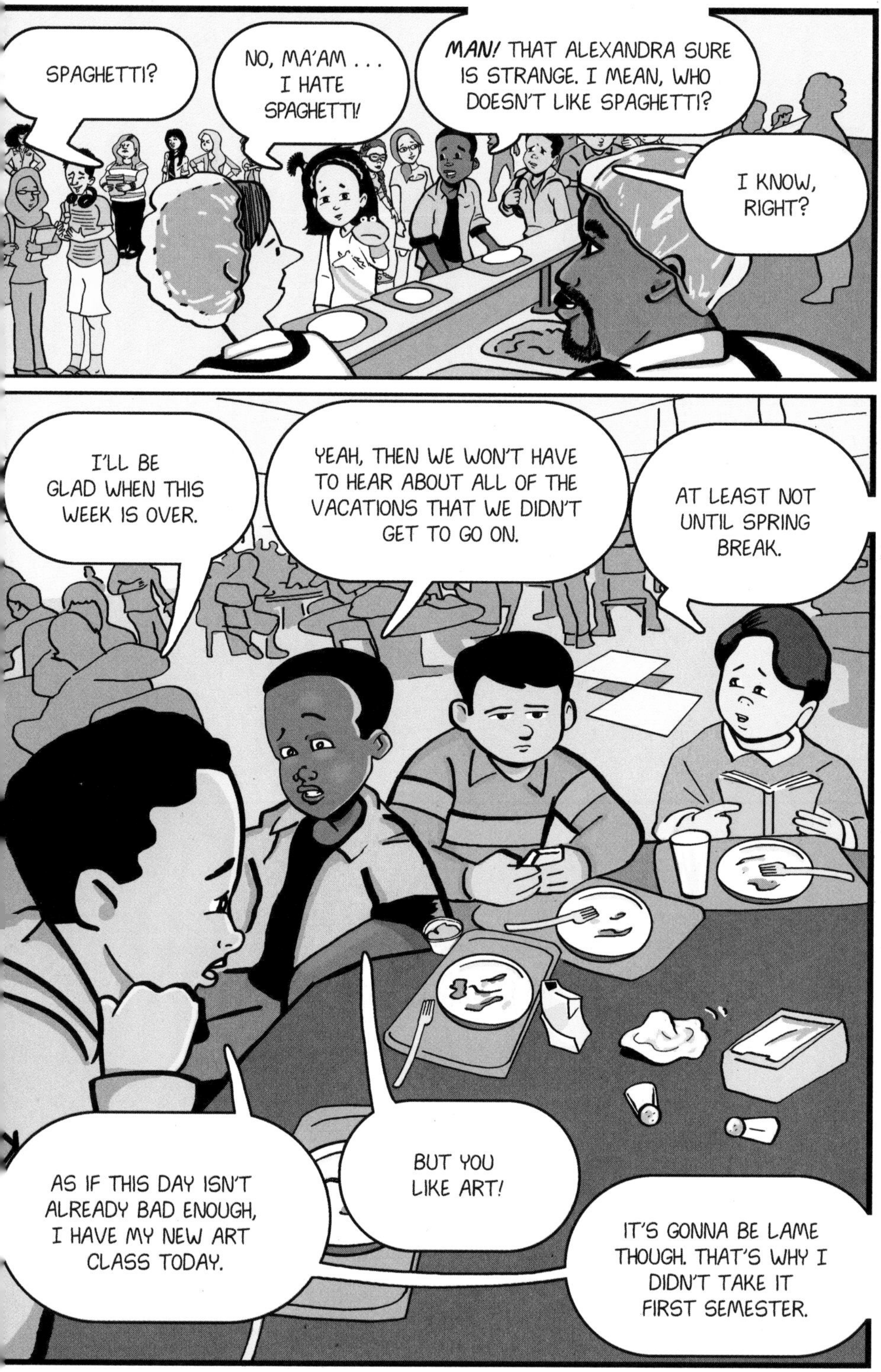
SPAGHETTI?
NO, MA'AM . . . I HATE SPAGHETTI!
MAN! THAT ALEXANDRA SURE IS STRANGE. I MEAN, WHO DOESN'T LIKE SPAGHETTI?
I KNOW, RIGHT?
I'LL BE GLAD WHEN THIS WEEK IS OVER.
YEAH, THEN WE WON'T HAVE TO HEAR ABOUT ALL OF THE VACATIONS THAT WE DIDN'T GET TO GO ON.
AT LEAST NOT UNTIL SPRING BREAK.
AS IF THIS DAY ISN'T ALREADY BAD ENOUGH, I HAVE MY NEW ART CLASS TODAY.
BUT YOU LIKE ART!
IT'S GONNA BE LAME THOUGH. THAT'S WHY I DIDN'T TAKE IT FIRST SEMESTER.

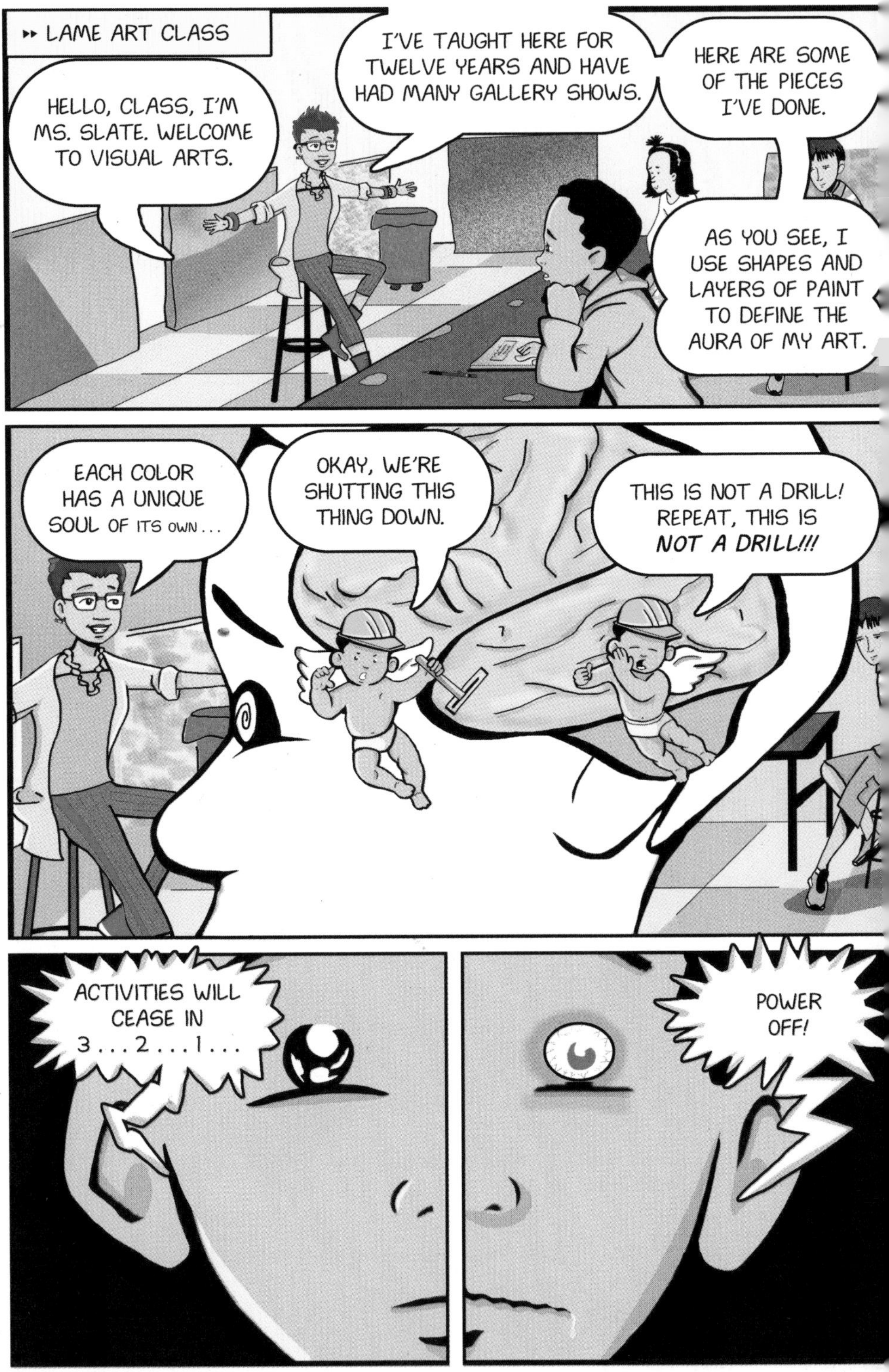

LAME ART CLASS
HELLO, CLASS, I'M MS. SLATE. WELCOME TO VISUAL ARTS.
I'VE TAUGHT HERE FOR TWELVE YEARS AND HAVE HAD MANY GALLERY SHOWS.
HERE ARE SOME OF THE PIECES I'VE DONE.
AS YOU SEE, I USE SHAPES AND LAYERS OF PAINT TO DEFINE THE AURA OF MY ART.
EACH COLOR HAS A UNIQUE SOUL OF ITS OWN . . .
OKAY, WE'RE SHUTTING THIS THING DOWN.
THIS IS NOT A DRILL! REPEAT, THIS IS NOT A DRILL!!!
ACTIVITIES WILL CEASE IN 3 . . . 2 . . . 1 . . .
POWER OFF!

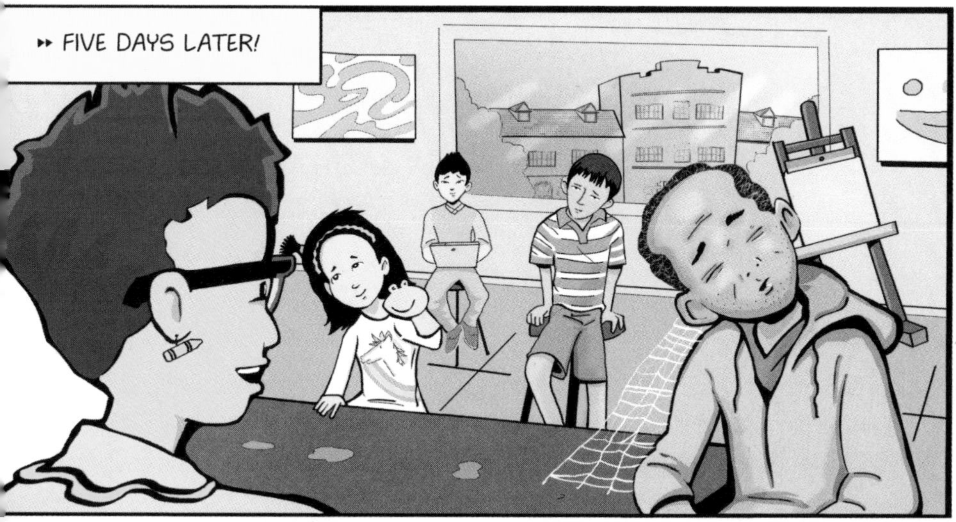
▸▸ FIVE DAYS LATER!

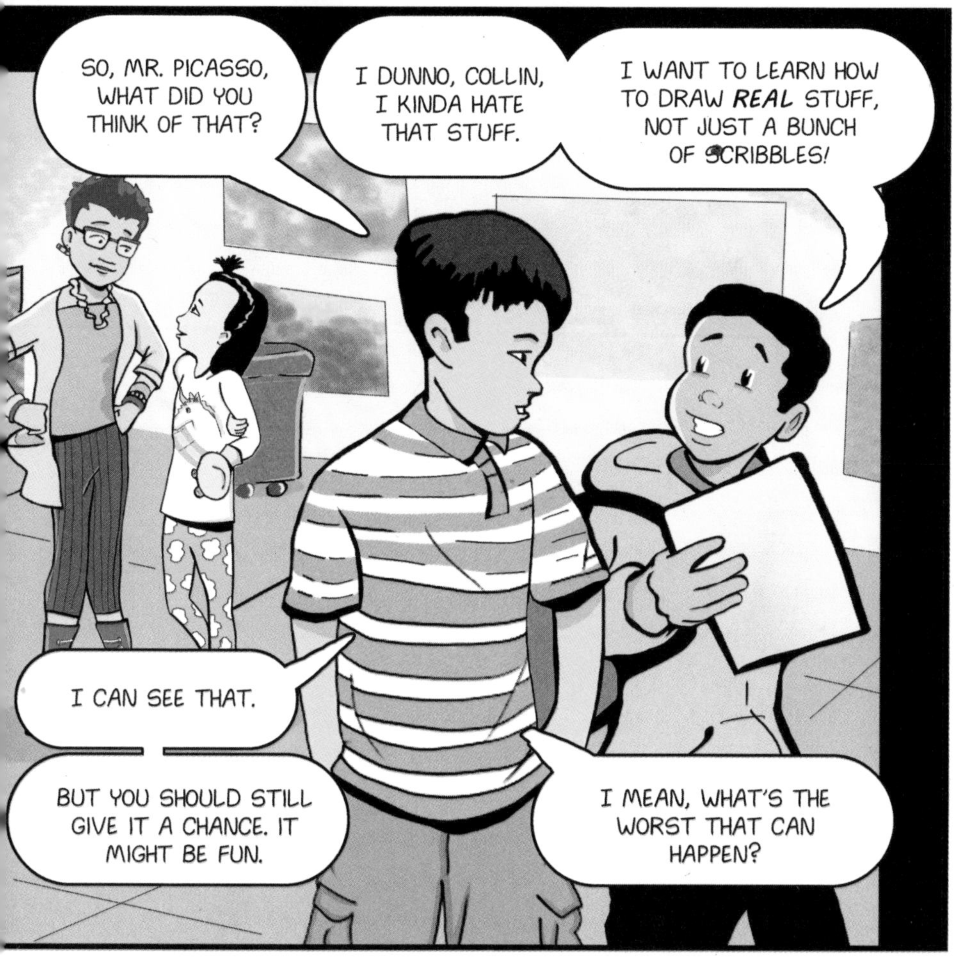
SO, MR. PICASSO, WHAT DID YOU THINK OF THAT?
I DUNNO, COLLIN, I KINDA HATE THAT STUFF.
I WANT TO LEARN HOW TO DRAW ***REAL*** STUFF, NOT JUST A BUNCH OF SCRIBBLES!
I CAN SEE THAT.
BUT YOU SHOULD STILL GIVE IT A CHANCE. IT MIGHT BE FUN.
I MEAN, WHAT'S THE WORST THAT CAN HAPPEN?

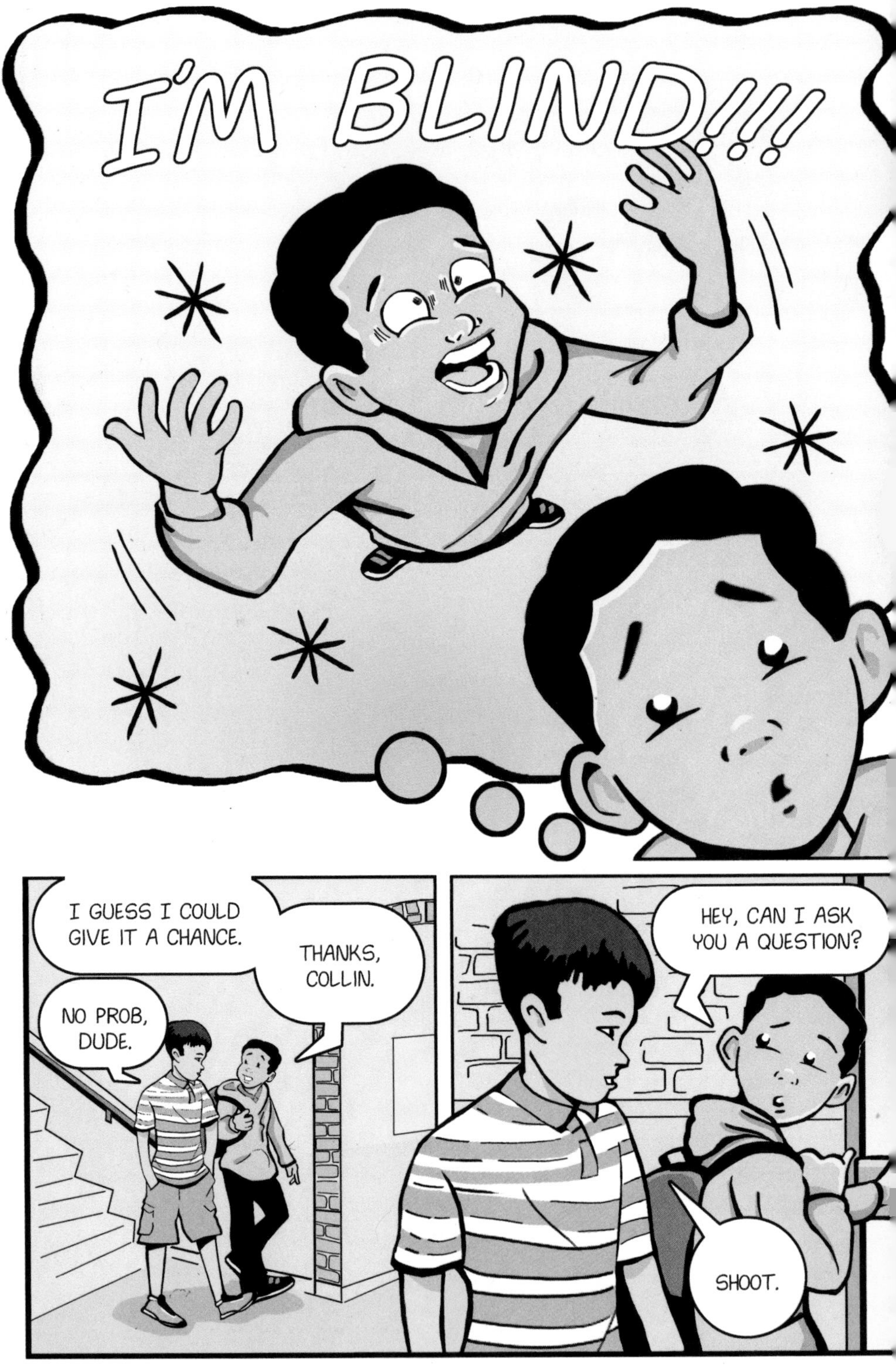
I'M BLIND!!!!
I GUESS I COULD GIVE IT A CHANCE.
THANKS, COLLIN.
NO PROB, DUDE.
HEY, CAN I ASK YOU A QUESTION?
SHOOT.

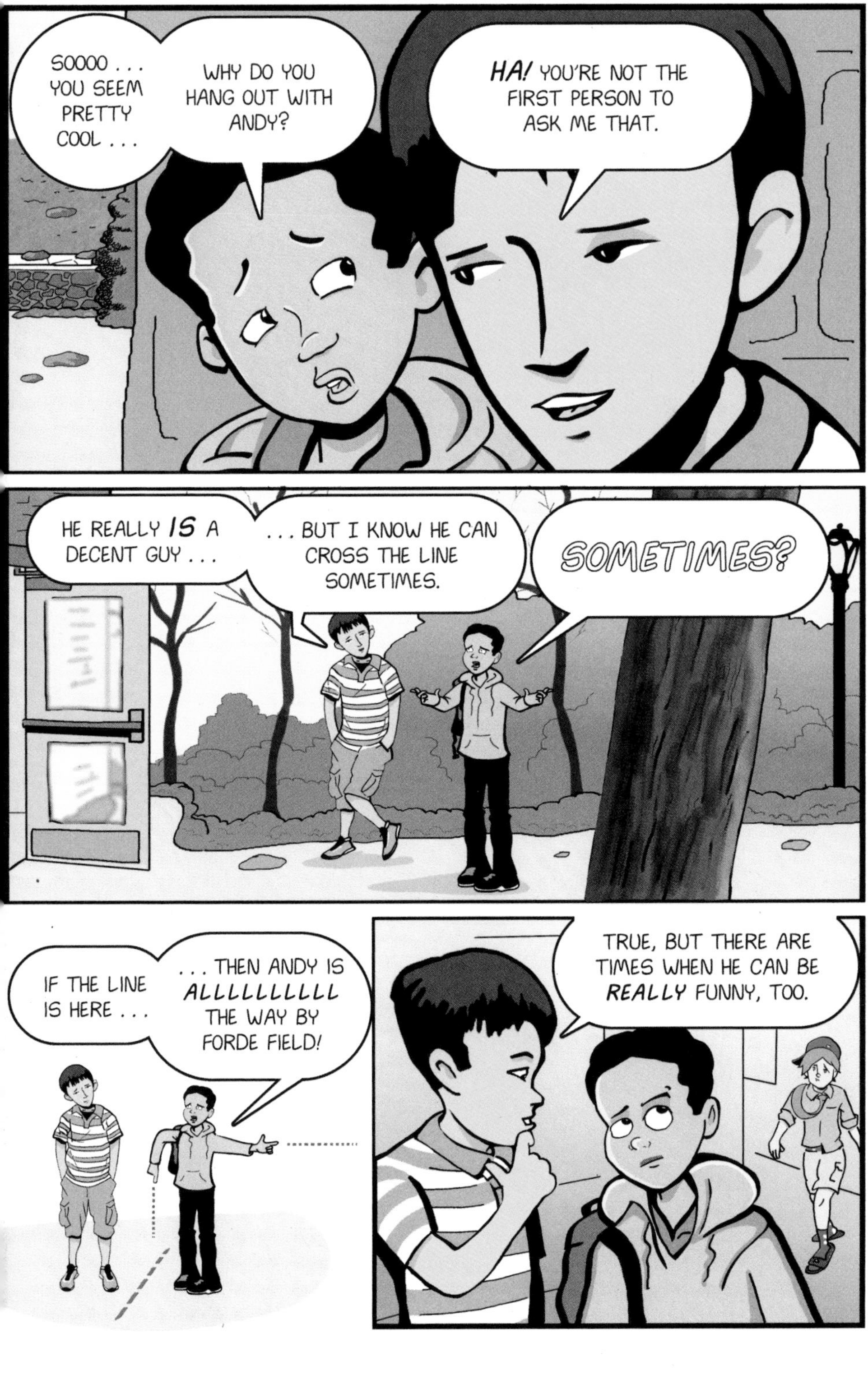
SOOOO . . . YOU SEEM PRETTY COOL . . .
WHY DO YOU HANG OUT WITH ANDY?
HA! YOU'RE NOT THE FIRST PERSON TO ASK ME THAT.
HE REALLY IS A DECENT GUY . . .
. . . BUT I KNOW HE CAN CROSS THE LINE SOMETIMES.
SOMETIMES?
IF THE LINE IS HERE . . .
. . . THEN ANDY IS ALLLLLLLLLL THE WAY BY FORDE FIELD!
TRUE, BUT THERE ARE TIMES WHEN HE CAN BE REALLY FUNNY, TOO.

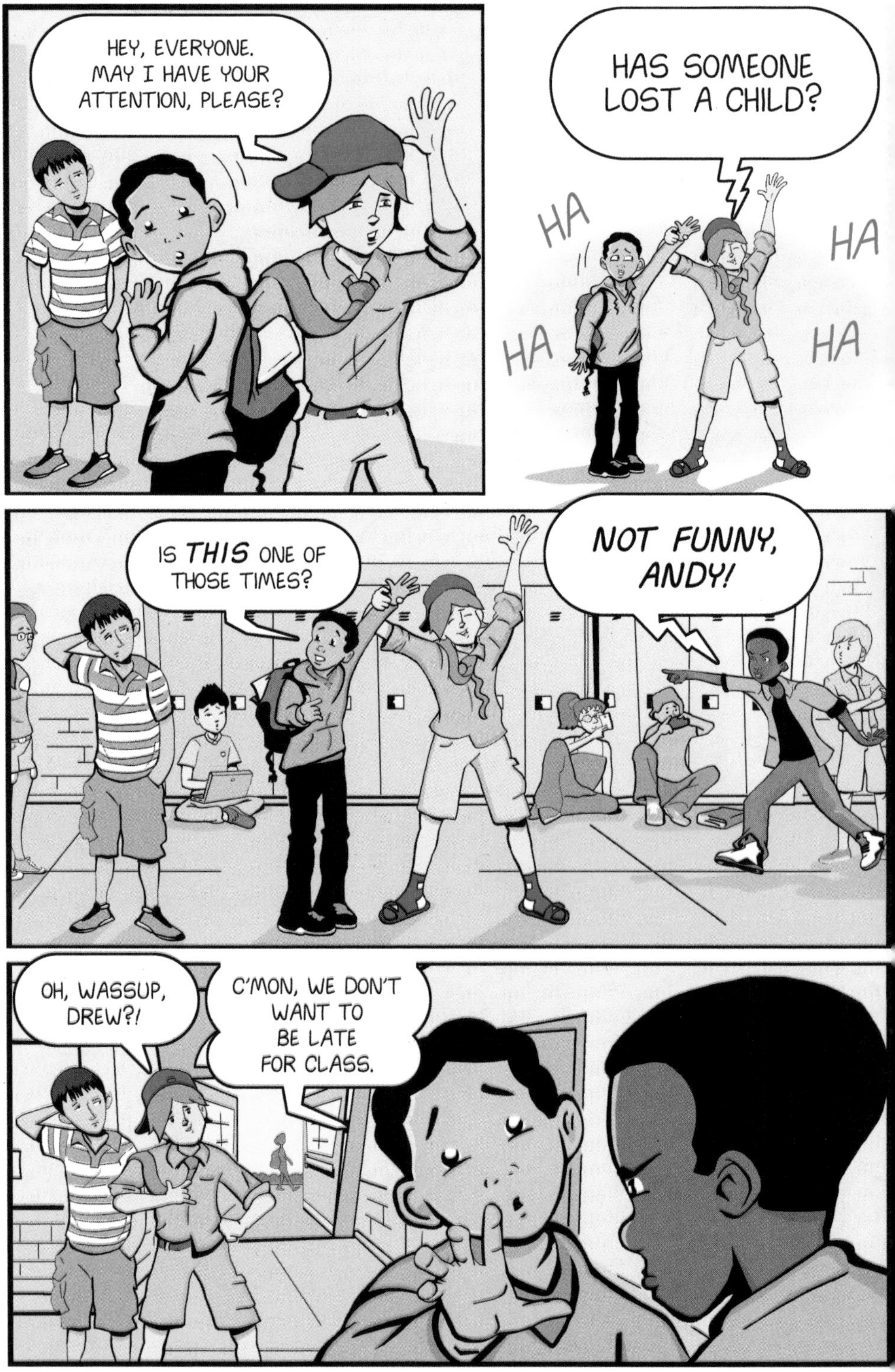
HEY, EVERYONE. MAY I HAVE YOUR ATTENTION, PLEASE?
HAS SOMEONE LOST A CHILD?
HA
HA
HA
HA
IS *THIS* ONE OF THOSE TIMES?
NOT FUNNY, ANDY!
OH, WASSUP, DREW?!
C'MON, WE DON'T WANT TO BE LATE FOR CLASS.

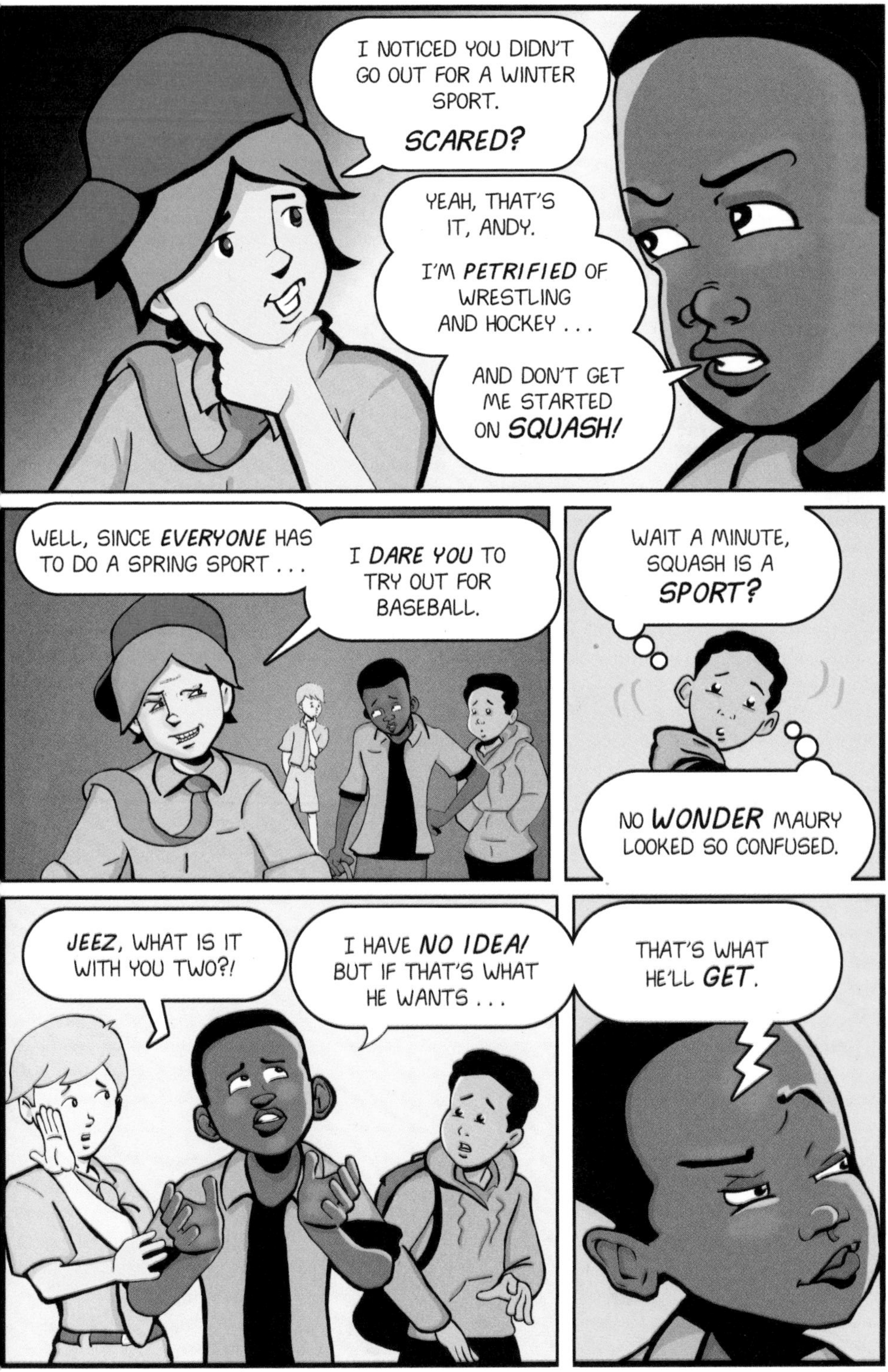
I NOTICED YOU DIDN'T GO OUT FOR A WINTER SPORT.
SCARED?
YEAH, THAT'S IT, ANDY.
I'M PETRIFIED OF WRESTLING AND HOCKEY . . .
AND DON'T GET ME STARTED ON SQUASH!
WELL, SINCE EVERYONE HAS TO DO A SPRING SPORT . . .
I DARE YOU TO TRY OUT FOR BASEBALL.
WAIT A MINUTE, SQUASH IS A SPORT?
NO WONDER MAURY LOOKED SO CONFUSED.
JEEZ, WHAT IS IT WITH YOU TWO?!
I HAVE NO IDEA! BUT IF THAT'S WHAT HE WANTS . . .
THAT'S WHAT HE'LL GET.

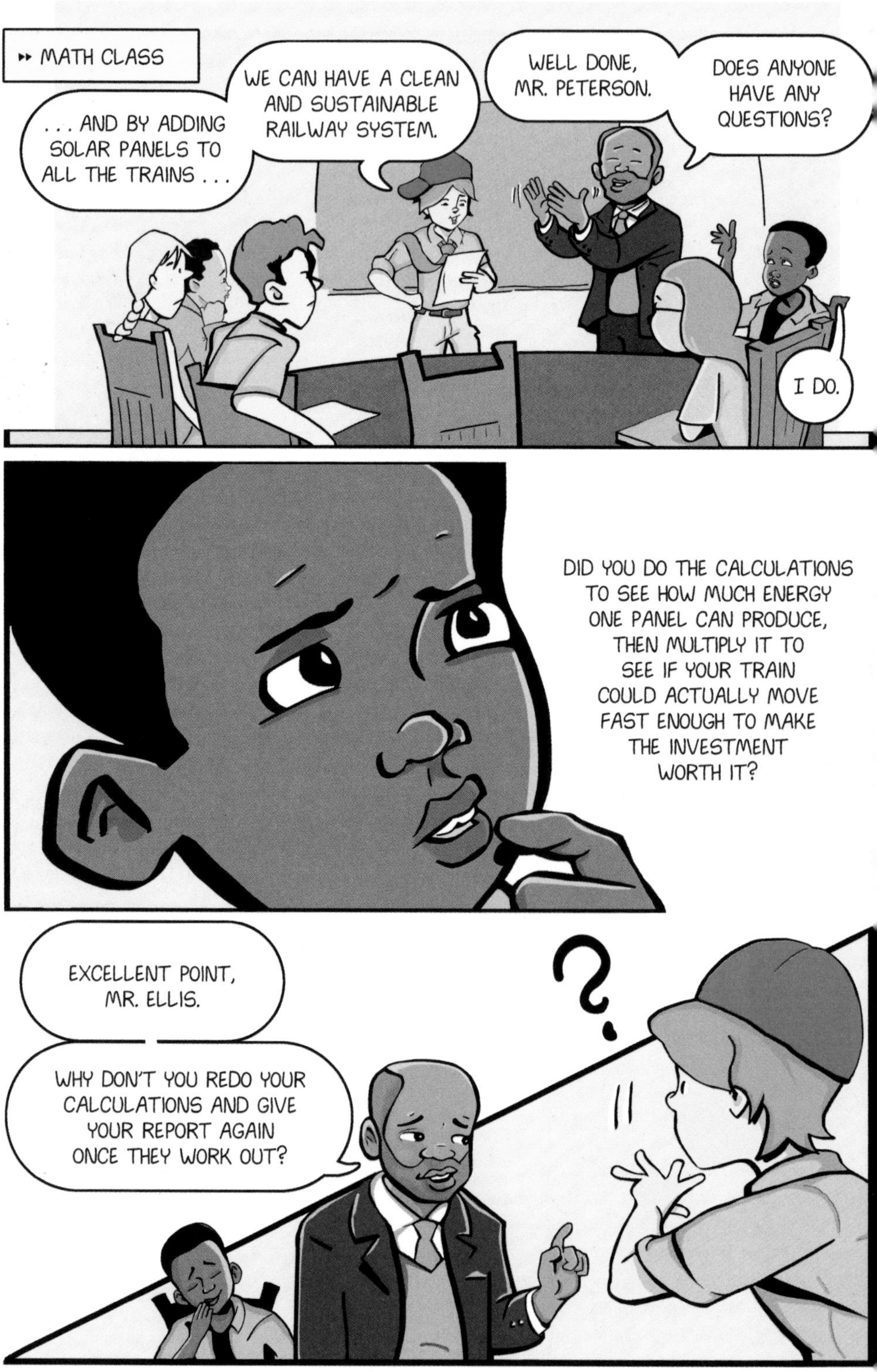
MATH CLASS
. . . AND BY ADDING SOLAR PANELS TO ALL THE TRAINS . . .
WE CAN HAVE A CLEAN AND SUSTAINABLE RAILWAY SYSTEM.
WELL DONE, MR. PETERSON.
DOES ANYONE HAVE ANY QUESTIONS?
I DO.
DID YOU DO THE CALCULATIONS TO SEE HOW MUCH ENERGY ONE PANEL CAN PRODUCE, THEN MULTIPLY IT TO SEE IF YOUR TRAIN COULD ACTUALLY MOVE FAST ENOUGH TO MAKE THE INVESTMENT WORTH IT?
EXCELLENT POINT, MR. ELLIS.
WHY DON'T YOU REDO YOUR CALCULATIONS AND GIVE YOUR REPORT AGAIN ONCE THEY WORK OUT?
?

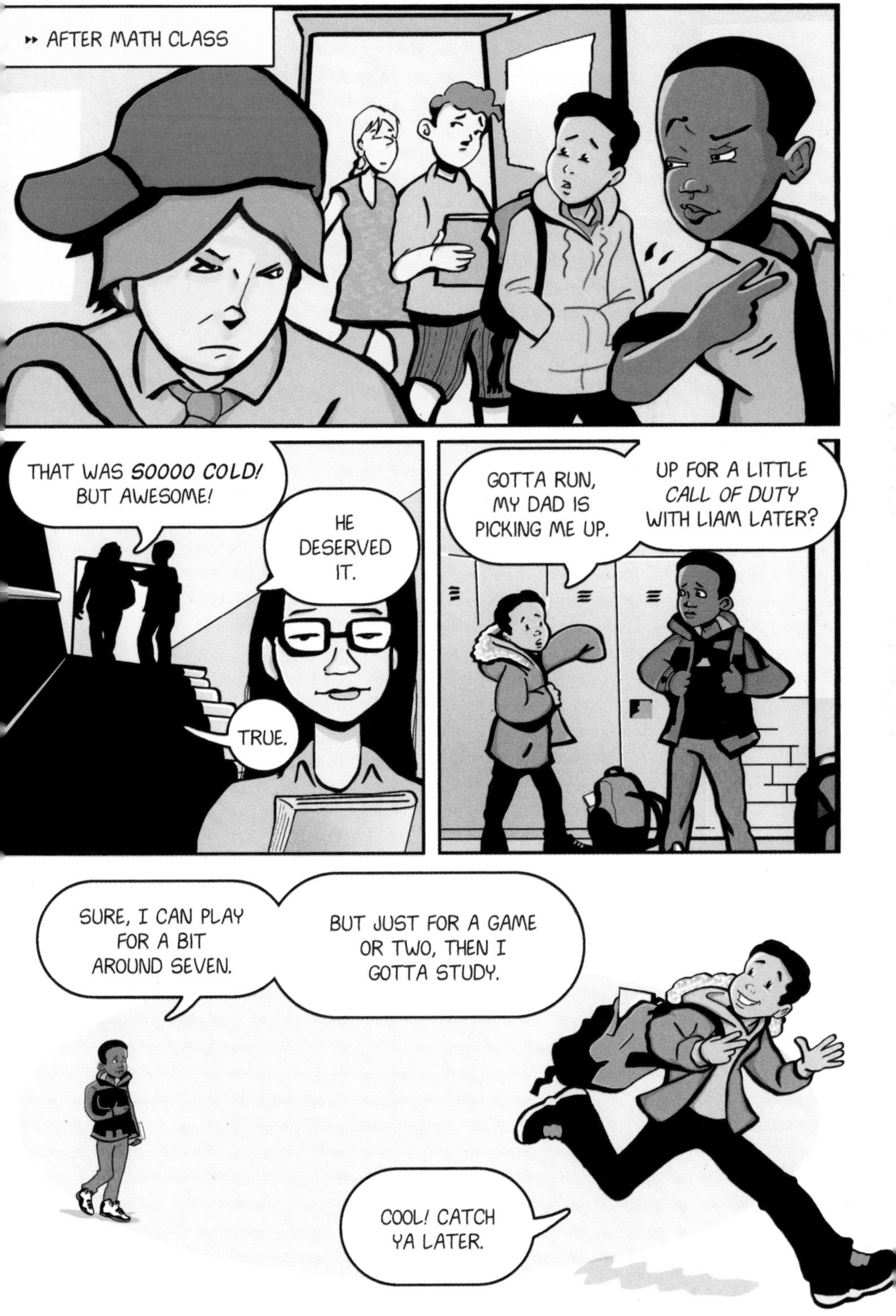
AFTER MATH CLASS
THAT WAS SOOOO COLD! BUT AWESOME!
HE DESERVED IT.
TRUE.
GOTTA RUN, MY DAD IS PICKING ME UP.
UP FOR A LITTLE CALL OF DUTY WITH LIAM LATER?
SURE, I CAN PLAY FOR A BIT AROUND SEVEN.
BUT JUST FOR A GAME OR TWO, THEN I GOTTA STUDY.
COOL! CATCH YA LATER.

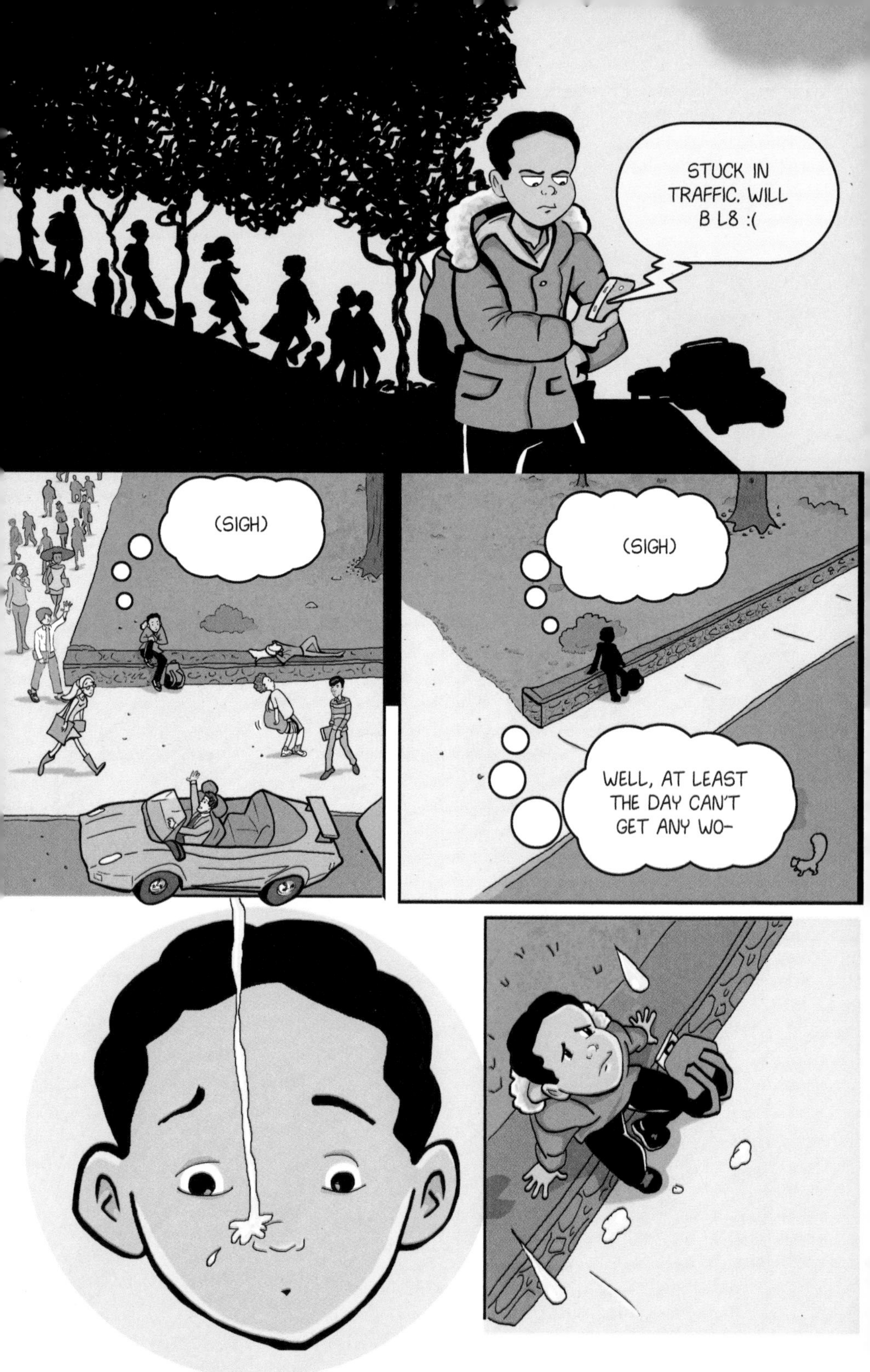
STUCK IN TRAFFIC. WILL B L8 :(
(SIGH)
(SIGH)
WELL, AT LEAST THE DAY CAN'T GET ANY WO-

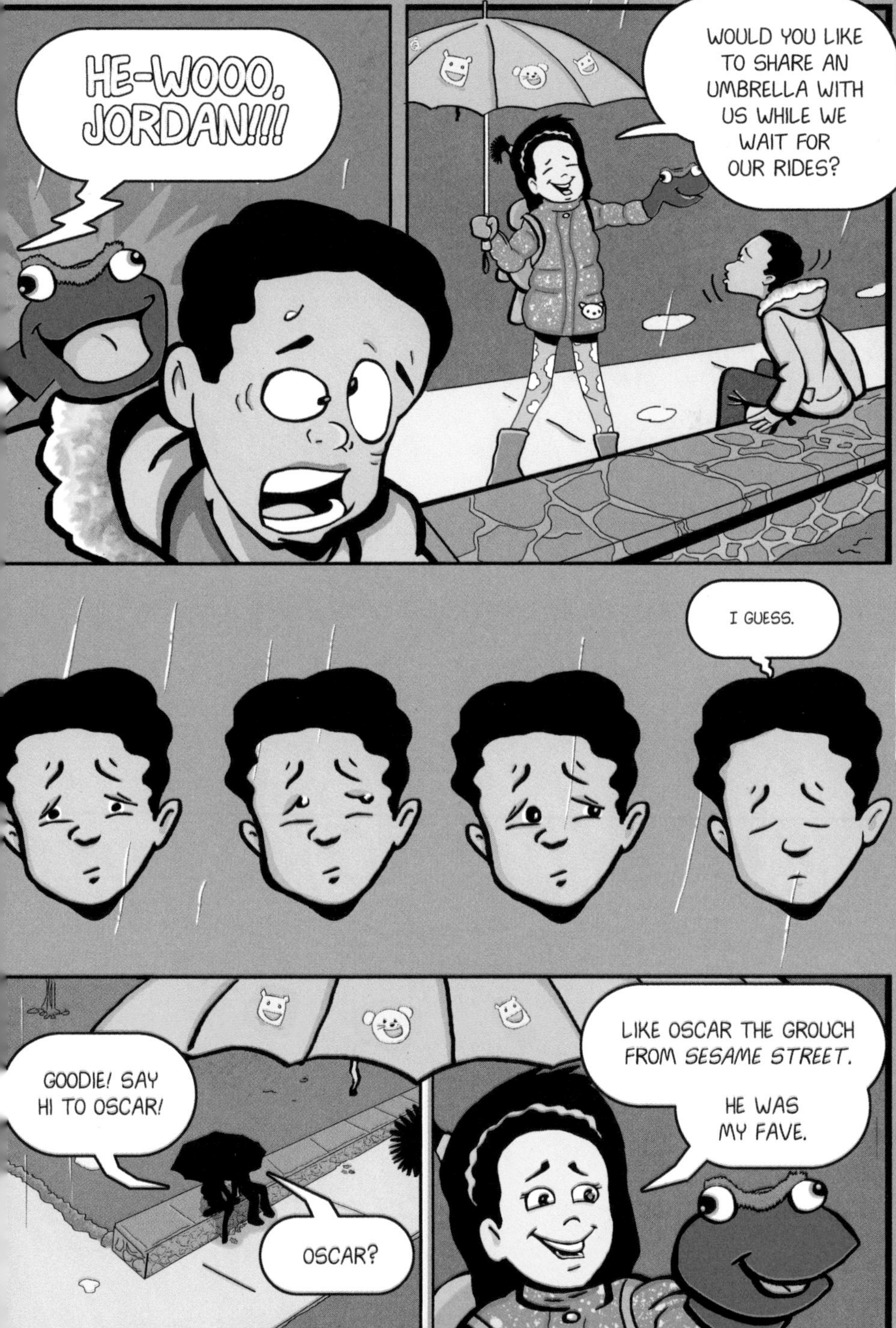

HE-WOOO, JORDAN!!!
WOULD YOU LIKE TO SHARE AN UMBRELLA WITH US WHILE WE WAIT FOR OUR RIDES?
I GUESS.
GOODIE! SAY HI TO OSCAR!
OSCAR?
LIKE OSCAR THE GROUCH FROM *SESAME STREET*.
HE WAS MY FAVE.

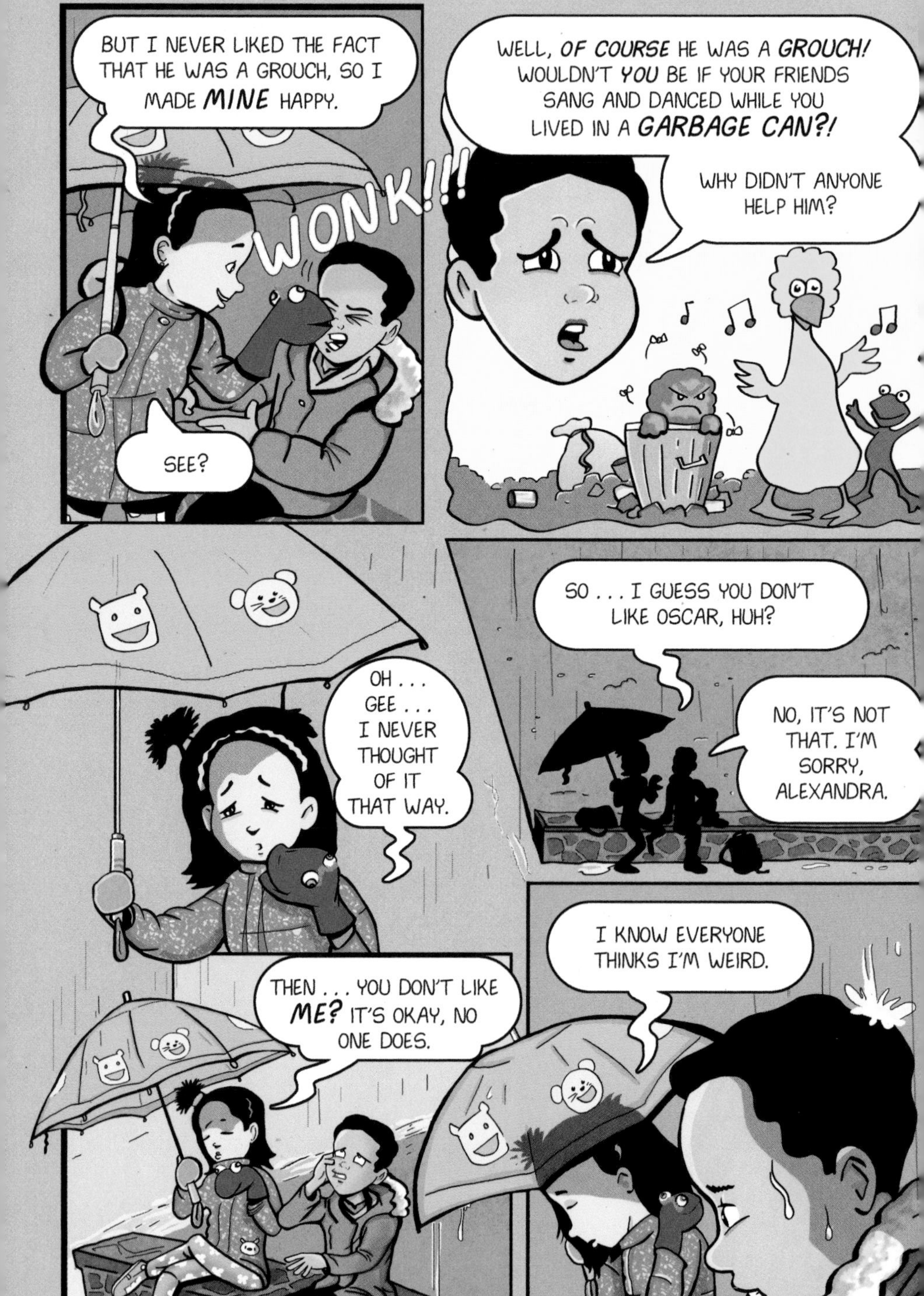
BUT I NEVER LIKED THE FACT THAT HE WAS A GROUCH, SO I MADE MINE HAPPY.
WONK!!!
SEE?
WELL, OF COURSE HE WAS A GROUCH! WOULDN'T YOU BE IF YOUR FRIENDS SANG AND DANCED WHILE YOU LIVED IN A GARBAGE CAN?!
WHY DIDN'T ANYONE HELP HIM?
OH . . . GEE . . . I NEVER THOUGHT OF IT THAT WAY.
SO . . . I GUESS YOU DON'T LIKE OSCAR, HUH?
NO, IT'S NOT THAT. I'M SORRY, ALEXANDRA.
THEN . . . YOU DON'T LIKE ME? IT'S OKAY, NO ONE DOES.
I KNOW EVERYONE THINKS I'M WEIRD.

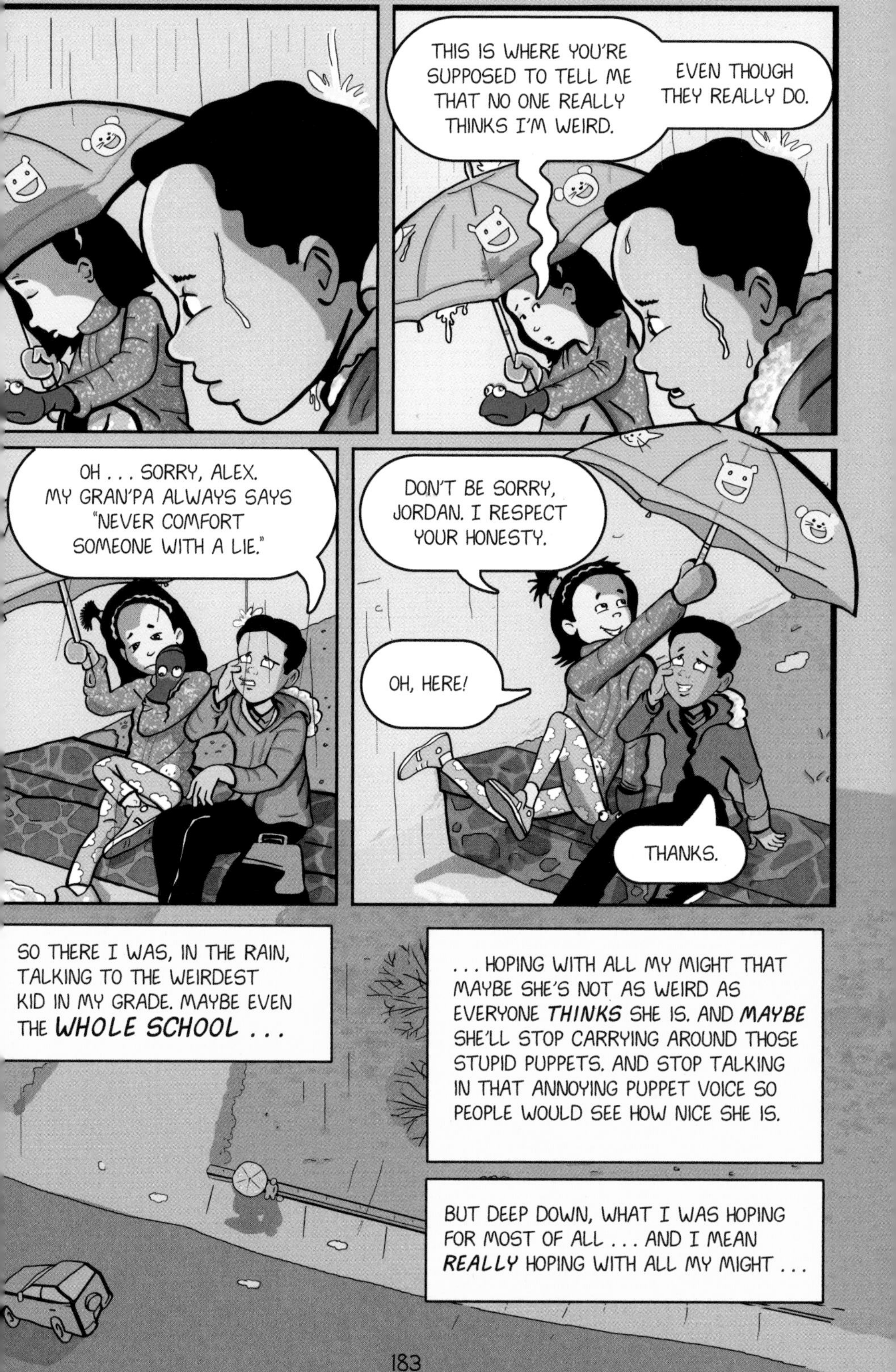

THIS IS WHERE YOU'RE SUPPOSED TO TELL ME THAT NO ONE REALLY THINKS I'M WEIRD.
EVEN THOUGH THEY REALLY DO.
OH . . . SORRY, ALEX. MY GRAN'PA ALWAYS SAYS "NEVER COMFORT SOMEONE WITH A LIE."
DON'T BE SORRY, JORDAN. I RESPECT YOUR HONESTY.
OH, HERE!
THANKS.
SO THERE I WAS, IN THE RAIN, TALKING TO THE WEIRDEST KID IN MY GRADE. MAYBE EVEN THE WHOLE SCHOOL . . .
. . . HOPING WITH ALL MY MIGHT THAT MAYBE SHE'S NOT AS WEIRD AS EVERYONE THINKS SHE IS. AND MAYBE SHE'LL STOP CARRYING AROUND THOSE STUPID PUPPETS. AND STOP TALKING IN THAT ANNOYING PUPPET VOICE SO PEOPLE WOULD SEE HOW NICE SHE IS.
BUT DEEP DOWN, WHAT I WAS HOPING FOR MOST OF ALL . . . AND I MEAN REALLY HOPING WITH ALL MY MIGHT . . .

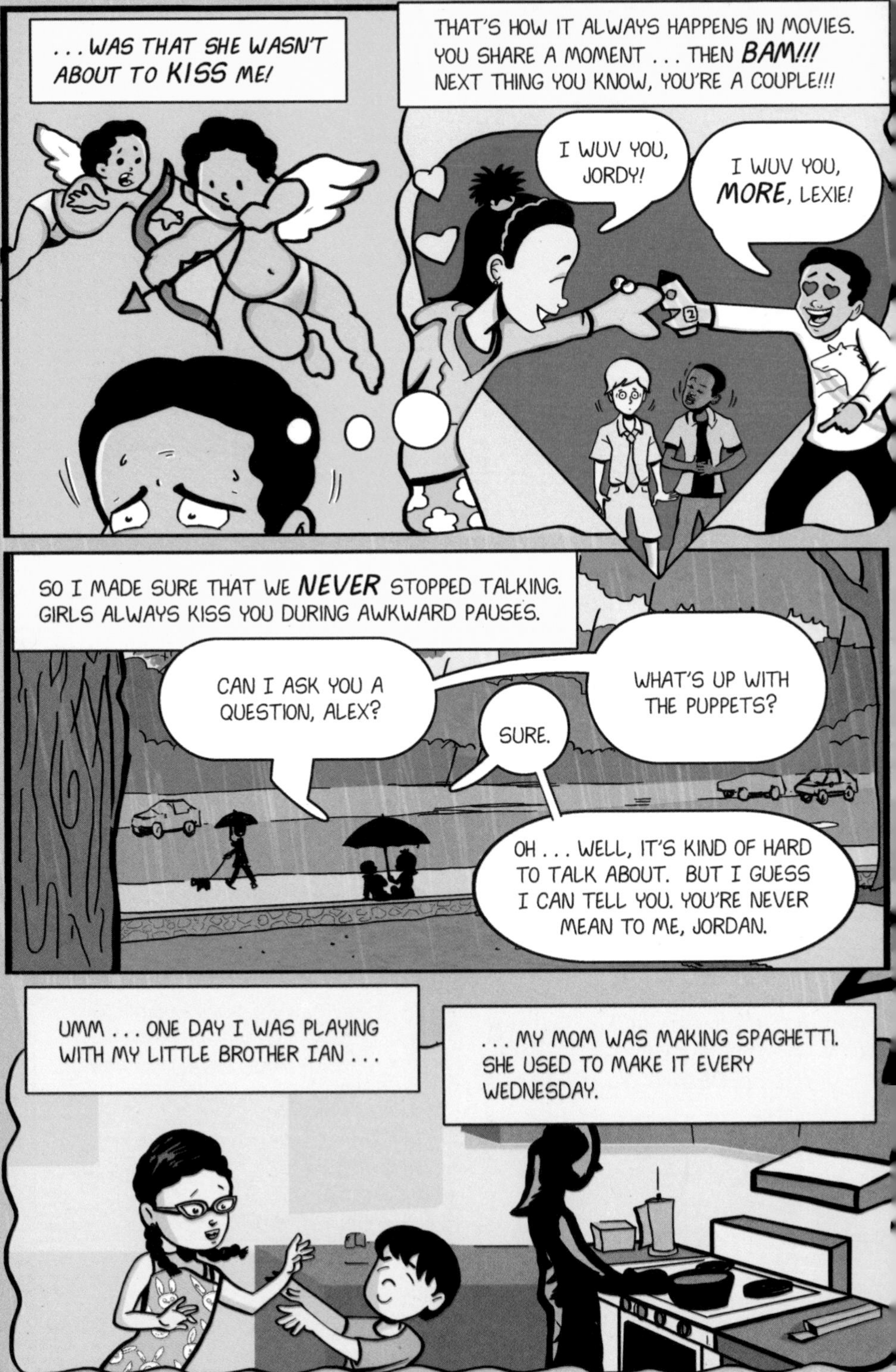

. . . WAS THAT SHE WASN'T ABOUT TO KISS ME!
THAT'S HOW IT ALWAYS HAPPENS IN MOVIES. YOU SHARE A MOMENT . . . THEN BAM!!! NEXT THING YOU KNOW, YOU'RE A COUPLE!!!
I WUV YOU, JORDY!
I WUV YOU, MORE, LEXIE!
SO I MADE SURE THAT WE NEVER STOPPED TALKING. GIRLS ALWAYS KISS YOU DURING AWKWARD PAUSES.
CAN I ASK YOU A QUESTION, ALEX?
SURE.
WHAT'S UP WITH THE PUPPETS?
OH . . . WELL, IT'S KIND OF HARD TO TALK ABOUT. BUT I GUESS I CAN TELL YOU. YOU'RE NEVER MEAN TO ME, JORDAN.
UMM . . . ONE DAY I WAS PLAYING WITH MY LITTLE BROTHER IAN . . .
. . . MY MOM WAS MAKING SPAGHETTI. SHE USED TO MAKE IT EVERY WEDNESDAY.

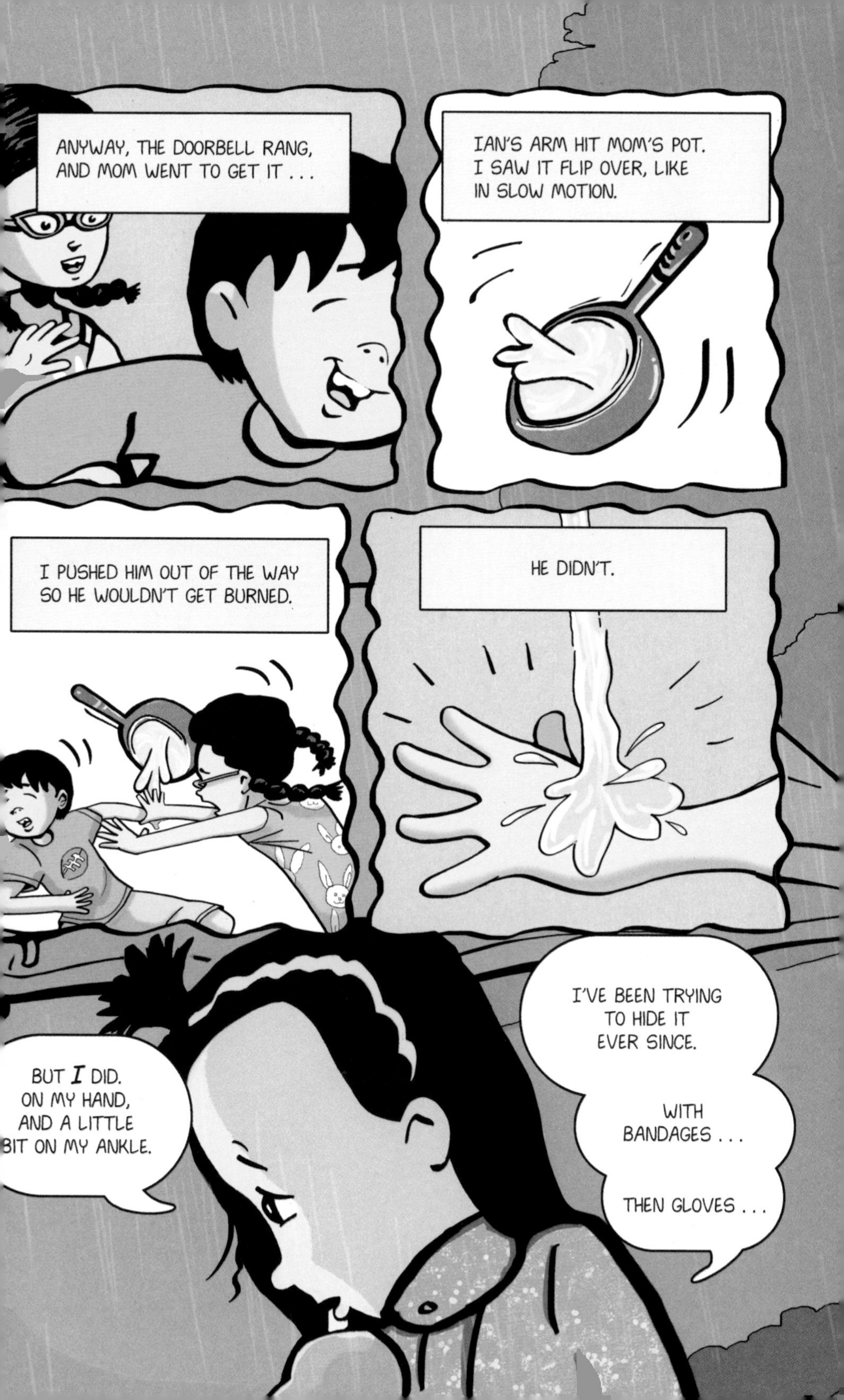
ANYWAY, THE DOORBELL RANG, AND MOM WENT TO GET IT . . .
IAN'S ARM HIT MOM'S POT. I SAW IT FLIP OVER, LIKE IN SLOW MOTION.
I PUSHED HIM OUT OF THE WAY SO HE WOULDN'T GET BURNED.
HE DIDN'T.
BUT *I* DID. ON MY HAND, AND A LITTLE BIT ON MY ANKLE.
I'VE BEEN TRYING TO HIDE IT EVER SINCE.
WITH BANDAGES . . .
THEN GLOVES . . .

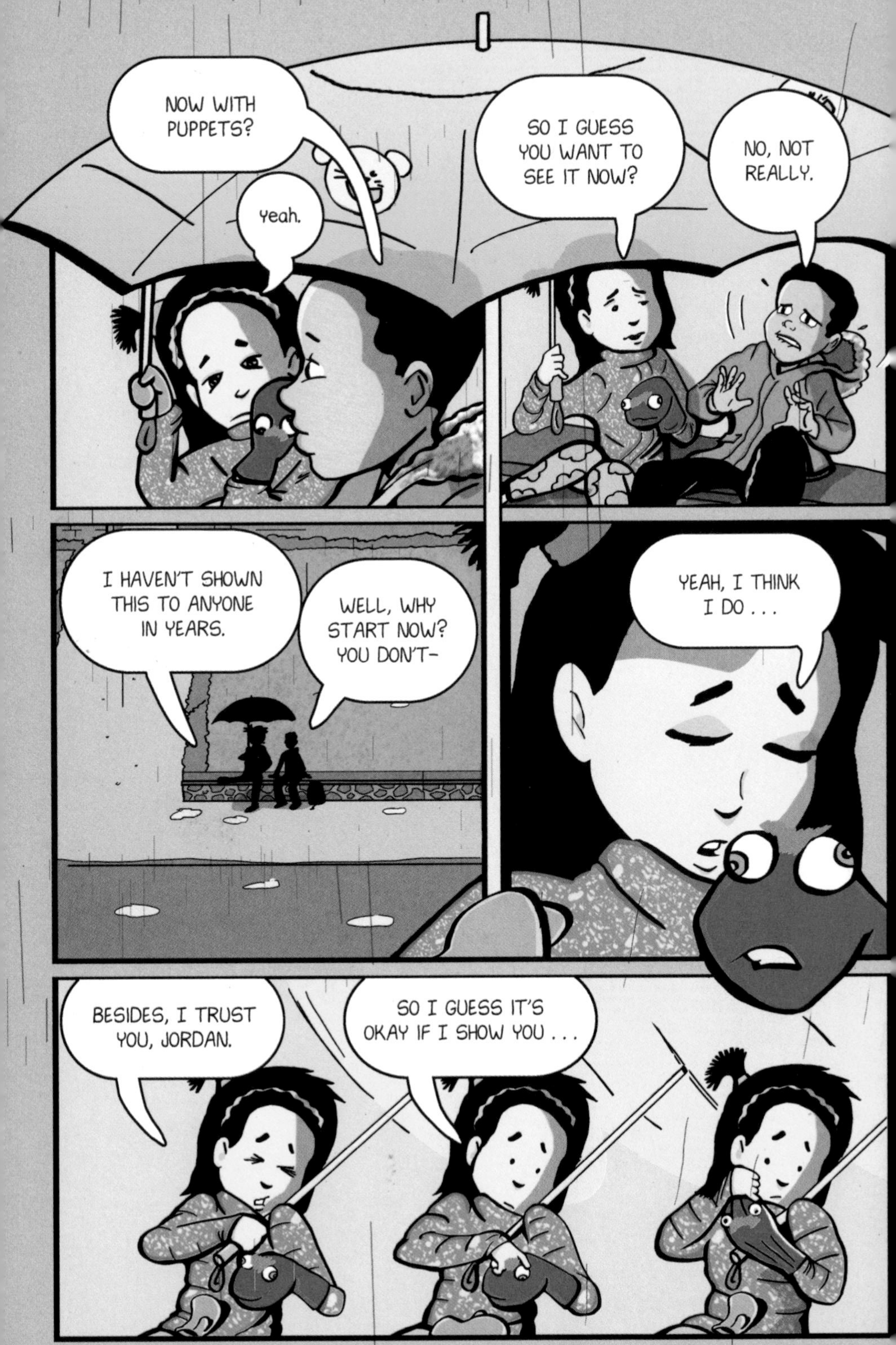
NOW WITH PUPPETS?
yeah.
SO I GUESS YOU WANT TO SEE IT NOW?
NO, NOT REALLY.
I HAVEN'T SHOWN THIS TO ANYONE IN YEARS.
WELL, WHY START NOW? YOU DON'T-
YEAH, I THINK I DO . . .
BESIDES, I TRUST YOU, JORDAN.
SO I GUESS IT'S OKAY IF I SHOW YOU . . .

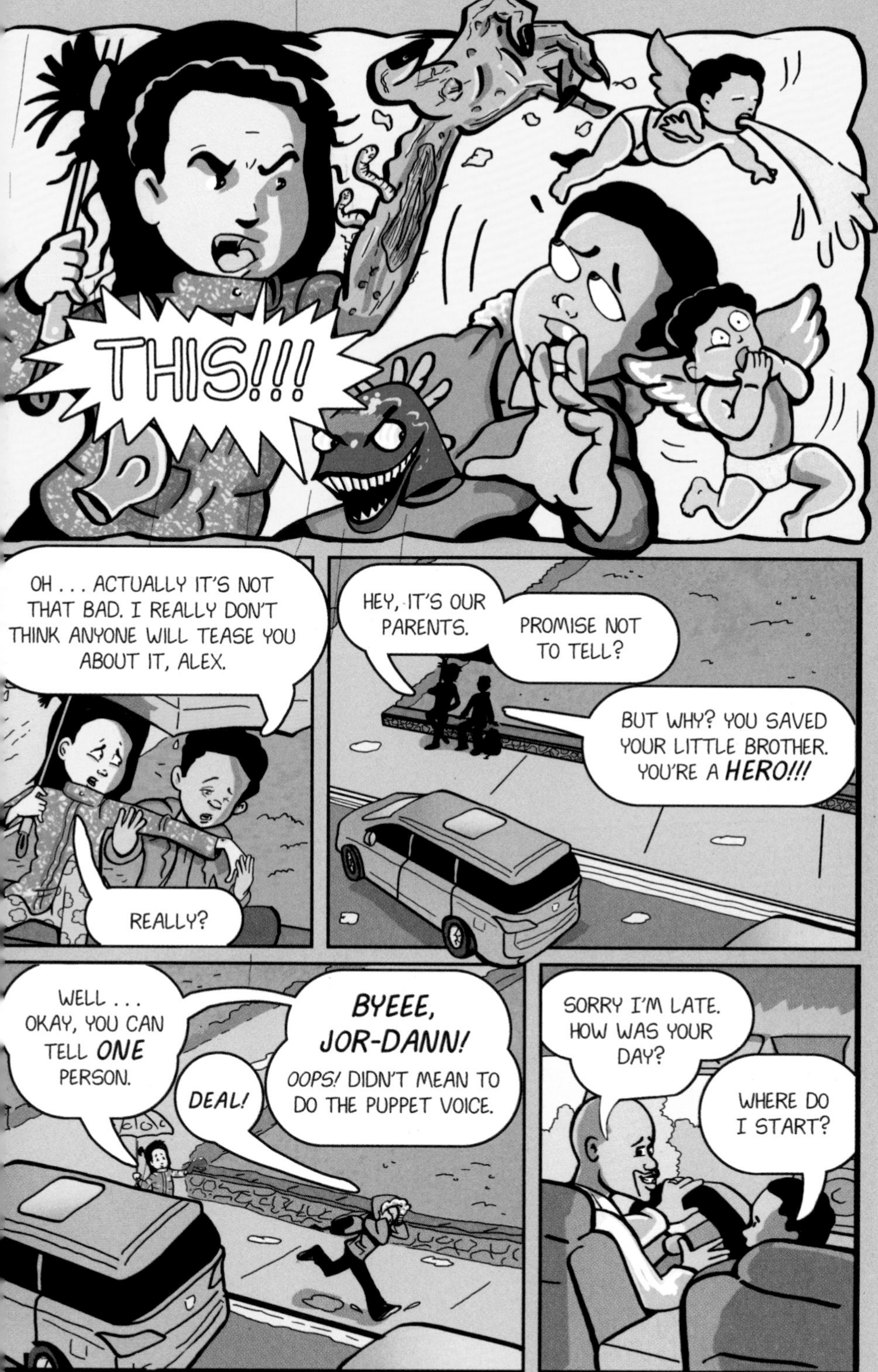
THIS!!!
OH . . . ACTUALLY IT'S NOT THAT BAD. I REALLY DON'T THINK ANYONE WILL TEASE YOU ABOUT IT, ALEX.
REALLY?
HEY, IT'S OUR PARENTS.
PROMISE NOT TO TELL?
BUT WHY? YOU SAVED YOUR LITTLE BROTHER. YOU'RE A ***HERO!!!***
WELL . . . OKAY, YOU CAN TELL ***ONE*** PERSON.
DEAL!
BYEEE, JOR-DANN!
OOPS! DIDN'T MEAN TO DO THE PUPPET VOICE.
SORRY I'M LATE. HOW WAS YOUR DAY?
WHERE DO I START?

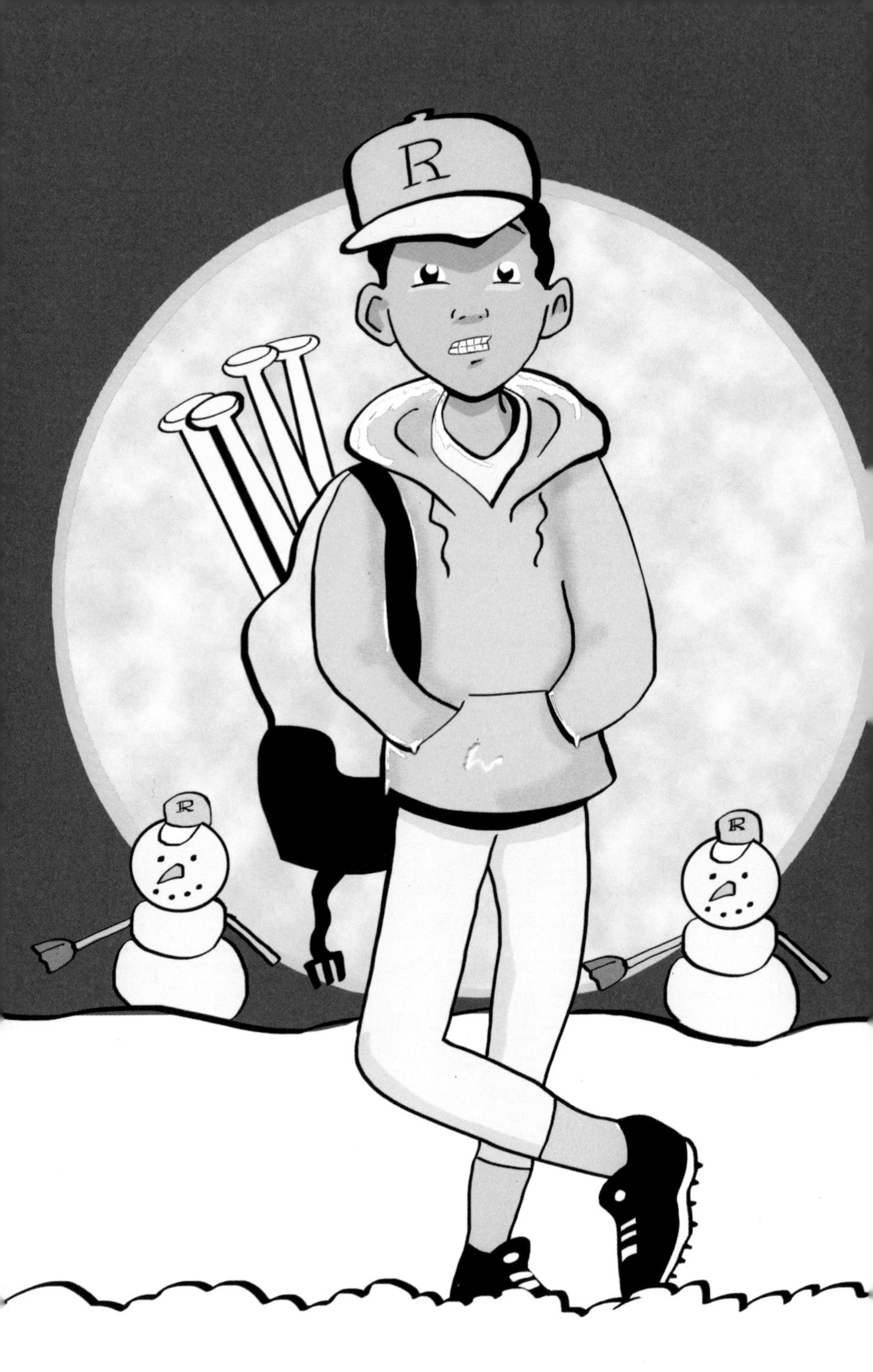

CHAPTER 11

FIELD OF SCREAMS

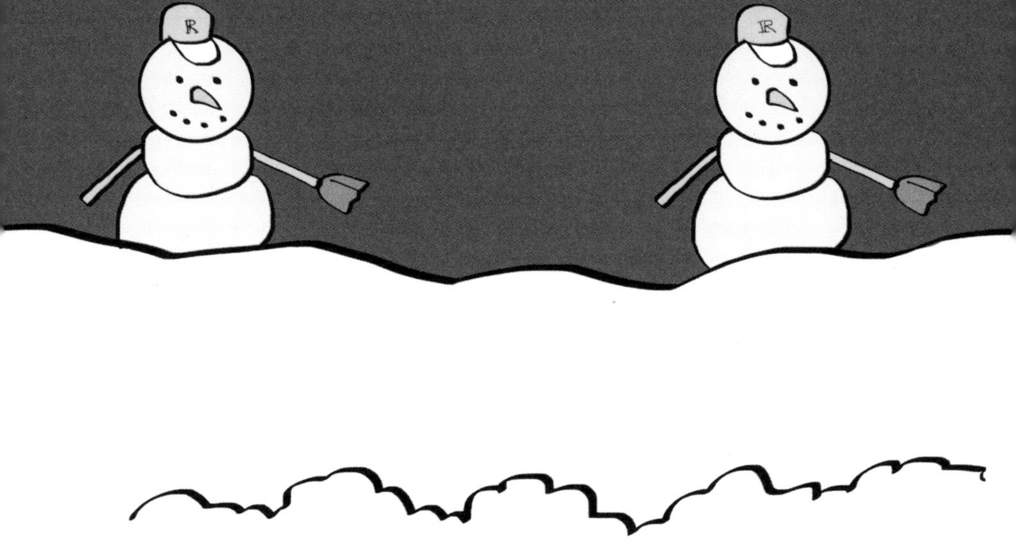

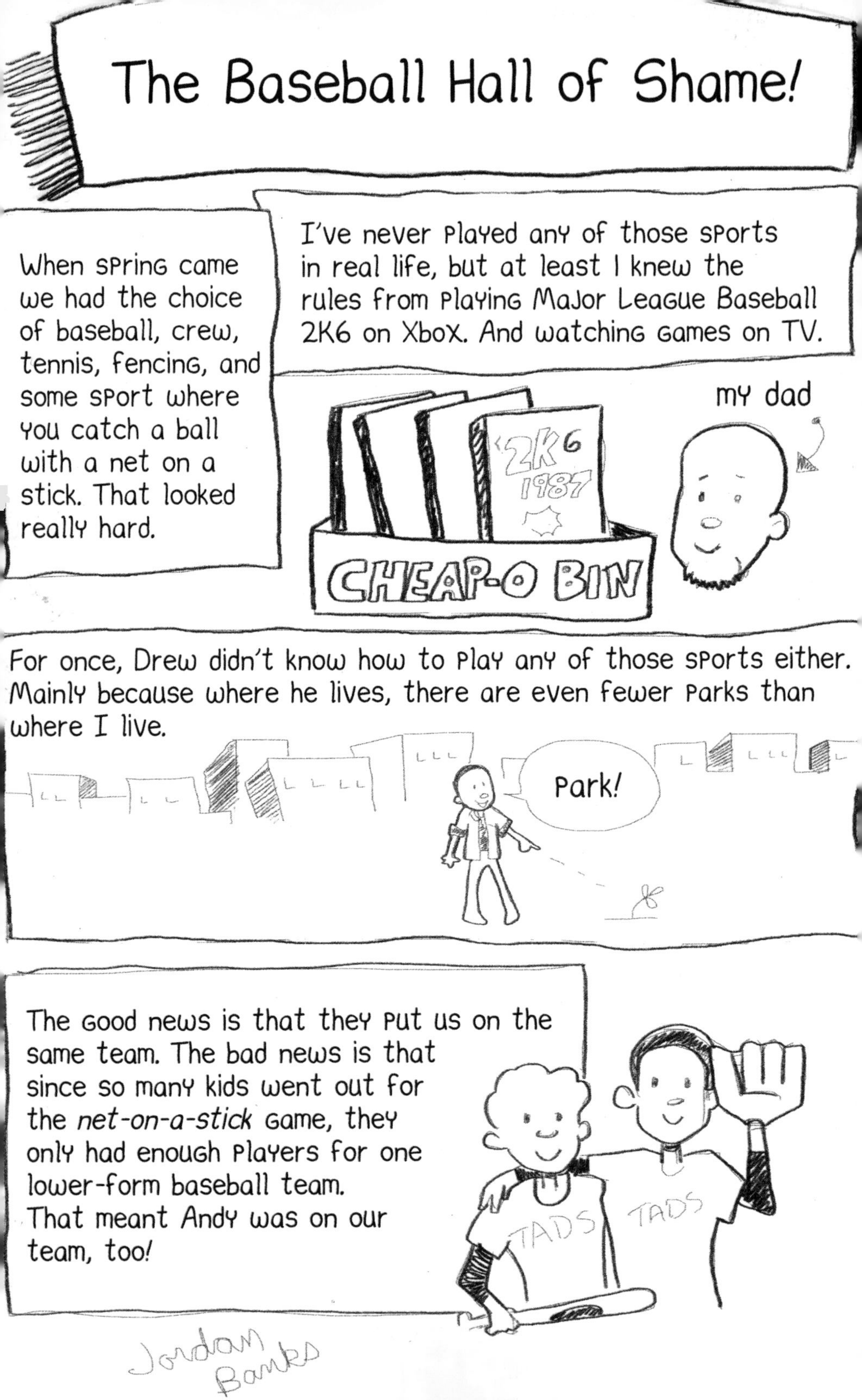
The Baseball Hall of Shame!
When spring came we had the choice of baseball, crew, tennis, fencing, and some sport where you catch a ball with a net on a stick. That looked really hard.
I've never played any of those sports in real life, but at least I knew the rules from playing Major League Baseball 2K6 on Xbox. And watching games on TV.
2K6
1987
CHEAP-O BIN
my dad
For once, Drew didn't know how to play any of those sports either. Mainly because where he lives, there are even fewer parks than where I live.
Park!
The good news is that they put us on the same team. The bad news is that since so many kids went out for the *net-on-a-stick* game, they only had enough players for one lower-form baseball team. That meant Andy was on our team, too!
TADS
TADS
Jordan Banks

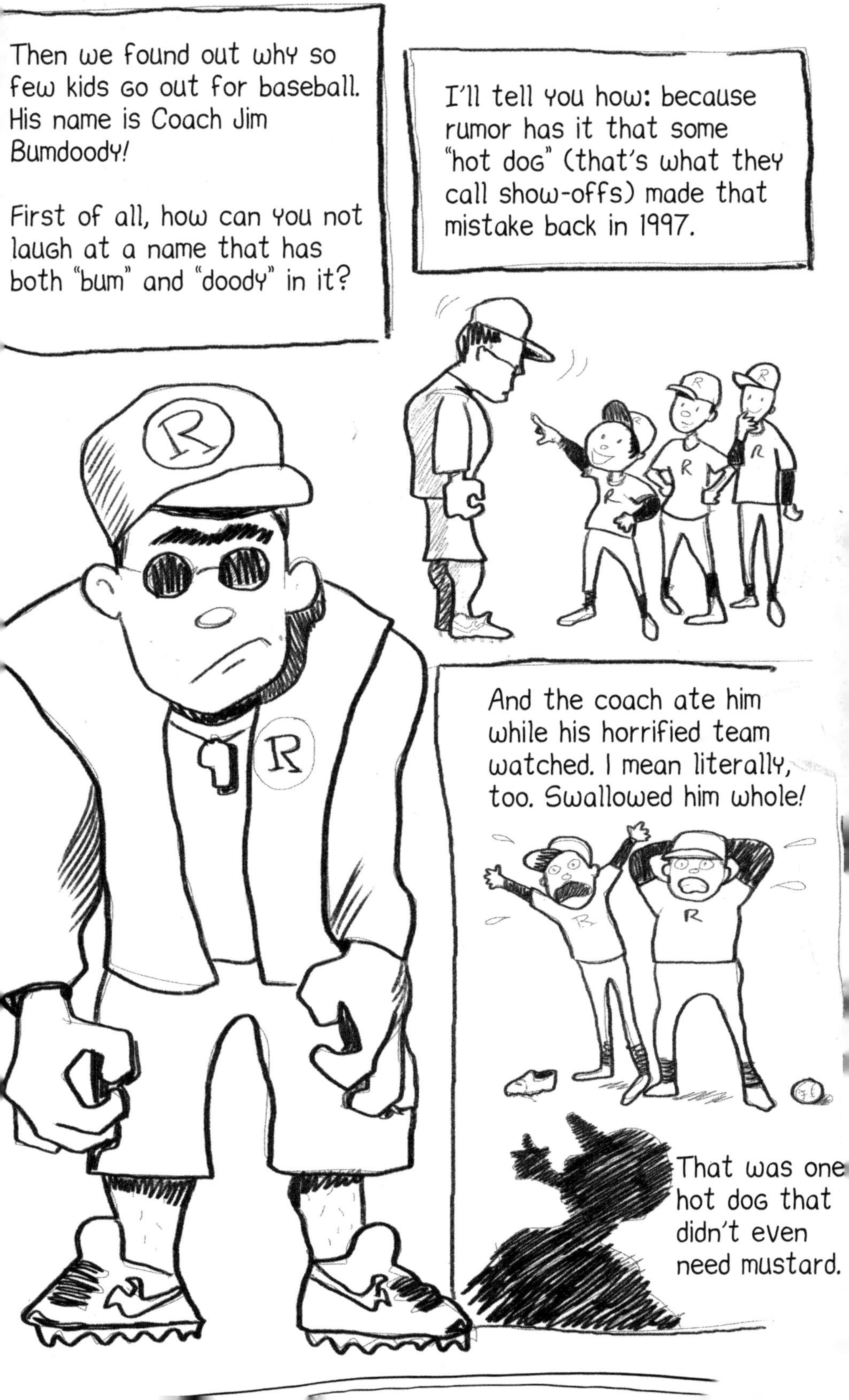
Then we found out why so few kids go out for baseball. His name is Coach Jim Bumdoody!
First of all, how can you not laugh at a name that has both "bum" and "doody" in it?
I'll tell you how: because rumor has it that some "hot dog" (that's what they call show-offs) made that mistake back in 1997.
And the coach ate him while his horrified team watched. I mean literally, too. Swallowed him whole!
That was one hot dog that didn't even need mustard.

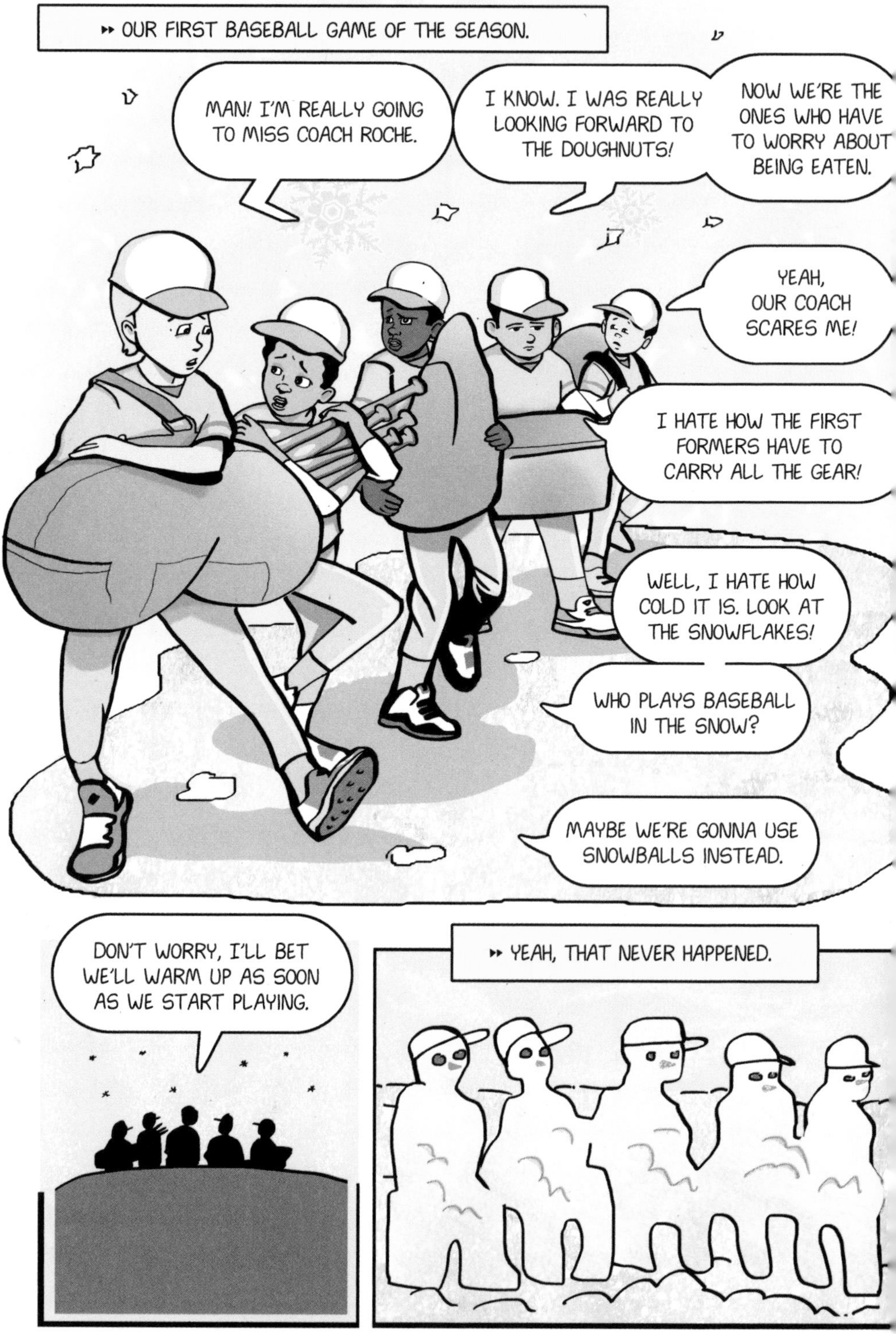

OUR FIRST BASEBALL GAME OF THE SEASON.
MAN! I'M REALLY GOING TO MISS COACH ROCHE.
I KNOW. I WAS REALLY LOOKING FORWARD TO THE DOUGHNUTS!
NOW WE'RE THE ONES WHO HAVE TO WORRY ABOUT BEING EATEN.
YEAH, OUR COACH SCARES ME!
I HATE HOW THE FIRST FORMERS HAVE TO CARRY ALL THE GEAR!
WELL, I HATE HOW COLD IT IS. LOOK AT THE SNOWFLAKES!
WHO PLAYS BASEBALL IN THE SNOW?
MAYBE WE'RE GONNA USE SNOWBALLS INSTEAD.
DON'T WORRY, I'LL BET WE'LL WARM UP AS SOON AS WE START PLAYING.
YEAH, THAT NEVER HAPPENED.

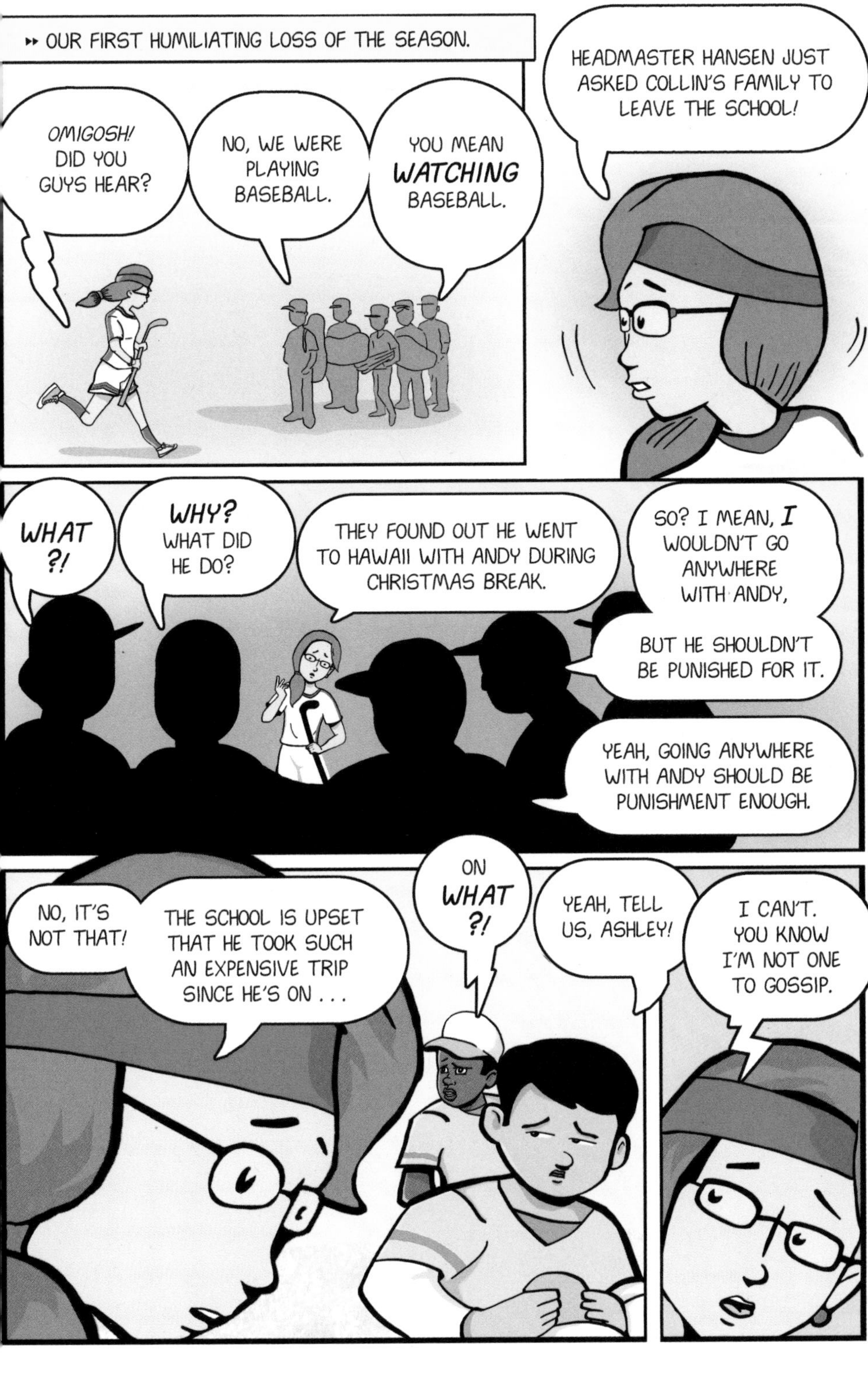

▸▸ OUR FIRST HUMILIATING LOSS OF THE SEASON.
OMIGOSH! DID YOU GUYS HEAR?
NO, WE WERE PLAYING BASEBALL.
YOU MEAN WATCHING BASEBALL.
HEADMASTER HANSEN JUST ASKED COLLIN'S FAMILY TO LEAVE THE SCHOOL!
WHAT?!
WHY? WHAT DID HE DO?
THEY FOUND OUT HE WENT TO HAWAII WITH ANDY DURING CHRISTMAS BREAK.
SO? I MEAN, I WOULDN'T GO ANYWHERE WITH ANDY,
BUT HE SHOULDN'T BE PUNISHED FOR IT.
YEAH, GOING ANYWHERE WITH ANDY SHOULD BE PUNISHMENT ENOUGH.
NO, IT'S NOT THAT!
THE SCHOOL IS UPSET THAT HE TOOK SUCH AN EXPENSIVE TRIP SINCE HE'S ON . . .
ON WHAT?!
YEAH, TELL US, ASHLEY!
I CAN'T. YOU KNOW I'M NOT ONE TO GOSSIP.

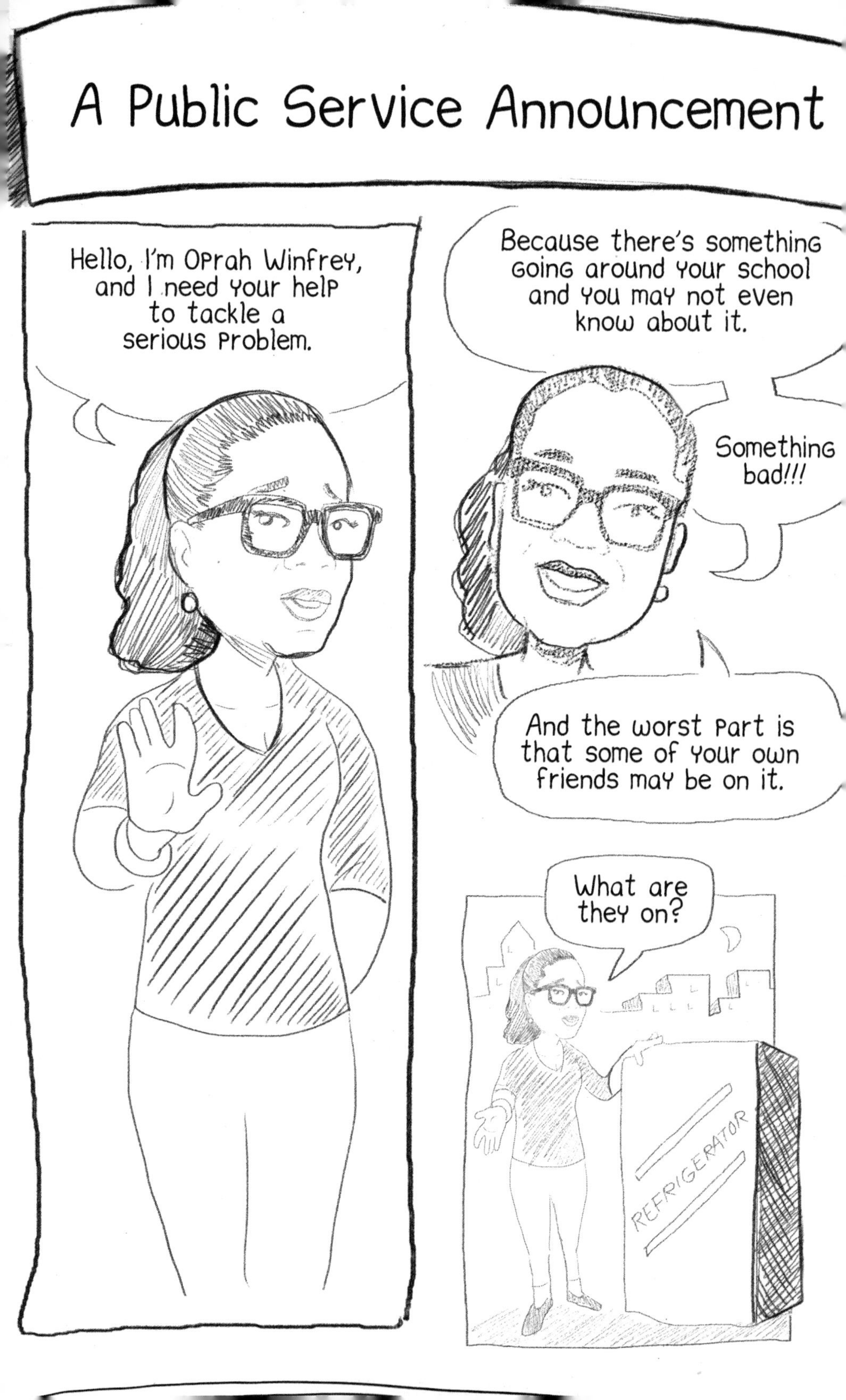
A Public Service Announcement
Hello, I'm Oprah Winfrey, and I need your help to tackle a serious problem.
Because there's something going around your school and you may not even know about it.
Something bad!!!
And the worst part is that some of your own friends may be on it.
What are they on?
REFRIGERATOR

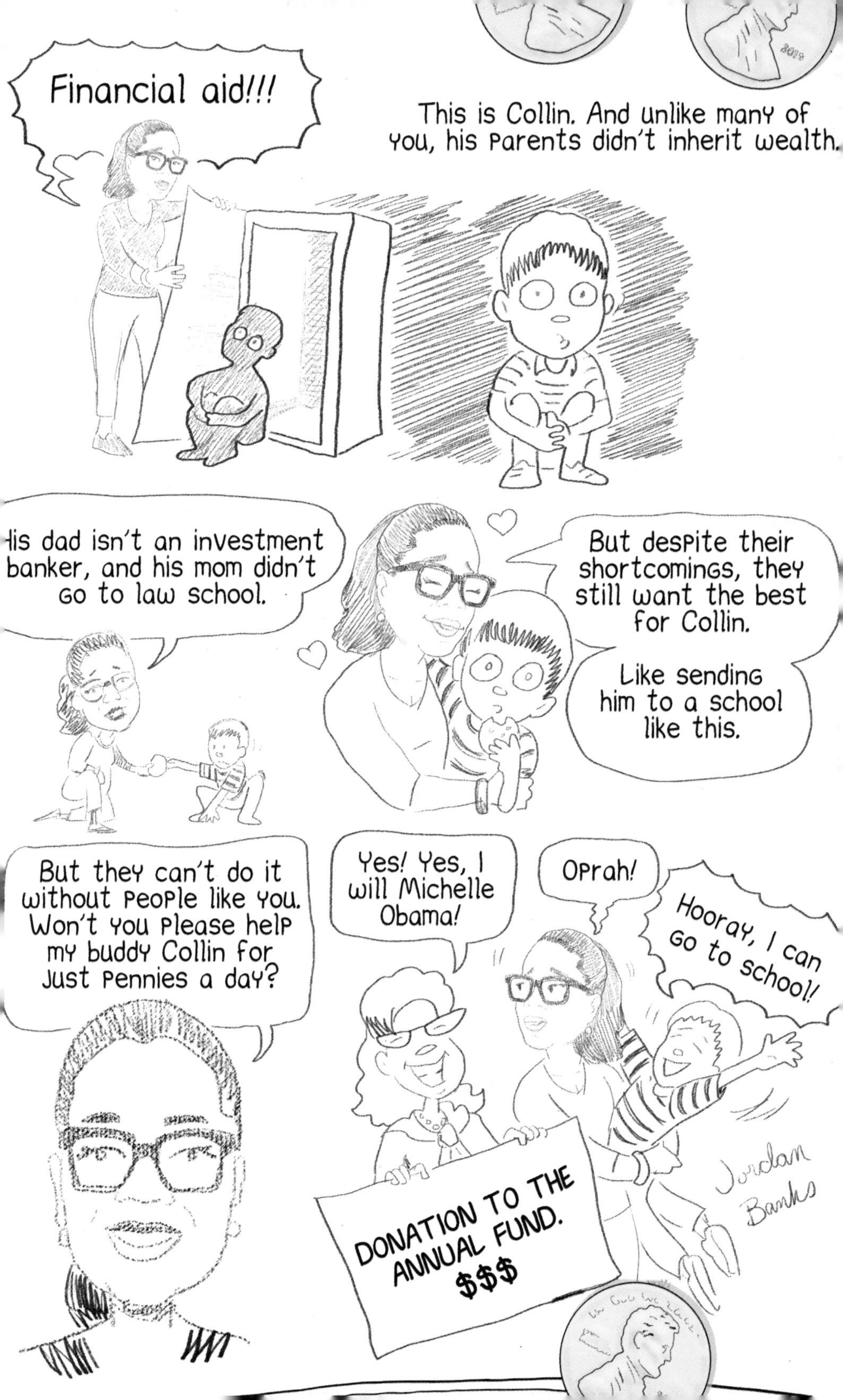
Financial aid!!!
This is Collin. And unlike many of you, his parents didn't inherit wealth.
His dad isn't an investment banker, and his mom didn't go to law school.
But despite their shortcomings, they still want the best for Collin.
Like sending him to a school like this.
But they can't do it without people like you. Won't you please help my buddy Collin for just pennies a day?
Yes! Yes, I will Michelle Obama!
Oprah!
Hooray, I can go to school!
DONATION TO THE ANNUAL FUND. $$$
Jordan Banks

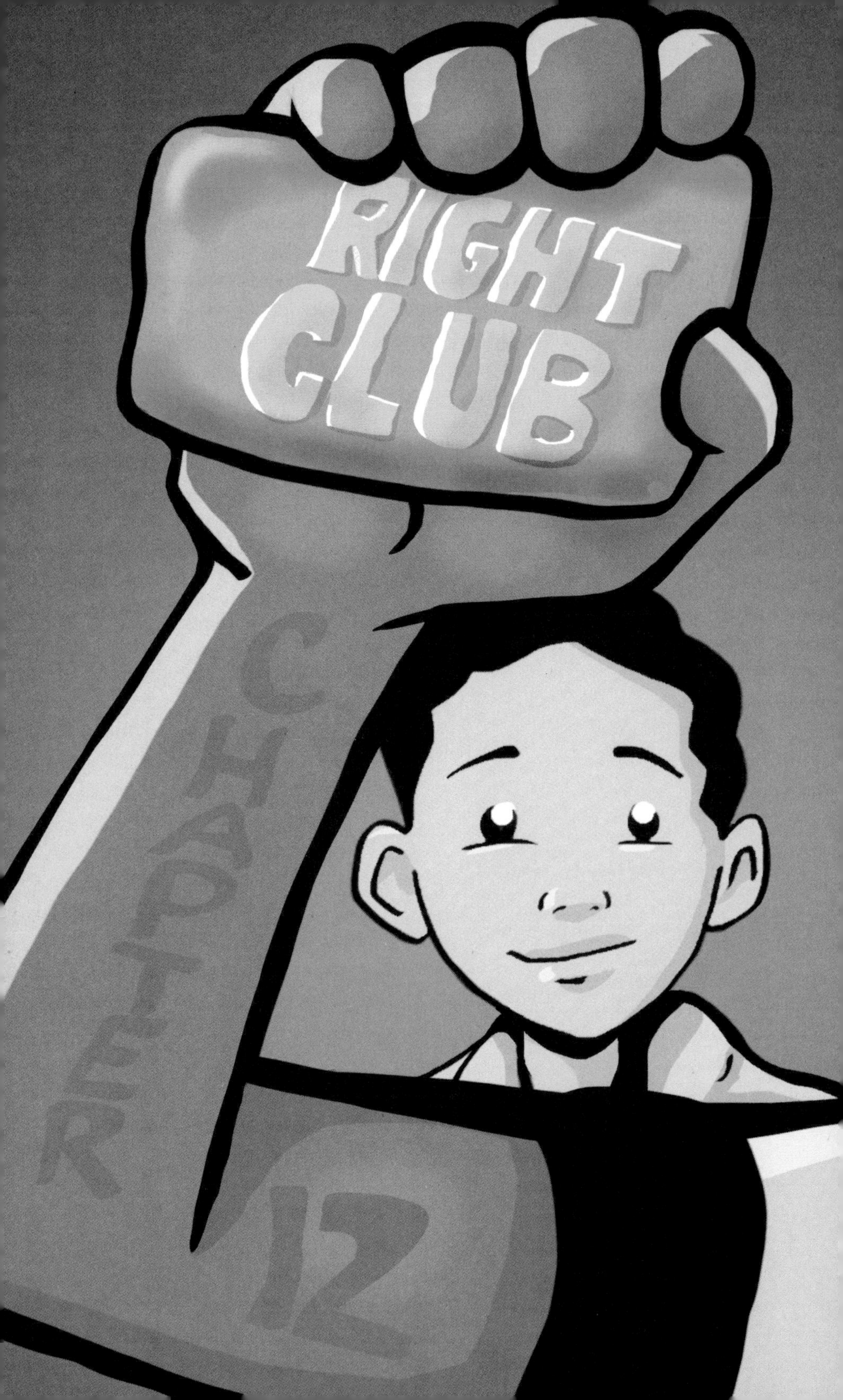
RIGHT CLUB
CHAPTER 12

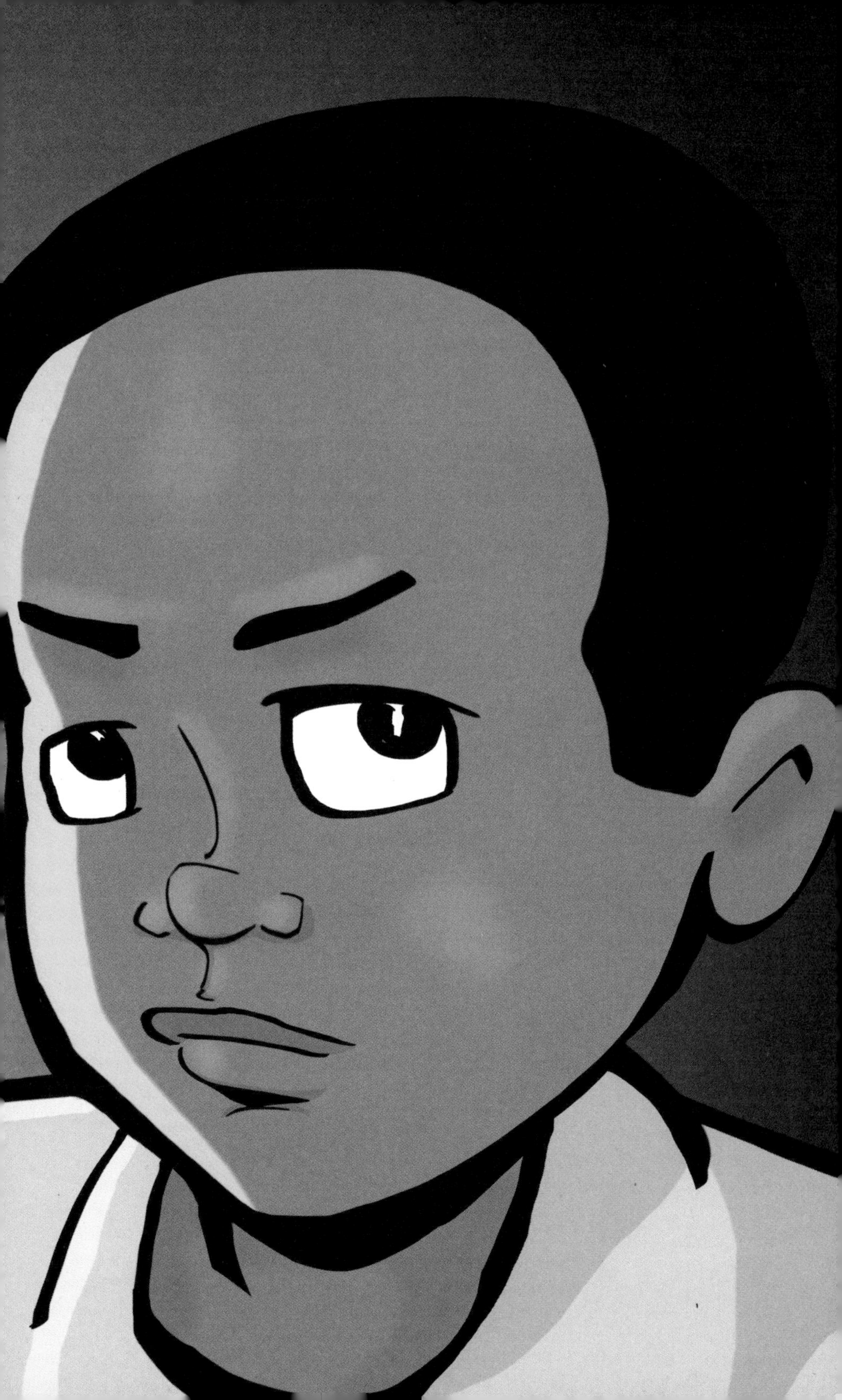

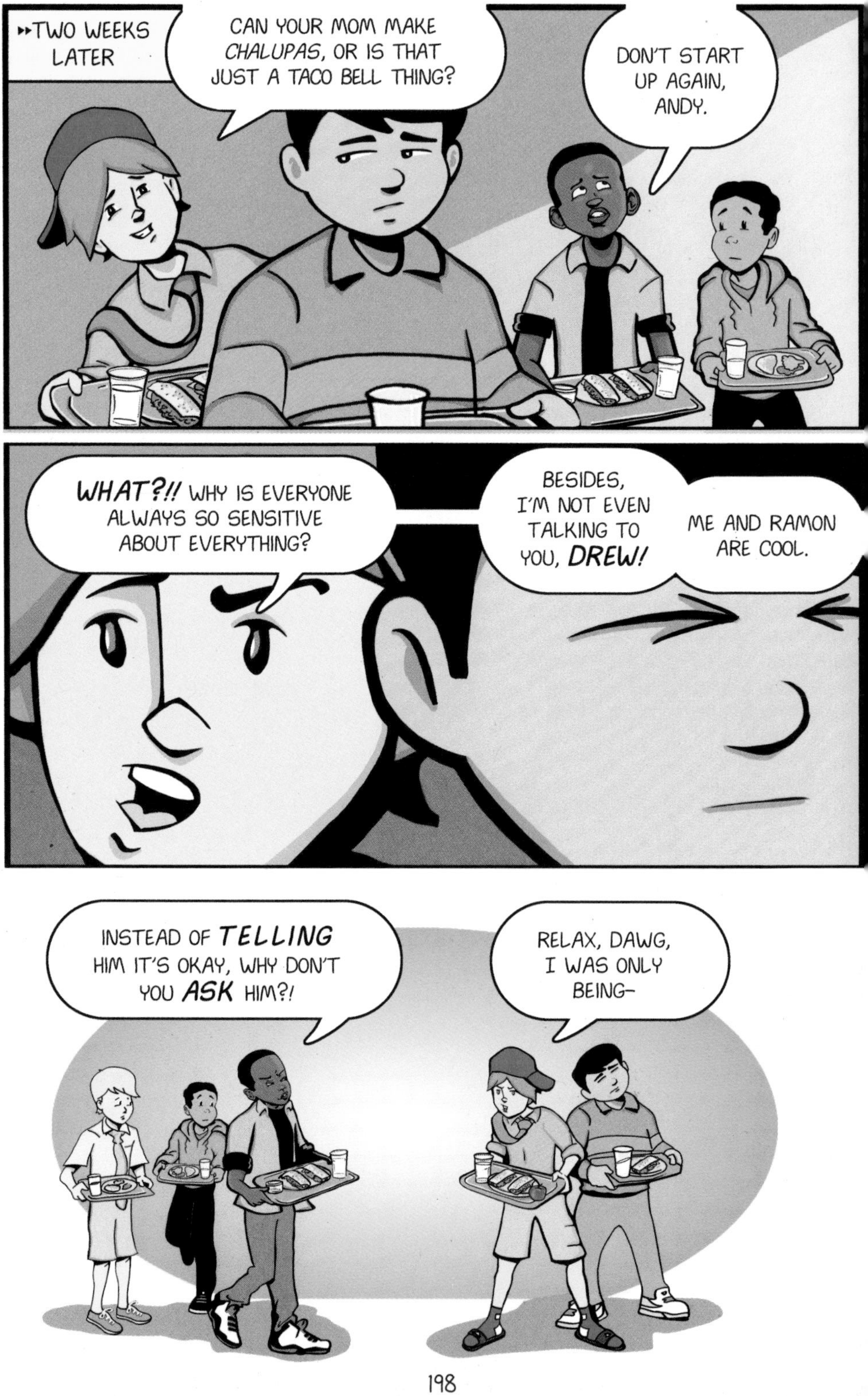
▸▸TWO WEEKS LATER
CAN YOUR MOM MAKE *CHALUPAS*, OR IS THAT JUST A TACO BELL THING?
DON'T START UP AGAIN, ANDY.
WHAT?!! WHY IS EVERYONE ALWAYS SO SENSITIVE ABOUT EVERYTHING?
BESIDES, I'M NOT EVEN TALKING TO YOU, **DREW!**
ME AND RAMON ARE COOL.
INSTEAD OF **TELLING** HIM IT'S OKAY, WHY DON'T YOU **ASK** HIM?!
RELAX, DAWG, I WAS ONLY BEING–

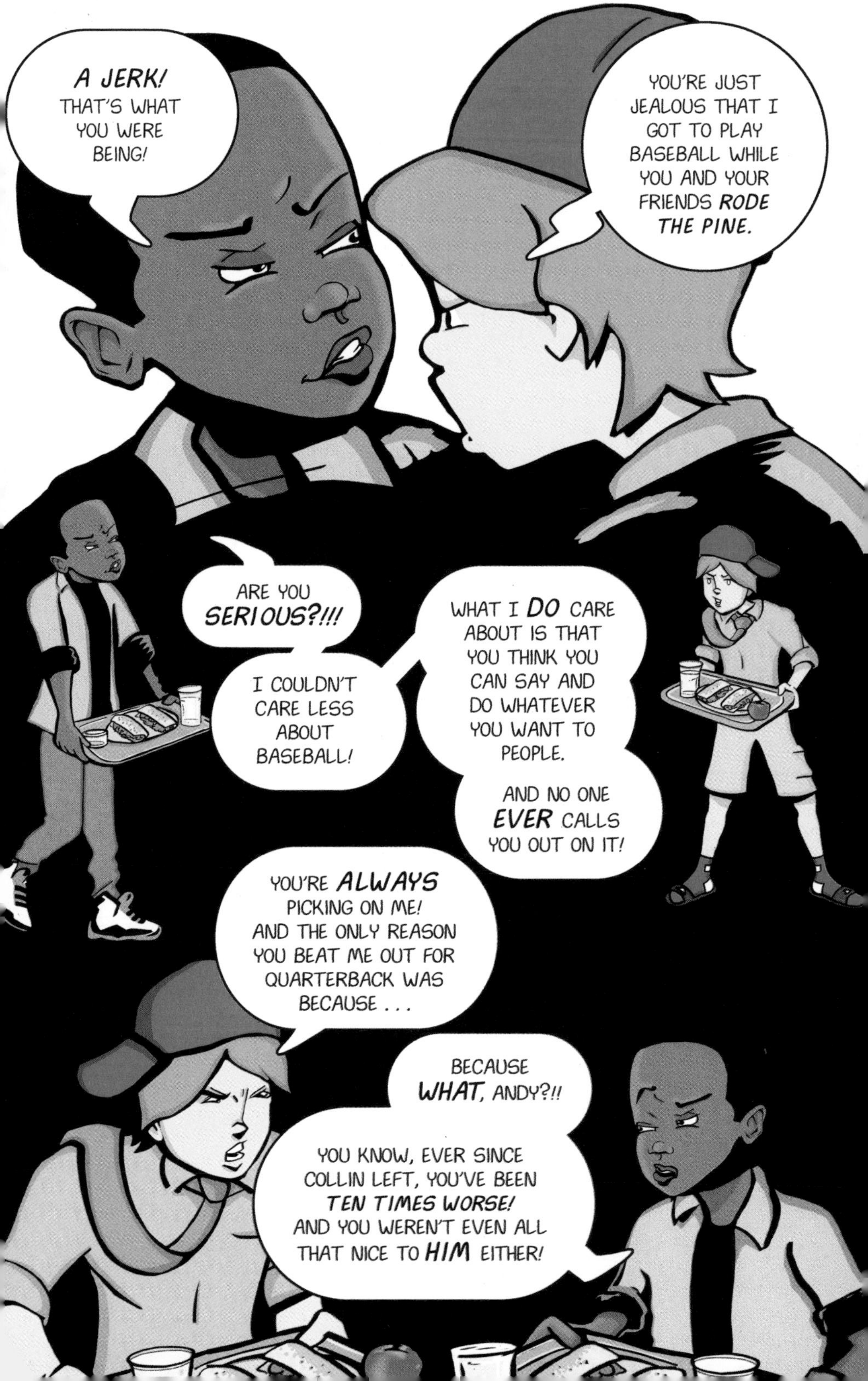
A JERK! THAT'S WHAT YOU WERE BEING!
YOU'RE JUST JEALOUS THAT I GOT TO PLAY BASEBALL WHILE YOU AND YOUR FRIENDS RODE THE PINE.
ARE YOU SERIOUS?!!!
I COULDN'T CARE LESS ABOUT BASEBALL!
WHAT I DO CARE ABOUT IS THAT YOU THINK YOU CAN SAY AND DO WHATEVER YOU WANT TO PEOPLE.
AND NO ONE EVER CALLS YOU OUT ON IT!
YOU'RE ALWAYS PICKING ON ME! AND THE ONLY REASON YOU BEAT ME OUT FOR QUARTERBACK WAS BECAUSE . . .
BECAUSE WHAT, ANDY?!!
YOU KNOW, EVER SINCE COLLIN LEFT, YOU'VE BEEN TEN TIMES WORSE! AND YOU WEREN'T EVEN ALL THAT NICE TO HIM EITHER!

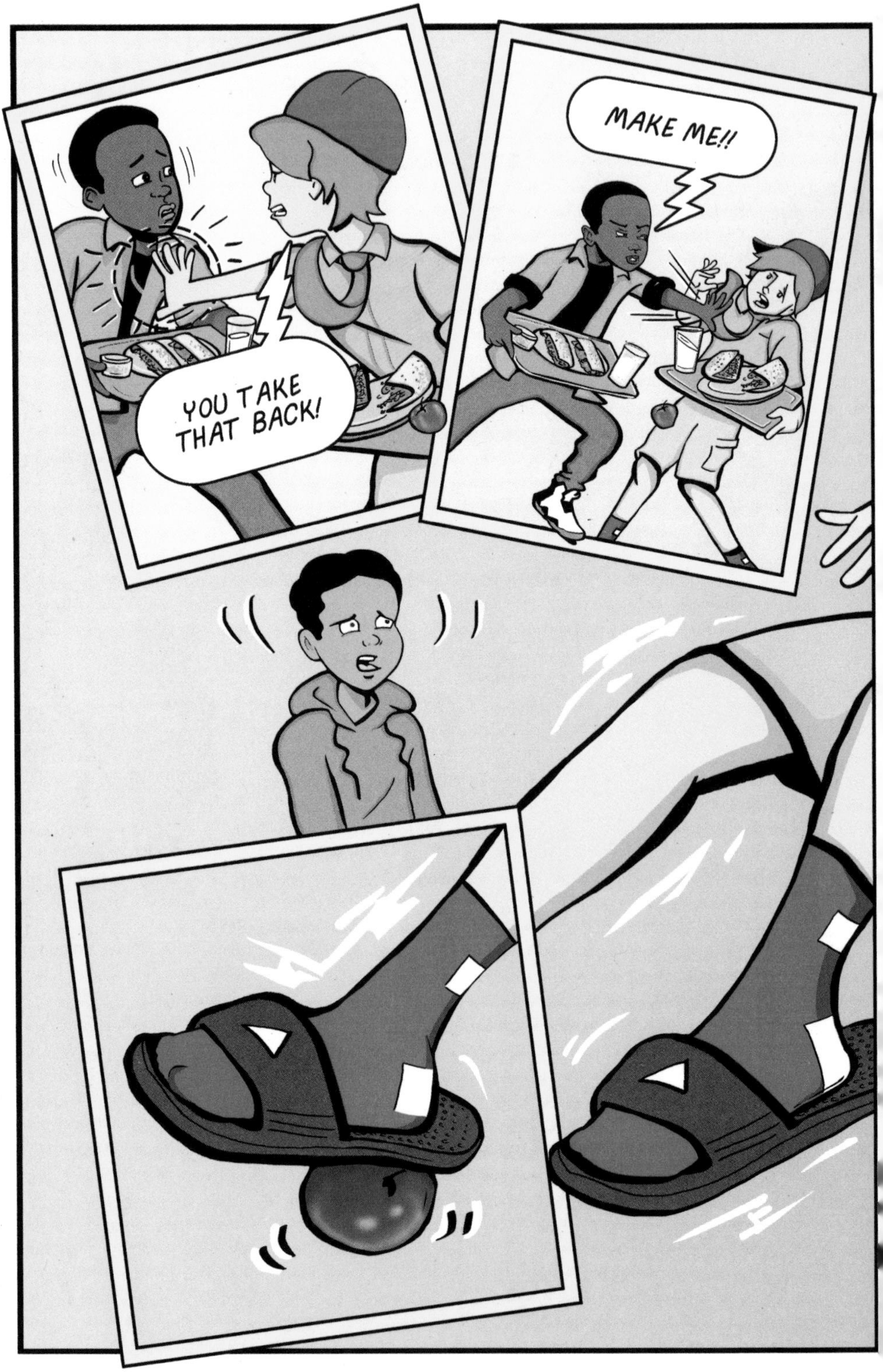
YOU TAKE THAT BACK!
MAKE ME!!

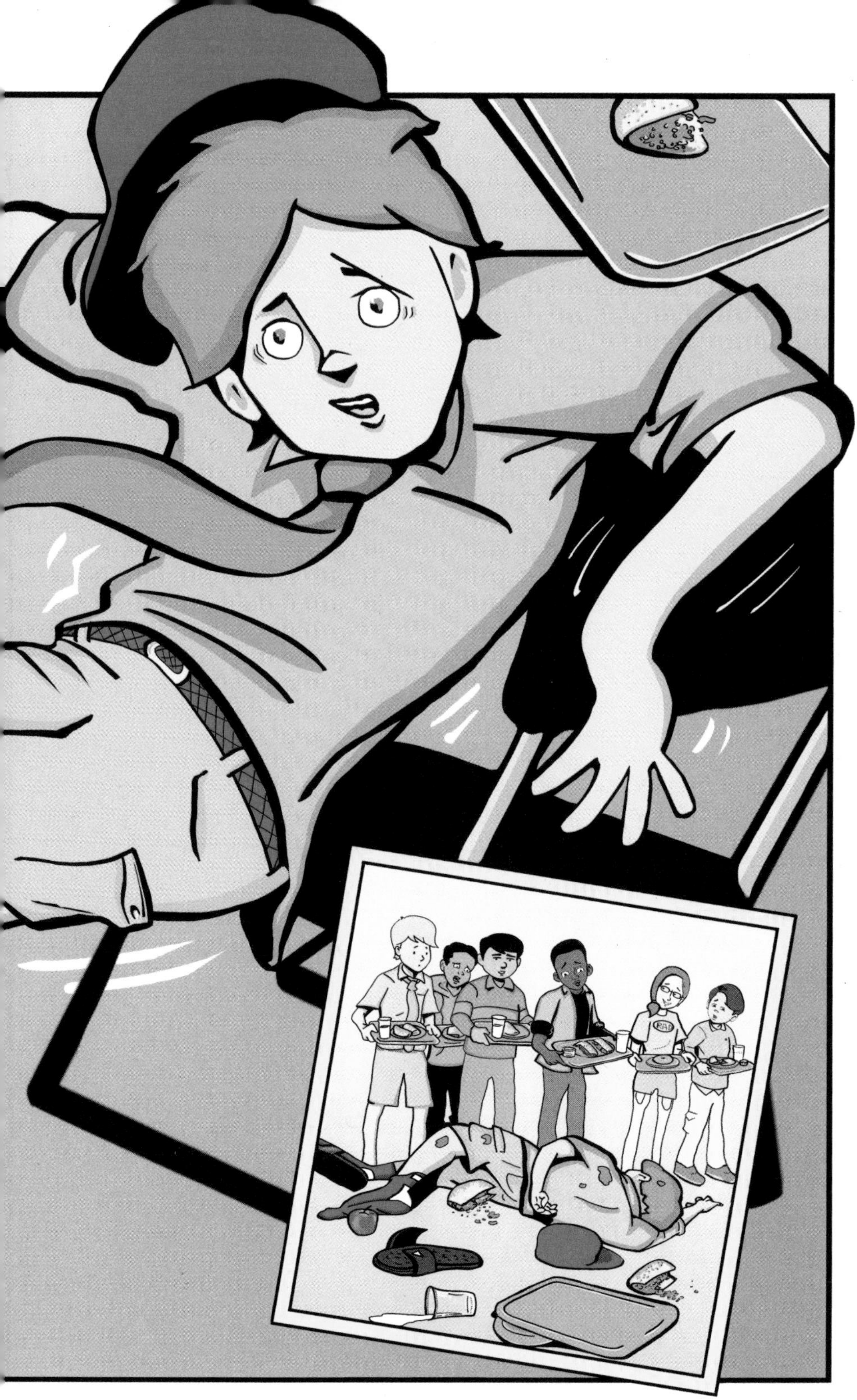

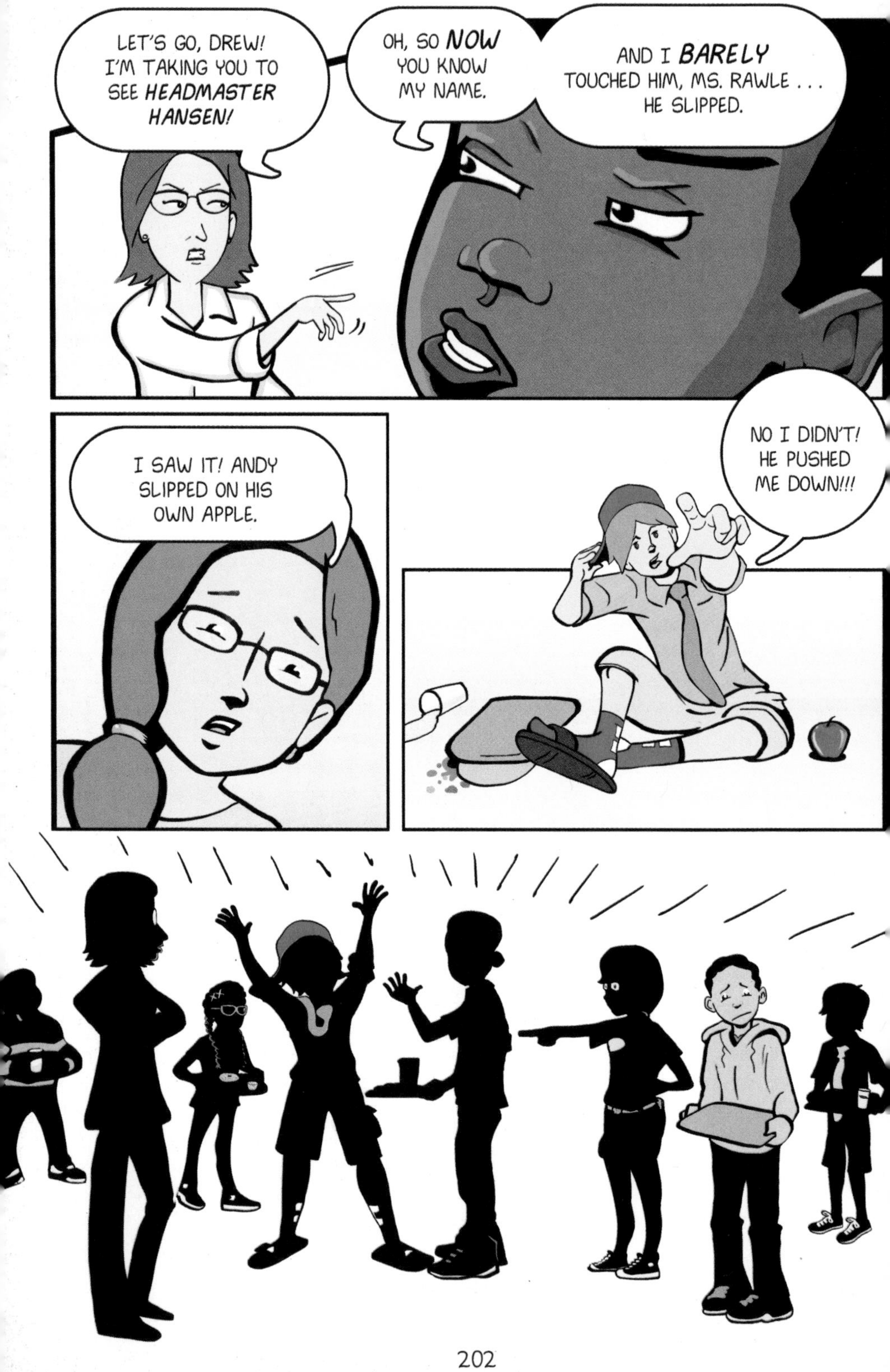
LET'S GO, DREW! I'M TAKING YOU TO SEE HEADMASTER HANSEN!
OH, SO NOW YOU KNOW MY NAME.
AND I BARELY TOUCHED HIM, MS. RAWLE . . . HE SLIPPED.
I SAW IT! ANDY SLIPPED ON HIS OWN APPLE.
NO I DIDN'T! HE PUSHED ME DOWN!!!

AND AT THAT
MOMENT, IT
ALL BECAME
TOO MUCH!

TOO MUCH OF KIDS
LIKE ME TRYING
TO FIT IN.

TOO MUCH OF KIDS WHO
SHOULD FIT IN TRYING
HARD NOT TO.

TOO MUCH OF GOOD KIDS
BEING BLAMED FOR
BEING BAD!

TOO MUCH OF BAD
KIDS GETTING
REWARDED FOR THEIR
MEAN BEHAVIOR!

AND WAYYYY
TOO MUCH
OF ME FEELING
LIKE I'M NEVER IN
CONTROL OF
ANYTHING!

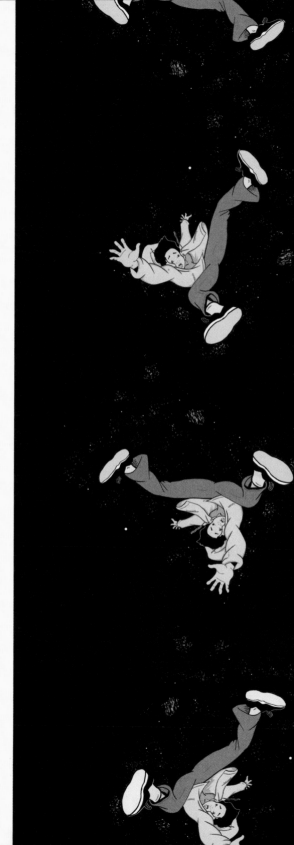

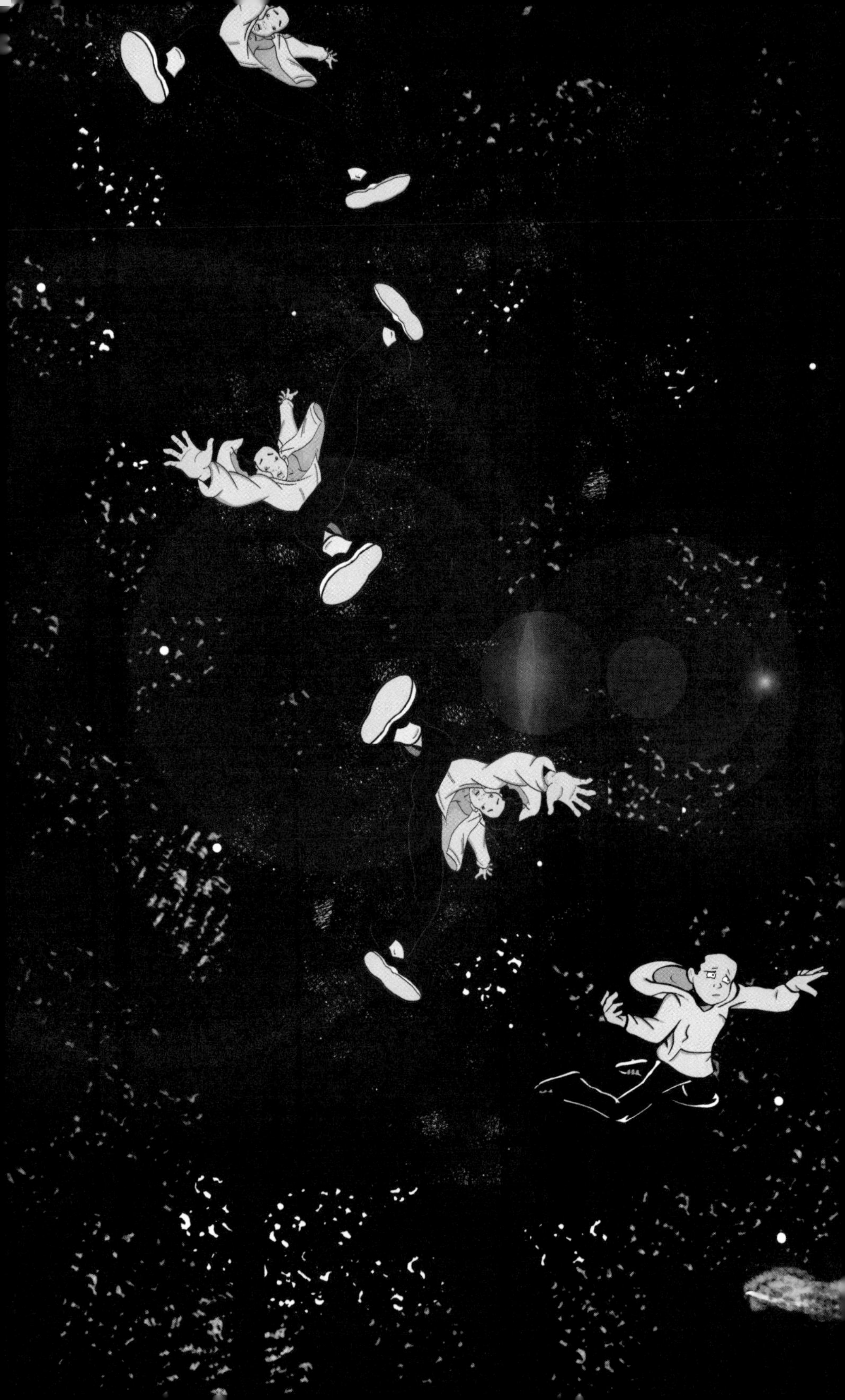

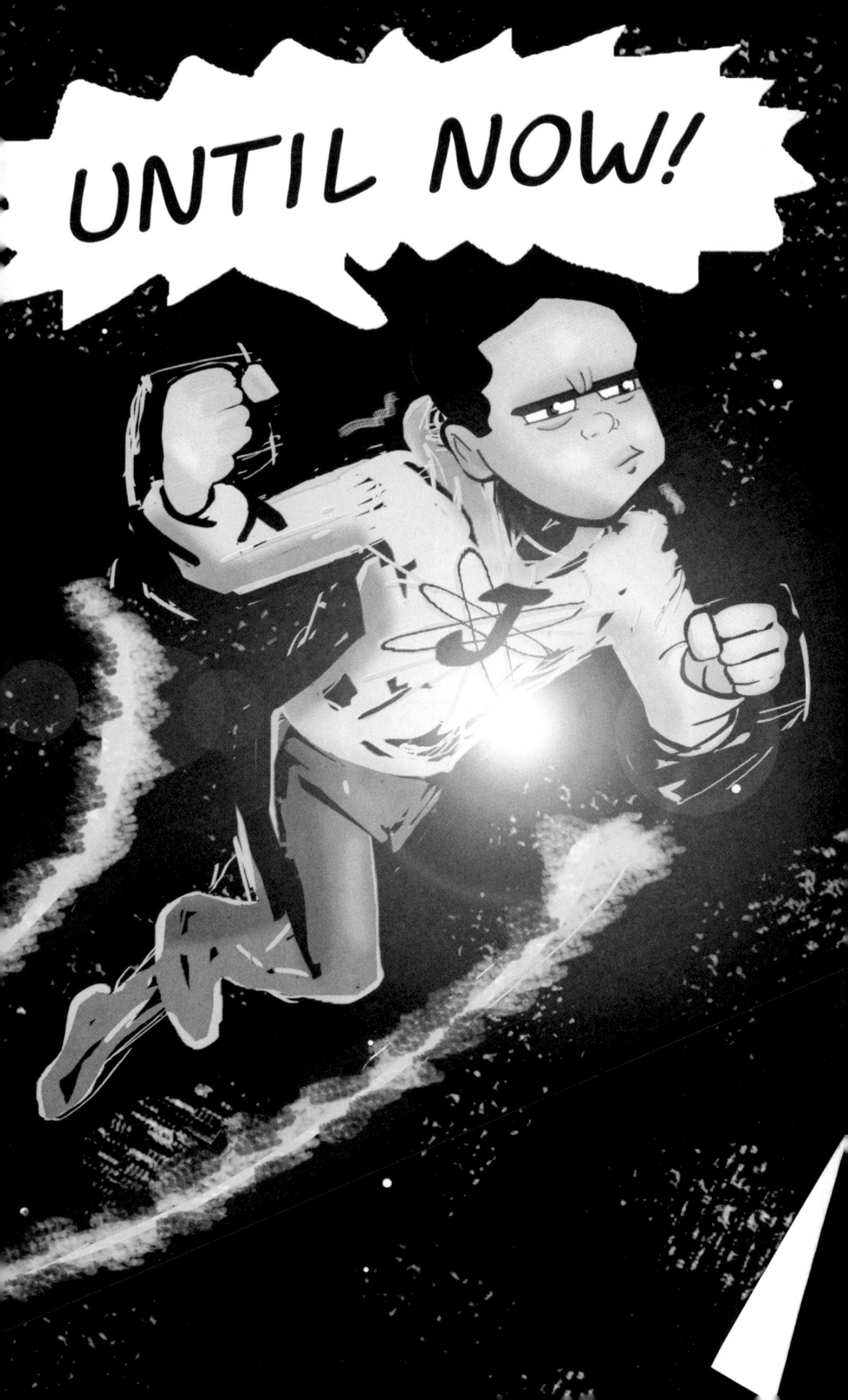
UNTIL NOW!

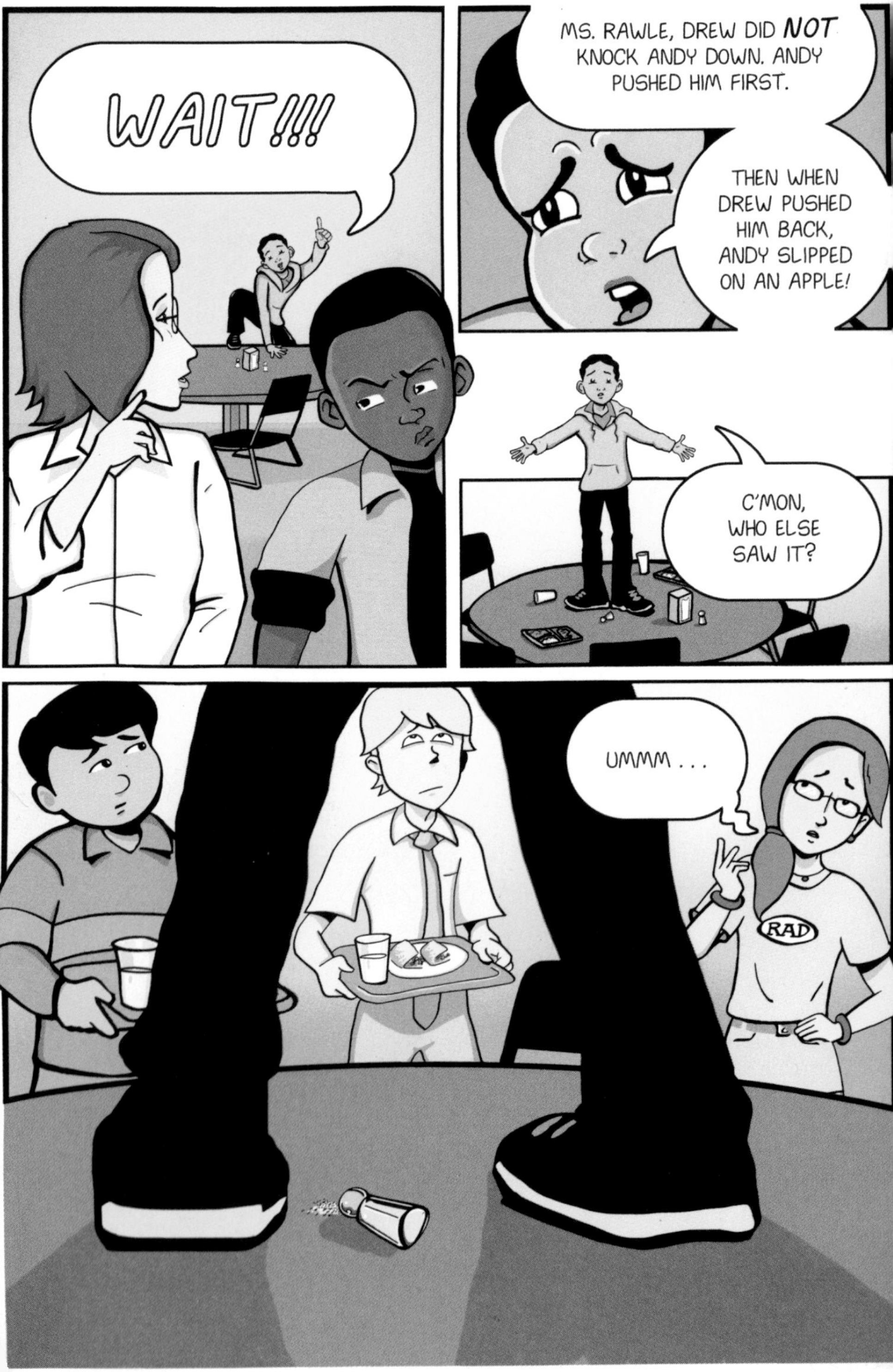
WAIT!!!
MS. RAWLE, DREW DID NOT KNOCK ANDY DOWN. ANDY PUSHED HIM FIRST.
THEN WHEN DREW PUSHED HIM BACK, ANDY SLIPPED ON AN APPLE!
C'MON, WHO ELSE SAW IT?
UMMM . . .
RAD

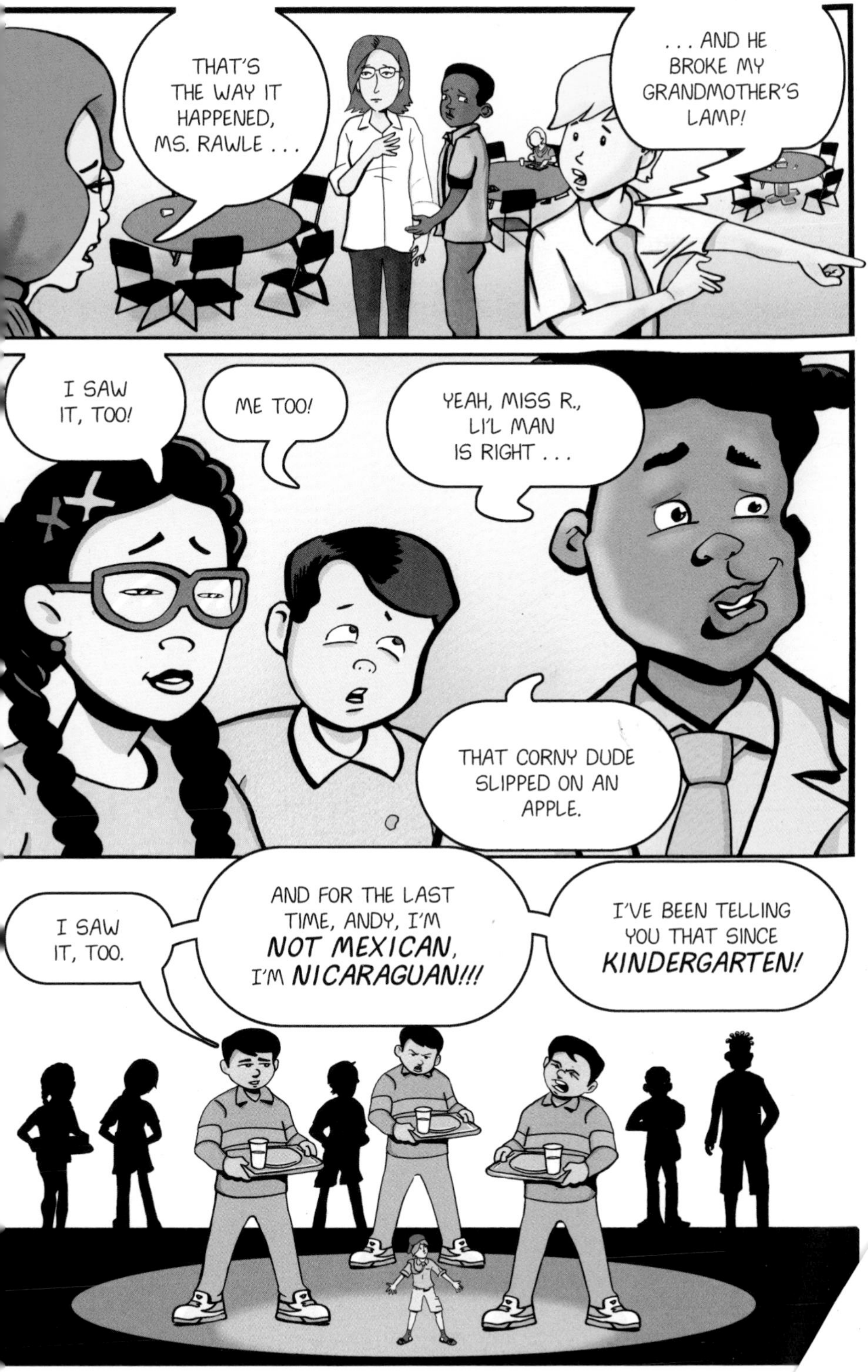

THAT'S THE WAY IT HAPPENED, MS. RAWLE . . .
. . . AND HE BROKE MY GRANDMOTHER'S LAMP!
I SAW IT, TOO!
ME TOO!
YEAH, MISS R., LI'L MAN IS RIGHT . . .
THAT CORNY DUDE SLIPPED ON AN APPLE.
I SAW IT, TOO.
AND FOR THE LAST TIME, ANDY, I'M NOT MEXICAN, I'M NICARAGUAN!!!
I'VE BEEN TELLING YOU THAT SINCE KINDERGARTEN!

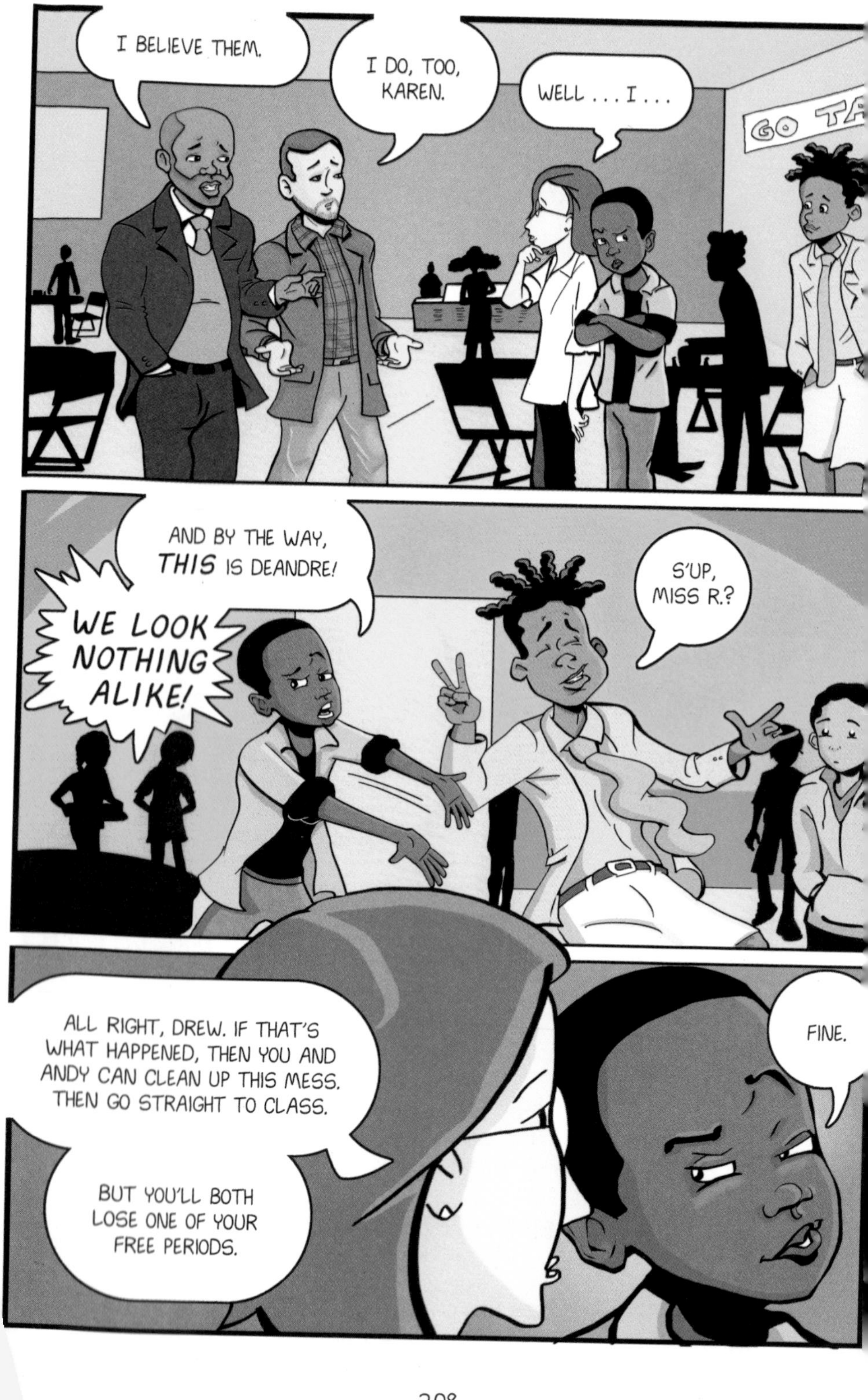
I BELIEVE THEM.
I DO, TOO, KAREN.
WELL . . . I . . .
GO TA
AND BY THE WAY, THIS IS DEANDRE!
WE LOOK NOTHING ALIKE!
S'UP, MISS R.?
ALL RIGHT, DREW. IF THAT'S WHAT HAPPENED, THEN YOU AND ANDY CAN CLEAN UP THIS MESS. THEN GO STRAIGHT TO CLASS.
BUT YOU'LL BOTH LOSE ONE OF YOUR FREE PERIODS.
FINE.

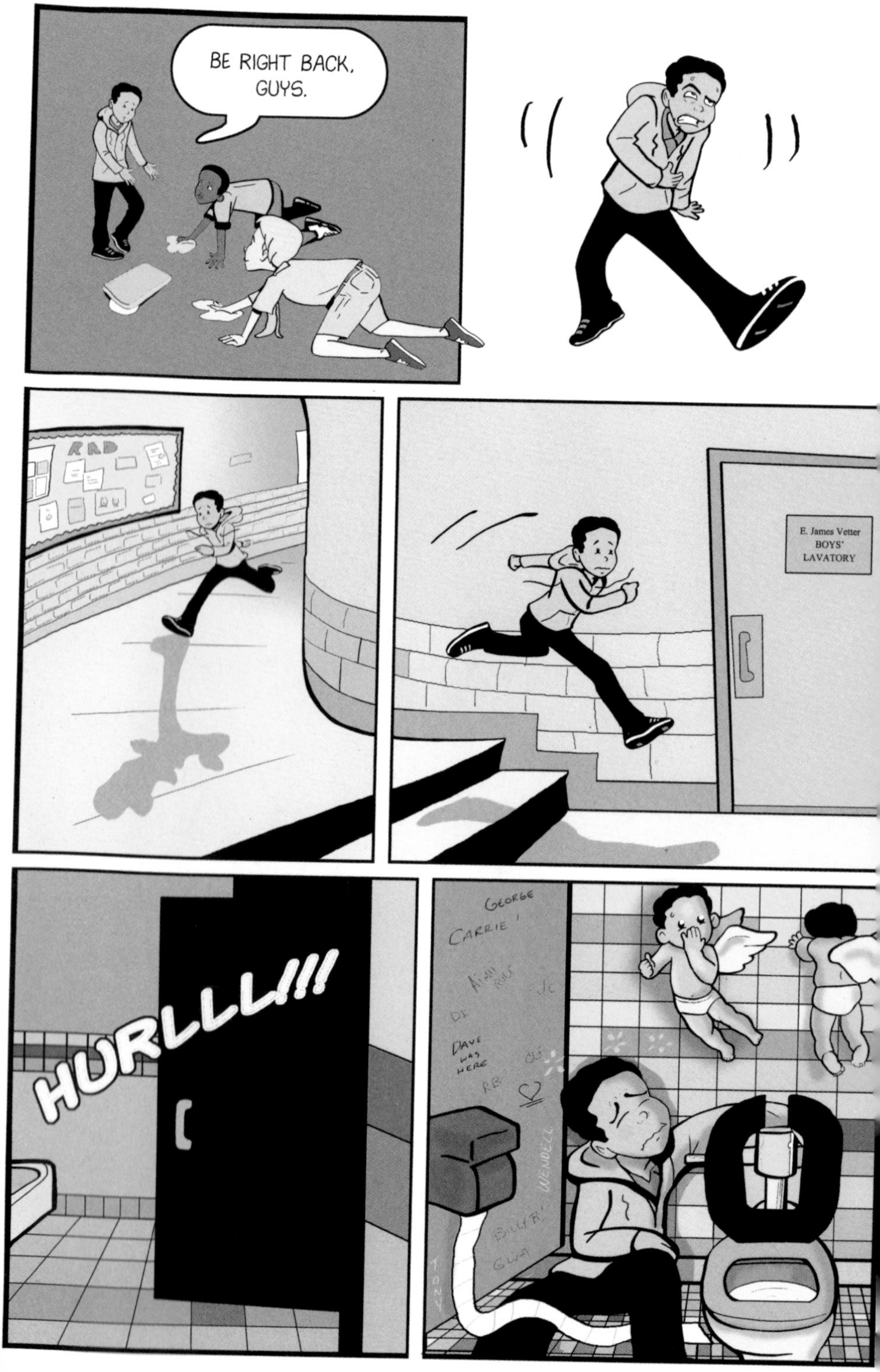
BE RIGHT BACK, GUYS.
E. James Vetter
BOYS'
LAVATORY
HURLLL!!!
GEORGE
CARRIE
DAVE WAS HERE
RB
WENDELL

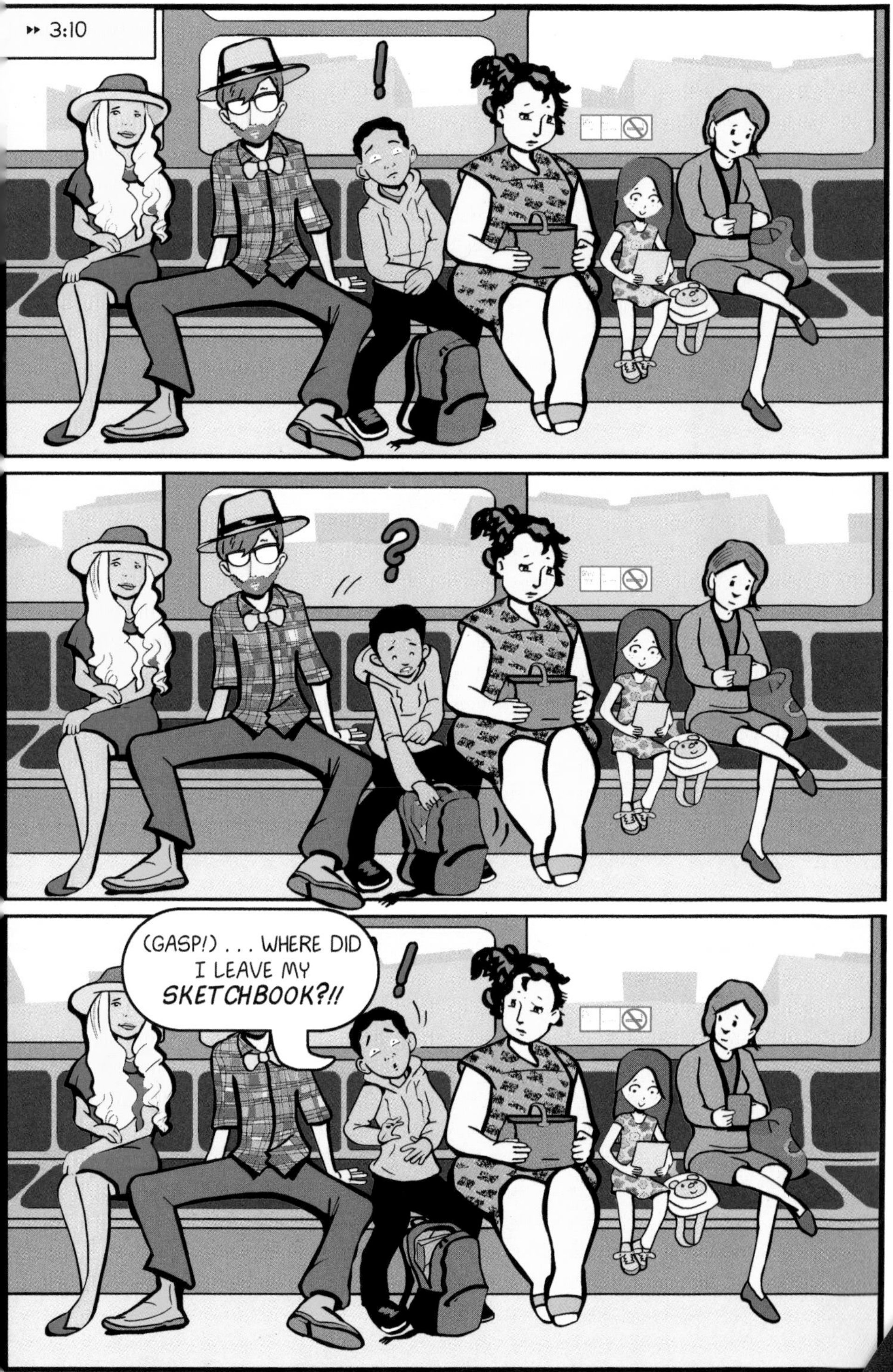
3:10
!
?
(GASP!) . . . WHERE DID I LEAVE MY SKETCHBOOK?!!
!

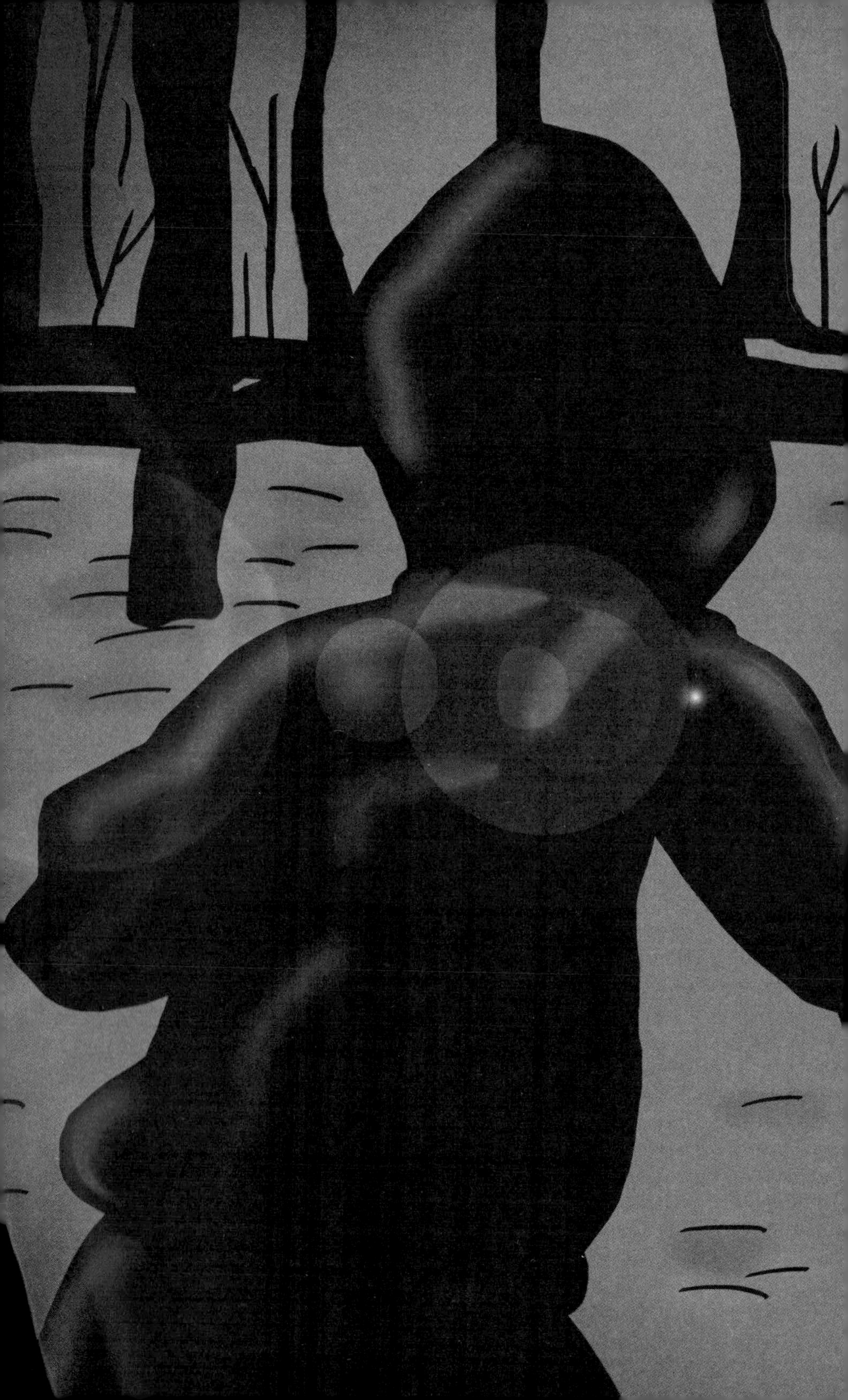

CHAPTER 13

THE FARCE AWAKENS

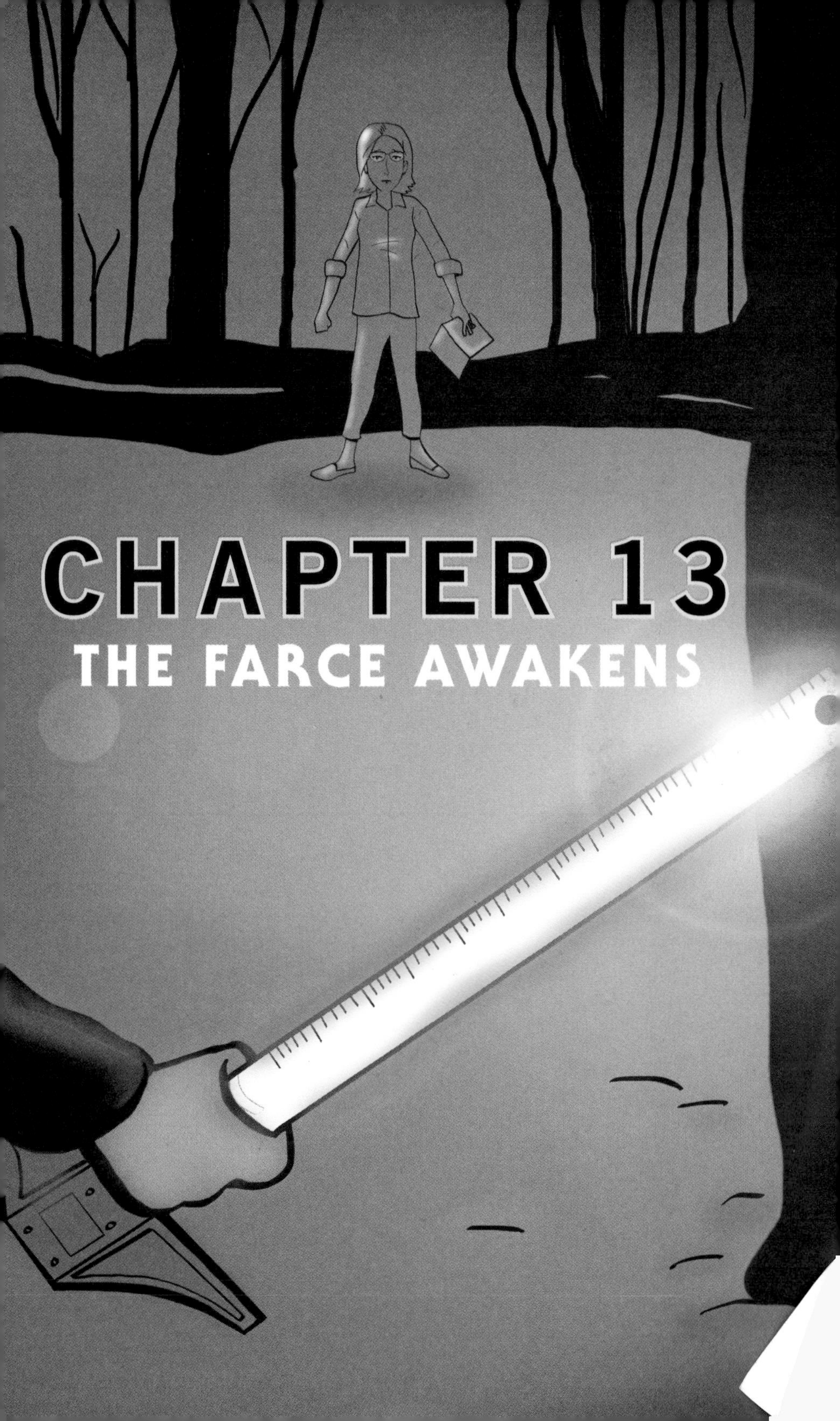

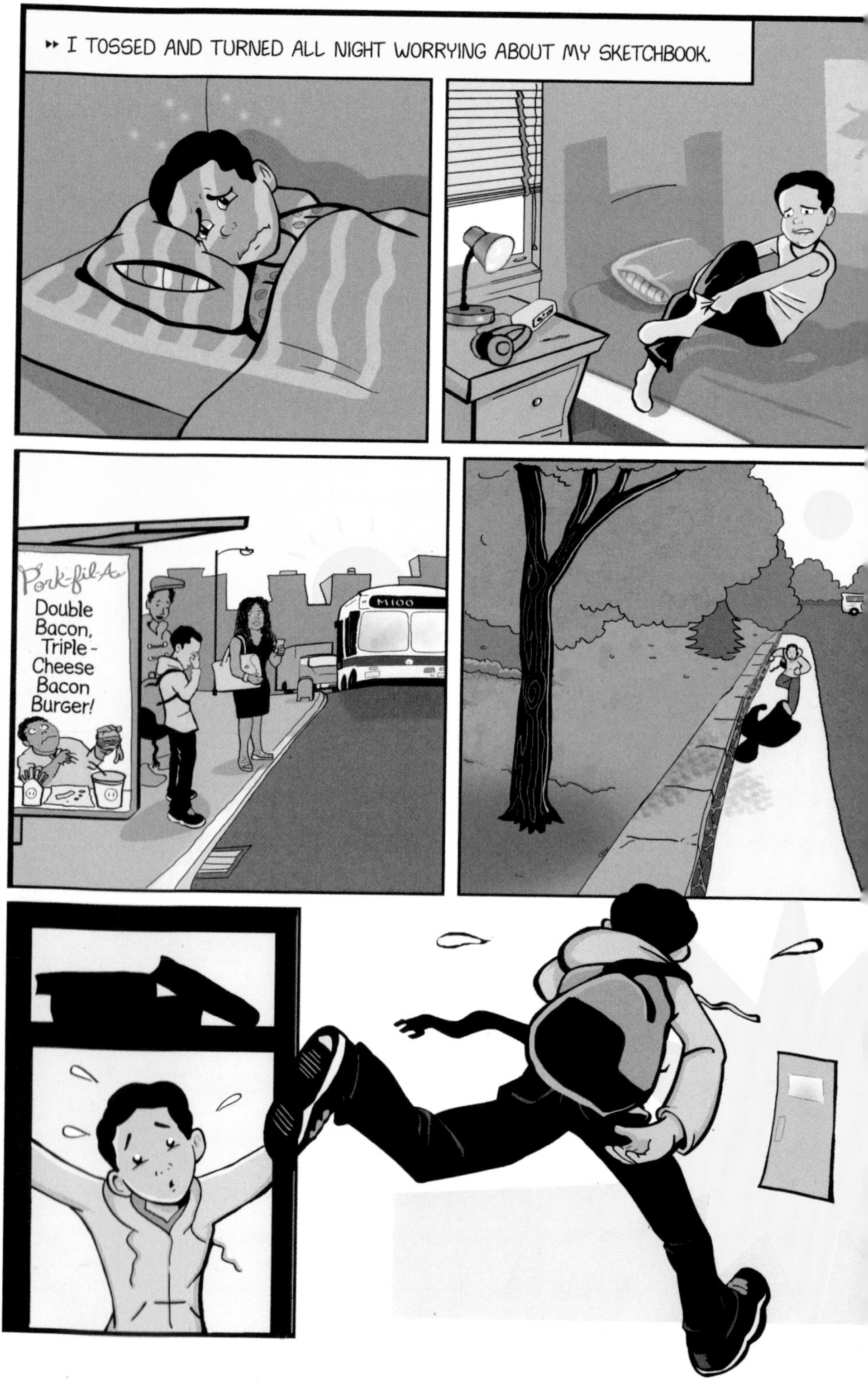
I TOSSED AND TURNED ALL NIGHT WORRYING ABOUT MY SKETCHBOOK.
Pork-fil-A
Double Bacon, Triple-Cheese Bacon Burger!
M100

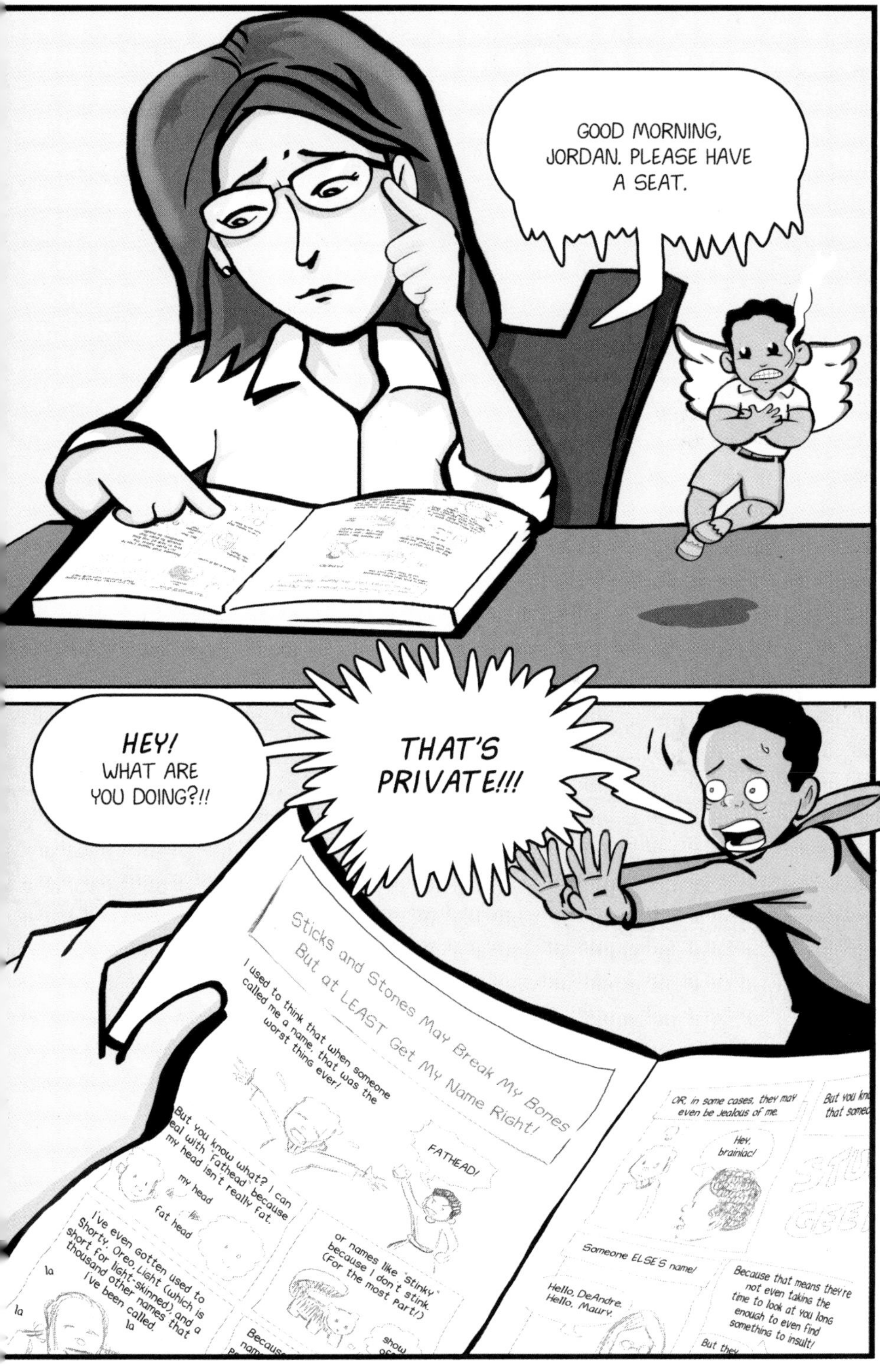

GOOD MORNING, JORDAN. PLEASE HAVE A SEAT.
HEY! WHAT ARE YOU DOING?!!
THAT'S PRIVATE!!!
Sticks and Stones May Break My Bones But at LEAST Get My Name Right!
I used to think that when someone called me a name, that was the worst thing ever!
FATHEAD!
But you know what? I can deal with "Fathead" because my head isn't really fat.
my head
fat head
or names like "Stinky" because I don't stink. (For the most part!)
I've even gotten used to Shorty, Oreo, Light (which is short for light-skinned), and a thousand other names that I've been called.
OR, in some cases, they may even be jealous of me.
Hey, brainiac!
Someone ELSE'S name!
Hello, DeAndre. Hello, Maury.
Because that means they're not even taking the time to look at you long enough to even find something to insult!

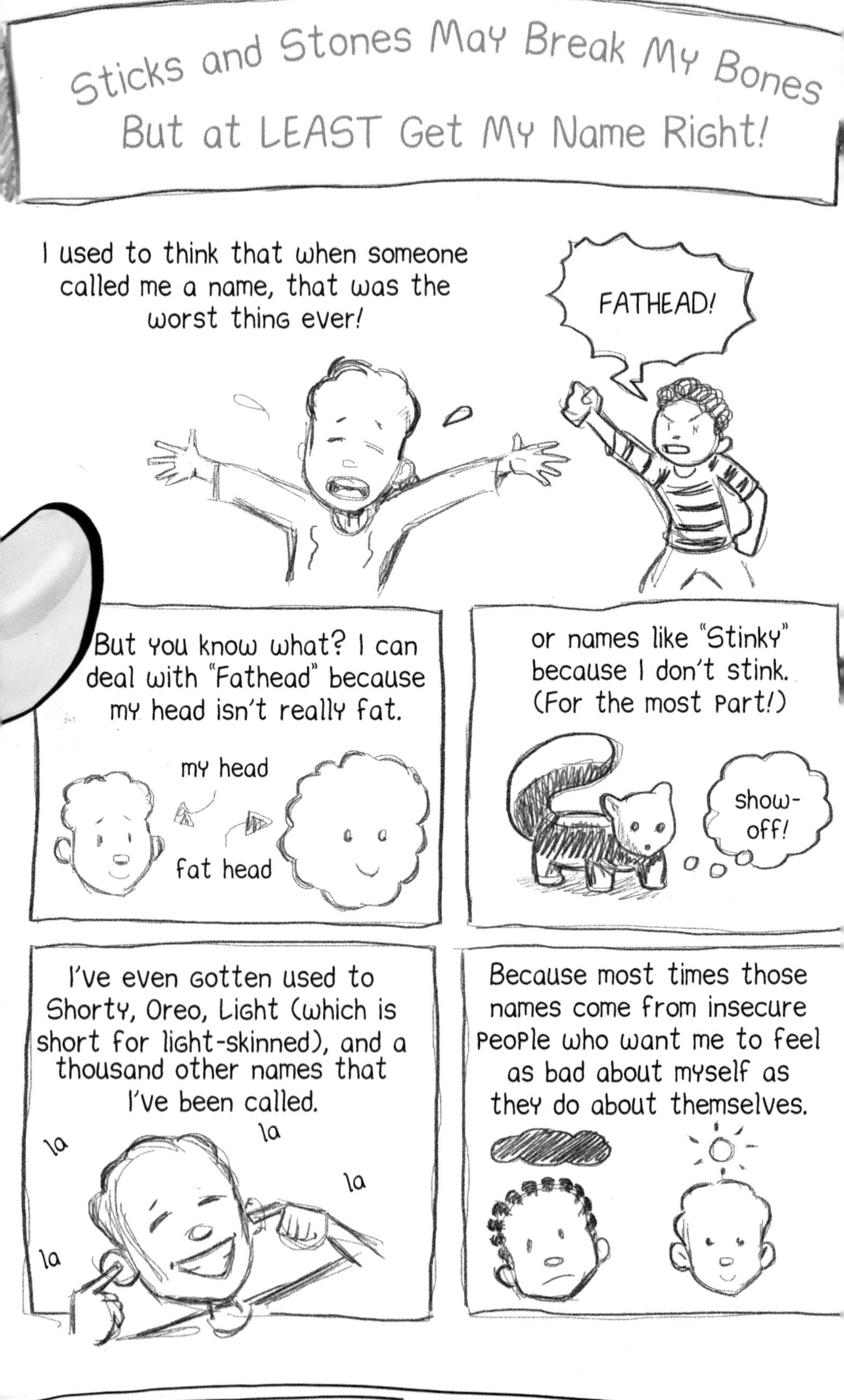
Sticks and Stones May Break My Bones
But at LEAST Get My Name Right!
I used to think that when someone called me a name, that was the worst thing ever!
FATHEAD!
But you know what? I can deal with "Fathead" because my head isn't really fat.
my head
fat head
or names like "Stinky" because I don't stink. (For the most part!)
show-off!
I've even gotten used to Shorty, Oreo, Light (which is short for light-skinned), and a thousand other names that I've been called.
la
la
la
la
Because most times those names come from insecure people who want me to feel as bad about myself as they do about themselves.

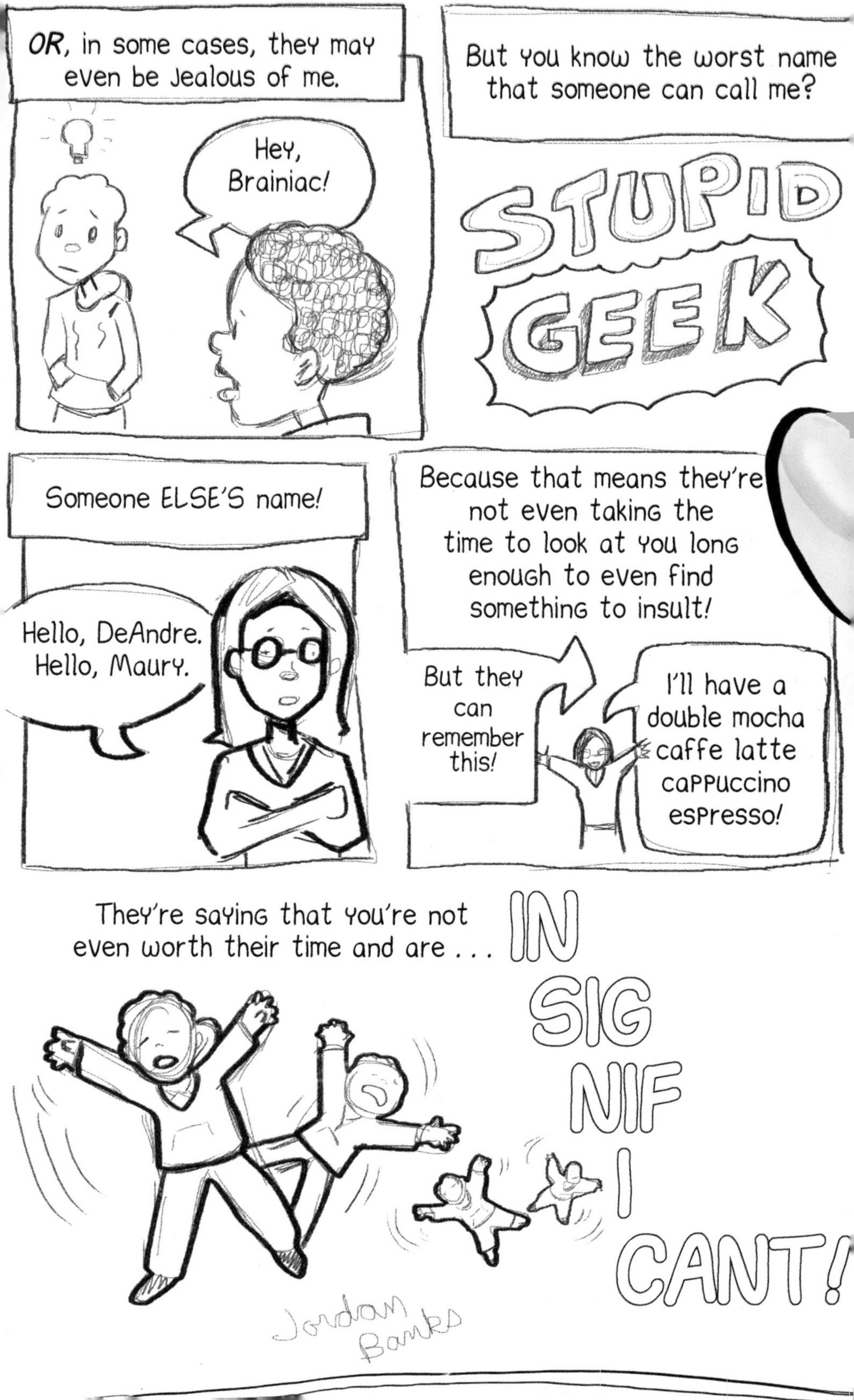
OR, in some cases, they may even be jealous of me.
Hey, Brainiac!
But you know the worst name that someone can call me?
STUPID GEEK
Someone ELSE'S name!
Hello, DeAndre. Hello, Maury.
Because that means they're not even taking the time to look at you long enough to even find something to insult!
But they can remember this!
I'll have a double mocha caffe latte cappuccino espresso!
They're saying that you're not even worth their time and are . . .
IN SIG NIF I CANT!
Jordan Banks

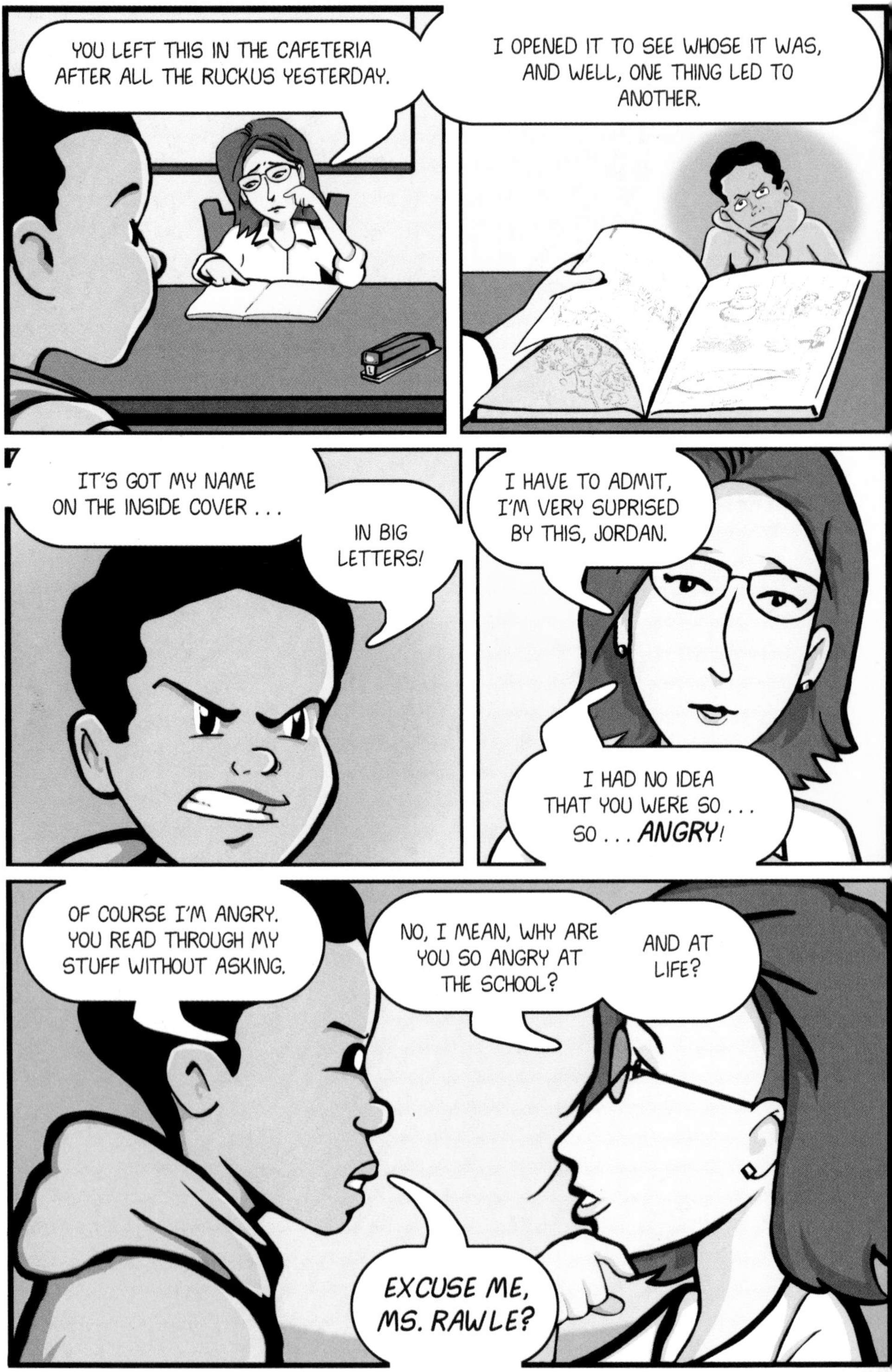
YOU LEFT THIS IN THE CAFETERIA AFTER ALL THE RUCKUS YESTERDAY.
I OPENED IT TO SEE WHOSE IT WAS, AND WELL, ONE THING LED TO ANOTHER.
IT'S GOT MY NAME ON THE INSIDE COVER . . .
IN BIG LETTERS!
I HAVE TO ADMIT, I'M VERY SUPRISED BY THIS, JORDAN.
I HAD NO IDEA THAT YOU WERE SO . . . SO . . . ANGRY!
OF COURSE I'M ANGRY. YOU READ THROUGH MY STUFF WITHOUT ASKING.
NO, I MEAN, WHY ARE YOU SO ANGRY AT THE SCHOOL?
AND AT LIFE?
EXCUSE ME, MS. RAWLE?

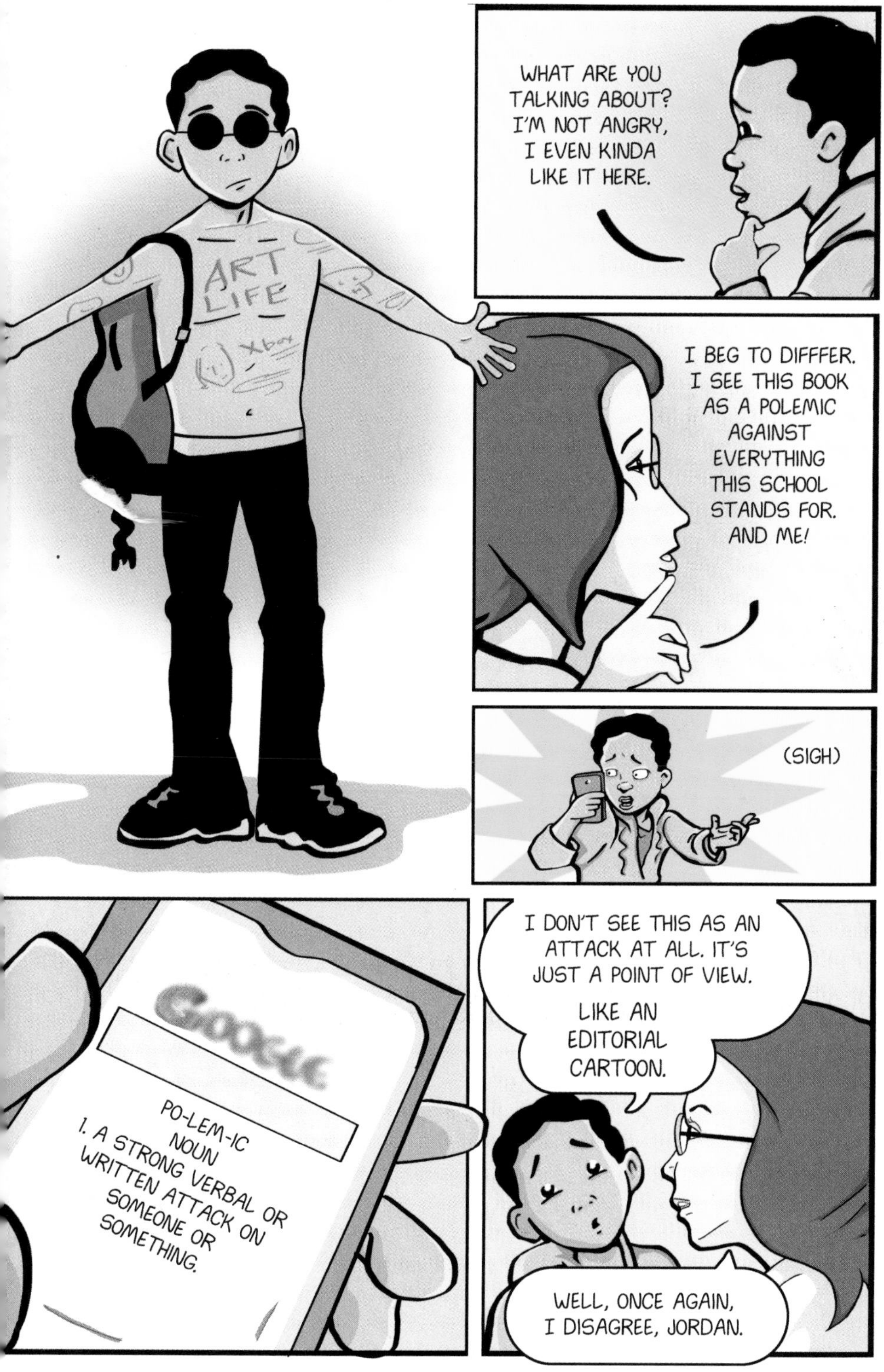

ART LIFE
Xbox
WHAT ARE YOU TALKING ABOUT? I'M NOT ANGRY, I EVEN KINDA LIKE IT HERE.
I BEG TO DIFFFER. I SEE THIS BOOK AS A POLEMIC AGAINST EVERYTHING THIS SCHOOL STANDS FOR. AND ME!
(SIGH)
PO-LEM-IC
NOUN
1. A STRONG VERBAL OR WRITTEN ATTACK ON SOMEONE OR SOMETHING.
I DON'T SEE THIS AS AN ATTACK AT ALL. IT'S JUST A POINT OF VIEW.
LIKE AN EDITORIAL CARTOON.
WELL, ONCE AGAIN, I DISAGREE, JORDAN.

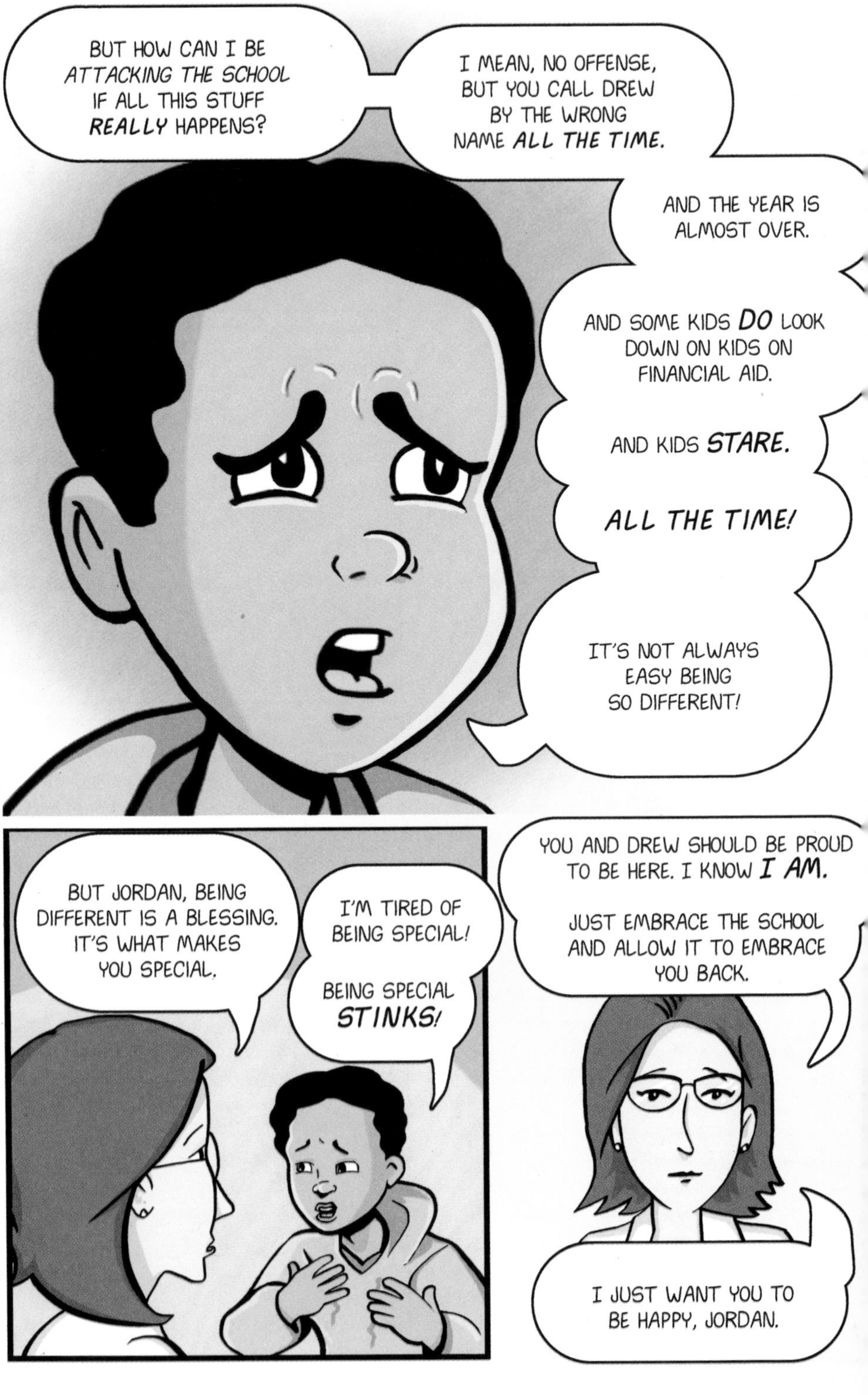

BUT HOW CAN I BE ATTACKING THE SCHOOL IF ALL THIS STUFF REALLY HAPPENS?
I MEAN, NO OFFENSE, BUT YOU CALL DREW BY THE WRONG NAME ALL THE TIME.
AND THE YEAR IS ALMOST OVER.
AND SOME KIDS DO LOOK DOWN ON KIDS ON FINANCIAL AID.
AND KIDS STARE.
ALL THE TIME!
IT'S NOT ALWAYS EASY BEING SO DIFFERENT!
BUT JORDAN, BEING DIFFERENT IS A BLESSING. IT'S WHAT MAKES YOU SPECIAL.
I'M TIRED OF BEING SPECIAL!
BEING SPECIAL STINKS!
YOU AND DREW SHOULD BE PROUD TO BE HERE. I KNOW I AM.
JUST EMBRACE THE SCHOOL AND ALLOW IT TO EMBRACE YOU BACK.
I JUST WANT YOU TO BE HAPPY, JORDAN.

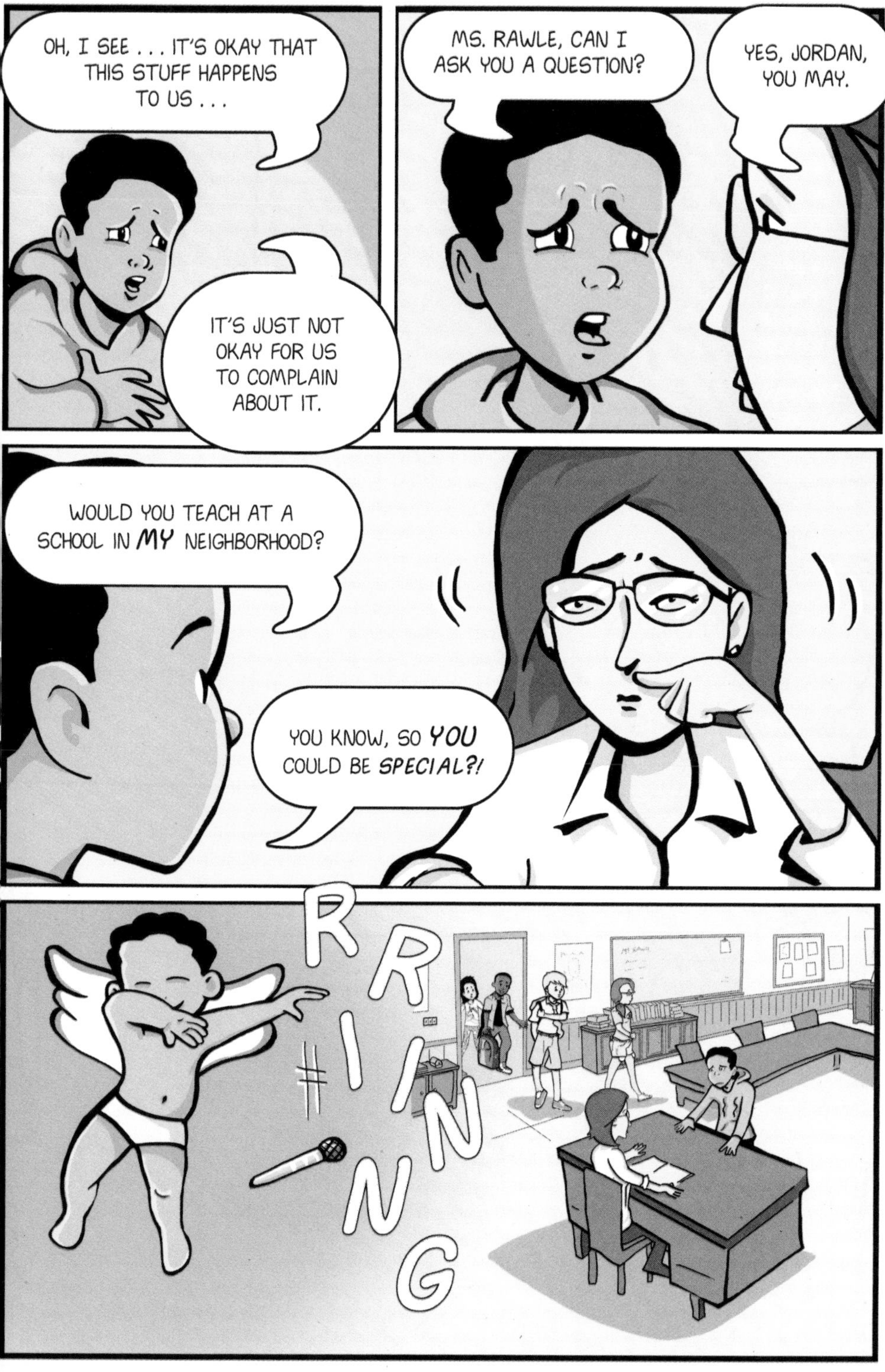
OH, I SEE . . . IT'S OKAY THAT THIS STUFF HAPPENS TO US . . .
IT'S JUST NOT OKAY FOR US TO COMPLAIN ABOUT IT.
MS. RAWLE, CAN I ASK YOU A QUESTION?
YES, JORDAN, YOU MAY.
WOULD YOU TEACH AT A SCHOOL IN MY NEIGHBORHOOD?
YOU KNOW, SO YOU COULD BE SPECIAL?!
RRING

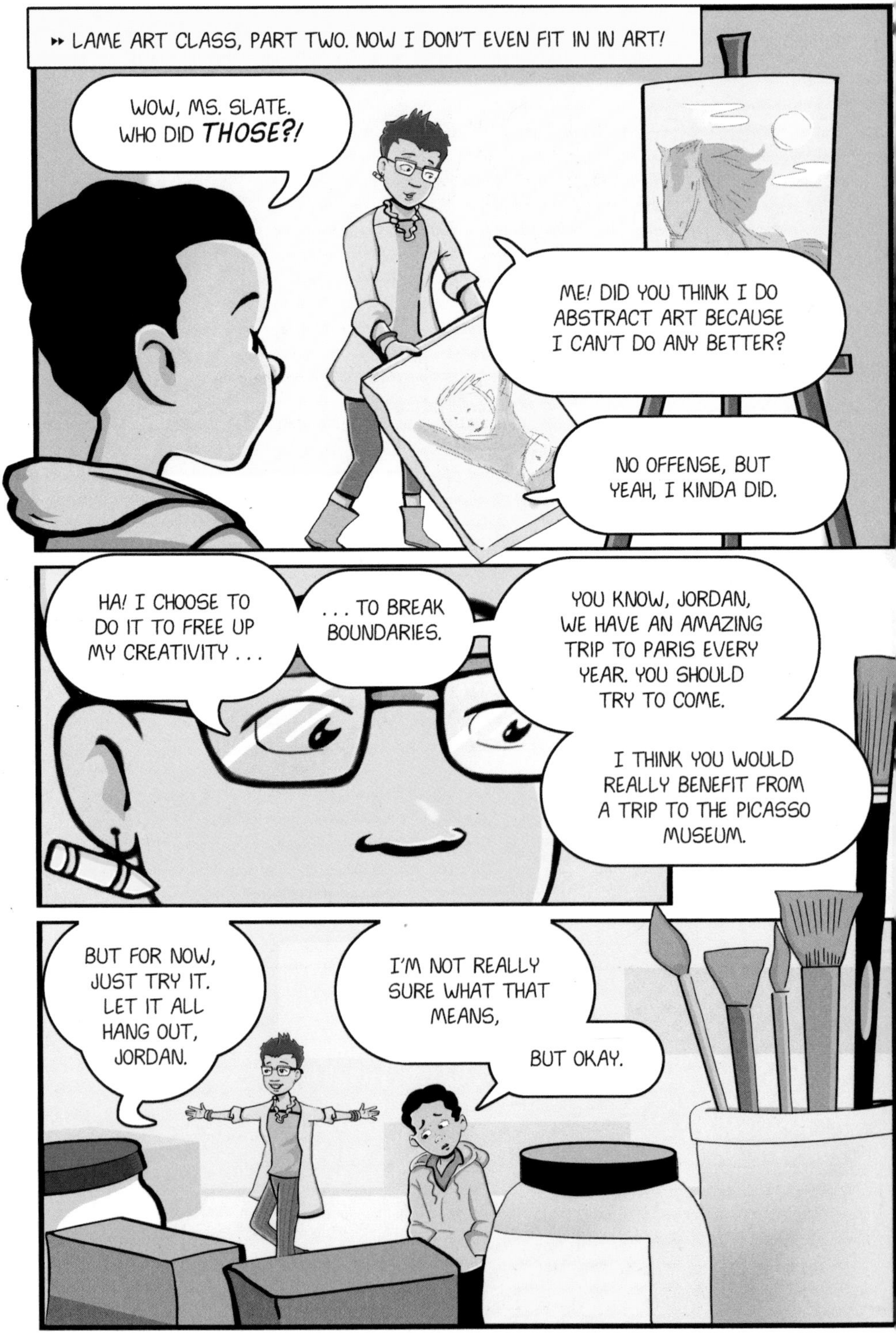
▸▸ LAME ART CLASS, PART TWO. NOW I DON'T EVEN FIT IN IN ART!
WOW, MS. SLATE. WHO DID *THOSE?!*
ME! DID YOU THINK I DO ABSTRACT ART BECAUSE I CAN'T DO ANY BETTER?
NO OFFENSE, BUT YEAH, I KINDA DID.
HA! I CHOOSE TO DO IT TO FREE UP MY CREATIVITY . . .
. . . TO BREAK BOUNDARIES.
YOU KNOW, JORDAN, WE HAVE AN AMAZING TRIP TO PARIS EVERY YEAR. YOU SHOULD TRY TO COME.
I THINK YOU WOULD REALLY BENEFIT FROM A TRIP TO THE PICASSO MUSEUM.
BUT FOR NOW, JUST TRY IT. LET IT ALL HANG OUT, JORDAN.
I'M NOT REALLY SURE WHAT THAT MEANS,
BUT OKAY.

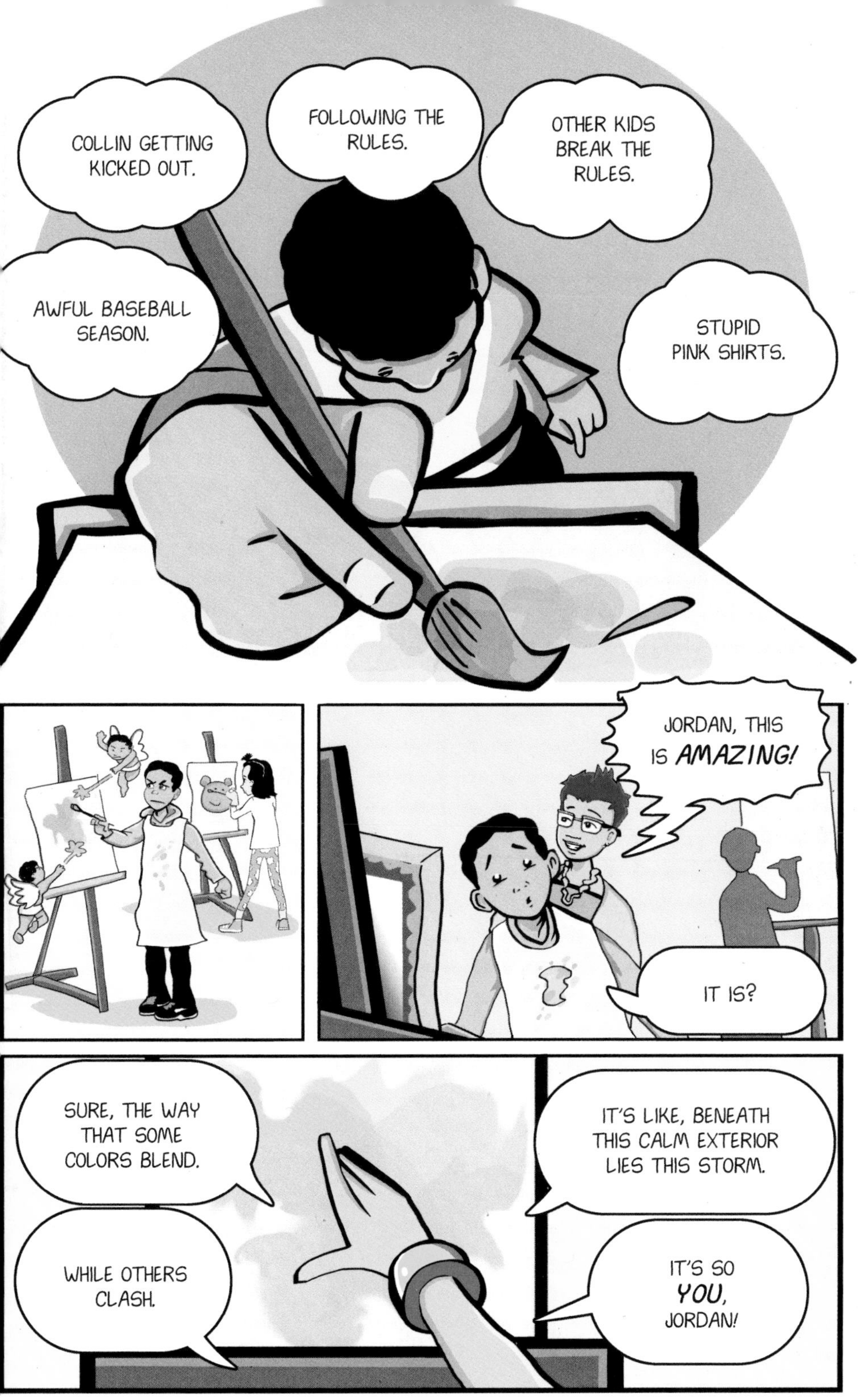
COLLIN GETTING KICKED OUT.
FOLLOWING THE RULES.
OTHER KIDS BREAK THE RULES.
AWFUL BASEBALL SEASON.
STUPID PINK SHIRTS.
JORDAN, THIS IS AMAZING!
IT IS?
SURE, THE WAY THAT SOME COLORS BLEND.
WHILE OTHERS CLASH.
IT'S LIKE, BENEATH THIS CALM EXTERIOR LIES THIS STORM.
IT'S SO YOU, JORDAN!

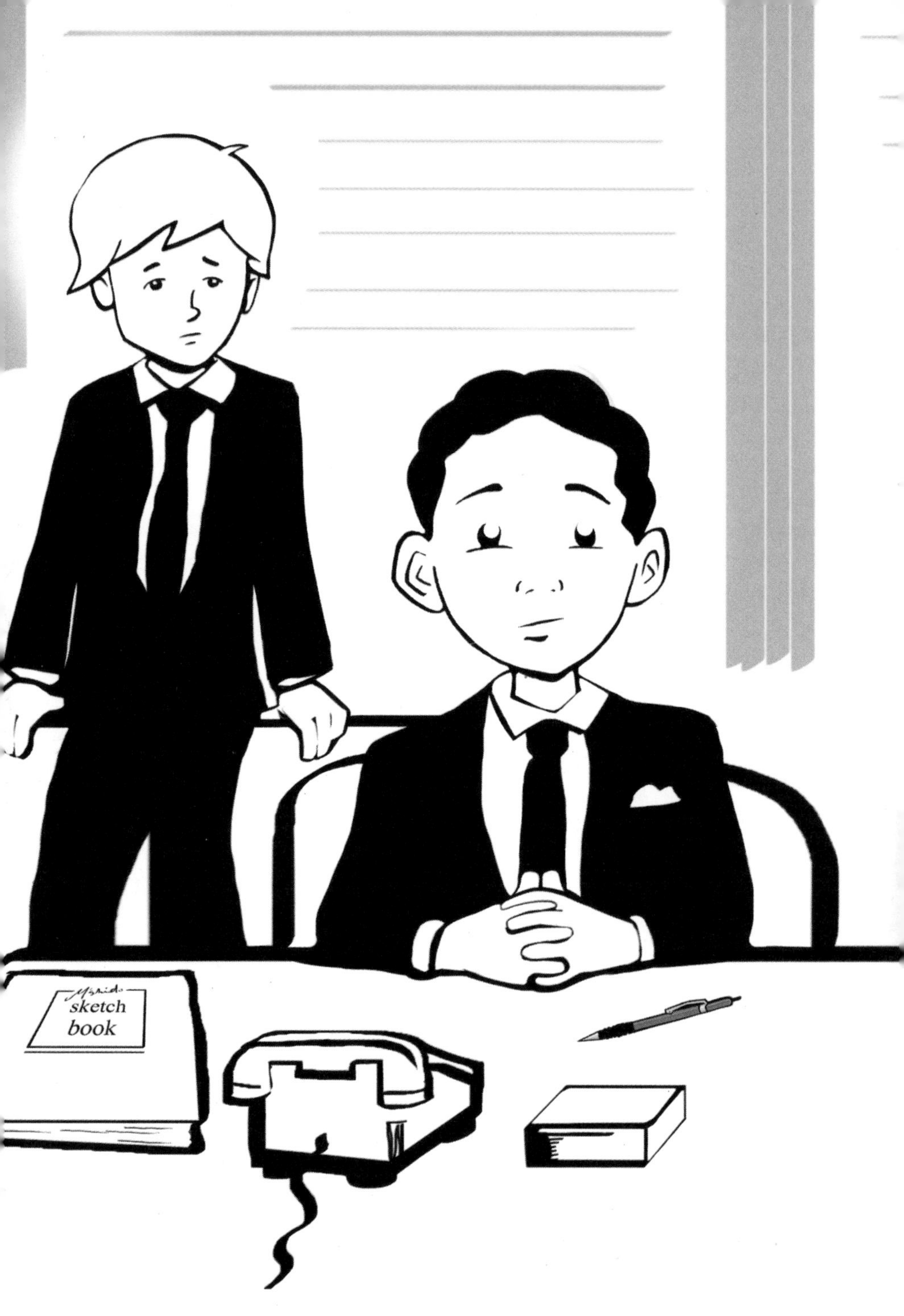
sketch
book

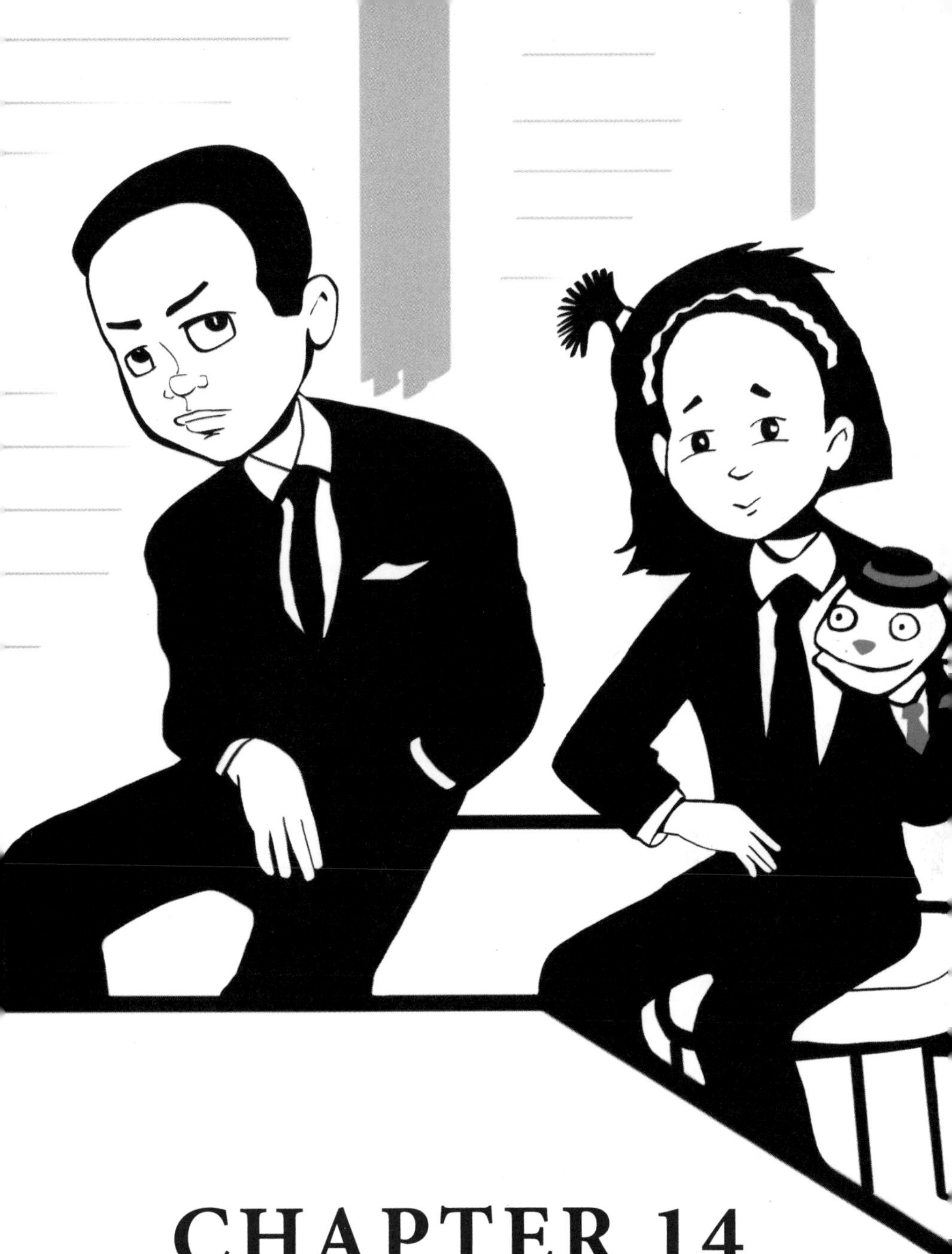

CHAPTER 14

RAD MEN

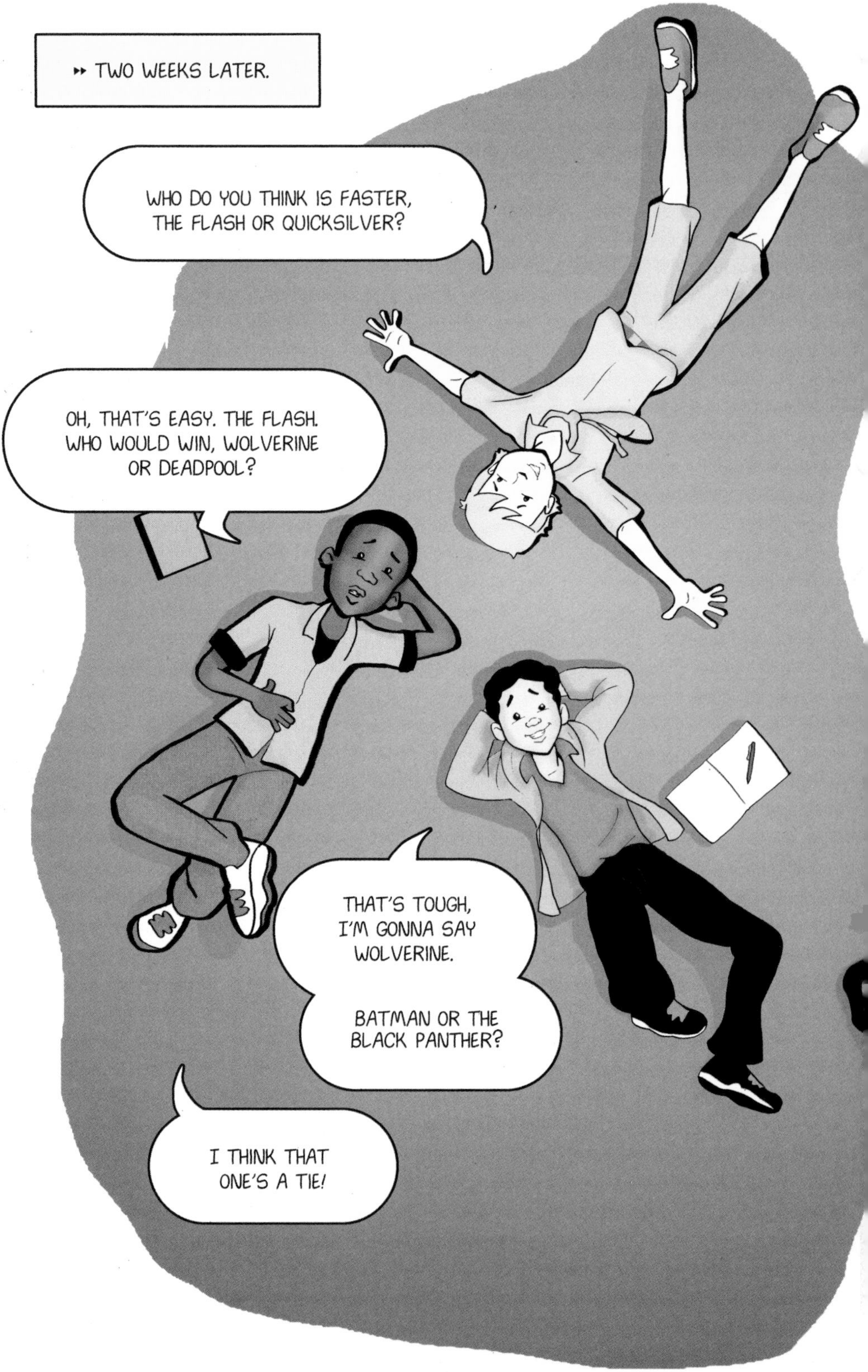
▸▸ TWO WEEKS LATER.
WHO DO YOU THINK IS FASTER, THE FLASH OR QUICKSILVER?
OH, THAT'S EASY. THE FLASH. WHO WOULD WIN, WOLVERINE OR DEADPOOL?
THAT'S TOUGH, I'M GONNA SAY WOLVERINE.
BATMAN OR THE BLACK PANTHER?
I THINK THAT ONE'S A TIE!

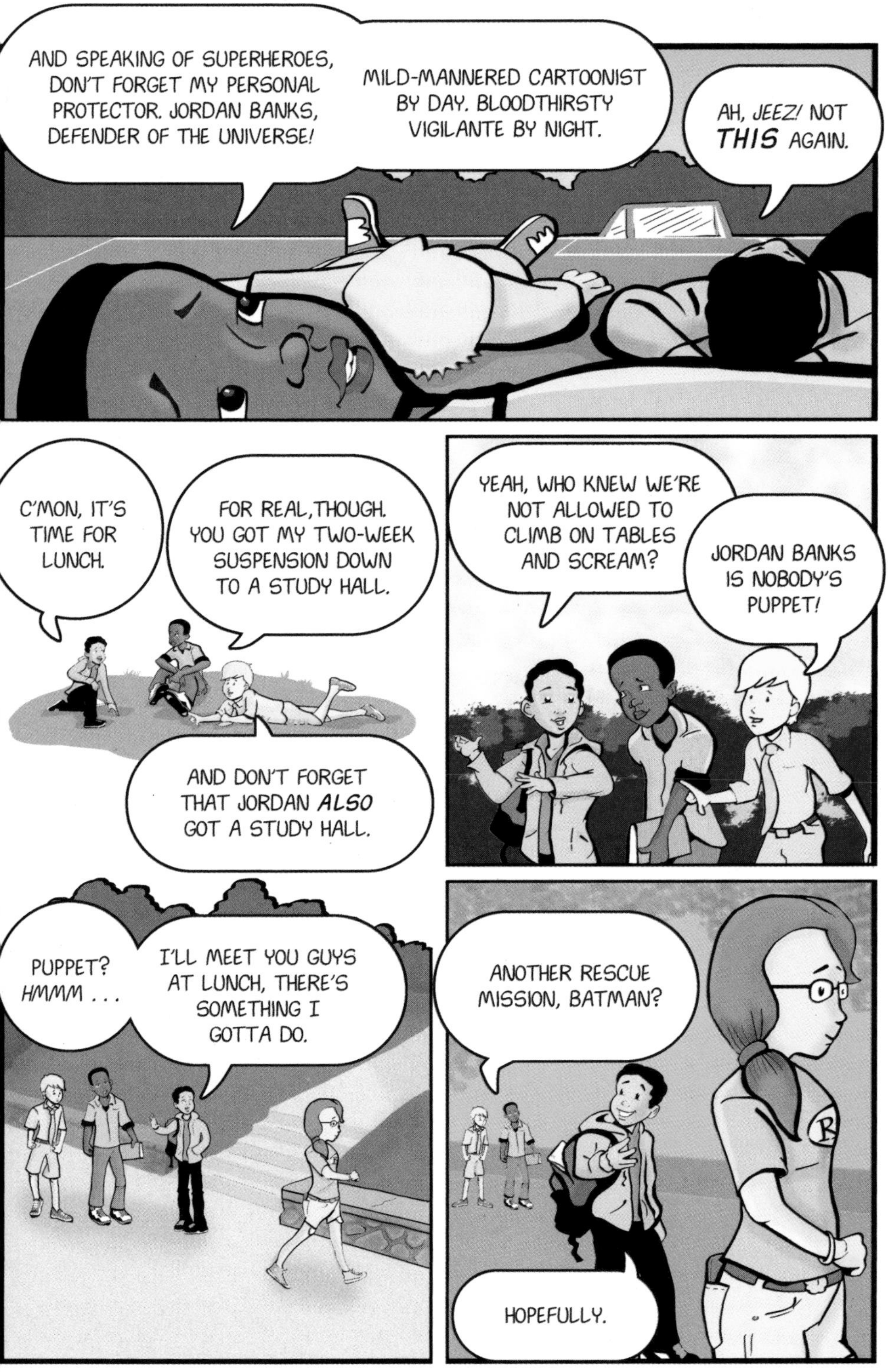
AND SPEAKING OF SUPERHEROES, DON'T FORGET MY PERSONAL PROTECTOR. JORDAN BANKS, DEFENDER OF THE UNIVERSE!
MILD-MANNERED CARTOONIST BY DAY. BLOODTHIRSTY VIGILANTE BY NIGHT.
AH, JEEZ! NOT *THIS* AGAIN.
C'MON, IT'S TIME FOR LUNCH.
FOR REAL,THOUGH. YOU GOT MY TWO-WEEK SUSPENSION DOWN TO A STUDY HALL.
AND DON'T FORGET THAT JORDAN *ALSO* GOT A STUDY HALL.
YEAH, WHO KNEW WE'RE NOT ALLOWED TO CLIMB ON TABLES AND SCREAM?
JORDAN BANKS IS NOBODY'S PUPPET!
PUPPET? HMMM . . .
I'LL MEET YOU GUYS AT LUNCH, THERE'S SOMETHING I GOTTA DO.
ANOTHER RESCUE MISSION, BATMAN?
HOPEFULLY.

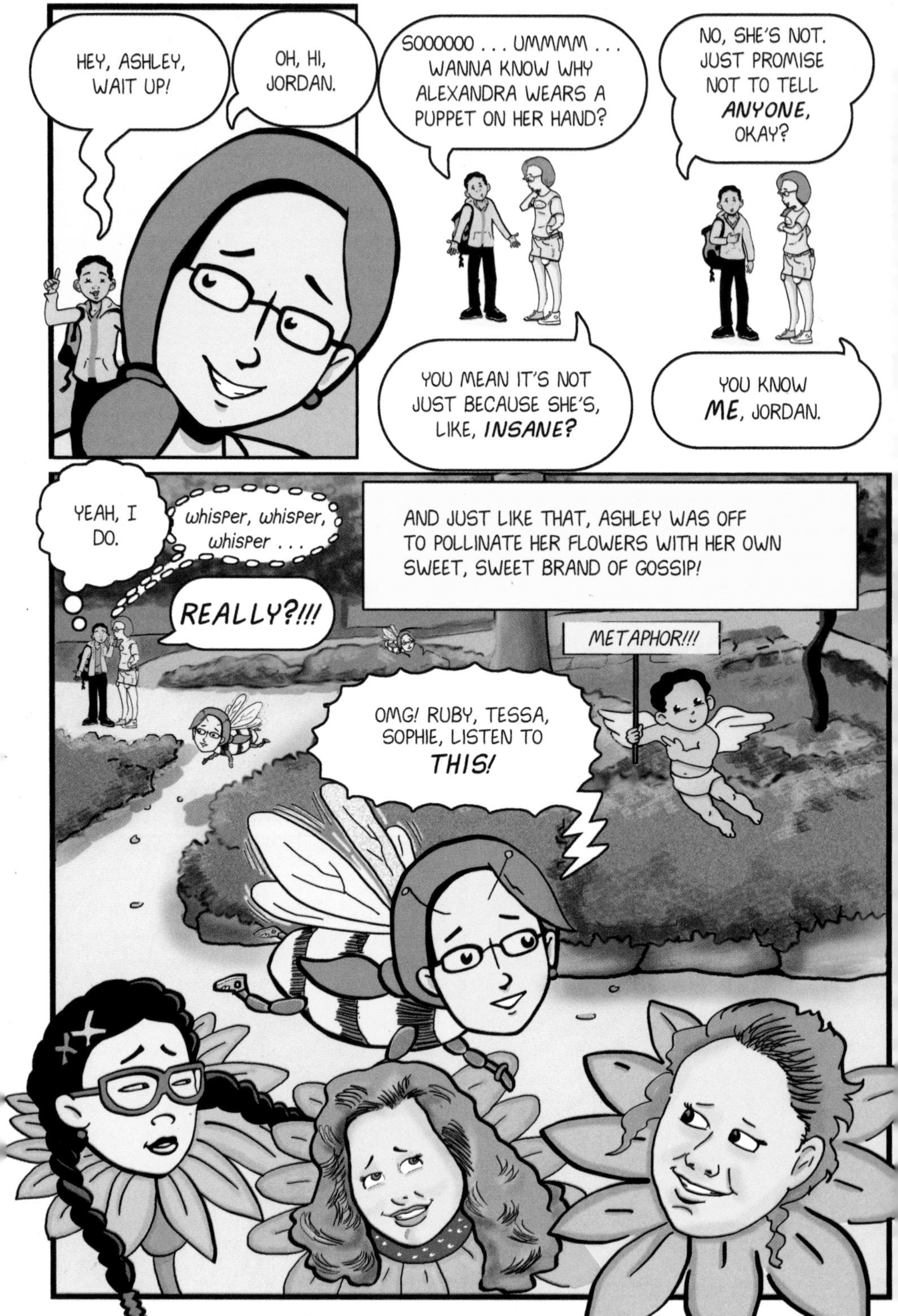
HEY, ASHLEY, WAIT UP!
OH, HI, JORDAN.
SOOOOOO . . . UMMMM . . . WANNA KNOW WHY ALEXANDRA WEARS A PUPPET ON HER HAND?
YOU MEAN IT'S NOT JUST BECAUSE SHE'S, LIKE, INSANE?
NO, SHE'S NOT. JUST PROMISE NOT TO TELL ANYONE, OKAY?
YOU KNOW ME, JORDAN.
YEAH, I DO.
whisper, whisper, whisper . . .
REALLY?!!!
AND JUST LIKE THAT, ASHLEY WAS OFF TO POLLINATE HER FLOWERS WITH HER OWN SWEET, SWEET BRAND OF GOSSIP!
METAPHOR!!!
OMG! RUBY, TESSA, SOPHIE, LISTEN TO THIS!

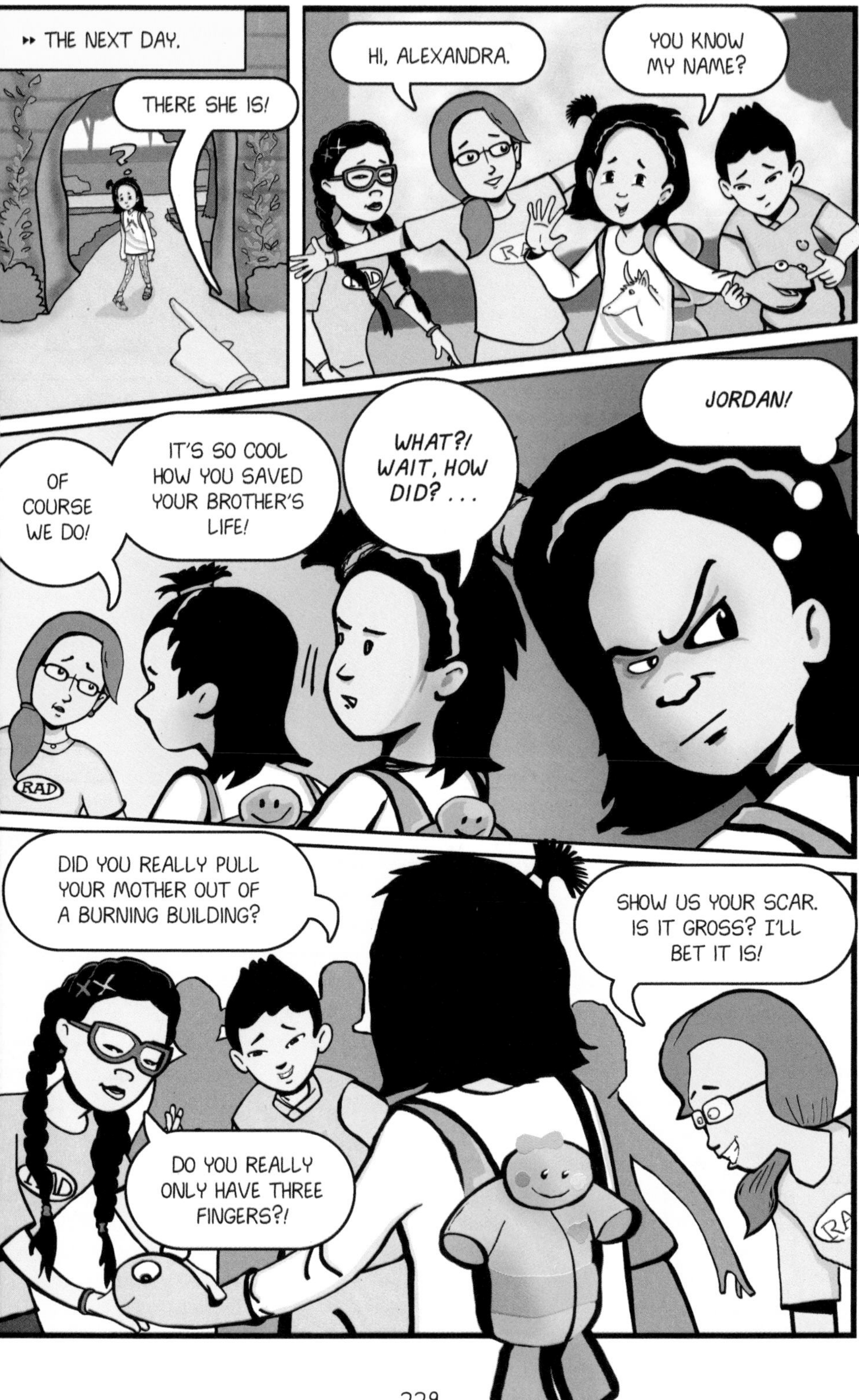

THE NEXT DAY.
THERE SHE IS!
HI, ALEXANDRA.
YOU KNOW MY NAME?
JORDAN!
OF COURSE WE DO!
IT'S SO COOL HOW YOU SAVED YOUR BROTHER'S LIFE!
WHAT?! WAIT, HOW DID? . . .
DID YOU REALLY PULL YOUR MOTHER OUT OF A BURNING BUILDING?
SHOW US YOUR SCAR. IS IT GROSS? I'LL BET IT IS!
DO YOU REALLY ONLY HAVE THREE FINGERS?!

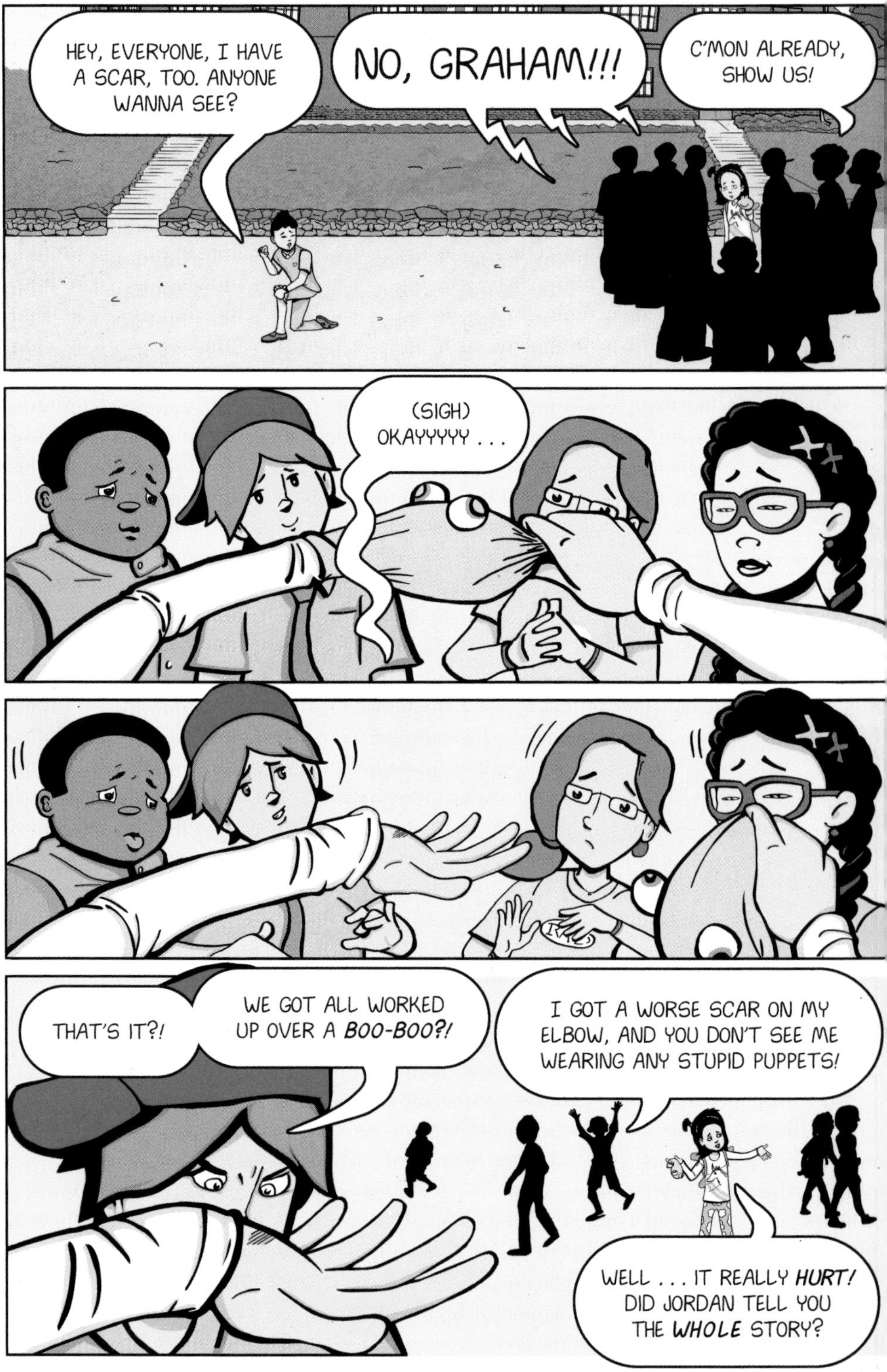
HEY, EVERYONE, I HAVE A SCAR, TOO. ANYONE WANNA SEE?
NO, GRAHAM!!!
C'MON ALREADY, SHOW US!
(SIGH) OKAYYYYY . . .
THAT'S IT?!
WE GOT ALL WORKED UP OVER A *BOO-BOO?!*
I GOT A WORSE SCAR ON MY ELBOW, AND YOU DON'T SEE ME WEARING ANY STUPID PUPPETS!
WELL . . . IT REALLY ***HURT!*** DID JORDAN TELL YOU THE ***WHOLE*** STORY?

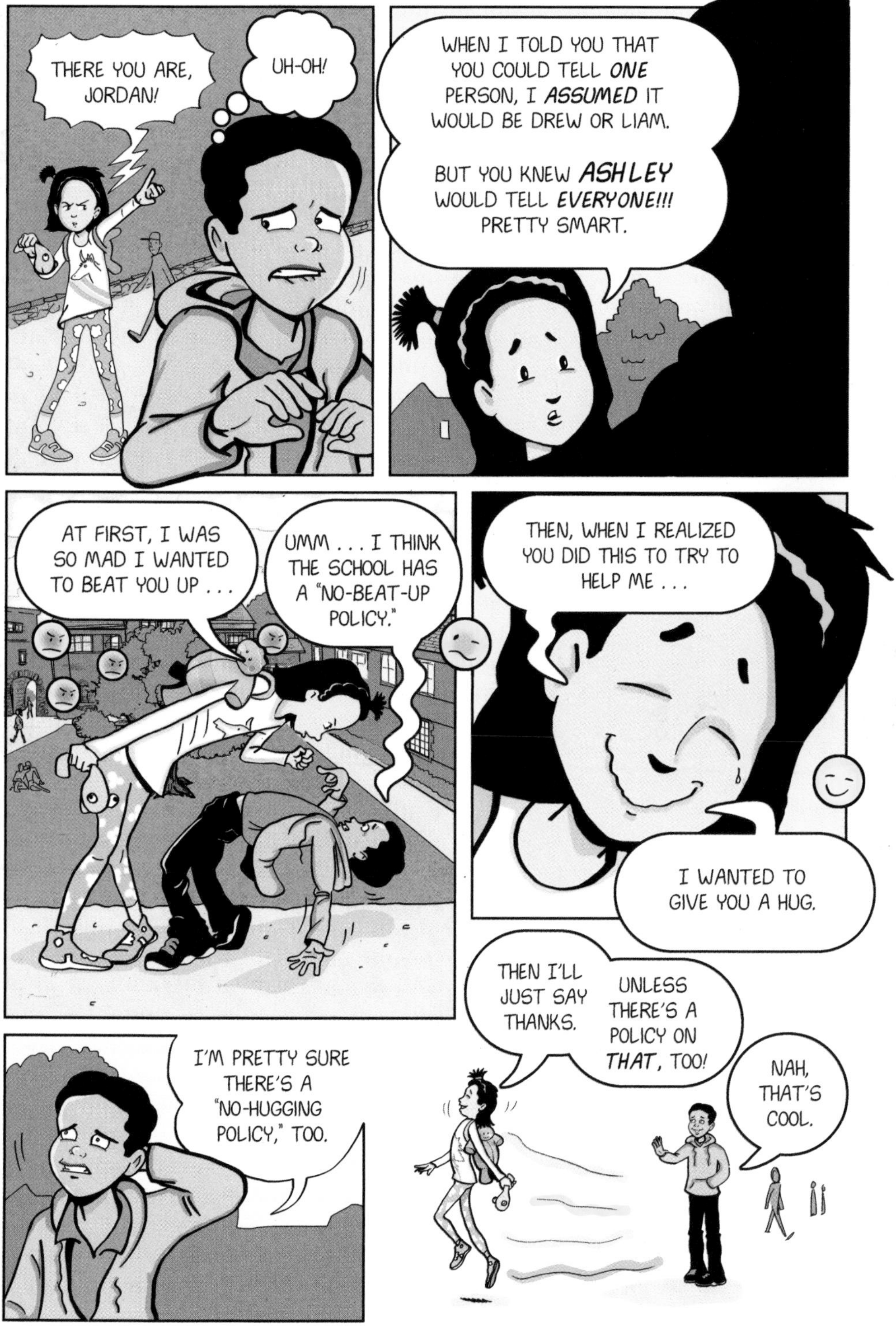
THERE YOU ARE, JORDAN!
UH-OH!
WHEN I TOLD YOU THAT YOU COULD TELL *ONE* PERSON, I *ASSUMED* IT WOULD BE DREW OR LIAM.
BUT YOU KNEW ***ASHLEY*** WOULD TELL *EVERYONE!!!* PRETTY SMART.
AT FIRST, I WAS SO MAD I WANTED TO BEAT YOU UP . . .
UMM . . . I THINK THE SCHOOL HAS A "NO-BEAT-UP POLICY."
THEN, WHEN I REALIZED YOU DID THIS TO TRY TO HELP ME . . .
I WANTED TO GIVE YOU A HUG.
I'M PRETTY SURE THERE'S A "NO-HUGGING POLICY," TOO.
THEN I'LL JUST SAY THANKS.
UNLESS THERE'S A POLICY ON *THAT*, TOO!
NAH, THAT'S COOL.

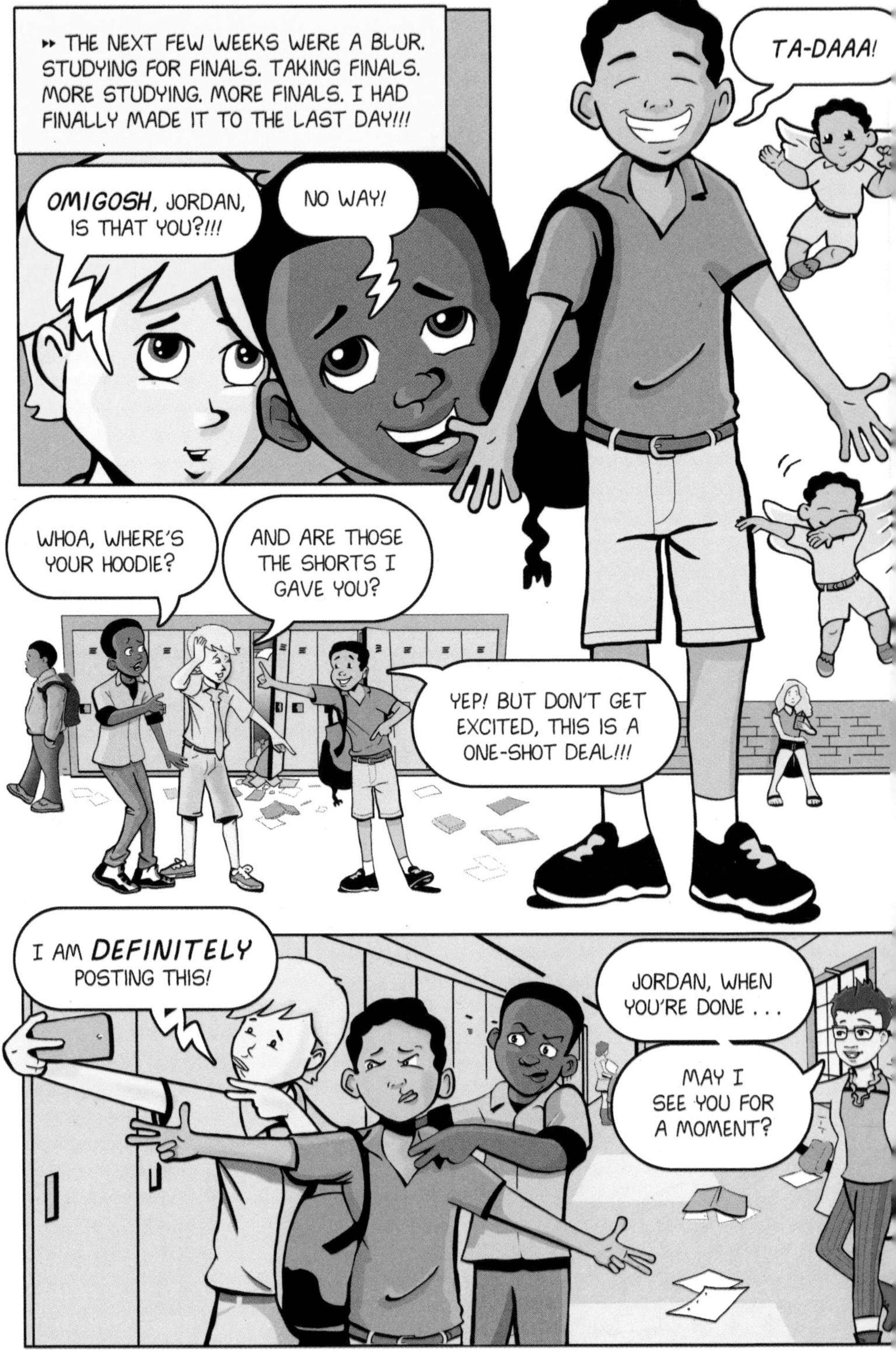
THE NEXT FEW WEEKS WERE A BLUR. STUDYING FOR FINALS. TAKING FINALS. MORE STUDYING. MORE FINALS. I HAD FINALLY MADE IT TO THE LAST DAY!!!
OMIGOSH, JORDAN, IS THAT YOU?!!!
NO WAY!
TA-DAAA!
WHOA, WHERE'S YOUR HOODIE?
AND ARE THOSE THE SHORTS I GAVE YOU?
YEP! BUT DON'T GET EXCITED, THIS IS A ONE-SHOT DEAL!!!
I AM DEFINITELY POSTING THIS!
JORDAN, WHEN YOU'RE DONE . . .
MAY I SEE YOU FOR A MOMENT?

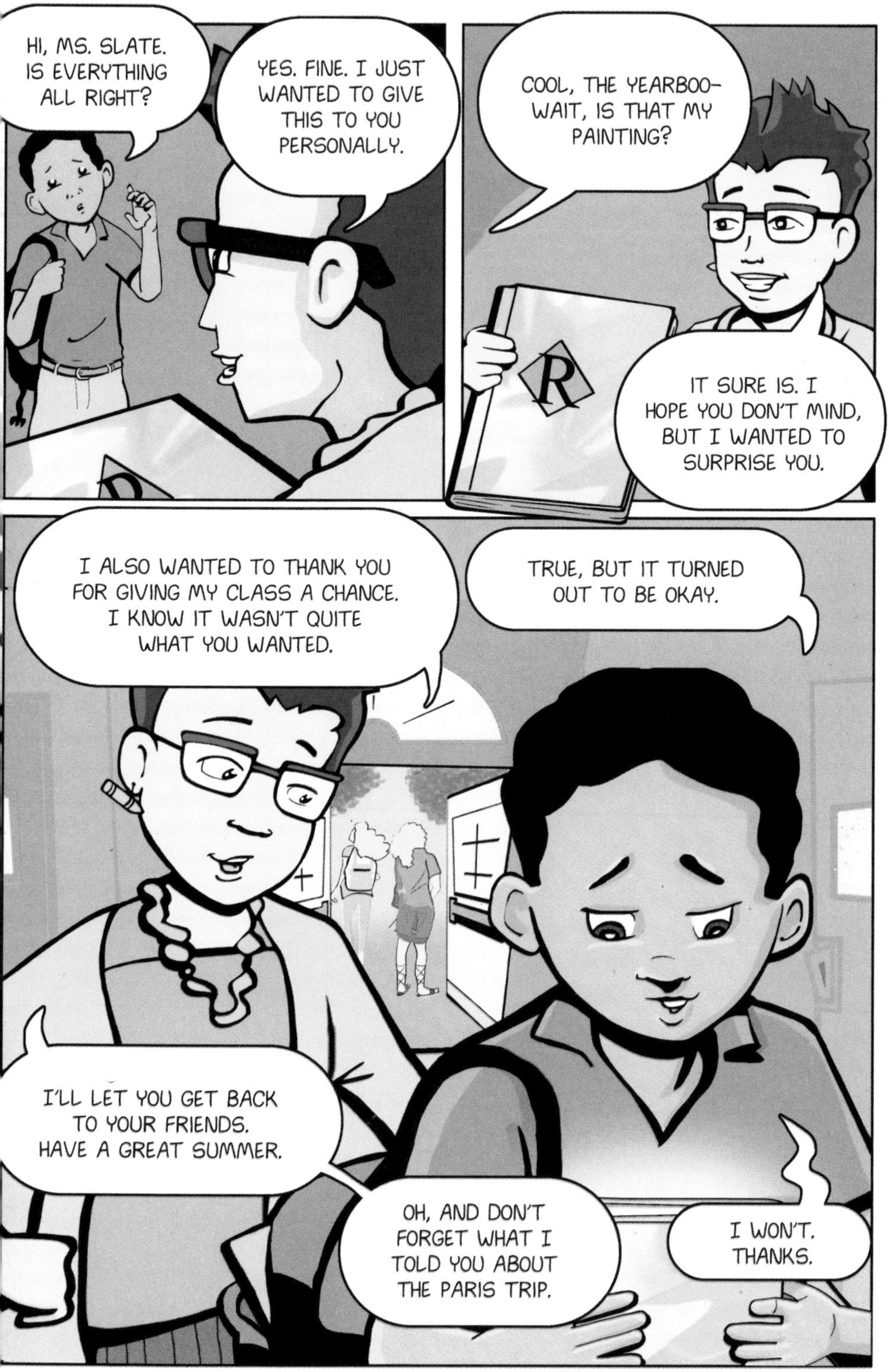
HI, MS. SLATE. IS EVERYTHING ALL RIGHT?
YES. FINE. I JUST WANTED TO GIVE THIS TO YOU PERSONALLY.
COOL, THE YEARBOO- WAIT, IS THAT MY PAINTING?
IT SURE IS. I HOPE YOU DON'T MIND, BUT I WANTED TO SURPRISE YOU.
I ALSO WANTED TO THANK YOU FOR GIVING MY CLASS A CHANCE. I KNOW IT WASN'T QUITE WHAT YOU WANTED.
TRUE, BUT IT TURNED OUT TO BE OKAY.
I'LL LET YOU GET BACK TO YOUR FRIENDS. HAVE A GREAT SUMMER.
OH, AND DON'T FORGET WHAT I TOLD YOU ABOUT THE PARIS TRIP.
I WON'T. THANKS.

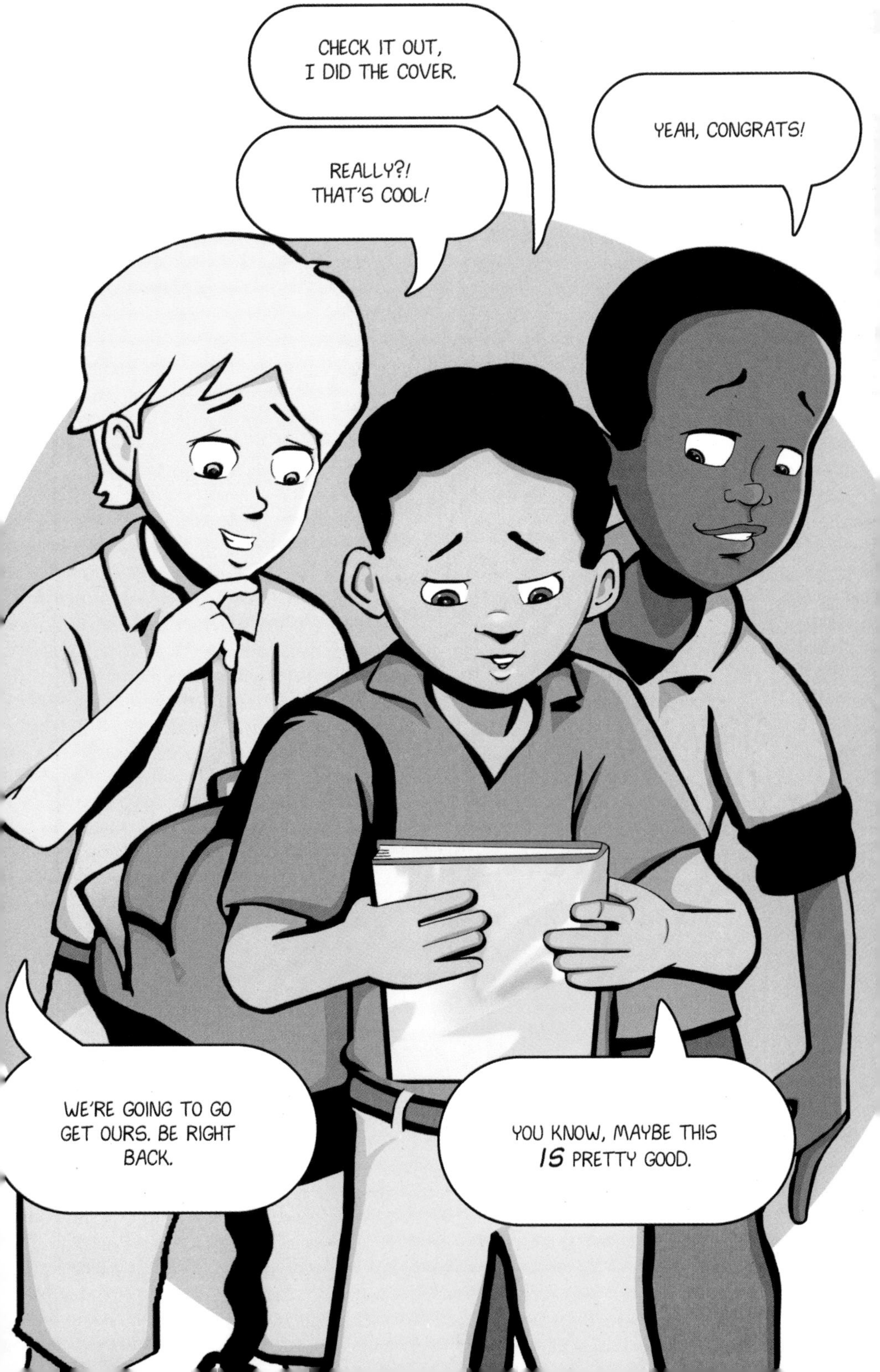
CHECK IT OUT, I DID THE COVER.
REALLY?! THAT'S COOL!
YEAH, CONGRATS!
WE'RE GOING TO GO GET OURS. BE RIGHT BACK.
YOU KNOW, MAYBE THIS *IS* PRETTY GOOD.

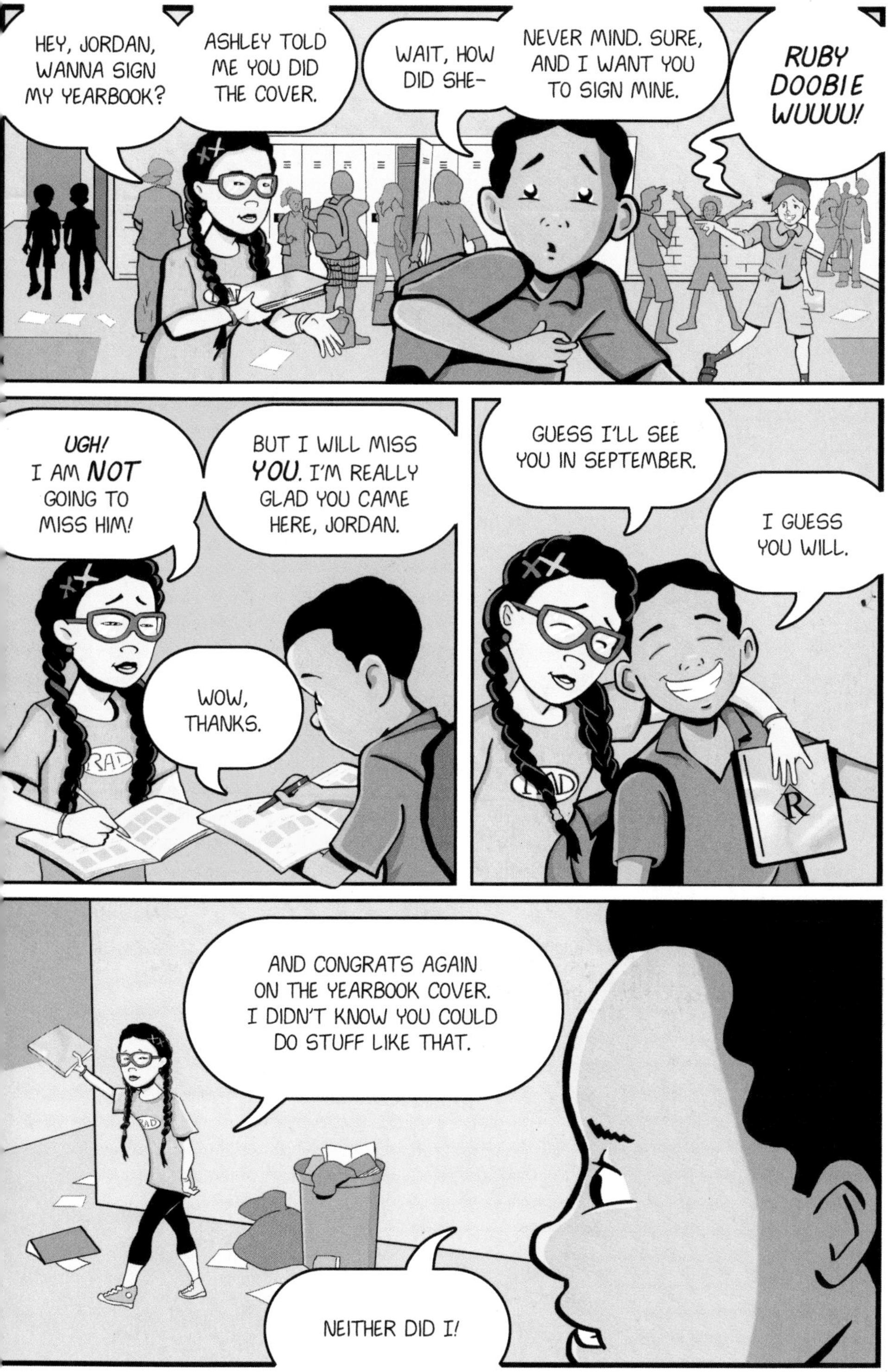
HEY, JORDAN, WANNA SIGN MY YEARBOOK?
ASHLEY TOLD ME YOU DID THE COVER.
WAIT, HOW DID SHE-
NEVER MIND. SURE, AND I WANT YOU TO SIGN MINE.
RUBY DOOBIE WUUUU!
UGH! I AM NOT GOING TO MISS HIM!
BUT I WILL MISS YOU. I'M REALLY GLAD YOU CAME HERE, JORDAN.
WOW, THANKS.
GUESS I'LL SEE YOU IN SEPTEMBER.
I GUESS YOU WILL.
AND CONGRATS AGAIN ON THE YEARBOOK COVER. I DIDN'T KNOW YOU COULD DO STUFF LIKE THAT.
NEITHER DID I!

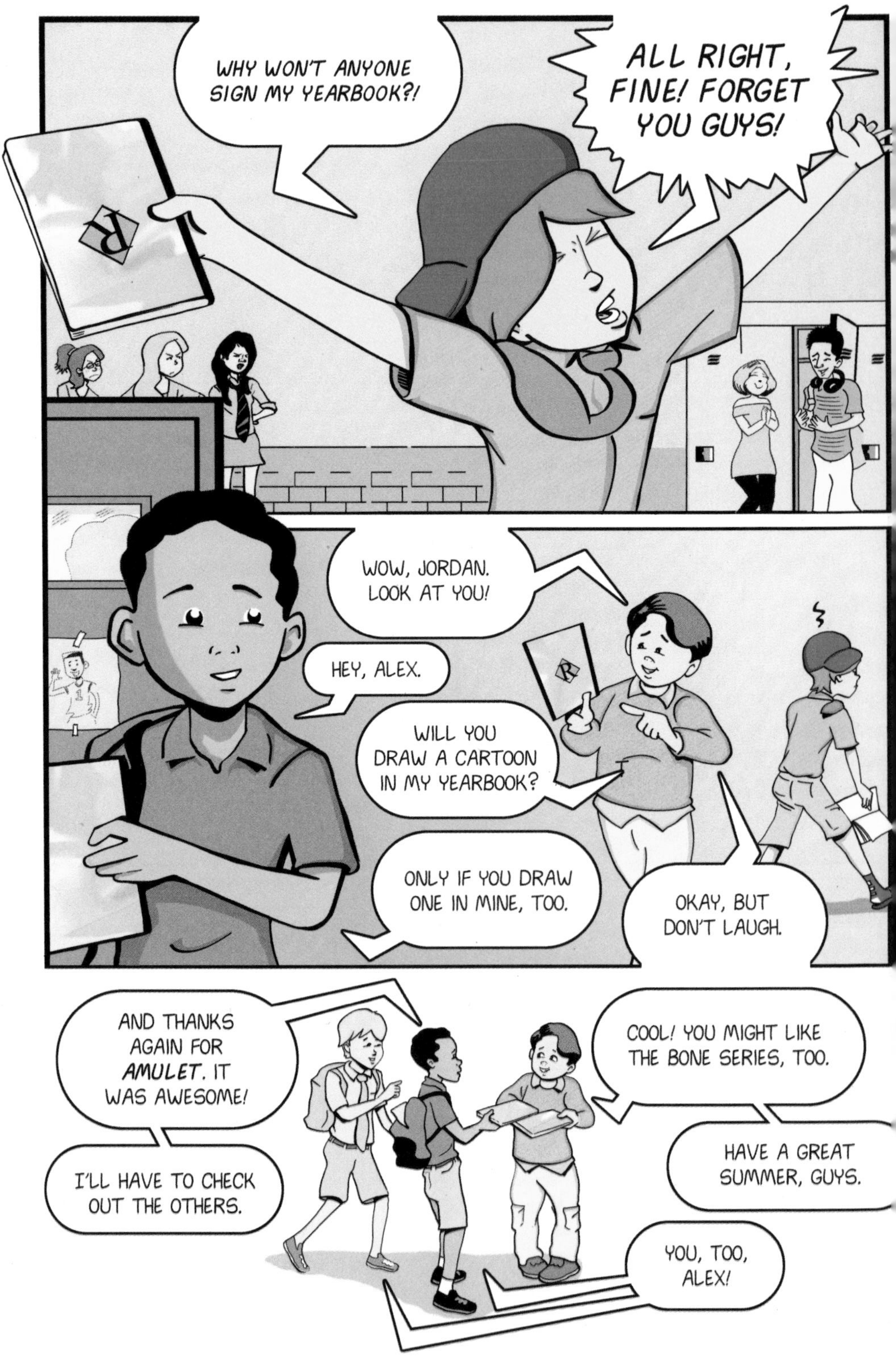
WHY WON'T ANYONE SIGN MY YEARBOOK?!
ALL RIGHT, FINE! FORGET YOU GUYS!
WOW, JORDAN. LOOK AT YOU!
HEY, ALEX.
WILL YOU DRAW A CARTOON IN MY YEARBOOK?
ONLY IF YOU DRAW ONE IN MINE, TOO.
OKAY, BUT DON'T LAUGH.
AND THANKS AGAIN FOR *AMULET*. IT WAS AWESOME!
I'LL HAVE TO CHECK OUT THE OTHERS.
COOL! YOU MIGHT LIKE THE BONE SERIES, TOO.
HAVE A GREAT SUMMER, GUYS.
YOU, TOO, ALEX!

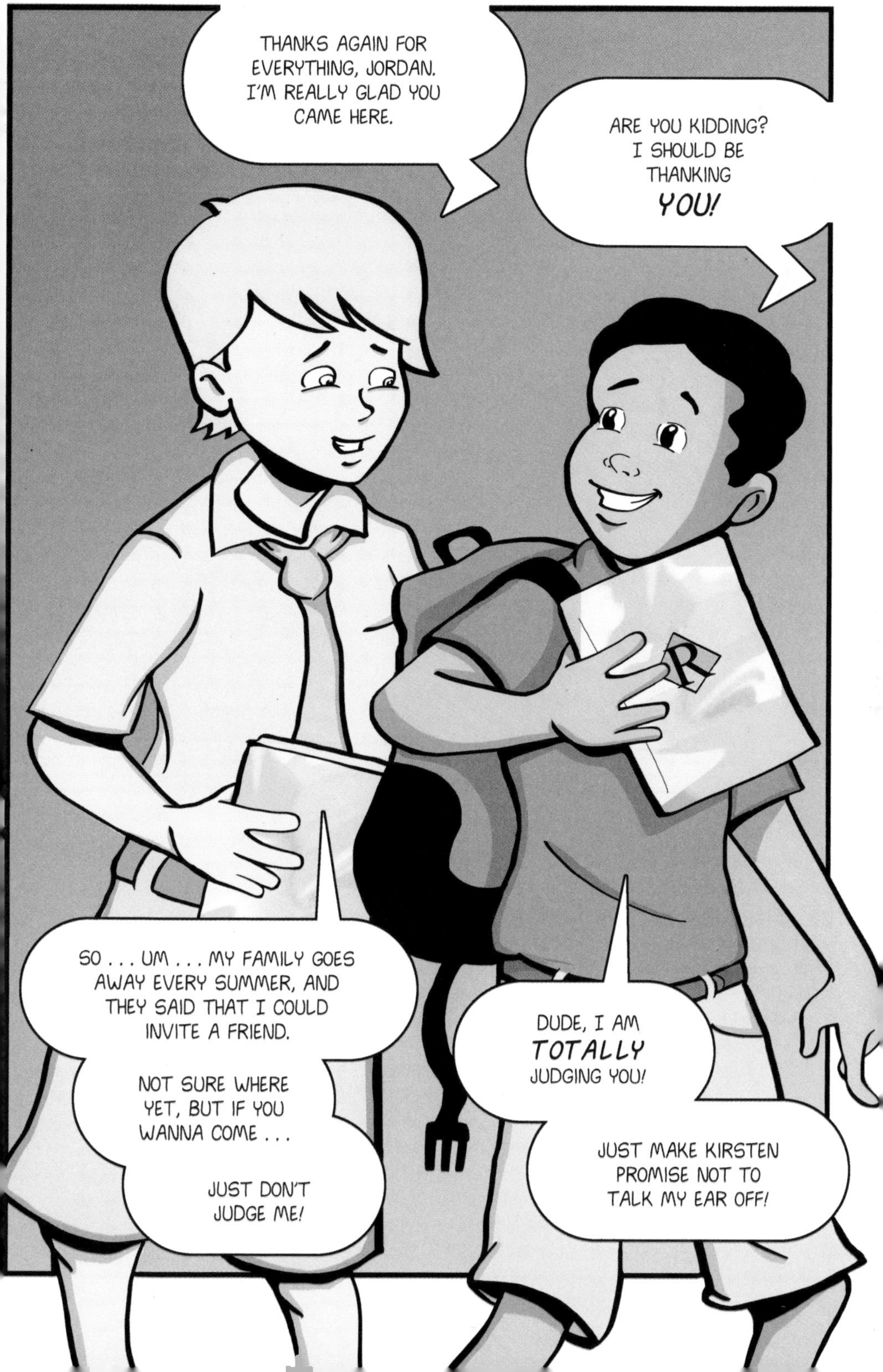

THANKS AGAIN FOR EVERYTHING, JORDAN. I'M REALLY GLAD YOU CAME HERE.
ARE YOU KIDDING? I SHOULD BE THANKING *YOU!*
SO . . . UM . . . MY FAMILY GOES AWAY EVERY SUMMER, AND THEY SAID THAT I COULD INVITE A FRIEND.
NOT SURE WHERE YET, BUT IF YOU WANNA COME . . .
JUST DON'T JUDGE ME!
DUDE, I AM *TOTALLY* JUDGING YOU!
JUST MAKE KIRSTEN PROMISE NOT TO TALK MY EAR OFF!

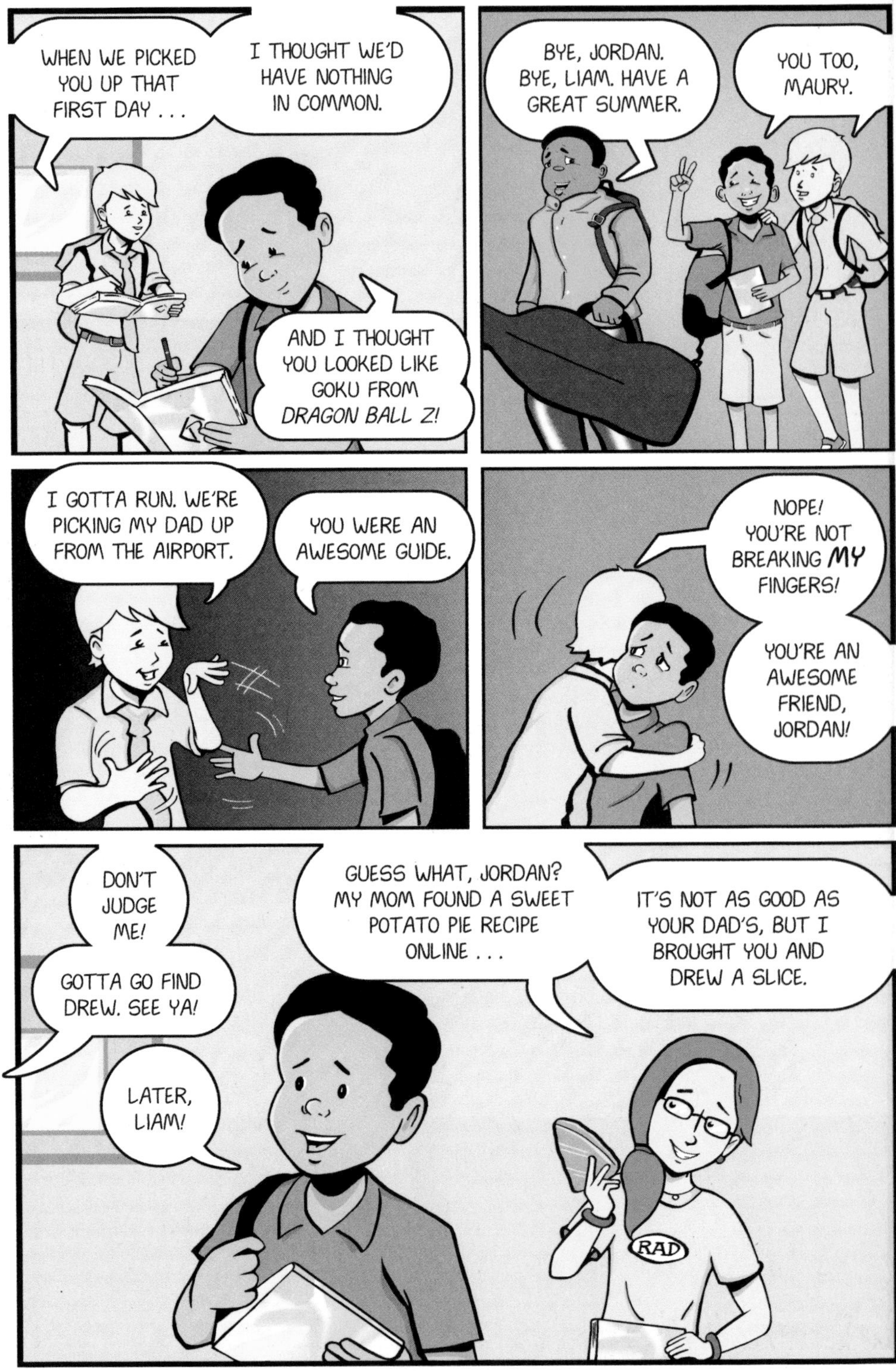
WHEN WE PICKED YOU UP THAT FIRST DAY . . .
I THOUGHT WE'D HAVE NOTHING IN COMMON.
AND I THOUGHT YOU LOOKED LIKE GOKU FROM *DRAGON BALL Z*!
BYE, JORDAN. BYE, LIAM. HAVE A GREAT SUMMER.
YOU TOO, MAURY.
I GOTTA RUN. WE'RE PICKING MY DAD UP FROM THE AIRPORT.
YOU WERE AN AWESOME GUIDE.
NOPE! YOU'RE NOT BREAKING **MY** FINGERS!
YOU'RE AN AWESOME FRIEND, JORDAN!
DON'T JUDGE ME!
GOTTA GO FIND DREW. SEE YA!
LATER, LIAM!
GUESS WHAT, JORDAN? MY MOM FOUND A SWEET POTATO PIE RECIPE ONLINE . . .
IT'S NOT AS GOOD AS YOUR DAD'S, BUT I BROUGHT YOU AND DREW A SLICE.
RAD

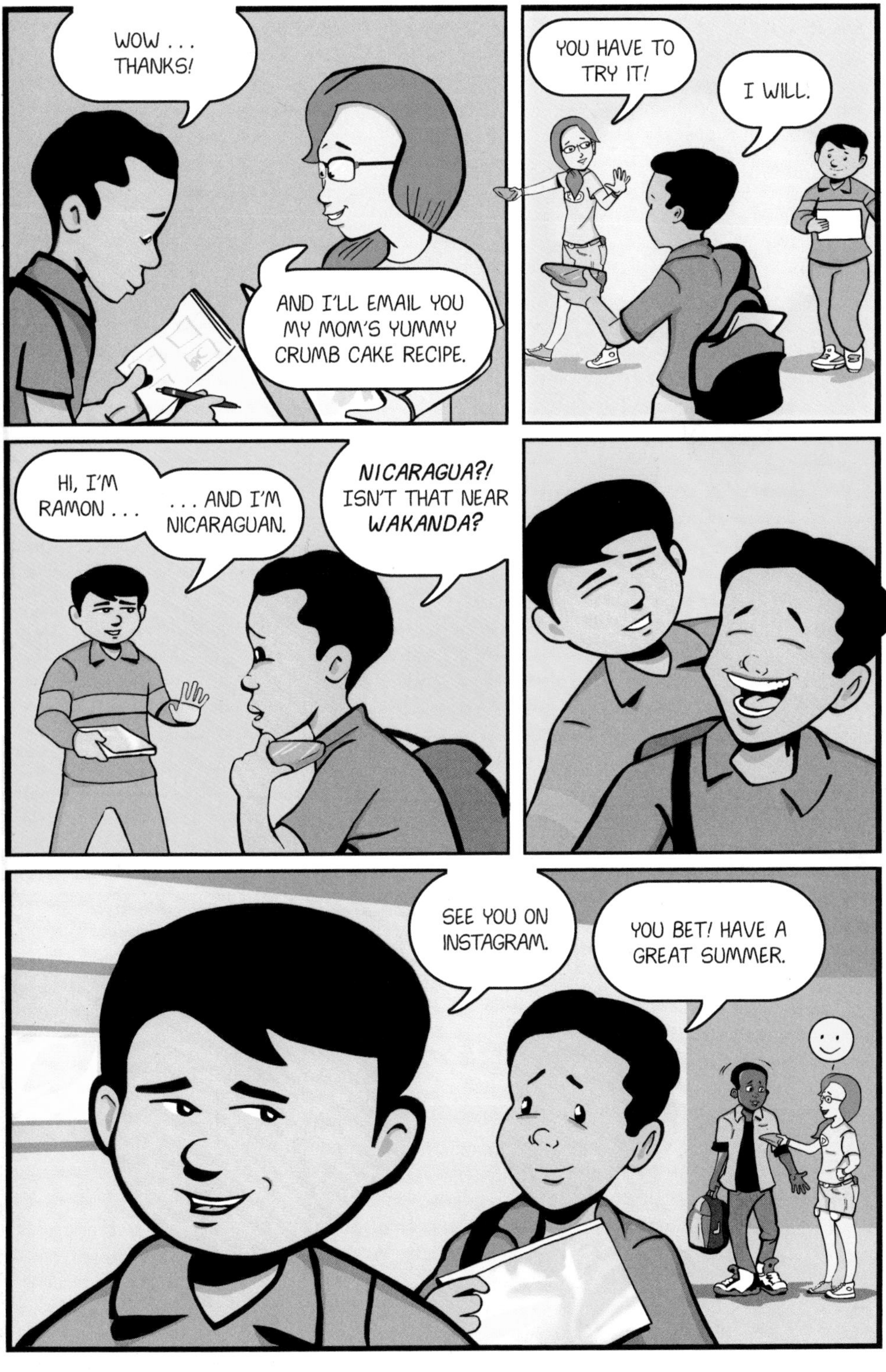
WOW . . . THANKS!
AND I'LL EMAIL YOU MY MOM'S YUMMY CRUMB CAKE RECIPE.
YOU HAVE TO TRY IT!
I WILL.
HI, I'M RAMON . . .
. . . AND I'M NICARAGUAN.
NICARAGUA?! ISN'T THAT NEAR *WAKANDA?*
SEE YOU ON INSTAGRAM.
YOU BET! HAVE A GREAT SUMMER.

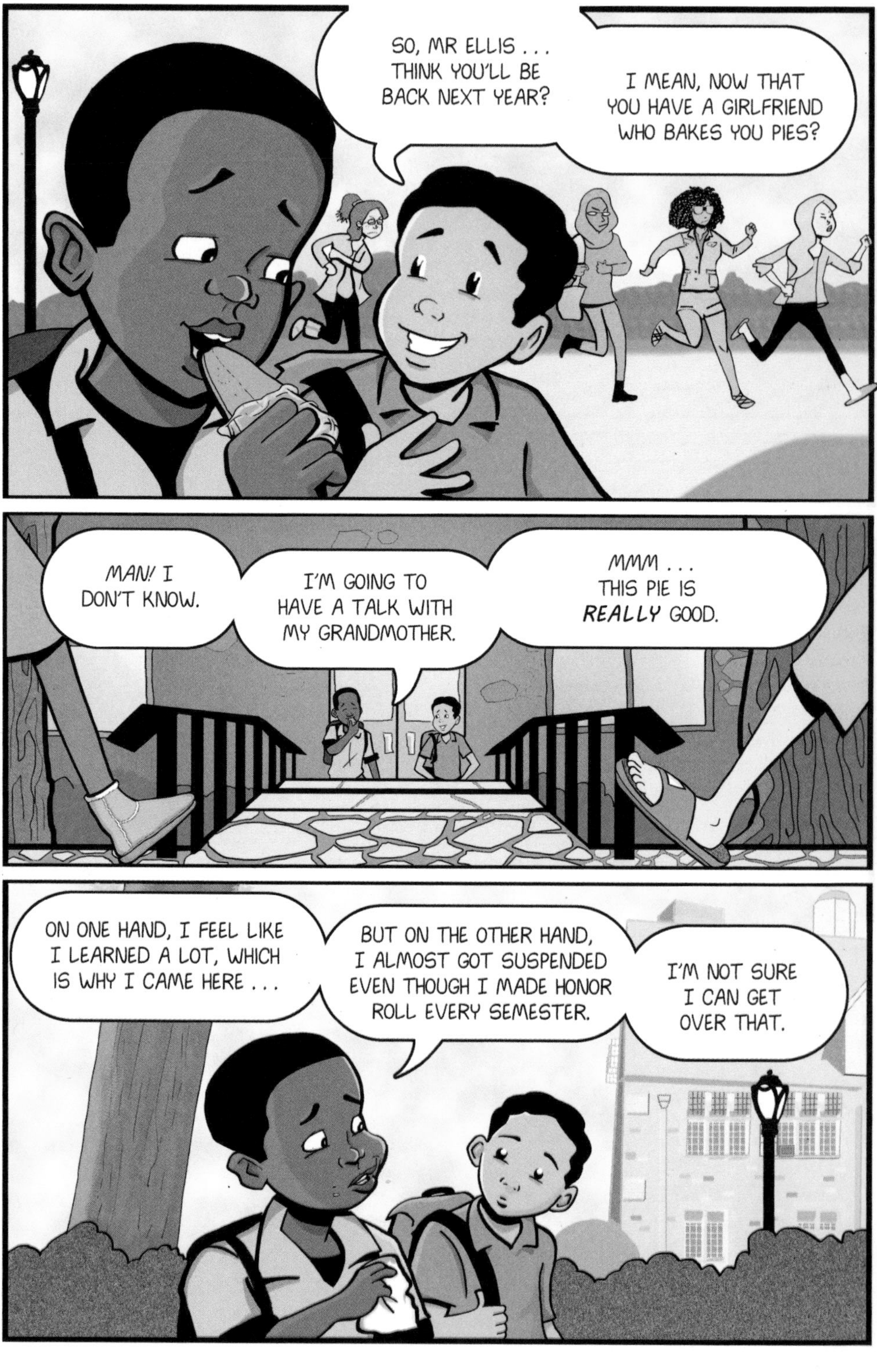
SO, MR ELLIS . . . THINK YOU'LL BE BACK NEXT YEAR?
I MEAN, NOW THAT YOU HAVE A GIRLFRIEND WHO BAKES YOU PIES?
MAN! I DON'T KNOW.
I'M GOING TO HAVE A TALK WITH MY GRANDMOTHER.
MMM . . . THIS PIE IS REALLY GOOD.
ON ONE HAND, I FEEL LIKE I LEARNED A LOT, WHICH IS WHY I CAME HERE . . .
BUT ON THE OTHER HAND, I ALMOST GOT SUSPENDED EVEN THOUGH I MADE HONOR ROLL EVERY SEMESTER.
I'M NOT SURE I CAN GET OVER THAT.

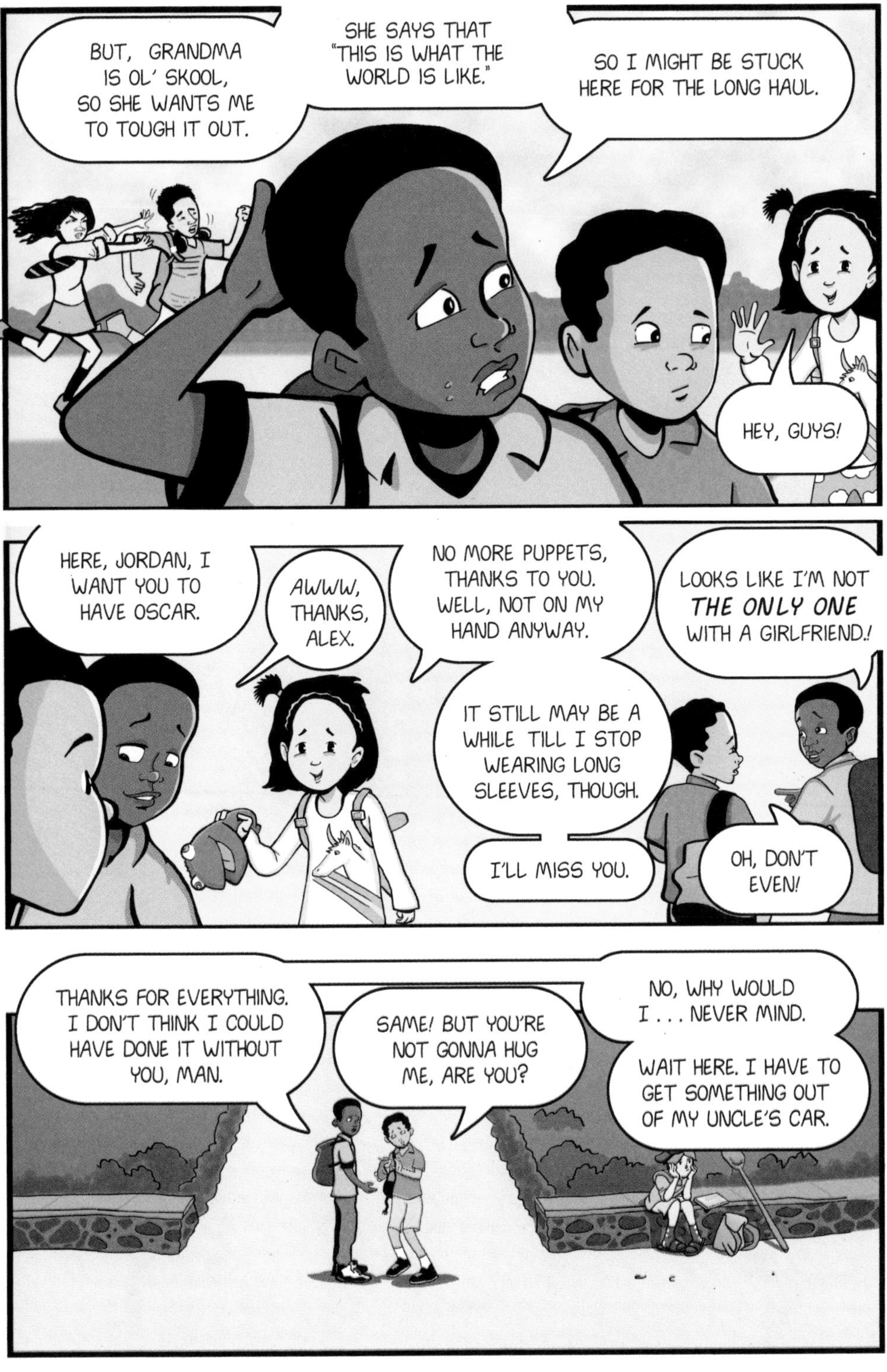
BUT, GRANDMA IS OL' SKOOL, SO SHE WANTS ME TO TOUGH IT OUT.
SHE SAYS THAT "THIS IS WHAT THE WORLD IS LIKE."
SO I MIGHT BE STUCK HERE FOR THE LONG HAUL.
HEY, GUYS!
HERE, JORDAN, I WANT YOU TO HAVE OSCAR.
AWWW, THANKS, ALEX.
NO MORE PUPPETS, THANKS TO YOU. WELL, NOT ON MY HAND ANYWAY.
IT STILL MAY BE A WHILE TILL I STOP WEARING LONG SLEEVES, THOUGH.
I'LL MISS YOU.
LOOKS LIKE I'M NOT ***THE ONLY ONE*** WITH A GIRLFRIEND.!
OH, DON'T EVEN!
THANKS FOR EVERYTHING. I DON'T THINK I COULD HAVE DONE IT WITHOUT YOU, MAN.
SAME! BUT YOU'RE NOT GONNA HUG ME, ARE YOU?
NO, WHY WOULD I . . . NEVER MIND.
WAIT HERE. I HAVE TO GET SOMETHING OUT OF MY UNCLE'S CAR.

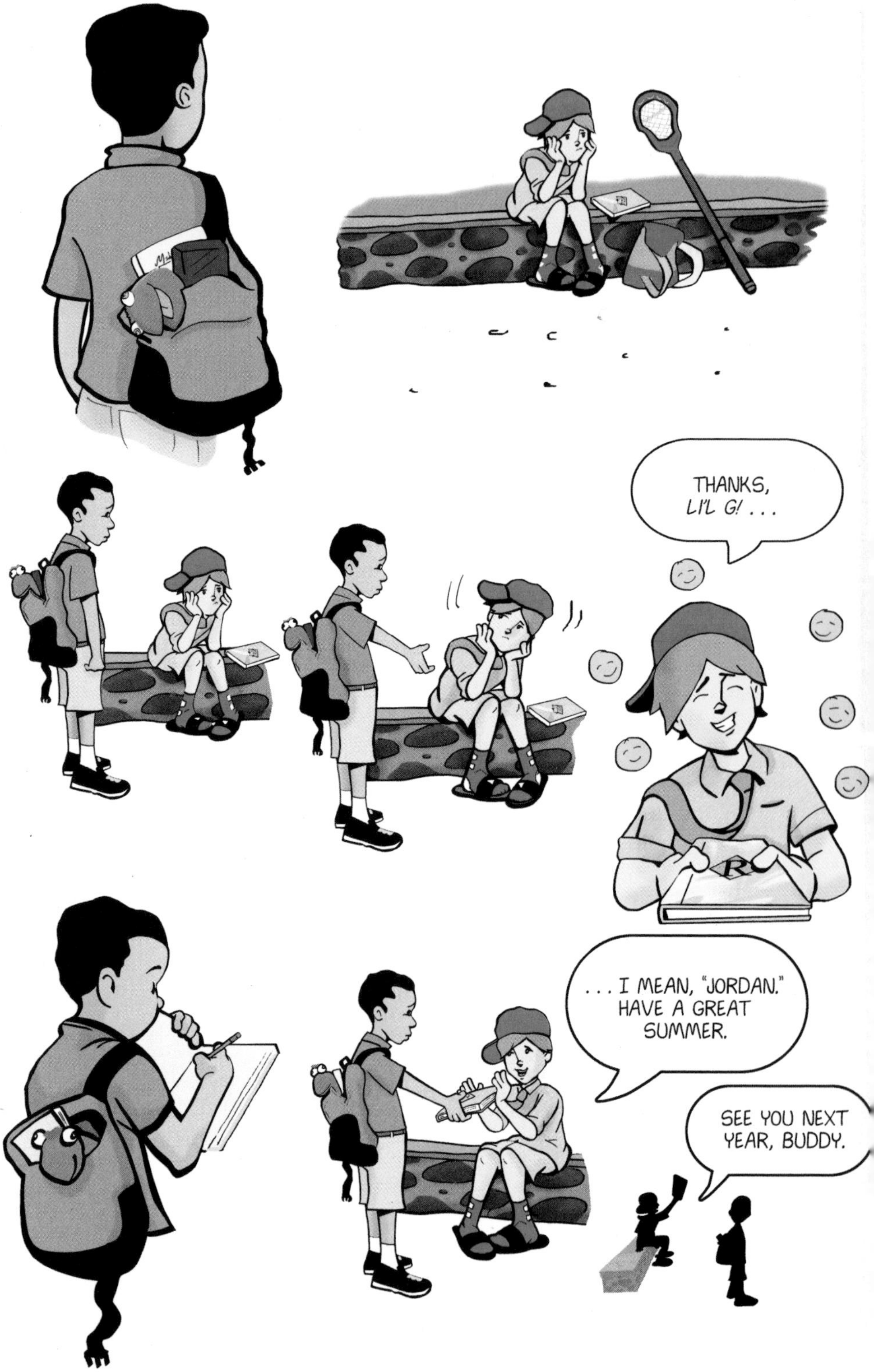
THANKS, LI'L G! . . .
. . . I MEAN, "JORDAN." HAVE A GREAT SUMMER.
SEE YOU NEXT YEAR, BUDDY.

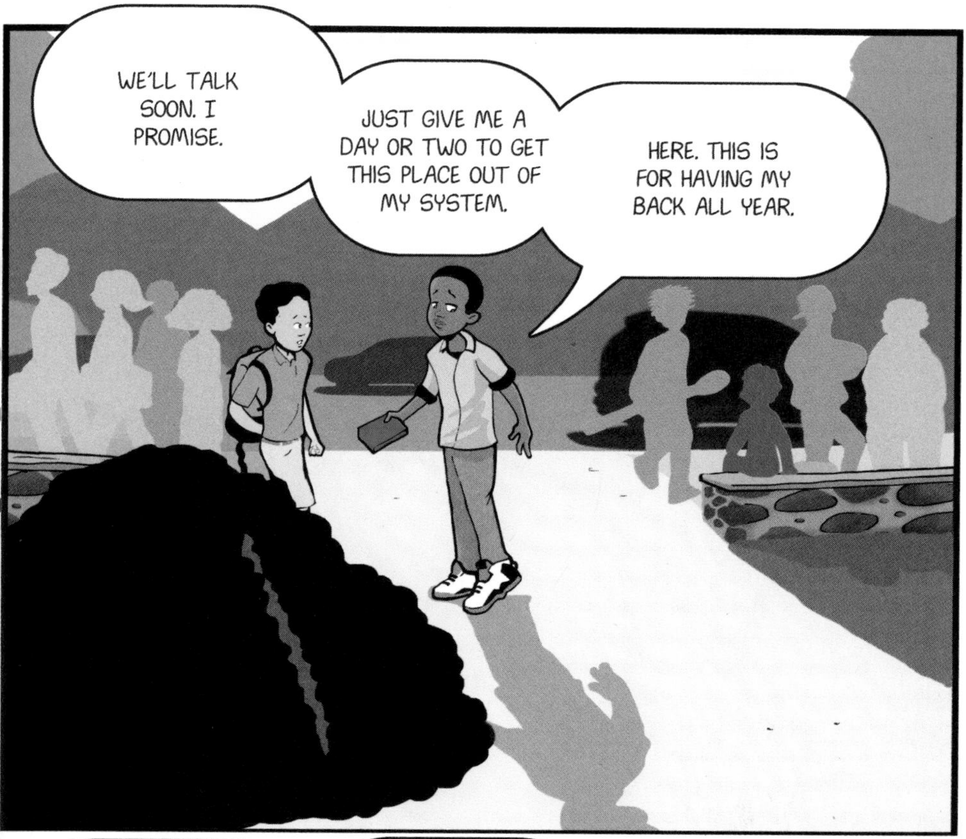
WE'LL TALK SOON. I PROMISE.
JUST GIVE ME A DAY OR TWO TO GET THIS PLACE OUT OF MY SYSTEM.
HERE. THIS IS FOR HAVING MY BACK ALL YEAR.

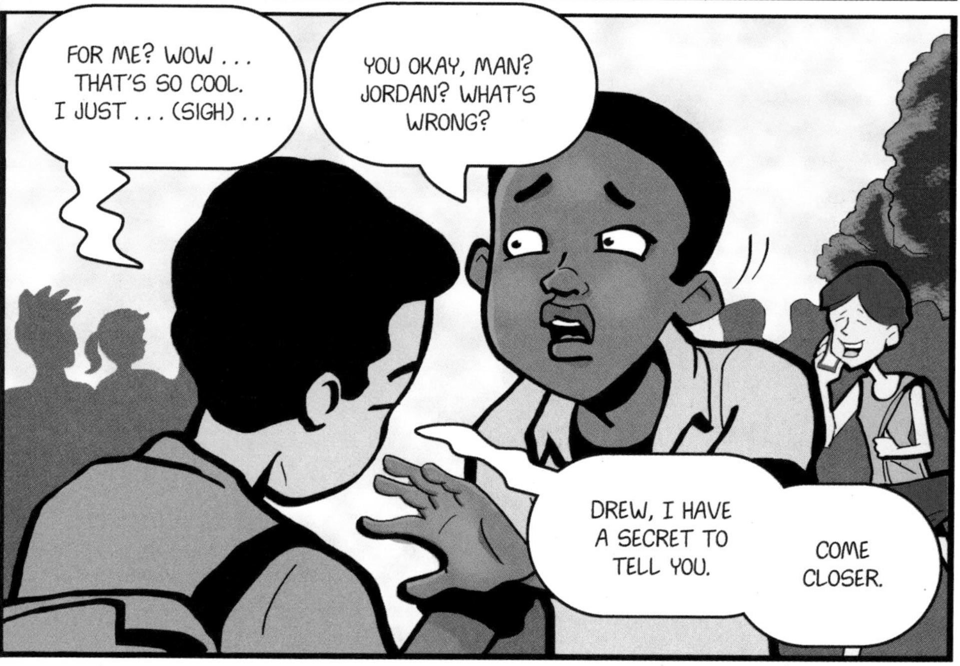
FOR ME? WOW . . . THAT'S SO COOL. I JUST . . . (SIGH) . . .
YOU OKAY, MAN? JORDAN? WHAT'S WRONG?
DREW, I HAVE A SECRET TO TELL YOU.
COME CLOSER.

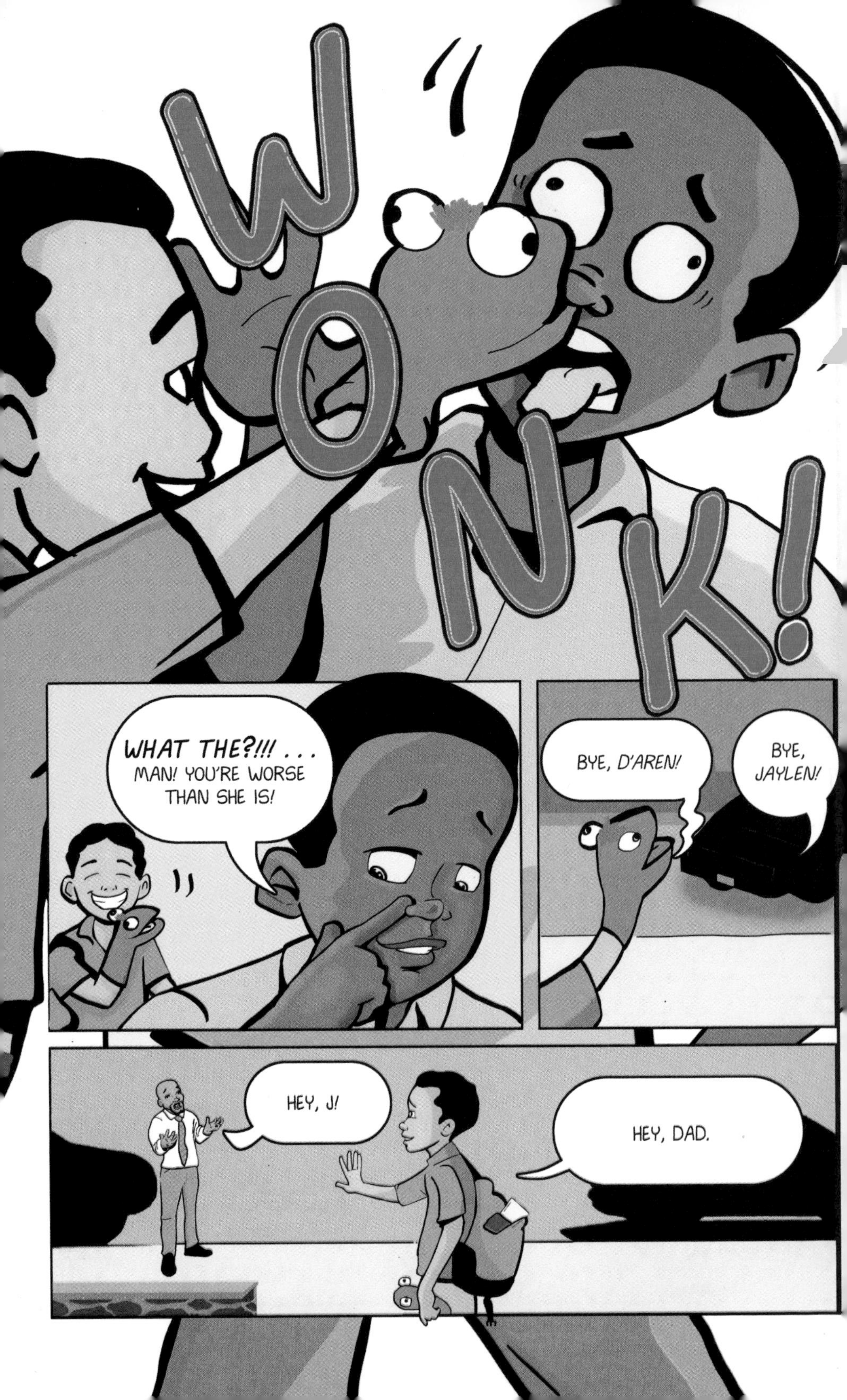
WONK!
WHAT THE?!!! . . . MAN! YOU'RE WORSE THAN SHE IS!
BYE, D'AREN!
BYE, JAYLEN!
HEY, J!
HEY, DAD.

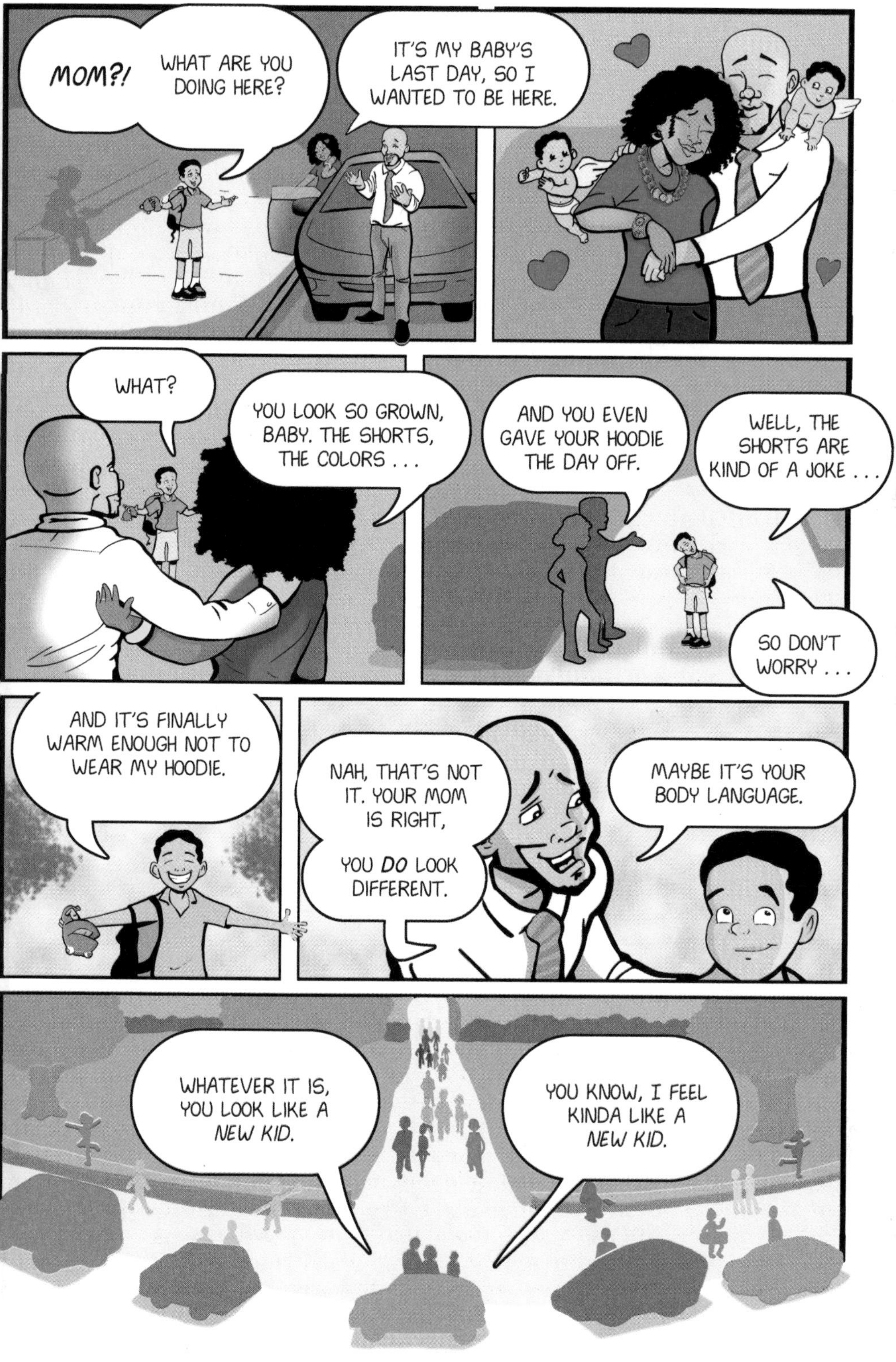
MOM?!
WHAT ARE YOU DOING HERE?
IT'S MY BABY'S LAST DAY, SO I WANTED TO BE HERE.
WHAT?
YOU LOOK SO GROWN, BABY. THE SHORTS, THE COLORS . . .
AND YOU EVEN GAVE YOUR HOODIE THE DAY OFF.
WELL, THE SHORTS ARE KIND OF A JOKE . . .
SO DON'T WORRY . . .
AND IT'S FINALLY WARM ENOUGH NOT TO WEAR MY HOODIE.
NAH, THAT'S NOT IT. YOUR MOM IS RIGHT,
YOU *DO* LOOK DIFFERENT.
MAYBE IT'S YOUR BODY LANGUAGE.
WHATEVER IT IS, YOU LOOK LIKE A *NEW KID*.
YOU KNOW, I FEEL KINDA LIKE A *NEW KID*.

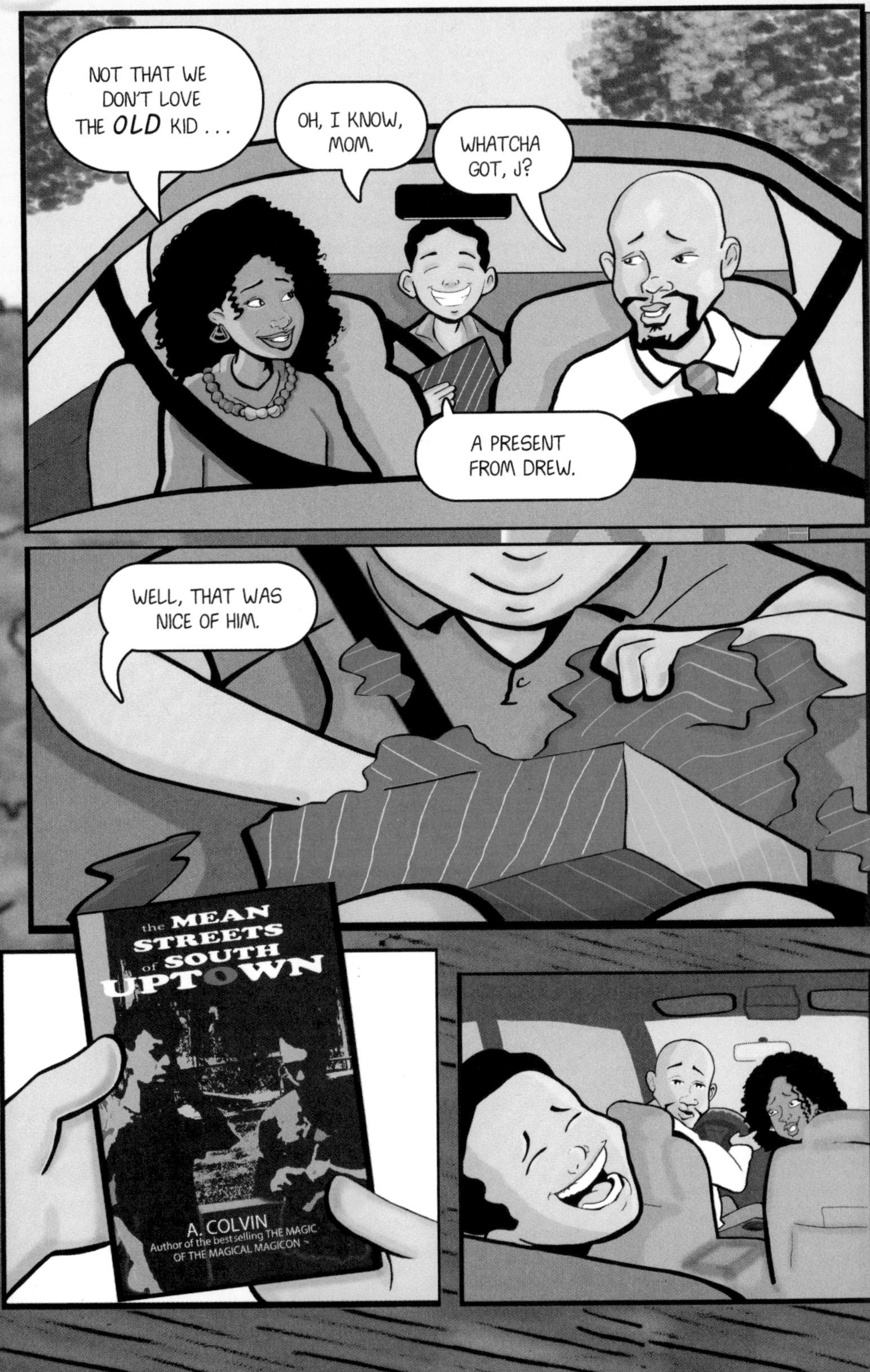
NOT THAT WE DON'T LOVE THE OLD KID . . .
OH, I KNOW, MOM.
WHATCHA GOT, J?
A PRESENT FROM DREW.
WELL, THAT WAS NICE OF HIM.
the MEAN STREETS of SOUTH UPTOWN
A. COLVIN
Author of the best selling THE MAGIC OF THE MAGICAL MAGICON ~

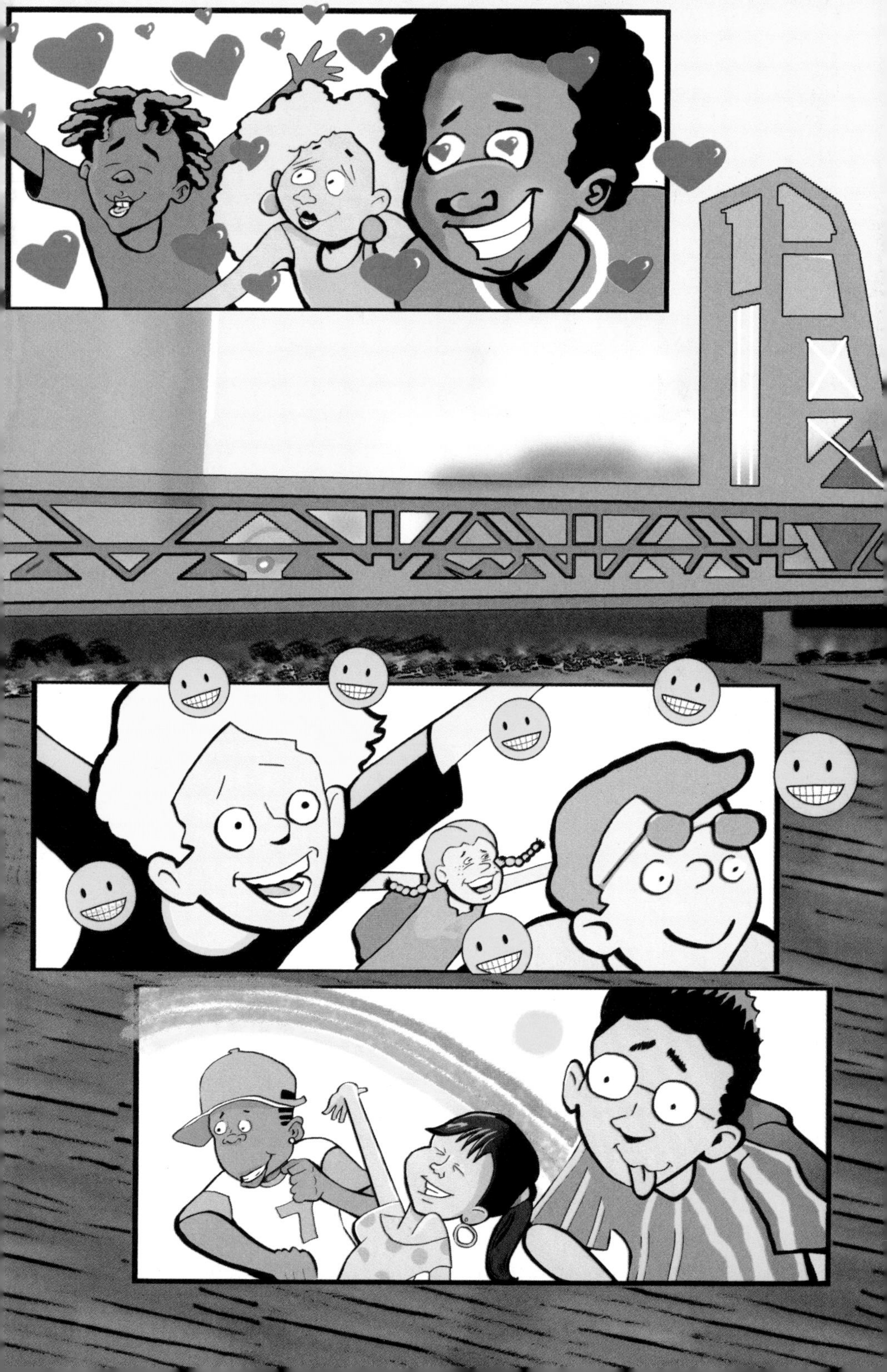

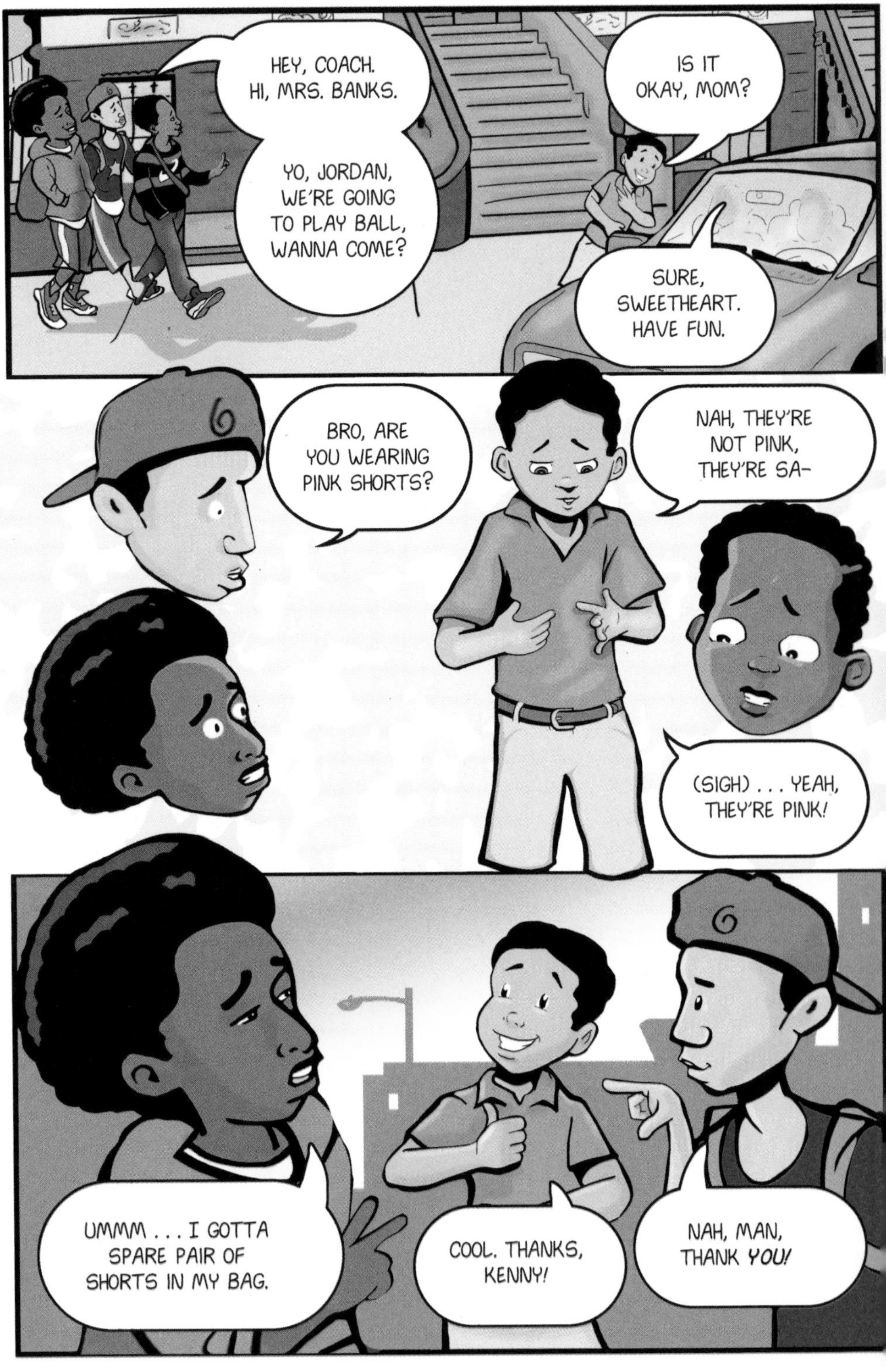
HEY, COACH. HI, MRS. BANKS.
YO, JORDAN, WE'RE GOING TO PLAY BALL, WANNA COME?
IS IT OKAY, MOM?
SURE, SWEETHEART. HAVE FUN.
BRO, ARE YOU WEARING PINK SHORTS?
NAH, THEY'RE NOT PINK, THEY'RE SA-
(SIGH) . . . YEAH, THEY'RE PINK!
UMMM . . . I GOTTA SPARE PAIR OF SHORTS IN MY BAG.
COOL. THANKS, KENNY!
NAH, MAN, THANK *YOU!*

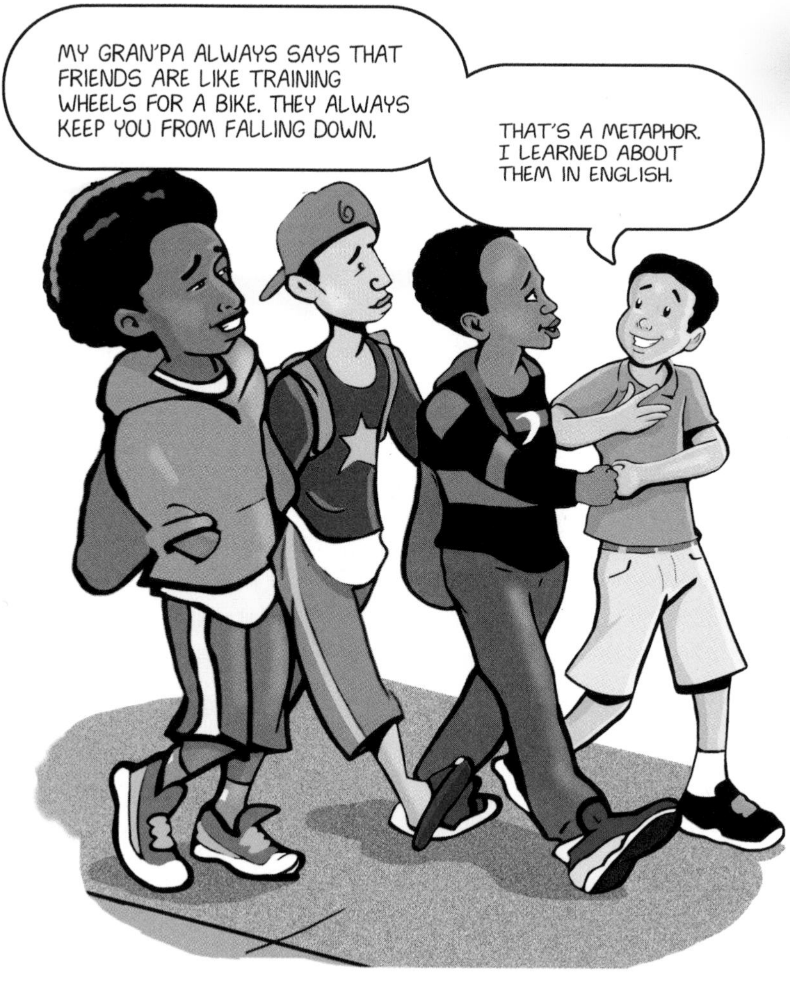
MY GRAN'PA ALWAYS SAYS THAT FRIENDS ARE LIKE TRAINING WHEELS FOR A BIKE. THEY ALWAYS KEEP YOU FROM FALLING DOWN.
THAT'S A METAPHOR. I LEARNED ABOUT THEM IN ENGLISH.

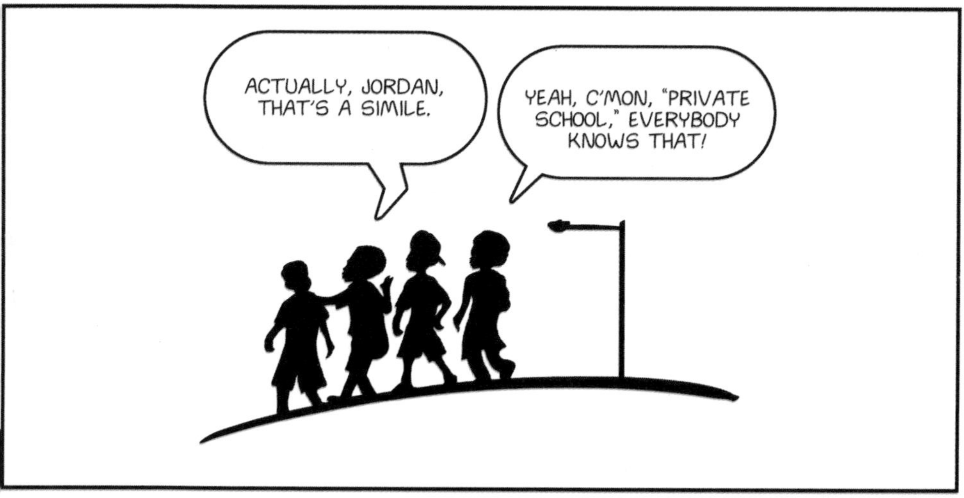
ACTUALLY, JORDAN, THAT'S A SIMILE.
YEAH, C'MON, "PRIVATE SCHOOL," EVERYBODY KNOWS THAT!

To my family, Jay, Aren, and Autier.
Thank you for making me a better person.

Thanks to my agent, Judy Hansen,
my editor, Andrew Eliopulos, and Rosemary Brosnan
and the team at HarperCollins for embracing my vision.

Thanks to Marva Allen, Pam Allyn, Debra Lakow
Dorfman, David Saylor, Andrea Davis Pinkney,
and Andrea Colvin for inspiring me along the way.

Special thanks to my amazing colorist, Jim Callahan,
and to Jacqueline Woodson, Jeff Kinney, and Kwame Alexander
for your kind words and inspiration.

And last but not least, thanks to Barbara Slate,
Jim Keefe, Ray Billingsley, M'shindo Kuumba,
Eric Velasquez, Danni Ai, and Jennifer Crute
for making me a better artist.